TRUE CONFESS

37
STORIES
OF
CONFESSION

TRUE STORY
and
TRUE CONFESSIONS
Magazines

True Story and *True Confessions* are the world's largest and best-selling women's romance magazines. They offer true-to-life stories to which women can relate.

Since 1919, the iconic *True Story* has been an extraordinary publication. The magazine gets its inspiration from the hearts and minds of women, and touches on those things in life that a woman holds close to her heart, like love, loss, family and friendship.

True Confessions, a cherished classic first published in 1922, looks into women's souls and reveals their deepest secrets.

Published by True Renditions, LLC

True Renditions, LLC
105 E. 34th Street, Suite 141
New York, NY 10016

Copyright @ 2020 by True Renditions, LLC

All rights reserved. No part of this book may be reproduced or transmitted in any form or by any electronic means, without the written permission of the publisher, except where permitted by law.

Visit us on the web at www.truerenditionsllc.com.

TRUE CONFESSIONS

37 STORIES OF CONFESSION

From the Editors
Of *True Story* And
True Confessions

BOOKS FROM THE EDITORS OF TRUE STORY AND TRUE CONFESSIONS

A Soldier's Family	More Miracles
A Turkey Day Gathering	One Winter Night
All The Scandalous Secrets	Our True Furry Friends
Always A Mystery	Painful Love
Becoming Cinderella	Parting Ways
Coming Home for Christmas	Real Heroes
Delivered Into Danger	Valentine Delights
Enchanting Easter	Second Chances
Faith, Hope, Love and Luck	Seriously Cheating
Young And Desperate	Shameful Secrets Revealed
Giving Thanks	Shattered Vows
Grandma Knows Best	Signs Of Angels
Hope For The Heart	Untrue
Jealous Obsessions	True Memories
Killer in the Shadow	Surviving The Unthinkable
Life Is a Lottery	Tales of Inspiration
Life-Changing	Tales of Inspiration: Volume 2
Little Baby Lost	Talk About Murder
Living Through Tragedy	Ten Greatest Love Stories
Married to the Military	The Day of the Jack-O-Lantern
Miracles: Volume 2	The Most Remarkable Mom

The Troubled Thoughts of a Teenager
The Very Best of the Best of Secrets Volume 1, 2, 3 & 4
The Very Best of the Best of True Confessions Volume 1, 2, 3 & 4
The Very Best of True Experience Volume 1, 2, 3 & 4
The Very Best of True Story Romance Special Volume 1, 2, 3 & 4
Thirteen Sizzling Confessions and Crimes of the Heart
Troubled Thoughts Of A Teenager
True Confessions Classic Novella Volume 1
True Ghosts—Stories from the Trues
Love After Loss—A Widow's Story
True Sisters Volume 1 & 2
True Story Romance Special 2017 & 2019
Twelve Tender Tearjerkers
Stroke of Midnight: A New Year's Eve Story Collection
Steadfast Love—Stories of Love and Devotion
Scandals, Secrets and Sensual Confessions
Finding The Way Out—Stories Of Addiction
Brides: From Blushing To Bawling
Editors' Favorites Volume 1 & 2
Miracles: The Greatest Gift of All

Contents

Confessions Of An Ice Queen..1
Confessions Of An Army Gal..13
Confessions Of A Sister..28
Confessions Of A Broken Wife..38
Confessions Of An Angry Teen...49
Confessions Of A Biker Babe..62
Confessions Of A Shopaholic..67
Confessions Of An ER Nurse..83
Confessions Of An Office Slut...93
Confessions Of An Abused Wife..107
Confessions Of A Runaway Teen...127
Confessions of A Survivor..135
Confessions Of A Kidnapper..144
Confessions Of A Heartbroken Mom......................................160
Confessions Of "The Other Woman".......................................178
Confessions Of A Drug Addict's Daughter.............................187
Confessions Of A Stalker..198
Confessions Of A Homeless Woman......................................217
Confessions Of A Fatherless Daughter...................................221
Confessions Of A Credit Card Junkie.....................................229
Confessions Of A Neglectful Mom...240
Confessions Of A Murderess..252
Confessions Of An Estranged Daughter.................................260
Confessions Of A 1-900-Number Girl....................................268
Confessions Of A Stepmonster...281
Confessions Of A Cover Wife..298
Confessions Of A Grieving Mother..310
Confessions Of A Disgruntled Employee...............................322
Confessions of A Suspicious Sister..333
Confessions Of The Worst Mom Ever....................................342
Confessions Of A Freewheeling Biker Chick.........................359
Confessions Of A Woman...362
Confessions Of A Postpartum Mommy..................................375
Confessions Of A Battered Woman..383
Confessions Of A Runaway..394
Confessions Of A Desperate Housewife.................................402
Confessions Of A Working Girl..412

CONFESSIONS OF AN ICE QUEEN
Why I Refuse To Fall In Love

"Wait 'til you see the new paralegal who's just been hired!" my coworker, Amanda York, panted, hurrying up to my desk. "He's hot, and he'll be here in a second."

"He can't be that great," I said wryly.

Amanda's eyes glistened with excitement. "His smile will curl your toes. And he's single, too."

I was still shaking my head when Mr. Cromwell brought the new employee over to me. Introducing him as Justin Fletcher. Mr. Cromwell, who did the hiring for the law firm where I worked, explained that Justin had just been added to our staff.

I was totally unprepared for the man in front of me. Justin Fletcher was tall and lean with dark hair and eyes the color of chocolate. His mouth, beneath his mustache, was wide and sensuous, his teeth flashing white. His warm smile crashed through the barriers I had erected between myself and the rest of the world like a bulldozer leveling an ant hill.

I had never permitted anyone to know me well, not even Amanda, who was my best friend. Lots of people have things in their lives they aren't proud of, but I was certain mine were so much more shameful than anyone else's. I prayed regularly they would remain hidden forever.

"Justin, this is Emma Holden," Mr. Cromwell said, his voice breaking into my thoughts. "She'll fill you in on our office procedures and introduce you around."

"I'm happy to meet you, Emma." Justin's deep, resonant voice and friendly smile gave the ordinary greeting new dimensions. His dark eyes stirred emotions in me that I had always managed to keep under control. "Is it Ms. or Mrs.?" he asked after Mr. Cromwell walked away.

"It's Ms.," I answered coolly. Ignoring Justin's gaze, I explained the way the office was run. After introducing him to the staff in the outer office, I took him to the head of the paralegal department.

Before we entered, he placed his hand on my arm. "Sorry if I came on too strong, but I couldn't help myself. You're a very pretty woman."

He was smooth, all right. Too smooth. But no matter how I tried to deny it, I felt an attraction toward him, too. "You're wasting your time," I told him. "I'm not interested."

1

I found it difficult to concentrate on my work for the rest of the day. My mind was on another level as I sat in front of my computer and printed out legal papers. Justin's face kept appearing on the monitor, and I had to redo two documents because I'd screwed them up.

It's difficult to comprehend the shame I've experienced since I was a child. Since as long as I can remember, I've wanted to crawl in a hole and hide from the rest of the world. Many times, I prayed lightning would strike me dead or that I would be run over by a Mac truck.

I lived in a rundown section of a large, midwestern city with my mother who drank and used drugs. She told me she had no family, that her parents were dead. From the little I learned from her, she had run away from home when she was sixteen and had been on the streets ever since. If she had any relatives, she wasn't aware of it or they refused to acknowledge her. She looked twice as old as her twenty odd years. Her complexion was blotchy, and she dyed her hair a harsh red. She dressed in skimpy clothes and went out a lot, leaving me to fend for myself after the ripe, old age of five. There was always men at our place. Some of them stayed overnight, some for several weeks. I was afraid to be in the same room with most of them.

Most of the kids I met when I started school had fathers. When I asked my mother where mine was, she emitted a brittle laugh. "Pick a city. I don't even know who your father is."

I stared at her, unsure of what she was saying.

"I've never been married," she went on. "There's been a lotta men in my life, as you've probably noticed."

Mom reached a new low when she brought "Rider" Garson home with her one night when I was fifteen. He was mean-eyed and beefy with a scar slicing across his cheek. I didn't like the way he looked at me and whenever he was around, I remained in my room. One night I woke up with him hovering over me, fondling me. I opened my mouth to scream, but he placed his hand over it and warned me not to cry out.

Then he raped me. I'll never forget the pain and degradation of it.

The next night, he crept into my room again. He continued to come into my room for several months, night after night. My mother was too spaced out to notice he wasn't with her. He warned me if I told her, he would kill both of us. I hated my lousy life and what my mother did to survive.

Then Rider and Mom got into a big fight over some drugs, and he left and never came back. After he was gone, because the door had no lock, I started shoving several knives across it and into the door frame. After that, if any man she brought home came close to me, dared touch me, I warned him to stay back or I'd kill him. They were much bigger than I was, but somehow, they sensed I meant it and stayed away from me.

I didn't tell Mom what had happened until several months after Rider left, after I was sure he was long gone and wouldn't come back to harm us. Although my mother was a hooker and druggie, I didn't want her hurt. She was all I had. She provided me with a roof over my head and food—when she didn't need the money for drugs.

When I finally told her what Rider had done to me, she didn't seem surprised. "You're young. You'll get over it," she said. Cocking a brow over one glazed eye, she asked. "Why didn't you say something about this before? I would have booted him out sooner."

Although I had learned not to expect sympathy or understanding from her, I couldn't believe what she was saying. "The reason I didn't tell you was because he said he would kill me and you," I told her. "But now that I think about it, it would have been better than the hell we're living in."

"Ungrateful brat," she muttered. Stumbling over to the broken-down sofa where she had tossed her handbag, she began to paw inside for a joint or a pill, anything she could find to feed her cravings.

Maybe she has something, I thought. Maybe I should use something that would kill the pain of living, just as she does. When she pulled out a packet of white powder, I held out my hand. "I want some of that, too."

She drew back, clutching the packet in her hand. "Get your own. This is all I've got."

That was the best thing she'd ever done for me. If she had shared with me I would have taken it and started using, too. Instead, I watched her stumble out of the apartment in search of another fix, her hair frizzed and ratted, and the cheap, skintight clothes she always wore clinging to her boney frame.

I vowed I would never look or be like her. Afraid someone would learn the truth about me and how I lived, I made few friends while I was growing up. What would they think if they found out about me? Would they think I was just like my mother?

Contrary to what she told me, I didn't "get over it." I was certain that all men were like Rider and Mom's other men, and I wanted nothing to do with them. I couldn't wait until I was old enough to leave the shabby apartment where I lived and get out on my own, away from the hell I lived in and the memories that haunted me.

Swearing I would never be like my mother whose only means of survival was selling her body, during high school, I took all the vocational and computer courses that were available. I studied hard and made good grades. Although I was often asked out, I seldom dated. My only goal in life was to get away from home—if you could call it that. I realized I couldn't change the circumstances of my birth and my childhood or that I'd been raped, but I was determined to make something of myself. Early in life, I resolved never to marry. I was certain no decent man would want me once he found out that I'd been molested—or that my mother was a hooker, and my father a john she had sold herself to for a quick fix.

After graduating from high school, I got a job at a law firm on the other side of the city where I grew up. Now, four years later, I was executive administrator for that firm. I made a good salary and lived in a nice, four-room apartment in a good neighborhood. When I looked in the mirror, I no longer saw a stringy-haired kid with solemn, gray eyes that had seen too much for her tender years, but a young woman with stylishly-cut hair and a trim figure clad in chic attire. After I'd left, I stopped at my mother's place from time to time to see how she was doing, but most of the time she wasn't home or was too spaced out to talk to me. A year ago she had been found dead in her apartment from an overdose.

The days following Justin Fletcher's arrival at the office, his face kept intruding into my thoughts while I worked, wracking havoc with my concentration. I was literally buried under a pile of legal documents a week or so later when my door opened, and I glanced up to meet his smiling, brown eyes.

"I hope I'm not intruding," he said.

"Not at all," I said tersely, my gaze sweeping over the papers stacked on my desk. "I don't have a thing to do."

Justin laughed. "Since it's break time, I was wondering if you would . . . if we could have coffee together in the cafeteria." I opened my mouth to refuse, but his next words came quickly. "I have some questions about the firm's benefits."

His voice was so sincere, his eyes so earnest—his excuse so flimsy and obvious. I felt my resistance fading no matter how hard I tried to hang onto it. Releasing a weighty sigh, I stood. "Since it pertains to business. . . ."

Every head in the outer office turned as we came out of my office together. A dozen astonished eyes followed our progress as we passed through on our way to the cafeteria.

"What was that all about?" Justin asked as we rode down the elevator. "Do I have on different colored socks or something?"

"It's not you. It's me they're staring at," I explained. "I usually don't socialize with men in the office." My avoidance of male relationships was a source of jokes and innuendo. Since I'd been working at Broberg and Renville, LTD, a number of attractive male paralegals had been employed there, but I had managed to keep a wide distance between them and me. Once I overheard someone saying I must be frigid, another time that I was gay.

Justin chuckled. "We're socializing? I thought we were going to talk about business over coffee—not that I would object to something more. Like the two of us having dinner together some evening."

"Coffee will have to do." I wasn't interested in becoming involved with any man, no matter how handsome and charming he was, for fear it might develop into something more. Even after all these years, I could smell the odor of Rider's foul breath on my face, feel the pain and humiliation I'd experienced as he raped me. If all men were like that, I wanted nothing to do with them.

Surprisingly, the coffee break with Justin went quickly. I discovered that he and I had similar likes and dislikes. In spite of my determination, I couldn't deny or understand the rapport between us. I found myself smiling at his wry sense of humor, laughing a time or two at one of his jokes. There was little of the old uneasiness or apprehension I usually experienced when I was with a man.

Justin told me he'd taken business law in college and was taking several more classes at night school. "Maybe someday I'll have my own office—if I live long enough." He laughed, then asked me what I did with my spare time.

My shoulders lifted in a shrug of indifferences. "I manage to keep myself occupied."

His eyes searched my face. "I suppose there's a guy you keep yourself occupied with."

I tensed, fearful of what he was leading up to. "There's no one."

He smiled. "Good. Then you're free to go out to dinner with me sometime."

"Sorry."

His disappointment was obvious. "Do I have bad breath, or aren't you in the habit of eating?"

Glancing at my watch, I pushed back my chair and rose to my feet. "We'd better get back to work."

The next few days, whenever it was break time or I went to lunch, Justin always seemed to be nearby.

"Have you changed your mind yet about having dinner with me some evening?" he asked as we rode up the elevator together after lunch one day.

I shook my head.

"You certainly are a stubborn woman, aren't you?" he teased.

"That's right." I jutted out my chin, daring him to try to break my resolve.

"We don't have to go on a date. We could go Dutch if you like. Or if you don't want to go to a restaurant, I could pick up some Kentucky Fried Chicken or Chinese takeout, and we can hang out at my place or yours." The hopefulness in his voice tugged at my heart, making me feel as if I were the meanest woman in the world.

I looked up at him as he stood beside me, his lean frame inches away and the fragrance of his cologne wafting around me. "You are persistent, aren't you?"

"How about pizza and conversation?" he suggested. "That's all. I promise." He made a cross over his heart.

I could feel my resistance melting as he looked down at me with a pleading, little-boy expression in his eyes. I held up my hands in a gesture of surrender. "Okay, okay. I give up." If I agreed to go out with him once, hopefully, he would leave me alone.

Our routine soon became an established one. Justin stopped over at my place a couple times a week after his night classes, sometimes on weekends. The apartment resounded with his laughter and lightheartedness, something I wasn't familiar with, for there had never been any laughter or good times in my life before. Sometimes he came with food and a bottle of wine. Occasionally, I prepared dinner.

I found myself looking forward to his next visit, cleaning my apartment until it sparkled and fussing over my appearance before his arrival. He told me about his childhood and his mother and father, who was a small-town doctor. Whenever the conversation shifted to me or my childhood, I quickly changed the subject. Justin had come from a wonderful home. He had a God-fearing, church-going family. I shuddered at what he would think if he learned about my childhood. Whenever he suggested we go out to a movie or to dinner, I made some excuse why I couldn't go. As long as we didn't date formally, I told myself we would be able to keep our relationship on a strictly friendly basis.

Many nights, after he left, I lay awake in bed, my whole being aching for his body beside mine, but I quickly reminded myself that I had to keep it light, keep him at a distance. If I permitted my feelings to go any further, I would be lost.

As the weeks passed, I realized Justin's feelings for me were deepening. One evening when he stopped by after his classes, it was all there in his eyes for me to see.

After he entered the apartment, I gestured for him to be seated. Instead, he placed his hands on my shoulders. His dark eyes searching my face, he said, "I think we should talk."

"Talk?" I said in bewilderment. "Haven't we been talking for weeks?"

"We need to talk about my being in love with you."

His were the words every woman dreams of hearing, but they frightened me to death. "You promised we wouldn't become involved in a serious relationship," I said. It was more of an accusation than a reminder.

"I didn't plan to fall in love with you. It just happened." He pulled me into his arms, and his lips sought mine. One hand clasping my shoulder, he gently took my chin in his other hand and turned my face up to him. "You care about me, too. I can feel it."

I drew back, out of his grasp. "I think you'd better leave." I could see Rider's face hovering over me, feeling him pushing into me. I cringed in horror.

"What have you got against falling in love?" Justin asked, frowning.

"Nothing," I said hastily. "It's just not for me." I told myself that you had to have been loved to know how to love. And love had always been absent from my life.

Justin wrapped his strong arms around me again, squeezing off my protests. "Everyone needs love."

"Let me go!" I protested as his lips crushed down on mine, cutting off my words.

"Let me show you how much I love you," he said. His hands moved slowly, sensuously over me. Gradually, his caresses began to heat my blood, send it surging through my veins. Whispering his love for me, he covered my face with hot kisses. I had never made love before, had never had anyone make love to me, but suddenly, starved for affection all my life, I wanted this man with a desire I couldn't deny.

Entwining my hands in his hair, I drew him close. I felt the heat of his passion, of his need for me. Nothing existed except the moment and the man holding me in his arms. All my vows, all the misery and pain I had endured were swept away. Forgotten.

Then reality returned and I drew away from him.

"This shouldn't have happened." My voice was harsh and filled with pain. "I shouldn't have let it to happen."

He stared at me, hurt and disbelieving. "Why not?"

"You have to leave." I couldn't let him love me. He was too good for me.

When I turned away from him, his shoulders stooped as if from a physical blow. "I don't understand, but I'm not giving up on our love no matter what you say or do. I know you feel the same way about me that I feel about you, whether you want to admit it or not."

After he was gone, the silence in the room enveloped me, making me feel lost and alone. Life was so unfair. Why had I been born? My mother hadn't wanted a child. She'd wanted a fix. Whoever had sired me didn't know I existed, and the man who had molested me had used me for his own sick purposes. Once Justin discovered the truth about me, he wouldn't want me, either.

The next morning, five minutes after I sat down at my desk, the door opened and Justin stuck his head in. "I'd like to stop by your place tonight. We need to talk."

I couldn't let him come to my place. I couldn't let him hold me in his arms and kiss me again. I didn't deserve him. "We have nothing to talk about."

"I think we do."

"I won't be home tonight," I said hastily. "I'm . . . I'm going to a movie."

"I haven't seen a movie in ages," he said, "Maybe I could go with you."

"No. I've made plans to go with somebody else."

His face fell. "With who? Amanda?"

Afraid he might check with her, I shook my head. "I'm going with someone else. You don't know her."

"Her?" he asked with relief.

For the next several days, I did my best to stay out of Justin's way. When he stopped by my office, I held up my hand. "I can't talk now. I'm swamped with work." If he tried to talk to me as I walked into the outer office for something, I brushed him aside by saying I was in a hurry.

One evening, as I waited for the elevator after work, he came up behind me. "Why are you avoiding me?" he asked. "Don't you know I care about you? I don't tell just anyone that I love them."

I blinked at the tears welling in my eyes. "I'm sorry, but I think it would be best if we didn't see each other outside the office anymore."

"Why?" he wanted to know as we stepped into the elevator. "Is there someone else in your life?"

I thanked God the elevator was too crowded for him to pursue his questioning. When we reached the lobby, I started to walk away.

Hurrying up behind me, he took hold of my arm. "I love you. Doesn't that mean anything to you? I want to marry you." His voice overflowed with emotion.

Stopping abruptly, I turned to face him. I loved him, too. But there was no way I could marry him and not tell him about myself. He had a right to know those things about his wife. Someone who had lived under the same conditions as I had might understand, but not decent, upstanding people like Justin and his parents. His mother probably baked cookies and went to church on Sunday. Mine had been a junkie with men passing in and out of our apartment like customers walking in and out of a supermarket. Justin had a loving family. A brother and a sister. Aunts and uncles. I was a stray cat no one wanted.

"I can't marry you." My voice was barely above a whisper, as though muting it, I could modulate the loneliness, the bleak future I saw ahead of me. "We don't know each other well enough . . . you don't know me. . . ."

"I know you well enough to know you're the woman I want to

marry. I want a family, a house in the suburbs, all the regular, normal things everyone else wants."

"Someday you'll have them, I'm sure. But not with me."

"I guess I'm thickheaded," he said, the pain of my rejection reflected in his eyes. "I really believed you cared for me as much as I care for you. I guess I was mistaken."

No, Justin! my heart cried. You aren't mistaken, but I can't tell you the real reason I won't marry you.

Turning away, I hurried toward the exit. Why didn't I end our relationship before it got this far? I had always been able to push away other men who'd been interested in me before. But you weren't in love with them, a voice inside me reminded me.

Instead of going home, I drove around in my car for hours. The sky overhead was as dark and brooding as my thoughts. Raindrops began to fall and slide down the windshield like the tears sliding down my cheeks. My vision blurred, and I pulled over to the side of the street. Leaning my head against the steering wheel, I let the teardrops fall unheeded. Much later, when I finally made my way home, I crawled into bed and cried myself to sleep.

The next week at the office was torture for me. Although we avoided each other, Justin and I were very much aware of each other's presence. When we ran into each another in the outer office or the cafeteria at lunchtime, I wondered if his heart ached as much as mine, if it, too, was shattered in a million pieces. I thought about asking for time off. I even considered quitting my job and finding another. But I had worked long and hard to get where I was, and I dreaded the thought of starting over.

"What's going on between you and Justin?" Amanda asked. "You seemed to be getting along so well."

"Nothing's wrong," I told her. "There never has been anything between us and there never will be."

She eyed me speculatively. "Are you sure about that?"

"I'm positive."

"Then you won't mind if he and I get something going?"

My heart plunged. "Of course not. Why should I?"

When Amanda and Justin started taking breaks together, I told myself I didn't care, that I couldn't condemn them. He wanted the normal things in life—love, marriage, a family. I knew Amanda wanted those things, too.

As the days passed, I grew more and more depressed. I had difficulty sleeping, and dark circles rimmed my eyes. One evening, when I stopped my car in the parking lot alongside my apartment building, I noticed a little, brown puppy being led across the lot. He was a mixture of breeds. One leg seemed shorter than the other, as if he had been injured by a car or had been born that way, but he was adorable. His eyes were bright and mischievous. His pink tongue lolled out of the corner of his mouth as he bounded and jumped about. I wanted to pick him up and hug him, take him home with me.

"Isn't he darling?" I said to the middle-aged man who had just pulled his car alongside mine.

"Looks like a gimpy mutt to me," he said with indifference.

"It's not his fault who his parents are, or that he's not perfect," I defended sharply.

Later that night, as I sat alone in my apartment after I'd eaten a light supper, I was once again surrounded by a sea of loneliness and despair. Then, unexpectedly, it came to me. I was like the puppy I'd seen in the parking lot. I wasn't responsible for who my parents were or what had happened to me. My imperfections and internal scars weren't my fault any more than that little dog was responsible for what had happened to him. Foolishly, I had spent my whole life punishing myself for the ugliness and disgrace of my birth and my childhood. I had worked myself up from a filing clerk to an executive administrator. I had moved from the wrong side of town into a beautiful apartment in a nice area of the city. I wasn't a thief or a murderer. I'd never deliberately hurt anyone. If Justin couldn't love me for who and what I was, he didn't deserve me.

Praying he was home, I lifted the phone and called his number. What if he wasn't there? What if Amanda was with him? What if he hung up when he heard my voice? I wasn't sure I would have the courage to call a second time. Yet I had to know if he still cared enough about me to listen to what I had to say to him.

"Hello?"

My heart leaped at the sound of his voice. I took a deep breath. "I'd like to talk to you. Could you come over?" I knew if I told him I was coming over to his place, I would probably lose my nerve halfway there and turn back. If he refused to come over, that would be the end of us. I would have to forget about him—if I could.

The pause on the other end of the line made my heart stop. "I'll be there in a few minutes," he said finally.

The next fifteen minutes were the longest of my life. The seconds dragged by slowly, like a freight train being towed by a turtle. I kept glancing at the time. I told myself I had to relax, but my nerves were taut as a watch spring. How could I relax when my future, and certainly my happiness, was hanging in the balance?

When Justin's knock sounded, I rose on unsteady legs. My heart pounding like a jungle drum, I gestured for him to be seated, then slid onto an armed chair across from him. What if I were too late? What if he had fallen in love with Amanda?

I ran my tongue over my lips to moisten them. "I owe you an apology."

"I agree." He waited silently, his eyes intent on my face.

Without omitting or embellishing on any of the details, I unburdened the secret that had haunted me for so long. By denying myself the privilege of loving someone, by not allowing them to love me, I had been half a woman. When I finished my explanation, my gaze searched his face.

"That's the reason you broke up with me?" he said, his voice hushed with disbelief. "That's the reason you refused to marry me?"

"I was afraid you wouldn't want anything to do with me if you knew about my background, about my childhood." My voice was low and uncertain. "I was afraid you wouldn't love me. . . ."

Rising from the sofa, Justin came over to me and drew me to my feet. With his hand, he lifted my chin and peered directly into my eyes. "I'm disappointed that you think I'm so shallow that I would judge you because of your mother's mistakes and what happened to you when you were fifteen. You had no control over that." As he spoke, I saw only love and acceptance in his eyes.

Tears oozed out from under my lashes.

"From the moment I met you I thought you were the prettiest, most wonderful woman I'd ever met," he said softly. "I haven't changed my mind one iota." Leaning down, he kissed away my tears. "I predict a wonderful future ahead of you, starting right now, this minute. But first, I'd like to ask you a question."

"What's that?" I drew back apprehensively.

"Will you marry me?"

I felt as if I were going to explode with happiness. "Yes! Yes! If you'll have me!"

"Nothing you've told me makes me love you any less. You're not responsible for what you mother was or what happened to you. You're only responsible for Emma. And I love who and what Emma is."

As his hungry mouth captured mine, the rapid hammering of my heart I experienced whenever I was near him intensified to a wild crescendo. His breath was warm and sweet against my face, his heart beating in unison with mine. His lips blazed a trail of kisses across my cheeks and down the side of my neck.

Finally he drew back and looked down at me with desire in his eyes. "I love you, Emma Holden."

"Are you sure?" I asked, still uncertain of whether what was happening was real or just a dream.

"I'm sure."

Reaching out, I caressed his face with the tips of my fingers. "I never thought I'd meet someone like you. I don't deserve you."

A radiance flickered in the depths of his brown eyes. "I'm the one who doesn't deserve you. All my life I've dreamed of meeting someone like you, someone who's caring and beautiful and totally honest. I can't believe I've found her."

Cherishing the thought of being his wife, of our making love to each other for the rest of our lives, I lifted my lips to his to claim the happiness and fulfillment that will finally be mine.

THE END

CONFESSIONS OF AN ARMY GAL
A frank exposé of what really happens in lewd war zones

Hoops and hollers came from outside my tent. I stepped out to investigate. My outfit, stationed in a remote area of Iraq next to the Syrian border, just got a long-awaited shipment: mail from home.

Next to going home, mail was one of the things we looked forward to most. That simple link to the people we love took the edge off the loneliness and the heat.

A crowd gathered around our makeshift post office. While the letters were being sorted, a soldier started tossing packages off the back of a truck. One guy came away with a big smile and a box that looked like a child had decorated with crayons. Someone else got a mangled envelope marked DO NOT BEND.

"Cpl. Kathy Williams!"

I sprang forward at the sound of my name. I reached up and caught a package from Mom, but things got even better. There was also a letter from my fiancé, Curtis. I hurried back to my tent and tore it open.

Dear Kathy, I hope you're safe and well. It took me three days to write this letter, because I didn't know how to say what I'm about to write. I guess the best thing to do is to come out and say it. I've found someone else. . . .

The sweat on my body turned cold.

I'm very sorry to hurt you this way. I wish I didn't have to do it while you were over there, but six months is a long time to wait until you get home. I never intended for things to turn out this way. It just happened. I still think that you're a fine person and I'll always remember you.

His name was scrawled carelessly at the bottom.

I reread the letter in disbelief. His last letter was signed, Love, Curtis. On the nights I laid on my cot wishing I could be in his arms, he was with someone else. A raw and painful lump formed in my throat.

Suddenly, I heard a giggle outside and the tent flap opened. Sheila, one of my tent mates, stepped in reading a humorous card that someone had sent her. When she looked up, her smile faded.

"Hey, girl. What's wrong?" Her gaze fell on the letter in my lap. "Bad news from home?"

"It's from Curtis. It's a Dear Jane letter."

"You're kidding. After all that talk about the future?"

I handed her the letter. A frown crossed her sun-darkened face as she read it. "Men. As if the Army isn't enough to sour you on them."

"I can't believe it," I said numbly. "Not a week went by that he didn't write at least once to say how much he missed me."

She sat down beside me and slipped an arm around my shoulder. "I'm so sorry."

I gave her a weak smile of thanks.

"Is there anything I can do?"

I shook my head. "I guess I just need to be alone for a while."

"Sure, I understand. I'll go get some chow. Want me to bring you some?"

"No, thanks."

After she left, I fell on my cot and bawled like a baby. That guy meant everything to me and I meant nothing to him. He didn't even bother to say who the girl was, not that it mattered anyway.

I got up and wiped my face. I was in such a state that I forgot about the package from home. I opened it to find several containers of homemade oatmeal raisin cookies, snapshots from my grandmother's sixty-fifth birthday party, some toiletry articles, and a letter. My younger brother caught a seven-pound bass, my sister made the high school honor roll, and the next-door neighbor gave birth to twin boys.

We miss you so much, Mom wrote. Stay safe. We love you and pray for you every night. Give our best to Curtis.

Just the sight of his name brought back tears. To soothe myself, I popped open one of the tins and started devouring cookies, one after the other. Poor Mom. She fell for Curtis's charms as well.

Curtis is a civilian construction worker at the base from which I'm deployed, but we actually met at a shopping mall. He was trying to pick out a sweater for his sister's birthday when I walked into the store with a couple of friends. All of a sudden, he came up and introduced himself. He said that his sister and I are about the same build and he asked if I'd help him select the right size.

One look at him and I couldn't say no, so I helped him pick out a lavender sweater set. A few days later, he called to say that his sister loved it. As a way of thanking me, he asked if I'd like to go out for a cappuccino.

We met at a coffee bar off base. It was only the second time I'd seen him, but pretty soon it seemed like I'd known him for ages. The more we talked, the more we discovered that we had in common. We liked the same music and we both come from small towns. He was in the Army, too, six years prior.

We began seeing each other as often as possible. We went hiking, camping, and cruising in quest of the ultimate Mexican restaurant. There was only one cloud hanging over us: There was a good chance that my unit would deploy to the Middle East, but that only made our relationship more intense. We savored every moment together.

The relationship grew serious enough that I took him home to meet my family and he introduced me to his. Then it finally happened. Six months into our relationship, I got my orders to go to Iraq. We talked about getting married when I got back.

As much as it hurt to leave Curtis, I had no right to complain. I joined the Army at nineteen with both eyes wide open. I joined to escape a dead-end retail job and my dismal hometown. I joined to get money to go to college. I joined to help my mother, who was struggling to raise my younger brother and sister by herself. The Army was good to me. It gave my life structure and meaning. Then comes payback time.

On the day that we left the base for Iraq, I watched through the bus window as Curtis faded into the distance. The last thing I wanted was for the men to see me cry. I didn't want anybody to think that I didn't have the guts to be a soldier, so I sat stiffly, holding in my sobs until my lungs burned. Despite our brave faces, I knew we all had to be thinking the same thing: We may never see our loved ones again. Once we were in Iraq, though, there was little time to brood. There were too many other things to worry about, like staying alive.

Our first mission was in an isolated setting. While we were away from the structure and oversight of a stateside base, one thing became painfully clear: Women were seen as sex objects instead of soldiers. We were surrounded and greatly outnumbered by macho, sex-starved guys constantly on the prowl for the enemy—and a bed partner. "Queens for a Year," they called us. We were rated on a "hotness" scale of one to ten, getting a couple of points just for being there. A woman who wouldn't get much notice at home could get more than she wanted in a war zone.

The first week I was there, I got a pat on the behind from somebody I didn't even know. A group of guys who'd been drinking actually offered me money to take off my T-shirt. Once I made it clear that I had a fiancé at home, they pretty much left me alone. I knew that they were under a lot of stress and enduring awful conditions, but their behavior was hard to excuse. It didn't help that some of the women were saying yes to just about anything they wanted. In fact, some were even sent home pregnant.

All of that took a backseat to the dangers that we face every day. There were roadside bombs and 130° heat, making everybody a little crazy at times. Some people let off steam by drinking; others by hooking up with somebody. What kept me going was my love for Curtis. Knowing that he was at home waiting for me made even the worst conditions more bearable.

I sat on my cot with his letter still in my hand. Anger started to take the place of shock. At a time when I needed him most, he'd abandoned me. All those letters filled with declarations of love and plans for the future are as worthless as the paper they were written on.

I threw open my footlocker angrily and grabbed them. There were dozens, tied together with an old bootlace. I borrowed a lighter from Sheila's personal things and stormed outside.

Following a dusty trail to the edge of the camp, I stopped in an area of cliffs overlooking a deep valley. Since it was evening, there weren't many people around except for a few soldiers on patrol. Using a small spade, I started chipping a hole in the dirt. Sweat poured down my face, mixing with tears.

When the hole was about a foot deep, I tossed the letters in and set them on fire. I stepped back and watched bitterly as they went up in a bright, orange blaze.

"What's going on here?" a male voice asked.

I whirled around to find Sgt. Rick standing behind me. "I'm disposing of some letters, Sir." There were tears in my voice.

"May I ask why you're going to all this trouble?"

"They're from my fiancé—my ex-fiancé. I got a letter from him today. He's found someone else."

"Sorry."

"Thanks," I said with a shrug.

With the toe of his boot, he kicked dirt into the hole, covering the dying embers. Suddenly I remembered that the last letter was still in my pocket. I picked up a small rock, dropped it into the envelope, wadded the envelope around it, and hurled it off the cliff. As it disappeared, along with my hopes and dreams, I crumpled into tears.

"Take it easy," Sgt. Rick said. "This isn't fatal."

"I'm sorry, Sir." As if this isn't bad enough, I have to cry in front of a superior.

"Listen, I've seen two-hundred-pound guys weep over the same thing."

Hearing that, I started to pull myself together.

He handed me a tissue. "Care to talk about it?"

"I don't know."

"Come on. Let's go to my tent. It's getting dark. You don't need to be out here alone, anyway."

Finding his presence comforting, I followed him down the hill. He had a large tent to himself. Inside were two cots and a picture of Osama Bin Laden that he'd used for target practice.

"Make yourself comfortable," he said, zipping the tent flap closed. "Care for a beer? It's not cold, but it's wet."

"Sure."

He pulled one out of a cooler filled with water and handed it to me. I drank deeply, not just out of thirst but a need to numb my feelings.

"Tell me about it," he said gently, sitting across from me.

Determined not to cry again, I spoke slowly. When I finished, I was into my third beer. "My ego feels like it's been hit by a five-hundred-pound bomb. It's like I'm some sort of discard."

He sat down beside me and slipped an arm around my shoulder. "I'm not going to allow you to beat up on yourself like that. He's the loser. Some men don't have what it takes to maintain a relationship with a strong woman, and a female soldier is about as strong as they come."

I looked up at him in mild surprise. "I've never thought about that before."

He shrugged. "I could be wrong, but. . . ."

I reached for a fourth beer. My head was buzzing from drinking the others on an empty stomach, but that night, I didn't care.

"You're very nice to listen to all this. You didn't have to."

"I wanted to. What affects my people affects me."

I noticed for the first time what a nice smile he had. Being career military, smiling isn't what he does much while he's on duty. Although he's somewhat aloof with women, he bonded with his men. He's a man's man, talking sports and occasionally passing out cigars. After hours, when it was too hot to toss a football around, he'd get some card games going. He's the type of leader who doesn't send his soldiers on a dangerous mission without leading the way himself. That got him a lot of respect.

"Has anything like this ever happened to you?" I asked.

"Yeah, when I was sixteen. I thought it was the end of the world."

I managed a smile.

"You'll live."

"I know, but I feel like dying."

He put both hands on my shoulders and looked into my eyes. "I don't know if it helps to hear this, Kathy, but you're very desirable."

I don't know what came over me, but I fell into his arms. I needed someone strong. I needed someone to make me feel wanted and he was there. The next thing I knew, his lips were on mine and he was unbuttoning my fatigues.

Half drunk and emotionally needy, I lacked the will to stop him. Boots and heaps of camouflage clothing hit the floor, one by one, until I was down to the one indulgence I brought with me—a matching set of pink cotton underwear. He pulled me against him and we tumbled to the floor, making love. In his arms, I took the comfort I so desperately needed.

After it was over, the realization of what I did hit me like a splash of cold water. I sat up suddenly.

"I'd better go."

He illuminated the dial on his watch. "It's only nine. Stay a few minutes longer. I'll make you glad you did."

"My tent mates will be concerned, Sir."

"Hey, when you're in my bed its Tony, not Sir."

"Thank you for being a good listener, Tony."

He nuzzled my neck. "I hope that's not all I was."

"No, not at all. You know how to make a woman feel wanted."

He kissed me one more time. "Go on, then. We'll pick up where we left off some other time."

I dressed hurriedly and smoothed down my hair. I stepped outside to a dark and quiet camp and an increasingly queasy feeling in my stomach. I just slept with my sergeant. In a weak moment, I not only violated Army principles but I compromised myself.

The truth is that stuff like that happens all the time. I don't want to make it sound like all female soldiers are for the taking, because they're not. But there are some who go wild in the company of all these men, some of whom wouldn't give them a second glance if they were at home. There are even tales that circulate from camp to camp about certain girls.

I certainly didn't want to be one of them, yet I understood what could make people act out in a war zone. Not knowing if they're going to survive, they live as if each day were their last.

One of the realities of being a woman in the Army is that some of the men are never going to accept you. They put you in one or two categories from the start: bitch or whore. A bitch is someone who won't give them sex. A whore is someone who will. Up until then, I would've gladly been a bitch. I had Curtis as a shield. Now, I wasn't sure what I was.

On the way back to my tent, I stopped behind a trailer and discreetly threw up. Getting the letter from Curtis was a full-body blow. Then I made things even worse.

I cleaned my face off with some bottled water before entering my tent. Lisa, my other tent mate, was sitting on her cot across from Sheila.

"Where have you been? We were worried. We've been looking for you."

"I went out and burned Curtis's letters." I was too scared and ashamed to tell them the whole truth.

Lisa put her arms around me. "I'm really sorry about what happened. This probably isn't much comfort right now, but it's better to know before marriage than after that he's the wrong guy."

"I know."

Exhausted and desperate to shut out everything that had happened that day, I collapsed on my cot and fell into a troubled sleep.

I was back on duty at eight o'clock the next morning, sorting out a supply shipment. Despite liberal doses of coffee and aspirin, my head still throbbed. Unless you've been wounded or are seriously ill, nobody in the Army calls in "sick."

It was the distraction of my work that got me through the day. Just like I was taught in basic training, I focused on my mission. But looming in the periphery were thoughts of the day before. Nothing I did could make them go away.

I felt like one big, walking wound. Worse yet, I'd poured salt into it and I wasn't going to be able to avoid Sgt. Rick. I saw him again that evening. I was coming back from taking a shower when he asked if he could see me in his tent. He looked like he'd just come off duty and was outfitted in full gear, including his rifle. Over six feet tall, he was an imposing sight.

On the other hand, I was in sweatpants and a T-shirt and my hair was dripping wet. As soon as I stepped into the tent, he swept me into his arms. His eyes were dusky with desire. "I've been thinking about you all day. How about an encore?"

A jolt of alarm went through me. I pulled away. "Sergeant, I'm sorry, but what happened last night shouldn't have happened."

His gaze darkened. "You mean because I outrank you?"

"It's not just that."

A muscle twitched in his jaw. "What do you mean? You were enjoying it as much as I was. Admit it."

"I was upset. I wasn't thinking clearly. I needed comforting and I got carried away."

"Hey, we were good together. Stop feeling guilty."

"I'm sorry, Sergeant. It was a mistake."

His expression hardened. "All right."

"Please don't take any offense."

"None taken. I understand."

I smiled stiffly. "Thank you."

He unzipped his tent flap. "Good night, Corporal."

"Good night, Sir."

I left the tent with a mixture of regret and mild relief. I wasn't able to undo the night before, but I did all that I could. Although I could tell by the expression on his face that he didn't like being rejected, that's understandable. At least he seemed to respect my decision. That's all I could ask.

Within a few days I started to get my bearings back. I made a big mistake, but no one would have to know—or so I thought. I was helping unload a supply truck when I noticed that the two guys I was working with were giving me the eye. One was Cpl. Garrison. The other was his buddy, Pvt. Anderson, who I knew only from the name strip above his pocket. Both were in country longer than I was. Garrison is a baby-faced guy who is well over six feet tall and built like a bear. Rumor was that a bad incident near Baghdad left him shaky and paranoid. Both were serving second tours.

"Corporal, did anybody ever tell you that you've got a cute little behind?" Anderson asked. His pale eyes glistened through the sandy grit on his tanned face.

Ignoring him, I kept working.

"Hey, Williams," Garrison said. "I'm not wearing any underwear today. Wanna see?"

Ignoring him also, I tossed him a box that must have weighed forty pounds. He barely caught it.

"I've got a hole in the front of my pants," he pointed out. "Come on, take a peek."

I feigned boredom. What he said wasn't any news to me. I saw some of them play a silly game in which they tried to throw pebbles through the holes in each other's pants.

"Oh, well, I tried," he said. "Word is that you prefer sergeants."

My gaze shot to his like an arrow as my heart scurried into my throat. "What are you talking about?"

"Oh, nothing," Garrison said nonchalantly. "But if you ever need comforting, the flap of my tent is always open."

My cheeks burned.

"So is the back of my Humvee," Anderson said. At that point, I noticed he was wearing a wedding band.

"You have no right to talk to me this way," I said, my voice trembling. "This is a military camp, not some stateside red-light district. I'm a soldier, not a whore. And even if I were, I'd draw the line at the likes of either of you."

"Wooooo!" Garrison mocked.

"If only your mothers could hear you now," I snapped. "Or your wife," I said, looking directly at Anderson. "They'd be so proud."

Their smiles faded.

"You can finish this job by yourselves," I said, stalking off.

I went to my tent and sat stunned, barely able to breathe. A lot of female soldiers were the targets of sexually loaded remarks, but that was different. It was obvious that Sgt. Rick let it be known that we'd slept together. For eighteen- or twenty-year-old male soldiers to make stupid comments is one thing, but for a sergeant to be so indiscrete is another.

I dropped my head into my hands. How could he? Couldn't he see that I've been through enough already? I know he wasn't pleased when I told him that I made a mistake. I could tell by the set of his jaw and the look in his eyes, but apparently he took it as an affront to his manhood. Telling about it must've been his way of getting even.

I was hurt, humiliated, and above all, mad.

Sheila walked into the tent. The dried sweat on her uniform left white streaks that revealed the outline of her bra. Needless to say, that was not anything that went unnoticed by some of the men.

"Feeling any better?" she asked.

"No, worse. And I didn't think it could get any worse."

She stripped off her gear and sat across from me. "How's that?"

"Have you heard anything about me and Sgt. Rick?"

"No."

"Before long, the whole camp will probably know, so I might as well tell you."

When I finished, her eyes narrowed with anger. "If I had the rank, I'd bust him down so far that there wouldn't be anything left but the soles of his boots."

"I know that what I did was stupid, but thanks for standing by me anyway."

"What he did was worse."

"On top of that, I've still got to work under him," I replied.

I told Lisa when she walked in.

"Yeah, I heard," she acknowledged reluctantly. "I told people that there was no way it could be true."

I felt my coloring deepen. "Sorry, I just kind of went crazy that night."

"It's all right. I understand."

Sheila got us some MREs—meals ready to eat—and came back to the tent. I managed to choke down some spaghetti. I was starting to feel my weight drop off and being thin already, I didn't have it to lose. Sheila and Lisa talked about what restaurants they were going to hit the minute they got home, but all I could think about was being the talk of the camp.

The more I thought about it, the more indignant I got. I don't believe that Sgt. Rick actually encouraged anybody to harass me, but I deeply resented the fact that he told some of his men what happened between us.

"What those soldiers said to me was illegal. I have a notion to file a formal complaint against them."

"I'd think twice before I did," Lisa said.

I felt a throb of surprise. "What do you mean?"

"In civilian life, it would be easier, but this is still a man's Army and it's a whole lot more complicated. I've heard stories."

"Like what?"

"You might not be able to count on these particular guys to help you if you ever take enemy fire. You might have to kiss your chances for a promotion good-bye. At the least, they'll come down on you for being too soft for the Army."

"But the rules are on my side," I argued.

"So are we," Sheila said, "but what we're trying to say is that it might not be worth it. They'll hang out every conceivable piece of dirty laundry that you've got."

"Half the camp has already seen it," I countered.

"You'll be leaving in six months. Maybe it would be easier just to lay low and ride it out. In filing a complaint your name is supposed to be kept confidential, but it gets out. If you're going to file one, save it for something big like rape."

I took a deep breath. I knew what they were really saying. I wasn't in the best position to complain. It would be next to impossible to discuss the soldiers' comments without revealing what prompted them. I really put my foot in it that time.

Ignoring the problem, however, didn't make it go away. The next day, another of Sgt. Rick's subordinates approached me as I was headed to work.

"Hey, how about coming to my tent tonight? I can make a girl forget all her troubles."

My stomach lurched as I looked at the smirk on his sunburned face. "Don't you ever talk to me like that again. Tell your friends that the same goes for them."

"What's the matter? Don't you like us?"

"Get out of here," I snapped.

"Let me know if you change your mind," he said, swaggering away.

A hot wave of anger engulfed me. I wanted to give Sgt. Rick a piece of my mind, but how could I dress down a superior? Taking it over his head through a formal complaint would have its own set of repercussions. Plus, it would take a lot of time to go through all the proper channels. I wanted it to stop. My only choice was to handle the matter informally and very carefully.

I took a deep breath to calm myself and walked to Sgt. Rick's tent.

I found him inside, cleaning his weapon. As I entered, he glanced at me with barely concealed interest.

"Hello, Corporal," he said smoothly. "What can I do for you?"

My heart pounded in my ears. "Sergeant, if some of your men were causing problems, would you want to be told about it?"

"Of course. What are they doing?"

"They've been making inappropriate remarks."

"What sort of remarks?" he asked with a tone of innocence.

"Remarks suggesting that I sleep with them just as I did you. I mean no disrespect, Sir, but how did they know about us?"

He leaned forward. "Are you suggesting that I told them?"

"They found out somehow," I said evasively.

He leaned forward. "This is a small camp. It's hard to do anything, even at night, without somebody getting ideas. Somebody must have seen you enter or leave my tent and jumped to conclusions."

I struggled to keep my voice steady. "It was more specific than that. Several of the soldiers offered to 'comfort' me just as you had."

"All right," he admitted. "Someone mentioned having seen you go into my tent. I told them you were going through a bad breakup and needed to talk. Period."

I looked at him warily. I wasn't sure if I believed him or not.

"Kathy, I'm sorry about my men. I'll see that it doesn't happen again. If any one of them so much as looks at you sideways, let me know and I'll take care of it."

I started to relax a little. "Thank you."

"About the other night. You might be sorry about what happened, but I'm not. Things are different out here. It's not a monastery. Rules are broken. People look the other way. I'm not afraid of getting into trouble. You shouldn't be, either."

"Yes, Sir."

"Remember, as long as you're in my tent, its Tony, okay?"

I nodded and then got up. I should've felt a lot better, but I didn't. I knew the look of lust in a man's eyes and despite everything it was still there.

A week passed and, just as he promised, I had no more problems with any of the men. In fact, some of them saluted me as they walked by. The three offenders apologized. One of them gave me a box of snack crackers from home as a peace offering. I did my best to forget the ugly incidents.

But my troubles were not over. One evening, when I saw Sgt. Rick outside, I stopped to tell him that things had improved. I thanked him for bringing his troops into line.

"My men will do anything for me. I've saved a few of their hides."

Uncomfortable in his presence, I turned to leave but he called me back. "I'd like to talk to you a few minutes."

My heart thumped.

"Privately."

Unable to refuse a superior, I followed him into an equipment building. He unlocked the door to an office and ushered me inside, closing the door behind us. "So, you appreciate the way I got my men to shape up."

"Yes."

"Show me you really mean it."

Before I could respond, he took me roughly into his arms and kissed me. When I tried to pull away, he pinned me to the wall.

"No, please!" I begged.

"Come on, we were good together. If you're worried about your career, don't. I'll take care of everything. I've got friends at the top. I can even get you a promotion."

He pushed against me, kissing me so hard that my lips felt bruised. "You won't believe what I can do for you," he murmured.

I twisted sideways, breaking his hold. "Leave me alone or I'll report you!"

A glint of anger appeared in his eyes. "Who's going to believe you? Let's not forget who's got rank here."

"You have no right to force yourself on me."

"You have no right to grant me one night of fun and then cut me off like that. You don't do a man that way."

"What we did wasn't right. You know that."

"What you're doing to me is not right. You just might regret it."

My stomach lurched. "What do you mean?"

His mouth twisted into a spiteful grin. "Just take my word for it." He pushed open the door. "Have a nice day, Corporal."

I was so distraught for the rest of the night that I couldn't sleep. My head pounded and my stomach was in knots. I refused to submit to his desires, but neither could I let him destroy me.

He made it clear that he had friends up the line. He made it sound like he was untouchable, but the only way I was going to get out of the corner he put me in was to fight my way out. I wasn't without friends, either. At least I hoped he was my friend.

Capt. Joe Murray always treated me with respect when he had occasion to come to the supply area where I work. Once, he showed me a picture of his wife and baby daughter, which he'd just received that day. He told me he had a sister who lived in my home state. Once, I managed to get some hard-to-find supplies for him.

I scheduled a meeting with him a few days later. With no small amount of embarrassment, I told him the whole story. He listened for a long time without saying anything.

"I'm surprised," he said finally. "Rick is considered to be a good sergeant. He inspires a lot of loyalty."

I experienced a sinking feeling. Is he one of the "friends in high places" that Sgt. Rick claims to have? "But you have to believe me. I'm afraid of what he might try to do to me."

"I'll look into it," he promised.

In the meantime, some of Sgt. Rick's men started harassing me again.

"Hey, Kathy," one of them said. "I heard you might be able to help me out. See, I'm going to get married when I get home and I've got this goal to sleep with fifty women before I do. Would you be number forty-eight?"

Because incidents like this happen periodically to women in general, it was hard to prove that Sgt. Rick had something to do with it. But the real shocker came when Garrison swaggered up.

"How about letting me see some of that pink underwear?"

My cheeks stung. No one knew about my pink underwear but my tent mates and Sgt. Rick. He'd told them everything, after all.

"I don't know what you're talking about," I fibbed.

"Like heck you don't," he said with a laugh.

I reported each incident to Capt. Murray.

In the meantime, it was impossible to avoid the sergeant entirely. He didn't speak to me, but his you-can't-touch-me smirk said plenty.

A few weeks later, Capt. Murray asked to see me again. "I thought you would want to know that Sgt. Rick is being reassigned," he said. He should be out of the camp within forty-eight hours."

I stared at him in surprise. "Thank you. This is more than I expected. He talked like he had too many friends in high places for any harm to come to him."

"This did go to a higher level. He did get off easier than he could have. He'll retain rank. There will be no disciplinary action at this point, at least not for the record. He's simply being reassigned. It was felt that was the best and quickest way to deal with it."

I took a deep breath and let it out slowly, but the rest of the news tempered my relief.

"He denies having threatened you in any way and says he broke off the relationship. He claims your charges were motivated by revenge over being rejected."

I was aghast. "But he's lying. He forced himself on me."

"Without witnesses, reassigning him was the best we could do," he repeated. "He's under orders not to have any more contact with you."

I got up slowly. "Thank you, Captain."

I left his office trembling. In a parting shot, Sgt. Rick had turned the tables and made me the perpetrator. I was grateful to be safe from him, but what about the next female soldier?

Word got around about what happened. The camp became quiet. I felt self-conscious, as though everyone was looking at me. Some of the men gave me cold glances, but one by one, the women thanked me. At least for the time being, the camp was free of sexually charged remarks. I was exhausted from my ordeal, but I was glad that I did what I did.

The new sergeant was all business. He didn't shoot hoops with his men or joke around with them. He went out of his way to treat women with respect. Needless to say, Sgt. Rick's buddies didn't like him.

One night, maybe as fallout from all the stress I'd endured, I woke up with stomach cramps. The latrine was about a five-minute walk from my tent. I didn't want to wake Lisa or Sheila, so I grabbed a flashlight and went by myself. Men and women were discouraged from going anywhere alone, but there were guards posted around the camp day and night.

Not far from the latrine, I approached one of the guards. To my dismay, it was Garrison.

"Well, look who's here," he said, glancing at his watch. "It's past two in the morning. My, my. Who's tent have we been to tonight?"

"I'm going to the latrine," I said, pushing past him.

About ten minutes later, as I started back to my tent, I heard rapid footsteps behind me. Just as I turned, a hulking form jumped me, knocking me to the ground. My flashlight flew out of my hand.

"This is for Sgt. Rick," he growled, kneeing me in the back. It was Garrison. His crushing weight left me breathless, unable to cry out beyond a whisper. All I could do was twist and flail, but I was no match for my assailant.

"Let me go!"

He clamped a gritty fist over my face. "Not until I get some justice for Sarge."

Keeping all his weight on me, he yanked me sideways and began ripping at the buttons on my pants.

I twisted my head furiously, managing to knock his hand off my face. "Help!"

To quiet me, he slammed his fist into the side of my head. There was a burst of pain followed by a shower of stars, but somehow I managed to stay conscious. Where are the other guards?

Suddenly, I heard footsteps running toward us. Garrison jumped up and tried to flee, but it was too late. I turned to see the unmistakable glint of a rifle in the moonlight.

"Stop!" a voice commanded.

Garrison dropped to his knees in the dirt and started crying like a baby. My head throbbing, I pulled myself upright.

"He tried to rape me."

As the man got closer, I could see that it was the new sergeant. He ordered Garrison to get up, but he was shaking so hard that he couldn't stand.

The sergeant aimed his flashlight at me. I could feel my eye starting to swell shut. "Are you all right?" he asked.

"Yes, thanks to you," I said weakly.

Suddenly, a couple of soldiers appeared who were on patrol.

"Get the MPs," the sergeant ordered.

As it turned out, Garrison had a complete mental breakdown that night. When they took him away, he was babbling incoherently and curled up into a fetal position. He was later deemed unfit for duty and sent home. The breakdown kept him from being charged with attempted rape.

Garrison, it turns out, had witnessed some of his friends being killed by a roadside bomb. He himself was hit in the neck by a piece of shrapnel. If it weren't for Sgt. Rick's immediate first aid, he would've died.

What Garrison did to me was out of some sort of twisted loyalty to the man who saved his life. Obviously, he had some problems to start with, but under the stress of war, he cracked.

There's no doubt that I helped set into motion the awful chain of events that happened to me. I used poor judgment in trying to drink myself numb, which in turn led Sgt. Rick to take advantage of me, but the price I paid was higher than I could've imagined.

Sadly, there's a greater chance of a female soldier being sexually assaulted by a comrade than by the enemy. To some scared, insecure, and sex-hungry soldiers, we'll never be more than sex objects on the battlefield.

My tour in Iraq is over, but now I'm engaged in a different kind of fight. I'm writing to congressmen and talking to anybody who will listen, especially female recruits. I want them to learn from my experience. I want to help improve conditions for women in the military. As long as women are dying for our country, we shouldn't have to fight for respect on our own front lines.

THE END

CONFESSIONS OF A SISTER
"My Brother's A Killer!"

I swallowed hard as a man near one of the white crosses folded his arms on his chest and glared at me.

Thank goodness Paul was holding tight to my arm. He didn't want to be there—didn't want me to be there either—but he wouldn't let me go alone. He's that kind of guy, and I love him so much for being there for me when it would have been so much easier for him to stay home.

A cold wind blew across the parking lot, stabbing my sweat-soaked back. Gray clouds hovered overhead, threatening to make the March day even more dismal, as if it was possible for things to get worse. My brother was a murderer.

He shot and killed three innocent school children and then turned the gun on himself. In typical Dean style, he'd left me to clean up his mess and deal with a town full of angry people. How on earth was I supposed to handle this?

My hands were shaking as we started the journey from my Civic toward the three tiny white wooden crosses that had been staked into the ground next to the elementary school swing set.

It was surreal to look at it in person after seeing it on the television news for the past forty-eight hours. The entire playground was surrounded by crime scene tape and three uniformed police officers were walking around.

"There she is," someone hollered from across the parking lot. But before I could tear my eyes off the playground to see who was yelling, a flash went off, blinding me, as a photographer jumped, seemingly out of nowhere, and took my picture.

Paul steered me away from the reporter as I tried to blink to clear my vision. "It's not too late," Paul whispered, leaning close, "we can go back home."

I shook my head and straightened my shoulders. I had to do this. I had to face the consequences of my brother's action. And maybe I had to take some of the blame for this, too.

"We don't want a killer's family here!" a woman cried out from the distance. Tears stung the sides of my eyes. I knew by coming here that I'd be facing the wrath of the town. They hated me just for being related to Dean. Truth is, I hated me for being related to him, too.

"Go home. You don't deserve to be here!" the woman cried again. This time I caught a glimpse of the face behind the barbed words. Joanna Johnson—a hard-working teacher who came into my restaurant at least once a week. She'd been outside with the children when the shootings had happened and broke her leg trying to dive in front of a bullet aimed at one of the boys.

I didn't want to cry, didn't want to show them their words hurt me so badly, but I couldn't stop the tears leaking from my eyes and down my cheeks. Mrs. Johnson must have noticed the tears, even from across the lot, because she pressed her lips together hard and glanced away as if she was holding back from saying anything else.

"I dumped your food in the trash! And I won't ever be eating in that filthy restaurant again!" the man with his arms crossed over his chest, Troy Tinley, said. He was referring to the meals I'd had my restaurant employees deliver to each of the victim's houses.

I shivered at the harsh tone of his voice, not because I was worried about the loss of business, but because I didn't know if I'd done the right thing by sending the food. Was I rubbing salt in the wounds of these families by trying to help? Why didn't I ever seem to know what to do to make things right? Especially when it came to my brother Dean.

Our God fearing parents had been strict, and I'm sure they did their best for us. At least that's how I liked to look at them. But maybe, as my younger brother Dean always said, I saw life through rose-colored glasses.

Dean hadn't always been a troublemaker. I'm not one to lay blame on other people—because really, what good does it do?—but if I had to pin a date on the event that changed him, it would be the day in second grade when the other boys teased him for being overweight. He did what he always did—ignored them, played by himself in the sandbox while the playground "monitors," the teachers who were supposed to be guarding the kids from harm, turned their heads the other way. But the words soaked through the thick skin my brother pretended to have.

And he didn't tell me about that playground episode. I heard about it from a friend—a friend whose younger sister had stood up for my brother. And that had made things worse. What boy needed a girl to come to his aid during recess?

And after she told the teacher on those boys, the teacher called all the parents. And when she'd phoned my house and told my parents what happened, my father decided it was time to teach Dean how to take up for himself by enrolling him in karate. Dean came home crying after the first class and refused to go back. I never knew why.

By middle school, things got worse for Dean. He made "friends" with the bullies by performing risky acts that made them laugh. Even if I hadn't been five years older, I would have known that when the boys stopped picking on him and started daring him to do things that would get him in trouble, it was just another form of bullying. They would run away laughing while he was being hauled off to the principal's office.

Through suspensions—for smart-mouthing teachers, throwing a desk out a window, and pulling the fire alarm—Dean considered those boys to be friends. By high school, his crimes escalated into destruction of property and assault, and Dean was kicked out of school.

When he turned eighteen a year later, my parents kicked him out of the house, trying to teach him to stand on his own two feet—their words, not mine. I wish I could have taken him in, especially now that I know how important it might have been. But I was only twenty-three, just out of college, had three roommates, and was starting my first job as a restaurant manager. I didn't have the time, the space, or the money to help him. And he had nothing. He disappeared and I didn't hear from him for three years. I didn't know if he was dead or alive.

A few months before the shooting he surfaced again, and I took him in when he showed up on our doorstep that rainy, cold night. Paul and I offered him coffee and a hot meal. Paul was actually the one who thought we should let him stay a while and that we should help him get a job. Paul saw the potential in my brother. Dean was smart, funny and had a great memory. He loved to watch Jeopardy and usually got most of the answers right.

I couldn't help thinking that he would have done really well in school if he'd only applied himself. But school had let him down, proved to be too rule-oriented and filled with turmoil. So, even when Paul and I offered to pay his tuition for a year, he wouldn't enroll at the community college.

But one day I came home to find the upstairs toilet running. Dean, who had been out looking for a job at fast food restaurants, wandered in behind me.

"Looks like this piece fell off here," he reached into the cold, toilet tank water and fiddled with a metal rod, "and it's supposed to fit in here." And with a quick flip of his wrist the water stopped running and the toilet was as good as new.

We looked at each other and Dean laughed. What a great sound it was, because Dean hardly ever laughed—it was hard to even get a good smile out of him. And at the exact same time, we both said, "Plumbing school!" It was our "a-ha" moment. He'd always loved to tinker with parts and fix things.

"I'm in!" he'd said with as much enthusiasm as I'd ever heard him muster up.

"Let's Google local schools," I said, smiling and hurrying down the steps to the computer, all the while whispering a silent prayer that there would be an immediate opening in the class. There was no time to waste. We'd finally found an interest for him and I, for one, was not going to let the chance slip away.

As I used the search engine, he hovered behind me, his breath close to my neck, his breathing heavy. He was actually excited! And I was excited that he was excited about something.

"Want me to do the search?" he asked, trying to conceal his excitement. In his mind, it wouldn't be cool to be excited about school.

And then we both saw it at the same time—a plumbing school that was only a mile from my house.

Again, he smiled. "That's the one," he said, holding a palm up so I could give him a high five.

So Dean started school the next week.

His first day of plumbing school was like a child's first day of kindergarten—he was nervous and excited at the same time.

I offered to drive him because he'd let his license expire, and couldn't have afforded insurance even if he could drive. But he wanted to walk the one-mile stretch of road.

For the next two and a half months, Dean seemed to be turning his life around. He started shaving regularly, taking care of his appearance, and was getting excited about having a paying job as a plumber's assistant. He'd even made a friend or two at plumbing school—real friends, this time.

Maybe I let my guard down. I had always been the one who looked out for him. But suddenly, he was looking out for himself. And it was such a great burden lifted off my shoulders that maybe I didn't notice something that I should have.

I've gone over that morning again and again—hundreds or thousands of times—since the shooting. Was there something I should have noticed? Was I in too much of a hurry to see that he needed someone to talk to?

But, as Paul said, "It's too late for regrets. They wouldn't change a thing."

The morning of the shooting, I'd been whistling as I made a hearty pancake breakfast. Dean poured a coffee and sat at the small, checkered table in my kitchen, just like he'd been doing for the past few months.

After Dean left the house that clear and windy morning, I'd been hurrying to wash dishes before I had to head to the restaurant to get ready for the lunch prep when I heard the sirens. Whenever I hear sirens, I always whisper a little prayer for whomever the emergency vehicles are heading for.

I knew Paul was safely at work by then, and Dean had walked to school, so nobody in my household could have gotten in a car accident. Little did I know, those sirens weren't for a car accident, they were police and emergency vehicles heading to the local elementary school.

Half an hour later, I grabbed my purse from the hook in the foyer and pulled open the door to find two policemen standing there.

"Tonya Billings?" the tall policeman asked.

My heart started beating double time. Why would the police be on my front porch?

All I could do was nod.

"Do you mind if we come in . . . ask you a few questions?"

Somehow, I found my voice. "What's this about?" I asked, stepping aside as they crossed the threshold and stepped in my small foyer.

"Is Dean Snyder your brother?"

Oh no! A car had hit Dean on his walk to school! I'd told him not to wear his iPod while he walked near traffic. Had he taken a chance, and tried to hurry across the road before it was all clear?

"D-Dean's hurt?" I felt my purse slip from my shoulder onto the floor and my legs felt like they'd give out at any moment.

One of the policemen—I couldn't even remember now which one it was—guided me to a chair.

"Ma'am, did your brother own a gun?"

At the time, I didn't notice that he used past tense when talking about Dean. I must have looked pretty shocked, and all I did was stare at them. A gun? Why on earth would they be asking me about a gun?

At that moment, I realized how my parents must have felt when the principal, or later the police department, would call about something Dean had done.

A sinking, completely terrifying feeling that made past worries I'd experienced pale in comparison to the possibilities of what Dean might have been involved with, started to eat away at my gut.

"W-what did he do?" My voice sounded shaky and weak, just like my whole body. "Should I get a lawyer?"

The dark-haired policeman blew out a sigh. "Ma'am, you're not in any trouble, and your brother. . . ." he threw a glance at his partner. "I'm sorry to inform you that it appears that your brother killed three children at the elementary school, then killed himself."

At first, I didn't say anything. It was as if the world suddenly stopped rotating and time stood still—nobody moved, nobody spoke and the policeman's words sort of hovered above us. "Ma'am?" one of the officers asked, squinting at me.

"With a gun?" After the words came out of my mouth, I realized that's what they'd been asking. But why was that the first thing that came out of my mouth? Why not something like, "No way! He didn't do that?" or "You've got the wrong guy!" But none of these words would come out. Because somewhere, deep in my gut, I knew he probably was capable of murder.

Where had he gotten the gun? Why would he shoot children?

The police let their words sink in, and, thinking back, they were actually very nice to me. They let me call Paul, and instead of looking at me with blaming eyes, they looked at me as if I could help them solve the puzzle—and the puzzle had been easier to solve once we found the letter in his room.

The police had been very nice, too, about keeping the press from trespassing. The reporters and photographers parked out by the curb, and stood on the sidewalk, but that was as close as they were allowed to come.

Paul and I quietly closed all the curtains after the police left that afternoon. We turned on the television. And for the past two days, that was how we learned how my brother's actions have torn apart the lives of hundreds of people in our town.

I lived with my brother—I even talked with him over pancakes that morning—and I had no clue what he planned to do.

Could I have known?

All these thoughts were running around in my head as I searched the school parking lot with Paul's steady hand on my arm. I needed to do the right thing. And deep in my heart, I knew that being here, showing my respects was the right thing to do. Would I be able to go to the funerals, too? Would that make things worse or better?

One step at a time, one agonizing step at a time, I kept repeating to myself.

I didn't think it was possible to feel any emptier than I'd felt the past few days, but as Paul and I started toward those little wooden crosses, my heart beat hard against my ribs and it felt like the echoes of that beat were bouncing around an empty chamber. There was nothing left to throw up, nothing left to think about, and nothing that might turn back time and take all this away.

I couldn't take my eyes off those little crosses. I knew their faces so well now: Tommy Crocker, six years old, a Little League baseball pitcher with blond curly hair that made his little cupid face look even younger than his age. Tears started to sting the sides of my eyes. The other little boy, Jimmy Johnson was the youngest of six children. The image of his brothers and sisters—the pained looks of disbelief on their young faces—was a picture I'd like to erase from my mind. And the last face—the face, according to Dean's letter that inspired him to do the deed—was a little boy named Oliver Owens, a boy who was getting picked on by the others at recess.

"We have to stand here. Can't go any further," Paul said softly, giving my arm a squeeze.

I blinked to clear my eyes and felt tears start to roll down my face and was surprised to see we'd reached the edge of the playground.

From the corner of my eye, I caught a movement and when I turned, a flash went off, throwing off my balance, blinding me for a minute—another photographer.

What made me think I could do this? What made me think I should do this?

"Fine, fine. You got your picture, now get out of here," I heard one of the policeman say, as he walked toward the reporter and shooed him off with his hand. The policeman glanced my way and I noticed he was the same one who came to my house to bring me the bad news—Officer Smoot. He touched the tip of his hat and nodded at me, then turned back to the reporter.

The guy threw a glance at me, shrugged, then replaced the camera lens and turned to cross the parking lot.

What did he care if the cops chased him off? He'd gotten what he came for, right? Is that what I got for coming here?

Dropping to my knees, facing the crosses, I suddenly knew why I'd felt so drawn to come here. A sudden calm fell over my fast-beating heart, and my tears dried up for the first time in days. Paul stayed beside me, still standing, with a hand on my shoulder as if he was keeping guard.

I folded my hands and closed my eyes. I wanted to pray, that's what I wanted to do. Say a prayer for the children. And that's what I started to do, until I heard a noise to my left, a choked sob.

My eyes flew open and I spotted the father of one of the boys standing close to the crime tape, holding it in his hands as if he wanted to rip it apart, as if that would make it as if the whole thing never happened.

I couldn't do this. I wasn't strong enough to see the devastation that my brother had brought to these people. And, as much as a big part of me wanted to say a prayer for the children, I also wanted to be at the place where my brother had taken his last breath, too.

I fell to the ground, no longer afraid of what anyone thought, no longer caring who took my picture or who thought what. I started to sob like I've never cried before. I leaned forward, face in the cold, trampled grass and let it out.

As sobs wracked my body, turning every bone into a quivering mass of sticks, I stopped worrying about what these people thought of me, stopped worrying about how I'd be able to face them knowing my brother—my own flesh and blood—had robbed their lives of any chance of happiness. I let myself give into the sadness that had been overwhelming me for so long. Three children dead. My brother dead. A whole town of people crushed beyond belief that such a thing could happen here.

"I'm sorry! I'm sorry," I sobbed, hitting the damp ground with my fist as if I could turn things around and make them better.

"Please God, take care of these children, they didn't deserve this. . . ." The words kept pouring out, as if not only the floodgate of tears had been opened, but that the words my heart had been holding onto so tight were now released into the world, too.

The ground was wet with my tears and I could feel Paul's hand stroking my back and I realized that even though I thought the reason I needed to come here was to pay my respects, I'd come to purge myself, too. I couldn't help Dean anymore. I couldn't protect him and I couldn't defend his behavior.

Sniffing the last of the sobs away, I wiped my hand across my eyes, clearing my vision as I sat up.

The parking lot and playground area had been busy with people gawking and wandering around earlier. Now, all eyes were pinned on me.

Paul stooped beside me.

"I guess I made a spectacle of myself, huh?" I said, sniffling as I tried unsuccessfully to lift the corners of my mouth into a half smile. He cupped my elbow in an attempt to help me to my feet.

"No," a deep voice said as someone gently grabbed my other elbow and helped lift me to my feet. I turned toward the voice, surprised to see Matt Owens—the father of the boy who'd been being bullied. "No," he repeated as I looked into his red-rimmed eyes and felt the tears start to form in my eyes again.

The man looked horrible. His kind face was wracked with pain, there were dark circles under his red swollen eyes, and he looked like he'd aged ten years since I saw him last week.

"None of this is your fault," Matt said, his face serious, his eyes sparkling with fresh tears, making me want to turn away in guilt. "You gave that boy every chance," he said, and then looked around at the angry parents who stood back glaring at me. If looks could kill, I'd be dead.

Keeping his hand on my elbow, he gave it a squeeze, sending a glimmer of hope through my entire body. Maybe things would be okay, eventually.

Turning to face the crowd, Matt said, "Tonya didn't do anything except get born into the same family as Dean and you all know it. She tried to help him. None of this is her fault."

Was it my imagination, or did the antagonism I'd felt since I'd stepped out of my car suddenly lesson? A photographer stepped forward, flashing a picture, but I didn't care as much anymore. Maybe I wasn't in this alone. Maybe, in time, there might be some understanding. Forgiveness was too much to ask, but understanding would be more than I could ever expect.

"Thank you, Tonya, for the pasta and salads you sent." I turned to face Cindy Owens—a petite blonde. She'd lost her son because of my brother, but she was standing here with swollen, red eyes, thanking me for food I'd sent.

"Cindy . . . I. . . ." but the words were choked back as a sob escaped my throat, and fresh tears started to spill. I didn't dare ask for forgiveness for all he'd done. But that's what Cindy was offering, and she and her husband were, through their actions, telling the rest of the town that they should forgive, too.

Cindy pulled me into her arms and I could feel her tiny body quiver with grief as we held each other and looked at those three tiny white crosses. Sorrow for the lives, for the boys, and what they might have lived to be washed over me. I couldn't imagine the pain that my brother's deed had brought on these parents. Pain they'd be living with forever. Again, guilt washed over me.

Life would never be the same for any of these people. But somehow, at least some of them could understand that life would never be the same for me either. It was more than I'd dared to ask for.

I could pack up and leave this town, start over. Paul had already suggested that. But that would be too easy and would be like running away from my problem. But would it be cruel to stay here? Was I going to be a reminder to all these people of what happened? Maybe it wasn't running away if I was doing it to spare them grief.

"Tonya," Cindy said, sniffling as she pulled away and threw a glance at her husband. "Do you think it would be okay to have the wake at your restaurant after tomorrow's funeral?" She sniffed and then wiped her nose with a tissue and looked toward the sky as if searching for her son. "We can't fit everyone in our house."

I opened my mouth, then frowned, closing it again. My throat was too tight to answer, so I just nodded several times. I'd give them the biggest feast I could pull together. I'd open my entire restaurant for them. I'd make sure these parents didn't have to worry about a thing. And they wouldn't pay for a thing, although I wouldn't address that right now.

Cindy nodded, then heaved a sigh as she glanced at the crosses again, reached for her husband's hand and started walking to their car.

More photographers moved forward, and a TV news van squealed into the parking lot as I stood by the taped-off area. But none of that mattered as I watched Cindy and her husband climb into their car, oblivious to the press. The other parents started talking amongst themselves, turning to their own conversations.

"Want to go, now?" Paul asked, his supportive hand still cupping my arm, making me feel loved.

With one last glance at the three crosses, and a silent prayer that

God might forgive my brother and keep the young boys in His care, I nodded. I turned, risking one more glance toward a group of parents, and caught the eye of the man who'd cried out to me when we'd left our car. I mouthed the words, "I'm sorry" to him and I thought I saw his chest heave with a deep breath before he blew it out and uncrossed his arms and nodded.

Breathing easier, I leaned into Paul as he pulled me close and we walked with our arms around each other's waists toward my car. I had someone by my side. Someone who would help me make it through this.

THE END

CONFESSIONS OF A BROKEN WIFE
"Bringing My Family Together"

My world couldn't have been more perfect. My husband, Steve, and I had been married for fifteen years. We had two beautiful, well-adjusted teenage children who were the light of our lives. Steve and I both held down good-paying jobs—Steve was an anesthesiologist and I was an assistant bank manager—and we lived in a well-to-do neighborhood. We were definitely enjoying the good life!

Then one day an unexpected phone call shattered our perfect lives.

Steve was working late at the hospital, the children, Melissa and Brandon, were both attending after-school functions, and I finally had an evening to myself to soak in the swimming pool in our backyard.

I was just sipping a margarita when the phone rang. Floating to the edge of the pool, I scrambled to the deck and reached for the phone on the lawn table.

"Hello?" I said breathlessly, while I dried my hair with the towel draped over the chair.

There was no answer, although I could hear someone breathing on the other end.

"Is someone there?" I asked, annoyed.

Heaving a frustrated sigh, I was just about to disconnect when a timid male voice finally responded. "Is this Margaret Wilson?"

I slumped down into the wicker chair. I hadn't been called Margaret Wilson in years.

"It's Margaret Dunn now," I answered, cautiously. "Who's calling?"

Another long pause ensued before he spoke again. "My name is Zack O'Dell. I'm the son you put up for adoption seventeen years ago."

The silence continued from my end of the line as I struggled for a suitable response to the astonishing news. What could I say to the child I'd been forced to abandon all those years ago? My heart palpitated from a myriad of emotions that I couldn't understand.

An unexpected chill snaked across my wet body, and I wrapped the towel tighter around my shoulders, and placed my elbows on the table. My free hand cupped my mouth as I fought back the tears that found their way down my cheeks.

"I know this is a shock," the voice claiming to be my son said. "I'm not calling to cause you any trouble."

I didn't miss the catch in his own voice as he spoke. He seemed desperate, lonely.

"I just want to meet you," he continued. "I need to meet you."

And I immediately knew I wanted to meet him. I wanted to finally see the child that I hadn't been allowed to see before he was whisked away to some unknown family.

Of course, Steve had always known about the child I'd put up for adoption during my high school years. While he'd been sympathetic to my situation during our early years of dating, I wasn't sure he'd understand my need to see my son at this time in my life. After all, our lives had evolved into a joyous family of four. Was there room for another, even if he was my own flesh and blood?

Some part of me wondered why he was contacting me. How did he even find me? Is his family life so horrendous that he suddenly felt the need to find his real family? Is he ill and in need of medical attention that only a blood relative can provide?

It was for those reasons that I decided to keep the meeting secret for the time being. Until I had more information, how could I be sure this young man really was who he claimed to be? Of course, my husband had to be told of the meeting, but not until I was sure there was something to tell.

We'd agreed to meet the following day at an outdoor park. I explained to my family that I had a business meeting to attend to after work. I promised to pick up dinner on the way home.

Since late meetings were not uncommon at my job, no one questioned my motive.

My heart beat with eager anticipation as I parked the car in the lot and killed the engine. My knuckles gripped the steering wheel as I fought back tears.

Would I recognize my own son? How would I feel seeing him for the first time? And even more importantly, how would the son I abandoned feel about me?

My legs felt wobbly as I exited the car and began walking toward the small manmade lake.

A young man was sitting on a park bench beneath a tall tree, shredding pieces of bread and tossing them to the ducks. His back seemed to stiffen as I approached, and at that moment I knew I'd soon be face-to-face with the son I'd wondered about for seventeen years.

He stood and turned suddenly, and my heart caught in my throat. I would have recognized him anywhere. His coal black hair, which he wore just slightly above his ears, complimented his tanned, chiseled complexion. He looked so much like his biological father, I felt like I had stepped back in time.

Blinking back tears, I sucked in a deep breath and walked closer until we stood just inches apart.

"Hello Zack," I said cautiously. The name felt strange on my lips.

This young adult before me was my own flesh and blood, but still we were strangers meeting for the first time.

A slight smile curved his lips, while his green eyes remained emotionless.

"Hello," he responded.

We stood close enough to touch, but while I wanted nothing more than to wrap my arms around him, I felt a sense of uncertainty.

"I'm glad you called," I finally said, breaking the awkward silence. "I've never stopped thinking about you, wondering what happened to you."

He hung his dark head low, fidgeting with his fingers, as if searching for the right words. I had so many questions to ask him, but I didn't want to push. He'd obviously gone through a lot of trouble to find me, and until he was ready to share that information, I knew I needed to back off.

"I had a pretty good life, you know," he finally said, his eyes still focused on his hands. "Like I told you on the phone, I'm not here to cause you any trouble."

The tears fell freely then, the long-buried love finally spilling forth. Wiping my eyes with the back of my hand, I reached over and cupped his hand in mine.

"Why don't we sit down?" I said.

We talked nonstop once that initial awkward moment had passed. Zack told me about the people who had adopted him and raised him as their own.

While he'd always known he was adopted, he'd never felt cheated or less loved than any of his friends.

The O'Dells had been the perfect parents—at least until they'd both been tragically killed in a car crash a few months earlier. That's when Zack's extended adoptive family hired a private investigator to help him locate his biological mother.

I couldn't have been happier. The son I had given away had suddenly come back into my life. The fear of resentment I'd felt all those years was no longer a concern. Zack didn't hate me. He only wanted to get to know me as well as his siblings.

Unfortunately, it wasn't going to be that easy.

Later that evening while both children were out with friends, Steve and I were sitting by the pool, enjoying the peaceful evening and sipping after dinner drinks.

"I have something to tell you," I said, finally gathering the courage to spring the news on my husband.

Steve set his drink down and nodded.

"I figured there was something on your mind. You've been uncharacteristically quiet since you got home. What's up?"

I swallowed a long sip of my drink, and then sucked in a deep breath. I had no idea how Steve would take the news I was about to share, but I did know that he had always been there for me whenever I needed him. I had no reason to expect anything different now.

"I got a phone call yesterday," I began. "From the son I gave away before you and I met."

The silence was deafening. I waited for a while, continuing to look down, as I drew an imaginary figure on the glass tabletop. I kept hoping Steve would say something, but when he didn't, I glanced up, searching his face for a sign of what he was thinking.

His eyes were closed, and I couldn't help wondering if he'd closed his mind as well.

"Steve? Did you hear me?"

"I heard you," he finally responded, in a voice barely audible.

My frustration grew. "Well, will you say something?" I demanded. "This came as a shock to me, as well."

Steve paused for a second longer, before he finally turned to face me, his expression firm.

"Okay," he said. "I'll tell you what's on my mind, but you're probably not gonna like it."

I braced myself for a letdown, while wondering what he could possibly have against me meeting with my biological son. The Steve I had married would have done anything to please me, as I would have for him. The man sitting across from me suddenly felt like a stranger.

"What?" I whispered, cautiously.

Steve took the last swallow of his drink, then leaned forward and placed both arms on the table.

"Our lives are already set," he said, plainly.

"What?" I screamed. "What does that even mean? Nobody's lives are set. Life is a huge cycle of unexpected events. Some good, some bad."

"And how would you classify this unexpected event?" he asked, calmly. "Good or bad?"

Tears stung my eyes. While I knew that this news would come as a surprise, I hadn't counted on this kind of reaction.

Swallowing the hurt, I managed to look my husband in the eye to utter my next words.

"He's . . . my . . . son!"

The simple statement came out harsher than I'd planned, even though Steve's callous attitude really hurt me. I didn't want to fight. I just needed my husband to be as supportive as he'd always been in the past whenever unfamiliar situations cropped up.

Reaching over the table, I placed my hand over his to soften the mood.

"He's not looking for anything other than a family," I said. "His adoptive parents were killed recently. He's just a lonely, confused seventeen-year-old boy who wants to connect with his biological family. Why can't you be happy for me?"

Steve's expression softened as well. Rubbing my hands across my eyes, I wiped away the lingering tears, and managed a hopeful smile. His next words touched my heart.

"I just don't want to see you get hurt. These kinds of things don't always end well."

I knew he was right. When Zack first called, I had mixed feelings. While one part of me longed to see my first-born son, another part of me worried about his real reason for locating me.

But Zack had seemed so sincere when we met at the park. I had no reason to think he had any ulterior motives other than trying to connect with a part of himself that he'd lost at birth. Didn't I owe it to him, and to myself, to try for a real relationship?

Meeting my husband's wary gaze, I offered an appreciative smile.

"I don't think I could possibly hurt any more than I did when I gave him up seventeen years ago," I said, with tears in my eyes. "But I do realize your concern. Believe me, I don't expect this to suddenly become one big happy family reunion."

"I'm glad you realize that," Steve said with a heavy sigh. "Because it probably won't."

Steve insisted on telling the children about their long-lost brother immediately. A part of me felt that he was secretly hoping their reaction would be unfavorable to having a stranger welcomed into our perfect family.

For a moment, I really thought he might get his wish, but fortunately I'd raised my children to be caring and supportive of family and friends.

We broke the news to them at breakfast the following morning. Since our teenagers always seemed to have plans with friends and after-school activities during the week, we always claimed weekend mornings for a huge breakfast and family discussions.

"We have something to tell you," I began nervously, as I set a stack of pancakes in the center of the round kitchen table.

"Sounds mysterious!" Brandon responded as he forked a couple of pancakes onto his plate and reached for the syrup.

"You're not getting a divorce, are you?" Melissa joked, rolling her large green eyes at her brother.

Melissa and Brandon always commented on how disgusting they thought Steve and I were in public. After fifteen years, we still held hands, exchanged soft caresses, and genuinely had eyes only for each other.

As my children continued their mockery of our perfect lives, my gaze drifted to Steve's. Tears filled my eyes as I realized his expression revealed only concern about the news I was about to share.

Lowering myself into my chair, I reached for my cup of coffee and savored a long sip before responding.

"Nothing like that," I said. "But it is something serious. Something that will affect our lives."

Melissa and Brandon exchanged frightful glances, before looking to their father for assurance. Steve didn't crack a smile.

He simply said, "I think we should let your mother explain."

I'd never felt so betrayed in my life. I felt that the man I'd loved for over fifteen years, the man I'd counted on to be there for me when the going got tough, had suddenly abandoned me when I needed him most.

Choking back tears, I held my head high, avoided my husband's demeaning gaze, and offered a reassuring smile to my children.

After another sip of coffee and a long drawn out sigh, I told my children the secret I'd been hiding for seventeen years.

"You have a brother," I began. "An older brother, named Zack."

Their silence only fueled my desire to tell them everything and hope they'd be able to understand why I'd done what I did all those years ago. Surely, my longing to have my firstborn join our lives wouldn't be enough to tear apart our perfect family.

"I was sixteen when I discovered I was pregnant," I said, softly. "I was still in high school and terrified."

"So where is he?" Brandon asked, his expression unreadable. "Why haven't we met him?"

"Zack has been living with another family," I answered. "I didn't know where he was until a few days ago."

Melissa seemed to be digesting this new information. "So you gave him up for adoption? You gave away your own baby?"

I looked to Steve for help in explaining my situation, but the husband I'd known and loved seemed in his own world of turmoil. I was on my own, just as I had been seventeen years earlier.

"What about Grandma and Grandpa?" Melissa asked. "They would have helped you."

Her words dredged up feelings I thought I had buried forever. My parents had been anything but supportive during that painful period of my young life. With that one mistake, I had suddenly become nothing more than a huge embarrassment to my parents. Within a month, I had been shipped off to live with a distant, unmarried aunt I barely knew.

I pulled my eyelids tight, as if that simple gesture could banish that awful time from my memory. Then, wiping away the single tear that betrayed my strength and courage, I raised my head, meeting my children's startled expressions.

"It was a different time then," I said, honestly, although secretly my insides cringed at my parents' insensitivity. I knew I would always be there, with unconditional love and understanding, to help my children through any difficulty they would encounter throughout their lives. They were my children, and they deserved no less.

"He found you." Brandon made the statement rather than asking the question.

"Yes," I said. "He found me." I took another sip of my coffee, realizing it had grown cold. "Zack had a wonderful life," I told them, realizing how grateful I was to say those words. Just knowing that I'd relinquished the care of my own child to loving parents gave me strength to confront the demons that haunted me for so long.

"Unfortunately, Zack's adoptive parents were tragically killed in an accident." I glanced up again, this time willing my husband to look at me as I uttered my next words. "He's young, alone, and scared," I said forcefully. "He's looking for comfort and understanding from a family he's never been allowed to know."

Melissa glanced at her brother and shrugged.

"So when do we get to meet him?" she asked.

With tears now flowing freely down my face, I sprang from my chair and embraced my two children. Glancing over their shoulders, I met Steve's gaze, his expression was less than enthusiastic about the impending confrontation. I tried not to let it bother me, although I really needed the support he'd always given me in the past.

An hour later, I punched in the phone number Zack had given me. We agreed he would come to the house for Sunday dinner where he would finally meet the half brother and sister he'd never known he had.

I awoke on Sunday morning to a jumble of nerves. Nightmares plagued my sleep.

In one scene, I'd dropped off my three children, Melissa, Brandon, and Zack, at school before going to work. Then, later that afternoon, I'd sent Steve to pick them up. Happily, the three siblings raced down the school steps toward their father. But Steve held his outstretched hand at Zack's chest.

"You're not coming with us," he'd said. "I'm supposed to bring my family home."

Tears had soaked my pillow throughout the night. Rubbing my palms against my eyes, I reached out for Steve, but my hand fell upon a bare, soft pillow. Sliding across the bed, I slid my feet into soft slippers and reached for my robe at the end of the bed.

I followed the aroma of freshly brewed coffee downstairs to the dark kitchen. Flipping on the light, I reached into the cabinet for a cup, and poured myself some of the enticing brew.

Steve was nowhere to be seen, but I knew from past experience where to find him. Whenever we had a problem or a situation that required some intense thought, we'd always end up on the patio near the pool in the early morning hours.

With my brew in hand, I gently opened the patio door and stepped outside.

"Good day to watch the sun come up," I said.

He didn't turn around. He continued sipping his coffee with his back to me.

Sucking in a deep breath, I crossed the patio and took a seat next to him.

"Let's talk," I suggested.

"What's to talk about?" he asked, continuing to look away.

Setting my cup on the glass tabletop, I reached over and stroked his face, pulling him toward me.

"I'll talk," I said. "And you'll listen."

He started to pull away again, but I refused to allow it. Choking back fresh tears, I finally told my husband how much he meant to me.

"When I met you seventeen years ago, I was a sad, scared young woman. You knew my deepest, darkest secret, and yet you still loved me. I was the luckiest girl in the world to have found someone so wonderful."

"You took away the hurt. Each time I began to feel lonely and depressed, you were there to pick up the pieces. You always listened when I wanted to talk, never judging. I knew I could always count on you."

Steve squeezed my hand, a simple gesture that I eagerly returned.

His brown eyes misted with a hurt I'd never witnessed in all of our years together.

"Do you think you can't count on me now?" he asked.

I raised his hand to my lips and placed a gentle kiss on his knuckles.

"I know I can always count on you," I replied. "But I want you to know that you can also count on me."

He raised his eyebrows.

"Do you think I'm not aware of the turmoil going on inside of you? For the most part, your life has been fairly uncomplicated until now. But my life has never been uncomplicated. There are times when I've looked at our two beautiful children and wondered whatever happened to my first child. That turmoil has never left me in the seventeen years since Zack's birth. But other than being there for me, you've never really had to deal with the confusion and anger I felt."

"And now it seems the tables are turned. Now it's your life that is being turned upside down. And I just want you to know that I'm here for you now. I know you have doubts and concerns. But I am here to listen and help you." My lips brushed his knuckles again as I pleaded. "Please tell me what you're feeling."

At first, I thought he wouldn't answer. After a long, uncomfortable silence, he finally spoke, his voice choking with emotion.

"I'm ashamed of myself," he admitted, looking toward the brightening sky. "I like our life the way it's been. I don't want anything to complicate it. And I know I'm a terrible person for feeling that way."

Leaning my head on his shoulder, I smiled at the sun rising above the distant trees.

"You're a wonderful human being," I told him. "You're feeling the same things anyone would feel under similar circumstances. But instead of shutting me out and trying to deal with these feelings yourself, you need to talk to me and let me help, just as you've done for me all these years."

We continued to sit in the quiet solitude of our back patio, enjoying the beautiful sunrise, as well as each other's company. Holding hands in comfortable silence sent waves of encouragement throughout my body.

Steve and I hadn't faced many obstacles during our marriage, and this newest one was certain to cause a few episodes of unease, but I knew, without a doubt, that the love we felt for one another could withstand any hurdle tossed our way.

We took great pains planning an elaborate home cooked meal for our first family meeting with Zack.

As always, in our home sit down meals were prepared with everyone's help. Steve and Brandon cooked pork chops on the grill, while Melissa and I made salads and twice-baked potatoes. For dessert, we decided on ice cream sundaes.

When the doorbell rang at noon, my stomach knotted, as my emotions bounced between excitement and dread. I desperately wanted this meeting to go well, but I knew things were rarely that simple.

"Come in," I said, with a smile that I knew must be gushing with pride and nervous energy.

Zack smiled back and stepped inside, his gaze settling with uncertainty on his two half siblings standing beside me.

"Zack, I'd like you to meet Melissa and Brandon."

"Hi Zack," Melissa said, quickly.

"It's good to finally meet you," Brandon added, a bit shyly.

The four of us stood in the same spot, unsure of what our next move should be, until Steve finally broke the spell.

"Maybe we should let Zack come in and sit down," he suggested with a slight grin. "I'm sure we'll all find that a comfortable dinner will make everyone feel more at ease."

I could have kissed my husband right then and there. Steve had always been able to make even the most awkward situation seem less intimidating, and he hadn't let me down this time.

"Of course," I agreed, moving aside to slip my arm around my husband's back. "Zack," I said, "this is my husband, Steve."

"Nice to meet you, sir," Zack said, extending his hand.

"It's Steve," he corrected him, giving me a gentle squeeze.

Steve was right. Dinner proved to be the icebreaker we all needed. Between eating, drinking, and laughing, we learned that Zack had received a scholarship to a local college, which he'd be attending in the fall.

Along with the money he'd received from his adoptive parents' estate, Zack would probably never have to worry about the financial strains some college kids faced.

Melissa and Brandon seemed in awe of their new older brother, asking him all sorts of questions about his life growing up.

Zack talked with sincere love about his adoptive parents. He told of his love of golf, and how he and his father, a college coach, used to play every weekend. He bragged about his mother's accomplishments as a schoolteacher for the physically and mentally challenged.

My eyes filled with tears as I realized the son I had worried about for so many years had been blessed with wonderful parents who loved him dearly as their own.

Melissa glanced up, catching my tear-stained face.

"Mom, why are you crying?" she asked. "These are wonderful stories."

Zack answered for me, and at that moment my heart experienced an insurmountable joy.

"Because she's felt guilty all these years," he said with determination. "And now she knows there was no reason to. I was lucky to have the life I had. I wouldn't have changed anything."

Steve reached across the table and cupped his strong hand over mine.

"You're right, Zack," he agreed. "There was no reason to feel any guilt over something she had no control over. Besides, it looks to me like she's given all of us a wonderful life."

Brandon, never the one to be overly emotional, broke the spell.

"I think it's time for a swim before dessert," he said, tossing his napkin onto his plate. "How about it, Zack?"

"I didn't bring a suit."

"I'm sure Brandon can find a spare one to fit you," Steve said, as he helped me clear the dishes. "We'll stack the dishes, then meet you kids outside."

As we stacked the last of the dishes into the dishwasher, Steve took me into his arms and pulled me close. "It looks like things are off to a great start."

"I know," I said, softly, glancing up at him with an unspoken question. "But I also know that our lives will never be the same."

"You're right," he agreed. "One day our kids will grow up, have families of their own, and maybe even move away." He held me at arm's length and looked into my eyes with the love that had warmed my heart throughout our entire marriage. "But as long as you and I continue to grow with each other instead of apart, I can handle anything life wants to toss my way."

I pulled him back into my embrace.

"I'm not going anywhere." I said.

THE END

CONFESSIONS OF AN ANGRY TEEN
I'll Live My Life The Way I Want

I've been in trouble all of my life, it seems like, and the really bad part is that I never caused any of it. If somebody else wanted to create a problem, then, sure, I'd step up to the plate.

But contrary to popular opinion, I myself was not the problem!

For example, the first time I had to go to court, I was only thirteen. Old Lady Norwood, our next-door neighbor, had come over—again—to complain about the weeds that were growing on our side of the property line. She didn't know why we couldn't get rid of them. She kept yelling that they were driving her crazy!

Personally, I thought she was already there, but Mom didn't like it when I actually said stuff like that, so I kept it to myself. That woman was always threatening to call the city's weed Nazis and get us a big fat fine. Like my mom needed any more bills! She already worked three jobs, and we still had bill collectors calling night and day. A year ago, Dad maxed out all the credit cards, then ran off and left Mom to deal with it. It had been one piece of bad news after another ever since.

I don't know what more our neighbor lady thought we should do. My little sister, Ginny, and I'd sat out there in the hot sun for two whole Saturdays yanking those stubborn weeds out of the ground, but it seemed like for every one we pulled up, twelve more popped up to take its place. And now the old pain in the butt was on our front porch again, about to make my mom cry.

"Would it kill you to give us a break?" I jumped in. "It's not like we sit up nights over here hatching plots against you."

"Hush, Chrissy," Mom said. "I'll handle this."

"White trash!" Old Lady Norwood spat out, turning to leave. "That's what you people are!"

"And you're about as nasty as that old muumuu you're always wearing," I called after her.

She whirled around—well, somebody her size can't really "whirl," I guess—but she turned around and called me a little slut. A slut just because some of my guy friends liked to hang out at my house after school!

That really made me mad, and that's when I did hatch a plot to drive Old Lady Norwood over the edge. My friend, Mika, stole a condom from his older brother's stash, and we stuck some squishy vanilla pudding down inside it. Then, once it got dark outside, we snuck next door and left the thing in her mailbox.

The next day was Saturday. Mika came over again and we hung out on the porch just waiting for Mrs. Norwood to come out and get her mail. It was worth the wait. When she saw what we'd left her, I mean, she went ballistic! She let out a scream you could've heard on the next block and slammed that mailbox lid so hard it's a wonder she didn't break something. Then she started hollering at us, but by then we were laughing so hard we couldn't hear a thing she said, not that we really wanted to. After that, she huffed and puffed her way back into her house, and the next thing I knew, a cop car was pulling up.

Anyway, that's how I wound up in court the first time. Mika and I had to pull all the weeds on my family's side of the property line and keep them pulled all summer. We also had to do a bunch of community service; plus we got put on probation for approximately forever.

Mika completed his probation just fine, but I got into trouble again, this time for failing to keep my appointments with my probation officer. At least that's how my P.O. saw it. I saw it differently. I showed up—usually. I was just late, that's all. But trust me when I tell you that he wasn't interested in hearing any of my very good excuses. For one thing, I told him, Mom couldn't miss work to take me to all of my appointments, and for another, in this city, you could have another birthday trying to get somewhere on a crosstown bus.

Anyway, before I knew it, I was back before the judge again. This time, people were using words like "defiant" and "willful" and talking about me like I was some kind of major problem child or something. My probation got extended, but when I asked what made them think I could make it on time to more appointments if I couldn't make it on time to the last ones, the judge looked at me over the top of his glasses and said, "You have a smart mouth, young lady." As I look back on it, it probably didn't help that I replied, "Thank you."

"Keep it up," he said. "We can always revoke your probation and find a bed for you at Rosecrest instead, if you'd like." Rosecrest was a lockup for juveniles, so I figured I'd better quit while I was ahead. I may have been "defiant," but I wasn't stupid.

That period of my life sucked big time, let me tell you, but not even half as bad as it did three years later, when my mom got hit by a car while crossing a city street. The guy who hit her didn't even stop to help! She was pretty messed up and was in the hospital for, like, forever. Ginny and I had to go live with our only other relatives, our dad's parents, who lived a couple of hours away in a place called Cold Spring. I think I'd seen them maybe once or twice in my whole life. They were basically strangers.

Grandma and Grandpa acted like people do when they don't really want to do something decent, but feel like they have to. They'd never liked Mom much. They blamed her for our dad being such a jerk. Go figure. Anyhow, it was clear that having us suddenly plopped down on their doorstep wasn't exactly a dream come true for them, either.

At first, Ginny and I thought this arrangement would be strictly temporary and we'd be going home again really soon, but when Mom was transferred from the hospital to a nursing home for months of rehabilitation, Grandma and Grandpa enrolled us in the local school system for the start of my junior year of high school.

It was awful. We missed our mom, but going to see her on weekends seemed to be out of the question, and the comments we got about running up the phone bill whenever we called her pretty well let us know that wasn't an option, either.

Ginny adjusted to her new school okay, I guess, but I was miserable. For one thing, I had absolutely nobody to talk to. Oh, some of the kids tried to start conversations with me at first, inviting me to sit with them at lunch and stuff like that, but the way I looked at it, it was a lousy deal that I was there in the first place. There was no use getting cozy with people who, when this was all over, I'd never see again.

After a while they stopped trying, which was okay by me. That is, most of them stopped trying. But there was this one guy, Gavin Perry, who just didn't seem to get the message. Gavin was a really good-looking guy, popular, sports hero—the whole package. Back home, I probably would have gone for him in a big way, but like I said, it made no sense to let myself get attached to someone I'd soon be leaving—no matter how blue his eyes or how deep his dimples were.

Gavin asked me out a couple of times, but apparently he didn't believe me when I told him I didn't want to date—not just him, but anybody. Finally, I had no choice but to get rude. "Look," I said, losing patience one afternoon when he offered me a ride home from school, "what's the matter with you, anyway? I'm not interested—not in-ter-es-ted. Get it? What do I have to do, hire an airplane to write it across the sky? Now, leave me alone!"

Gavin just stood there looking at me for a long moment, along with a few other people who'd stopped to gawk. "Okay," he said quietly, "I can do that." He turned away as if to leave, then seemed to change his mind. "You know, Chrissy," he said, turning back toward me, "I don't know what you're so mad about. All any of us wanted to do was get to know you, that's all." Then, his head down and shoulders slumped forward, Gavin turned and walked away.

Just when I thought it was impossible to feel any worse, suddenly I did.

"That was cold!" one girl snapped who'd seen the whole thing.

In a flash, feeling bad about what I'd said to Gavin was replaced with fury. This girl didn't know all the stuff I'd been through. Where did she get off criticizing me? "What is it with you people?" I yelled. "Jeez, get a life, will you!"

That episode pretty well tore it. From then on, I was only slightly more welcome around Cold Spring High School than an outbreak of Ebola. With every passing week, my grades fell a little further, and I cared a little less. The only thing that helped was thinking that any minute now, Ginny and I might be getting that call from Mom telling us we could come home.

Well, we got a phone call all right, but not the one we'd been hoping for. Mom wasn't healing up the way the doctors wanted, she told us. She was facing at least two more surgeries. Even after she was as good as they could make her again, she still faced more months of painful rehabilitation. It looked like we were going to be stuck at Grandma and Grandpa's for the rest of the school year.

The next day, I begged Grandma not to make me go to school. I couldn't face another day there feeling like a prisoner who'd just received a life sentence. I'd go the next day, I promised her, if she'd just let me stay home today. But Grandma wasn't having it, and so off I went.

I tried to stay out of everybody's way that day, I really did. I was just staking out a spot in the back of the classroom and trying to pretend I wasn't there. But that must be the equivalent of daring the universe to mess with you, because I got called on for answers to homework assignments I hadn't done by virtually every teacher I had that day.

Finally, it was last period. All I wanted to do was get through it by being as invisible as possible. Unfortunately, Mr. Kramer had other ideas.

Kramer was one of those teachers that nobody respects, but nearly everybody fears—everybody but me, anyway. I mean, what more could he do to me? I already felt like I'd died and gone to Hell. Kicking me out of his class would be an improvement, and expulsion, if it came to that, would be the answer to my prayers. Anyway, he asked me something I had no clue about, so I admitted it, hoping he'd move on to his next victim. No such luck.

"What do you mean you don't know?" he barked. "That was the assignment—to find out!"

"I didn't do the assignment," I said.

"Gee, what a surprise!"

Some of the other kids snickered, some hunkered down in their seats looking like they wished they could disappear. That's when I heard Gavin Perry's voice in my ear. He sat directly behind me. "Just tell him you're sorry and it won't happen again," he whispered.

"No," I said, a little louder than I meant to.

"What was that?" Mr. Kramer snapped.

"Nothing, I wasn't talking to you," I said.

Those must have been the magic words or something, because Kramer's face turned bright red, and he looked like he was about to fly around the room backward. "I asked you a question, Miss Hicks."

"And I answered it," I replied. "I wasn't talking to you." I'm not sure what would have happened had I left it at that, but when I get tense, my mouth sometimes moves faster than my brain. This was one of those times. Suddenly every frustration I'd had for the last four months came surging forward. "But since you seem so set on hearing from me," I pressed on, "then I think I should tell you that you're a bully and a lousy teacher. You can't scare people into learning."

"Should I be taking notes?" he sneered.

"You see, that's what I mean!" I practically yelled. "You think that because you're the teacher you can talk to us any stupid way you want to, but you can't!"

"Really?" he replied. "Because it seems to me that I can, and I am."

I rose to leave. "No, you're not," I said. "You can't talk to me that way." I started for the door.

"Sit down, Miss Hicks!" Kramer shouted.

I ignored him and kept right on going.

"I'll have you marked truant for the day!" he threatened.

"Do what you gotta do, Special K."

My hand was on the classroom door when I heard a commotion behind me. Then, someone grabbed me by the back of my collar and spun me around. I think what happened next was pure instinct on my part. I didn't think, I just reacted—and the next thing I knew I'd popped Mr. Kramer one in the jaw, sending him toppling backward across some kid's desk.

That's how I wound up at Rosecrest.

I know this will sound strange, considering that Rosecrest was basically a jail, but at first I felt relieved to be there. At least I wasn't back in Cold Spring with Grandma and Grandpa and a whole high school full of people who hated me. I felt guilty for leaving Ginny there without me, but it was a little late to worry about that now.

My public defender did a pretty good job, bargaining my case down a few notches due to "extenuating circumstances," as he called them, meaning, I think, that we all knew Kramer had had it coming. But still, I'd slugged a teacher, and you don't just smile, offer up a sweet "I'm sorry," and then skate out from under something like that. So, for the time being, Rosecrest was my home.

Don't get me wrong. By "home," I don't mean that we were all just one big, happy family. Rosecrest had more than its share of weirdos, troublemakers, and drama queens, but I kept to myself and managed to avoid most of the daily disasters. If anybody even looked like she wanted to be friends, I made it clear I was just passing through. I wasn't interested in becoming anyone's buddy. After a while, most got the message and left me alone.

There was a school right there in the facility, and they made us go every day, which was okay, I guess. It beat sitting around the dayroom watching cartoons. Plus, when my time there was up, I'd be able to return to my old high school back home and graduate with the rest of my class.

This next part, though, was a total crock. The only thing I'd done was protect myself, but because I was a minor and Kramer was a teacher, I had to go to anger management classes! Talk about unfair, but there was no way out of it.

"What if I refuse?" I asked my case manager, Mr. Cleary.

"Then, for starters, you'll lose all your freedoms—phone calls, visits, and commissary privileges."

"I can live with that."

"You didn't let me finish," Mr. Cleary said. "You'll also lose your good time. Right now you're getting days off your sentence for every month that you work your court-ordered program. Screw that up, though, and not only won't you get any more good time, you'll lose what you've built up so far. I hope you love it here, because if that happens, you could end up staying a whole lot longer than we originally thought."

"This sucks," I said, seeing it as one more example of how life was stacked against me.

"Maybe," Mr. Cleary replied, "but all the same, that's how it is. I'd advise you to be smart, buckle down, and do what you've got to do to get through this experience. And who knows? Miss Reynold is a good teacher. You might actually learn something!"

I can't wait, I thought.

Anger Control class, as it was called, started the next day. I showed up along with about ten other girls.

"How many of you think you have an anger problem?" Miss Reynold began by asking. Not a single girl raised her hand.

"Has anybody ever lost her temper at work and then lost her job?" Miss Reynold went on. One hand went up.

"Have any of you ever lost a boyfriend because of something you said or did while angry?" Four more hands were raised.

"Has anyone here ever physically hurt someone else or themselves while angry?" Up went a couple more hands.

"Anybody ever get locked up for acting on an angry impulse?" Some of the girls laughed and rolled their eyes as if to say, "Why do you think I'm here?" By now, everyone but me had raised her hand.

"Now, does anyone still feels she doesn't have an anger problem?" Miss Reynold asked.

I raised my hand. "Chrissy Hicks," I said, identifying myself. "Other people—they're the ones with the problem. All I did was defend myself, but I'm the one being punished!"

"I see," Miss Reynold said. "No matter who was right and who was wrong, though, you're the one suffering because of the actions you took. Isn't that correct?"

"I'm suffering because of the actions he took. I only did what I did because of what he did first."

Miss Reynold paused for a minute, as if I'd given her something to think about. I sat back, feeling pleased that I'd made my point.

"Where is your victim now, Chrissy?" Miss Reynold finally asked. "Did he get in trouble, too?"

"Hardly," I said, rolling my eyes. I looked at the clock on the wall. "He's a teacher, so right now, he's in the middle of third period, terrorizing another roomful of kids. And please," I added, "don't call him the victim, okay?"

"You feel the actions you took were justified, yet you're the only one whose life has been disrupted," Miss Reynold summed up, ignoring my last remark. "Meanwhile, your teacher's life is going on pretty much the same as before. That doesn't sound like a very satisfying outcome to me."

"Yeah, well, what can I say? Life isn't fair."

Miss Reynold was silent for a few seconds, pacing back and forth at the front of the room. Then she said, "Chrissy, what would you say if I told you that I can only have a good day so long as everyone around me is in a terrific mood and agrees to let me have a good day?"

"I'd say, 'I hope you enjoy bad days, because you're probably going to have a whole lot of them!'" I replied.

"Exactly, yet that's pretty much what I'm hearing from you this morning. If even one person who crosses your path is in a bad mood, then it sounds as if you feel you have to respond negatively and risk ruining your own day."

That wasn't what I'd said, was it? Because when she put it like that, it sounded really immature—even stupid!

"When we go around living our lives purely in reaction to others, we're like puppets," Miss Reynold continued, "controlled completely by other people's moods. Like you pointed out, Chrissy, life isn't fair. But here's what many of my students overlook—it never has been! Many people complain when they think they've been treated unfairly, as if fairness were a guarantee in life and somehow they were cheated out of their share. But a wise adult knows that fairness is never a given, and justice is often nowhere to be found. That's why a truly powerful woman is one who controls her own emotions."

Miss Reynold moved on and told us about the ideas and

techniques we'd be studying in Anger Control class, things like assessing consequences before we act, taking responsibility for our choices, and noticing when our anger is rising too fast, putting us and others at risk.

I raised my hand a second time. "But what if you just react?" I asked. "Who takes time to notice their—what did you call them—'anger cues'? I went from zero to sixty in about two nanoseconds. I didn't think; I just went off, period." I saw several heads nodding out of the corner of my eye.

"Are you sure?" Miss Reynold asked. "Because I'm willing to bet that your body was sending you anger signals for several minutes before you snapped, and you ignored them. And for that to have happened, you had to have been feeding those signals with some pretty angry thoughts. So, what kind of thoughts were you having just before you lost control?"

"I was thinking how much I hated that place and what a jerk the teacher was."

"And where did you notice those thoughts in your body?"

I was totally lost, and it must have shown on my face.

"Your thoughts create your emotions, not the other way around," she explained, "and angry thoughts always show up physically. Our bodies are excellent early warning systems. They tell us right away when something is going on with us emotionally, usually way before our brains have it figured out. When we learn to pay attention to our anger cues, we can interrupt the process before our feelings overwhelm us and we lose our ability to think straight.

"Now, as you look back on the moments just before the incident that brought you here, Chrissy, do you remember noticing any tension in your jaw or your neck or shoulders? Was your stomach tight or uncomfortable in any way? What was going on with your heart rate and your breathing?"

Now that I thought about it, I told her I remembered a shooting pain in my forehead as I got up and headed for the classroom door.

"Ever notice that sort of thing before when you were upset?"

I was feeling more and more uncomfortable. "I noticed the same thing the morning my mom told my sister and me that our dad had moved out," I said, remembering. "He didn't even say good-bye!" All of a sudden, tears were stinging my eyes. I blinked really hard, trying to hold them back.

"Good work, Chrissy!" Miss Reynold cheered. "Way to tune into yourself!"

Apparently I'd done something great just now, though I didn't have a clue what. All I knew was that I felt embarrassed and really lousy. Suddenly, I noticed that my jaw was clenched so tightly it was starting to ache. Was anger control class literally going to be this big a pain every time? I shifted restlessly in my seat and waited for class to be over. I needed to go back to my room and think.

After each class, Miss Reynold gave us homework. We were supposed to practice relaxation exercises every night before going to sleep, write about our feelings in journals she gave us, and practice taking deep breaths to calm ourselves down whenever we felt stressed or angry. I had to admit some of it worked pretty well. The relaxation exercises, for example, helped me sleep better, especially after I got a letter from Mom saying that she was recovering nicely and had returned home again. Ginny was back home, too. I was really glad and relieved for both of them, but at the same time, the news made me feel even lonelier and more homesick than before.

Anyway, while I appreciated the ability to get a good night's sleep now, some of the other techniques Miss Reynold taught us just didn't seem powerful enough to cope with all the rest of the crapola Rosecrest could dish out. I could see trouble coming, and its name was Josie Berkshire. No amount of deep breathing was going to help me handle her!

Josie had been in and out of places like Rosecrest most of her life and acted like she owned the joint. She was always pushing people around. I'd already decided that when she finally got around to me, I was going to push back!

As luck would have it, the day that happened, we were in Anger Control class. Miss Reynold hadn't arrived yet, and we were all just getting settled in. I'd noticed that whenever two people got into it, it was usually over something really stupid. This time was no exception.

"Move it, Hicks," Josie said, towering over me, "that's my chair."

I got up and made a show of inspecting the thing. "I don't see your name on it," I replied, sitting back down again.

Josie made a grab for the chair and tried to unseat me just as Miss Reynold walked in.

"Whoa!" she called out just as I jumped to my feet. "Not in my classroom, ladies! In here we practice better methods of dealing with our problems!"

Josie backed off, and I sat down again.

What happened next was probably right out of the Anger Management Teacher's Handbook or something, because I figured that out of all the lame things I'd ever had to do, this was shaping up to be the lamest! We all sat in a semi-circle, and Miss Reynold made Josie and me face each other in two chairs out in front of the group. Then, with her leading the way, we had to tell each other what the problem was from our point of view. We couldn't interrupt each other, and there would be no name-calling or sarcasm, Miss Reynold said.

We were to speak to one another respectfully, which was going to be a challenge, if you asked me, considering that neither Josie nor I had the slightest bit of respect for each other. Anyway, with Miss Reynold steering the dialogue, it was soon clear that our conflict had nothing to do with the chair.

"Josie," Miss Reynold said, "please tell Chrissy why you felt so angry at her that you wanted to challenge her over where she was sitting."

"I don't like her."

"Tell her, Josie; don't tell me."

"I don't like you," Josie said to me.

"Back at you," I replied.

"Wait your turn, Chrissy," Miss Reynold directed.

"You think you're better than everybody here," Josie added.

"Okay, Chrissy," Miss Reynold said, "you know what to do next."

I did because I'd seen this exercise acted out at least ten times between other feuding girls in the group. "So, what you're telling me is that you think I'm stuck up; is that right, Josie?" I hoped I sounded as bored as I felt. I told you it was lame!

Josie allowed that I'd heard her correctly. "You don't talk to anybody," she elaborated, "you don't play cards or watch TV with us. You just stay in your room and act like you're above the rest of us."

I might have expected Josie to get it all wrong, but to my amazement, I saw everybody else's heads bobbing in agreement as the other girls listened to Josie's comments. It was Cold Spring High School all over again!

"Now can I tell my side of it?" I asked Miss Reynold.

"Not yet," she said. "And how do you feel when you run into the wall that Chrissy's built around herself, Josie?"

"I feel mad."

"Anything else?" Miss Reynold prompted.

Josie thought for a minute. "And left out," she added. "It's like you're judging me all the time," Josie said to me. "People have been calling me a troublemaker all my life, and it's like you've made up your mind about me, too. You're no different than me. I mean, you're here for doing something bad, too, but you won't even give me a chance. You won't give any of us a chance."

"Now, Chrissy, reflect back what you just heard," Miss Reynold directed.

For once I was having trouble coming up with something to say, and yet at the same time, I didn't really need to think about it at all. Somehow, Josie's words felt as familiar to me as if I'd spoken them myself. "You're telling me that my behavior makes you feel bad about yourself, like I'm just one more person in your life who can't see past your label of troublemaker. And because of that, you feel like getting even with me so I'll have to deal with you, like if I'm going to judge you anyway, then you might as well give me something to judge you for—is that right?"

Josie's eyes widened in recognition. She nodded.

How many times had I done the same thing, I wondered now. I'd felt Mrs. Norwood's judgment, and, since she seemed to have it in for me, anyway, I'd decided to earn her low opinion of me. I'd had a chip on my shoulder for years, I now realized.

When it was my turn to tell my side of things, all the justifications I'd been holding back while Josie was talking seemed to have drifted away. I ended up telling her—and the rest of the group—that my standoffishness wasn't meant as anything against them. I felt mad at the world—and at myself—because I was here instead of at home with my family. The plain fact was that, outside of my mom and my sister, I didn't trust people anymore. Heck, I didn't trust life, period! If my own dad could walk away and throw his family to the wolves, why should I assume anyone else cared about me? And if my mom could be mowed down in the middle of a crosswalk, no less doing nothing but minding her own business, then the only conclusion that seemed reasonable to me was that life was out to get us! All things considered, it seemed to make more sense to keep to myself and avoid trouble. Why try to make friends with people who, I was convinced, probably weren't going to like me, anyway?

When Josie and I were finished, Miss Reynold summed up the day's lesson by saying how she'd heard both Josie and me talk about feeling like victims of life. She cautioned the class that thinking this way makes us feel weak and powerless, which, in turn, takes away our motivation to do anything constructive. Plus, thinking like victims makes us angry at the way the world treats us and gives us permission—at least in our own minds—to act out and get even. Then she asked us all to make a list of three positive actions we could take to make us feel better about ourselves and our lives. Taking action in a healthy way, Miss Reynold said, was a good way to leave passive victim thinking behind and slip into the driver's seat of our own lives. It wasn't enough simply to list these positive actions, though. We actually had to do something about them.

I guess my behavior must have begun to change after that because one day I noticed that there was now a lot less friction between me and the other girls at Rosecrest. I'd even developed a taste for a nightly game of hearts with the girls in my housing unit. Socializing more and letting people get to know me was item number one on my list of positive actions. And right next to it was a big, bold checkmark, a visual reminder that I was carrying out my goals and making progress.

Item number two was to work things out with Josie Berkshire whenever we had a conflict—which was, like, at least once a day. After we had butted heads, I'd give us both some time to cool off, then I'd go back and try to talk things over with her face to face, like we'd learned to do in class. It was amazing to find out how many of our disputes came from simple misunderstandings. I don't think Josie and I will ever really be friends, but at least we're not enemies anymore, and that's a big improvement. That's why, if you were to look, you'd see another big checkmark on my list, right next to item number two.

One Sunday a few weeks later, I was hanging out in the dayroom, watching a movie with some of the other girls, when the guard began calling people down to the door.

"Hicks," the voice boomed over the loudspeaker. "You have a visit."

My heart jumped into my throat. Mom and Ginny had been here earlier in the week, so I was pretty sure it wasn't them. I hurried to join the line of girls forming at the door.

Visitors were already seated at the visitation tables when we arrived. My eyes scanned the room, searching for a familiar face. And then I saw one.

Gavin Perry stood up when he saw me coming. I tried not to grin from ear to ear, but it was hard. He looked so darned good! I just hoped he hadn't come all this way so he could tell me off in person or something.

We stood on opposite sides of the visitation table for a few awkward moments and then sat down.

"How've you been?" we both said at the same time.

"You first," Gavin said.

"I'm glad to see you," I said sincerely.

"Are you? Well, that's different!"

"Yeah, about that," I said quickly, scanning his face for a hint of a smile and finding none, "I'm really sorry. I was a pretty big jerk to you. You know how people always say, 'It's not you, it's me'?"

Gavin nodded.

"Well, in this case, it goes double. It was me. You didn't do anything wrong. As a matter of fact, you did everything right. I'm really sorry about the way I treated you. Can you forgive me?"

Gavin hesitated for what seemed like an eternity. Then a slow smile spread across his face, revealing those gorgeous dimples. "Okay," he said. "I can do that."

I don't remember too clearly what we talked about after that. My heart was singing so loudly that it drowned out almost everything else. I do remember, however, that Gavin said he'd come back again soon.

"Are you sure?" I asked. "What would your friends say if they knew you were coming to see me?"

"Are you kidding? You're the girl who decked Mr. Kramer. It doesn't get any cooler than that. You're a legend!"

"I'd rather be free, if it's all the same to you and everybody back in Cold Spring."

Gavin reached across the table and squeezed my hand. "I wish you were free, too," he said softly. Then we talked about how, in a few months, he might drive up to spend the weekend with me, Mom, and Ginny, once I was back home again. I couldn't wait!

All too soon, it was time for Gavin to go. "Think anybody would mind if I kissed you good-bye?" he asked.

"Didn't you read the rules before you came in?" I teased. "It's a requirement."

The feel of Gavin's soft, sweet lips on mine lingered as I watched him leave the room. He turned and waved when he reached the door, and then he was gone.

I joined the line of girls heading back to our housing units, feeling warm and happy inside. I knew I'd be daydreaming about every moment of my visit with Gavin and anticipating the next one for days to come. But first, there was something important I had to take care of back in my room.

Once there, I went to the bulletin board above my desk and carefully took down the piece of paper taped there. Then I laid the paper on the desk in front of me. Item number three, the paper read, write to Gavin Perry. I'd checked off that completed goal more than a week ago.

Now, I took out a pencil and wrote: Item number four—beg for Gavin's forgiveness. I smiled as I placed another great, big checkmark out in the margin.

I kind of liked this little ritual. Maybe I'd come up with a few more items to add to my list, but right now, my friends were waiting. It was time for our nightly game of hearts.

THE END

CONFESSIONS OF A BIKER BABE
Life's a highway & I ride it hard & fast!

I had to laugh at my nervousness. I'd gotten four tattoos in the last ten years, so why did another one bother me?

I met this new tattoo artist through Pete, my boyfriend (at the time). Pete had only recently gotten interested in body art, so I wasn't sure if I could trust his judgment when it came to the caliber of a tattoo artist's work. Granted, I've been around tattoo shops ever since my teenage years of running with biker boys, but I didn't get inked myself until I was almost thirty.

Friends or biker brothers of mine did all of my tattoos. I rode with them, trusted them, and their tattoos represent things that are truly important to me. They all mark a certain passing phase of my life, so a tattoo on my tailbone for my fortieth birthday seemed like the perfect thing to do. The only thing that made me nervous was that I didn't know the artist, Carver, very well. In spite of what you might think, showing my ass to a perfect stranger actually isn't an easy thing for me to do, but Pete convinced me that Carver would be gentle.

Oh—

He was gentle, all right.

When I first met Carver, he reminded me of all the old-school bikers I've ever known. His long hair, scruffy beard, leather vest, and ink-covered arms were familiar to me and made me feel at ease right away. He was very quiet, but his eyes spoke volumes; you know the type—gray at first, then green, then blue. Immediately, I not only wondered if he had an old lady, but I also wondered if his chameleon colors were indicators of his moods. Of course, I found all of that out later on.

He said nothing, but gestured to his apprentice, a bull-dyke lesbian he was trying to break, to get me "ready." She had the Celtic knot I wanted all ready and stenciled out to put on my tailbone; nevertheless, I admit I was a little disappointed that Carver, himself, did not "unveil" me. But as my red, leopard-skin pants dropped to the floor, I could feel his eyes burning a look at his "next canvas."

Already, I was getting a bit tense, and yet I was thrilled to have a new conquest in front of me, so I asked my boyfriend, Pete, to go to the store and get me something to drink.

Knowing that the nearest convenience store is a few minutes away, I also knew I suddenly had Pete-free time. So I settled in to check out this Longhair before he got lost in his work. I mean, as much as I like the time I spend with Pete, this tattoo guy was interesting . . . and quite attractive! You see—I'm a sucker for artists . . . and a slave to bad boys. And Carver was a bad boy, all right. Just one look at him would tell you he has years of hard life written all over him. But the energy he gives off is positively addictive. Without even so much as speaking a single word to me, he captured my soul. And even before the tattoo gun started buzzing, I knew I'd be buzzing from his touch alone.

He set his equipment up, checked the stencil transferred to my back, and invited me to lie down on the table. I was glad for the big pillow he gave me to rest my head on. Hey, don't get me wrong—I'm pretty tough. But it'd been a little while since I last got tattooed, so I wanted to have something to squeeze. And as Carver gave me a soil-spoken pre-tattoo spiel, I felt myself drawn to him. He spoke very quietly about how it might sting a little—or something like that. To tell you the truth—I was too lost in his eyes to pay attention.

I'm not sure if it was the sound of the tattoo gun, or the power of his eyes that hypnotized me, but either way—I was captured. As he got ready to bless my ass, I turned away to the comfort of the fleece pillow, just as the sting of the needles sizzled into my tailbone.

He drilled for a minute and then stopped to raise his head. Our eyes met, and I knew in that one beautiful instant that I was going to enjoy this work more than any I ever had before. We both grinned. The guy has magic in his hands and the devil in his eyes and I was his for the next few hours—

And, I decided, probably for a hell of a lot longer than that, too.

As the tattoo gun drilled its ink into me, I couldn't help but get lost in its sound and sting. The pain turned to a sweet, painful pleasure that moved from my tailbone throughout my whole body. I was glad I was tucked away in the back of the shop where other customers wouldn't see me, for I figured my face was most likely contorting in some pretty interesting facial expressions.

Indeed, I admit I was really glad that Pete had, apparently, gotten lost in the city, for he was gone for some time. And in that time, I decided that I would be jumping this tattoo artist as soon as I had a chance. If his sexual prowess is half as talented as his touch with a tattoo gun, then pissing off Pete by messing around with Carver will be well worth it! I determined with devilish anticipation and delight. Anyway, who says Pete ever even has to find out? This could be the beginning of something secret . . . and infinitely sensual. . . .

As Carver worked on my tailbone tattoo, he worked me into a frenzy of feelings I truthfully hadn't experienced in a long while—too long, if you ask me! Granted, I was a little embarrassed and hoped he wouldn't notice, but I was getting quite moist in certain . . . areas (if you know what I mean), and it was only getting worse (or better, depending on how you look at it). As much as I wanted to talk to him to get my mind off the excitement, he clearly didn't seem to be in the mood for conversation. Indeed, he was lost in the masterpiece he was creating, and I was lost in the masterpiece of sensations building in my loins.

We took a break when Pete returned with my pop. Ironic as it seems, it was actually perfect timing, because I had to excuse myself to clean up in the ladies' room. The men went out for a smoke, and in the meantime, I gathered my wits so Pete wouldn't pick up on my sudden attraction to his buddy. I mean, clearly—paying a dude to steal his girlfriend's affections is not what Pete had in mind when he brought me to Carver's shop!

When we all returned, I have to say that I was disappointed that Pete and Carver were in the midst of a conversation that lasted most of the rest of my tattoo session. Don't get me wrong—I completely enjoyed myself! The sensation of the needles on my tender back was delightful and painful, all at once, and I actually had to excuse myself two or three more times to hide the fact that this tattoo was arousing me more than sex with Pete ever did! And as Carver put his finishing touches on me, I couldn't help but want some more. I realized then that I wasn't only growing rapidly addicted to his work, but that I was also yearning for his hot biker bod!

A few days later, I went back to the shop to see if Carver was around. His bull-dyke apprentice was there—and she was not interested in finding Carver for me. So I told her (in no uncertain terms, mind you) that I wanted Carver to look at my tattoo—which she immediately did, telling me that it was "fine."

How was I to tell her that I wanted to make love to her boss right there in the shop on his tattoo table? After all, I considered, despite first impressions, she may or may not be his lover, too. Indeed, she seems to be very close to him.

I don't care, I quickly decided. And, anyway—Carver wasn't even there for us to fight over. So I turned to leave—only to find myself face to face with the biker himself.

And his eyes are green.

He welcomed me with a hug that felt much too warm to be anything but an invitation. Then we stepped into the back room and he drew the black, velvet curtains as I told him that I wanted him to look at the tattoo. He teased me about Pete giving me "too much action in the bedroom" and rubbing it too hard, but his joking only enticed me more.

I simply had to have him.

He ran his hand softly over my tailbone, gently caressing his fine

work. As I turned to talk to him, I couldn't help but lean in and kiss him.
That was it.
I let my pants drop, grabbed that long hair—
And lived in the moment.

I completely forgot about the rest of the shop—forgot about the lesbian on the other side of the gently swaying, black, velvet curtains—and gave my body to this artist to use me as his sexual canvas. We locked eyes and souls and I could see a spontaneous spark between us. Without words or sounds, I unzipped his jeans and explored the great goods the gods blessed him with. My mouth went to work all over his body, which he definitely enjoyed.

Silently, we turned as one as he bent me over the table. My tattoo was a little sore still, so a little sound escaped my lips as he pushed on the small of my back. His one hand went to my mouth to quiet me as his other hand brought back the sensations of the day when he tattooed me. He didn't need his tattoo gun this time, for his weapon of mass pleasures was loaded and ready for drilling—no electricity required, save for the sparks flying between us.

We made love fast and powerfully. I almost forgot that there was a shop full of people on the other side of the curtains, so it amazed me that we were getting it on so . . . quietly. Carver was masterful and, I dared to hope—a potential lifelong friend.

I wanted every touch he would offer me, but I didn't want him to know it, so when we finished, we cleaned up, and simply "reentered the real world." Nevertheless, my head was so buzzing with endorphins, I must've given away our adventures with my spacey behavior because suddenly, everyone in the shop started smiling at us as we reentered the central parlor. I was embarrassed to be found out, so when Carver asked me for my number to call me about the "touchup work," I had to shut him down by telling him that I would contact him when I had "the chance."

It wasn't until a few weeks later that I picked up the phone in a drunken haze and called Carver. I was lonely, horny, and wanting to see those eyes in front of me. As it was, we'd exchanged a few emails back and forth, but I needed to feel his touch, and I was going to have it.

My son was gone for a few days, so I invited him over to my apartment. We had some drinks, got comfortable with each other, and made love in every room in the house . . . in every possible position. For an old-school biker guy, I was impressed by his regenerative abilities, and stamina. Pete and most of the older guys I've dated are good for one session, maybe two, in a night, but Carver was unstoppable. I loved our rendezvous and I was beginning to have real feelings for him.

For several months, we met and made love, or just had a few drinks and talked for a while. He fascinated me, and I him, apparently. We shared our similar pasts and spoke of riding motorcycles together the following spring. The long winter dragged on and I found I simply could not wait to steal Carver away from his shop. I love to ride and, for a woman, I'm pretty damn good at it, if I do say so myself!

Then finally, the day arrived when he pulled into my driveway on his old, precious, wonderfully maintained Harley; I hollered a rebel yell and started up my crap bike and we rode off and fooled around by the roadside, and then rode some more. Our time together was priceless to me, and the quiet energy that flowed between us only assured me that this tattoo artist would be the brother of a lifetime. Oh, I didn't think he could ever be the faithful old man I wanted, but he certainly had great worth in my life.

Then one day, he actually invited me to be a part of his business, and as much as my lifestyle couldn't fit into it just then, I somehow knew that eventually, our relationship would be an everyday adventure.

Indeed, this past summer, we opened another tattoo studio! I'm the shop manager, as well as one of the artists. Carver and I blessed the shop with a lovely lovemaking session over all tables and chairs (How else would we know their strength?). Pete and I still see each other and he still gets tattoos—and brings his other girlfriends to get tattoos. The lesbian and I are great friends, but as much as I love her, I don't want to do anyone in the shop except my Carver.

We don't have rules or rhyme or reason with each other. We do have a shared, spontaneous zest for living that remains eternal, burning bright and strong as each day passes. Indeed, I often say that I've run away with the circus and I'm never coming home!

Well, Carver is certainly the ringleader of us all. Besides finding a lifetime love and sometime lover, I realized I've finally found my real family. The artists, apprentices, and regular hang-around folks are all reminders to me that quite often, the gods hand you your destiny in interesting packages.

I simply wanted a nice birthday present when I turned forty, but the old adage is true: "Life begins at forty."

In this case, the life I have now started at forty—and it should keep me happy till my time is up.

Beautify America—get a tattoo!

THE END

CONFESSIONS OF A SHOPAHOLIC
Choosing Between Diamonds Or My Husband?

My eyes opened wide when I saw the necklace in the jewelry store display case. "Ooh," I sighed in appreciation. "Laura, look at that necklace! Isn't it the most beautiful thing you've ever seen?"

Laura frowned at me. "Ooh, Courtney," she mimicked sarcastically. "Look at that price tag. Isn't that the most outrageous thing you've ever seen?"

I ignored her sarcasm. "It's a lot of money," I agreed. "But just look at how smooth the gold is. If I was wearing that necklace . . ."

"You'd have spent way too much money—again," Laura finished for me. "I hate to bring you back to the cruel world of reality, but you can't afford it. You and Brian are saving to buy a house, remember? You can't spend money on frivolous things anymore."

I shrugged. "I have cut back on my spending," I answered calmly. "I haven't bought anything new in months."

Laura just stared at me until I laughed. "Okay, okay, I've bought a few things," I admitted. "But I've tried to be good. I don't see what the big deal is anyway. Brian is doing really well at his job, and I'm working too. He's just being way too cautious about this whole money thing."

Laura looked shocked. "Are you crazy?" she demanded. "You almost lost Brian once with this kind of behavior. When he found out how much money you owed on your credit cards, he went nuts! Don't you remember how you sat in your apartment and cried for a week until he accepted your apology?"

"I remember," I said quietly. "Of course I remember." That had been an awful time in my life. Brian and I had been so in love, but my spending had almost ruined everything for us.

Even now, I cringed as I remembered the look on his face when I showed him my bills and he added up the totals. He had accused me of lying to him and said we couldn't get married. I had been stunned that he reacted that way.

All the trouble had started simply because I volunteered to pick out his mother's birthday present for him.

Brian and his two brothers had wanted to get his mother something really special for her fiftieth birthday. They were thinking of a sweater or a new set of dishes, when I came up with a brilliant idea.

"I saw a beautiful set of earrings on my lunch hour," I told them eagerly. "They're white gold and emeralds. Emeralds are your mother's birthstones, and these are absolutely gorgeous! She'll love them."

They all agreed that the earrings sounded perfect, and reached into their wallets for the cash to cover the cost. "Thanks, Court," Brian said gratefully. "You saved the day. We wanted something that she'd really love."

I had every intention of buying the earrings the next day on my lunch hour, but when I got home that night, there was a message on my answering machine from my landlord. My last rent check had bounced and she wanted the money immediately, or she would call the manager of the building to report my late payment.

I knew I had to pay my rent, so I ran down to the building office with the money right away. I was nice, but Mrs. McLeod was downright snippy when I handed her the cash to cover the bounced check. "You should really be more careful when you pay your bills," she said sternly. "A bad credit rating can follow you around for years. And you don't want to get kicked out of the building. You'll have a hard time renting another apartment if you lose one this way."

The funny thing was, I didn't think I really had a bad credit rating. I spent a lot of money, but always managed to make at least the minimum payment on my credit card. Sometimes, though, I slipped up, and that's why the rent check had bounced.

But now I had a new problem. I had covered the rent check with the cash, but how was I going to buy the earrings? I had no choice but to put the earrings on my newest credit card. I would have gotten away with the small deception, if I hadn't left the credit card slip on my kitchen counter. Brian saw it when he came to pick me up for the birthday dinner.

"Honey, what's this?" he asked, puzzled. "You charged Mom's earrings? Why?"

Brian hated credit cards, and thought people who used them were foolish. "Oh, no big deal," I said airily. "That card gives me cash back at the end of the month, and all kinds of rewards when I use it."

"Well, I hope you're paying it off completely every month," he warned. "The interest rates..."

"I know, I know," I interrupted impatiently. "I'm not stupid! I know how interest rates work."

"Sorry, honey," he apologized quickly. "It's just that my brother, Ken, is always getting into financial trouble by buying things he can't afford and doesn't need. I'm so used to lecturing him, I can't stop myself."

The truth was I was tired of thinking so much about money and credit. It just didn't matter that much to me. I worked hard as a secretary five days a week, and I thought I deserved some reward for that. I liked nice things and I didn't see any harm in buying them before I had all the money saved up. That's why credit cards had been invented in the first place.

"Well, that's your brother, not me!" I snapped. I had done Brian a favor by getting the earrings and now he was acting like I was some wayward child.

"Okay, honey," he said, but he was frowning slightly. "I just want you to be careful." I could tell he thought I was overreacting over his simple questions, and I was. But I couldn't tell him that I had four credit cards, and three of them were almost maxed out.

Brian's mother loved the earrings – just as I'd known she would. Brian kissed me happily, and whispered that I had excellent taste.

"A woman knows good jewelry," I answered back. But it was more than that, I thought. A woman likes to be appreciated and have the people she loves recognize how important she is in their lives.

We got engaged at Christmastime, and Brian bought me a beautiful diamond ring. I knew when I accepted it that I should tell him about the money I owed, but something stopped me. I didn't want to spoil the most important moment in my life, discussing how much money I owed.

And there never seemed to be a good time to bring the subject up. I knew Brian would be very upset with me, and I couldn't bear the look of disappointment I would see on his face.

But Brian and I were spending all our time together, and it was inevitable that one day he would discover my secret. Sure enough, one Saturday, he happened to look through the pile of mail I had left on the dining room table.

"Courtney, what are all these?" he asked, frowning deeply. "They look like bills from credit card companies."

I could have kicked myself for leaving them out on the table, but I tried to cover quickly. "Oh, maybe they are," I said, trying to sound casual. "I bought some things on sale last month and I got a 10% discount if I opened up an account."

He threw the bills down on the table angrily. "Well, you need to close them right away," he said sternly. "We're going to be married soon and we aren't going to start out by having a whole bunch of credit card bills to worry about."

"Brian, you need to stop treating me like I'm ten years old!" I snapped. "I've managed to run my life pretty well without you for the last twenty-three years!"

Brian looked surprised at my outburst, and then he laughed. "Sorry, Court," he apologized. "You're right. I didn't mean to come on so strong. I trust you to take care of this."

I felt guilty for making Brian out to be the bad guy. I knew he was sincerely worried about me spending too much and paying outrageous finance charges. Still, I was a big girl and responsible for my own money.

And, so, I talked myself out of canceling the credit cards, or limiting my spending to necessities. I suppose a psychiatrist could have found some troubling reason that I was overspending, but the simple truth was that I liked nice things. I enjoyed dressing well and having pretty things around me.

My real weakness was jewelry. It was no accident I had seen the emerald earrings for Brian's mother – I window-shopped at that jewelry store all the time. It was one of those beautiful stores – with lush carpeting and soft lighting. The diamonds, rubies and emeralds glimmered in the display cases, and the salespeople were wonderful about allowing me to try on whatever I wanted.

I didn't want to wear rhinestones – I liked real gems. My favorite, of course, was diamonds.

After I had purchased my second pair of diamond earrings, Laura spoke up: "You know, Courtney," she said quietly. "That's a lot of money for a pair of earrings."

"Diamonds aren't cheap," I answered breezily. "Besides, this pair is white gold. It's completely different than the pair I bought last fall."

"Will Brian think they're completely different?" she asked pointedly. "I thought he told you to stop charging on your credit cards."

"What do men know about jewelry?" I asked, shrugging my shoulders. "Anyway, he spent more on my engagement ring than I did on the earrings."

Laura tilted her head to look at me. "You buy an engagement ring once," she said calmly. "At least, that's the way it's supposed to work."

I should have taken Laura's warning to heart, but I didn't. Frankly, I was irritated that everyone was always trying to tell me what to do. And I didn't really see what was so wrong about buying a few things. I wasn't using illegal drugs or stealing, for heaven's sake!

But it turned out to be a big problem – at least for Brian. He found out that I was still using the credit cards and he freaked out. He demanded that I bring out all my bills and show them to him immediately.

"Don't be ridiculous," I said, trying to smooth the situation over. "You're making a big deal out of nothing at all. Let's go grab a bite to eat and we'll talk about this."

"I don't want to talk about this," he said angrily. "And I don't want you to treat this like some sort of inconvenience to you. The very fact that you still have credit card bills means you lied to me."

"I didn't lie," I replied hastily. "I tried to pay off the balances. . . ."

"Don't make it worse by making up excuses," he interrupted,

sounding furious. "You knew I'd be upset about this so you deliberately didn't tell me! That's the same as lying."

The next hour was the most humiliating of my life. I brought out the bills for Brian to go over. With every one that he opened, I could see he was getting madder and madder. Finally, he exploded.

"Courtney, how could you let this happen?' he demanded. "Do you have any idea how much money you owe?"

"Brian," I began quietly. "I know this seems bad right now, but…"

He didn't let me finish. "You have a real problem," he said hotly. "I mean, your spending is way out of control. There's no excuse for living so irresponsibly."

I started to cry then, but Brian was unmoved by my tears. "Courtney, under the circumstances, I don't see how we can get married," he said coldly. "I need a mature woman – someone I can trust. I feel like you've deliberately been untruthful."

I couldn't believe that our relationship was over that quickly. "Brian, don't say things like that," I pleaded. "I can do better, but you have to give me a chance."

He shook his head. "I gave you a chance, Courtney," he said. "I feel like I don't even know you."

He walked out on me, and I burst into tears. I sobbed myself to sleep that night, and woke up with a pounding headache, and the feeling that my life was over. When I called Laura to come over, she was sympathetic, but couldn't resist saying; "I told you so."

"Courtney, I tried to warn you," she said. "You've always liked to spend too much money."

"Laura, he doesn't want to marry me," I said, still stunned. "I can't believe it! He doesn't love me anymore! It's just over."

"It's not over," she assured me. "Brian still loves you. He's just upset right now. Give him a few days to cool off. But you have to convince him you're going to change Courtney, and you have to really mean it. You saw how important this is to him."

I stopped crying then. "You really think I have a chance of getting him back?" I asked hopefully.

She nodded. "I think you two have something special going," she answered. "I think he probably already misses you. But you've hurt him pretty badly, and he's not going to get over that easily. You have to give him some time and space."

I hoped she was right. I loved Brian with all my heart, and nothing I had ever purchased seemed worth the cost of losing him.

"Tell me what to do," I said urgently. "How can I get him back?"

She took a deep breath. "You need to show him something concrete," she replied. "A plan of how you're going to pay off these balances."

"Will you help me do that?" I asked, feeling the tears starting to flow again.

"Yes," she answered slowly. "But only if you make me the same promise that I want you to make to Brian. I want to see you out of this mess for your own sake, not just because Brian won't marry you."

"I promise," I said quietly. "Just help me get Brian back."

And, so, Laura had helped me figure out an actual budget plan to show Brian. In addition, I cut all my credit cards in half, except one that I promised I would use only for emergencies.

After a week of silence on Brian's part, I called him. "Courtney," he said, the moment he heard my voice. "We don't really have anything to talk about right now."

"Yes, we do," I said firmly. "Look, Brian, you had every reason to be mad, but I've spent this last week thinking of ways I can prove myself to you. I made up a budget for myself. I cut up the credit cards."

There was a long pause. "That's a good start," he agreed. "But . . ."

"I think you owe me a chance to prove myself," I interrupted. "I admit I hid the bills from you, but it wasn't like we were married already. In fact, if you think about it, it's still really my problem."

To my surprise, he laughed. "I've missed you, Courtney," he said warmly. "Let's have dinner tonight and talk."

We ended up getting back together. Brian was impressed that I had actually put together a budget and agreed that he had overreacted when he saw my credit card bills. "But I want us to be secure," he said, kissing me gently. "And I don't want any nasty surprises like that again."

That night, our lovemaking was special. We'd only been apart for a week, but it felt like a year. I fell asleep, snuggled in Brian's strong arms, and determined to be the kind of wife he wanted.

And it was pretty easy at first to stick with my budget. Brian and I were busy planning our wedding, but my parents were paying for most of it. And, whatever Brian and I were paying for, we discussed together.

Our wedding was beautiful. I don't suppose every detail was perfect, but it seemed that way to me. Brian and I exchanged vows, and I thought I was the luckiest woman in the world.

Brian's apartment was bigger, so we moved in there. Since we were only paying rent on one place, I had lots more spending money than before.

Brian had already planned out what to do with the savings. "In about a year, we should have enough money to make a down payment on a house," he told me. "It's foolish to keep paying rent, when we could own."

I wasn't used to making plans so far in advance. On one hand, I was glad that Brian was so organized. I knew he was right about owning a house, and I did want one. On the other hand, I missed the freedom of just going out and buying things that caught my eye. I wasn't exactly on an allowance, but Brian even wanted to know how much I spent for lunch every day.

"Brian, stop," I told him more than once. "You have to relax a little about all this money stuff. We're doing fine."

"Courtney, do you realize if you gave up your morning latte, you'd save twenty dollars a week," he answered. "And if you packed your own lunch…"

"I'd be really crabby," I answered truthfully. "Besides, I don't see you packing your lunch."

"I have business lunches," he replied. "I can't very well ask clients to share a tuna fish sandwich and a cupcake with me."

And it seemed like Brian had a reason for everything he spent money on. He needed nice suits for work and a reliable car to drive. But he always thought I spent too much money on clothes and argued that I should take the bus to work.

"You want me to take the bus?" I asked indignantly. "But you drive a car to your job!"

"That's different," he replied patiently. "I have to drive to pick up clients or to show a house. I need to have a car."

His explanations were always reasonable, but I resented it anyway. Brian was only a few years older than I was, but he treated me like I was a child.

Feeling the way I did, it was only natural that I would start spending money again – even though I had promised Brian I would cut back. It was pretty easy to fool Brian; he didn't really know how much women's clothing cost and I always told him I got things on sale. When I bought a designer purse for over three hundred dollars, I managed to convince him it was only twenty dollars.

Just as I promised, I paid off the credit card bills and showed Brian the zero balance. What I didn't tell him is that for every card I paid off, I opened a new one. It was so easy. Every store I went into offered me a card with a discount for my first purchase.

It was a race every day to get the mail before Brian did. Fortunately, he didn't have much real interest in getting the mail, and he trusted that my spending problem had been taken care of.

When I got my yearly raise, I simply didn't mention it to Brian. It wasn't a lot of money, but it gave me more to spend every month. I felt guilty about that, but I told myself that a lot of married couples kept tiny secrets from each other.

Now, as I stood looking at the necklace in the window of the jewelry store, I knew I had to have it. "Come on," I pleaded with Laura. "Let's just go in and look at it. That can't do any harm."

"Courtney," Laura said, shaking her head. "Are you kidding? It's like putting a drink in the hand of an alcoholic."

"Oh, that's ridiculous," I said, grabbing her hand. "I just want to look at it. It's a beautiful piece of jewelry."

Laura had no choice but to follow me in. I felt better the minute I stepped inside the store. That probably sounds stupid to most people, but it was exhilarating just to be surrounded by so many beautiful things.

A saleswoman came up to us immediately. "May I help you?" she asked.

"I was interested in the necklace in the window," I said. "The diamond one."

She smiled. "Oh, yes," she said, walking towards the display case. "It's very lovely, isn't it? We just got that in on Saturday."

The moment I tried it on, I knew I had to have it. It felt so good around my neck, and it looked so wonderful! The diamonds sparkled against my skin and the gold was as smooth as butter. I touched it gently and sighed.

"It's spectacular," I said softly.

Laura cleared her throat. "Courtney, we just stopped to look at it, remember?" she asked. "It is a beautiful necklace, but you don't need anything that expensive."

I nodded, but my eyes remained glued to the mirror. "I have a dress that has just the right neckline for this," I said, almost to myself.

The salesclerk smiled. "We have several different payment plans," she said. "And, of course, if you open a store credit card, the first purchase would have a ten percent discount."

"Of course," Laura murmured, a bit sarcastically.

"Courtney, you're going to be late for work," Laura said urgently.

"Yes, I suppose," I said reluctantly. I took off the necklace and handed it back to the clerk."

"Thanks for letting me try it on," I said.

"Come back any time," she answered. "My name is Debra and we're open until eight tonight."

"Don't even think about it!" Laura hissed, as soon as we were outside.

"Think about what?" I asked.

"About coming back before eight and opening another credit card and getting that necklace," she replied. "And I know that's exactly what was going on in your head."

"I don't know why I go to lunch with you," I grumbled. "You're no fun at all."

"I keep you out of trouble," she corrected me. "You'll thank me for it later."

All afternoon, I couldn't concentrate on anything but how beautiful that necklace had looked on me. As soon as I left work, I headed right back to the jewelry store. Debra looked up and smiled when she saw me.

"I was hoping you'd come back," she said warmly. "I could tell how much you loved that necklace."

"I did," I answered. "I'd like to open an account and charge the necklace."

At that moment, I couldn't think about anything but getting the necklace. In the back of my mind, I knew both Brian and Laura would be upset with me, but I simply didn't care.

It took less than ten minutes for my new card to be approved. "Would you like to wear it home?" Debra asked.

That question stopped me. I wanted to wear it more than anything else in the world, but I couldn't risk Brian seeing it. "No, just wrap it up," I said, a bit sadly.

Brian wasn't home when I got there, so I quickly rushed to the bedroom so I could try it on one more time. It was so pretty! There was no way of explaining to Brian just how happy I was with a new piece of jewelry. When I heard his car door slam, I took off the necklace and pushed it to the back of one of my drawers. By the time Brian walked in, I was just opening a beer for myself.

"I'll have one of those," he said. "How was your day?"

I loved my husband, and I suppose I should have felt guilty about the necklace I had just hidden, but I didn't. It was up there, waiting for me, just like a kid's Halloween candy or an unopened Christmas present.

"Fine," I replied, handing him a cold bottle. "Nothing out of the ordinary."

All the while, my mind was working on what to tell Brian about the necklace. It didn't take me long – my birthday was three weeks away. I would simply tell him my grandmother had given it to me as a gift.

Laura, of course, was horrified. "You told Brian your grandmother gave you a diamond necklace for your birthday? What's going to happen if he asks her about it?"

"My grandmother is eighty and lives in Arizona," I said, shaking my head. "What are the chances Brian is going to ask her about it?"

"That's not even the point," Laura replied, frowning. "You lied to him about it."

"I wouldn't have to lie to him if he didn't make such a big deal out of everything," I said defensively. "I don't know why I can only buy the things that he thinks are important."

"You need to talk to him," she urged. "But if you don't have any truth or honesty as a basis for your marriage . . ."

"I'm hiding a necklace, not a drug habit," I snapped impatiently. "I don't really think I have anything to be ashamed of."

It was easy to justify my behavior. I thought Brian was being unreasonable with his attitude about spending money. It seemed to me that when he needed something, he didn't have to justify it at all.

And my deception worked. Brian thought that the necklace was beautiful and that my grandmother was incredibly generous. "She really knows you," he said, smiling. "That looks just like something you'd pick out for yourself."

I looked at him sharply, but there was nothing sarcastic in the comment. "Yes," I said, relieved. "Well, all the women in my family like nice jewelry."

As the months went on, I became more relaxed about my spending. I didn't have any problem making the minimum payments for the credit cards and Brian even complimented me several times on how nice I looked in a certain outfit.

"See?" I said to Laura triumphantly. "And how does he think I get these clothes if I don't spend money?"

She looked uncertain. "Well, sometimes men don't realize how much things cost," she answered weakly.

"Exactly!" I said triumphantly.

"Courtney, that doesn't mean you can just lie to the poor guy," she replied crossly.

I knew Laura was mad at me, but I wasn't too thrilled with her attitude. Brian was a "poor guy," and I was a "liar." She was supposed to be my friend!

Of course, it was only a matter of time before Brian figured out what was going on. He had gone to the bank to ask about financing a home, only to find out that I had five credit cards in my name that he didn't know about. He was so furious I was surprised he hadn't had a car accident on the way home.

"Do you know how embarrassed I was?" he demanded. "I kept insisting that we didn't have any credit cards and he had to print off a copy of our credit report so he could prove it to me."

I sat down heavily on the couch. "Oh," was all I could manage.

"Is that all you can say?" he yelled. "Oh?"

I looked at him. "Brian, what do you want me to say?" I asked evenly. "That I'm sorry and it won't happen again? The truth is, I'm relieved you found out about the credit cards. I'm tired of hiding the things I buy. I don't really think I'm doing anything wrong."

Now it was his turn to be speechless. "Are you kidding?" he asked. "You lied to me! You spent money you had no right to! You jeopardized our chances of buying a house!"

"So what?" I shot back. "Why are we in such a hurry to buy a house? Why can't we just enjoy life for a while? Why does everything have to be on your timetable?"

Everything I said just made Brian angrier. "I'm leaving!" he announced, slamming the door. He was so mad I could even hear the outer door to the apartment building slam.

I did start to cry then. I loved Brian and I didn't want to lose my husband. Still, I had enough pride to realize that he had walked out on me because of something I just didn't think was that important. His attitude hurt my feelings.

I didn't tell Laura until the next day. She gasped in shock as I told her how Brian had just walked out the door.

"Look, call him and tell him that you . . ." she began helpfully.

I shook my head. "I'm not calling to apologize," I interrupted firmly. "He didn't want to hear anything I had to say yesterday. He's the one who decided to walk out on me, not the other way around."

Her eyes grew wide. "So the marriage is over just like that?" she asked. "You're not even going to fight to save it?"

"I don't know," I said wearily. "But I don't think everything that's happened is my fault. I don't know if I want to be married to someone who has to control money this way."

As I said the words, I realized I'd been thinking them for a long time. As much as I loved Brian, I was tired of the way we were living. I was tired of looking over my shoulder and hiding things from my husband.

Over the weekend, Brian arranged to come over and pick up some clothes he needed. When I came back to the apartment, I started to cry again. I guess as long as Brian's things had been there, I could imagine him coming back home. Now, it looked like I was really losing him.

Still, I couldn't bring myself to call and apologize either. Maybe we hadn't been as happy as I thought. After all, he had left me pretty quickly.

About two weeks after our fight, I looked up to see Brian standing at my desk. I could feel my heart pounding in my chest, and I knew my face was flushed. "Hi," I said softly.

"Look, we need to talk," he said quietly. "Can you get away for lunch?"

I nodded. "Sure," I agreed. I didn't exactly know what Brian wanted from me. Did he want to get back together, or did he want to tell me that our marriage was over?

We went to the coffee shop near my office. All the way there, I couldn't think of a single thing to say, and neither could Brian. It was like we were complete strangers. My stomach was bouncing up and down, but I ordered a sandwich and coffee. When our food was in front of us, Brian finally spoke.

"I've missed you," he said gently. "How have you been?"

"Fine," I said automatically. "I've missed you, too."

He nodded. "I've been doing a lot of thinking," he said. "I love you, Courtney, and I want our marriage to work. I was mad the other day, and I'm still upset, but I want us to work on the problem."

I sat back in the booth. "The problem?" I repeated. "You mean my problem, don't you?"

Brian frowned. "Courtney, I didn't mean to hurt your feelings," he replied. "I . . . I got the name of a counselor – someone who specializes in this kind of thing."

"What kind of thing?" I asked, starting to get angry.

"Well, money problems," he answered. "Look, do you want us to stay married or not?"

"Yes," I said reluctantly. "But I don't know that I want to go to some guy who's just going to tell me everything I'm doing is wrong."

Brian laughed. "Well, if it makes any difference, this counselor is a woman," he said.

I had to smile at that. "It makes a difference," I replied. "At least, I think it does."

Brian's face grew serious. "Will you try, Courtney?" he asked. "The counseling, I mean? I made an appointment for tonight."

"Tonight?" I asked, alarmed. "You made an appointment without asking me?"

"Yes," he said firmly. "I thought it was important."

"So you just went ahead and did it," I said flatly.

Now, he sat back angrily. "Well, at least I was thinking of ways to get us back together," he replied coolly. "What ideas did you come up with?"

"None," I said. "I didn't know we were having a contest."

"Courtney, if you don't want to go, just say so," he replied. "Do you want a divorce?"

Those words stopped me cold. "No," I said.

"Okay, well, she gave me some forms for the both of us to fill out before we get there," he said, sounding smug.

"So I have to fill these out at work?" I asked, glaring at him.

Brian reached for my hand. "Please?" he asked. "I know it's short notice, but I think it's worth a try."

"Fine," I said, gathering up the papers. "I'll see you at . . ." I looked down at the forms to find a name. "Libby Lawhorn's office at five-thirty."

By the time I got back to the office, I felt totally confused. Brian had made the first move, and had told me he loved me. I suppose that was a good start, but I still felt like I was the naughty child, going with an angry parent to meet with the principal.

I looked at the papers and sighed. It was pages and pages of questions about how I felt about spending money, what goals were important to me, how I spent my spare time, etc. Fortunately, my boss was at a meeting out of the office for the afternoon. I flipped through the pages and sighed. It would take me until five-thirty to finish all this.

I was right on time for the appointment. The secretary took my forms and Brian's and told us it would only be a few minutes. There was an awkward silence between us and I picked up a magazine.

"I'm sorry, Courtney," Brian said quietly. "You were right – I should have told you about this."

I put the magazine down. "Yes, you should have," I replied. "Doesn't this seem kind of silly – telling a perfect stranger about our problems because we can't figure it out by ourselves?"

He frowned. "No," he said shortly. "She's an expert. Maybe if someone else tells you what I've been saying . . ."

I was about to say something mean, but just then, the receptionist interrupted us. "Dr. Lawhorn will see you now," she said.

I was nervous when I walked in, but Dr. Lawhorn wasn't anything like I'd imagined. Her office looked like someone's living room.

"Hello," she said warmly. "I'm glad you're here. Please make yourselves comfortable. And please call me Libby."

Brian and I sat down on the couch, not looking at each other. She smiled at us, and looked down at the papers in front of her.

"I asked both of you to fill out these forms so I could get to know a little bit about the both of you," she said. "And it only took me a few minutes to see where I think the problem might be."

Brian spoke up right away. "I've talked to Courtney about her spending," he began, sounding triumphant. "And she says she's tried to stop, but . . ."

Libby held up her hand to quiet him. "Brian, the first thing both of you need to do is listen to each other," she interrupted. "What you think the problem is, and what Courtney thinks the problem is, could be two completely different things."

He looked surprised. "But the reason we're here is because of Courtney," he said in confusion.

She shook her head. "The reason we're here is to help both of you try to understand each other," she corrected. "And to save your marriage."

"But, but," Brian sputtered. "I don't understand."

"I'm here to help you understand," she replied. "I'd like to hear what Courtney thinks about this."

I swallowed hard. "I lied to Brian about my spending," I replied quietly. "I can't stop shopping and I don't know if I can change – even to save my marriage."

Libby didn't seem surprised in the least. "And why did you lie about your spending?" she asked. "Are you ashamed of the amount of money you spend?"

I thought about that for a minute. "No, not really," I answered. "It's just that he gets so mad when I buy something for myself. I can't talk to him about the things I want to buy. He wants us to save for a house."

"And you don't agree with that?" she asked.

I had to think again. "I don't know," I answered honestly. "I mean, I want a house, but I don't see why we can't wait for a while."

"See?" Brian broke in. "That's the problem right there. There's no thought to the future."

"And you want a house, so you think Courtney should share that opinion," Libby said. "But lots of people wait to buy, or are perfectly happy in an apartment. There is no right or wrong answer here, you know. What you need to decide is whether you want Courtney enough to compromise on the things you want."

Brian looked offended. "Why do I have to compromise?" he asked, sounding like a spoiled child.

"Because this is a marriage," she replied easily. "You're asking Courtney to change her way of thinking for you, but you aren't willing to change for her. I've looked over Courtney's spending habits. It doesn't appear to me that she has a spending problem."

Now, it was my turn to be surprised. "But I lie to cover up my spending," I replied. "I know that's not right."

"That isn't right," she agreed. "But I think you've felt like you had to. I asked both of you to write down your major purchases for the last few months on these forms. Now, Brian, when you bought a set of golf clubs two months ago, did you discuss that purchase with Courtney?"

"You bought golf clubs?" I asked, staring at him.

"Well, that was for business purposes," he said defensively. "And, no, I didn't tell Courtney."

"You bought golf clubs?" I repeated.

"Brian, my point is this," Libby said. "Marriage is a partnership – in every sense of the word. If you want Courtney to be honest about money, then you have to be honest too."

"Golf clubs for business?" I asked angrily. "And you were mad about what I spent?"

"See, she doesn't understand," Brian said. "I have to take clients out, and some of them like to play golf."

Libby smiled again. "Brian, Courtney's purchases probably seem just as silly to you as golf clubs do to her," she replied. "That's what we need to work on."

"I think what's happened here," she continued gently. "Is that you two have fallen into the habit of playing roles. Brian has taken charge of the financial matters, as a parent would, and that leaves Courtney to play the part of the child. Unfortunately, that doesn't make for a happy marriage."

"So where do we start?" I asked.

"Relax, it's not going to hurt," she said. "At least not much. I want the two of you to start from ground zero. That is, you're going to sit down with the finances and a clean slate. The rules are that you have to listen to each other, and not get angry. You may decide you need separate checking accounts, or to do the bills together every single month."

"But nothing can be taken for granted," she continued. "Brian, you can't assume owning a home is the right thing for right now. Courtney, you have to be honest about how much you spend and why. I'm here to help you get through this, but the majority of the work will be up to you."

Brian looked decidedly unhappy, and I didn't feel any better. Libby looked at both of us. "You've made a good first step in coming here," she said gently. "You both recognize that there's a problem. Now, you need to solve it."

Libby sent us home with the assignment of figuring out a budget we could both be happy with. We made a follow-up appointment for the next week.

"Remember," she cautioned us. "No one is right and no one is wrong."

Brian and I walked to the elevator in silence. "Well, that wasn't what I expected," Brian finally said.

"Yeah, really," I added. "Golf clubs?"

Brian managed a small smile. "No one's right and no one's wrong, remember?" he said.

"Yeah," I said.

Brian turned to me. "I'm sorry, Courtney," he said softly. "The doctor – what she said – it was like a slap in the face. She's right. I always have to have things my way. I didn't realize how it all looked til it was right there in black and white."

I frowned. "Brian, you lied to me," I said slowly. "You walked out on me, but you did exactly the same thing you accused me of. . . ."

Brian kissed me then. "Yes," he said. "I'm sorry. Can we do what she suggested? Can we start over with a clean slate?"

I hesitated. I was mad at Brian, but not mad enough to say no to a chance at saving our marriage. "Okay," I said softly. "But we really have a lot of work to do."

"Let's go home and talk," he said. "After I make love to you. I've missed you desperately."

"That sounds like a plan," I agreed. "I've missed you too."

It wasn't easy for Brian and I to change our patterns of behavior, but we did. It took hours of talking—and listening—to agree on a budget plan. The main thing is, we discuss every purchase over twenty dollars. That might sound ridiculous to some, but it's saved our marriage. We've started saving towards a house, but that won't happen for a couple of years at least.

We don't have separate checking accounts, but we do allow each other "mad money" to spend on anything we want. I still have a weakness for diamonds, but I really think about something before I buy it.

Brian and I are closer than we ever were. I guess it's because we really feel like partners now, and that's what a good marriage is all about.

THE END

CONFESSIONS OF AN ER NURSE
"I Stole Another Woman's Life"

I hadn't planned on wrecking a marriage. I hadn't planned on destroying a family.

Colin and I had met by accident at a local coffee shop where I often stopped for a huge to-go coffee after work. I would have had to be blind not to notice someone as good-looking as he was. Thick brown hair shaped his handsome dark complexion, while deep blue eyes offered a sadness that anyone with any compassion at all would want to erase. Including me.

"We've gotta stop meeting like this," I said one morning as I accepted my Styrofoam cup and turned to leave, almost bumping into the man I'd been noticing for over a week. "People will talk."

"I know," he said, his mouth curving into a slight smile. "But the hospital's coffee isn't as good. Besides, I needed a break."

"Hospital?" I asked, wondering why I'd never seen him there. "Do you work at the hospital, too? I'm surprised I haven't seen you around."

"I don't work there," he said, taking his turn at the counter. "Just visiting a sick relative." Something made me wait until he'd received his coffee instead of simply exiting the building as I usually did.

Although I didn't want to pry, he almost seemed to want to unburden himself, so I simply hung around for moral support.

We'd been running into each other at this same coffee shop for the past three weeks, so it was obvious that whomever he was visiting wasn't responding to treatment very quickly.

"What about you?" he asked, as he turned to face me again. "You asked if I worked there, too? Meaning you do?"

"I'm an ER nurse," I said, proudly. "I rotate shifts, and this past month has been my turn to work the late shift. I'm just getting off work."

"Rough night?"

"It's always a rough night in the ER. You wouldn't believe some of the things I see."

But something in his eyes made me realize that he did know.

"If you're not in a big hurry," he said, softly, if not a bit nervously, "would you like to sit and talk a while?"

Truthfully, I was in a hurry to go home and get some much-needed sleep, but something about his pleading look made me reconsider. Maybe it was the nurse in me that made me want to offer comfort whenever I saw fit. And this poor man definitely needed a comforting shoulder. I'd seen enough grief-stricken family members to know that this man needed a shoulder.

"My name is Colin," he said, as he slid into a booth. "Colin Larsen."

"Tara Wells," I responded, sliding into the opposite side. "Wanna talk about it?"

Colin stared down at his cup for a long time, rubbing his hands across the warmth of the cup. "My wife, Connie," he said, softly. "She's brain dead, and I'm the reason for it."

Working as an ER nurse, I realized that Colin probably wasn't as bad as he thought. Many people blamed themselves for the terrible things that happened to loved ones. "If only" was a terrible phrase to have to live with the rest of one's life.

"I'm sure you're not the reason," I told him. "Tell me what happened." Reaching across the table, my hand closed over his.

"We had a fight," he said, with a shrug of his shoulders that seemed to say that was all the explanation needed. "We'd only been together about a year when Connie got pregnant with our child, so we did the expected thing and got married. We both knew it was a mistake, but we wanted to make our families happy."

"I understand," I said.

"We fought constantly about anything and everything. And then finally I'd had enough. One night during one of our arguments, I told her I was done. I wanted a divorce. It wasn't working and it was never going to work. I just wanted out."

"And she didn't?"

Colin sipped a bit of his coffee, and then seemed to consider his answer. "I think she knew it was hopeless. But she wanted to try longer for the sake of our child. She'd come from a broken family, and she didn't want that for her baby.

A single tear slid down his face and he made no effort to brush it away. "But I refused," he said with genuine remorse. "I told her I was moving out. She took the baby, stormed out—"

"And she had a wreck," I finished the sentence for him. I'd seen this kind of thing too many times in my line of work. Anger did terrible things to people. They never considered the consequences and then it was too late.

"Except that she didn't die," he choked out softly, with more tears in his eyes. "She didn't die, but she didn't live, either. She's on life support and will be for the rest of her life unless I decide to end her suffering."

He hadn't mentioned the baby. I was curious to know what

became of the small child, but was almost afraid of the answer.

As if sensing my curiosity, he finally gave me my answer.

"The baby lived," he said with genuine relief. Sucking in a deep breath, he raised his eyes as if thanking God for saving his child. "Miraculously, Sammy survived with only a few scratches."

My hand tightened on his. "I know that has to be a blessing," I said. "It's always amazed me how some people walk away with hardly a scratch while others are mangled, maimed, and even killed."

Colin wiped at tears. "I am very lucky to have my son," he said. "Deciding to give our son life was the best decision Connie and I ever made. Too bad we couldn't agree on anything else."

"So what will you do about your wife?" I asked. "You said that the doctors don't offer any hope of recovery."

He shook his head in sorrow. "None at all. She's totally brain dead. They've suggested that I should discontinue the life support."

"I'm sure that's a hard decision."

Colin actually laughed, but the humor didn't reach his eyes. "That's just it," he said. "I do want to end it. We were friends before she became pregnant. While we were terrible partners, we were best friends. And I know she wouldn't want to live like this. I know I wouldn't want to live like that."

"Then it's her parents who are holding back," I said, knowing I was right.

"Exactly," he admitted. "They can't face the fact that their only daughter is gone for good. They're holding out for a hope that isn't there. But if I allow the doctors to pull the plug, then I'm doing it for selfish reasons. At least, according to them I am."

It all happened so innocently. I doubt either of us realized what was going on at the time.

We continued to run into each other at the same coffee shop each morning for the next several weeks. A few times we'd even managed to sneak away to a quiet restaurant for a relaxing dinner before we both had to return to the hospital.

As much as I hated to admit it, Colin and I became very close after that first meeting. We hadn't planned it. We certainly hadn't expected it. It was just something that simply happened.

During that time, I'd come to look forward to the end of my shift in anticipation of seeing Colin again. And the way his eyes lit up as I entered the tiny shop each morning told me the feeling was mutual.

"Good morning," I greeted Colin as I entered the coffee shop one Friday morning.

He rose from his seat in the same booth we always chose and held up two cups of coffee. "One Mocha Surprise just for you!" he said with a twinkle in his eyes.

"How thoughtful," I said, sliding in beside him and accepting the hot Styrofoam cup. Taking a much-needed sip of the delicious brew, I exhaled a sigh of appreciation. "You seem more relaxed today," I said. "Has something changed?"

"You might say that," he admitted, as he smiled and slid his hand across the table to embrace mine.

A chill snaked through my body at his unexpected touch. I wanted to say something, but I wasn't sure what it was. Had his wife died during the night? Or had a miracle actually occurred and she'd gotten better?

There was no denying my attraction to Colin, but I didn't want to force my way into a situation that could prove to be difficult for Colin.

But his next words removed any doubt I might have had. "I think you know how I feel," he said, softly, his trembling hand still on mine. "I've been honest with you from the start. My marriage was over before this accident. I wish I could change what happened. I wish there was some miracle drug or operation that would bring Connie back, but I know there isn't.

"But I also can't pull the plug and give up the only hope her parents have of getting their daughter back. And honestly, I don't think Connie would want that either. At least not until they're ready to give up the fight, as well."

"I understand," I told him, tears filling my eyes.

But he continued. "I don't know how long my wife will last as she is. Unfortunately, experience has indicated that it could go on for years, and I don't want to end my life because of it."

My own hand trembled, realizing what he was leading up to. My feelings for Colin had escalated over the week, and if things were different I was sure we would have already settled into a wonderful relationship.

But things were what they were, and because of that, I also felt as if my future was on hold.

"I know how you feel," I told him.

Colin's eyes bore into mine in a pleading look. "I truly hope you do," he said, "because I'm telling you that I really like you. I'm trying to say that I want us to move forward with this relationship and see where it goes."

My eyes misted. "I feel the same way," I told him. "But what about your wife? What will people say? And what about your son?" I asked, as an afterthought. I'd yet to meet Sammy since he was staying with Colin's parents while Colin visited his wife in the hospital. But I couldn't help but wonder what they would say about their son becoming involved with another woman at this troubled time in his life.

Colin must have considered the same possibilities because his eyes closed tightly as he heaved a weary sigh. "That's where it gets complicated," he admitted, rubbing his hands through his hair. "Believe me, if I thought there was even the slightest hope that Connie would recover, I would never abandon her at such a time. But I know she won't. And deep down, I also believe that her parents realize that their daughter will remain a vegetable until the day she finally breathes her last breath."

"I'm sure it's hard for them to let go," I said, softly.

"Of course it is," he agreed. "I understand that. And maybe if our marriage had been stronger, I'd feel the same way. I honestly don't know. All I know for sure is that she's medically gone. But I still can't pull the plug."

He grew silent for a moment, as he seemed to consider his next words carefully. His silence, along with the pained expression on his handsome face told me that whatever was on his mind was tearing him apart.

"I can't just walk away," he finally said, his voice so low, I could barely hear the words. When he finally raised his eyes to meet mine, I noticed the moisture pooling around his lids.

I smiled and reached my hand across the table to wipe away his tears. "Let's get out of here," I suggested, grabbing my handbag and sliding from the booth. "Let's go somewhere more private where we can talk."

We ended up at my apartment.

After putting on pot of coffee, I showered and changed into something more comfortable. Then I pulled out a large frying pan and a cutting board. Colin and I worked side-by-side cutting onions, mushrooms, and green peppers to make two huge omelets.

"I knew you wouldn't be able to just walk away," I finally told Colin when we sat down at the kitchen table to eat. "It's probably one of the reasons I grew to love you so quickly and easily."

Colin exhaled a long sigh, which seemed to relax the tension he'd been feeling. His broad shoulders lowered dramatically as if a giant weight had been removed.

"Somehow I knew you'd understand," he said, a warm smile spreading across his face.

We continued our breakfast in a companionable conversation. Colin told me about his job as a paralegal at a huge law firm, and his wish to further his education and graduate from law school.

I admitted my desire at a young age to work in the medical field where I could truly make a difference in people's lives.

For a brief time, it seemed as though Colin and I were the only two people in the world that mattered, as we shared our desires and wishes for the future.

Since I worked the night shift and hadn't slept yet, I fell asleep on the sofa in Colin's arms. When I awoke several hours later, I found myself in my own bed, snuggled comfortably beneath a light blanket.

Colin was in kitchen, where an enticing aroma of beef stew simmered in the Crock-Pot.

"Good afternoon," he greeted me, flashing me a warm smile. "I hope you don't mind that I made myself at home in your kitchen," he said, bending over the steaming pot and carefully sipping the stew from a wooden spoon.

"Of course not," I told him. Somehow his being there in my apartment felt so right, so comfortable. The thought that we might not be able to continue to live this way was disheartening, to say the least.

"You carried me to bed." It was a statement rather than a question, since the answer was obvious.

"I didn't want you to wake up with a stiff neck," he said, flashing a warm, sincere smile. "Besides, as wonderful as it felt having you lying so close to me, I needed to leave for a while." He sat two plates of biscuits and gravy on the table and pulled out a chair, then kissed me on the forehead as I slid into my seat. "Anyway, you were pretty wiped out. I didn't think you'd miss me."

But I did miss him. I missed him not being there beside me when I woke up. Although I knew I had no right to ask the next question, I asked anyway. "So how did you spend your day while I slept?"

Lowering himself into the chair opposite me, he picked up his fork and shoved a bite of egg into his mouth. "Moving on," he said with an air of confidence I hadn't noticed before.

"Moving on?"

He leaned forward, reaching for my hand. "Tara, we've already admitted to each other that there's something going on between us. I've been honest with you from the start. My marriage to Connie was over long before the accident."

He put down his fork and reached for his cup of coffee, taking a long drink before continuing. "I want a more permanent relationship with you, and I don't want to wait forever. I spoke with Connie's parents this morning, and told them I needed to start going back to work and spending time with my son."

"Were they upset?"

"They were surprised, but not upset. To be honest, they were never aware of why Connie was driving her car on that awful night in the first place. And thankfully, they realize that I still have to make a living. But we did work out a schedule so that someone will always be there with Connie. I'll be there during the late evening hours."

I smiled, realizing what he was saying. "You'll be there during my shifts, which means maybe we can steal a few minutes for a coffee break now and then?"

"Exactly," he said. "But it's more than that. I want to spend every waking moment with you as well. I want you to meet my son. I want us to be a real family."

Tears were spilling into my eggs, but I made no attempt to brush them away.

From the moment I first talked to Colin, I knew there was something special about him. Falling in love with him had been too easy, probably because of his need to do the right things in life, whether it being marrying his pregnant girlfriend, or refusing to walk away and leave her alone in her vegetative state. Either way, there was no way I couldn't fall in love with someone as wonderful as Colin Larsen.

Our new life began quickly. Colin and his son moved into my apartment, since remaining in the one he once shared with Connie, would have been a bit awkward.

Sammy and I soon settled into a comfortable relationship as well. He was too young to realize that his biological mother would never return, but with his father's love and my growing love, Sammy would never know the loss of his mother.

Colin's parents continued to watch Sammy during the times Colin and I worked.

While it was hectic for a while, with Colin and I both surviving on many sleepless nights and entertaining a small baby, my love and admiration for Colin grew even stronger. He was truly devoted to his son. No matter how tired he was from a long day at work and keeping vigil over his wife's hospital bed, he always found time to spend with his son.

At least once a week, Colin also managed to take his son in to see Connie. Although Sammy was too young to understand any of what was happening, the obviously thoughtful gesture obviously by their son-in-law proved therapeutic to Connie's parents.

Colin talked to Connie as if she were simply asleep. He told her about the cute things Sammy had done during the day, as well as how much their son missed her. He allowed Sammy to sit on his mother's hospital bed, while Colin cupped his wife's lifeless hand into Sammy's.

As a hospital nurse, it was easy for me to wander through the hospital on my breaks to witness these acts of kindness. My love for Colin grew more each day.

It wasn't long before my first encounter with Colin's parents occurred without warning.

Colin and I were sitting in the hospital cafeteria late one evening, sipping coffee and enjoying each other's company when Mr. and Mrs. Larsen spotted us and approached our table.

"Good evening," Mrs. Larsen said, with a raised eyebrow. "Mind if we join you?"

I had a feeling something was up, but I remained silent and let Colin do the talking.

"Of course," he told them. "Have a seat."

After ordering two cups of coffee, they slid into the two remaining chairs. "Is there something the two of you want to tell us?" Colin's mother asked.

Colin and I glanced quickly at one another, our faces reflecting each other's surprise. We'd gone through great pains to keep our relationship secret from our families. The stress Connie's accident had caused was stress enough for anyone to have to endure. We had no intention of adding to it.

Although Colin's parents continued to watch their grandson while Colin and I worked, they were unaware that the two of us had set-up house together. At least that's what we thought.

"What do you mean," Colin asked, innocently.

Mrs. Larsen sipped her coffee, and then placed her hands on the table. A slight smile curved the corner of her mouth. "I'm no fool," she said. "I've seen the way the two of you look at each other."

Colin flashed a furtive glance in my direction, the expression on his face revealing the decline of his calm composure.

Mrs. Larsen broke the awkward silence. "Don't worry," she said. "Your secret is safe with us. I just wanted you to know that you don't have to hide from us anymore. We've noticed that something was happening between the two of you for quite a while."

Colin's father finally spoke his mind as well. "We're not upset," he said. "We've known all along that Colin and Connie weren't happy together. But keep in mind that Connie's parents are having a terribly difficult time dealing with all of this." He heaved a heavy sigh before continuing. "Heck, if the situation were reversed, we'd probably feel the same way they do. Letting one of your children go can't be easy for anyone."

"We'd never do anything to hurt them," Colin said, reaching for my hand. "We didn't mean for this to happen. It just did."

"I know," Mrs. Larsen said. "Life and love are rarely as easy as they seem. And we do admire the way the two of you have acted through all of this. I know it can't be easy."

Suddenly, I wanted Colin's mother to hear my side. "Believe me, we'd never do anything to hurt Connie's parents. I just hope they haven't been as observant as the two of you have been," I said. "I can't even begin to imagine what they're going through, but I'd never do anything to cause them more grief."

Mrs. Larsen shook her head. "Don't worry," she said, softly. "The only thing on Connie's parents' minds right now is their daughter. Nothing else matters to them at this point."

"I won't walk away from Connie," Colin told his parents. "Tara and I have already discussed this, but I've decided that I won't pull the plug on Connie's life support unless her parents are in total agreement." Colin shrugged his shoulders. "And I know they will never agree to that."

"You're right," Mr. Larsen said. "They never will."

I was more careful after that meeting with Colin's parents. I no longer meandered up to Colin's wife's room while he sat with her, for fear that Connie's parents might wander in and realize what was going on between Colin and me.

Instead, Colin and I met as promised in the Cafeteria during my breaks until we could both leave the hospital together to return to our apartment.

We spent the next three months of our lives following this same routine. While it wasn't an ideal situation, it was the only one that made sense for now.

Connie's health continued to deteriorate during those months.

Many times, Colin confided to me that he was so tired of watching his former best friend die in what appeared to be an agonizing death, that he was tempted to revoke his original promise and remove her from life support after all.

But I knew he wouldn't. He'd made a promise to Connie's parents, and Colin was a man of his word.

After hearing Colin talk of how Connie seemed to deteriorate daily, I decided to take a risk and peek in on her myself while no one else was around.

I walked slowly to the floor where Colin's wife lay, making sure no family members were nearby as I entered the room.

In my years as an ER nurse, I'd seen enough death to realize that Connie Larsen was not going to last much longer in this world. Her pale face had sunk in so that her cheekbones protruded in a skeletal manner, and her eyes remained closed as they had since the time she was brought into the hospital on that fateful night so many months ago.

Casting a quick glance at the door, I sat in the chair next to her bed, and took her frail hand in mine. Speaking softly and from the heart, I promised her that I'd always take care of her young son. I also told her that I'd make sure her parents always had access to their grandson.

Then I squeezed her hand as I told her good-bye. In my heart, I knew she wouldn't last much longer.

It was during my ER shift the following night, that I received a message from Colin, asking if I could meet him for coffee in the cafeteria.

Explaining to my supervisor that I had suffered a family crisis, I ended my shift early and joined Colin at a small table in the hospital dining area. I pulled out a chair and sat down, pulling Colin's hands into mine and raising them to my lips.

"I'm so sorry," I said, sincerely.

He actually laughed, although the humor didn't reach his pained expression. "I don't know why I'm so sad," he admitted. "I really thought I'd be relieved when this finally happened."

I reached up and wiped a tear from his cheek. "It's because you never wished her to die," I told him. "You wanted your marriage to end, not Connie's life."

He shook his head in agreement. "I never wanted that," he said. "Connie was a good person." He fidgeted with his fingers for a moment, then swallowed hard, as if searching for the right thing to say. "You know what's really weird?" he asked.

"What's that?" I said.

He looked up, meeting my gaze. "Just before Connie quit breathing for the last time, she actually opened her eyes and smiled at me. I mean, I had just said something to her, and then she opened her eyes and smiled. That's weird, don't you think? It's almost as if she wanted to let me know that everything was okay."

"What did you say to her?"

"I told her that I'd always make sure Sammy remembered her."

I took his hands in mine again and squeezed them tight. "It's not weird at all," I told him.

And I knew it was a promise we'd both keep.

THE END

CONFESSIONS OF AN OFFICE SLUT
I used T & A from 9 to 5 to seduce my boss—just for thrills!

I slipped the silky, black dress over my hips and twirled around. "Well? What do you think?" I asked Marisa, my best friend. "It feels sensational!"

Marisa made a face. "Truth? You look like you should be working on a street corner downtown," she said matter-of-factly. "Seriously, Brandi—you can't possibly be thinking of wearing that to work! It's . . . practically obscene!"

"Oh, please," I replied, twirling again. "You sound like my mother! I think it's perfect!"

She frowned. "Brandi, seriously," she said sternly. "You know I don't approve of this whole thing with you and Jaden. It's wrong and you know it as well as I do! He's a married man—and he's your boss. It's a recipe for disaster, if you ask me."

"Well, I didn't ask you about my 'thing' with Jaden," I replied lightly. "I asked you about the dress. Come on; I look good in it, don't I? It's sexy, right?"

"I'm sure Jaden will love it," she answered grudgingly. "But that doesn't change my mind about what you're doing. He's not going to leave his wife for you, you know. They never do."

"I don't want him to," I said truthfully. "Jaden has two kids. Do you think I want to be a stepmother at my age? I'm just having some fun with him. And sleeping with the boss makes my job a whole lot easier. He wouldn't dare let anyone fire me!"

She shook her head. "That's ridiculous," she replied, looking upset. "You're tearing apart this guy's family for a fling! And you're even making stupid jokes about it, for heaven's sake! Have you given any serious thought to what will happen when his wife finds out about you?"

"That's not my problem," I replied calmly. "Look—I like Jaden. But I'm not in love with him." I shrugged and smiled easily. "We have a good time together, that's all. And I'm not doing anything wrong. He's the one who's married, not me."

Marisa rolled her eyes. "Do you really believe all that? You think you're just some innocent bystander in all of this?"

"In all of what?" I asked stubbornly. "You make it sound like some sort of big scandal! Who are we hurting, Marisa? Tell me honestly. We both like the sex and it's up to Jaden to keep it from his wife if he doesn't want her to find out."

"So it's just sex for you?" she pressed. "You're not emotionally involved at all with this guy?"

I shrugged. "I like Jaden," I repeated matter-of-factly. "He's smart and funny and amazing in bed. But he's twenty years older than I am. I don't want to marry him or be engaged to him or anything even remotely serious like that. I'm just having a good time with him."

"You can't just fool around with people's lives that way," she persisted, still frowning deeply. "Even if you're not in love with him, it sure sounds like he loves you. You're going to end up hurting him if you're not careful."

I was starting to get really angry with Marisa. "He's a grown man, for Pete's sake!" I snapped. "He's not a teenager with his first crush! Jeez, Marisa—I hardly think I'm the love of his life!"

"You know what I mean," she replied patiently. "I think Jaden is wrong to cheat on his wife, but he doesn't deserve to be used by you, either. You should make sure he knows that you don't feel the same way about him."

"Marisa, you're making this soooo much more complicated than it really is," I answered, slipping out of the dress and folding it neatly. "After all, it's not like I planned an affair with Jaden—it just . . . happened. It's so totally not a big deal."

Fortunately, Marisa decided to change the subject after that. She didn't understand the way I felt about Jaden—or my job, for that matter—that much was patently clear. Indeed, nothing was what I planned for myself; I was just trying to make the best of it.

I guess I expected that when I graduated from college and got a job with Woodbridge Incorporated that my life would suddenly change completely . . . and be wonderful! I guess I thought I'd be all grown up—or something like that. Instead—

I just felt . . . trapped!

The salary was good and I could afford my own apartment at last, but the job was deadly boring! Instead of being involved in the advertising department like I wanted, I was stuck in Personnel, reviewing charts, entering data on the computer, and analyzing reports. I had my own office, but it was small and had no windows. The weekly meetings I attended were so dull, I dozed off in them a bit practically every time.

When I complained to Marisa about being bored at work, she just laughed. "Don't be silly. You should be glad you have a job at all! So what if it's boring? Just work really hard and you'll be promoted to something interesting soon enough."

"You like your job," I pointed out. Right after college, Marisa started her own photography business, specializing in weddings and children's portraits. I've never heard her question whether or not she made the right choice.

"Yes, I do like my job," she agreed. "And I work about twice as many hours as you do for half the pay! And you have health insurance and benefits."

I knew I was lucky, but I guess I just expected . . . more from working. I liked being in college—going to classes and staying up until all hours. Now, though, I was stuck in the routine of an eight-to-five job for the rest of my life!

I wanted more and I wanted it NOW!

Of course, with an attitude like mine, it wasn't long before my work started to slide. I was reading so many reports, all the names and numbers started to look alike to me. Soon, I was handing in work that I'd barely glanced over.

And, inevitably, I was called into Jaden Silver's office.

This was the first time I had a face-to-face meeting with my boss, so believe me—I knew I was in trouble! Even so, I couldn't help but notice that the man sitting across from me was very attractive. I guess I never looked at him that closely before, but I was noticing him right then!

He gave me a stern look. "Ms. Harper," he began quietly. "Your supervisor, Mrs. Carole, just showed me some of the reports you've been working on. Frankly, I'm very disappointed. This isn't the quality of work we were hoping for when we hired you."

I knew instantly that I had to think fast if I wanted to save my job. "I know," I replied, hoping I sounded sincere. "It's just that, well . . . my grandmother—she's . . . been pretty sick. I—I've been helping my mother take care of her. I guess I've been distracted at work because of that. I'm really sorry."

Instantly, his expression changed to one of sympathy. "I didn't realize." He paused, evidently considering the situation. "Mrs. Carole recommended that we let you go, but I'll . . . have a word with her on your behalf. If you feel you need to take some time off for your grandmother's—"

"Oh, no," I interrupted quickly. "She's actually doing much better, thank you. I'll—I'll try harder from now on. And please—tell Mrs. Carole I'd be more than glad to work extra hours if that will help."

"I'm sure that won't be necessary," he replied, smiling. He handed me back the pile of reports. "Just go through these more carefully from now on and give them back to Mrs. Carole when you're finished."

That old cow, I thought to myself, I'd like to throw them in her face! But I just nodded and smiled at Jaden. "I will," I told him. "Thank you very, very much."

Jaden looked at me for a long moment before continuing. "I know this job can be boring," he said finally. "But Woodbridge is a good company and you could have a very bright future here, if you want it."

I frowned slightly. Until that morning, I hadn't really thought much about my "future" with Woodbridge—or any other company, for that matter. But I lied pretty quickly to keep my job because I knew I couldn't afford to lose it. And suddenly . . . this Jaden dude was looking pretty interesting to me. . . .

I nodded. "I'll keep that in mind, Mr. Silver," I replied lightly. "Thanks again."

I went into my office and spent the rest of that day correcting the mistakes I made on my reports. When I put them on Mrs. Carole's desk, she looked up at me in surprise.

"I didn't expect these back so soon," she said, arching an eyebrow. "Mr. Silver told me all about how you've been helping your mother care for your sick grandmother. That must be very hard on you."

I could tell from the tone of her voice and the look on her face that she didn't believe my story about my grandmother for a millisecond, but I didn't really care; after all, I managed to save my job and Jaden Silver took my side against hers. She lost the battle and she knew it as well as I did!

"Well, you know how it is as you get older," I continued casually. "More and more things just go wrong as your body wears out and starts on its inevitable course of gradual breakdown followed by total collapse. Of course, you're not quite as old as my grandmother is, but I'm sure you have your share of aches and pains."

She turned bright red and for a second, I almost regretted my words. After all, I suppose she was just doing her job, but she's also the one who wanted me fired! So I flipped my long, black hair back and walked away.

Later, when I was about to leave for the day, I decided I'd thank Jaden again. I knocked on his office door and waited.

"Come in," he said.

He looked up when I walked in and I felt suddenly shy. "Uh, I just—wanted to thank you again, Mr. Silver," I said a bit awkwardly. "And I thought maybe you'd like to, oh—I don't know—go out for a drink or something sometime? My treat?"

"Ms. Harper," he began uncertainly. "That's very nice of you, but. . . ."

"It's Brandi," I interrupted. "You don't have to call me Ms. Harper, you know. I work for you, after all."

He smiled. "Okay, Brandi. But the thing is, well, you see—I'm married, Brandi, and. . . ."

I was amused. "I kind of guessed that," I interrupted again. "I mean, I got the clue from your platinum wedding band and the pictures of your wife and kids all over your office—like on your credenza over there. Anyway, I wasn't asking you on a date or anything like that—I guess I just thought it might be nice for the two of us to grab a quick drink some evening after work and just—you know—talk. And I really do want to thank you for today; you were very, very nice to me, and I really, really appreciate it."

"Brandi," he began slowly, "I'm sure you did mean it as an innocent invitation, but, well . . . you know how office gossip goes. It wouldn't look right—make that, seemly—for us to be seen leaving the office together and heading off to some bar."

"So meet me at The Chain Link bar in half an hour," I replied easily. "I'll leave now, and you can wait twenty minutes to follow me."

Jaden hesitated for a long time, and I knew that he was weighing all of the pros and cons of going out for an "innocent" drink with an office assistant. Finally, he nodded.

"Okay; maybe just a quick one," he agreed. "It's been a long day, after all."

I really didn't have an affair in mind when I invited Jaden out. Honestly.

At the time, I was really only thinking that he was a good person to have on my side in the office. And after the way I'd just humiliated Mrs. Carole with my remarks about her age, I figured I was going to need all the friends I could get at work.

I waited in my car until I saw Jaden drive up. Then I got out and walked over to him. "No one from work ever comes here," I assured him. "It's more of a hangout for college kids."

He frowned slightly. "I feel like I'm sneaking around," he replied darkly. "I shouldn't feel guilty, but I do."

"Relax," I said softly. "I won't bite."

He looked at me then, and his expression changed slightly. "Oh, but I bet you would," he replied, smiling. "Under the right circumstances."

I smiled back at him. "So you do have a sense of humor!" I said merrily. "That's always good to know."

Two drinks turned into dinner—without us really even talking about it, much less acknowledging it. Jaden excused himself at one point, and I knew that he was probably calling home—making up some lame-ass excuse to his wife. I felt a little funny about that, since I knew he would never tell her where he really was—much less who he was with.

"Everything okay?" I asked, all innocence, when he returned to the table.

"Not really," he replied, scowling a bit. "I just told Claire that I'm . . . having dinner with a client." He grimaced slightly, looking embarrassed, uncomfortable—and guilty as sin. "I'm really not in the habit of lying to her—about anything. I felt pretty funny doing that. Pretty lousy, actually."

"You're not doing anything wrong," I answered simply.

"No . . . not technically," he conceded uncertainly. "But I'm having drinks and dinner with a beautiful, young woman. That might be, shall we say—misunderstood—by even the most open-minded wives."

"And is she?" I asked bluntly. "Open-minded, I mean?"

He laughed. "Not where other women are concerned, that's for certain," he replied. "Especially other women half my age. Who are flirting with me."

After two glasses of wine, I couldn't deny that that's exactly what I was doing. "I like you," I told him bluntly. "You're kind and interesting."

"That sounds pretty deadly," he said, smiling. "Like I'm your father or great-uncle or something."

I grinned. "Not at all. You're very handsome, too, and smart and funny. And very successful, clearly."

We talked for a long time that night, and I could tell that Jaden was attracted to me. I liked being with him, and I was intrigued by the idea that a married man could be interested in someone like me.

In the parking lot, I stood on tiptoe to kiss him on the cheek. "That was nice," I said.

"Are you okay to drive home?" he asked. "Should I follow you or call a car service?"

I shook my head. "I'm fine. And if you follow me home, you'll want to come inside my apartment."

He didn't smile. "I know," he agreed solemnly.

The next morning, Jaden was all business at work, but I could feel his eyes linger on me every time we happened to walk by each other. By this point, I'd been with enough guys to know that Jaden wanted me. For that very reason, I deliberately played it cool with him. I was polite, but I made no attempt to seek him out.

A few days later, he appeared at my office door. "Um, I was thinking," he began slowly, "how about lunch today?"

"How about it?" I teased. "Are you asking me to go out to lunch with you?"

He laughed. "Yeah," he admitted. "I guess so. Did that sound as stupid to you as it did to me?"

"Yes," I told him honestly. "But it's okay; I understand."

"Do you want to have lunch with me, then?" he asked softly. "I need to talk to you."

"How about you leave first this time?" I suggested. "I'll meet you at the Chinese restaurant in the mall. The booths are quiet and secluded."

"I know the place; I'll order for both of us."

I smiled at that. "You think you know me well enough to order for me?"

He smiled. "Let's just wait and see how well I know you. I bet I get it exactly right."

"You're pretty sure of yourself," I answered. But deep down, I liked his confidence—and I mean, really liked it.

I've always liked a man who takes control!

Jaden did get it exactly right: spicy orange chicken and egg rolls, with pork fried rice on the side. "Good job," I said, taking a huge bite of my egg roll dipped in duck sauce. "Gosh, I'm starved."

Jaden wasn't eating. "Brandi, I haven't been able to stop thinking about you," he said quietly, taking a sip of his Dewar's on the rocks. "This is crazy—and I damn well know it, believe me. . . . I vowed to myself that I would keep my distance, but . . . I can't."

I put my fork down and considered him over the rim of my martini glass as I sipped delicately. "Jaden, we haven't done anything yet," I finally answered truthfully. "I mean, we've had a few drinks, and eaten together a couple of times, but that doesn't—"

He shook his head. "I know we haven't done anything," he interrupted impatiently. "The point is, I—I think I . . . want to. I hate guys who cheat on their wives, but now. . . ." He drank more Dewar's. "Now, I'm beginning to understand how it happens. It's not . . . something anyone plans, but it does happen, just the same."

I felt a twinge of guilt at how Jaden was reacting to what was going on between us. "You know, Jaden," I began slowly, "I haven't been entirely honest with you. . . . My grandmother . . . she—really wasn't really sick. She isn't sick at all, in fact. I just—told you that so I wouldn't get fired."

Jaden laughed. "I know that. But you were so cute when you said all that nonsense, I let you think that I believed you. Truth is, I knew damn well you'd been slacking off. But I also believe you're capable of doing terrific work. I think you just need motivation."

I leaned forward. "What kind of 'motivation' did you have in mind?" I asked huskily.

He groaned. "Don't do that to me," he said gently. "Don't flirt with me. I don't know how to handle it right now."

I sat back in the booth. "Look—nothing has to happen, you know. We can just have lunch and go back to the office. We can be friends, and that can be all there is to it."

"I know," he said unhappily, nodding. "And that's exactly what should happen. At least, that's what my head is trying to tell me. But I . . . I'm afraid I want . . . more. . . ."

I took another bite of my egg roll. "Don't think so much," I advised. "Just relax and enjoy the food and the booze. Enjoy yourself."

"It's more complicated than that," he persisted, shaking his head grimly.

"No, it isn't. Look—if something happens between us, it's going to be okay, all right? I mean, I am totally not looking to break up your marriage or anything like that—understand?" I shrugged simply and signaled to our waiter for refills on our drinks. "Maybe you just need a change of pace right now."

"That's not how marriage works, Brandi. It probably sounds old-fashioned to you, but I really meant what I said on my wedding day; the vows truly meant what they're intended to mean, as far as I'm concerned. Even the idea that I'm thinking of some other woman besides Claire makes me sad."

I'm half Jaden's age, but somehow, some little, intuitive part of me realized then that I had the power to make all of this okay. I realized that I could just tell him that I wasn't really interested, anyway, and so he should be faithful to his wife. And part of me really wanted to do just that—for his sake. But I also found myself really liking—relishing, in fact—the fact that Jaden was so attracted to me.

So I didn't discourage him.

Not in the least, in fact.

Oh, but nothing happened that day—or the next time we had lunch. But still, we both knew we'd "started something that couldn't be stopped." There were phone calls and brief meetings in the hallways at work and all throughout the workday we were constantly sending each other playful emails and instant messages. Yes, indeed—we were playing with fire and it was exciting.

For instance one day, I wore a skirt that was short enough to make Mrs. Carole do a double take when I walked in. I know she was dying to say something about it to me, but she didn't—which is to say, she didn't dare. I also know that all of the men in the office definitely appreciated me wearing it!

Jaden took one look at my outfit and frowned slightly. A few minutes later, he appeared at the door to my office. "That's quite a skirt you're almost wearing," he remarked, arching one eyebrow in critical consideration—no doubt even appreciation.

I giggled. "You noticed?" I asked innocently. "Good. After all, I wore it just for you, you know."

"Damn," he muttered under his breath. "Brandi, do you know how you look in that outfit? Do you know what every guy in the office is thinking about when they look at you?"

I stared up at him all wide-eyed and fluttering, black, lustrous lashes. "Why don't you tell me?" I asked, tilting my head. "What is every guy thinking when they look at me?"

"They're thinking about what it would be like to make love to you," he said softly. "And it's all I can think about, too."

"Really?" I asked in a teasing tone. "And so . . . what are you going to do about that, then?"

Jaden looked around quickly, then came in and shut the door behind him. "We've been dancing around this for a while," he said evenly. "Are you serious about the two of us?"

I was surprised. "Serious? No; probably not."

He frowned. "What does that mean?"

I sighed. "I don't know, Jaden, I mean . . . you keep talking about your wife and your marriage vows. . . . I don't have those . . . problems. Understand? I mean, I'm not even dating anyone else right now."

Jaden looked disappointed. "So you don't have any feelings for me, then? Have you just been leading me on because you're bored or something?"

"I have . . . feelings for you," I said slowly. "But I don't think they're the same as yours. And, more important—I'm not risking anything by seeing you. It makes a difference."

"So what are you saying, then?" he demanded.

I looked at him plainly. "Jaden, if we made love, it would be wonderful," I replied, sighing. "But if you're really honest with yourself, for you, part of the thrill of being with me is that I'm 'forbidden fruit.' You can't really have me because you're married, and of course, that only makes you want me more. Do you see what I mean?"

He frowned. "That's not it, Brandi. I really . . . like you—I think I could even be in love with—"

"Don't say it, Jaden," I interrupted gently. "You don't love me—at least, not yet. But you want me. You want me something fierce."

"Yeah, he agreed, smiling for the first time. "I do. Very much so—very . . . fiercely, it seems."

"So come on over to my place tonight," I replied, looking straight at him, my eyes never wavering, never leaving his molten, hungry gaze. "I'll make you dinner."

"Okay."

I grinned. "And we'll see if my theory is correct."

I stopped at the corner deli on the way home from work and picked up cold cuts and pasta salad. When Jaden came over, I poured him a glass of wine and asked him what kind of sandwich he wanted for dinner.

"I thought you were cooking for me," he said, grinning playfully.

"I was hoping to find out what kind of domestic skills you have."

"Is that what you really came here for?" I asked, taking a sip of my wine. "To find out if I can cook?"

His expression became serious. "No," he said quietly. "You know that isn't why."

I put my wineglass down and stepped into his arms. "Why don't we go into the bedroom?" I suggested in my silkiest voice.

Jaden kissed me then, and I felt myself melting in his arms.

"Wow," I murmured. "Do that again."

"I've been wanting to do that ever since you first came into my office," he said huskily. "God, you're so incredibly beautiful. . . ."

"You talk too much," I whispered. "Kiss me again."

Jaden kissed me, then led me into my bedroom. He pulled me down beside him on the bed. "This is scary for me," he said, frowning slightly. "I . . . haven't been with another woman since I got married."

I chuckled gently. "Not only do you talk too much," I said, pushing him back onto the big pile of velvety pillows, "you think too much, too. Just make love to me, big boy. . . ."

He didn't need to be asked twice.

Let me just tell you this much—

Jaden definitely knows his way around a woman's body! His hands and mouth and tongue and manhood teased and tortured me until I thought I would burst with pleasure. He's definitely the most experienced guy I've ever been with—

And I loved every minute of it.

Afterward, I snuggled in his arms. "That was really nice," I told him.

He laughed and tenderly kissed the tip of my nose. "Nice? No man wants to be reviewed as, 'nice' in bed."

"Wonderful, then. Terrific! Exciting," I replied, nibbling on his ear. "The best sex I've ever had in my life!"

"That's much better," he said, sounding smug.

"Hey, now—don't go getting all conceited on me," I replied, wrapping a sheet around my body. "Come on; I'll make you a sandwich and you can check out my amazing 'domestic skills.' "

"I've seen the skills I'm interested in," he teased. "But—what the heck? I'm starving, too. Let's just say I . . . really worked up an appetite. . . ."

Right from the very beginning, Jaden and I both always knew the limits of our relationship. We both knew we had to be very careful at work, and that Jaden could never spend the night with me, or just drop by my apartment unexpectedly. I knew that my sneaking around bothered him, but I was actually fine with the situation; after all, I wasn't ready for a commitment by any means, so Jaden was perfect for me.

I didn't tell many people about our relationship, but Marisa's my best friend, so I ended up telling her everything. Of course she didn't approve at all, but that didn't bother me in the least. As it is, I've always thought she's just too straitlaced for her own good.

In fact, back then, I pretty much thought I knew everything about, well—everything! Jaden was in love with me, and that made my job easier; the work was as boring as watching paint dry (if not more so), but having an office romance sure wasn't. I got such kinky thrills out of flirting with Jaden whenever no one else was around, and whenever I wore tight skirts—which is often, believe me—I loved the idea that he was watching my every move, fantasizing about the sex we had—and had yet to have. . . .

Plus, another super bonus: Jaden just loved to buy me presents—pricey jewelry, adorable stuffed animals, gorgeous flowers, fancy perfume, designer clothes, and so many cute cards and other "sweet nothings" like that. Sometimes, he'd even get to talking about "the future" when we were lying in my bed together and he was all sweaty and sated and woozily tender with orgasmic release, and he always talked as though we could actually truly be together someday. But I always stopped him after a while.

"Let's just enjoy 'the right here, and the right now,' " I'd tell him firmly. "After all, your kids are still so little, Jaden; you know you're not getting a divorce, so stop talking like that's even a possibility. We're doing the only thing we can do right now to be together, so you should just stop worrying about anything else."

Looking back, I can see now that I was behaving like a selfish, spoiled brat. Hindsight is twenty/twenty, after all—right? But it's hard to be objective about things when you're right in the middle of them, I guess. Back then, all I knew was that I was having a good time with Jaden, and I honestly didn't see our affair coming to an end anytime soon.

But, boy—

Was I in for a nasty surprise.

Bright and early one Monday morning, I was called into a meeting in the human resources department. When I saw Mr. Conklin, the vice president of the company, and Mrs. Carole already seated in there and apparently waiting for lil' ol' me . . . let's just say that I knew something was very, very wrong. To this day, I get a sick feeling in the pit of my stomach, just thinking about it.

I went in and took a seat across from them at the conference table, and that's when Mr. Conklin looked down at some papers he had laid out in front of him. "Ms. Harper," he began sternly, "I've recently been informed of a very unfortunate situation involving you and Jaden Silver. It seems that your relationship has become . . . less than professional."

I felt my face grow hot. "I don't think my personal relationships outside of the office are anyone's business," I began angrily. "Jaden and I—"

"You and Mr. Silver are both employed by this company—is that not correct, Ms. Harper?" Mr. Conklin broke in icily. "Which makes what the two of you do on company time my business. Under the circumstances, I have no choice but to let you go."

I was stunned. "You're firing me? You can't fire me just because I'm having an affair with Jaden!"

His face remained serious. Honestly—the old fart barely even blinked. "You might just be correct about that, Ms. Harper," he continued in the same icy tone. "Fortunately, your so-called 'work' history has given us another option. It seems you were warned three months ago about the quality of your work. Mrs. Carole here has just informed me that you've done nothing to improve either the quality or quantity of your output since the aforementioned—and, I might add, duly noted in your personnel file—warning."

I turned to glare at Mrs. Carole and saw her smug, plug-ugly smile. She was obviously enjoying every single millisecond of my humiliation and I have to tell you—I've never hated anyone as much as I hated her at that moment!

"We've drafted a letter of resignation for you to sign," Mr. Conklin continued brusquely, pushing a very formal-looking, typewritten sheet of paper across the table at me. "It will indicate that your decision to leave the company was of your own choosing. That should at least make finding another job that much easier for you, considering the circumstances."

"And if I don't sign it?" I challenged defiantly.

He shrugged. "We will simply proceed onward to document every single instance of tardiness, poor work quality, and other dubious behavior on your part," he replied matter-of-factly. "And believe me, Ms. Harper—we already have more than enough grounds on which to fire you, so I hope that's not the option you choose. It would get very ugly for you."

"So I have no choice?" I asked bitterly, flatly.

He stared at me for a moment. "If I were you," he proceeded calmly, "I would use this as a learning experience. Maybe you'll take your next position just a little more seriously."

I signed the letter and received my check for two weeks' pay on the spot. When I went to clean out my desk—that's when I realized I had no one to say good-bye to. I never made any real friends at the office at all and realizing that fact, well, in a strange way . . . that made me feel worse than anything else that happened that day. You see—no one even cared that I was leaving. In fact, I realize now that they were probably glad to see me go.

When I got home, I called Marisa to tell her everything that happened. She was sympathetic, but I could tell by the tone of her voice that she thought I should've listened to her in the first place.

"What about Jaden?" she asked me finally.

"What?" I asked in confusion. "What about him?"

"What did he say about all of this?" she asked impatiently. "Did he get in trouble?"

As it was, up until that moment—I hadn't even thought about Jaden once since I was called into the meeting.

"I don't know," I finally replied honestly.

"Are you serious?" she demanded. "You didn't even try to call him to find out?"

"I'm the one who got fired," I grumbled.

"Yeah—from a job you didn't even want," she replied coolly. "But Jaden—he likes his job, and he has a family to support. What if his wife finds out about all of this?"

"I don't know," I repeated.

"Look—I'm sorry about this mess you're in," Marisa said. "It sounds horrible, and I know you weren't expecting it. I'm really swamped this week, but I can help you with your resume this weekend if you want. I know of a couple places that are hiring."

"Thanks, Marisa," I told her sincerely.

"Are you okay?" she asked, concerned. "Do you need me to come over so we can talk?"

I smiled. "I'm going to eat a pint of Cherry Garcia and go straight to bed. Honestly—I'm just going to feel sorry for myself for a while."

"You didn't deserve this, you know," she said gently. "You just made a mistake, that's all."

"Maybe I did," I admitted grudgingly. "I mean, I did hate the job, and I wasn't very good at it, anyway. . . . So maybe it's really for the best that I was fired."

The next morning, there was a knock on my door. I groaned when I turned over to look at my alarm clock and saw that it wasn't even seven in the morning.

I opened my door to find Jaden standing there, looking haggard and lost. He looked worse than I felt.

"Hi, Brandi," he said quietly. "Can I come in?"

I nodded. "Sure, Jaden; I'll—make some coffee."

"I can't stay long," he said unhappily. "Look—I know you got fired, and I'm sorry. I—I just wish there was something I could do; after all, it's all my fault."

I shrugged. "They let me resign," I told him blankly, rubbing sleep from my eyes. "So at least I can say it was 'my' idea. Anyway, that old witch, Mrs. Carole, was pretty happy about the whole deal—believe me."

He sighed. "I've been transferred to Portland," he said, sitting down heavily. "I leave in two weeks."

I whirled around to face him. "What? But—why do you have to go?"

He gave another long, labored, jaded and weary sounding sigh. "Brandi, Woodbridge prides itself on being a 'family' organization. What we did rubbed a lot of people the wrong way. . . . I've seen it happen before—and I, of all people, certainly should've known better. I didn't lose my job officially, but they've made it plainly clear to me in terms that I understand as a senior professional that they . . . don't want me around."

"But you could quit," I began. "You could—"

He sighed again. "It took me most of the weekend just to convince Claire that going to Portland is a wonderful opportunity for us," he said, sounding tortured. "I . . . tried to make it sound like a promotion, instead of what it really is."

"You knew on Friday?" I asked, frowning. "Then—why didn't you tell me?"

"I wanted to call you, but I was in shock myself. Brandi, listen—I'm so sorry. This whole mess is all my fault, and I feel the worst about what's happened to you."

Suddenly, the reality of everything hit me like someone kicked me in the gut—and then threw me a down a flight of stairs: I lost my job because of Jaden—and it was all for nothing! And to think I was never even in love with Jaden—that I could've stopped the affair at any time and saved Jaden—and myself—from all of this heartache! But, no—I was too self-absorbed to even think of the consequences of my harebrained, slutty actions.

I drew a deep breath and let it out slowly. "No, Jaden . . . I'm the one who's sorry," I told him honestly. "I could've said no . . . and I should have. But you . . . you still have your family and your career to consider. . . . at least we know you're going to be okay."

"I love you, Brandi," he said softly. "If things were different, we could, maybe . . . have a life together. . . ."

I nodded. "I know. But it isn't enough, is it? And it never was. . . . When you're in Portland, you should concentrate all of your time and energy on your marriage and your family. Soon enough, you'll stop thinking about me. I know you will."

I kissed Jaden good-bye that morning, knowing I did the right thing—

For once.

THE END

CONFESSIONS OF AN ABUSED WIFE
"Why I Keep Taking Him Back"

"Isabel! Man, that woman can't do anything right!"

Jake slammed the refrigerator door shut with teeth-jarring force, his furious outburst abruptly shattering the fragile peace I had tenaciously hung on to these past few weeks. My stomach clenched painfully.

The sound of my husband's voice, so full of anger and hostility, was enough to unleash the fear in me, a fear that was as much a part of me as was my skin or my hair. This was a familiar routine of ours. We'd been through it countless times before, and I felt a sick dread for what I knew was coming.

"I told you to buy beer," he yelled, storming from the kitchen and into the living room where I was folding clothes. He was red-faced and bloated from the beer he'd already consumed that day, and the clock hands were minutes shy of noon.

"But, as usual, you don't remember a thing I tell you, do you?" he raged on. "I don't ask for much. A little beer now and then, but do you care? Of course not!" He shot me a hateful look of disgust. "You're so dumb."

Ever since my husband, Jake, had been laid off from his job six months ago, those scenes had become more frequent and increasingly violent.

"Jake, honey, I didn't forget. Really. But it's just that I had to buy groceries, Tyler's teacher sent a note saying that he needed his own crayons and scissors, and then, then there wasn't enough money left. . . ."

I knew that my stammering only made him angrier, but I couldn't help it. When he got like this—angry, yelling, accusing, his eyes and words like daggers pinning me to the wall—I stammered, and my voice went weak and high-pitched, like a cornered mouse's fearful squeak.

"Who am I here?" he raged on, knuckles as white and tight as the leather of a new baseball stretched across balled fists, his eyes narrowing to thin slits. "You made sure there was enough money to get food to feed your face and buy junk for that kid, but for me—the man of this house—nothing. Nothing!" he shouted again, and with one arm, made powerful by many years working physical labor jobs, swept the carefully folded piles of clean clothes off the coffee table and kicked them all over the room. The look in his eyes said he wanted to do the same to me. I clutched my son's small, red T-shirt to my chest for what little protection it offered. I knew I should run, but the floor was like a thick layer of sticky tar beneath my bare feet.

"Jake, I . . . I'm sorry, I'm sorry about the beer," I said quickly. "I'll go next door and get you some right now; Lou probably has some." Keeping my eyes on him, I managed to pry my feet loose from the floor and slowly began making my way around him toward the old screened front door flapping and creaking in the breeze.

"I'll just go right now and ask her and be right back?" I said a quick silent prayer that I'd make it out the door. But it wasn't to be.

"You're not going anywhere," Jake snarled, grabbing my hair and jerking me backward. The carpet offered no cushioning as I landed on its threadbare surface with a bone-jarring thud. I lay sprawled on the floor, as defenseless as a cockroach on its back, gasping, struggling to take in a big enough gulp of air. The stench of ingested alcohol invaded my nostrils when Jake knelt over me. A knee on each side of my body, he pinned me to the floor like a butterfly to a board.

"You're going to stay right here and get a lesson in respecting the boss of the house," he threatened.

The mid-spring sun stretched broadly, throwing off the soft blanket of clouds from its shoulders, and sending thick bands of light slanting across the room where my neighbor, Lou, and I sat a few hours after I had received my "lesson." As the TV characters on an afternoon soap opera babbled in the background, I focused on trying not to wince as Lou applied antiseptic to the cut on my rapidly swelling cheek.

"When are you going to wise up and leave that beast you call a husband?" Lou asked me, dabbing the wound gently with a medicine-soaked cotton ball.

Luella Martin was more than my neighbor and friend; she was the closest thing I had to a mother. She made me feel as if I really were her daughter. Lou and I didn't do things or go places together like most friends did; there just wasn't the money for that. But she was always there to help me bandage or ice whichever part of my body was swollen, bruised, broken, or cut.

Despite the closeness we shared, I couldn't bring myself to divulge the whole truth about the troubles that plagued my family, though I had a feeling she already knew. But still, she wasn't family, and I had been taught that you don't hang the family's dirty laundry for all to see. Besides, I knew well the punishment for talking to the neighbors about private matters.

"I told you, Lou, I left the cabinet door open and ran into it when I turned around," I lied, and jumped up from the couch to put the first aid kit away in the bathroom cabinet so as not to have to face Lou's knowing eyes.

"Why do you keep covering for him, letting him get away with it?" she demanded of me, loudly enough to make sure I could hear her from where I was in the bathroom. "As long as you let him beat you, he's gonna keep doing it. You gotta get away from him." She wagged her finger insistently at me to emphasize her words as I came back into the room.

"He doesn't beat me, Lou," I said, picking up the pot of coffee from the table near us. "He yells and, well, sometimes pushes me, but that's only because he's so upset at not having a job and at not being able to give us the things we need. He gets frustrated, and kind of crazy," I said, refilling Lou's cup with coffee, then reaching for my own cup. "He doesn't mean anything by it. He loves me"

"I don't know who's crazier—him for acting the way he does, or you for putting up with it. Nothing gives him the right to hit you—not being out of work, not being drunk, and not liking something you say or do. Nothing. Why can't you see this? Does he have to kill you or Tyler before you understand that?"

I slammed down my mug, sloshing hot coffee onto the table and my hand.

"Lou, that's enough. Jake's never laid a hand on Tyler," I insisted, quickly wiping up the coffee with a paper towel. "And he never will. He loves his son. If he ever did touch Tyler, I would leave. Even if we had to live on the streets."

"That's the first sensible thing I've heard you say, but why wait till it gets that bad? You can go to the women's shelters. They'll let you and Tyler stay there for a while, till you can find a job and get on your feet."

I got up and began straightening the already neat-as-a-pin room. "I have a home. I'm not going to any shelter," I said over my shoulder. "Jake is just going through a rough time right now. He needs my support, not talk of leaving."

My eyes caught sight of the family photograph sitting on the shelf. The three of us sat close together in the traditional family pose, wearing our happiest faces for the camera, smiling like our life really was picture-perfect.

"Everything will be fine, just as soon as he finds a job. Everything will be fine. Besides," I said, turning away from the fairytale pose to meet Lou's eyes. "How would I take care of Tyler and me if I left? With Jake we have a place to live, food to eat, and clothes to wear. They're not the best, but. . . . What happened this morning was just a fluke." I angrily switched off the TV characters. Why did I need their fantasy story when I had my own going on right in this room?

"So, tell me," Lou said. "What did you do this time to deserve being slapped around? The sheet on the bed was wrinkled? Cooked the wrong breakfast? Said good morning? Looked at him funny?"

"Please, just drop it, Lou," I moaned, dropping down beside her, onto the couch.

But she wasn't going to drop it until she was good and ready.

"And what was that excuse you made up for him last month, huh?" She took my chin in her hand and turned my face toward her. "That cut on your forehead is still not completely healed from the bottle he smashed over your head because you bought the wrong kind of beer." At my shocked look, she continued. "You didn't think I knew about that, huh."

"No, you're wrong," I insisted. "It was an accident."

"Yeah, right. There was so much screaming, cussing, and crying coming from the house that night, sounds of glass breaking. . . . It was like a war zone. It was no accident. I know it. Everybody knows it." Lou reached over and laid her hand on mine, and her voice, when she again spoke, was kinder, less harsh. "Why didn't you tell the cops the truth? They could have helped you, they could have taken him away so he couldn't hurt you."

"That's enough, Lou. And I mean it. I told you then and I'm telling you now: it was an accident. They were all just accidents. What can I say? I'm clumsy. Now, would you just drop it? I don't want—"

The opening of the front door and a youthful, excited voice interrupted my sentence.

"Hi, Mom, Hi, Aunt Lou! What do we have to eat? I'm starving!" It was Tyler, home from school. The six-year-old bundle of energy tossed his backpack onto the table and made a beeline for the refrigerator.

"Hey, baby, where's my hug?" I called from the living room. Tyler charged out of the kitchen, chomping noisily on a crisp, red apple and skipped over to me.

"Mom! I told you I'm not a baby," he said, throwing his arms around me. "I m a big dude. Thanks for the apple. They're yummy!"

"You're welcome, dude." I looked down at his sweet face. I was glad I had bought the apples, even though they had been too expensive and one of the reasons I hadn't bought Jake's beer. How I love this child. I'd do anything for him, anything to keep that happy look on his face, even take the beatings so he can have a shot at a decent life. But as Tyler looked up into my bandaged face, his happy expression changed.

"Mom, what happened to your face?"

Self-consciously, I covered my bandaged cheek with my hand and quickly turned away, my eyes colliding with Lou's dark brown ones that seemed to say, explain it to him, if you can.

"Oh, it's nothing, hon," I said, with a dismissive laugh. "I ran into the cabinet door this morning." Seeing that he wasn't entirely convinced, I tried to further convince him by adding, "If you think this is bad," I joked, pointing at the bandaged cheek. "You should see that—"

"Mom, have you and Daddy been fighting again?" Tyler interrupted me, asking the question in a voice that said he already knew the answer.

I brushed the too-long fringe of bangs away from my son's eyes. "Hey, why don't you go play outside for a while until dinner," I said softly, changing the subject.

"No, Mama, I want to stay with you," he said solemnly, hugging me to him. He always wanted to stay close to me after one of his parents "arguments." I'm not sure why. To protect me, maybe. Or maybe the fights made him sick to his stomach, like they did me, and he was the one in need of protection.

"I'm fine, baby. I mean, dude. Really," I said softly, cupping his face in my hand. "Go on and play with Luke, now." At his reluctant nod of agreement, I tacked on, "Love you."

"Love you, Mom," he answered, mimicking my soft voice. "Yell if you need me, okay?"

"You bet I will. And don t go anywhere but Luke s."

"Okay." He gave me one last huge hug.

"I'm going, too," Lou announced. "Call if you need me, Isabel. Wait up, Tyler. I'll walk out with you." She patted him on the shoulder as she walked through the door Tyler held open for her.

"Bye, Mom," Tyler said as he followed Lou out the door, on his way over to play with his best friend, Luke, who lived a few houses down the street from ours.

I stood at the window, shading the sun from my eyes with my hand, watching them, hating to let them go, until they disappeared in opposite directions. Only then did I turn my attention to the empty room where the echo of Lou's words taunted me, and my mind tried in vain to counter them with denials.

My eyes again fell on the photograph, the three happy faces smiling up at me, almost as if they were waiting for my decision. I picked up the photograph and gently brushed away minute particles of dust off the glass with my sleeve.

Are things ever going to get better, or am I just trying to convince myself of it so I won't have to make the hard decisions, so I wouldn't have to be alone? I clutched the photo to my breast, against my heart, wondering how it had gotten this bad.

When Jake and I had started dating in high school and after we got married, he was good to me, but he was also insanely jealous, always afraid that some guy was going to take me away from him.

He never hit me, just threw things, pushed me a bit, and blew up over things anyone else would consider trivial.

At the time, I thought his behavior, though bordering on the obsessive, showed how much he cared about me. His attention made me feel special, loved. Love and attention were two necessities of life I had grown up without, so when I got them from him, I refused to let go, even if things between us were less than perfect, and even if I glimpsed, now and then, the harsh blinking red of the danger signs in the road up ahead. In our seven years together, the pushes had progressed to slaps and punches, and my love for him had changed into out-and-out fear.

I looked at the photo and sighed. "We can make it through this," I said, as if saying it loud would make it so. Then I gently placed it back on the shelf.

A couple of hours later, I had given up wrestling with my thoughts and had moved on to more constructive housecleaning activities. I was up to my elbows in a sink full of soapy water and dishes when I heard the telltale creak of the screen door opening, then banging closed against the doorjamb. When I didn't hear any footsteps or voices, I called out.

"Tyler? Is that you?"

At the lack of response, I left the dishes and walked into the living room. I halted in mid-step, my body cringing into a tight ball of tension at the sight before me. Jake stood in the doorway, shifting from one foot to the other, an awkward half-smile on his face. In one fist was a small bouquet of yellow daffodils, flowers he had obviously swiped from someone's early blooming garden, judging by the little clods of dirt still clinging to the bottom of the long stems. The other hand he rubbed repeatedly against the leg of his faded blue jeans as if he were desperately trying to get something off his palm.

Besides the little nervous gestures, he appeared sober, even gentle and loving. But, as he had shown me more times than I could count, appearances were deceiving. I often found that it was best to not say anything at all until I knew what kind of mood he was in, so I remained quiet and just watched him through my one good eye.

"Hi." His voice cracked. He cleared his throat and repeated his greeting a little louder. I didn't respond. I was afraid to. But watching him approach, he didn't appear threatening. He was more cautious, the way he would approach a small child so as not to frighten it. As he slowly closed the distance between us, I had to fight back the impulse to run from him.

"Isabel, honey, I'm sorry about earlier today."

I'm sorry. He always began this way. It sounded so trite, so insincere, so meaningless to my ears, after having heard it so often.

It carried the same weight as the overused, but still popular, sayings, Have a nice day, or How are you?

"Isabel, I . . . I didn't mean to. You know how much I love you, don't you? You know how upset I've been, you know, not being able to find a job to take care of you and Tyler, give you the things you deserve. It just hurts me that I can't. But things will start looking up for us, I promise. And I want to make another promise. I won't hurt you again, Isabel. Please forgive me." Then he held out the flowers timidly, a peace offering, their yellow heads nodding up and down as if trying to do their part to persuade me to accept Jake's apology.

I knew that forgiving him would buy Tyler and me a few days of peace. Even though I knew he would hit me again, I wanted to believe him when he said he wouldn't. I wanted the old Jake back, the Jake I had fallen in love with, the Jake I had a child with, the Jake I had taken as my lifelong husband for better or for worse. How could I ever have that Jake back if I gave up? I took his flowers, his apologies, and his promises.

The days that followed were tense, but relatively uneventful. I tried to relax and enjoy the peace while it lasted. But I couldn't relax; living with an abuser is like playing Russian roulette. You never knew when the madness would roll back around to face you, yet you still try.

Jake had been out all day, following up on what he called "some pretty strong leads" for jobs. Tyler was spending the night with Luke, so I planned a nice evening for Jake and me, a sort of a twofold celebration: because we had been getting along so well for the past few weeks, and just in case he had received a job offer.

Delicious aromas drifted through the house, setting the foundation for a relaxing evening. Dinner warmed on the stove. Several small, scented candles borrowed from a neighbor bathed the cozily set table in soft, flickering light, their scent floating above the table like a light fragrant cloud.

I was ready, too. I wore my only nice dress, the black one I had bought in better years when money hadn't been so scarce. My hair was swept into a high, loose bun. My makeup, just mascara and lipstick, was lightly applied; just the way Jake liked it. Yes, everything was perfect. And waiting for him. I wanted so much to please him, to maintain the fragile peace we had been enjoying.

The hangdog look on his face and his slouched-over walk when he came through the door a short time later told me that he hadn't gotten a job offer from any of the leads, only another pocket full of maybes or rejections. But I asked anyway.

"Those losers." He growled his response through his teeth. "They all say the same thing. 'We don't have anything now, but we'll keep you in mind. Or, 'thanks for applying with us, we'll let you know soon.'"

Determined to keep the evening light and enjoyable, I began massaging his shoulders and neck. "Well, they didn't say no, and that's good, right?" I countered, continuing the kneading and trying to erase or at least diminish his frustration.

"I guess," he admitted hesitantly.

"I bet someone will call you soon about a job. In fact, they'll probably all call at once and then you'll get to choose the best job."

"Wouldn't that be something," he said, his bunched muscles relaxing beneath my fingers. "Have all them begging me to work for them. And me getting to be the one to say 'I'll let you know.' Ha! That would be great. Let them know how it feels to be left dangling."

On this somewhat positive note, we started dinner, but as the evening progressed, the notes soured considerably. I can't pinpoint the exact moment it started to go wrong; it was a series of little, unrelated things that got the ball rolling until it was thundering downhill out of control.

"How much money did you waste on these candles?" he demanded a few moments into dinner.

"Oh, I didn't buy them. Heidi from next door let me borrow them," I answered quickly.

"You been talking about our private stuff to the neighbors?"

"What do you mean?"

"Telling them we don't have any money to buy candles."

"No, I . . . I just mentioned that I was making a special dinner tonight. She offered the candles." I tried in vain to curb the stammering that was already creeping into my speech. He eyed me suspiciously, but he seemed to accept my explanation.

"Make sure you keep our private life private." It was an obvious warning, one that I always heeded.

"I do, of course, always." I muttered, bobbing my head up and down.

"Any beer left?"

"Um, I think so. I'll check." I could feel his stare burn me every step of the way into the kitchen.

"Um, there's two left," I called back to him.

A glimmer of anger shone in his eyes when I returned with the beer and began pouring it into his glass.

"You been wearing that all day?" he sneered, looking me up and down. "Parading yourself around in front of the neighbors?"

"No, I put this on just before you got here."

"You better be telling the truth." The threat hung thick, heavy, and menacing in the air, the way my father's leather strap had hung in plain sight on the nail on the living room wall to remind me of how accessible it was, to remind me to, as he put it, "Watch your step, missy."

"Cause if I find out you're not. . . . Isabel! How many times I gotta tell you, tip the glass and pour the beer slowly so you don't get all head. For crying out loud!" He shoved the glass away then pushed back in his chair. "I can't drink it like that." He slung his hands up.

"Sorry, Jake. Sorry. I thought I was doing it right. I'll take this one and get you the other one."

"Oh, never mind. Never mind, I said! Just sit down and leave it alone." He chugged what was left in the can and belched loudly before resuming the meal. After a few moments of silence, I tried to start the conversation again.

"Having the place to ourselves reminds me of when we were first married."

A sliver of a smile actually touched one corner of his mouth. Encouraged by that one gesture, I leaned toward him and put my hand on his arm.

"We had a lot of fun, didn't we? Remember when you used to call in sick from work and we'd order pizza—a large, cheesy one with sausage and onions—and rent a couple of videos and just stay in all day, snuggled up together in bed?"

His smile vanished as quickly as it had appeared. "Yeah, well, that's when I had a job to call in sick to and we had money to waste on stupid things like movies and pizza," he spat out.

"Oh, honey, we will again. I just know it. One of those jobs will come through. Just don't give up."

He slammed down his fork onto the table, making me jump back in surprise at the sudden explosiveness of the action. "You think it's easy? Going out day after day, having doors slammed shut in my face, being told, 'no, no, no. We don't want you.' How do you think that makes me feel?"

"I know it's hard."

"And just how do you know how hard it is? Huh?" He was slinging his arms, now, and his hands were balled into fists. "I don't see you out there. If you did, maybe you'd be a little more understanding and helpful instead of being so pushy."

"I'm sorry." He wasn't listening. He was already an avalanche thundering down the mountain and there was no way anybody was going to stop it.

"Push, push, push, that's all you do. That, and nag me all the time. Why did I even marry you? What good are you to me? All you do is complain and spend money we don't have. There's always something you and that boy got to have, but whatever old Jake needs comes last. You don't help me, or support me. You don't do anything but cause me trouble."

I could read his mannerisms as easily as I could read the stop sign at the corner of our road, and his beet-red face and the bulging veins in his forehead and neck spelled trouble in big, bold, flashing red letters. And I knew that if this conversation continued, he would start punctuating his sentences with his fists.

This dinner was over. I got up from the table and started carrying our dishes, the food on them only half eaten, to the kitchen to scrape and wash them. But I waited too long to act; Jake was already too far into his tirade to let me go.

"Don't you walk away from me while I'm talking to you."

He jumped up and knocked the dishes out of my hands, sending them crashing against the wall. He sent the rest of the dishes on the table sailing after them, the little scented candles followed; their waxy, blood-like liquid splattered all over the floor was already hardening, the way my body was hardening itself to deflect the blows it knew were coming.

The first blow, a sound slap across the face, sent me reeling backwards. The pile of shards and slivers of broken glass that I landed in sliced and gouged my hands, legs, and other exposed areas of my body. Blood flowed from the numerous cuts and gashes.

I remember holding up my hands, staring, almost mesmerized, at the jagged shards protruding from them, looking like crystals had sprouted from my hands, and all the blood—so much blood—and wondering why I didn't feel any pain.

Though the sight of my flowing blood stunned me, it only seemed to incense Jake. Like a hungry wolf that smells life flowing out of its victim's wounds, he moved in. I sat motionless in the sparkling mosaic of blood-covered glass, pieces of baked chicken, and bits of potato and broccoli, thinking how odd it was that I could still smell the sweet scent of those little candles.

One of the neighbors must have complained about the commotion, because soon the place was in a whirl: police were bursting through the door, paramedics were treating my wounds, and Jake was being taken away in handcuffs to jail. The doctor at the hospital who treated me said I was lucky that the broken glass hadn't sliced a vein. Yeah, I sure felt lucky, with my black eye, a matching set of bruised and swollen cheeks, a split and bloody lip, cuts all over my body—several requiring stitches—large bruises on my arms and legs, and two broken fingernails.

At Lou's insistence, I pressed charges against Jake. He spent very little time in jail, but the judge did issue a restraining order against him, so when he did get out, he wasn't allowed to come near Tyler and me, or our home. What a joke that piece of paper was for all the good it did.

Jake phoned constantly, calling me names, screaming that he would "make me pay" for sending him to jail. I hung up as soon as I knew it was him, but there were times that the phone calls would come every half hour, all during the day and night.

When it got to the point that I wouldn't even answer the phone, it would sometimes ring for five minutes straight.

When I just couldn't stand the shrill, tortuous sound, I would pick it up, slam it down, and then take it off the hook.

When he realized the calls were not an effective threat, he began showing up at the house, giving us the same treatment in person.

Tyler and I were both having trouble sleeping since Jake had begun harassing us. Tyler had taken to sleeping with me; we both felt a bit safer that way. One night, we were awakened by loud and insistent banging noises at the front of the house. Groggily, I looked at the clock. Three-thirty in the morning. Who is banging on the door at this hour? I was too sleepy to be afraid at that point, so I got up to investigate, thinking it might be Lou in trouble.

As I moved along the hallway that led to the living room, the banging stopped. The house held an eerie silence that I could almost feel as I moved through it, like the feeling of silky spider webs brushing against you as you walk past. I moved cautiously into the living room and let the dark shadows by the wall facing the door hide me. The stark, white light of a full moon beamed through the living room windows and pooled onto the floor.

I saw no one. I walked over to the windows and peered out. Suddenly, a face appeared in the window from outside. I screamed and jumped back. From the dim glow of the porch light, I could see Jake—crazed and obviously drunk—and he saw me, too, because he started banging on the door again, against the windows, and then on the side of the house.

"Let me in my house!" he yelled in an angry, but slurred, voice. "Let me in or I swear, I'll get you. I'll make you pay. This is my house."

I ran to the bedroom and grabbed Tyler, who by that time was awake and crying in the middle of the bed. I punched out 911 on the phone. We could still hear Jake outside yelling, cussing, running around to all the windows, and banging against them. Tyler and I huddled together in the deepest, darkest corner of the bedroom closet, crying, silently praying that Jake would go away, and terrified that he was going to get in and kill us. Soon there was just quiet. Then, later, knocking on the door.

I didn't move an inch from my cavern until I heard the person at the door identify himself as a police officer. Still knitted together, Tyler and I moved as one to the door. I peeked out. There were two officers standing on my front porch and a squad car in front. I flung open the door and collapsed at their feet, a sobbing and trembling pile of relief.

The officers looked around the neighborhood for Jake, but they didn't find him. They suggested I stay with family or friends for a while. Lou insisted we stay with her at least until my wounds healed and until they had "thrown Jake back in jail where he belonged," she added. For once I didn't argue with her, and just accepted her offer gratefully.

After we moved in, I made a special point to stay inside the house, not leaving unless it was absolutely necessary; I even kept Tyler home from school and in from playing. Jake was making us prisoners in this house, but for our safety, I had to make it look like we were nowhere around.

Days passed with no trouble from Jake, but soon enough, he found us. Lou called the cops out twice to enforce the restraining order, but they said they couldn't do anything unless they actually caught him on the premises and in the act of doing something to us. Unrestrained, Jake kept up the harassment. One night, they caught him as he was running away from Lou's and put him in jail. Since this was only his second offense and he hadn't threatened us, he was only in for a short time.

After weeks of not seeing or hearing from Jake, I was feeling pretty safe; so safe, in fact, that I ventured outside long enough to hang out some just-washed clothes on the string line at the side of Lou's house. It had been so long since I had been outside in the fresh, sun-warmed air. The sun was smiling on everything, making even the shabby neighborhood look halfway pleasant. The birds were out, chirping and teasing each other. The few trees in the small yards were open umbrellas of bright green, which shaded and cooled the ground underneath. Kids were outside, running around, laughing, and playing. Just being out in it all made me feel better and more cheerful than I had in a long time.

Half of the laundry was drying on the line, and I was reaching up to hang a shirt when Jake appeared on the other side of the curtain of clothes from me. I don't know how long he had been standing there watching me. The shirt in my hands never made it to the line. It fell to the ground and was already forming a muddy puddle in the dirt when I turned and ran toward the house. Unfortunately, Jake was faster. He grabbed my arm, and though I pulled and yanked frantically, trying to get away, he held fast. "Isabel! Isabel, don't go, please."

"Let me go, let me go," I squeaked, trying to keep my back to him to ward off any blows. I just knew he was going to make good on his vow to "make me pay" for letting them put him in jail and because I told them to keep him away from us. I didn't think my abused body could take even one more blow.

"Isabel. Honey, I just want to talk."

"You're not supposed to be here. I'll call the cops. I mean it."

"I just want to talk, that's all. I'm not going to hurt you. Isabel, look at me."

He used his superior strength to force me to turn toward him. His eyes flew open wide and so did his mouth, and he stepped back a bit. He hadn't seen me since the night of the beating, so he hadn't witnessed the effect of his handiwork on my face and body.

I had only seen Jake cry once, and that was the day Tyler was born. But, to my astonishment, tears welled up in my husband's eyes as he took in the full image I presented before him: puffy eyes, colored in shades of red, purple, yellow, and blue, were so swollen they were almost completely shut. A barrage of both large and small white and tan bandages covered various cuts on my body. Lips, split and swollen, looked more like those of a boxer than a housewife. Huge, purple-yellow bruises stained my flesh in a Dalmatian pattern.

"Isabel, I'm. . . ." Tears and emotion choking back his words, he pulled me gently into his arms and cried against my shoulder.

I heard him mumbling, "I'm sorry," over and over through the tears. I couldn't return his affection, nor absolve his guilt, but neither could I push him away.

"I love you so much, Isabel," he said finally, wiping his eyes that were red and wet from crying. "I know that I don't always show it, but I do love you. This time. . . ." He paused, hung his head, and again wiped his eyes. "This time I've learned my lesson. I can't believe I did this to you. I know I don't deserve it, but please, I'm begging you, give me one more chance to make it up to you, to prove what a good husband and father I can be. It's been hell without my family. I promise, I swear, I'll never, ever hurt you again. I need you and Tyler. I'm completely lost without you guys."

At my silence, he continued. "I know, you're probably thinking, 'How do I know this time will be any different? All I can tell you is that spending time in jail and being kept away from you and Tyler made me realize how horrible it is being without my family. I love you guys so much, and I need you. Tyler needs his father and you need a husband, one who treats you good, who loves you and takes care of you. I can do that. I haven't had a drink in weeks. Give me another chance to prove how good I can be. I won't disappoint you again."

His pleading eyes, his soft and gentle touches to my arm and my head, matched his words, but I couldn't honestly say I believed that a short stint in jail had changed him as dramatically as he claimed. Yet his words, so sincere sounding, turned my resolve to jelly. Without Lou right there beside me, without her strength, I didn't have enough of my own to oppose him, to ignore his promises, to scoff at his assurances that he was going to be different . . . this time. "This time." If I only had a nickel for all the times I had heard him say that to me. Well, I'd be a rich woman and could buy my way out of my mess of a life.

To Jake s credit, he had never acted that contrite before, or so tender and genuinely remorseful for what he had done. And I agreed with him on one issue, and that was that Tyler needed his father and I needed a husband. My brain was logically advising me not to believe him, but my heart was screaming, Give him another chance. Very much against Lou's advice and pleading, I agreed to move Tyler and me back to our home with Jake.

Months passed. Jake was looking for work every day, going on interviews, following leads. He still came home frustrated and yelling sometimes, but he didn't take out it out me. And he hadn't taken a drink since we had all gotten back together. Things weren't perfect, but they were better. I was actually beginning to believe the worst was behind us.

A steamy summer breeze blew into the kitchen from the open window, barely cooling the sticky beads of perspiration dotting my face and neck and running down my back. It was an uncomfortably warm night, made worse by the fact that the oven was raging on high, ready to accept the cornbread I had mixed up for dinner. Jake was expected home any time now.

Tyler was watching a cartoon show on TV in the living room. Every once in a while, his carefree laughter floated in, making me smile with pleasure at the sound I didn't often hear in this house.

I heard the screen door creak open, then slam shut. An involuntary rush of fear sprinted through my body. Jake was home. I couldn't figure out, though, why he kept slamming the door against the jamb, again and again and again. What is he doing? I thought. He knows the door won't stay closed unless it's locked.

I came out of the kitchen and was going to comment on it until I got a good look at him. His clothes, which I had neatly pressed this morning when he left the house for the job interviews, were now stained and badly wrinkled, looking like he had dug to the bottom of the dirty clothes basket for them. His hair equaled his clothes in appearance; it stood out every which way from his scalp.

A foul odor surrounded him like a cloud; it was one I knew well. My father had come home every night of my life wearing that stench like cheap cologne. The stench that had lingered on me long after the old man had passed out on the floor after overexerting himself while delivering my nightly beating. The stench that lingered in my nostrils and in my brain, although I scrubbed my skin nearly raw under the stinging spray of the hot shower to eliminate it. Jake smelled like that; an obnoxious, blending of stale liquor, vomit, and sweat. That smell evoked a deep-seated fear within me; I tasted, smelled, saw, and felt fear and pain.

I slunk back into the kitchen to continue preparing dinner, but carefully watched his every move out of the corner of my eye. Jake stumbled into the kitchen and plopped down into one of the wobbly dinette chairs and stared at me. I tossed a light, "hi" over my shoulder to him, which instead of making him feel welcome only served to open the floodgate of nastiness.

He started with "Where's my dinner?" progressed to "Gimme a beer!" Then he threw in a number of other epithets I couldn't understand because the liquor had slurred his words so badly. I didn't dare tell him that more liquor was the last thing he needed. Instead, I took a single can out of the refrigerator, opened it, and placed it on the table in front of my husband.

"Dinner will be ready in a few minutes," I said quietly as I slipped the cast iron skillet filled with the cornbread batter into the oven. "The cornbread's in the oven now and the beans are already ready."

"Cornbread! I want tortillas with my beans, not cornbread!" Jake's words were still slurred, but I had no problem understanding their tone, that sarcastic, combative, hostile tone I knew so well.

Here it comes. Another fight. I mentally steeled myself, hunching my shoulders and gripping the scarred and peeling edge of the countertop. He only grabbed his beer, mumbled another obscenity, and taking a big swig, staggered out of the room. On his way to the bedroom to pass out, I hoped.

I stood stock still, heaving a huge sigh of relief that maybe, just maybe, that was as bad as it was going to get. When I realized no attack was coming, my hands released their death grip on the countertop. I released the breath I had been holding, and my tense body uncurled and relaxed a bit.

Maybe he's really serious about keeping his promises this time, I thought. In another time, he would have already started the punching.

Then Tyler's voice came from the living room. "Dad, I was watching that show! Come on, Dad. Put it back, put it back on my channel!" he pleaded.

"It's my TV, and I'll watch what I want. I don't want to watch a cartoon show," came Jake's hateful, slurred answer. Then, "where do you think you're going? Get back here and sit down!"

"I'm going to my room," came Tyler's stormy reply. "Since I can't watch my show, I don't want to watch anything."

Sensing the rapidly heating tension, I dashed out of the kitchen just in time to see Jake jump up from the couch and leap after Tyler. He grabbed Tyler's arm and swung him around to face him. Then, gripping him tightly by the lower arms, Jake stuck his face right up to Tyler's and snarled, "I told you to come sit back down. You don't listen any better than your mother does, so I guess it's time I give you the same lesson I give her!" And with that, he slapped Tyler's little body across the room where it bashed against the wall with a sickening thump.

I watched this scene play out before me like a movie being run in slow motion, the knot in my stomach growing bigger and bigger until it felt as if it were completely filling my stomach and ready to burst into my heart, lungs, and throat. I was in motion in a second, running toward father and son, but like in a dream where you run but your legs just won't go, I hadn't been fast enough.

"No!" I screamed and crossed the short distance to where my son lay in a crumpled heap. "Tyler! Oh, Tyler, honey, can you hear me?" I murmured to my son, shaking him gently, trying to make him wake up, but he didn't respond.

Frantically, I pressed my fingers to a spot on his neck just below his ear, the way I saw people on TV do, but I wasn't sure if I felt a pulse or not, nor was I entirely sure that I felt his breath on my cheek as I leaned closer toward his pale face. I'd heard of CPR, but I didn't know how to do it or even if it was needed. Weakness and ignorance bound my hands, rendering me useless to my son. The realization hurt worse than any beating I had ever received. I lifted his head into my lap. My fingers felt wetness.

"He's bleeding!" I moaned, and watched my son's blood trickle down my fingers, crawl across my hand, and be sucked up by the sleeve of my T-shirt

I could see Jake hovering over us, as still as a statue, just looking down at his blood-covered wife and son on the floor. A small wave of sanity must have sluiced its way through his liquor-fogged brain, because he staggered forward, bent down, and reached out his hand to touch his son's still body.

"Tyler."

"Don't!" I yelled. "Don't you dare touch him, or even say his name!" I had never in my life spoken to Jake that way. I had never raised my voice to him. I had never before had the courage to speak out against him. But now it wasn't a matter of courage, it was more a matter of full-blown rage at his treatment of Tyler, of the years of physical and mental abuse he had heaped upon me, on us.

I gently picked Tyler up off the hard floor and cradled him in my lap. I rocked him and crooned to him like I did when he was a baby. I didn't hear Jake on the phone to the emergency operator, but he must have called. The next thing I knew, Tyler was being taken out of my arms despite my protests. The cops were there, and paramedics began working on Tyler, pumping oxygen into his body, putting him on a gurney, and wheeling him into the gaping mouth of the waiting ambulance. I climbed aboard, too, and we sped off to the hospital in a blur of sound and motion.

All through the long night at the hospital, I passed the many hours pacing up and down the small corridor in the emergency room, staring blankly out of the window into dark nothingness, or sitting in the waiting room on an orange, flowered chair, dying inside all the while not knowing if my baby was going to be okay. They wouldn't let me see him, which tripled my worry and fear.

It's amazing what thoughts of dread can swim unwittingly through your mind at a time like this. Is he okay? Is he dead? It must be bad because they're taking so long. If he dies, it'll be my fault. I allowed him to be around a man who I knew was abusive and dangerous. I let my baby down. He is hurt because of me. I'm a horrible mother, a horrible person. On and on my mind spun and prodded and stung.

It was blessed relief when I got some word after waiting what seemed like an eternity.

Tyler had a slight concussion and was expected to recover in a few days. His doctor wanted him to stay in the hospital overnight for observation. He must have hit his head on a nail in the wall because there was a puncture wound at the heart of a very large bump. The way he was bleeding, I was sure that his injury was much worse, but the doctor assured me that head wounds bleed a lot. Tyler's broken wrist, however, was going to take a little longer to heal, but he was going to be okay.

He is going to be okay! I collapsed into that hideous orange chair that had been my constant companion since arriving to the hospital . . . how long ago was it? I didn't know. Tears of relief, of guilt, of happiness poured out of my eyes. I leaned my face on my hands and sobbed into them, my shoulders shaking. I cried for my son, for myself, and for our unknown future.

Lou came by early the next morning to check on us. She found me curled up in a chair pulled close to Tyler's bed. Tyler was still asleep, but I couldn't leave his side. I had been given a new chance with him; I wasn't going to risk losing him again. Lou put her arm around my shoulder and motioned for me to come out of the room. She led me to a waiting room just down the hall from Tyler's room and sat me down on the couch.

I knew I must look a sight. I had washed my hands earlier, but my clothes were still smeared with dried blood. I could feel that my hair gave me the appearance of having just barely survived a windstorm. I turned red, swollen eyes to her as she sat down next to me on the couch and pulled me into a comforting hug. The loving touch of another human being can be such powerful medicine.

"How are you two?" she asked, stroking my head gently.

"The doctor says Tyler's going to be fine," I said against her shoulder. "He has a concussion and a broken wrist, but he's going to be okay."

"And you?"

"Last night I almost lost my baby," I managed to choke out. "It's all my fault." Tears rolled down my face and were absorbed by the soft sweater covering Lou's solid shoulder.

"Shh," Lou crooned. "It's not your fault. Tyler's going to be all right. That's the important thing."

"Oh, yes, Lou, it is my fault. If only I had left Jake when he first started beating me. If I had just been a stronger person to stand up to him, he never would have been able to do this to Tyler."

"You didn't know he would hurt him, Isabel."

I pushed away from Lou. "I knew! I knew that someday he might hurt Tyler, too, but I just kept giving him another chance. Another chance to hurt us and that makes me as guilty as he is for Tyler's injuries." I sobbed. "I put Tyler in danger time after time. He could have been killed! Oh, Lou, what am I going to do?" I took refuge in Lou's loving embrace again until, finally, my wracking sobs subsided to whimpering hiccups.

The sounds of the hospital swirled around us, two huddled figures in the middle of a field of orange flowers. Figures passed, but I couldn't have said what they looked like, what they wore, whether they were male or female, young or old. A chorus of noises—soft-soled shoes squeaking on the floor, the ticking of a clock somewhere, a constant mechanical beep, beep, beep in a nearby room, phones ringing and voices answering them—all blended into one melodic hum that acted like a lullaby to lead me into a light daze. For one blissful moment, I didn't feel a thing, just sweet numbness.

"Mrs. Tanner." I heard the name spoken as if from a dream, somewhere above me, but it was awhile before I realized the voice called for me. My eyes opened against their will and looked up. Two police officers, a woman and a man, stood near Lou and me, their gray uniforms, black weapons strapped to their side, silver glasses reflecting a distorted view of my own face back at me—all in all, a picture of power, intimidation, and authority.

"Are you Mrs. Tanner?" one asked again.

I nodded my head and wiped my tear-stained face and runny nose with the back of my sleeve. Not very ladylike, but decorum was the last thing on my mind after all the barbarism I had experienced in the last few hours. The tall female officer removed her sunglasses and identified herself as Officer Donnelly and the male at her side as Officer Carson. Officer Donnelly asked if I would mind answering a few questions for the record. I nodded in acquiescence.

"Mrs. Tanner, your husband alleges that he and the boy were wrestling in the living room when the boy tripped on the rug and fell against the wall, losing consciousness." Her voice was calm and direct, without a hint of judgment—not harsh, just direct.

"That's a lie." The accusation was out before I realized what I said.

The officers looked at each other, then back at me. "Is there anything you can add to the report?" asked Officer Carson while removing a pen and a small, spiral-bound notepad from his pocket. Though his voice held the same calmness and no-nonsense attitude as the female officer, it carried just a hint of that smile that never seemed to completely leave his face.

I stared at him, then at her. I knew that if I started down this road, there was no turning back. If I say what really happened and Jake will be ripped from our lives, probably forever. Is this what I want? Am I ready to admit that the marriage is dead, and give it a proper burial? Now is the time to decide.

I turned to Lou and whispered, "Lou, am I strong enough?"

Lou nodded, gave me a warm smile, and a strong hug for courage. "I'll be here to add my strength to yours."

Officer Carson's pen was poised over the white, lined paper in that incredibly small black notepad, ready to take down my every word. I hope he has plenty of paper in that thing, I thought. Then I took a deep breath.

"Yes, there's quite a bit I'd like to add."

I told the officers everything that had happened that night, and the many nights and days before. Officer Carson was writing fast and furiously in his notebook while I went on and on. Occasionally Officer Donnelly interrupted with a question.

Jake was sentenced to time in jail; Tyler and I were on our own for the first time in our lives. We got by on government assistance at first while I went to school and learned a marketable skill, and it wasn't long before I got a job that allowed me to take care of us. Lou was a big help, too, watching Tyler after school while I was at work, sharing her meals with us, and offering a shoulder for us to lean on when the road got rocky.

I filed for divorce. Surprisingly enough, Jake didn't contest it, but signed the papers right away, even giving up his rights to see Tyler. He seemed rather disinterested in us, but to play it safe, Tyler and I moved out of state as soon as I had enough money saved. Saying good-bye to Lou was the hardest part about leaving, but leaving was the best thing I ever did for myself and for my son.

Tyler and I are settled in our new home now. I have a job that lets me pay the bills, and Tyler has made friends in his new school. It's hard being on our own, knowing what to do. Jake had controlled everything throughout our years of marriage—the bills, the money, everything. But I'm learning.

It's crazy, I know, but having to do it all myself, I can empathize with Jake a little, understand his frustration all those years at there being too much month left at the end of the paycheck. I understand the anguish at having to tell my son that I don't have ten dollars to give him so he can go to a movie with a friend, or that we have to have beans again instead of steak.

Though I understand and empathize, I also understand that frustration, fear, or whatever negative emotion he was feeling, never justified his beating me. It took me months of counseling to realize that Jake beat me not because I was a bad person or because I did anything to deserve a beating, but that because he was sick. This realization has helped me become a stronger person. I'm also a happier person because I'm safe, and because my son is safe. Now, love—for my son and for myself—battles life's challenges, not fists and hateful words. Love feels much better.

THE END

CONFESSIONS OF A RUNAWAY TEEN
It's the only way to save myself from my druggie parents

The old blackberry bramble that my granddad planted was the place I always went to cry. I wouldn't let anyone—especially not Mom or Dad—see tears on my face. I sat amidst the untended grass and weeds, the sobs finally dying away, and munched the ripe, dark berries that always reminded me of my grandfather. Why did you go away and leave me? I miss you so much!

Granddad died a year ago and with him vanished the last bit of sanity in my family. He was my mainstay, the one who kept me going, and he'd said the same for me. "I don't know why your dad turned out the way he did, Kylie," he told me only a few days before his fatal heart attack. "We did the best we could for him, your grandma and me, but he got mixed up with drugs and alcohol when he was just a boy and we never seemed able to pull him away."

Then he smiled down at me. "But you're not going that way, Kylie. You're my hope and joy. I can go to your grandma and tell her that our lives weren't wasted, that we have a granddaughter to be proud of."

It wasn't just Dad, but Mom and my older brother, George, too. Everybody at school, everybody in town, knew the Prices were just no good. They respected my granddad and felt sorry for him and they knew I worked hard at school and tried to keep myself clean and decent-looking in spite of my hand-me-down clothes, but I guess they're just waiting to see what would happen next.

Now that I'm fifteen, I'd probably follow the family path and turn to wild boys and booze. Everybody knew about the kind of crowd George ran with, the kind of druggies that kept company with my parents. Every day I resolved that I'd turn out differently and there I was down at the blackberry patch, thinking about Granddad and missing him something awful, while up at the house Mom and Dad were drinking and yelling at each other. Before long they'd be hitting and hurting each other and me, too, if I didn't stay clear of the place.

Trouble is, when the drinking and the drugs stopped even for a little, when Dad said he wouldn't hit Mom anymore and Mom said we'd have a regular home, they're sweet and lovable people.

People sometimes wonder why abused kids keep on loving their parents and I can tell them that it's because underneath the drinking and drugs, they're lovable people. And it's just nature for kids to love their folks.

Stuffed with blackberries and the tears dried on my face, I waited until the sun set and the sky was darkening to head back up the hill to our little farmhouse.

Dad was sprawled sound asleep with his mouth open on the worn-out old sofa in the front room. I could hear Mom in the kitchen puttering with the dishes. "Kylie, is that you? Come and help me get something together for supper. George is bringing some friends over for a little party."

"I've got to study, Mom. I've got an essay due tomorrow."

She came in from the kitchen, glaring at me. "Kylie Marie Price, did you just say no to your mother?"

Dressed in fitted blue jeans and a tight knit top, she teetered on high heels looking more like she was dressed for going out than for cooking supper. She was more than a little high; I could tell that from the glazed look to her eyes and the way she had to grab on to a chair to keep her balance.

It won't do any good to argue, not when she's like this. "I'll help some, but I've got to do my homework."

My teachers told me that I could be a top student if only my work wasn't so uneven. It's uneven because of nights like this when I couldn't even get to my homework, or the even worse nights when I fell asleep late, hiding under the covers to keep out the yelling and noise outside my door.

We put together tacos for supper and by the time we finished, George was home with half a dozen of his friends, boys and girls just about his age, which was close on nineteen.

"My little sister, Kylie," he introduced me, grinning in my direction. George is a good-looking boy and when he grins at you like that it's easy to forget how much trouble he can be. I guess Dad must've looked like that when Mom fell in love him.

George dropped out of school when he was not much older than I was and he worked in town at a garage. He likes fixing cars and might have done all right if he could stay away from the drugs. His boss gave him one more chance after the latest bender and I prayed that he'd be able to hang on.

He wasn't thinking about his troubles as he woke Dad up to make room on the sofa and then started some music playing on his boom box.

"What's to eat?"

"We made tacos," Mom said. "Kylie and me."

We fixed our plates and then found places to sit in the kitchen and living room. I settled over in the corner with my pen and paper and a plate full of food, trying to do school work and eat at the same time.

I was only halfway through my tacos when one of the boys came over and sat on the arm of my chair. "So, you're Kylie. I'm Nick."

"Hi, Nick," I said a little shyly. Until lately George's friends didn't pay much attention to me.

"He didn't tell me what a good-looking sister he has."

I squirmed uneasily; not answering back, but within minutes his friendly manner had me chatting with him as though I'd known him for years. I found out he just moved into the area and is working with George at the garage.

Then the booze and the weed began to move around the room from person to person and when Nick offered me a joint he'd roiled himself, I was tempted for the first time. The sweet, aromatic scene seemed unthreatening, especially when compared with the liquor and the meth that would soon he circulating.

No big deal if I just take a few puffs to relax. I don't want this sweet-faced boy to think I'm just a kid.

"No way!" George's deep voice interrupted the moment. "Kylie, what do you think you're doing?" He grabbed the joint from my hand and tore it into bits, staring at his friend.

Nick flushed angrily. "Come on, dude. What are you doing? She can make up her own mind."

"Not my little sister," George told him angrily, grabbing Nick's shoulder. When George is under the influence of something or other, he always gets belligerent and normally I stay out of his way.

I stood up, pushing his hand from Nick. "You're not my boss."

"But I am." Daddy stood swaying behind him. "You just go on to your room, Kylie, and lock the door. This isn't a place for you."

"Of all the two-faced hypocrites," I protested loudly, but then Mom's arm circled my shoulder.

"You listen to them, baby girl," she whispered in my ear. "We want better things for you."

Feeling like a five-year-old being sent to bed early, I went back to the little room that's my own. After a few minutes I calmed down enough to get halfway through my essay, then put it aside to lie down on my bed and listen to the increasingly loud sounds of the party going on in the rest of the house.

I felt lonely and confused as I looked around at the little room I decorated as best I could, with a comforter and curtains from the thrift shop. My schoolbooks were stacked neatly on a box next to my bed and the rag doll Grandma made me when I was a toddler lay next to me on my pillow.

It wasn't fair. Because of my clothes and my family, I wasn't accepted at school. I couldn't keep my grades at more than average because it was such a struggle to get my homework done. I might as well give up and find what fun I could the way my parents and brother did.

I had half a mind to go out and get another joint from Nick and join the party, but inside I seemed to hear Granddad's voice reminding me that he hoped for better things from me.

"The good Lord doesn't mean for any of us to throw our lives away," he'd told me once and I heard in his voice the deep grief he'd felt at what had happened to his family.

So instead I slipped on my Batman nightshirt and lay down next to the rag doll. It was a long time before I fell asleep.

I awoke to total darkness as a hand touched my hair. "Move over, baby girl," a slurred voice told me, followed by low laughter. "It's old Nick, come to keep you com . . ." he stumbled over the word, finally going on, "com . . . company." He laughed again.

I tried to move away, but a strong arm gripped me. "Nick, go away. You're in my room and you're so drunk or whatever that you don't know what you're doing."

He laughed once more. "Sure do. Know exactly what I'm doing—coming to keep a pretty girl company. Girl named . . . named. . . ."

I sat up in disgust. He doesn't even remember my name. The seemingly pleasant, rather attractive boy of early in the evening is someone else now. "I'm Kylie Price, the sister of you friend, George, who's gonna come running and kick your butt if you don't get out of my room."

"Naw," he said lazily, fingers fumbling at my sleep shirt, touching my breasts. "George's too wasted to even get up. Reckon he'll sleep the day out."

I pushed his searching hands away. "I'm going to scream."

"Go ahead," he returned good-naturedly. "Nobody'll hear."

We struggled until I found breath to scream as long and loud as I could.

He rubbed at his head. "Give me a headache yelling like that," he accused as though I was unaccountably rude.

There was no sound from the rest of the house. Nobody seemed to hear. Nobody was coming. The family that seemed so anxious to protect me earlier in the evening was too under the influence to come when I really needed them.

Feeling more furious than anything else, I pulled away from those fumbling hands and jumped up, running out of the room. I had two advantages over Nick. I wasn't high and I knew my way through the house, even in the darkness.

He followed me, calling loudly. "Little girl. Pretty little girl. Don't mean no harm. Just want a little com . . . company. . . ."

I heard muttered oaths from George where he was sprawled across the sofa, but he didn't move. It was too dark to see if Mom and

Dad were anywhere about, though I did trip noisily across someone sleeping on the floor as I headed for the kitchen, slipping quietly out the back door.

If that drunken lout caught me, there'd be nobody in shape to help me out. Knowing I had to take care of myself, I headed for the trees in back of Granddad's blackberry bramble and in the cool darkness of the last hours of the night sought refuge against the trunk of a big, old oak.

Anger was quickly replaced by shaking, sobbing fear as I settled against the ground. Most girls my age would've been afraid to be out there in the night with wild animals creeping through the night and the sound of coyotes yelping in the distance, but I was more afraid of what lay inside my home. My sobs gradually died away and, tired out, I slept.

When I awoke, the shade of the oak was protecting me from the bright sun of early morning. It must be nearly time for school. My heart in my throat, I went back to the house, creeping among sleepers dead to the world to get to the bathroom for a quick wash, then pulled on fresh clothes just in time to get out the door to catch the school bus. It wasn't until I was on the bus that I realized I'd left my half-completed essay behind.

Feeling too sick inside to eat breakfast, by noon I was starving. It wasn't a good morning. In history a twig, one I'd failed to notice when I'd hurriedly brushed my hair after sleeping on the ground, fell out of my hair just as I got up to leave class. Naturally one of the other girls noticed and made a few public remarks about my lack of good grooming.

I felt less than clean, having been forced to skip my morning shower at home. In algebra, I feel asleep at my desk and was sent, humiliatingly, to the office where the principal lectured me about paying attention to my teacher. I wondered how she'd feel if she spent an uneasy half of the night at the foot of an oak.

At lunch I ate by myself as usual, an experience too common to make me feel more than a stab of resentment. It was a small community after all and they discouraged their sons and daughters from associating with members of my family, even though I was trying so hard to be different from the rest.

I wanted to be different. I would be different.

I knew that I came really close to taking that first slipping step the previous night that would take me down the path that my brother was following. But I felt so alone and so hungry for some good moments in my life that Nick's warm smile and sweet-looking face enticed me almost beyond refusal.

I wanted to take the weed and the alcohol, to forget for a little that I was the outcast Kylie Price and just have fun and acceptance, to have a good time with a boy not too many years older than myself.

But the sweet face and the engaging personality changed quickly enough, as did my parents and my brother when they're on something.

Nobody can be trusted, I told myself, pushing my plate away after only a few bites and going on with a heavy heart to freshman English, which was my next class.

As the teacher made us read parts from Romeo and Juliet, I hoped against hope that she'd forget to ask for the essays to be turned in. But not Mrs. Pendergrast. She never forgot.

I sat still, hoping she wouldn't notice that I hadn't turned in my paper. Oh, I wouldn't be the only one. There were always two or three boys who always made excuses and wouldn't actually come up with the work until she called their parents to put the pressure on.

I sat, my heart pounding, while she leafed through the papers, frowning. The bell rang and I got to my feet, prepared to dash out, but she looked over the other heads to me.

"Kylie, will you stay a moment, please."

No help for it now. I sank back down in hopeless dejection while the other students fled the classroom.

Mrs. Pendergrast is the kind of teacher who scared freshmen to death, but from what I heard of the older students, by senior year she transformed to most kids' favorite teacher. That was a puzzle I didn't understand.

She waited until everyone else left the classroom, then glared at me. "Kylie, sometimes I could just shake you."

I looked down at my feet. "I did get half of it done, but I forgot and left it at home."

"I expect better than excuses from you."

In a way it was a compliment. I raised my gaze to her face. "It's the truth."

"Why only half finished?"

I might as well be truthful. "We had company last night, it was hard to study."

She nodded, accepting that. "And why leave that half at home?"

I stared at her, daring her to look at me with pity. "I didn't sleep in the house last night and I woke up late and almost missed the bus."

"Where did you sleep?"

"On the ground in back of the blackberry bramble Granddad planted. It was safe there."

Her face suddenly looked older, but the only thing she said was, "Your grandparents were fine people, Kylie."

"I don't remember Grandma much. I was too little when she died, but Granddad was really good to me."

Mrs. Pendergrast wearily went over to sit behind her desk. For a moment, she put her face down, propping it with both hands, and then she looked up. "I have no choice but the report this to the authorities, Kylie. You have a right to some protection, even from your own family."

I stared at her "I'll tell them it didn't happen."

She stared right back. "At my advanced age, Kylie Price, I have some credibility. I feel that I'll be believed."

My heart pounded. I couldn't tell on my own family and yet I knew things couldn't go on that way. Something really bad was going to happen to me. "Let me take care of it," I begged, tears in my eyes.

She looked down again, and then sighed. "You're only fifteen, Kylie."

I managed a grin. "I've had to grow up fast."

She nodded. "I'll give you until tomorrow at this time if you will then confide your plans to me."

"Okay." After she left me in the classroom to gather my books for the next period, I was breathing hard. If only I actually had a plan.

Instead of going to class, I went instead to the library and asked to be allowed to use the computer. "Mrs. Pendergrast sent me," I told the librarian. Even the other teachers stood in awe of the formidable English teacher. After a moment's hesitation, I was waved to a seat at one of the computers.

The Internet. The place to go for almost anything. We don't have a computer at home, but I was used to using the ones in the library for my schoolwork.

Home. I entered the word and everything came up from decorating tips to poems about home. Not nearly close enough.

Homes for homeless children, I typed in. Still not close enough, I realized, as I saw lists of articles about the homeless throughout the world.

Homeless teens in Oklahoma, I tried again.

This time one of the listings was from a group of homes in my state. They're run by the same church group that Granddad and Grandma always attended and where they took me when I was little.

I entered their site, where I saw photos of cottages and young people, lots of them. Groups of teens lived in a cottage with a set of house parents. There's a ranch for boys in one town, a girls' school in another, and several for both boys and girls. It said all admissions are voluntary. That meant I got to choose.

I emailed them, trying to be very business-like. I am a fifteen-year-old girl in need of a place to live. I would like more information about your school.

Then I noticed there was a toll-free phone number. I wrote it down on a little slip of paper and, heart pounding so hard I could hardly breathe, I went barging into Mrs. Pendergrast's class. She looked up, obviously startled, and then when she saw my face, quickly told the class to continue reading silently and then joined me out in the hall.

I blurted it all straight out. "I looked up a girls' home on the Internet. I sent a message, asking if they could take me in, but then I thought I'd maybe better call. . . ."

For at least the second time that day she stared at me. "You are a girl of decisive action, Kylie." She went back into the classroom, came back with her purse, took out a cell phone, and thrust it at me.

I made the call and the action was started. It took a few weeks. I couldn't just volunteer myself, my parents had to agree. Dad swore and Morn cried, but they both decided it was best at least until things got better, as Mom said.

One weekend Mrs. Pendergrast drove me to my new home. At the home, I was taken to a cottage to meet my house parents and the seven other girls who lived there.

Balloons decorated the front porch and inside cake and punch were waiting. I couldn't help being a little shy as my new family members greeted me, but I worked hard at hiding it.

My housemother—a tall, slim woman—smiled at me. "Kylie Price, the girl who referred herself."

Mrs. Pendergrast took her measure in one sharp glance. "You can expect great things of Kylie. I certainly do."

I've been at the girls' home for six months now. It isn't perfect. I was used to running my own life and the rules are really strict there. I like some of the people and others I don't like. We all go to the public high school and I'm a good student and making friends there, too.

Sometimes at night I cry because I miss Mom and Dad and George, but when they come to visit I love showing them around.

I have girlfriends and a boyfriend and I was just voted president of the sophomore class. Mrs. Pendergrast said she never expected anything less. She said Granddad would be proud of me.

THE END

CONFESSIONS OF A SURVIVOR
"I Finally Took Control!"

"Why don't you just leave him?" my coworker flippantly said.

Everyone at the table was looking at me and thinking the same thing—they all wanted to know why I didn't just leave my husband if he was so mean to me. How could I explain?

Things in a marriage are never simple, I guess. It's not the sort of thing that is easy to understand.

I just nodded because I didn't know what to say to that question. They wouldn't understand anyway.

Over the past couple months I had started telling everyone how my husband, Bill, beat me up. I hadn't intended to start talking about myself, but when I kept coming to work with bruises and once a black eye, they started asking questions. It just seemed easier to tell the truth than try to cover it up.

At first, my coworkers had been so nice and sympathetic that I'm afraid I talked too much, basking in their concern and the attention. Now that several months had passed I could tell that their sympathy had been exhausted.

In fact, I felt their disapproval so strongly that it was almost as if they had spoken these exact words: If you do nothing to get away from Bill or to help yourself then you are partly responsible because you are letting him get away with it and you are not doing anything about it.

They used to be so nice; I couldn't help but miss that.

I couldn't explain why I stayed with Bill or the terror he inspired in me.

Writing the words down makes it easier to explain, though I am still ashamed.

The first time Bill hit me I was too surprised to do anything at all. It was so unlike him and I thought it was just a fluke, one of those things that happen for no rhyme or reason, because Bill was a sweet man when I met him, very considerate and polite.

We had been talking about how he needed to replace the breaks on the car and he just went nuts.

"Why am I always the one who has to take care of things?" Bill yelled. "I have to do everything around here!"

It was odd because it was almost as if he had been trying to work himself up into losing control. It was like he wanted to hit me, but had to get emotional enough to do it, if that makes any sense at all.

He slapped me hard across the face and turned away from me

with a look of such disgust. He hits me and then I disgust him?

"If that's the way you feel about it, I can take the car in myself!" I said, coldly.

"That will cost too much and you know it. No, I'll have to do it myself."

"You know you didn't want me to get a job, but I can get one. I can help pay for the brakes. I can pay for my half of everything, or even better, I can move out and you won't have to worry about fixing anything that belongs to me," I said.

I had been so angry then and so not afraid of him at that time.

It was like he collapsed suddenly when I said that.

"I'm so, so sorry," he said, and then he humbled himself. "I don't know what got into me."

It was a complete change from the way he had been just seconds before that. I knew that he was afraid that I would leave him.

It wasn't much of an excuse that he gave for hitting me, I even thought so myself at the time. Still, you don't walk out of a marriage just because of one mistake.

He looked so miserable, so absolutely contrite. He even cried a few tears. I found myself comforting him when I guess it should have been the other way around, but I still loved him.

I got a job and though working on an assembly line could be pretty boring, I really liked the people I got to know.

Bill didn't like to see my family, he didn't talk to his family, and we couldn't afford to go out, so that meant I didn't get to socialize much. The people I saw at work were the only people I got to see at all, and I grew to like each and every one of them.

My best friend was a short girl with red hair and freckles named Pam. We used to act like we were afraid to make her mad because of her red hair—we were always doing silly stuff like that at work to help pass the time.

The first day I went to work with bruises—one on my left arm and one on my cheekbone—everyone was asking me what happened.

So, I just told them the truth. I figured that if I lied about it and tried to cover it up they'd just gossip about it and I'd rather be up front with it. It wasn't like I had done anything wrong, it was Bill who did.

They were so nice to me, and called Bill a jerk and a louse. I felt much better afterward, but Pam said something to me so seriously that I'll never forget it.

"If he hit you once, he'll do it again," Pam said. "Men that hit women never stop, trust me."

She went on to tell me about her own mother's abuse and what her father put the whole family through.

It was an amazing story, but I didn't think Bill was like her dad.

Her dad sounded so cruel and beastly, my husband could be so loving and considerate of me and so kind that I didn't think my situation was like hers at all.

She didn't know me that well, and more importantly, she didn't know Bill.

Bill was honestly sorry for what he had done. He had bought me a charm bracelet with tiny ballet shoes as a charm, remembering how I had once wanted to be a ballet dancer. Then he took me out to eat at a nice restaurant and had even sprung for a bottle of wine.

He had listened, really listened, to me when I talked about us. I felt very hopeful for the future. We had even talked about having children.

Besides, everyone loses their temper now and then, and Bill knew that it was something he needed to work on, I reasoned.

Bill had scared me badly, but then he swept me away with small kindnesses and tender lovemaking.

I felt like no man could make love to me the way he did and be a bad person.

As summer faded into fall and there were no more incidents, I started to relax.

We began talking about starting a family.

I felt an ache within me, and I knew I was hungry for a child, a baby of our very own.

I started talking about all of the dreams I had been having—how we could add another bedroom onto the house and how we could buy one of those beautifully carved Victorian cribs I had seen in a catalog.

You know when you think that you are on the same page as someone? You think you know what your husband is thinking, and then you find out that you never really did know at all.

While I was still talking about all the stuff we could buy for the baby, I walked by where Bill was sitting on the couch and he stuck his foot out and tripped me.

When I fell, he fell on top of me. He was yelling, but I couldn't understand the words, I couldn't understand what in the world was happening to me. I couldn't adjust. One minute I was off in the clouds talking about my sweet dream of becoming a mother, and then he was on top of me punching me.

I curled up into a ball so he just hit my back and shoulders. When he grew tired he stood up over me and told me to get up.

I got up and he called me names and told me to go to bed.

I went to bed with tears falling down my cheeks.

I heard his car start and I knew he was leaving, but all I felt was relief. I was just glad that he was gone. I felt like I had gotten off easy, but what was so devastating was that it had been so unexpected and so sudden.

Bill reminded me of Dr. Jekyll and Mr. Hyde, because he would go from being so nice to being so violent so very, very fast. It was the stuff of fiction, not real life, and I felt as though I were living in a horror novel.

Later, he was very apologetic and even I could see a pattern in his behavior.

"I promise I will never do it again." He sobbed.

I thought of what Pam had said many times before and realized that she had been right—I was a battered wife. I should have recognized myself as one, but when it's your own life surrounding you and your feelings that are all over the place it's hard to take a step back. I would think that I hated him, I would think that I loved him, and then I didn't know what I felt or what I thought anymore.

When you see something on television or when you see how other couples relate to one another it's far enough away from you that you can focus on it and see it for what it is. When it is your own life you're not objective. Your life surrounds you in every direction and it is too big to focus on.

It was all a jigsaw puzzle, but when I finally put the pieces together it was too late. I was much too afraid to do anything at all.

I would feel a sense of wonder or more like total weirdness. How did I end up like this?

I was so bewildered by my husband's transformations that seemed to be set off by something I said that I became frightened of saying anything at all.

I went to work and hid the fact that I loved to go to work. It was the one place where I could be myself, and it was the one place where I was not afraid. We had a routine, I would go to work and come home, and then Bill would go outside for a few minutes while I fixed dinner.

After a while I started to wonder why he had to step outside every time I came home.

One night, I slipped out the backdoor and crept around the corner of the house and I saw him with one of those tiny spiral notebooks writing down the mileage numbers off the odometer of my car! I was amazed. Here I was never going anywhere, going to work, and coming straight home afterward, and he still found it necessary to write down the mileage on my car. Obviously, he was suspicious that I was going somewhere other than work.

Not long after, he asked me if I was cheating on him—like I would tell him if I was! I avoided a fight by telling him how much I loved him.

Dating was really the last thing on my mind.

Bill became super-critical. I couldn't do anything right.

Something seemingly unimportant, like not putting the little twist tie on the loaf of bread, would set him off. Then I would hear a sermon about how I wasted food and how we were not rich and how I made things difficult for him because he had to follow after me and correct my mistakes. He said I needed correction.

I can't remember exactly when he first started saying I needed to be corrected, but it would become something that he would say many times.

One night, I cooked a casserole I had cooked many times before, made of hamburger, seashell macaroni, and tomato sauce.

"What do you mean cooking this slop?" he demanded as I sat down to eat.

"You like it. Remember, honey, my mom used to cook it for us and you said that you liked it," I said as tactfully as I could.

I was ignoring the way he was glowering at me with his head down and his eyes starting to look wild. I didn't have to have a crystal ball to know I was in for it.

He threw the plate of food against the wall and red tomato sauce went everywhere.

I jumped up quickly and said, "No problem, I'll cook something else."

Trying to hide the fact that my hands were shaking, I hurriedly grabbed the bag of potatoes and started setting some out by the sink.

I don't know exactly why, but it always seemed important for me to hide how very frightened I was even though he knew well enough that he could scare me. I guess I didn't want him to know how completely demoralized I was, like if he knew the way I was in my head, he really would murder me and carry my body somewhere and dump it. I didn't put anything past him.

Anyway, he grabbed me that night and threw me on the floor. That night started the worst few weeks of my life and it was the night Bill went completely crazy.

"Let me cook you something else," I said, with Bill on top of me.

"It's too late now!" he growled.

"Please, please, stop," I moaned, half out of my mind.

"If you would just put a little effort and do right we wouldn't have to have these CORRECTIONS!" he yelled.

I remember I actually shivered, he sounded so crazy.

"When you do wrong you have to be corrected. I have to do this because stupid people never understand. You have to beat it into their heads 'cause you don't have any brains!"

He had rolled me over on my back and was punching my face. I covered my face with my hands, so it was my hands that got the worst of it. They swelled up, and I called in sick for a couple of days until the swelling went down.

The morning after that fight, Bill cooked my breakfast and I had to smile and tell him what a great husband I had, but inside I felt like death. He was going to kill me, and there was not a thing that I could do about it.

He would get angry and tell me again I needed correction. This word, correction, seemed to be a keyword for him and he used this word all the time.

He said that he was teaching me when he beat me, but what I was supposed to learn I didn't know.

One thing I did gain was an overwhelming fear, until there was nothing else—no other emotions and hardly any thoughts in my head but this terrible, terrible fear. It is like your world was once very big—the size of the real world—but it is all the time getting smaller.

At the end, it was like my whole world was this tiny room and within it was very little space for me to move. This tiny room you could look out of and see people living normal lives and doing normal things, but they are so far away.

At the worst times, you feel as though you cannot speak, like some nightmare where you try to scream and nothing will come out of your mouth. My world was only this tiny room. Oh, I was so jealous of other people who were not living with the fear that each day might be their last. My body hurt so badly from being hit, but I feared doctors and hospitals. I did what I could to placate Bill, I would tell him I loved him over and over, but sometimes it was like he couldn't hear me at all.

I hoped that Bill and his bad temper would get in a fight with someone else, and they would kill him. I had lost all my fine objections against harming him or taking a life, but I was much too afraid to attack him.

I prayed he would have a heart attack and fall over dead. I did. These fantasies crossing my mind were like an oasis in the desert, the delicious possibility that something could happen to him.

But deep in my heart, I somehow knew that salvation would not come from that quarter. Bill was careful and though he often got into nasty arguments, he always backed down when it looked like things might get physical. No, there was really no hope there.

The last time he beat me it was over a trivial thing. I had forgotten to put the twist tie back on the loaf of bread, an automatic thing you do after getting bread out to make a sandwich, but somehow I had forgotten.

"Don't you know the bread will go bad? Don't you know that bread costs money?" he yelled at me, and I cried and cried thinking of how many times I had gotten into trouble over that very thing.

I was feeling hysterical. How could I have forgotten to close the bread?

I heard these strange whimpering sounds and wondered where they were coming from for a few seconds, and then suddenly realized they were coming from myself.

"Oh, no! Oh, no!" I started saying over and over. I felt I was losing my mind.

"Now you need CORRECTION!" he shouted, and I started to whimper.

If anything, crying just made Bill hit me harder. He had no mercy and he had no tender feelings that you could get to in the middle of his anger. He usually slapped me at first and then he would use his fists. He bruised me up, but he never went so far as to break bones or put me in the hospital.

I know that other battered women have been hurt worse than me, but it was the psychological effect on me that was so devastating.

I couldn't think coherently, much less make plans to get away. I knew I had to escape. Anything was better than what I was going through—even homelessness if it came to it.

I was losing myself. I wasn't me, but I didn't know who else I could be. I had been pared down until all that was left was my silent soul. This is what I could not explain. This is what I want people to understand. It is another universe and you are observing life from some far off planet when you are with other people. At other times you are in this tiny room that is by infinite degrees getting smaller and smaller.

One Friday, I was driving home with my paycheck in my pocket, and suddenly I could not face going home. Why was I going home? I could just go.

I remembered all the threats Bill had made.

"If you leave me, I will find you and cut your face with a razor," he threatened. "I will make you so ugly another man would never have you."

I wanted to tell him that if I ever got rid of the man I had, I never wanted another man for my entire life, but I didn't.

He had threatened my family, too, but I had a feeling that if I wasn't at any of their houses he would leave them alone.

I figured the best thing that I could do to keep them safe was to stay away from them. I headed North, the opposite direction of my family. It was as good a direction as any. He would search for me among my coworkers and my family, he would search for me in places that I had lived in or visited. That was why I had to go to a whole new, unknown place.

I drove for miles before I stopped at a motel. I was becoming so sleepy that I was afraid I'd fall asleep driving. I stopped, but I could not sleep and I kept on peering out the curtains into the parking lot.

I felt that Bill would show up, that somehow he would find me.

He didn't seem human to me anymore and I felt like he could feel my fear and find me through supernatural means of some kind. I know it sounds crazy, but that first night away from Bill I didn't feel safe.

I moved the chest of drawers in front of the door, but I still didn't sleep until the sun came up. With daylight, I began to feel more normal and I drifted off to sleep and slept for ten hours.

I woke up and my head was pounding. I wanted desperately to call my sister and my mother, but I didn't. There was little I could do for them anyway if Bill decided to attack them. I prayed that they were safe.

I had to pay the motel for another night because I had slept past the deadline for checking out, and I wondered how long my money would last.

I continued driving the next day and stayed in a motel in a town I can't remember the name of. I didn't know where I would end up.

The following morning was Sunday, and I was driving aimlessly through this little town when I saw this beautiful church with people going inside. It looked so beautiful I decided to go in. I wasn't dressed properly, but I waited until the service had begun and I snuck in and sat in the last pew.

The minister gave a lovely sermon and I felt my spirits rise up. I felt the healing power of that church that day. The minister looked so kind I decided to speak with him after the service.

He told me about the little town and his ministry and right then and there I decided to stay there. I wanted to go to the little church again, there was something there I wanted more of. In fact, the longer I was away from Bill, the better I felt. It was like every mile away from him, every hour of time was an improvement. The tiny room I had lived in was getting bigger and bigger every day.

My life changed from that very day, and I am so happy now.

Bill never caused my family or me any more harm. After all the threats he had made that he would find me and make me sorry, the divorce from Bill was surprisingly easy.

All his big threats turned out to be nothing but hot air. He had me so terrorized that I had foolishly believed him.

Now I look back and I am filled with wonder that such a thing had happened to me. Why would someone want to marry someone and tell them they love them and then want to make them as miserable as possible?

I don't know, even though it happened to me. I would guess that maybe Bill felt small and helpless in the world, and beating me up made him feel big and powerful. Like if he was making someone else afraid, then he could forget how afraid he was. I just don't know. I'm just glad that all of that is over.

I have a job now. After doing some flower arrangements for the church, I was hired by a florist. I love working with beautiful, fresh flowers every day and I am amazed to find that I have a talent for something. I am so glad to see my family now as often as I want. I had missed them so much. I have such a wonderful life, such wonderful friends and family.

I hope my story will give other women strength to do what may seem impossible. I hope that battered women will be brave enough to escape a man who bullies them and can believe that there is a better life waiting for them.

No matter how black things may seem to you at one time, things can get much, much better.

THE END

CONFESSIONS OF A KIDNAPPER
A Reader Reveals His Shocking Story

"You guys up for the zoo?" I asked once I had my two children strapped into their seats and we were on the road to my weekend.

Although it was barely winter, the wind held a bit of a chill. The sun was shining brightly, and it promised to be a beautiful afternoon—a perfect day to pack in as many activities as a divorced father possibly could.

Being a weekend Dad has always been a difficult task for me. I felt guilty that I didn't get to spend much time with Kaylee and Joey, so I overcompensated and tried to do two weeks' worth of activities in two days. Come Monday morning I felt guilty that I let them do everything they wanted and more, but by my "off" Saturday, I was back to the guilt of not enough time.

I had expected a chorus of "yahoos" to my question. Kaylee and Joey love the zoo. But instead of a resounding "Yes!" I got only incoherent mumbles mixed with shrugged shoulders.

I looked at them in the rearview mirror. They exchanged a look that I didn't recognize.

"Come on," I cajoled. I tried to keep my tone easy when I felt anything but. This was not like them. "We'll get to see the polar bears."

They nodded slowly and forced smiles on their tiny faces. The gesture was better than nothing, but it still didn't make me feel any better. Something was up and before I returned them to their mother on Sunday, I was going to find out just what that something was. Knowing Charlotte Whitman-Taylor, it was an endless monologue of how worthless their father really was.

Now, I might not have been CEO of a fancy company or run the town's only factory like her father did, but I think I did all right. I'd joined the military so Charlotte could "see the world." But it only took a few years in countries that she didn't even know existed before she hightailed it back home to Daddy's. I guess she thought that she'd be an officer's wife and go to balls and organize charity functions to benefit the needy. Instead it was two kids and living paycheck to paycheck in base housing. Yet despite our differences, the two absolute best things in the world came out of our relationship: Kaylee and Joey. Now Kaylee was eight and growing into quite a young lady. Joey was six, my little man. I loved them so.

We did all of their favorite things at the zoo. We rode the train through the park. I bought them hot dogs, nachos, sodas, and cotton candy—all guilt-assuaging foods for their weekend Dad. But the pair was still uncharacteristically reserved.

I know that the divorce had been hard on them both, but it had been close to a year since it was final. I would have liked to think there was time enough to adjust, but the fact was, they seemed to be going backward. They were more reserved than they had been the week I moved out. I tried every way that I could think of to get them to talk to me and tell me what was on their minds, but no dice. "How's school?" "How's T-ball?" "Dance lessons?" "Your mom?" "Your grandparents?"

All of my questions were answered with a mumbled, "Fine."

Despite my best efforts, by Sunday evening, I was still none the wiser. I hated taking them back to their house without knowing what was bothering them. Even more, I hated the invitation that I received from Charlotte.

"Come in, Jesse. I need to talk to you." Damn, I really hated when she said things like that to me. It's how she told me that she was leaving me—or rather that I had to move out. It was the same phrase that she used to tell me that she had filed for a divorce. I had no cause to believe that good news would follow the words this time.

"Sure," I said, hoping my casual tone hid my trepidation. I followed her through the house, then plopped down onto one of the kitchen barstools. Nonchalantly, I fished into the bowl of fruit sitting on the counter and tossed a grape into my mouth. I did it more to annoy Charlotte that out of hunger. Plus it gave me something to do with my now-shaking hands. I was a little weirded out, being invited into what had once been my house.

She took a deep breath and, for the first time, I noticed that she was even more nervous that I was. She rubbed her hands together in front of her and shifted from one designer shoe to the other. "I need the children weekend after next."

"No," I flatly replied. The court had ordered her to let me have them every other weekend and there was no way I was letting her have them on my time.

"Jesse—"

"I said no." I grabbed a handful of grapes this time.

We just stared at each other, both of us so quiet that it seemed like the sunlight coming through the ceiling windows created noise. We were at an old standoff, an impasse that we both knew all too well.

"I'm seeing someone," Charlotte finally said, dropping her gaze to stare at her clasped hands.

My gut hit my cowboy boots, but there was no way in hell I'd ever let her know that. It was all part of the game we played. "Good for you," I said, not meaning it at all. "But you're still not getting the kids on my weekend."

She took another deep breath. "We're getting married on that Saturday."

I was on my feet in a nanosecond, all games aside. "What!?" I didn't take the time to figure out what made me angrier: the fact that she was getting married again or the fact that she was only telling me about it two weeks before the wedding. It wasn't like I would have found out any other way. The town we lived in was small, but we didn't run in the same circles—not even close.

"Isn't this sort of sudden?" I gritted out from between my clenched teeth. I hated when she got me like this and I hated it even more than she knew it.

Charlotte sniffed, a sure sign that I had hit a nerve of my own. Score one for poor Jesse Taylor.

"We've been seeing each other for a while now."

"Pick another Saturday."

"We can't get the church any other time." She stopped to gauge my reaction. I stood there, hands braced on my hips, and snorted my disbelief.

"Jesse, it's the first weekend in June. It's wedding season."

"And that makes it okay to intrude on my time with the children?"

She stared at me as if she didn't understand why I was so upset. "Jesse. . . ." she said in that whiney, pleading voice that I hated so much. It was the same voice that she used to get what she wanted from her father and, once upon a time, from me.

"I want to meet him."

She rolled her eyes.

"Oh, come on, Char. Surely it's not too much to ask to get to meet the man who's going to be taking care of my children."

"Our children."

I nodded, my jaw tight. "You know what I mean." But I couldn't help being possessive of Kaylee and Joey. I was the one who pushed for us to start our family. I was the maternal one. I know it sounds strange—me, an ex-Army ranger, currently a macho cop, maternal.

"So what's it going to be, Jesse?"

"That depends. When do I get to meet Romeo?"

"His name is Anthony. Anthony McDaniel."

A McDaniel. I should have known. Charlotte wouldn't marry beneath her twice. The McDaniel family was very prominent where we lived. Even more so than my ex-in-laws.

"Jesse. . . ." she whined

"Charlotte. . . ." I mocked.

"Fine." She sighed with a pout on her lips. "You can meet him next Friday night. Now can I have the children for the wedding?"

I nodded slowly, a bitter taste filling my mouth. Something told me this marriage wasn't going to be a good thing. But what really had my insides twisted into knots was the fact that there was nothing that I could do about it.

The weekend before the wedding, Charlotte called to let me know that I could come over for cocktails that evening. It was my chance to meet the new love of her life.

I arrived on her doorstep five minutes early, but rang, anyway. If Charlotte held fast to the habits she had when we were married, then she wouldn't be ready for another twenty minutes, anyway.

But surprise, surprise—Charlotte answered the door after the first ring. "Hello, Jesse. Come in."

I stepped into the house, still marveling at the fact that not only was Charlotte dressed, but she had on her makeup as well. Shaking my head, I followed her into the living room, where Anthony McDaniel waited.

As much as I would have enjoyed seeing my children, Charlotte had arranged for them to go to her parents' house for the evening.

The blond-haired man stood when we entered and reached out a hand in greeting.

"Jesse Taylor. Anthony McDaniel," Charlotte said by way of introduction.

I instantly disliked the man.

We all lived in the same town, but that's where our similarities ended. He was influential, well groomed, and probably had someone buff his nails once a week. He was crab cakes and liqueur. I, on the other hand, was a beer and potato chips kind of guy.

I shook his hand, even though a part of me—a big part—didn't want to. Call it a cop's instincts. After all, I hadn't been on the force these last five years and not learned anything. There was something wrong about him. His smile was a little too toothy, his hair a little too perfect, his eyes a little too cold. No, I definitely didn't like him. Not one bit.

Charlotte fixed me a drink and settled down on the sofa beside him. I sat in the chair opposite them and tried not to stare as I wondered what I should say. After all, it's not every day that I meet the man who's going to marry my wife. My children were going to be living with him. I thought it best to be nice to him, no matter how much I distrusted him.

It was his eyes, I finally decided. He was one of those people who looked you straight in the eye with too much intensity. It was as if he were trying too hard to make me think that he was sincere. All it did was make me suspicious.

"You look nice tonight," I told Charlotte, hoping that it would help break the ice.

"Thank you." She smiled prettily and smoothed the crease down one leg of her designer slacks.

"I'm amazed that you're ready on time. Early, even." I chuckled across the awkward silence.

"Well. . . ." Charlotte stammered, then glanced nervously toward her fiancé.

"I like promptness. Isn't that right, darling?" McDaniel answered instead, and something about his tone made my skin crawl. I mean, all men like promptness, but very few of us actually get it. He seemed like he thought it was his God-given right.

"Anthony is in politics," Charlotte said, looping her arm through his and smiling up at him as if he had hung the moon. It was enough to make me nauseous.

"You don't say," I murmured and took another sip of my Scotch. That was an unnecessary bit of information. All the McDaniel's were involved in politics. The two words were practically synonymous. Maybe that was why I thought McDaniel wasn't on the level. Most Americans just naturally mistrust politicians. Yeah, that had to be it.

Mistrust and jealousy. Yes, I admit that I was jealous. After all, this man was going to be living my life. Raising my children. Sleeping with my wife. I had a great deal to be jealous about. That had to be why I was concerned about his integrity. Just that and nothing more.

I missed the kids even more the weekend of the wedding. Knowing that it was my turn and I wasn't able to spend it with them was murder. I wasted the day watching ESPN, drinking beer, and feeling sorry for myself. I tried to be happy for Charlotte and the kids, but I couldn't make myself feel anything other than mild anger mixed with a little sadness. Anger that Charlotte had found someone else and sadness that my life—the lives of my children—would never be the same.

I asked Charlotte if I could have the children for an extra weekend to make up for the one that I missed. She said she would do what she could, but her tone sounded preoccupied.

I had hoped that she and Romeo would take a nice, long honeymoon and I could get Kaylee and Joey all to myself for a few weeks. No such luck. The newlyweds didn't even spend one night in a hotel. When I mentioned this to Charlotte she said that they were just so anxious to start being a family that they postponed their trip until next year.

Great. Just great.

"Are you guys settling into the new house okay?"

Kaylee gave me a hesitant nod. We were seated at the kitchen table in my small, two-bedroom apartment. It was a far cry from the houses they were living in, but they didn't seem to mind.

My weekend had finally rolled around again, and I had envisioned two days of nothing but fun. Instead, I got two sullen children who seemed to not know the meaning of the word "fun" any longer.

"Is McDaniel taking you to T-ball after school?" This question I directed to Joey. "Because if he's not, I can take you."

"We have a nanny now," Joey blurted.

"He's not a nanny," Kaylee corrected. "Only girls are nannies. He's a tutor."

I skipped the opportunity to be politically correct and instead went straight to the heart of the matter. "Tutor? Are you guys having trouble in school?"

They both fell silent.

"Spill it," I demanded in that tried-and-true father tone that works every time.

It was Kaylee who finally broke. "We're not going to school anymore."

They're not going to school anymore?

"Mr. Gilmore comes every day to tutor us."

I was going to have to speak to Charlotte about this. She might have full custody, but I was still their father. She should have discussed it with me before she took the kids out of school.

"And this Mr. Gilmore—he takes you to practice?"

Again the children were quiet.

"Tell me," I commanded. "'Cause you know I'll find out."

"Joey ain't playing T-ball no more," Kaylee said with a frown on her tiny, pink lips.

"Isn't playing T-ball anymore," I automatically corrected.

Another blow. Charlotte and McDaniel had only been married for two weeks and yet so many changes already. Wasn't it enough that the children had been moved out of their home and across town? I was definitely talking to her about this. It's important for children to have fun activities.

"Are you still taking dance lessons?"

Kaylee shook her head, her platinum blond hair brushing across her shoulders. Charlotte had always kept Kaylee's ultra-fine hair tied in braids, but today. . . .

Way too many changes. No more school, no more dance lessons, no more T-ball or little girl hairstyles. Something was up, and I needed to find out what it was.

I called Charlotte on my lunch break on Monday afternoon, but she didn't have time to talk to me. She continued to put me off until I felt even that was suspicious. Then I made up my mind to confront her face to face in a place where she couldn't avoid me.

Since coming back home again, Charlotte had taken a job with her father—doing heaven only knew what. Kent Whitman was so ecstatic over his daughter's return to the family fold that he most likely invented a position just for her. Just one more triumph over the lowly Taylor clan.

Her secretary was not at her desk when I arrived at Charlotte's office a week later. That's how I planned it. That way I could ask her about the changes the children were experiencing without having an audience for the evitable confrontation that usually followed when Charlotte and I were in the same building.

"Knock, knock," I said, entering her office without an invitation.

Her head jerked up, and she dropped the file that she had been reading. "Jesse," she squeaked. "What are you doing here?" She stood and tried to move away from me—tried to hide the purple-black bruise on her left cheek.

My instincts went on high alert. "What happened to you?"

She shook her head and managed not to meet my gaze. "Racquetball," she said, gingerly touching the ugly-looking mark.

I hadn't lived with her for twelve years not to know when she wasn't telling the truth, and this time she was definitely lying. That left only one explanation: she had been hit. Hard. And it didn't take a genius to figure out who did it.

"Charlotte," I said quietly and calmly, when my insides were churning like a stormy sea. "You should go down to the station—"

She lifted a hand and cut me off mid-sentence. "I cannot jail my racquetball partner for my own carelessness."

"Everyone else around here might believe that bull crap, but I don't. And if that jerk so much as breathes wrong on Kaylee or Joey—"

"Did you come here for a reason, Jesse? Or just to pry?" As usual, we'd have to play this by Charlotte's rules.

"I want to know why you pulled the children out of school."

She shrugged. "You know how hard it is to find good education."

"The best private school in the state wasn't good enough?" Our town might be small, but our education system was first rate.

Once gain her gaze didn't meet mine. "Anthony thought it would be beneficial for them to be home schooled."

I didn't bother to point out that one of the many arguments for home schooling is to keep the family unit together with the mother as the teacher, not some hired stranger.

"What about T-ball and dance lessons? Why aren't they going to their after-school activities?"

Charlotte's expression hardened and just like that, she shut me out. "Listen, Jesse. I told you why we pulled them out of school. That's all you need to know."

"No, you listen, Charlotte. Something's going on here and I intend to get to the bottom of it."

"Don't be ridiculous."

"I mean it. If he hurts Kaylee or Joey. . . ." I let my words trail off, unable to actually voice what I would do.

"Don't be ridiculous," she repeated, but her hand shook as she waved me out of her office.

But the matter wasn't over. Not by a long shot.

I couldn't stop thinking about that terrible bruise on Charlotte's face. I didn't for one minute believe that she had hurt herself playing racquetball, and she was a fool to think that I would buy her lame story. Though I no longer held a romantic love for her, she had once been my lover, my wife. She was the mother of my children. I hated beyond anything to know that McDaniel would do something like that to her.

But what scared me the most—what sent chills down my spine every time I thought about it—were Kaylee and Joey. They lived with an abuser, and I was terrified that he would do something like that to my children. I tried to keep a professional outlook on the situation, but I'm a man and a father, not just a cop. The man in me wanted to protect Charlotte as my onetime mate. The father in me wanted to kill McDaniel, chop the body into tiny pieces, then throw them into the nearest body of water. But the cop in me knew that I had no proof and I had to follow protocol.

Friday before my weekend with my children, I knocked on my captain's door. "Can I talk to you a minute?"

Captain Michael Collier looked up from the report he was reading and nodded his head toward the chair that sat in front of his desk. "Take a load off," he said, but his gaze shifted back to the papers that he held.

I eased into the chair and tried to find words for what I needed to talk to him about. I must have taken too long, for he tossed the papers onto his desk and leaned back in his own chair. "That's quite a serious look you've got there, Jess."

I nodded. "It's a serious matter, Mike." I leaned forward and braced my elbows on my knees, trying to dispel some of the tension in my back. "This goes no further."

He nodded.

I took a deep breath and plunged right in. "Charlotte got remarried a few weeks ago, and I think her new husband is abusing her. I'm afraid that my children are next. Naturally, I want to nail the guy."

"I see." Michael folded his arms on his desk and eyed me carefully. "That's some accusation."

"I've seen the bruises on her, and he's pulled the children out of school and all of their extracurricular activities. He has to be hiding something."

"Has she contacted us?"

I shook my head. "She told me she got it playing racquetball."

"Did anyone else see it happen?"

"Not that I know."

"That's a pretty shaky case, Jess."

"I know. I know."

"Then drop it. She's a big girl. If she wants to be a punching bag—"

"But my children live with this dirt bag."

"It doesn't matter. You're a cop. You know the rules. Unless something happens to the kids, there's nothing you can do."

The hardest part of being an ex-soldier and a police officer is the loss of trust in the human race. Day in and day out I only saw the bad side of humanity. I'll admit it: I've become jaded by the ways of the world. I always expect the worst. It's sheer habit, ingrained from years of training, but maybe—just maybe—this time I was overreacting.

Friday night after my talk with the captain, Charlotte called to tell me that I couldn't have Kaylee and Joey for the weekend. I tried to remain calm, tried to keep a positive spin on the situation. Just because she wanted them for the weekend didn't mean. . . .

"That's two weeks, Char."

She sighed into the phone. She hated when I shortened her name, and I knew it. "I know, Jesse. But Anthony has this family thing. You know how it is."

I didn't, but I didn't say as much. My parents had long ago traded in their house for an RV and a post office box in Florida. I saw them once a year and got a box from them on birthdays and Christmases.

But I couldn't help think that if our family had been as important to Charlotte as what "Anthony wanted," then maybe we would have had a chance. "Then I want them the following weekend."

She got really quiet, and I knew that she was struggling. With what, I didn't know. "I'll see what I can do."

"I want to talk to them, Charlotte."

"Now?"

"Yes, now."

"They're in bed."

I wanted to demand that she wake them, but I was being irrational. After all, it was after nine on a school night—not that they were in regular school anymore. They still had "classes" in the morning.

"Tomorrow, then," I said. Even to my own ears, it sounded like a threat.

As I hung up the phone, dread coursed through my veins. I had the terrible, terrible feeling that I was never going to see my children again.

The weekend came and went and then another. When it was my turn to have the children again, Charlotte called, her voice sounding defeated as she made up yet another excuse as to why I couldn't have Kaylee and Joey. This one was worse than the last. My suspicions mounted.

"You can't do this," I said, my teeth clenched in barely-controlled rage. "That's three weekends this year. The court said I am to have them every other weekend."

"Then sue me," she gritted in return and slammed down the phone.

I sighed heavily, then replaced my own receiver.

My captain's words kept coming back to me: "Unless something happens to the kids, there's nothing you can do." I hadn't seen my children in over a month, hadn't even talked to them on the phone. As far as I knew something could have already happened. It didn't look like Charlotte was going to let me see them anytime soon. So I did the only thing I could do: I staked out their house.

It took me two days and twelve passes before I had the proof that Charlotte had lied to me. She had told me that they were going out of town, but I saw them leave for church Sunday morning. I saw something else during my impromptu investigation: the children were never seen outside at any time of the day. No school, no dance lessons, no T-ball, no fresh air. I wasn't overreacting. It was over eighty degrees outside—sunny and beautiful—and my children were locked inside their home.

I went to see Michael again the next day.

"People change their minds all the time," was all he said when I told him about Charlotte's lies. I knew he had a point, but deep down, I knew there was something more to this story.

"But—" I started, even though I had no more words to continue. "I'm afraid," I finally whispered. "I'm so afraid that he's hurting them."

My captain nodded solemnly. "I know it's hard, but without visible proof. . . ."

He trailed off, but I understood what he was delicately trying to say. I didn't have a leg to stand on unless I could prove that McDaniel had physically abused them. Bruises, cuts, burns. The mere thought turned my stomach.

"How am I supposed to get proof? I don't even get to see them anymore. I haven't seen them in almost two months." Suddenly I was more agitated than I had been the day Charlotte told me that she was getting remarried. I stood and paced across the office.

"I don't mean to pry, Jesse, but if you have court ordered time with the kids, then take her back before a judge."

I snorted. "Yeah, like that would do me any good. The Whitmans have half the judges in this town in their hip pockets. And the ones they don't own surely belong to the McDaniels."

"McDaniels?"

I nodded. "Charlotte's new husband is none other than Anthony McDaniel."

He whistled through his teeth. "That's not good, Jesse. I hate to be the one to tell you this, but with those kinds of odds, you're going to need more than proof to get your children back."

Despite knowing the chance I had of getting my children away from their mother—or even being able to see them on the already court-specified times, I called my lawyer first thing Tuesday morning.

"Tony, it's Jesse Taylor."

"Jesse. How are things on the beat?"

"Not bad," I said, not bothering to tell him that I'd made detective some months ago.

Maybe it was the tone of my voice. Or maybe it was the simple fact that I had the best lawyer the influential families in my town didn't already hold on retainer, but Tony Decker knew immediately that I had something on my mind. "I take it this isn't a social call."

"No," I said. "No, it's not." I quickly filled him in on the events of the last few weeks, including the fact that Charlotte had married Anthony McDaniel. "So what do you think?"

"Proving that she's been deliberately keeping the kids from you is going to be your word against hers. As for the other allegations. . . ." He trailed off. "Well, the fact of the matter is that you don't have any proof. Just speculation. At this point, the best you can hope for is getting back your regular visitations."

Not exactly what I wanted to hear, but it was better than nothing.

"Jesse." I could tell from his tone that I wasn't going to like what was coming next. "People like Anthony McDaniel have money and power. Even if you get proof that he's guilty of this abuse, he can delay things in court until you run out of money and are forced to give up. Are you prepared to launch such a war?"

"I have to. They're my children. I have some company time and vacation days saved up. I could use them for court dates."

"And money?"

"I'll sell my car if I have to." The cherry-red, vintage Mustang was the only thing I got to keep out of my marriage. And that was only because it was mine before I married Charlotte. I had rebuilt the car the year I turned seventeen. And I'd kept her in mint condition ever since. I loved that old car, but I loved my children even more. I'd gladly sacrifice her for them.

"Jesse—"

"Let me guess," I interrupted Charlotte before she could finish yet another excuse about why I couldn't have the children yet again. "I can't have the kids."

"Jesse. . . ." There was that whiney voice again. But in the year since our divorce had become final, I had grown immune to it.

"What is it this time? Another family emergency? Lunch with the governor?"

"Benefit picnic."

I hated the fact that McDaniel felt that my children could—and should—help him further his career. Mostly at mine and their expense. "When's the picnic?"

"Saturday."

"I want them Sunday."

"Well, you see . . . Anthony thinks it's a good idea if we attend church as a family."

I felt my anger rise. "I don't care what Anthony thinks. The court ordered you to let me have the kids every other weekend."

"I know, Jesse, but a set schedule is good for Kaylee and Joey."

"So is time with their father."

"Jesse—"

"This is the last time, Charlotte."

"But—"

"The very last time, and I mean it." I slammed down the receiver and ran my fingers through my hair, trying to get a grip on my temper. I just felt so helpless, smothered by the fact that she held all the cards. All I wanted was to see my kids. Was that so much to ask? Was she hiding the children from me in order to hide their injuries, intentional burns and bruises? The thought made me sick.

Michael was right. I needed more than proof. But there was no way I could even get that much unless I was allowed to see my children. And until our court date arrived, seeing my children didn't seem to be an option any longer. They weren't enrolled in school or any of their extracurricular activities anymore. They weren't even allowed to go outside. I didn't have a prayer until Charlotte relented.

Prayer.

The thought sizzled through me. Charlotte had mentioned they were going to church on Sunday morning as a family. It was my only hope, my only chance to make certain that my children were safe.

It was a big church with hundreds of followers calling it their home of worship. The chances were in my favor that no one would even notice me. All I had to do was sneak in between the services and mill around until I found them. I would be able to talk to them, make certain they weren't being hurt, then I could head on back to my apartment. After all, even as jaded as I had become, I couldn't allow myself to believe that Charlotte would knowingly allow our children to be abused. But I just had to see them for myself and ease the gnawing feeling I carried in my gut.

"Psst," I whispered to Kaylee as she passed by me in the hallway of the church. Joey followed behind her as she led him to his Sunday school class.

"Daddy!" Her face split into an ear-to-ear grin when she caught sight of me. I pulled them both into my arms, but shushed Kaylee to keep from drawing any more eyes than necessary.

"I've missed you both so much." I closed my eyes and inhaled the sweet scent of them, of orange-smelling shampoo and fabric softener.

"You have?" Joey asked, pulling back just enough so he could look at me.

I could see both doubt and hope in his eyes. "Of course I have."

"See?" Kaylee asked in that superior tone that only a big sister could produce. "I told you so."

"But Mom said—"

"Kaylee," I interrupted, aware that soon we would be drawing attention, and that wasn't part of my plan. "Do you know someplace where we can talk? Then you and Joey can tell me everything that your mom has said."

She nodded her blond head and led us to a small Sunday school room that wasn't being used.

"They're painting in here," she said with an adult tone, no doubt repeated like the leaders of the church. "Soon it will look like the deserts of Arabia."

I smiled to myself at how grown up she sounded. God, I missed her so much. And Joey, too. It seemed like they had grown a foot since the last time I had seen them. I reached down and tussled Joey's hair, but he pulled away with a wince. My alarm bells went off immediately.

"What's the matter with your head, Joey?" I tried to keep the fear and trepidation out of my voice, but it was there just the same. Don't jump to conclusions, Taylor, I told myself, but I felt as if I was preparing to take one giant leap.

Joey and Kaylee exchanged a look.

"He fell." Even in those two little words, I could hear the borrowed tone of an adult. Of her new and powerful stepfather?

I dropped to one knee and gently searched his small scalp for the contusion. "How did you fall, son?" I tried to keep my tone as calm as possible, but my hands started to tremble. Instinctively, I knew that my life was about to take a sharp turn.

Another look passed between brother and sister.

"I was playing . . . outside."

I briefly closed my eyes, trying to gather the shreds of my self-control. I felt the tears biting behind my lids. I couldn't give in to the weakness. Not now.

I took a deep breath and slowly reopened my eyes. My son was lying to me. And there was only one reason why he would feel that he should have to do that: fear.

My hands were outright shaking as I placed them on his shoulders. I gave him a gentle squeeze to gain his attention. "Tell me the truth, 'cause you know I'll find out if you don't."

I've never been much of a praying man, but as the seconds ticked by and I waited for Joey's answer, the words tumbled around in my head. God, please, please let him say that he just got confused, that he was really playing inside. Let him say anything but—

"He pushed him down the stairs."

A shrill buzzing started in my ears.

"Kay-lee," Joey whined, tears streaming down his sweet, little face. "You weren't supposed to tell."

She bit her lip, clearly fighting an inner struggle.

"He"—I swallowed hard—"pushed you down the stairs." I repeated the words, the humming in my ears growing louder. I didn't need to ask who "he" was. "Has he hurt you other times?"

Kaylee and Joey exchanged another of their looks.

"Tell me," I commanded, my teeth clenched. I tried to keep my voice low, fighting a maelstrom of swirling emotions, but it wouldn't do if we were overheard.

The children slowly, solemnly nodded.

I should have seen it immediately. The signs were all there from the way they had trouble looking me in the eye to their long-sleeved shirts in the summertime.

As quickly as I could, I examined them. I was running out of time, but I had to see for myself. My agitated state impeded my search, and seeing the marks on their tiny bodies, mixed with smelling the paint fumes in the room, made me light-headed. Nothing in my police training had prepared me to search for evidence on my own children.

Seeing the bruises, cuts, and burns on them was almost more than I could bear. I pulled them close to me, as if by simply holding them to me I could take away the pain that they had suffered.

"I'm sorry," I whispered. "So, so sorry."

Kaylee, tears flowing across her cheeks, laid her hand on my shoulder. "It's okay, Daddy. You're here now."

I felt Joey squeeze me a little tighter and I knew what I had to do, I had to get them away from their stepfather. And I couldn't wait, not a moment longer. I couldn't wait until a court date. I couldn't be positive that the system would work in my favor. Even with the apparent signs of abuse, people like Anthony McDaniel are slippery enough and sly enough to slide their way through the legal system. There was no way I could fight the combined power of the McDaniels and the Whitmans. I had spent all of the money I had squirreled away to gain what little custody I had of Kaylee and Joey. Michael's words kept echoing in my head: "You're going to need more than proof to get your children back."

But I couldn't let my children live with a monster.

"That's right," I croaked, my voice thickened by my tears. "I'm here now and you never have to go back to him again. I'm here and you're safe now. Safe."

Getting them out of the church was easy—almost too easy, and that in itself had me worried. I knew the rest of the day wouldn't go so smoothly.

We had only an hour and forty-five minutes before church was over and Charlotte would realize that the children were missing. We only had a few minutes after that before she realized that I had taken them.

My palms were sweating as I pulled out of the church parking lot and into the street. My heart pounded in my chest, but I knew that this was the only way. Charlotte wasn't going to just hand over the children without a lengthy court battle, and McDaniel surely wouldn't stand to have his name dragged through the courts with the charge of child abuse attached. Without money and power of my own, I didn't stand a chance. My children didn't stand a chance.

"Daddy, is everything going to be okay?" Kaylee asked, her voice taking on the little girl quality I instantly recognized. She felt safe with me. She might be afraid, but she felt safe. She was, no doubt, picking up on my nervousness, but she knew deep down that she was in good hands.

"Everything's going to be fine, sweetheart." I pulled the car into the bank parking lot, painfully aware of how little time we had. "We're just going to stop here for a couple of minutes and get us some money. Then we're going to take a little trip. Isn't that going to be fun?"

"And you want us to go, too?" Joey asked.

"Of course I do."

It took three ATM stops to clear my accounts and get what little money I had for our escape. I had to drop by my apartment and pick up our passports to get us across the border. Everything else I left behind. It hardly would have been fair of me to get my own personal items when my children were leaving behind everything they held dear. No, it was a time for a fresh start for all of us.

I headed away from my favorite campsite at the lake, figuring that would be the first place they—Charlotte and McDaniel—would look for us. I drove north for a couple of hours, used my credit card to leave a false trail, then headed south like the devil was on our heels. In a way, I guess he was.

Last year, I read an article about a tiny country in Central America, where with only a thousand or so American dollars, a person could live like a king. That's where we were going.

Just before sunset on the first day of our trip, I traded my car and prayed that McDaniel wouldn't find out until we were so far over the border that they'd never be able to find us. We had to be careful, especially at the border. We didn't have fake IDs or passports, just the ones we had for military purposes. I surely didn't want us to get busted so close to our goal.

I know it sounds extreme. I could have taken them across the country and hid out in the mountains somewhere, but how long would it have been before our faces turned up on milk cartons or in one of those ads in front of Wal-Mart? That was just too risky. The McDaniels' power was growing every day. Before long they would have political ties nationwide. This was the only way—the only way that I had to protect my children.

We have a small house on the beach now. Our life is simple and wholesome and filled with fun and color—lots and lots of color. The children are doing better every day. They miss their mommy, but have grown to understand that she and Anthony McDaniel are a package deal. They'd rather live without her than with the both of them.

I'm just so grateful that I found out what I did before it got worse—before the children were damaged beyond help. As it is, they grow stronger and more confident every day. Their scars—both inside and out—are fading as the days turn into weeks and the weeks into months. They have a dog now and they take him running on the beach every morning. I have a job as a handyman in a small beachfront resort. There's a lady in the village who cares for them while I'm at work. I gave up my career as a policeman to save my children.

I don't know if I'll ever forgive Charlotte for the danger that she placed our children in, but I know that I would never have forgiven myself if I hadn't taken them when I did. And each day that I see their smiling, happy faces turned so brown by the ever-present sun, I know that I did the right thing.

THE END

CONFESSIONS OF A HEARTBROKEN MOM
"I Raised An Angel, But She Turned Out To Be The Devil"

The door was slammed so hard I felt the floor under my feet quiver and several pictures on the living room wall tilted crookedly, as if to sympathize with the sudden disruption of my small world. From my position in the middle of the room, I could see outside to the street, where Austin sat in his car, waiting for Amber, my daughter, to join him. Of course, he didn't have the guts to join her in the declaration just delivered to me.

I looked on, too stunned to move, as Amber hopped into the convertible without opening the door, and they sped off with a squeal of tires.

I took deep breaths to try and still my shaking body, placing a hand over my heart, which actually hurt. Amber's words still rang in my ears.

"Brenda and I are moving into an apartment with our boyfriends, and there's nothing you can do about it, Mother—so don't try. I'm eighteen now, and I can do as I please!" Her voice was shrill and charged with defiance, her dark eyes blazing at me.

I gaped at her, incapable of speech. Amber and Austin had been dating for a year, but I never thought the attachment very serious—certainly not mind-shattering like this announcement. Finally, I squeaked, "You mean you're going to live together without the benefit of marriage?"

"Oh, Mother!" she sneered, her lip curling. "Get a grip! Who in this day and age gets married? What's the point?" She glared at me, her whole demeanor bristling defiance.

"That's strange," I murmured. "No one gets married, yet last month we went to two weddings."

Amber swung her shoulder purse in an exaggerated attitude of nonchalance. "Well, Austin and I are not getting married and neither are Dan and Brenda. I'll be around to pick up my things tomorrow."

"What things?" I asked stupidly, unable to comprehend so quickly this drastic turn of events. After all, Amber was accepted at the state university to continue her education, even though she never made up her mind about a major.

"My bedroom, of course," she said, giving me a pitying glance at my stupidity.

By her "bedroom" I assumed she meant everything in the room.

Her bedroom set was an antique inherited from my mother, and she from her mother. It was worth a lot of money.

"See you tomorrow, Mother. Austin will be bringing his dad's pickup." Out the door she went, slamming it as hard as she could—making a statement, I guess.

I collapsed onto the nearest chair, too shocked, too stunned to cry. My brain refused to function properly. It couldn't seem to get beyond the disdain and contempt of Amber's expression. Why have I never seen it before? Was I blind, deaf, and dumb to my own daughter's behavior? Her character? Did I live in denial and didn't even know it?

I sat thus for a half hour or so, a thousand images flashing through my mind, all pictures of Amber from the day she was born. She was a beautiful baby, child, teenager. Too much so? Did her beauty blind Mark and me to her character flaws? Greg said so once, when Amber was sixteen, and he was twenty-six, the older brother who could look at his little sister with a sibling's perspective.

I rose from my chair suddenly; I had to talk to someone, and it had to be someone familiar with Amber, and with me, her mother. Mark was out of town. He wouldn't be any help, anyway, since Amber was the apple of his eye. She could do no wrong.

Greg had to be the one. I walked to the kitchen, picked up the cordless phone, and dialed the number to the place where he worked as a computer programmer.

At the sound of his voice the tears gushed suddenly. "I have to talk to you, Greg," I sobbed. "Someone... I have to talk to someone."

"Is it about Amber?"

How on earth did he know? "Yes... yes—she just left—permanently, I guess."

"Look, Mom, I'll take an early lunch hour and come to your house. Fix me a sandwich, something easy."

Relief coursed through me as I placed the receiver in its cradle. Greg had so much common sense, was so down to earth. He would tell me what to do—what both Mark and I should do. I opened the fridge door to get the food for a lunch for my son.

"Any iced tea, Mom?" Greg, like my husband, prefers iced tea as a hot weather beverage. I like lemonade, spiced.

"You didn't see this coming, Mom?"

I sat down after getting the jug of tea, and stared at my son across the narrow table. "You mean with Amber? What was there to see?"

"You and Dad have been too trusting with her. She's not the innocent, little girl you both think she is. She runs with a pretty fast crowd. Her best friend, Brenda, is a wild, little thing—a bad influence."

"She's always been very polite and respectful here in the house when she's visited Amber."

Greg looked at me with pity in his eyes and shook his head in disbelief. "And that's all you go by? How she acts in your home? Ever question Amber as to their doings—where they hang out, where they get their booze?"

I felt my eyes widening in shock. "What are you talking about?"

"Are you aware, Mom, that Amber has come home drunk on several occasions and safely stumbled to her room, while you and Dad slept?"

I took a sip of lemonade, then pushed my sandwich away. I was no longer hungry. I remembered suddenly several occasions when Amber spent most of Sunday in bed, complaining of not feeling well. I thought she had a touch of the flu, while she really had a hangover. I felt outraged, betrayed, my trust and love taken advantage of. The prick of tears hurt behind my eyes, and I blinked to ease the pain.

"How do you know all this, Greg? You and Amber have never been close. You hardly know each other."

"I have connections, Mother. Amanda hears things through some of her friends." Amanda is my daughter-in-law.

I looked at Greg with accusing eyes. "Why didn't you tell us?"

He snorted. "And you would have believed me? Fat chance! Dad never wants to hear a word against my little sister. She could do no wrong. Amber actually believes the world revolves around her and her wishes. She does, Mom. And right now she wants to live with her boyfriend, so she can do it—excuse the vulgarity—any time they damn well please, without any adult saying no, or looking on with disapproving eyes."

I was appalled at the images his words conjured up. "Your dad will be shattered."

"Dad deserves to be shattered. Maybe he'll finally get his eyes open to reality. Maybe you both will."

"You don't think we should stop her?"

Greg rose abruptly. "Mother, she's eighteen. She can make her own choices now. Let her, and make her responsible for them as well." He placed his dishes in the sink, then sat down beside me. "Amber expects to come tomorrow and haul everything out of her bedroom—in masse—except for the carpet; expects use of your credit cards, probably; expects a monthly allowance. Oh, who knows what else she expects!"

I cried into a Kleenex as his words hammered against me, making me see my cherished daughter in a way I'd never seen before. It was heartbreaking. "I don't think she's as bad as you picture," I sobbed.

"I think she's even worse," he said coldly and got up to leave.

I wiped my eyes, blew my nose, and rose to my feet. "What do you think I should do?"

"You don't want to hear it." His blue eyes were hard and cold, so much like Amber's in their intensity, but hers were dark and beguiling.

"Tell me, anyway."

He counted his suggestions off on his fingers. "One, change all the locks on the doors. Two, pack her belongings—the ones you think she should have—in boxes. Three, place them on the front porch for her to pick up tomorrow. Four, let her know the house is off-limits to her from now on. Write that it's so in a note and tape it to one of the boxes. She has chosen a different lifestyle. To some of us, marriage is sacred. Five, don't give in to her tantrums—and there will be some, believe me."

No, I didn't want to hear such drastic measures. They all seemed so cruel, so hard, so . . . ending.

After Greg left, I found myself going to Amber's bedroom and looking around. She hadn't cleaned the room in some time, and it was messy and cluttered. Keeping her room clean was her only chore, but she rarely did it.

Suddenly, a small smile tugged at the corners of my mouth. I could see Amber cooking, or rather, trying to cook. The poor, little fool! Did she have any idea of all the tasks she would now be responsible for? Of course not. She and her friends were thinking only of the excitement of living together. They knew absolutely nothing of the real issues of life. Nothing . . . nothing. . . .

I went to the basement to collect some boxes and, on the way, stopped to phone a locksmith to get the locks changed. "It's an emergency," I insisted. "It must be done this afternoon."

I couldn't sleep that night and finally gave up and got out of bed. I had come to grips with what must be done, even accepting the heartbreak that went along with it. What preyed on me now was Mark, my husband. Was I too hasty in accepting Greg's advice? Would Mark return home and in anger, reverse what I did? After all, Amber was his golden girl, his little angel who could do no wrong. That's the way it had always been; why would he change now?

I paced the floor of my home in the dim nightlights. "I should have waited," I moaned aloud. "Mark is the head of this house, not Greg. He is going to be so angry. I know he will be angry with me . . . angry with Greg for interfering . . . angry because I acted in haste."

A sudden thought jolted into my mind. Gosh, he won't even be able to get into his own house because the locks are all changed, which means. . . .

Well, it meant I had to stay put until he arrived. I had planned on leaving for the day. I didn't want to be a witness to my daughter's tantrum when she found herself denied access to the house. The boxes I packed were still on the front porch, with her name on them and a note.

I flung myself in the nearest chair, a bundle of overwrought nerves, then shot out of it again to continue my pacing. I could not sit still. I put a CD of classical music in the stereo and did my pacing and my weeping to it.

The early dawn of the day chased away the darkness of night, as I sat at the kitchen counter nursing a cup of strong, black coffee. My face felt puffy from crying, and my temples pounded with a tension headache, in spite of the aspirin I had swallowed. The pain in my breast was like an instrument of torture, scraping, probing, hurting incredibly.

The doorbell pealed through the house, its suddenness making me jump so violently I sloshed coffee all over the counter. I left the mess and jumped to my feet. Surely Amber wouldn't be here at this hour! Of course not. Greg maybe . . . or the police. . . .

I peered through the long, narrow window alongside the door. It was Mark! Thank goodness it was Mark. I turned the lever that operates the bolt and threw the door open.

"Thank goodness you're here!" I cried. Only then did I notice how disheveled and tired and drained he looked.

He plunked his suitcase on the floor, then gathered me tightly into his arms. "Greg called me," he said brokenly.

Thank God. Thank God for Greg who went through all the hassle of contacting his father when he was out on his route.

"I hope you have some coffee made. I feel like an absolute wreck."

"I didn't sleep all night," I said as I led the way to the kitchen. My sloshed coffee had dripped to the floor, and I got a paper towel to clean up the mess.

After I poured him coffee Mark said, "Now tell me exactly what happened."

I did as succinctly as possible, so glad he was home, so glad I no longer had to bear the burden alone. I finished by asking, "Do you think I acted too hastily? I was beside myself, Mark; I had to talk to someone, and there was only Greg."

I distinctly saw my husband's lips quiver—big, strong Mark, who was quite unemotional about everything, very logical, factual in his thinking, except where his daughter was concerned.

He brushed a hand over his eyes and, as he did so, his expression changed. "Poor fool," he murmured. "Poor, little fool. She's made a terrible choice, but she'll have to live with it. You and I are out of her life as of now."

Is this Mark speaking? My husband, who would move mountains for his golden girl?

"It breaks my heart that she has given herself, body and soul, to this worthless scamp, Austin. He flips hamburgers at a fast food joint,

Susan. Flips hamburgers! He has no plans for further education."

"Do you know his parents at all?"

"Not really, but I've heard about him. He's the habitual troublemaker, who has run circles around his parents, and they buy him off with money. The convertible he drives was a birthday gift, on his eighteenth. At least I had sense enough not to do that." He shook his head, lost in thought. Then he said, "Two unmarried couples, all eighteen, living together in an apartment, thinking they have the world by the tail. Mere babes in the woods who haven't a clue about life. Not a clue, Susan. Why, Amber has never even held down a job, because we wanted her to concentrate on her schooling, get good grades, prepare for college."

He rose abruptly from his chair and went to stand by the French doors that open onto the deck. "What's wrong with today's kids, Susan? You think you're doing what's best, you want to help them so they're not deprived like you and I were when we were growing up—and look what happens. They turn and stick a knife in your back."

I rose quickly and took him in my arms. "We did too much, Mark. Hard times are good for children as well as adults. Amber's difficult times started as of yesterday. She will have to find work. She's qualified for nothing. Maybe she will join Austin flipping hamburgers. There won't be any more hundred-dollar sneakers, no more Abercrombie outfits. She'll be shopping at a discount store. It's time she grew up, Mark, and learned what real life is all about. We did a good job raising Greg. We weren't as affluent then. He always had to earn his own spending money. We gave Amber everything and only now she will have to work for what she wants. We helped make her what she has become."

Suddenly, I felt strong, assured we were making the right decision, that Amber had to learn the hard way. After all we had done for her, she had only contempt for us, her parents. It's part of being overindulged. "Do you have the strength, Mark, to remain firm when she comes begging?" I asked as I stepped away from him. "She will, you know."

I saw the suffering on his face, the terrible hurt in his eyes. "Something broke in me, Susan, when Greg relayed the news to me. I can't describe it. Something broke and splintered and snapped that used to bind Amber to me in an unrealistic way. It's like my eyes were suddenly opened to her faults, that she could be cruel, uncaring, spiteful—my little princess, who I would gladly have died for!" He shook his head in disbelief. "Well, I'm going to shower and change clothes, then I want us to go away for the day. I want to sit by a lake and drink in its beauty and forget the trauma of the last few hours."

As he left the room I opened the French doors and stepped out onto the deck, which was still wet from early morning's dew. The sun was up now, already shining warmly, and the sky was cloudless. It was going to be a gorgeous day, but hot, just the kind to relax by a lake and do nothing.

I picked up the garden hose and turned on the spigot. Might as well water all the flowerpots that are so attractively scattered across the deck. I'd do it and get it over with, then I'd shower, too, and get ready for the day. Mark and I had Saturday and Sunday to spend together, to prepare ourselves for what future days might hold. I shut my mind to Amber and concentrated on my watering.

We were ready to leave the house when the phone rang.

"Should we answer it?" I asked apprehensively.

Mark, who was carrying our luggage, said, "Of course you answer," and set down my overnight case to lock the French doors and pull down the shades.

"Hello," said a shrill, feminine voice. "This is Karen Kinsey, Austin's mother. Have I called you at a bad time? I know it's very early."

Austin's mother, my brain registered, as I watched Mark leave the room to take the luggage to the car in the garage.

"Hello, are you there?"

"Yes—yes," I stammered, wishing I had the other woman's poise and self-assurance. "I—I . . . you took me by surprise, that's all."

"Well, I called to see what you're giving Amber to set up housekeeping so we don't duplicate. They need everything, you know."

What they need to set up housekeeping? Is the woman suggesting some kind of bridal shower for a girl who isn't going to be a bride?

"Hello!" Karen sang out.

Anger coursed through me in an overpowering surge, the adrenaline finally kicking in so my brain would operate again. "We're not giving Amber a darned thing!" I rasped. "This is her decision totally to move out, forget about her education, forget about everything that's decent and sane. And my husband and I are not helping her one bit in this insanity!"

Silence greeted my explosion—silence that went on and on, until I felt like asking, "Are you there, Karen Kinsey?"

Finally, "Well . . . I didn't expect such a reaction as this. Personally speaking, Ted and I are so glad to be rid of Austin. We have paid the first month's rent and deposit on the apartment and letting Austin take some furniture."

"That's your choice," I said, my voice dripping ice. "Personally speaking, my husband and I happen to believe in marriage, not living together, and this business of two teenaged couples sharing an apartment is the most ridiculous thing I have ever heard of. Do you plan on supporting the foursome financially as well?"

"No. . . ." Now the woman's voice held some doubt. "We're just helping them get established."

"Amber was to go to the university this fall. She was accepted, and the down payment was made on the first semester. And she's throwing it all away for this." I repeated, "For this! Well, she's made her choice, as she so arrogantly told me yesterday, and she can live by her choice. When she walked out the door, she walked out of our lives!" I slammed the receiver down as Mark walked into the room. I was trembling from head to foot.

"Who was that?" he asked sharply.

"Austin's mother, Karen Kinsey."

"Is that his last name? Kinsey? What did she want?"

I told him.

"She's got the nerves!" he exploded. "They paid the rent and the deposit, did they? And what were we to give them? Furniture for the apartment? It isn't enough, of course, that Austin has our daughter, but we are to help them? We are to help them?" He slammed his fist on the counter, his face red with rage.

"Let's get out of here. Please, Mark, before someone else calls."

"Wait. I'm writing a note to stick on Amber's boxes."

"I already did," I said.

"She'll get two notes then, won't she?"

I looked over his shoulder as he wrote:

Amber,

These are the clothes and personal belongings your mother and I decided we would let you have. The rest of the furnishings in the bedroom belong to us. They were for your use as long as you lived with us, but since you have chosen to leave, they are no longer for your use.

We are devastated by your choice and know the day will come when you realize you made a terrible mistake. Regrets always come too late, and the damage can't be undone.

In the meantime this decision of yours will force you into facing the realities of everyday living, with all its difficulties, which you've never had to contend with before.

Good luck looking for a job! Your mother and I will be thinking of you, but don't expect any kind of support from us—moral or financial. You're on your own, girl!

Dad

"What do you think?" Mark asked as he folded the paper and wrote Amber's name on the envelope.

"It's a good letter; states facts, without being vindictive. It's so sad, Mark, so terribly sad."

"Where's the Scotch tape?"

I got it from the junk drawer, and he grabbed it and left the room to tape the note on one of the boxes on the front porch.

What would Amber's reaction be? Stunned disbelief that her father isn't going to support her in her decision? Yes, I thought so. She had been led to believe in her eighteen years of life that she could do no wrong that wouldn't be forgiven on the instant. Which proved she didn't know her father, and I didn't know my husband. She had outraged his moral integrity by her choice and uncovered iron in Mark's character.

"There's one more thing I have to do before we leave," Mark said as he entered the kitchen again. "I just thought of it."

So I sat down at the counter and tried to wait patiently as he faxed the state university, requesting Amber's enrollment be cancelled because she had changed plans. He asked them to kindly return the tuition payment that had been made.

"I wouldn't want Austin Kinsey to get a hold of that money," Mark explained as we finally got in the car. "Wouldn't he have a lark!"

Yes, I agreed silently, as Mark backed out of the garage. The lark would be shared by all four, as long as the money lasted.

I thought to the days ahead, when Amber would have to get herself out of bed, get her own breakfast, look for work—all these responsibilities foreign to her. Who would cook dinner? Or would their food be from a fast food joint? Yes, I acknowledged sadly. We had been remiss in the way we raised Amber. All she ever had to do was clean her bedroom, and that wasn't enforced. What were we thinking?

Well, that day Mark and I were paying for the choices we made as well—and it was a bitter, bitter payment.

I leaned my head against the closed window of the car and closed my eyes. I needed some sleep, where I could forget the trauma of the past twenty-four hours—and the guilt.

"Let's stay another day, Susan," Mark said Monday morning over breakfast. "It's been a long time since we got away like this, just the two of us."

"What will McCormick say?" Mark is an engineer and does bid work for McCormick, Inc., a heavy construction company, which builds bridges and that sort of thing.

"I haven't had a decent vacation in several years. McCormick owes me a lot of time."

I sniffed delicately. "They may owe you a lot of time, but that doesn't necessarily mean you're going to get it."

"If I insist, I will. I'm tired, Susan—tired of everything."

He looked tired, too. Normally Mark is an intense, high-energy person, raring to go, whatever the occasion. This is probably why, at fifty, he's as thin as a lath, with no hint of love handles around his middle. But now his face was shadowed and lined, and puffy bags hung under his eyes. I had never seen him sit in a lounge chair for hours, as he had done the past two days.

"My pots need watering," I reminded him.

"Forget the pots! Call your neighbor; she'll water them for you."

Our neighbor is Mary Holman, a sixty-year-old widow whose hobby is her vast flower garden. Yes, she would water my pots with pleasure. She was always telling me I never give them enough fertilizer.

"I never expected you to react in this way," I ventured presently, when the waitress had taken our plates and we were enjoying third cups of coffee.

Mark's frown was quick and fierce. "You thought I'd condone immoral behavior?"

"According to Greg, Amber has been a pretty wild girl this past year."

"Funny, isn't it, how parents can be so blind to their children's behavior? But of course, she was always on her best behavior around us."

"We never taught her to do anything, Mark. Nothing! How could we be so remiss? Of course she's expecting us to support her."

"I don't see why, after all our conversations at the dinner table about living together without benefit of marriage. For some reason, kids seem to think if there's no marriage, there's no broken hearts, either, no kids, no nothing—just fun, pleasure, partying." He stopped abruptly and brushed lean fingers over his face. "Two teenaged couples living together. . . a lark, Susan, is how they view it. Just thinking about it makes me sick." He rose abruptly from the table and stalked from the room, leaving me to pay the bill. From the astonished expressions of the other patrons, I'm sure they thought we had a fight. Mark, in his anguish of heart, didn't even realize the café had other customers.

We didn't stay the day, but we did take our time driving home and arrived there at five.

Of course, the first thing we saw when we walked into the kitchen was the blinking light of the answering machine. The messages were probably all from Amber; I wasn't going near it. Mark had more courage. He went to it immediately and pressed the button. After a long silence of rewinding, Amber's voice filled the room.

"Hi, Dad. Just wanted you to know I've had a change of plans. College is out, for the time being at least, and Austin and I are going to share an apartment. Mom, of course, doesn't approve. See you when you get home." The message was dated the day she made her announcement to me. In my distress, after her visit, I hadn't even noticed the message. Her voice was happy-go-lucky, as though her momentous decision was one of little importance.

"What a fool!" Mark muttered as he leaned against the desk in the office nook, as we called it, where desk, telephone, answering machine, and fax were all conveniently located. "What a blind, little fool!"

"Dad." This time the voice held some urgency; the put-on gaiety was gone. "Austin and I came to the house this morning and couldn't get any of my furniture. And we couldn't get in the house. My key wouldn't work in any of the locks. Mom"—here her voice turned to one of outrage—"had all my clothes packed in boxes on the front porch! What is going on? Please call me as soon as you get home. I need five-hundred dollars right now—desperately, Dad. I know you won't let me down."

Sick rage boiled through my entire body. I had been sipping icy water from the fridge dispense, and I now threw the glass, not caring where it landed, or caring that it broke into a hundred shards and the water ran down the wall. I ran from the room, refusing to listen to any more of Amber's pleas.

In our bedroom I threw myself on the bed, in the middle of all the ruffled pillows, not caring if I damaged them. At the moment I hated my daughter with an intensity that was frightening.

How dare she! How dare she expect financial support from us, when she's deliberately going against everything we believe in? And Austin—that scumbag, that loser—why is she giving herself to him, thinking it's going to work, when the union never had a chance? How dare she inflict such pain and suffering into our lives? I sobbed uncontrollably into a lace-covered pillow.

Mark came, lay on the bed beside me, pulled me into his arms, and held me tightly. "Don't, Susan. Don't cry so, darling. One day she will get her senses back, or she will get some sense, at least. This is a phase she has to go through; she has to, dear. Maybe it's partly our fault. I don't know, but it's mostly hers. She has chosen, as I just told her, and now she lives with her choice."

"You talked to her?" I stopped crying long enough to ask.

"Yes. At first she was quite subdued, then stunned at my refusal to give her money. Then she called me every filthy name in the book. Where do you suppose she learned such obscenities?"

"From her precious friends . . . all those wonderful kids we don't know anything about. Oh, Mark." My arms tightened around him. "At least we have Greg and Amanda."

"Yes, we do, and I think we have neglected them shamefully, all our attention taken up with Amber, our golden girl—who isn't golden at all, but a dirty tramp."

So the next morning Mark went to work, and I stayed home in an empty house. Oh, it was a house filled with furniture and pictures on the wall and mementos scattered around the rooms, but it was empty of Amber's presence. The stillness hung around me like a dark cloak, pressing, pressing on me.

I'll houseclean her bedroom, I decided midmorning and got out the vacuum cleaner, window cleaner, lemon oil, and rags. Armed, I went to her room. It looked terribly bare and empty, too. It would be this week's project to redo the room and make it beautiful.

I started by stripping the bed and carrying the bedding to the laundry room, put a load in the washer, then returned to the room to take down the swag that hung over the duet-type shade. Everything was covered with dust, and I sneezed and sneezed as it tickled the lining of my nose. When, for heaven's sake, was the last time the room had been really cleaned? When Amber was fourteen, and we moved in the antique bedroom set? Probably.

I decided to turn the mattress since I was doing such an in-depth job. To my astonishment several magazines were neatly laid out between the box spring and mattress, and an envelope which contained money. Mystified, I drew out the bills and counted them: one-hundred and fifty dollars. Now, where did that come from?

The magazines were all porn. I hated even touching the evil things, but gathered them up and took them outside to the garbage can. I didn't want such trash in my house.

As I reentered Amber's room, I realized I didn't know my daughter at all. She led a double life and to her parents, she revealed only the good side of herself. Even in the privacy of her bedroom she was a different person. The money I placed on the desk in the kitchen. Maybe Mark would know where it came from. The room held no further surprises—thank goodness—aside from candy bar wrappers under the bed.

By late afternoon I had the room thoroughly cleaned, the furniture polished to a soft glow, clean bedding on the bed. The next project was a new bedspread with matching drapes, or swag, and some plants or silk flowers. The demands of physical labor kept my mind from brooding over Amber, which was a relief.

But as I walked to the kitchen to begin preparations for dinner, I couldn't help but wonder what kind of bedroom Amber had now . . . and if she even had a bed to sleep on. Are Mark and I being too harsh?

"A thought occurred to me this afternoon," Mark said over dinner, which we were eating on the deck. The air was wonderfully warm, the scent of flowers tantalizing to the senses.

"What's that?" I asked as I cut my grilled chicken breast, in a show of eating. Appetite had fled under the constant pain in my heart.

"Austin might try some vandalism—as a revenge, you know."

I paused with a morsel of food halfway to my mouth. "What gives you this idea?" I was horrified.

"Well, part of his delinquent record has to do with vandalism: mailboxes, cars in parking lots, city parks. He has quite a record."

"Why isn't he in jail?"

"Juvenile detention, you mean," offered my pragmatic husband calmly. He was certainly relishing his dinner.

"So why isn't he?"

"He's mostly gotten a slap on the wrist. I don't know why, but I think he's on probation."

I gave up all pretense of eating and said sarcastically, "Maybe we'll have a rock flying through our window around two A.M. tonight? Is this what you're telling me?"

"It will be something much worse than a rock breaking a window. I'm thinking of hiring a night patrol . . . guard—whatever you want to call it."

"And this is the young man our daughter chose. I can't believe it, Mark; I just can't believe it. Am I dreaming all this? Is it for real?" I paused for long moments. "Maybe we should be like the other parents: help the kids out, give them money, give them all the things they need."

He quirked an eyebrow at me. "You're willing to be blackmailed? Do what I say, or else?"

"At least the other parents won't have to hire a night watchman to protect their property."

"You don't know what they'll have to do, or already have done."

"I wonder why dangerous, young men attract decent, young girls."

Mark threw down his napkin and rose from his chair. "They're more exciting, that's why. I'm calling Grizzly Security."

"You can't get someone that soon, Mark. You probably have to make an appointment and have an interview." Left alone, I sipped my lemonade and thought of Amber. I wanted to know how she was coping, if living with three other teens was as fun, as exciting, as she thought it would be. How long would it take her to come to her senses, if ever? Suddenly I was crying again. Would I ever run out of tears?

Mark returned to the deck and told me I was right. We couldn't hire security just like that. "I'm going to call the police station and ask them to patrol the area, especially the alley."

We carried our dirty dishes into the house and put them in the dishwasher. Mark went into the living room to watch the news while I cleaned up the kitchen. The news was so depressing, I wasn't interested in watching it. I had enough negative happenings in my life. At eleven we went to bed and tried to get some sleep.

Mark called the police station early next morning before breakfast, and was told there had been activity in the alley at two A.M., but the two males fled the scene when the cop car came driving down the alley. They were driving a small sports car. The description fit the convertible Austin drove. Suddenly I was afraid to be alone anymore.

"Let's sell this place and move away," I said impulsively.

"Really, Susan!" Mark snorted. "Think I'm giving up my home because of a punk like Austin?"

"He scares me."

Mark patted my shoulder as he walked by my stool. "You'll be fine in the daytime, and you'll never be alone at night, not for a while, at least. I'm working in the office right now, remember?"

"That's small comfort," I said. "Houses are broken into every day, in broad daylight."

"Austin's kind do it in the dead of night, when everyone is sleeping."

I had to take what comfort I could from that.

I met Brenda's mother a week later in the supermarket near my home. She introduced herself. I didn't ask how she knew me.

"You're Amber's mother, aren't you?" she asked. "I'm Brenda's mom." She was quite an attractive woman, blond hair that looked real, sky-blue eyes, slim, and attractively dressed. Not the type of woman I expected Brenda's mother to be. But what does outward appearance signify? Not much.

I acknowledged her introduction with a slight smile, a mere show of politeness, and waited for her condemnation.

"You haven't been to visit the kids yet, have you?" She smiled as she asked the question, but a steely gleam shone in her eyes.

"No, I haven't." My tone did not encourage further questions, but my aloofness did not faze this woman.

"They are having a ball."

"Teenagers generally look on life as a ball, don't they? But the 'ball,' as you view their decision, isn't very long-lasting."

A frown creased her smooth brow. "What do you mean by that?"

"I mean that eventually the realities of life, apart from Mom and Dad, will catch up with them, and their glorious, little bubble will burst. They will find that minimum wages don't stretch very far, even with four of them working. Has Amber found a job yet?"

"No. She has been looking, of course, but all the summer jobs have been taken. She has given an application to several places, so she will find something—perhaps late summer, when the college kids go back to school."

"Yes," I agreed, "when the college kids go back to school, as she was supposed to do. Great future, isn't it, working in a hamburger joint? Her father is an engineer, her brother is a computer programmer, and I'm a teacher. Amber is going to flip hamburgers for a living." I brushed past the woman, trembling with anger, forgetful of the groceries I wanted to buy. There were other stores, where I wouldn't run into the likes of Brenda's mother.

I tried to remember what Amber had said about Brenda and her family. I had pried a few times, but Amber hadn't been very forthcoming. There was no dad, this I knew, the woman worked, but Amber never said where, and she wasn't home, which gave Brenda a lot of free time to do whatever she pleased. That's all I knew, but this brief revelation should have set warning bells clanging inside me, but it hadn't. How could I have been so incredibly stupid, so incredibly trusting?

I told Mark over dinner about meeting Brenda's mom. "I don't even know her name!" I stormed. "I don't even know Brenda's last name."

"It's Keller," Mark said. "Brenda Keller, but that's not her mother's name. She has been married several times and has a live-in boyfriend at the present time."

"How do you know?"

"Amber told me, when I asked her once to tell me about Brenda."

I stared at him in amazement. "And you never told me?"

"You never asked."

Isn't that just like a man? Never share specific information unless asked for it. "Amber must have snickered over our blindness."

"I'm sure she did," Mark agreed calmly. "I'll bet she had a regular lark over our gullibility. But once gullible parents' eyes are opened, there's not much laughing going on."

"No. Now she's cursing us."

It was Monday morning two weeks later. Mark and I were eating breakfast when the phone rang.

"Well, Mother, have you heard the latest?" It was Greg.

"The latest what?"

"Obviously you don't have the radio on. Amber and her friends were arrested last night. They were having a drunken party in their apartment, neighbors complained about the noise and antics, and everyone there was arrested—possession of alcohol by minors, drug-use, you name it! So now our name will be smeared in the papers, over the radio and television. I'd like to choke the life out of my little sister! She's nothing but a tramp!"

I handed the receiver to Mark, too distraught, too sick at heart to even make a comment to my son.

"Well, it won't go well with the Kinsey kid," Mark said as he sat down. "He has a record. I don't know about the other two, and Amber. . . ." He shook his head. "How did she ever get mixed up with such a crowd? She might get off with a warning, since she's never been arrested before."

I had nothing to say; I had no idea what to say. If I knew Brenda's mother's name, I'd have called and asked her if she thought the whole thing was still a ball. Stupid woman! "Who supplied the booze?" I asked Mark.

He shrugged. "If kids want liquor, there's always a way to get it. Probably one of the parents supplied it. Boy, is Greg ever mad. I've never heard him so angry."

After Mark left for work, I called the police station, asking for particulars, telling them I was Amber's mother. I explained the situation briefly, and how sick my husband and I were over everything.

"Some kids are determined to rebel against all authority, cause their parents untold grief, but they have to learn there's a price to pay for such behavior. The foursome has been given notice to get out of the apartment. Is your daughter returning to your house?"

"Not as long as she's associating with that crowd!" I snapped.

"Well, at least there's one set of parents with some standards. The other parents are trying to get all charges dropped, but it isn't going to work this time. The other three have records."

I hung up the phone feeling sicker than ever, not just because of my own daughter, but because of the behavior of the other parents. Wanting all charges dropped, indeed.

Later in the week we learned what the punishment was. Amber had a fine and had to do ninety hours of community service, as a first-time offender. Austin Kinsey would be leaving the area for jail time. Brenda got a huge fine and was required to do three hundred hours of community service, as this was her third offense. What her boyfriend got, I never heard and didn't care.

Mark and I agonized over our role in all this. Where did our responsibility end? Did it end when Amber walked out of the house, against our wishes? We sought the counsel of others. Getting such a wide spectrum of advice, we ignored it all and tried to use our own common sense.

When she phoned several days later, we were ready for her.

"Yes, you can come home," Mark said, "but it will be under our conditions. Otherwise, you can find your own place to stay."

I was at his elbow, listening. This was Mark, Amber's father speaking, the man she thought she could wrap around her little finger.

"Do you want to hear the conditions?"

Obviously she said yes because Mark continued, "You will drop all association with Brenda Keller, Austin Kinsey, and Dan. You will get a job and pay your fine. Your mother and I will not pay it; we were not the ones arrested. Whether you decide to further your education is up to you. You could enroll at the community college this fall."

I heard Amber's voice crackling over the line, but could not distinguish the words. "So be it," Mark said brusquely and hung up. He turned to me. "Well, that's that, I guess."

"Tell me."

"Our daughter informed me very emphatically that she is eighteen and no one is going to tell her how to live her life. Brenda is the best friend she's ever had, and she is not giving her up just to please us."

Unshed tears pained behind my eyelids as I turned away from Mark. "How can she be so blind, Mark? Brenda is a terrible influence in her life. Why can't she see it? I don't understand it. Talk about the blind leading the blind!"

I stumbled to a chair and sat down, letting the tears flow. "She's gone, Mark . . . probably forever."

"Oh, not forever, I don't think, but certainly for the time being. I never realized before what an arrogant, know-it-all Amber is. She has no more realization of the realities of life than a baby!"

"So where is she staying?"

"With Brenda Keller, of course, and her mother will expect a monthly check from us to pay for her keep."

"Maybe," I began timidly, "maybe we've done everything wrong, Mark. Maybe we should have chipped in with financial help from the very beginning."

Mark gave me a cold, disgusted look. "Maybe we should have, but we decided on this course, and we will continue on it. Sure, we could have opened our home to the foursome, Susan; they could have set up housekeeping in the basement—two couples living together, not married. We could have aided and abetted their delinquency."

"I suppose you're right," I agreed reluctantly, "but it certainly brings no satisfaction."

"I had a conversation with one of the cops who brought the four into the police station. He said most problems with teenagers is the result of parents not caring enough to set boundaries for their kids, no punishment when they do wrong, too much freedom, giving too much that they haven't earned. Then when the kids get in trouble, Mom and Pop show up, bound and determined to get the kids off with no consequences. Money is the answer for everything. He said they're even bribed by some of these parents, that it's disgusting. I told him that's how we raised our daughter, but I got my eyes opened when she moved out of the house, and she was going to live with the choice she made." Mark's voice became grim. "Well, Susan, Amber has chosen Brenda Keller, not us, and we'll have to live with that. Now I'm going to work; I'm only two hours late."

I sat curled up in Mark's recliner in the TV room, musing over what he had just told me. Our precious daughter had chosen, and it was not us. We gave her the freedom to choose, and now she would have to live with it.

The telephone shrilled suddenly in the kitchen. I let it ring. The answering machine clicked on, then Amber's voice broke the silence of the house. "Oh, Mom and Dad, just thought I'd let you know—I'm pregnant. And I'm scheduled for an abortion next week." The click was very loud as she hung up.

I pushed the recliner back further. The message was meant to hurt us, of course, since she knew we do not agree with abortion. It was a deliberate act on her part, and she probably expected us to phone back immediately and beg her not to do it, that we would pay for everything. Could one even believe Amber anymore? I stretched out on the recliner, feeling utterly drained and tired. A nap would do me good.

There was no point agonizing over Amber anymore. She would live her life as she saw fit, and Mark and I would live ours. And we still had Greg and Amanda, who were expecting their first child in three months. I smiled for the first time in days.

We still had a lot to live for.

THE END

CONFESSIONS OF "THE OTHER WOMAN"

I may be a low-down, dirty sleaze—but I have feelings, too! And no matter what his wife says or does—I will not be denied the love of my life!

I was thirty-five, single—
And seriously bummed.
I'd never been married.
In fact, it'd been six years since my last relationship with a man.
As it was, I never dated.
I wasn't even sure as to why that was the case.
I honestly wasn't sure about what, exactly, was so wrong with me.

I know, I know—I suppose I could've asked men out instead of waiting for them to do it. And I could've spent a few more evenings out than I did at home in front of the TV. But everyone needs "alone time"—right? Besides, as it was, I worked every day as a receptionist at a golf club, and I actually met quite a few men that way. They just never became anything more to me than friends. Indeed, back then, I had more male friends than I had female ones, actually—just because, I suppose, there are more male golfers out there than female golfers.

Anyway, by the time Garrison started as our new golf pro, I was seriously in need of male companionship of a, well . . . at least romantic nature. My body and spirit needed it; my ego needed it.

"Neela, this is Garrison," RJ, my boss, told me when he brought him around for introductions.

At the time, Garrison was the best-looking guy I'd seen in ages. About thirty or so, with sandy hair that he'd let grow long enough for its edges to curl over the collar of his hunter-green golf shirt, his amber eyes looked straight into mine as he shook my hand, sending a jolt of fire down my spine. My eyes went wide and I wondered if he felt it, too, but he just laughed and said, "I'm very pleased to meet you, Neela." Then, leaning conspiratorially toward me, he whispered, "I'll bet you really run the place, huh?"

This was pretty close to the truth, but I was too stunned by his charismatic presence to answer. Instead, I pondered whether my hair was still in place, or had been flattened by the telephone headset I so often wore. I glanced down at my clothes—glory be, that morning I had on the royal blue, silk blouse that matches my eyes—and decided I looked acceptable. Maybe even attractive. Realizing Garrison was still looking at me, I managed a small smile and said, "Welcome aboard."

He grinned, then turned away, giving me the opportunity to examine his taut, muscular ass—definitely a wonder of anatomical perfection!

He came by my desk again early the next morning with a cup of coffee for me—not the cheap coffee I brewed in the lunchroom for everyone, but an expensive Colombian coffee from Starbucks.

"I took a guess based on your creamy, luscious skin," he said, "and added a lot of cream and a little bit of sugar."

He handed the cup over and I sipped it. I usually take my coffee black with three teaspoons of sugar, but in that instant, he converted me. "Yum," I purred, smiling. "What did I do to deserve this?"

"You just flashed me that beautiful smile of yours and made me feel welcome," he replied, and the look he gave me convinced me that, as far as I was concerned, Garrison would not be "just another guy friend."

Indeed, he took to coming by my desk between students. We'd chat for five or ten minutes until the appearance of yet another middle-aged man with a roll of fat bouncing over the waistband of his golf pants. Garrison would always give me a wink as he led the man outside to the golf carts. Then he'd wave to me as he brought the man into the pro shop later, proudly displaying the expensive clubs that just might help improve the gentleman's swing.

Then, when Garrison had been working with us for about two weeks, my boss dropped by my desk and remarked, "That Garrison's selling more equipment than anyone else on staff, and the members totally love him!" He shook his head admiringly. "Jeez! I sure wish I could follow him around and find out how he does it."

"Hmm," I said, thinking. "Well, I can tell you why women like him, but I can't guess what he does for the men."

RJ looked at me strangely. As it was, I figured he'd probably never heard me express "feminine" opinions about any particular guy before. Indeed, maybe it wasn't even professional for me to say such a thing to my boss, but I couldn't help myself. Apparently, though, RJ found my statement helpful, for I noticed that more and more female golfers were assigned to Garrison as the weeks went by. In fact, every time an attractive, young coed came in for lessons with Garrison, I found myself gritting my teeth until she finally left. Then Garrison would turn right away from her to perch, once again, on the corner of my desk and ask me what I had planned for the weekend.

At first, realizing that my real plans were too embarrassingly boring to even mention, I made up things—a party with friends who were visiting from out of town, or a date to the theater. But as we got to know each other better, I finally started telling Garrison the truth about my real—albeit, dismal—plans.

"You're so good to your parents," he said one day after I told him that after work, I planned to drive an hour each way to take a hot dinner to my parents, seeing as my mother had just had minor surgery to biopsy a mole. He rejoiced with me when the mole was determined to be benign.

Another time, he smiled appreciatively when I explained to him that my weekend plans were to care for my sister's two young children so that she and her husband could celebrate their wedding anniversary alone. "You're so giving," he remarked admiringly. "But do you make sure to take time for yourself, too?"

I shrugged. "I guess so. I mean, I live alone, so normally, I guess you could say I'm the most important person in my life!" I chuckled.

"I don't believe that for a second," he countered, shaking his head sagely. "Sounds to me like you're always doing more for others than you do for yourself." He turned and swept his arm across the reception area. "Even around here. I mean, the guys can certainly make their own coffee and schedule their own appointments, and yet—you take care of us all."

"Hey," I said, playfully poking a finger into his ribs, "if guys like you did all of those things yourselves—I'd be out of a job!"

Garrison held up his hands in protest. "No, wait—please; don't go anywhere. Things would be very bleak around here without you to talk to. Consider us absolutely and utterly helpless. Please?" he kidded.

Outwardly, I laughed. Inside, though, I admit I ate up the attention and compliments, thinking, What a warm, wonderful man Garrison is! He's not afraid to say nice things or give credit where credit's due, and he really seems to care about my well-being and like having me around. As it was, I couldn't remember the last time anyone other than my parents had felt that way about me.

And, as time went by, so it became that my last thoughts before I went to sleep each night were inevitably of Garrison. These fantasies always began with him perched his usual way on the edge of my desk . . . and ended with him gently lowering me across it, kissing my neck, kissing lower. . . . I always fell asleep before we got any further than that, darn it, but even then, I knew that if such things were ever to truly happen, I would be happy forever.

Then one Monday morning, Garrison handed me an envelope just as a student arrived to drag him away. Alone at my desk, my heart started to pound as I opened it. Inside were two tickets to Orlando, Florida! The names on the tickets were Garrison's and mine, and they had us leaving that coming Friday and returning Sunday night!

I didn't know what to think. I didn't dare hope that this meant we'd be taking our relationship "to the next level," and yet, all at once, I was so curious about Garrison's "intentions" with regard to me that I could hardly sit still in my chair! I took off my phone headset, threw it onto my desk, and walked briskly to the lunchroom. We didn't really need it right then, but I made another pot of coffee. Then I scrubbed the counters to diffuse my nervous energy.

For the next hour adrenaline flowed through me like a raging, storm-churned current, giving me the jitters. By the time Garrison finally reappeared with his latest ingénue in tow, the top of my head was about to blow off from the pressure of waiting for his return. As he approached my desk, I waved the tickets at him and cocked my head questioningly.

"I hope you don't think I'm out of line," he said, giving me a sheepish look, "but, well, you see—" He shrugged. "I go to Florida periodically to play the Disney courses—students expect their pros to have played the most popular courses recently so they can give them relevant, helpful pointers—and I just thought. . . ." He took a deep breath as though gathering his nerve. "Well, since you spend so much time helping other people, I thought it's time for you to have some fun yourself. Plus, I'd like to take care of you, for a change."

He looked down at his hands, then back up at me. "Look—there're absolutely no strings attached. We can get separate rooms. I just want . . . to help you have some fun."

He looked so earnest, and like he needed approval so badly, that it was all I could do not to throw my arms around his neck and kiss him silly. Fortunately, I restrained myself. But I did reach out for his hand.

"Thank you so much, Garrison. What a wonderful idea! I'd love to go. And, please—feel perfectly free to go about your business as much as you need to when we get there. I can always take care of myself."

He smiled warmly, nodding. "I know you can. That's why I want to take care of you for a while. I mean, you can definitely count on me playing a few rounds of golf, but other than that, you may expect my guaranteed, full, undivided attention. And for all of your expenses to be paid."

"Oh, but that'll be very expensive, I'm sure. I can pay my way—really." With my salary, I knew it would be a strain, but I figured I could manage it.

Garrison shook his head. "Nope. I won a couple of important tournaments a few years back, so I can definitely afford to lavish you with the best getaway ever. Don't worry."

And with that, he rose and strode off before I could protest.

That Monday to that Friday made for my longest workweek ever, as I waited almost breathlessly to leave with Garrison. At work I was antsy, waiting for any glimpse of him that I could get, hoping he wouldn't change his mind. Joy swelled in my chest at every wink and knowing look he gave me, letting me know he was anticipating the trip as much as I was. At home, I packed and unpacked, changing my mind every five minutes about whether I should take the gold, silk teddy I'd bought with high hopes at the beginning of my last relationship so long ago, or wear my usual long T-shirt and sleep in my own room. Finally, I decided to pack the teddy and decide when the dilemma truly presented itself.

When my parents called that Thursday evening for our weekly chat and asked nonchalantly about my plans for the weekend, I panicked. I certainly couldn't tell them that I was going eight hundred miles away on a trip paid for by a male coworker—and potential new boyfriend. You see, my parents are very conservative and I knew they would never understand. To them, a "date" is going to a Saturday matinee and, at most, maybe holding hands during the suspenseful parts.

So, I lied and told them that I would probably be "in and out all weekend," as I had "a lot of errands to run." I figured that way, if they called, even multiple times, and didn't get me, they wouldn't worry. And I vowed to check my answering machine for messages at least once during the weekend.

I left early for work on Friday, hiding my suitcase in the trunk of my car. All day long, Garrison patted my shoulder each time he passed by my desk—like he was getting himself comfortable with touching me. He left a spot of heat behind with each touch that made me quiver.

At quitting time, I gathered up my purse and jacket, as usual, and went out to my car to wait for Garrison. We hadn't talked about it, but it seemed that we were both keeping our trip together a secret from our coworkers. That was just fine with me; I didn't need to hear any admonishments about how "dating a coworker never works out" or other related horror stories about such relationships.

About five minutes later, Garrison pulled up next to my car in his red Ford Ranger. While he got out I popped my trunk, and then he pulled out my suitcase and shoved it behind his seat as though it weighed mere ounces. He opened the passenger door for me with a flourish and took my hand and helped me in.

"Thank you, kind sir," I said, settling myself inside.

Once he was behind the wheel, he gathered my left hand in his right one and didn't let go until we reached the airport. I remember thinking, It's a good thing his car's an automatic so he doesn't have to relinquish his hand for shifting gears!

Once we boarded our flight, to my delighted surprise, the flight attendant led us to posh seats in first class and served us free drinks. Garrison had a Seven and Seven, and I chose white wine. After he'd quickly downed his drink in one long chug, Garrison whispered to me, "I still can't believe you're really here with me! I was afraid you'd suddenly decide that I'm a creep and back out on me."

I was shocked. "Why would I ever think that you're a creep? You've been nothing but kind and friendly to me, right from the get-go."

He shrugged. "I guess maybe I don't have a whole lot of self-esteem."

Again, I was shocked—even more so, in fact. "What? Garrison—you've won big tourneys—you told me so yourself—and all of your students worship you. They spend more money through you than through anyone else at the club!"

"Aw, shucks; thank you, ma'am," he said in a fake, Southern accent. "Keep it up, though, and I may get a swelled head!"

"Well, if anyone deserves one, it's you. You're wonderful, Garrison, and don't let anyone ever tell you otherwise," I told him emphatically.

Garrison just smiled, settled back into his seat, and wrapped his arm around my shoulders. We stayed that way for almost the entire flight.

Orlando was hot and sunny, just like it's supposed to be. Garrison had reserved adjoining rooms for us at the Dolphin that were the lushest and most luxurious I'd ever even seen, much less stayed in. At his suggestion, I changed quickly into the bright sundress I'd brought, and then he called us a cab to take us to dinner.

He chose a candlelit bistro that serves everything from sushi to spaghetti. "I don't know much about what you like to eat, but I want to learn," he explained.

I chose the filet mignon and he ordered lobster. We laughed about having created a "surf and turf" for our table and much later, after a lovely dinner and the finest champagne I've ever had the pleasure of enjoying, we strolled the five blocks back to our hotel rather than getting another cab. A balmy breeze tickled my skin and ruffled my skirt against my legs as we strolled along languidly; stars twinkled in the sky, seemingly just for us. Even the slight traffic noise didn't drown out the calls of seagulls and the eternal, gentle, lulling, hypnotic roar of the surf. All my senses seemed so heightened that when Garrison took my hand, I nearly jumped and yet . . . wished for . . . more. So much more. . . .

Garrison looked at me then, smiled his crooked smile, and I knew—

Housekeeping won't need to make the bed in my room tomorrow morning.

Somehow, Garrison was well aware of my "decision," and when we reached the hotel, he guided me to his room, not my own.

Neither of us questioned it; I didn't even think of running into my room for my lingerie. Indeed—it wouldn't have been worth the trip, considering the few seconds I might've spent in it. No—our bodies, our bare skin—that's all we needed.

And so it was.

We woke late on Saturday morning. So late, in fact, that lunch was on the menu by the time we thought of food. Apologizing profusely, Garrison rose, dressed, and left me. His tee time for that day was at two, but he promised to return as soon as he possibly could for a room-service dinner, so I didn't really mind. I stretched out across the king-sized bed and relived the previous night's finer, more sensual nuances over and over again in my mind, thinking, with great pleasure and satisfaction, of how every moment I spent with Garrison was so unbelievably precious to me. Physically, of course, his lovemaking was enormously satisfying after I'd spent so many months alone. But the best part was when I realized: I'm not questioning anything at all. In fact—I have no second thoughts whatsoever. Our being together just feels so . . . natural. So right in every possible way.

Garrison returned at six, and I was all ready and waiting for him in a short, hot-pink miniskirt and a white tank top—with my teddy hidden underneath! We ordered grilled salmon, steamed asparagus, and rice pilaf for dinner, with strawberries and cream and champagne for dessert. Garrison had played well that day, he told me, and had successfully mastered several changes that had been made to the course since his last visit. I congratulated him with a lingering, hungry kiss.

"And what did you do while I was away?" he asked.

"I thought of you," I replied with a dreamy smile.

His eyebrows went up. "The whole time?"

"Every second," I said. And it was the truth.

"And just what did you decide about me?" he asked with a smile sparkling in his eyes that let me know he was kidding around—playing with me.

But I didn't kid back.

"I decided that you make me very happy, Garrison," I told him earnestly, coming close to wrap my arms around his tan neck.

His face went so serious suddenly that I was afraid I'd scared him off. What I said, shouldn't, though, I told myself reasonably. After all, at least I'm smart enough to know not to tell him that I love him—even though it's true.

"You make me very happy, too," he said finally. "Which is why . . . well, I'm afraid to . . . to tell you what I need to tell you. . . ."

Instantly, I was scared, wondering frantically, Is he dying—and coming to Orlando with me is his last wish? My gosh—is he about to be incarcerated for some heinous crime or miscarriage of justice? I should've seen it coming, I guess. But, damn it! As usual, I was too hopeful and too trusting to see what I should've known all along: Good-looking, charismatic, successful men don't make it to Garrison's age unencumbered.

"What is it?" I finally managed to ask him, despite the painful lump of unshed tears that had built up in my constricted throat.

He put his hands over his face. "I don't want it to . . . to change how you think of me. . . . How you treat me. . . ."

I knew then that—no matter what—I had to comfort him.

"Nothing you could ever say or do would make me think any less of you, Garrison—much less feel any less for you."

Finally, he lifted his head and showed me a wan smile. "I hope that's true," he said softly. "Because, well . . . how's this? I'm married."

My mouth dropped open and my stomach went all queasy as it dawned on me:

I made love with a married man. He's taken. He isn't mine. He's pulled one over on both his wife and me.

When my vision cleared I realized that he was looking at me hopefully—waiting for the verdict, praying it would be in his favor. He looked like a little boy who broke his mother's favorite vase and was ready to be beaten for it. Like a dog whose owner had the rolled-up newspaper in his hand.

That look just about broke my heart.

And I realized then: I can't break Garrison's heart.

"Tell me about her," I said, trying to keep judgment out of my voice.

Garrison still seemed to be holding his breath, waiting for my reaction, but finally, he spoke. "Her name is Alessandra. . . . We went to high school together—we were . . . sweethearts. Married soon after graduation. The usual story, I guess. We were too young; we started growing up and changing, growing apart. . . ."

"Are you saying it's not going well?" I asked, excitement and hope building inside me despite my shame and fear.

His lips formed a thin, gray line in his dour face. "She filed for divorce two months ago."

I grinned at him—instantly relieved, almost beyond measure. "Then—you're not really married," I gasped, breathless with renewed hope. "You're separated."

Garrison hung his head and shook it slowly. Sadly. "Not really. You see . . . the house is mine—I inherited it from my grandparents—but Alessandra . . . she doesn't have anywhere to go, so . . . I'm letting her stay there. . . . With me."

I tried to remember the logistics I'd learned from the daytime soaps I taped while I was at work. "But—you have to be living in separate households for a certain amount of time before the divorce can be finalized, right?"

Garrison winced. "She didn't go to college—because we got married. She can't get a really good job, like I have. I can't kick her out. Plus. . . ."

I gaped at him, instantly stunned all over again. "There's more?"

Garrison nodded grimly, his eyes meeting mine warily. "She's pregnant."

"With—with . . . your baby?"

He nodded. "We found out right after she filed for divorce."

Carefully avoiding the plate of strawberries and cream, I folded my arms onto the little room service table and dropped my head onto them. My emotions were churning; I couldn't decide whether to be angry with Garrison for his deception, or to feel sorry for him for the awful circumstances he found himself in.

No one wants to pay for the mistakes of youth for the rest of their lives, I realized then. No one wants a baby to be the only reason to stay married. He must be torn between doing what he thinks is the right thing to do and making his own life livable. And to think: He accused me of being too giving and not looking out for myself—but that's surely the pot calling the kettle black! When will he take care of himself above all others?

And what about what I want? Garrison practically dragged me into this relationship. Don't my feelings even count?

"I want to help you," I told him finally in a stern, but calmly determined tone of voice. "How can I help make your life bearable, Garrison?"

He smiled, then—the biggest grin I ever saw him wear. "Just be here for me," he replied simply, gratefully. "Talk to me. Make me feel like more than monetary support and a father to an unwanted child."

"I can do that," I said.

And I have.

Garrison still stops by my desk to chat and flirt.

We still secretly fly off together to all the wonderful places that have world-class golf courses.

We still make love and eat strawberries and cream with the finest champagnes.

But nowadays, Garrison tells me about how large his wife is getting—how she's making up the baby's nursery all in yellow because she doesn't want to know its gender in advance.

Garrison tells me how excited he is that he'll soon be a father, but also about how he wishes someone else could be the mother. And I know that he wishes the child were mine, and that we could share a life together, in the open—in public, for all the world to see.

He promises me that as soon as his child is old enough to understand, that will happen. After all, he'll finally be free, then, and then we can truly be together, openly and forever.

I can't wait.

THE END

CONFESSIONS OF A DRUG ADDICT'S DAUGHTER
"How I Broke The Cycle"

To say I was flattered by the attention that Tyler Steele gave me would be putting it mildly. I'm not especially pretty or smart, or flashy in the way I dress. I'm not very outgoing. In fact, I'm pretty average.

Tyler could've dated any number of beautiful girls in our high school, but he zeroed in on me.

He liked me because I was genuine and serious, and I applied myself to my studies. The other girls, he said, were silly gossips who played head games with guys.

Little did he know how much I envied the girls who seemed so carefree and happy. I had no choice but to be serious. I couldn't afford to waste time or money. I had to take advantage of the opportunity to finish high school, because it was certain I wouldn't get a chance to further my education. I had to do my best in school or my life would really be doomed.

"When are you going to let me come to your house?" Tyler asked, resting his shoulder against the wall while he flirted with me. We were in the library studying for a chemistry exam.

"I told you that my mother works in the evening and she doesn't like me to have company over when she isn't home."

Tyler put his arm around my shoulder. "Will you go to the movies with me this weekend? You can meet me at the movie theater in the mall. I'll be getting off work at five o'clock. I'll see to it that you get home safely. I promise."

"Uh, I don't know. I might have to babysit this weekend."

"There you go again, putting me off. You always have an excuse." He regarded me with frustration. "You and I have been studying together and having lunch for weeks, but every time I suggest we go out together, you put up a wall between us. What gives?"

I hated the look of rejection in Tyler's eyes. The last thing I wanted to do was hurt him. I really liked him a lot.

"Don't take it personally. I would love to go out with you, but it's just not a good time for me. My mother depends on me to take care of the house and the kids while she works."

"I see," he said, giving me a sad smile. "But the first chance you get to have some time on your own, I want you to let me know. Tell your mom there's this really great guy dying to take you out."

He smiled, covering my hand with his. His smile was so warm and attractive. It was irresistible. It lit up his whole face, including his wonderful blue eyes. My heart was going from liking Tyler to a growing affection that took my breath away.

I stayed in the library with him until it was time for him to go to work. Being with him always eased my mind and gave me a needed relief from the problems I faced at home. As usual, he volunteered to take me home. As usual, I begged off, explaining that I had some extra work to do in the library. Tyler leaned over and brushed his lips gently over mine. Then he lavished me with one of his fabulous smiles before rushing off to his job in the mall.

Our first kiss took me by surprise and I felt warm all over. My heart ached because I knew I couldn't enjoy the kind of relationship I wanted to have with him. My life was too much of a mess for a sweet romance to develop with such a great guy like Tyler.

With a heavy heart and a feeling of misery, I gathered my books and headed for home, wondering what kind of turmoil would be awaiting me there.

My poverty-stricken neighborhood was dreary. A police cruiser passed through the community every thirty minutes, the officers keeping an eye on young men who looked suspicious as they lingered outside vacant houses or in the shadows of alleys. At night gunfire rang out and cars careened around corners with loud music blaring and curses filling the air. The sounds of sirens sliced through the evening and there never seemed to be a moment of peace.

Crime is rampant in our neighborhood and I certainly had no desire to introduce Tyler to what had become routine to me, although I never let down my guard. Our house sat in the middle of the block, white flecks of paint still clinging in spots but mostly rotting wood exposed. With its sagging porch and leaky roof, it could barely be considered shelter, let alone refuge from the violent elements lurking outside.

The door was unlocked and I entered our pitiful residence, greeted by my little sister, Peyton, who was six years old. She threw her arms around my waist and smothered her tear-stained face against me.

"What's the matter?" I asked, setting aside my books to comfort her, kneeling to eye-level with her.

"She got a bad spanking," Cameron, my nine-year-old brother announced, his voice quivering.

"Where's Mom?" I asked Cameron, staring at his sad eyes.

"She's in her room. She slammed her door. She said Peyton was making too much noise singing. Mom said she's got a headache and her nerves are bad," he explained somberly. "Peyton wasn't singing loud, though. She was keeping it low like you told her to do when Mom is in one of her moods."

I patted Peyton's head. "It's all right, sweetie. But you'll have to keep quiet," I told her, reaching in my pocket to retrieve a pack of gum I'd bought for them.

Splitting it between them, I hugged them and said, "Go watch television, but keep it down as low as you can. I'm going to see what we have so I can fix supper." Smiling at them, I let them know everything would be okay now that I was home.

Once they were out of sight, I took a deep breath and braced myself. Hating the tension that knotted my stomach at the thought of facing my temperamental mother, I approached her room with caution, wondering how I would be received.

Sometimes she would want to talk about things she wanted to accomplish for my siblings and me when she got herself straight. Other times she would accuse me of things I hadn't done.

She called me cruel names because I hadn't done enough to please her, or just because she felt like being mean to me. Often she accused me of thinking I was better than she was because I was determined to finish school. Whenever she'd see me with a book or studying, she'd tell me I was wasting my time. Life would turn out badly for me, she would gleefully predict, and I hated her negative words.

Opening her door, I found her lying on the bed with the lights out and the curtains drawn to keep out the streetlights just outside her bedroom window.

"I'm home, Mom. Is there anything I can do for you?" I stood in the doorway, my legs trembling with fear.

"Keep those stupid kids quiet," she snapped. "Come in here and get my blanket out of the closet and throw it over me. I can't get warm in this old, drafty house. And bring me a beer when you're done. I don't feel like hearing any foolishness from you."

"Yes, Mom," I replied.

While I obeyed her commands, I longed for her to greet me with a smile and ask about my day like she used to when I was a little girl. I remembered my mother as a happy, pretty woman who worked as a teller in a bank.

She used to keep a clean house and she loved to cook all kinds of delicious dishes. She and I used to do all sorts of fun things until she met Donnie Matthews, who came to live with us.

She loved him dearly. Whenever he was around, she shoved me aside and made me feel like I was intruding on their happiness. Though they never married, Donnie was the father of my sister and brother. For a while, Donnie made my mother happy with his quick wit and hot kisses. But all that changed.

He used to work as a welder, but he was fired. He blamed my mother for the problems in his life. He beat her and took her money, leaving us with barely enough to get by. Donnie hung out with scruffy looking people who were in and out of the house, partying to all hours of the night. My mother didn't like it, but because she loved Donnie she overlooked it.

After a while, my mother started joining the party with Donnie and his dirty, sunken-eyed friends. Soon, she lost weight and then she lost all interest in her regular life and quit going to work.

Donnie just took off one day. I'd hear Mom crying in her room because he was gone. She was never the same. She walked around like a zombie. She finally got another job working as a maid in a hotel.

"Don't just stand there letting in all that light, girl. Close the door," she roared, breaking my reverie.

I jumped at the sound of her harsh tone and did as she said. Heading to the kitchen for a beer, I opened our nearly empty fridge, found a package of hot dogs, a few eggs, and some milk. There was the six-pack of beer. I searched the shelves to find only a can of pork and beans, a can of peaches, and a couple of cans of spaghetti. There was also a package of crackers.

I made hot dogs and beans for supper. Mom had promised that when she got paid she was going to stock up on food for a change, but as usual, she didn't keep her promise. Beer and other needs always came first with her.

After placing the hot dogs in a pan to boil and pouring the beans in another pan to heat, I took a beer from the fridge for my mother. As I was on my way to her room, there was a pounding on the door. I whirled around to move quickly and answer it so Mother wouldn't be disturbed.

When I saw who was at the door, I didn't want to open it. It was that no-good, lowdown Rocco, looking for my mother.

"Hey, beautiful. Where's your old lady?" he asked, leering at me as if he was undressing me. He had a toothpick jammed in the corner of his mouth.

"She's asleep," I answered, hoping he would go away.

"That figures. She needs to see me. I've got something that will pick her right up and give her energy. You'd love to see your old lady up and moving around, wouldn't you?" He swept past me, jostling me aside, disregarding my reluctance to let him in.

"Give it to me. I'll see that she gets it." I tried to keep him from going any further.

"No, baby. This is between your old lady and me. Besides, she promised to pay me for my kindness from the last time."

I stood there glaring at the tall, lanky man, wishing I could make him disappear off the face of the earth.

"Are you trying to come on to me, baby?" He chuckled, meeting my cold stare with a grin. I whirled away from him to go get my mother. Just as I did, he grabbed my waist and held me to him. "You're blossoming into a fine, sexy woman, Ashley. You're filling out nice for a girl of seventeen. I could make a pretty, young thing like you mighty happy. All you would have to do is treat me nice."

I wriggled free and moved away, horrified and repulsed by the way he was holding me. He laughed at me as if playing a game. I stormed off, my heart pounding with fear.

When I told my mother that Rocco wanted to see her, she bolted out of bed and dashed for him. From the kitchen, I saw her hand over some folded money. Then Rocco handed her a brown bag. Soon, there was the sound I had come to hate.

Tears misted my eyes when I saw her, squeezing her nostrils and looking euphoric. I knew my mother had given Rocco the money she was supposed to use for groceries and the electricity bill that was already overdue. The exchange was for the drug that was controlling her and ruining our lives. Cocaine.

Despite all that was going on in my life, I managed to do well in school. If it weren't for my studies and my goal of finishing high school, I think I would've gone nuts. Just getting away from home for a few hours was a lifesaver. Other kids complained about our assignments, but I worked hard on them and was grateful to have something that took my mind off my home life.

Not only was I going to school, but Tyler also helped me get a job working in the music store where he worked in the mall. I was thankful for the opportunity. The money was badly needed at home. My mother's addiction made her oblivious to her responsibilities to her children.

"I like having you work with me," Tyler told me, leaning on the counter near me while the store was empty. "At least I get a chance to see you and be near you some of the time."

I smiled at him. "I like working with you, too," I said, leaving him to stock the shelves.

Tyler trailed along behind me. "I think about you a lot. Even though you won't give me a chance to be with you, I'm in love with you, Ashley."

Surprised by his bold revelation, I swung my gaze to meet his.

He took my hand. "Ashley, please give me a sign that you like me. Go out with me. Can't you see how much I care for you?"

I squeezed his hand, enjoying the way his simple touch made my heart melt. "Tyler, I'm not trying to tease you or anything like that. I like you a lot, too. It's just that I have some family problems that make it impossible for me to have the kind of relationship you deserve."

I told him how afraid I was for my brother and sister and most of all, my mother who couldn't overcome the drug habit that was destroying her, and us.

I told him that we had no lights because my mother used the money for drugs to put up her nose. I'd long since given up on having a telephone. I'd never said a word to anyone about my problems before, and I made Tyler swear not to say a word. I explained why I had no close friends and didn't date—because I was so ashamed they would find out my secret.

Tyler sat there stunned and looking sympathetic.

"Ashley, I had no idea. And to think you come to school with a smile on your pretty face every day. I understand now why you kept giving me excuses when I asked for your phone number or wanted you to go out with me."

He took my hand and squeezed it. "You make me feel so selfish. I use my money from my job to buy things I don't really need, but just see in the mall and want. And here you are taking care of your family without a thought to your own wants or needs."

He became pensive. "This is too much for you to deal with. Don't you have any relatives who can help you?" His brow was furrowed with concern.

I shook my head. "No, there's no one. My mother has sisters, but they gave up on her when they learned she was using the money for her habit instead of us. There's nothing they can do. They have their own problems, and they live clear across the country."

Since I trusted the details of my life to Tyler, I allowed him to take me home that evening. Thankfully, he didn't make any comment about the neighborhood, but I saw the anxious look on his face. We sat in his car and talked. I snuggled close to him, my head resting on his shoulder, his arm draped around me.

"I want you to be my girl," he said, slipping the gold chain he wore over his head. He placed it around my neck. "I want you to wear this and think about me and the special feelings I have for you."

Leaning toward me, he gave me a lingering kiss that thrilled and warmed me. "Ashley, I'm here for you whenever you need me." He kissed me again gently and tenderly.

When I entered the house, I learned the kids were by themselves and had been that way since they got out of school. My mother hadn't been home for hours. Thankfully, I had hidden a key for Cameron and told him to keep it hidden from our mother. I had arrived far too many evenings to find the place dark, my sister and brother huddling together. My mother would be off on one of her excursions that ended up with her drug binges.

I went to the ice chest and retrieved a pack of bologna I had bought and made sandwiches for the kids and gave them soft drinks.

While we sat in the glowing candlelight at the kitchen table, talking and giggling as we ate, my mother came home. She acted like demons were on her heels.

"Ashley, give me some money, girl. I know you got it because you just got paid," she demanded of me.

I ignored her because I didn't want to give her my hard-earned money. My intentions were to spend some of my money for food. Plus, I wanted to buy much-needed new sneakers for the kids.

"I don't have it anymore," I lied, not looking at her.

"Don't lie to me!" she shouted. "Where is your bag? I'll get it myself," she snapped, flying from the kitchen, waving the flashlight she snatched from the kids.

I leaped up from the table and dashed after her. I didn't want her to use my money for her drugs, her poison. I spotted my bag on the sofa and quickly sat on it. My mother walked over to me and tried to shove me away. I wouldn't budge.

Suddenly, she gave me several open-handed slaps across the face. I squealed from the pain. When I did, the children came running to me, crying with fear. They begged her not to hurt me. My mother yanked them off, slinging them to one side.

"Give me that money!" she shouted at the top of her lungs.

I still wouldn't relinquish the bag. She hit me again and again. She was crazy with frustration. She grabbed my blouse and her fingers encountered the gold chain at my neck—the precious token of Tyler's love for me.

"Where in the world did you get this?" She swung the flashlight beam, aiming it at the necklace, studying the fine quality of the piece of jewelry.

I pulled away from her. "You can't have it. Someone special gave it to me."

"So, you've got a boyfriend? He must have some money. That's nice," she said, smoothing her hand over the gold chain.

"Mom, please don't take it. If you want money, I have a few dollars to share with you. Just let me keep enough so we can eat."

I grabbed my bag and dug into it, handing her ten dollars, hoping to distract her from the necklace.

She snatched the money out of my hand. Then she reached up and yanked the gold chain. It broke away from my neck, leaving it bruised with her brutal assault. I couldn't believe her cruelty.

I gasped and tried to struggle with her to get it back. Though she was scrawny, she was stronger than me. She pushed me to the floor.

"Your boyfriend will get you another one. I've got a debt to pay. Tell your man that he was a lifesaver." She disappeared through the door and into the night.

I sat on the floor and wept. My sister and brother came and hugged me, trying to comfort me. At that instant, I hated my mother and the awful creature she had become. I was so tired of her always taking and never giving. I was tired of her placing all her responsibilities on me while she took off to get high.

As soon as I got to school the next morning, I went looking for Tyler. I was glad to find him standing outside his homeroom, talking with some of his friends. When he saw me coming, his grin spread.

"I need to speak to you alone," I said.

Tyler could see that I was upset, so he left his friends and led me to the end of the hall where we could have some privacy.

"My mother took your chain from me. I'm sorry." I couldn't look at him. I clutched my books to my chest and rested my chin on them. Tears spilled from the corners of my eyes.

Tyler cupped my chin and used his thumb to gently brush away my tears. "Forget it. It's not important. Are you all right?" he asked in a soothing tone.

"I'm okay. She needed money to pay off her drug dealer. She even took some of the money I'd been saving for food."

He draped his arm around my shoulder and kissed me. "I have some extra money. I want you to take it."

"No, I can't do that."

"I want you to. I believe you would do the same for me if I were in trouble." He dug in his pocket and thrust some money into my hand. "You're not alone anymore, Ashley. Come on; let's go to class. We're going to be late."

Having Tyler in my life made it so much easier. I no longer felt as though I was carrying a load on my shoulders. My little sister and brother absolutely adored him. They looked forward to the Saturday afternoons when he came and took us out for a day of fun. He had no qualms about spending his money on them to play video games at the arcade, or miniature golf followed by a meal at the restaurant of their choice.

When we were alone, I savored the tenderness in his gaze and the warmth of his love. He always made me laugh when I was feeling low and he filled me with hope when I thought all hope was gone.

Tyler even bought me a cell phone. "If you ever need me, call."

As the school year came to an end, I was proud of the grades I'd earned. I managed to make the honor roll. I looked forward to the summer because I was going to be able to graduate and be able to work full-time. I'd made arrangements at the community recreation center for my sister and brother to be a part of the summer daycare program, so I wouldn't have to worry whether or not they were fed or safe until I got off work.

My mother was still on an emotional roller-coaster because she was constantly using drugs. One minute, she was all hyped up from cocaine, talking fast and full of promises for a better life for us all. The next minute, when she was crashing down from her drug, she was depressed and hated everyone and everything. She managed to get to work at the motel most days, but the money she made went to Rocco, the drug dealer.

One night, when I got in from a wonderful evening with Tyler, I found Rocco sitting in the living room with my mother, who was slumped over her chair.

"Hey, angel." He greeted me like someone important to him.

I didn't speak to him. I went to my mother to see what was wrong with her.

"Your old lady is all right. She needs some stuff, but she owes me too much money for me to let her have anything." Rocco shoved my mother's shoulder to stir her.

"Yeah . . . what?" Her face twisted with confusion, her cloudy gaze settling on me. "Where have you been, girl? Rocco's been waiting for you."

"Waiting for me?" I asked, puzzled.

Rocco settled back on the sofa and grinned at me. "Tell your daughter about the arrangement we made."

My mother struggled to get off her chair and grabbed me by the arm, leading me away from Rocco.

"What's all this about, Mom? I don't have any money to give him."

"He doesn't want your money. He . . . he wants you, baby. He told me I could get all the . . . all I want. He likes you. He wants you. He can give you things and me things, too, baby. Don't you love your family?"

I snatched my arm away from my mother and backed away. I couldn't believe what her drugs were driving her to do. She wanted me to give myself to a drug dealer to make her life easier.

Rocco got up and blocked my path toward the door. "I wouldn't try that if I were you, Ashley. Your mother made a deal and if you don't keep it, you'll lose her and maybe your sister and brother, too." Rocco's voice was flat and cold. I looked to my mother, but her gaze fell away from mine. Rocco stepped up to her and yanked her across the floor like she was a rag doll.

"Speak to your daughter, woman. Make her understand what's going down."

My mother's face was streaked with tears, a hint of shame, and some desperation. Her lips quivered, but no words came.

"Tell her! Tell her, woman!" Rocco slapped her across the face, making her yelp in pain.

"Ashley, do this for me, girl," my mother said, finding her voice at last. "I'm sorry, angel. I'm sick, baby. I'm sick and I can't help it."

Tears clouded my vision and I trembled, realizing I had been traded off for drugs. Suddenly, Peyton and Cameron appeared in the room in their pajamas. Their eyes were wide with fright and confusion. Seeing them, Rocco had no mercy. He held onto my mother, ordering her to make me do right by him.

"You kids get out of here. This is grown people's business," he growled.

Cameron and Peyton dashed out of the room, whining and calling for me.

"Go with him. It's only one night, baby," my mother continued to plead.

My lips pursed as I glared at her. She shriveled from my gaze and then Rocco took hold of her, bracing her up.

"You're my only way out, girl," she snapped. "Don't you care about your mother?"

Rocco cut in at that point. "Can't you see she's craving her drug? Look at her. Ain't she a pathetic sight?" He released his hold on her and she crumpled to the floor. "Well, she's not getting any more of my stuff. I don't have time for this foolishness."

My mother crawled along the floor, reaching for the leg of a chair and pulling herself upright. "Ashley! Go with him! I need to get high!"

Scrambling to her feet, my mother staggered toward me and began slapping me. She was strong as she pushed me toward Rocco.

Peyton and Cameron hovered in the doorway, crying and begging Mom to stop hitting me. Bile rose in my throat. I couldn't bear the thought of the kids witnessing such horror. I pulled away from my mother.

"Rocco, let me take the kids to their bedroom and tuck them in," I said stoutly. "Then I'll . . . be with you."

His scowl turned to a leering grin and he crowed with glee.

Wasting no time, I hurried to the kids and guided them down the hall.

"No funny business, now," Rocco called after me. "Don't even think of calling the police."

I smiled then, feeling for the cell phone in my pocket.

"We don't have a phone," I heard my mother assuring Rocco.

Quickly getting the kids into bed, I kissed them good night and told them everything would be fine.

I crept into the bathroom and latched the hook; dialing Tyler's number on the phone he gave me. He answered immediately. "I need help," I whispered. "Call the police."

Thankfully, Tyler didn't ask questions or wait for an explanation.

"Got it," he said, letting me know he understood before disconnecting.

"Come on, sweetness, the party's on," Rocco called from the living room. "What's keeping you, angel?"

I could hear him lurching down the hall, no doubt seeing the light on in the bathroom. He began to beat on the door. Still holding the cell phone, I hesitated. Should I place a call to 911? Just before Rocco broke the door in, I hid the phone among some dirty towels.

He found me huddled in the corner behind the toilet. Without remorse Rocco picked me up and slung me over his shoulder, eager to have his way with me. Hauling me into the living room, he threw me on the sofa and when I fought him, screaming, he punched me in the face with his fists. He was in the process of ripping off my clothes when the police burst in and knocked Rocco to the floor, handcuffing him and reading him his rights.

Tyler made his way into the house and as soon as the police and paramedics were finished with me, he took me in his arms and consoled me.

Incredibly, the kids slept through the whole thing.

My mother was sent to prison, and Rocco as well. Peyton, Cameron, and I were all placed in foster care, but it isn't so bad. The folks we live with are nice. They're helping me apply for assistance so that I can attend college. I've decided I want to be a teacher.

I'm working part-time at night while I take classes during the day. Tyler understands why the kids and I need counseling. I couldn't get the trauma of what happened with Rocco out of my mind. Tyler knows I need a little more time before I can agree to a relationship.

Tyler saved me from Rocco and I truly love him. He's a wonderful guy. Just spending time with him was a big step toward normalcy for me. The future looks bright for all of us.

THE END

CONFESSIONS OF A STALKER
"I'll Do Anything For Him"

I thought I could make Dylan love me if I only tried hard enough. As the police officer led me away from Dylan's house in handcuffs, though, I finally had to admit that we weren't meant to be together. It was embarrassing how I had let things go so far before figuring that out.

People watched me through the windows and doors of their homes to gawk at the scene I made. The windows of Dylan's house, though, remained empty although I knew he was inside. I ducked my head as I walked toward the police car, hoping that none of Dylan's neighbors could see the mortified look on my face in the flashing lights.

When I first met Dylan it was love at first sight, just like in the movies. I worked as a waitress at the local diner and it was another typical Friday evening with a steady but not too busy crowd. Working weekends always made me feel a bit pathetic, because it was clear I had no social life. Weekends were supposed to be for dates and romance, and yet there I was, wasting the best years of my life serving burgers to high school students so I could pay the rent. Even they had a better social life than I did. I always felt like I was meant for a better, more exciting life, but I didn't know how I could make it happen.

I was making a fresh pot of coffee when Shelly, one of the other waitresses, nudged me as she headed to the kitchen window to pick up her order.

"Psst, Marcy. Check out the guy at Table 5. That's your table, isn't it?"

I looked over my shoulder, expecting to steal a quick glance and get back to work. Shelly was always telling me to look at this guy or that guy in the diner, trying to fix me up. "You're so cute," she often said to me. "I don't know why you don't go out more."

"Cute doesn't pay the bills unless I find some rich Prince Charming, and I doubt that guys like that eat at a dive like this."

Shelly's heart was in the right place, though. And, not to brag, but she was right about me being cute. Being blonde, thin, and twenty-one years old had its advantages when it came to getting male attention. The problem was that most guys I met weren't anything special. They weren't the Prince Charming I longed for.

The guy at Table 5, though, was different. Even from a distance, you could tell he was no ordinary guy. He was a real man; the kind that I thought only existed in movies. It wasn't only the way he looked, either.

Sure, he would've turned any woman's head with his movie-star good looks. His white T-shirt couldn't hide the muscular planes of his chest. But it was the graceful way he sat at the table, one arm casually draped over the back of the booth, that made him stand out. His body practically invited you to slide next to him. He posed like a cat, oozing confidence, an animal sexiness. I was dying for him to stand up so that I could check out the rest of his body.

I watched as the hostess placed a napkin and silverware in front of him. When he smiled, he lit up the whole diner. My knees turned to Jell-O. I could tell that he was having the same effect on the hostess because I saw the menus in her hand trembling as she walked back to her hostess desk.

Shelly gave me a gentle shove. "Marcy, go! Don't keep him waiting."

I licked my lips and smoothed my damp palms down my apron. Here we go. Relax, he's only another customer.

I approached his table as gracefully as I could and put on my best waitress smile.

"Hi, I'm Marcy, and I'll be taking care of you tonight," I said, trying not to talk too fast from nervousness. "Will anyone be joining you?"

He seemed to be checking me out by the way his eyes lingered on my face and then drifted down my body. I felt like he was undressing me with his gaze. I never had a guy look at me quite that way before. I immediately felt attractive and womanly under his stare.

"Hi, Marcy," he said. The sound of his voice saying my name sent ripples down my spine. "I'm Dylan. No, it's only me tonight."

"That's too bad," I blurted. "I mean, unless you wanted to be by yourself tonight. Not that there's anything wrong with that or anything." So much for playing it cool. I gave up trying to be charming and yanked a notepad out of my pocket. "May I take your order?"

Dylan laughed, a deep, masculine rumble that sounded more intimate than he probably intended. "I'll have a chicken sandwich and a black coffee."

"Will that be all?"

"Well, I'd like to have you join me as well."

He certainly didn't waste any time picking me to flirt with. His friendly banter gave me some of my confidence back, enough to make me decide to play hard to get.

"I'm sorry, but I'm not on the menu," I said. I winked and walked away, forcing myself not to look back at him until I was well out of sight by the order window.

When I brought him his dinner five minutes later, he asked, "Can I at least get your number?"

"I'll think about it. I don't normally give my number to strange men."

"Do you think I'm strange?" He tried to look offended, but his smile gave him away.

"Strange to me," I said.

A crowd of high school students filled up the rest of my section, making it impossible for me to talk any longer. I placed his check on the table and hustled over to my other tables to get their drink orders. By the time I returned to Dylan's table, he was already gone.

At first my heart sank, and then I saw his tip. He had left me a ten-dollar bill, more than the cost of his meal, along with a slip of paper. My fingers felt clumsy as I unfolded it.

Are you free tomorrow night? Call me. Dylan. He'd left his phone number.

I stopped myself from jumping up and down and clapping. This unbelievably gorgeous man wants to go out with me. Me! He puts every other guy I've ever dated to shame.

Forget playing hard to get. I had to call him immediately because miracles like that didn't happen every day. I pulled my cell phone out of my purse as soon as my shift ended. My fingers were shaking so much that I had to redial twice because I kept hitting the wrong numbers. As I waited for him to answer, I felt an electric surge through my body. This is the start of something special. I know it.

The next two months were the most amazing ones of my life. Dylan and I bonded right from the first date. We met for coffee at our first meeting to keep things casual, and we ended up talking for hours until the coffee shop kicked us out. I learned that he was from the nicer part of town and had come back after college to work at his family's bank.

I know it sounds a bit shallow to think about a man's money, but it's one of those things you can't ignore. Even though I came from a much different background than Dylan, he always made me feel like a princess and made sure I was comfortable wherever we went. He bought me new clothes and took me to the nicest places in town, showing me off to his friends and attracting envious stares from both men and women. I felt classy, elegant, and far, far away from the reality of my dumpy life.

The royal treatment didn't end when we were alone, either. We spent lots of nights out on the town, but my favorite moments were when we spent the evening in. He was a wonderful cook, and there were many nights when I would help him make dinner.

It was during one of those quiet evenings that I knew for sure he was my true love. We were in his kitchen making a French beef stew, capping off a lovely, relaxing day with most of the hours spent in bed. Dylan opened a bottle of wine and poured me a glass while I sliced mushrooms for him. With jazz music floating through the house, I felt like Carrie in Sex and the City, with Dylan as my own Mr. Big. It was a fairy tale come true. I wanted it to last forever.

While I watched Dylan stir the pot, I must have had a huge grin on my face because he asked, "You look so happy, babe. Why are you smiling?"

"I'm just thinking of how much I love you."

Dylan's hand paused, the spoon skipping a beat mid-stir. He gave me a stare that seemed to last for hours. Although he still kept smiling, it no longer seemed to reach his eyes. My heart dropped to somewhere near my feet.

"What did you say?" he asked.

"I said I was thinking of how much I love being with you."

He chuckled. "That's so sweet. I like being with you, too."

Whew, I dodged a bullet with that one. I reminded myself to be more careful about what I said around him in the future. I didn't want to break the spell. I couldn't imagine life without him, didn't even want to let that horrible thought enter my head for a second. Even though he'd initially frozen up when he heard my careless confession, he relaxed as the night went on. He even fed me bits of stew from his own fork.

It was nearly two o'clock in the morning before we fell asleep. Dylan spooned against me with his arm wrapped around my waist. I snuggled deeper into the cocoon of his body. Even though he never said he loved me, I knew that he did. After all, actions speak louder than words, and Dylan's actions that night were all the proof I needed.

I had to work an extra shift at the diner the next day, so Dylan dropped me off at my apartment so I could change into my uniform before heading out. He planted a quick kiss on my lips.

"Call me," I said before I closed his car door. He winked at me, and then waved as he drove off.

Thank goodness I had to work for most of the day. My life had fallen into a steady cycle of work and seeing Dylan, and not much else. Keeping busy at the diner made the stretches of time without Dylan bearable. Dylan normally called me at least once during my shift, but when I checked my cell phone a few hours later, the screen didn't show the little envelope indicating that I had a new message.

I dialed my voicemail password to make sure. There were no new messages.

I tried not to worry. *Maybe he's tied up with errands or taking care of things at the bank. I know he's a very busy man, so I certainly can't expect him to call me every time I want him to.*

An hour later, I checked my phone again. Still no calls from him. I must have looked distressed, because Shelly came up and asked me what was wrong.

"Dylan didn't call," I said. "He usually calls by now. I'm afraid something bad has happened to him."

"I'm sure he's fine. He's probably extra-swamped today. I wouldn't sweat it."

I tried not to think about Dylan as I served the customers, but every person I saw reminded me of him. This one ordered black coffee like Dylan always did. That one had Dylan's smile, and the other one wore a jacket that Dylan had. He wasn't even in the diner, and yet he was everywhere.

Dylan still hadn't called by the time my shift ended. I had no plans for the evening for the first time in months, and I felt momentarily lost.

I dialed his work number, thinking that maybe an office emergency kept him from calling me. I got his voicemail. I didn't have any luck with his cell number, either, even after calling it four times. I finally decided to leave a message.

"Hey, hon, it's me," I said, forcing a cheerful lilt into my voice. He always hated it when I seemed the least bit down, so I made sure I acted energetic around him even when I felt dead-tired. "Is everything all right? I tried your work number and you weren't there. I'm a bit worried about you. Call me."

I snapped the phone shut, then stood still, thinking. "Should I call him back and tell him to meet me here or something?" I asked.

Shelly shook her head. "You don't want to look desperate and freak him out."

"Shelly, I am desperate."

"No, you're not." She gave my shoulders a firm shake. "Look, let's have a girls' night out tonight. That will help get your mind off of him so you can stop worrying. How does that sound?"

I agreed reluctantly. It was nice of Shelly to suggest hanging out together, but what if Dylan called with plans at the last minute? I suggested going to a bar that Dylan and I went to a lot. That way, if he did call, he'd know where to find me. Of course, I didn't tell Shelly any of that. I didn't think she'd understand.

As I got ready that night, I picked a slinky, silky purple top that Dylan bought for me a few weeks ago and black jeans that he really liked on me. If we ran into him, I wanted to be sure I looked hot. I also thought that if I chose clothes with some history of our time together, it would magically draw him back to me. That's what all those positive thinking gurus say, anyway: your thoughts are like a magnet. I was ready to try and believe anything if it meant keeping Dylan in my life.

The dance music thumped through the speakers, a pulsing backdrop to the well-dressed crowd around us. Shelly leaned against the bar and took a dainty sip of her pomegranate martini. She wrinkled her nose.

"Now I know why I don't come here. Twelve bucks for a watery drink? I'd better make this last for at least an hour."

I agreed. I never had to pay attention to drink prices when I was with Dylan, but I still wasn't surprised that the prices matched the bar's atmosphere. It was a place where the area's in-crowd and hangers-on went. Without him by my side, I felt a bit out of place even though I knew I was still pretty enough to hold my own against the girls around me, who all seemed to be wearing shoes that cost as much as my monthly rent. I was thankful that guys didn't notice things like shoes. They tend to look elsewhere.

My mood lifted as I sipped my drink. Maybe I'll meet a new guy tonight. It can't hurt and he might even be a welcome distraction for the evening. I scanned the crush of people surrounding the bar to see if I could catch the eye of someone promising. I searched among the sea of male faces, almost all of them handsome in that generic, unexciting kind of way. So many men, so few options.

Then I saw him.

Dylan stood about ten feet away, far enough so I wasn't even sure it was he at first. But then I saw him walk toward the bar in a slow, confident stride, effortlessly parting the crowd as he moved past. It had to be him. No one else moved like he did.

It looked like all of my positive thinking actually worked.

"Shelly," I said. "Dylan's here."

"What?"

"There, at the corner of the bar. I'm going over to say hello."

Shelly grabbed my arm. "Wait." She pulled me away from the bar, letting the crush of people shield us from his line of sight. "Let's see what he's doing here first."

I watched him flash that familiar, charming smile at the girl next to him. Correction: she's no girl. Everything about her screamed "woman." She tossed her head and laughed, making her dark curls dance around her shoulders.

I clenched my teeth. Why is Dylan talking to her? Worse yet, why does he seem to be enjoying himself so much with her? He belongs to me, not her. I'd do anything for him. She looks like the type that eats men alive. She won't treat him as well as I did. She'll string him along and break his heart.

"Wasn't he with you this morning? What a jerk!" Shelly said. "C'mon, let's go before he sees us."

We wove our way through the crowd and out the door. I swallowed hard, but that didn't stop the tears from coming.

"What does she have that I don't?"

"He's not worth crying over," Shelly said. "You should just forget about him now and move on. He's a two-timing jerk."

I wished I could believe her, but she didn't know Dylan like I knew him. He was the closest thing to a perfect man that I'd ever known. If he was cheating on me, it was certainly because of something I did. And if that was the case, then I could change whatever was bothering him about me. The challenge was letting him know that. I was sure that if he knew how willing I was to improve myself, he would welcome me back.

Even though it was late, I drove to Dylan's house and parked half a block away. I turned off my headlights so that he wouldn't see my car. While I waited, I replayed all the tender, dream-like moments Dylan and I had together over the past two months. I soon realized that mentioning "love" probably scared him off. Most guys freak out when they heard that word. I vowed that when we got back together, I'd try even harder to be his dream girl come true, one that didn't make any demands of him.

I saw his car pass mine and pull into the driveway. I held my breath as the door opened to see how many people came out.

Only Dylan appeared.

I sighed with relief. The mystery woman didn't come home with him. That meant that I still had a chance with him. I made a mental note to call him the next morning. And evening.

Despite my efforts, the weeks stretched on without Dylan returning my calls, even after I sent him a card marking what would have been our three-month anniversary. I called him at different times of the day on his cell phone and his work phone, hoping that he might answer in person. Sometimes I left messages. After the first week, I made sure I didn't call too often so he wouldn't know when to expect my calls. I also didn't want to freak him out with too much pestering on my part. I wanted to lure him back, not scare him away! I considered getting a new phone number in case he was blocking my current one.

I also checked Dylan's house every few days. I saw the dark-haired woman from the bar visit his house on my second visit. Seeing her was like a stab to my heart. I nearly broke down crying when I saw her disappear through his door the way I used to. To calm down, I reminded myself that he would break up with her soon and then I could come back into his life as if nothing ever happened.

But two months stretched into three, then four. Every time I saw her go up to his house, I became angrier. I couldn't believe that he kept her around longer than he had kept me, even though he knew how devoted and faithful I was to him. I wrote him a letter telling him that I haven't even looked at another guy since him, that he never told me what went wrong in the first place, and that I was willing to change whatever he didn't like about me to make him happy. He never wrote me back.

I eventually had to admit that all of my letters, cards, and phone calls weren't doing the trick. It was time to change tactics. What's the girl doing to hold on to him so tightly? Regardless of what she was doing, I knew that if I was going to win Dylan back, I needed a better strategy.

I tossed my head, flipping my hair over my shoulder, and checking out my reflection in the mirror. Even I had to admit that I looked good as a brunette. I changed my hair color to match Dylan's girlfriend's. I even got it cut in a style similar to hers.

I stepped back from the mirror, admiring the way I looked in the business casual clothes that I would be wearing at my new job as a bank teller. I had applied for a job at Citizens Bank the previous week, the same bank owned by Dylan's family. It took a little homework to figure out which particular branch office Dylan worked at, but when I found it, I was thrilled that there was a job opening there. It was another sign that I was meant to be with him.

I gave my notice at the diner and told Shelly about the new job.

"So, that's why you dyed your hair," she said. "I don't blame you for wanting a real job in an office and everything. This waitressing gig gets old really fast. Where are you going?"

I hesitated. "Citizens Bank, the one on the north side of town."

"Citizens Bank? Isn't that the one that Dylan guy works for?"

"Uhm."

Thanks, Shelly, for your incredible memory. I hadn't mentioned Dylan for months, not since we ran into him at the bar, because I knew she would give me a hard time about trying to contact him.

"Marcy, you're a great girl and it's too bad that he can't see that. Let him go."

"I can't. I love him so much, and this new job lets me see him again." I sniffled and swiped a tear away from the corner of my eye.

"No, you don't love him. You only think you do. He's not worth chasing after, not like this."

I wished I could believe her, but she was all wrong about him. It wasn't worth arguing over, though. She already said how great I was. Dylan only needed a little more time to realize that, too, and doing that meant getting close enough to him where I could spend that time with him.

Shelly touched my shoulder. "Please don't take this the wrong way because I'm saying this as a concerned friend, but. . . ." She bit her lip and looked at the ground, then back at my face. "I really think you should get some help."

Get some help? I jerked my shoulder away from her hand.

"What, you're saying that I'm crazy now?" It took a huge effort for me to keep my voice low so the other waitresses wouldn't hear.

"I didn't mean it like that."

"I know what you meant. I heard you loud and clear."

Shelly sighed. "I'm sorry if you feel that way. I'm really worried about you, that's all."

"All because I got a new job at the bank?"

"You know the new job isn't what I'm worried about. I think it's great you're moving up in the world. It's where and why you got the job. And it explains your new hair, too. Now that I think of it, you look more like that girl at the bar. If I didn't know you better, I would've thought you were stalking him."

Stalking. I clenched my fists at the sound of the word. Despite Shelly's protests, it was crystal clear she thought I was crazy. Otherwise, she wouldn't have suggested that I get some "help." Everyone knew what people meant by the word "help," no matter how much they tried to sugarcoat it.

"I'm not stalking him," I said. My throat choked up and tears spilled onto my face. I couldn't look at Shelly anymore. "I can't believe you think that I'm even capable of such a thing. I thought you were my friend."

"I am."

"No, you're not. If you were, you'd understand how much Dylan means to me. I'm not some psycho chick who's going to kill his pets or anything. I got a better job, and if it makes it easier for me to see him again, then that's a bonus."

A confused look crossed Shelly's face. "But you just said you got the job because you loved him and wanted to see him again."

"No, that's not what I said. You're twisting my words around, and I don't appreciate it. I had hoped you'd understand, but I guess I was wrong."

I ran to the bathroom, vowing never to speak to Shelly again. I splashed cold water on my face, hoping that it would stop my eyes from puffing up.

Who does Shelly think she is, accusing me of being a stalker? Stalkers are crazy, ugly older women who chase after married ex-boyfriends. They're stupid girls who have pictures of celebrities plastered on every flat surface of their homes. Stalkers have stringy hair, wild eyes, and they don't take "no" for an answer. None of those things describe me, and I was offended that Shelly even dared to lump me in the same category as those kinds of women.

Shelly didn't understand that Dylan never broke up with me. He never said he didn't want to see me again. Sure, he may have faded from my life a bit over the past few months, and I did see him with another girl, but that didn't mean that we were over. Lots of guys date more than one girl at a time. I was fine with that, but I worried that he would forget about me completely if he didn't see me at least once in a while. Working at his bank would be the little nudge he needed to get us back together again.

I took a few deep, cleansing breaths and immediately felt calmer. Shelly's words echoed in my mind, hinting that I got mad at her because she was telling the uncomfortable truth about me. I pushed that negative thought out of my mind. No, Shelly was wrong. I thought she was the kind of person who wanted to see me happy, but I had obviously misjudged her. Oh, well, it's good I found that out sooner rather than later. That would make it easier to leave her off our wedding invitation list.

I checked my reflection in the mirror, and then pulled out my makeup bag. I studied the dark eye shadows that I had bought a few weeks ago, still unsure of what went where. Dylan's new girlfriend wore a lot of makeup, enough for me to even notice it from my car when I watched Dylan's house. I planned to spend more time perfecting my technique so I could show up at the new job on Monday with the perfect smoky, sexy eye—the kind that Dylan would find irresistible.

I dressed as nicely as I could at my new job. In every outfit, I included a piece of clothing or jewelry that Dylan had given me, both for good luck and to show that I still appreciated everything he'd given me, in case I ran into him. It was great to go to work dressed in nice clothes rather than a waitress uniform. Not smelling like grease at the end of day and not having to work nights were welcome changes, too.

Unfortunately, I didn't see Dylan right away. The first three days were spent filling out forms, meeting people, and getting trained on everything. It felt overwhelming at first, but I knew that if I could handle a Friday night dinner rush, I could handle working as a bank teller.

Still, even though the work itself was coming along well, I hated getting ready each morning, looking forward to seeing Dylan and then never catching a glimpse of him. I knew he worked in the same building as me, so I thought I'd at least run into him by pure chance.

By the middle of the second week, I decided to take matters in my own hands and started asking around discreetly. On my first day at the teller's window, I had made it through the lunchtime rush with no mistakes. Debbie, my supervisor, had hovered beside me the entire time to make sure I kept everything under control.

When the crowd subsided, Debbie patted me on the back.

"Nice work, especially since it's your first day handling customers. I can see that you're going to do great here."

"Thanks," I said. "Hey, I was wondering whether you knew anything about Dylan Thompson. It's his family's bank, right?"

"That's right. Mr. Thompson works on the fifth floor. He manages all the branches in this region. He seems very nice, sometimes even mingles with us little people here on the main floor when he feels like doing his banking in person. You know him?"

"No," I lied. "I read something about him in the paper the other day and wondered what he was like."

"I see his picture a lot in the society pages. His family is really involved in charities and stuff. I don't know much about him personally, but I love reading about the beautiful people in town. It's better than TV."

I wasn't particularly interested in Debbie's reading habits. I wanted to tell her that I used to be one of those beautiful people, hanging out at the best clubs and living the kind of life that Debbie only read about. But, wisely, I didn't. She was my boss, after all.

"He always used to have a pretty girl on his arm," she said "Makes me wish I was fifteen years younger. He's quite good-looking."

That was the understatement of the year. I tuned out Debbie's voice as I thought of possible excuses for visiting the fifth floor. I soon realized that I needed to learn more about my job before I could come up with plausible reasons. That meant another delay before seeing Dylan. Oh, well, I'd waited this long. I could wait another few days.

Debbie studied me for a moment. "You know, you look a little bit like his fiancée."

My thoughts came to a screeching halt.

"Excuse me?" I said.

"You look like Dylan's fiancée. Her name's Candace something. You have similar features, the same hair. She's quite pretty."

My heart felt like it was being ripped apart.

"I didn't know he was getting married," I said, struggling to keep my voice even. It felt like the air left the room.

"Oh, yes, the announcement was in last week's paper," she said. "Some of the girls here want to throw them an engagement party. Isn't that sweet?"

Sweet enough to make me want to gag. "I really should get back to my station," I said, even though the bank was empty.

I didn't speak to anyone for the rest of the afternoon. I arranged my pens so they faced the same direction, stocked up on paper clips, reviewed the notes from my training, and fussed with the computer—anything to avoid thinking about how Dylan had moved on without me.

At first, I was angry. Then I realized that if he had announced his engagement only last week, the wedding date was still a long way off. Anything could happen to change his mind before then. Engagements break up all the time.

As if on cue, Dylan emerged from the hallway where the elevators were. I smoothed my blouse and stood up a little straighter. The other girls seemed to burst into a flurry of activity as well, straightening up their already neat stations. To my delight, he headed toward my window. I told myself to stay cool and calm.

"Hi, there," he said. "Could you look up my account balances for me?"

"Hello, Dylan. I'd be happy to do that for you."

He did a double take. "How'd you know my name?"

Then he saw my nametag. A slow grin spread across his face. The warm feeling that washed over me when I saw his smile was indescribable. It was like no time had passed since I last saw him.

"Marcy?" he asked.

I nodded and smiled back.

He shook his head. The grin was still on his face, and then he studied me again, looking at me with the kind of gaze that I had dreamed about for so many months.

"I'm sorry I didn't recognize you," he said. "You look so different. Good different. I like what you did to your hair. It's very sexy."

My whole body tingled, every nerve taking in the fact that he was only a few feet away. It was amazing how he could do that without even touching me.

"It's good to see you, too," I said. I longed to reach for him so I could kiss him, but I forced my fingers to start typing on the keyboard. "Did you want the balances on all of your accounts?"

"Yes," he said.

I typed a few more commands and sent the information to the small printer next to my computer monitor. I handed him the slip of paper. His fingers brushed against mine as he took it from me.

"Well, it's good seeing you again. Let's meet for coffee sometime soon and catch up."

He gave me a wink, just like old times. Before I could answer, he stepped away from my window and headed toward the front doors. I watched him maneuver through the parking lot before disappearing in the sea of cars.

There was hope for me yet. He seemed happy to see me again, he said I looked sexy—not simply good, but sexy—and, most importantly, he had asked me out for coffee. All were good signs. Still, I didn't have much time to convince him that I was the right one for him and not that Candace girl. I didn't know whether they'd even set a wedding date. I needed to figure something out, and soon. I hoped checking out his office would give me some ideas.

"Debbie, is it okay if I go on break now?" I asked. When she nodded, I grabbed my purse as if I was heading to the ladies' room.

The restrooms were past the elevators, so I knew that the other girls wouldn't think anything was amiss as I headed in that direction.

As I passed the elevators, I hit the "up" button, then kept walking toward the restrooms so no one would see me waiting. I turned right back around when I heard the telltale "ding" of the elevator arriving, I glanced over my shoulder to make sure no one was around, and then slipped inside. When the doors opened at the fifth floor, I hesitated at the threshold; concerned that anyone who saw me would immediately know I didn't belong there. I shouldn't have worried. The hallways were empty.

Dylan's office was easy to find since his nameplate was next to the door. I closed the door partially so no one could see me from the hallway if they walked by. The early evening light streaming through the windows was enough for me to see everything without turning on the overhead fluorescents.

The first thing I noticed was the faint lingering scent of Dylan's cologne. I closed my eyes for a moment and breathed in the scent, remembering all those nights when I smelled it on his warm skin.

Dylan's office was large and filled with heavy, dark wood furniture, a perfect backdrop for him. Everything in his office reflected his impeccable taste, from the modern artwork on the walls to the plush leather chair behind his desk. I sank into the chair, letting it envelop me. I couldn't believe that I was there, the same place where Dylan spent most of his waking hours. I smoothed my hands over the arms of his chair, trying to absorb any leftover energy from Dylan, thinking of subtle ways that I could let him know that I hadn't forgotten about what we'd shared together.

Then I saw the picture on the corner of his desk. It was Candace and Dylan together, both of them laughing with their arms embracing each other. I picked up the heavy silver frame and stared at the picture. The girl in the picture was supposed to be me. My reflection from the glass created a ghostly shadow over their smiling faces. Even though my reflected face was faint compared to Candace's, I could tell that we looked a lot alike. The problem was that she was in the picture and I wasn't. I stroked a finger over Dylan's chin, and then clenched the frame in both hands. He belonged to me.

I slipped the frame in my purse, and then I got out of the chair and arranged it at the same position that I found it. Mission accomplished. I couldn't help smiling all the way back to my station.

"You must have needed that break bad," Debbie said. "You're glowing so much."

I kept the smile on my face as I stashed my purse under the desk. I gave it a gentle pat, feeling the frame underneath.

"Yeah, it's amazing what a short walk can do to perk you up," I said. "You should try it sometime."

As soon as I got home, I took the picture out of the frame and carefully cut away all evidence of Candace, leaving only Dylan's face smiling back at me. I searched my junk drawer for a smaller frame and slipped his picture inside, then placed it next to my bed. I regretted not taking any pictures of Dylan when we were together, but now I could look at him anytime I wanted.

Dylan invaded my dreams that night. In my dream, he was upset that Candace broke off the engagement. I comforted him, telling him that if she didn't recognize how wonderful he was, she didn't deserve him. He kissed me, then got down on one knee and presented me with the biggest diamond ring I'd ever seen.

When I woke up, the dream felt so real that I knew it had to be a sign of my future. Our future. I was sure Dylan had had the same dream. I checked my finger, almost expecting the ring to be there. Of course it wasn't, but it was only a matter of time before it would be.

"Marcy, can I talk to you for a moment?"

Debbie had given me more responsibilities over the past few days because I was learning everything so quickly, so I wasn't surprised when she wanted to talk to me yet again. As she led me into her office, I secretly hoped for a raise.

"Please," she said, motioning toward the chair across her desk. That was strange. Normally, she hated visitors in her office. Most of the time, they never even got a chance to sit before she kicked them out.

Debbie folded her chubby hands on her desk. "Marcy, did you visit Mr. Thompson's office last week?"

How did she find out? I swallowed and said, "Yes, I did."

"May I ask why?"

Think fast, Marcy. "I wanted to take a look around," I said. That was the most truthful, yet innocent, answer I could think of on the fly.

"Right in Mr. Thompson's office? He said that you took something of his. He didn't say what, but he said it was valuable. He also said that you were caught on the security tape."

Oh, no. I didn't even think about surveillance cameras. And I had thought I was being so sneaky. I couldn't say anything in my defense. The words stuck in my throat.

After a few moments of silence, Debbie sighed. "I'm really disappointed in you, Marcy. You're a really bright girl, and I thought you had a lot of potential."

I stared at my lap. What could I say? No fancy talking from me could change the fact that I had been caught red-handed, on tape, my silly decision saved for posterity.

"You know I'm going to have to let you go immediately," she said. "We can't have thieves of any kind working in a bank. I'm sure you understand."

I nodded, still not looking at her. I was not going to let myself cry in front of her, no matter how humiliated I felt.

Thankfully, Debbie escorted me out of the bank herself, sparing me the embarrassment of being shown the door by a bunch of security guards. I guess she was still willing to treat me with a little dignity because I didn't steal money. She continued to follow one step behind me across the parking lot. Neither of us said anything.

I knew I should have thanked Debbie or said something to let her know that I appreciated all the time she put into training me. All that wasted time. Instead, I got into my car and drove off without another word. I was too lost in my thoughts, trying to figure out my next move.

I had to let Dylan know why I was no longer at the bank. We still had a standing coffee date, and I wanted to take him up on it. I didn't want Dylan to hear whatever gossip the other tellers were saying about me the next time he visited the first floor. He needed to hear my side of the story. I had to apologize for doing something so immature.

The more I thought about it, the more I was convinced that he had nothing to do with me getting fired. He's more understanding than that. I knew that if it were only up to him, I would still have my job. He cared about me. I also knew, though, that even he had to follow the rules at his own bank. I felt a wave of compassion for him. It must have been rough for him to be bound by rules that he couldn't ignore even if he wanted to help someone he loved. I really needed to meet him for coffee so I could ease any lingering guilt he might have about what happened to me. I had to let him know that I wasn't angry with him, not one bit.

As I drove home, I imagined what our coffee date would be like. I would return the frame to him and tell him I was sorry for my poor judgment. I'd soothe his conscience by telling him that I didn't take my firing personally, that I knew he had no part in the stupid strict rules he was forced to follow. He would laugh, take my hand, and tell me that he was relieved I understood, maybe even say that he was having second thoughts about his engagement. He'd tell me that he wished Candace were as understanding as me. I would tell him that I would be around anytime he wanted to talk.

So many wonderful possibilities, yet all of them required me to take the first step and call him.

It took the rest of the day for me to gather enough courage to call him. I still had his number programmed on speed dial in my cell phone, but it still felt strange to be actually calling him after so many months.

"Hello?" The female voice that answered the phone sounded shrill and not the least bit friendly. Is she always this annoying? If so, Dylan needs rescuing even more than I had thought.

I took a deep breath and made my voice sound as smooth as possible. "Hello, is Dylan in?"

"Who is this?"

"This is Marcy, from work. I need to speak with him about something." That wasn't exactly a lie. Yes, I was from work. She didn't have to know more than that.

There was a long pause on the other end. "He's not here."

"May I at least leave a message?"

"No."

I bit my lip. I knew Dylan was home. Seeing him for two months made me an expert on his routine. Fine. If she was going to be that way. . . .

"Well, he asked me out for coffee a while back, and I'd like to take him up on the offer."

She hung up on me.

Good. Now she knew that I was out there and waiting in the wings. Judging from her reaction, though, I had to be more discreet about contacting Dylan in the future. I didn't want to make his life even more difficult for him. Trying to get Candace out of the picture was still a priority, but I cared about Dylan too much to make things hard for him in the process.

I had suspected that Candace was a witch. Now I knew it for sure, and it was up to me to save Dylan from a lifetime of misery with her. The problem was that I knew Dylan wouldn't get my message about coffee. The only hope I had of explaining myself to him was to somehow run into him in person. I knew it wasn't going to happen by chance anytime soon, so I decided to take matters into my own hands yet again.

I drove to Dylan's house the next day and parked at my usual spot half a block away. His BMW was parked in the driveway.

I listened to the soft rock station as I waited, letting my imagination float along with the love songs that streamed into my car. Those songs fueled my energy and reminded me why I was there. It was a labor of love.

My patience was eventually rewarded. Dylan and Candace emerged through the front door, both of them looking fashionably casual in jeans and leather jackets. They hopped into Dylan's car, and then backed out of the driveway. I waited a few seconds before I pulled behind them, letting one car slip in between us.

I followed them to the gourmet store, parking at the far end of the lot so I would remain out of view. When I entered the store, I felt a stab of nostalgia as the clean scent of fresh produce greeted my nose. Dylan and I used to shop there before making dinner together. The memory fueled my heart as I kept searching the store.

I found Candace browsing the cheese section with a shopping

basket hanging from her forearm. I didn't bother pretending that I was there to check out the Brie as I approached her.

"Why did you hang up on me?" I said. "That was really rude of you."

Her eyes grew wide. "Excuse me?"

"I asked you to leave a message for Dylan and you hung up on me. Didn't your mom teach you any manners?"

Candace looked behind me and then turned around as if searching for someone. Her forehead crinkled with worry, which made me feel even more powerful. She seemed afraid of me. I hoped she was scared enough to realize that as long as she was with Dylan, I would always be waiting in her shadow. Maybe that would convince her to leave him.

"Marcy, what are you doing here?"

The deep, familiar voice sent a delicious shiver through me. The sound of my name on his lips felt like warm chocolate through my veins. It had been far too long since I heard him say it.

"Dylan!" I said. I threw an arm around him, giving him one of those formal hugs that people gave in public, affectionate but not close enough to make anyone feel uncomfortable. His body remained stiff. I figured he was as surprised to see me as Candace was.

"What a coincidence running into you here," I said. "I actually called just yesterday and tried to leave you a message, but she—" I flicked my chin in Candace's direction. "Hung up on me. I assume you didn't know I called."

Dylan looked at Candace, then at me. The expression on his face was unreadable. I couldn't tell whether he was confused, annoyed, or amused. "I'm sure it was an accident," he said after a long pause. "What was the message?"

"I wanted to take you up on that coffee date invitation." I didn't care if Candace heard me. If they were truly close, she would have already known that Dylan had recently asked me out. And if she didn't know, their lack of communication was yet another sign they shouldn't be together. Either way, I won.

"Oh, that," he said. He touched Candace's sleeve and stepped away from me. "We can talk about that later. We're kind of in a hurry right now."

They were halfway down the baking aisle before I could respond. I saw Dylan glance over his shoulder at me before whispering something in Candace's ear. She looked back at me with a poisonous stare. His hand was still on her sleeve, probably to hold her back from lunging at me like an angry dog. She obviously saw me as her competition, which was exactly what I wanted. It was time to show her how serious I was about taking Dylan away from her.

I got the restraining order a few days later. When it arrived, I was shocked that Dylan would do such a thing to me. I was positive that Candace put him up to it. Maybe confronting them in the grocery store wasn't the smartest move, but I never thought that Dylan would want me to stay away from him, let alone do something so drastic.

I read the restraining order again. It all looked so official, and at first I was intimidated. I wasn't allowed within a hundred feet of either of their workplaces or their home. I couldn't call them, email them, or contact them in any way. Well, that'll make it a bit difficult setting up that coffee date, I thought with a wry smile.

I tossed the restraining order on my bed, and then sat on top of it as I reached for Dylan's picture on my nightstand. His face still beamed through the glass, his eyes kind, and his expression assuring me that everything was still okay between us.

I took Dylan's silver picture frame, the one I'd swiped from his office, out of my dresser drawer. I knew I should return it to him to show him that I was willing to admit my own mistakes so we could start again with a clean slate.

When I stopped by Dylan's house to return the frame, the restraining order didn't concern me. It was a meaningless piece of paper. I knew that once I spoke with him, he would wave all that away as a simple misunderstanding. Besides, it wasn't like he would call the police on me if I showed up on his doorstep. As extra insurance, I bought a huge flower arrangement as a peace offering.

I was relieved when Dylan, and not Candace, answered the door. As always, the sight of him gave me goose bumps.

"Dylan! Sorry for the surprise drop-in, but I wanted to return this to you and also give you a little something extra." I said. I held out the picture frame and the flowers. "No hard feelings, okay?"

The frown on Dylan's face worried me. He didn't even reach out to take anything from my hands. I'd hoped he would give me a hug to let me know that the restraining order was all Candace's idea and not his. I wanted to hear him say that he wished I were sharing his house instead of Candace.

"Who is it?" Candace's voice yelled out from the back of the house.

"It's her again," he said, his eyes not leaving my face. He didn't even say my name.

Dylan still stood in the doorway, motionless, his expression looking less than welcoming. I straightened my shoulders and held out the frame and the flowers again, a few inches closer to him, hoping the motion would act like a rewind button to cover up my earlier awkwardness.

"Here, take them. They're for you."

"Leave them on the porch," Dylan said. "I'll get them later."

What? This isn't the way things are supposed to happen. He's supposed to take me in his arms and tell me he wants me back. Where's the hug? Where's my happily ever after? I looked away. There was no way I was going to let him see me cry.

"Well, ah, I better get going," I said.

I'd barely stepped off the porch when I heard the door close behind me. When I turned around, the frame and the flowers were exactly where I had left them. Dylan hadn't even bothered to pick them up. He also didn't say good-bye.

I was halfway to my car when the police car arrived. An officer leapt out and headed right toward me. Instinctively, I knew that any sudden moves on my part wouldn't be a good idea. At that moment, whatever shreds of dignity I still had after my embarrassing encounter with Dylan disappeared. All the energy left my body, making my legs feel like they couldn't support me another second. I sank to the curb and hugged my knees to my chest.

"Are you Marcy Michaels?" the officer asked.

I nodded, rocking back and forth.

"You're going to have to come with me. Get up."

I looked up. Despite his harsh words, the officer had a kind look on his face. It felt like it would be last bit of kindness I'd see for a long time.

He gripped my arm firmly and led me toward the car. He didn't need to be so rough. I didn't have anywhere else to go. Without Dylan, I didn't have a direction in my life anymore. Even getting arrested felt like it gave me some sort of purpose. At least I knew where I was going. I needed something, anything, to fill the huge hole in my life that Dylan had left.

As the police car pulled away from the curb, I took one last long look at the home Dylan now shares with Candace, the woman he chose over me. I saw the shades of one of the windows move apart. I squinted and thought I could see his face peeking through the crack. With tears streaming down my face, I blew a kiss to the face in the window, my last tribute to the love I felt for Dylan. He had made it clear that he didn't want me in his life, and I loved him enough to let him go for good.

THE END

CONFESSIONS OF A HOMELESS WOMAN
"How I Got Here"

I'm squatting in an abandoned hotel, sleeping next to junkies and drifters, sharing what food I can steal with crack-addicted prostitutes in hopes that a candy bar will loosen a tongue, praying that one of these outcasts can help me find my daughter. Another day begging for spare change brings me another day closer to finding my little girl.

Maybe I wasn't the best mother, but it wasn't for lack of love or trying. Molly's father, Dale, took off with his barfly girlfriend when Molly was three days old, leaving me alone in the hospital without even a car seat to take my daughter home in. We moved in with my mother for a while, but her excessive drinking was unbearable while I was growing up. I decided I wasn't going to expose my little angel to the gin-soaked monster I call Mom.

I saved every cent I could from my job at the supermarket checkout and got us an apartment on the west end of town, the bad side of the tracks. I painted our living room purple and her bedroom pink, just to make it seem more like our home. I took her to church every Sunday, and got both of us baptized—something my own parents never did. As you can imagine, we didn't have much extra money, but we found a lot of fun, free things to do together. I took her to the park to feed bread heels to the ducks and to the playground to soar for hours on the swings; we built blanket castles in her bedroom and had campouts, complete with s'mores, in the living room. I loved her so much and I just wanted the best for her.

When she was old enough to go to school, I enrolled her in Girl Scouts and after-school sports so that I could take on a second job as a happy hour waitress while she was out of the house. Molly was a wonderful student who excelled in reading and math; I used to let her count up my tips to help her practice her numbers. Our fridge was covered with her A+ tests and crayon artwork. It seems like she brought me something new to hang up every day.

I made sure that Molly had a warm winter jacket even if it meant I walked to work for two months to save my bus fare. She ate fruit for a snack even though potato chips were cheaper. I wanted her to grow up healthy, so that she might have a chance of escaping my overworked, underpaid fate. It's the dream of all parents that their child will exceed the life they were born into. When my feet hurt from standing all day and my mind raced with the thoughts of unpaid bills, I imagined her growing up to be a doctor, a lawyer, or a college professor; someone who never had to worry about paying rent or going into debt.

Somewhere along the line, my love failed her. Maybe it was the rotten neighborhood, maybe it was just bad genetics, but by the time she was in seventh grade, she was stealing from the corner store and getting drunk with the boys on the stoop. Imagine the pain of slaving all day and coming home to find your beloved child puking her guts out, intoxicated beyond all recognition.

We fought constantly and every day it seemed like she came home with a new drug in her system. I started searching her room, throwing out liquor bottles, bags of marijuana, and glass pipes. Once I even found a syringe. I tremble whenever I recall that moment when I knew my baby was out of control. I think about it all too often.

Soon I was getting frantic calls at four in the morning to come pick her up because she'd been in a fight or she was hiding from the cops, pleading, "Please, Mommy. I'll be good, I promise, just please come get me!" Of course I'd swoop to her rescue and rush to whatever street corner pay phone she was huddled in, covered with cuts and bruises, blood in her mouth and booze on her breath. Her pleas were all empty promises, however; words she forgot when she woke up the next morning with a screaming hangover and self-hate in her heart. We'd fight and she'd leave again while I sat crying, praying for a way to heal my broken baby girl.

I tried to get her help. I tried to talk to her teachers and I dragged her punching and screaming to several counselors and recovery programs, but it wasn't until she got arrested for beating a fellow student with a broken board that her problems got any sort of recognition. My face has never burned so red as when I sat in that courtroom, humiliated that the daughter I tried to raise so well turned out so wicked. I knew all eyes were on me, trying to dissect what kind of awful mother I must be to let my little girl turn out this way. I wanted to scream at them, whose child do you think she's drinking with?

Molly was sentenced to six months in a juvenile facility and I thought she'd finally get her life back together. I visited every chance I was allowed, driving two hours upstate, but all she did was blame me for "doing this to her." I tried to remind her that I still loved her, but it felt like she didn't care. I cried into my pillow every night, wondering if I really was to blame. Do I not love her enough? Do I spoil her too much? Do I overwork her with after school activities and pressure her too hard for good grades? Am I just not home enough? All these thoughts plagued my every waking moment, making the hard life I used to be able to cope with almost unbearable.

Six weeks intro her incarceration, I got a midnight phone call from the warder telling me that she and another girl had escaped. The police had already been notified. I sat up all night, half-expecting and mostly praying for her to come home and beg me to forgive her for all the pain she must know she caused me, pain I would forget in an instant if she would just return to my loving arms. When she didn't arrive at my door, I pleaded with the police to widen the search.

"We're doing all we can, ma'am," Captain Davidson told me over and over again. "I promise, we're searching as hard as we can."

I knew he was lying. I knew another runaway delinquent junkie wasn't a high priority for them; after all, he knew his men would catch her doing something illegal sometime, and I'd find her then. What I knew he wasn't telling me is that they expected to find her, only instead of a call to post bail at the police station, I'd get a call from the morgue to identify her battered, drug-ravaged body.

I couldn't wait around for someone to find her for me, so I took to the streets. I asked her friends and they just laughed at me, not willing to betray Molly.

"Why the hell would she want to come back to you?" one girl sneered. "You don't let her have no fun!"

I never imagined that the same little girl who called me "The Greatest Mommy in the World" would paint such an awful picture of her mother to her friends, but it didn't deter my love or my willingness to do whatever it took to find her. I prayed nightly for her safe return, and asked the members of my church to pray for her to find her way back to myself and to the Lord.

I asked at stores I knew she stole from, knowing they'd be extra vigilant for a former shoplifter. Nothing. I finally realized that if I were ever going to find Molly, I'd have to join the world I tried so hard to keep her from. I gave up my apartment, took all my money out of the bank, and joined the thousands of vagrants in the city. I slept in shelters and in doorways for a month before I made a friend, a mentally ill drug addict named Shelby, who showed me a picture of the son Social Services took away. She invited me to live with her and a few others in the forlorn Augusta Hotel.

It's been a year and I've followed every lead I've been given. For the first few weeks, I thought I saw her everywhere—on the subway platform, getting off the bus, standing in line at the newspaper stand, through a polished, plate-glass window, selling beautiful clothes. Some prostitutes told me she was hooking at a truck stop outside of town, but when I showed her tattered school picture to the waitresses, none of them recognized her. I found a drug dealer who said he sold her crack-cocaine, but when I waited for her to make another score, she never showed.

Every night, I shiver myself to sleep under dirty blankets,

wondering if I'd even recognize her face anymore. Has she grown so gaunt and scarred with drugs that she no longer bears any resemblance to the beautiful girl I used to push on the swings? I often dream that I find her and she always looks as precious as I remember her, in pink dresses and lace-trimmed socks, running toward me with her arms outstretched, joyfully crying, "Mommy, Mommy!"

I'm so happy when I dream. When I awake to the shriek of a police siren, I take a moment to weep for waking from the peaceful beauty before I remind myself of my quest and resolve myself to go on another day.

In the year I've walked these streets I've been harassed by police, spit on and sneered at by businessmen, beaten and robbed by teenage thugs, and nearly raped twice. I've gone hungry many nights, and my face has become so old I sometimes don't recognize myself when I catch sight of my reflection in a store window. Every day is a fight to survive, not just physically, but spiritually and emotionally as well. There have been many days when I've wanted to give up, but I look at Molly's smiling photograph and strengthen my resolve. I've spent my whole life doing everything I could for her. I won't stop now.

It's a mother's duty to protect her child in times of need, and if that means enduring all I've endured, I'll thank Heaven for every moment. Perhaps all my searching is in vain. She might be dead for all I know, but until I either bury her body or tuck her into bed, I'll never stop looking for my baby.

THE END

CONFESSIONS OF A FATHERLESS DAUGHTER
My Mom Kept My Dad From Me!

No one could have been more surprised than I was when I learned that my father had named me executor and primary recipient of his estate. I had not seen him since the day my mother and I stood in the driveway and watched him pack his clothes into the sedan. I had just started second grade that year and had not even received my first report card.

After packing the car, my father squatted down in front of me, and then gathered me into his arms in a long hug that I thought would crush out all of my breath. I thought I saw him reach a finger under his glasses and wipe a tear away from the corner of his eye as he stood, but I didn't understand then that I would never see him again.

"He doesn't love us anymore," my mother said as my father drove away. She had her arms crossed under her breasts, and her face drawn up in a tight pucker that I saw all too often in the following years. "Doesn't love us at all," she continued.

My mother repeated the refrain throughout my childhood and well into my teens. She convinced me that my father had abandoned me and, since I never heard from him, I believed her. Christmases passed without presents, birthdays passed without cards. At first I cried, but as I grew older I slowly accepted my mother's version of what had happened. For reasons I never understood, my father had walked out of my life.

As I grew older, I met other children of divorced parents. Nearly all of them lived with their mother or with their mother and their stepfather. Most of them saw their real father on weekends, or spent summers with him if he lived far away. Their fathers remembered Christmases and birthdays, and some of them even remembered the other holidays like Thanksgiving and Valentine's Day—not my father.

Before long, I started telling people my father had died because it was easier to lie than to explain why I never heard from him. How could I tell people my father didn't love me when I didn't even understand why?

Twenty years after my father drove away, I received a phone call from an attorney claiming to represent my father's estate. I met with the attorney in his downtown office two days later, and then I followed him from his office to my father's home, less than ten miles from where I'd spent my childhood.

I followed the attorney up the walk, past a neatly manicured lawn and flowerbeds in full bloom, and soon we stood in the living room of my father's two-bedroom brick home.

"He never remarried," the attorney said. He was a thin, bald-headed man wearing an expensive but ill-fitting suit. "And he's left nearly everything to you."

"But why me?" I still didn't understand why my father would leave everything to me.

The attorney ignored the question and continued, "No one's been in here since he passed, so it's a bit dusty."

"But. . . ."

The attorney placed the house keys in my hands. "If you need anything, phone the office. Otherwise, I'll contact you if there's any additional information we need to probate the will."

We shook hands, said goodbye, and then I was alone. I felt like I was violating a stranger's home. I didn't know the man who had lived here, and had only vague memories of who he had been when I was a child.

I stood exactly where the attorney had left me and slowly looked around. Although everything was covered in a thin layer of dust, nothing appeared to be out of place. It reminded me of my father's workbench in the garage, where the painted outlines of each of his tools remained on the pegboard long after his departure.

Hanging on the wall in front of me were three framed certificates and I stepped closer to examine them. Two named my father as "Employee of the Year," and the third certificate appeared to have been given as a joke because it named him as the employee with the "Neatest Desk."

His organizational skills had been recognized by his co-workers, yet my mother had always referred to my father as "fussy."

"He would yell at me if I folded the towels the wrong way," she'd told me one day during my senior year of high school, and indeed everything in my father's house seemed to have a place and be in it.

I slowly made my way through the house, poking my nose into the bathroom where every item in the medicine cabinet had been placed label-forward, the hall closet where the towels were neatly folded and organized by color, and the master bedroom where the bed was so neatly made I expected to find a mint on the pillow. Instead, I found a pair of reading glasses on the nightstand along with a well-thumbed King James Version of the Bible and my first grade school photo in a gold frame. I picked up the frame and stared at the photo for a long time, noticing how it had yellowed with age.

After replacing the framed picture on the night stand, I crossed the hall into the guest bedroom, and was even more surprised. A teddy bear exactly like the one I'd had as a child sat on the day bed. On the dresser sat a silver jewelry box and, when I opened it, a tiny ballerina began to twirl to the music it played. Stacked in the closet were unopened Christmas presents, each with my name neatly penned on the tag in what I presumed was my father's handwriting.

The dresser drawers were all empty. Perhaps they waited my arrival for a weekend visit when I would shove my clothes haphazardly into one of the drawers before rushing off to the park or the Bijou with my father.

In a filing cabinet in the garage I found dozens of unopened envelopes addressed to me that had been returned to my father. On the front of each was a handwritten note that said, "Return to sender." The handwriting was my mother's.

In a desk drawer in the kitchen I found a savings passbook with both my name and my father's name on it. The account had been opened the same month he had moved out of our home and each month my father had deposited one hundred dollars. He had stopped making deposits the month I turned 21—there were no withdrawals.

On a bookshelf in the living room I found a photo album containing nothing but photographs of me as a child, a clipping from the local newspaper mentioning the time I won the seventh-grade American history essay contest and another mentioning my high school softball team's losing trip to the state championship. I'd been the relief pitcher that year, the starting pitcher the following year.

After a few hours of poking through my father's belongings, I carried everything I found to the living room and sat on the floor surrounded by it all. Rather than forgetting me, it seemed as if my father had done everything he could not to forget me.

First, I looked through the photo album again. He'd placed all the photos in chronological order, from the first one taken at the hospital the day of my birth, through various birthdays, Christmases, and visits to the park. Underneath each photo was a neatly written caption naming each person in the photo, the event pictured, and the date the photo was taken. After he'd left us, there were fewer photos, but these included pictures taken at my softball games and my high school graduation. He'd been there and I hadn't known it.

I found copies of all of my report cards, a crayon and watercolor landscape of mine that had sold at auction for four dollars and seventy-two cents when my school was raising money for new playground equipment, and a photograph of my date and me taken at my Senior Prom.

There wasn't much in the album after my high school graduation. I'd had a series of jobs in fast-food restaurants before finding my current position as a sales clerk at a local department store, but nothing I had done since high school had gotten my name or my picture in the paper—the last few pages were empty.

When I finished looking though the photo album, I opened

all the Christmas gifts, finding twenty-year-old Barbie dolls, record albums by groups popular during my junior high years, and books too numerous to mention. I found two watches, a make-up case, wallets, belts, T-shirts, and board games.

Then I read all the letters. In some he told me he loved me and he missed me. In others, he congratulated me for my good grades, or for being named to the softball team, or for graduation. In letters written during my last two years of high school, he asked about college and told me how important he thought a good education would be to me as I grew older. He mentioned his regret at not furthering his own education and emphasized how lucky he had been to find a good job with a good company willing to train him.

By the time I finished reading all the letters, the morning sun had begun to peek through the open shades. I still sat cross-legged on the living room carpet, fighting back tears.

My father had tried to contact me and my mother had prevented him from doing so, yet not one of his letters said anything negative about my mother.

She'd returned every present, every letter, and every child support check he'd ever sent. Yet, throughout it all she'd told me that my father didn't love me and didn't ever want to have anything to do with me. I can't say that she'd taught me to hate him, but I'd certainly stopped loving him. He had gone and I just never thought much about him.

Now, sitting on the living room floor of his house, two weeks after his cremation, surrounded by all the evidence that he had loved me, I didn't know what to think or do.

I stopped trying to fight back the tears and just let them flow. They streamed down my cheeks and onto my blouse, leaving black streaks of mascara across my face.

I returned to my own apartment later that morning and caught a short nap and a shower before I reported for the afternoon-shift at the department store where I'd been working for nearly two years.

"You look beat," Angela said as we stood at the time clock together waiting to punch in. We worked together in House Wares and had been friends ever since we'd first met. "What happened?"

"I met a ghost," I said. "I met my father."

"You told me he was dead." Angela punched her time card and placed it in the rack.

"He is," I said before clocking in. As we walked together to the house wares department, I told her about everything that had happened to me the previous twenty-four hours.

"You really thought he didn't love you?" Angela asked.

"I thought he'd abandoned me completely," I told her. "Now maybe I think it wasn't him at all."

We arrived in House Wares to find Ethel and Marge serving a line of customers seven deep at the counter. We immediately pitched in and helped clear out the customers. We didn't get to talk again for nearly an hour.

"What was he like?" Angela asked.

"I remembered him as a big man," I said. "That must have been just because I was so small when he left, but he really wasn't. I found a picture of him standing next to my mother and she was holding me."

I told Angela about the picture. It had been taken my first Easter. I wore a bonnet and my parents were dressed in their Sunday clothes. In her heels, my mother stood nearly as tall as my father.

"I remember him reading me bedtime stories," I told Angela. After my father left, I never heard another bedtime story. "He must have loved to read, or he thought it was important for me to read."

I told Angela about all the unopened presents I'd found. "There were so many books," I said. We were interrupted again by another rush of customers.

Later, Angela asked, "You have any idea what those dolls are worth, unopened in their original boxes?"

"It doesn't really matter," I told her. "It isn't about the money."

"I know that," Angela said. "It's just that, well, between the dolls, and the savings account, and your father probably having insurance and all, you could really change your life."

Just discovering that my father had loved me all those years had already changed my life. I was completely confused. Everything I thought I knew about my father had turned out to be a lie.

After work, I stopped at my apartment and stuffed an overnight bag full of the things I would need to spend the night away from home, then I picked up a burger and fries at a fast-food joint, and returned to my father's house.

I turned on all the lights to drive away any dark shadows, and then I sat at the kitchen table eating my dinner and wondering how he had managed to live alone for so many years.

After I finished eating, I wiped off the table and the kitchen counters, and then I cleaned out the refrigerator, removing leftovers that had grown moldy in my father's absence. I carried a plastic bag filled with garbage to the can outside the garage, and then I returned to the kitchen.

As soon as I felt confident that I had the kitchen as clean as I thought my father would have kept it, I began dusting and vacuuming the rest of the house. He had obviously kept a clean home and I needed to do the same.

After I'd given the house the once-over, I carried my overnight bag into the guest bedroom. I unloaded my things, arranging them neatly in the dresser drawers. After I showered and changed into my nightshirt, I made the day bed with clean sheets from the hall closet, selected a book from all the gifts my father had left for me, and settled into bed to read.

I wondered if this is how my father had imagined my visits. Would he have read to me, or helped me select a book to read? Would he have kissed me goodnight and tucked me in? Would he have crossed the hall to his own bedroom, secure in the knowledge of his daughter's love?

And if this is what he imagined, how had he lived all those years without it? I wondered.

The next afternoon I sat with my mother in her kitchen, in the house where I'd been raised, sipping at a hot mug of coffee. The yellow linoleum floor had not changed since my father had left, though my mother had recently mopped it to a brilliant shine. The kitchen table and four chairs were less than a year old, my Christmas gift to my mother.

I remembered the kitchen as the place where my mother had bandaged my scrapes and kissed my bruises as I grew up; the place where she'd told me about the birds and the bees and the teenaged boys; the place where nearly every one of our heart-to-heart talks had ever taken place.

Without preamble, I said, "Dad died two weeks ago."

"Good riddance to bad news," my mother said. She had both hands wrapped around her coffee mug, griping it tightly, and I could see the veins in the backs of her hands throbbing. She squinted at me accusingly. "How'd you find out? I didn't see it in the paper."

I told her about the attorney's phone call and how it had led to my spending the previous afternoon in my father's house. I told her about everything I'd found, including all of my father's undelivered letters to me.

"He had a lot he wanted to tell me over the years," I explained. "It took hours to read through everything."

At first my mother seemed defiant, but the more I told her, the less defiant she became. Her shoulders slumped and she stared down at her now-empty coffee mug.

"He didn't love you," she insisted without quite looking at me. As she said it, she suddenly seemed older, like all the years of her life had just caught up with her. "He just did all that to spite me."

"For twenty years?" I asked.

"Sure," my mother said, but she didn't sound like she believed it herself. "Your father was like that."

I swallowed the last of my coffee, and then retrieved the pot from the coffee maker on the kitchen counter. I refilled both our mugs, and then returned the coffee pot to its place. As I returned to the kitchen table, I asked a question I had not asked in years, which my mother had never truly answered. "Why did he leave?"

"The marriage was over," my mother explained after a prolonged silence. "It had been over for a long time, but we still lived in the same house. We tried to hide it from you, but we fought all the time, about everything. We hadn't slept in the same bed for years. Every night after you went to sleep, your father would get out a pillow and make a place for himself on the couch."

"I never knew," I said. I remembered coming home from school and having my mother meet me at the door with a snack. I remembered helping my mother prepare dinner each evening so it would be on the table when my father arrived home from work. I remembered the weekends when my father would take me to the park or to the Saturday matinee at the Bijou downtown. But I did not remember them fighting, and I told my mother so.

"That's the way we wanted it," my mother continued. She looked down at the coffee mug as she spoke, not lifting her gaze even once. "We stayed together for you. That's what we told each other, but it just kept getting worse. We couldn't stand each other and it finally got so bad that we couldn't even pretend anymore."

"But. . . ."

She looked up at me finally. "Your father and I never should have married, but we had to. You were born two months after the wedding. If we had been more careful, we would have realized that we weren't right for each other, but we weren't careful. When I told your father I was pregnant, he insisted that we do 'the right thing' and get married. He gave up a college scholarship."

"So it's my fault?" I asked.

My mother shook her head. Wisps of gray hair floated around her head. "It was never your fault," she explained. "Your father and I were young, and stupid, and just didn't take precautions. That's all."

I said, "So you married young and became parents, and. . . ."

"And we just weren't prepared for any of it," my mother continued. "Your father found a job working as a janitor at one of the office buildings. Then he took a job on the assembly line at the bottling factory. We saved enough for a down payment on this house, and after we moved in things really got bad. We had everything we thought we had ever wanted—a house, a car, a family—but we didn't love each other. Before long we didn't even like each other."

My mother sipped from her coffee mug and we both sat in silence for a moment. Then she continued.

"Your father found out I was having an affair with . . . well, his name isn't important now," she said. She gripped her coffee mug so tightly her knuckles were turning white. "He worked the nightshift at the same factory where your father worked. He would come over during the day when you were at school and your father was at work. He made me feel alive, like a whole woman again."

She finally looked up, watching me carefully and studying my reaction. "Then your father found out. He left the next day. When I told the other man that we were divorcing and that I would be free to marry him, he dropped me—stopped coming by, and stopped calling."

I had just learned more about my mother than I ever really wanted to know, but she still hadn't told me what I most wanted to know. "That doesn't explain why you drove my father away."

"I couldn't stand the thought that you might love him more than you loved me," she said. "So I wouldn't let him talk to you when he phoned and I returned all of his letters. I told you he didn't love you. The truth was, he didn't love me and I didn't love him. It was my way to hurt him, to take the one thing away from him that he actually cared about."

"But when you took me away from him, you also took him away from me," I said.

"I didn't see that at first, and by the time I realized it, it was too late." My mother shook her head and looked down at her coffee mug again. "Too late."

We sat together for a long, long time after that, not speaking, not even looking at one another. My mother finally broke the silence sometime later when she asked, "You have dinner plans? I could make a salad."

That summer I moved from my one-bedroom apartment into my father's house. I used the money from his life insurance policy to pay his medical bills and the cost of his cremation. I used the rest of the life insurance settlement, the money from his retirement fund at the plant, and the child support money he had diligently saved for me, to support myself when I entered college that Fall. According to his letters, it had been my father's dream to see his daughter go to college, and in this, I could not disappoint him.

He had done far more for me than I had ever imagined, had loved me even when he received no love in return, and had left me with a house full of memories I had yet to explore.

My mother and I never spoke about my father again.
THE END

CONFESSIONS OF A CREDIT CARD JUNKIE
"I Can't Stop!"

"Look, Janice! They sent me my new charge card! Isn't it pretty? Now I can buy that new dress I've been wanting."

My sister frowned. "How many cards do you have, Heidi? Couldn't you use one of the others?"

I smiled; blissfully unaware of the hole I was digging for myself. "I have five other cards, but they're all maxed out. How can I stay sexy for Carl unless I keep myself up? He likes me to look hot." I laughed and danced around, waving the card. "And a girl can't do that without a little help from her friends."

Janice shook her head at me. "You're heading for trouble, I hope you know that. How much more do you think you can charge and still be able to pay your bills?"

"You worry too much. My husband gives me plenty of money for the bills and I pay the minimum payment on each one. There's no problem that I can see."

How I wish I'd listened to Janice's warning. I might have saved myself some grief if I had, but I'm hardheaded and a slow learner to boot. I didn't bother worrying about details, as long as everything went smoothly and I got what I wanted.

I paid all the bills and knew that unless he checked, Carl would never find out. He had no idea what was going on and I didn't plan to tell him, either. Why ruin a good thing?

It only took a few weeks to reach the limit on the latest card. Meanwhile, another offer arrived in the mail and I greedily applied for it, too. You'd think my husband would've questioned me about all the expensive clothes stuffed into my closet, but poor Carl was so busy at work that most stuff slipped by him. If he did ask, I lied and told him Mom or Dad bought it for me. Mom had recently received an inheritance from an aunt. Carl believed it was a sizable sum and he knew my parents liked to spoil me.

Of course it helped that I started tucking away most of my clothes in other closets that Carl never used. He had no idea what was in them and I always kept them closed.

In addition, I had enough earrings to supply a small army, but he didn't know about those, either. I grew obsessed with making purchases. The more I made the better I felt. I guess you could call me a shopping junkie.

Six months and three credit cards later, Carl came home early one evening and brought the mail with him. Tossing it aside, he stood there watching me. My pulse began to race wildly. Are you on to me, Carl?

"Hi, honey. I got off work early and thought I'd surprise you." He grinned and handed me a bouquet of pink carnations. "Thought you might like these."

"Thank you, Carl! You're such a sweetie," I gushed, hoping he didn't notice my hands shake as I took the flowers.

He retrieved the stack of white envelopes from the coffee table. "Here's the mail. Are all these banks trying to get us to open an account or something?"

I took a deep breath and forced a smile. "I'm sure it's just garbage."

"Good. I'll toss them in the trash for you."

"No! Don't do that!"

"What's wrong?" he asked, looking at me strangely.

"Nothing. Sorry. I've had a bad day. Janice called and you know how she can upset me sometimes. Here, let me take the mail. I need to go through each item and make sure there's nothing important inside. You never know, honey." I laughed. "Someone might be sending us some money."

I ran to the post office the next morning and opened a box. It was the only way I could make sure that Carl didn't get his hands on the bills again. What if he'd opened one and read it? Back at home I busied myself with making out change of address forms to mail in to the credit card companies. The doorbell rang and I left the cards lying on the kitchen table while I ran to see who it was.

"Lisa, what are you doing here? You usually call before you come over."

"I thought I'd surprise you. You have an odd look on your face, sis. What's going on?"

She pushed her way into the house before I could stop her and she headed for the kitchen.

"Put some coffee on. We haven't had a good chat in a while."

I hurried ahead of her and stood in front of the table, trying to block her view, but she glanced over my shoulder and spotted the credit cards.

"What on earth? Don't tell me all those credit cards are yours. Is this the reason you don't act pleased to see me? Are you trying to hide them?"

"No, of course not, silly."

Lisa strode over to the table where she proceeded to rifle through the stack of cards. I heard her give a low whistle.

"Put those down!" I demanded.

Lisa ignored me. "Nine cards! Why do you need so many?"

"Some of them are Carl's. I'm going through them to decide which ones to keep. The rest I'm going to cancel."

"Funny, I don't see Carl's name on any of them. Are you in trouble, Heidi? What does Carl say, or does he not even know about this?"

She stared hard at me for several long moments. "That's it, isn't it? You've kept this from Carl and you're worried I'll tell him."

"No, of course not," I lied. "Carl knows about them. We don't keep secrets from each other. The reason you don't see his name is that I'm using my cards. He has the same ones and I'm going to cut them up as soon as I write the letters."

"You're lying. I can tell by the fidgeting and the way you avoid looking at me. Please take a step back and see what you're doing. I don't think Carl will tolerate this and it could ruin your marriage. This sounds like an addiction, Heidi, and I know someone you can talk to. He's a therapist, and a friend of mine. Can I call him?"

"Absolutely not!" My voice grew shrill. "I'm not addicted to anything. How dare you imply I am?" I gathered the credit cards and tucked them away in a drawer, refusing to make coffee. My tone was icy. "I want you to leave."

I almost had to push her out the door, but Lisa finally left. "I'll be back," she promised as I closed the door and locked it.

I knew what would happen next. Lisa would run to Janice and the two of them would gang up on me. If they got Dad involved, I was in for trouble. Dad believes in honesty and he'd feel Carl should know the truth. Knowing Dad, he'd go straight to Carl and then my husband would know my ugly little secret. I could only guess what he'd do next.

I shook all over as I raced to the medicine cabinet and took a sedative I'd taken from my mother's prescription bottle. There was only one left and I knew I'd have to swipe some more soon. Mom didn't know that I took a few out here and there. A few minutes later I had calmed down and almost forgotten about my sister's visit. I'd figure out a way to deal with my family. I had to. Meanwhile I picked up the phone and punched in a few numbers.

"This is Heidi Lewis and I'd like to make an order, please. I rattled off the product number of the outfit I'd seen in the catalog. It was green, my favorite color, and I knew Carl would adore me in it. I thanked the person who took my order and hung up feeling a whole lot better.

That night I put on a sexy, new nightgown I'd purchased the week before. I wanted to have my husband admire me in it. Keeping him busy like that helped divert his attention from other matters.

I called Lisa a few days later.

"Hi, sis. I want to apologize for the other day. You were right and

I want you to know that I've made an appointment to see a therapist."

"That's wonderful, Heidi. Who is it?"

I rattled off a name from the phone book and after chatting a few minutes, I hung up. Lisa sounded convinced about my seeing a therapist and if I were careful, that would be the end of it. The lies were starting to pile up and I felt a twinge of guilt over it, but I quickly pushed it away. If people minded their own business I wouldn't have to lie.

My credit card debt grew larger and larger. I kept charging. I couldn't help myself, but I refused to believe I had a problem, or find help. Carl still hadn't caught on, but things changed one evening when I got a phone call from Dad.

"I've taken your mom to the emergency room."

I called Carl and told him, then raced over to the hospital. Daddy got up from his seat in the waiting room, took me in his arms, and held me.

"What's wrong with Mom? Is she going to be all right?"

My sisters arrived before he could answer and we shared a group hug.

"Your mother had a mild heart attack. They're running tests right now, but the doctor thinks she'll be okay."

We stayed at Dad's side until he finally ordered us to leave. "Go home, girls. Your mother needs her rest. Don't worry; I'll call if anything changes."

"But, Daddy. . . ." Lisa sputtered.

"I'll be fine. Get out of here."

Carl sat in the living room waiting for me when I got home. "Why didn't you come to the hospital?" I asked. "I missed your support and so did Daddy."

"That's not what he said. Yes, I called; I guess he forgot to tell you. He told me to stay home, that your mother is going to be fine. He said it'd be better if I went over tomorrow to visit."

"Oh. Well, I'm tired. I think I'll go to bed then."

"Why do we have so many credit card statements?"

"Pardon me, what did you say?" My heart thudded against my chest. I remembered Dad calling just as I'd come home from the post office and in the confusion I must have forgotten and left the bills on the table.

"We have five credit card bills here and every one of them shows they've reached their limit. What's going on?"

"Oh, it's nothing. We only have five cards, honey, and I'm sorry. I've been buying all the groceries and paying bills with them. I pay the minimum payment on each one, so there's nothing to worry about."

"You need to start paying more on them and pay them off. I don't like being in debt like this. I mean it, Heidi. Stop making all these charges or I'll cancel your cards."

Carl stomped away. He was angry with me and I couldn't blame him. Why did Mom pick today to get sick? A fresh wave of guilt washed over me. What am I doing blaming my mother for this? And why is Carl checking on me? Doesn't he trust me?

I hurried into the bathroom and locked the door. There was a new supply of pills I'd stolen and hidden in my vitamin bottle. I popped one, washing it down with a glass of water. There. I'll be fine, I promised myself. No use getting upset. I have this all handled. I just have to make sure my husband never gets his hands on one of the bills again.

With that in mind, I drove to the local hardware store the next morning and purchased a fireproof metal safe. I could store the bills inside, lock it, and hide the key. I knew Carl wouldn't force the lock open, but he might question its contents. I hid the safe on the floor in back of one of the spare closets as an added precaution. Then I piled stuff on top of it. I stepped back and surveyed my handiwork, feeling pleased with myself for being so clever. Carl will never find it there. As a final measure I stowed the keys inside one of the socks in my underwear drawer.

We were sitting at the dinner table one evening when Carl first quizzed me about the bills again.

"What's happened to all the credit card bills, Heidi? I looked in the file cabinet for them, but all I could find was utility bills. Do you have a special place where you keep them?"

Evading his question, I asked, "Are you planning on taking over the job of paying the bills, honey?"

"No, I just wanted to see if you're paying them down like I told you to."

"Of course I am. In fact I paid one off the other day and am working on the others. With any luck, we'll be debt-free by the end of the year."

"So, where are the receipts?"

"I keep all that stuff ground up in the shredder, Carl. Experts say not to keep it around in case a thief might get hold of it. You don't want to deal with identity theft, do you? I've heard some real horror stories about that."

Carl frowned. "The next time you receive a bill I want to see it."

I didn't say anything, hoping I could figure out a way to stall him when the time came.

The phone rang and I let Carl answer it, hoping the call would distract him so he'd forget about the bills for a while. It worked because he dropped the subject.

I spent the next few weeks working hard to come up with phony bills that would convince Carl I was telling the truth. After hours of trial and error I managed to take one of the old bills and make a copy that looked reasonably real. Pleased with my success, I printed out a few more bogus bills and filed them. Carl must have found them because he never said another word about it. I pushed my guilt aside, pleased that my cleverness had fooled my husband. Now that Carl's off my case I can get back to having fun again.

I still refused to realize I was in trouble and kept busy buying anything that caught my fancy. At Christmas and on birthdays I usually charged elaborate gifts and gave them to friends and family. Deciding to avoid arousing further suspicion, I cut back on spending, giving fewer and less costly gifts. That action alone worked to convince Carl and my sisters that I'd cleaned up my act. How easy it was to fool them.

Shopping had become a drug to me, but it wasn't the only one I needed because I was still using tranquilizers a couple of times a week. Mom's bottle kept me supplied with enough to get me by. Life was becoming a blurry haze of packages arriving in the mail and searching the Internet, TV, and catalogs for new items to buy.

One evening I prepared a large dinner to surprise Carl. I'd been feeling guilty about deceiving him and decided to make his favorite lasagna. It sat on the counter ready to serve, but Carl didn't come home at his usual time. The meal was starting to get cold and I began to worry that something had happened.

I picked up the phone, but the front door slammed and I put it down as Carl walked into the kitchen.

"You're late, honey. I made lasagna for dinner and it's getting cold."

"Thanks, but I'm not hungry. You can go ahead and eat, Heidi, and then put it away. Maybe I'll eat some later."

"I went to a lot of trouble tonight. The least you can do is eat some of it. It ticks me off that you didn't call and let me know you'd be late."

Carl sat down at the table and stared at his hands. "I have some bad news, Heidi. They laid me off today."

I walked over and put my hand on his shoulder, but he shrugged it off. "You've been drinking, haven't you?" I accused, as my voice grew shrill. Then it hit me. "You're fired? But how can they do that? You've always been a good worker for that company. Can't you make them change their minds?"

My heart was sinking fast. What will I do about the bills?

"No. They laid off half the workforce today. They told me as soon as business picks up again they'll hire me back, but there's no guarantee of when that will be. We're going to have to scale back our spending until I can find something else. I'm sure glad you've been paying down the credit card debt."

He must have seen the panicked look on my face. "You have been paying the bills, haven't you?" His face grew redder. "How much do we owe, Heidi?"

I ran to the bathroom, closed the door, and threw open the

medicine cabinet. The few pills I'd stolen from Mom were gone. I'd taken the last one the other day. The pounding on the door made me drop the bottle and it skittered across the floor.

"Open up! You and I need to talk!" Carl roared.

When the door banged open, I realized that I'd forgotten to secure the lock. My angry husband stood there glaring at me with his fists clenched.

"I asked you a question. Tell me how much money we owe."

"I don't know," I yelled.

"You've been lying to me all along, haven't you? What's this?" Carl stooped down and picked up the empty bottle.

"I was going to take some valerian root to help calm me down."

"Why doesn't it say that on the bottle?"

"I don't know. Stop quizzing me. How can I think when you're accusing me of stuff I didn't do?"

"Shut up! Just shut up!" he hollered.

I realized I'd pushed Carl over the edge with my lies. I'd never seen my husband so angry before. I considered sprinting for the door and trying to escape, but knew it was futile because I'd have to face Carl sometime. I figured I might as well get it over with. I followed him out of the bathroom and through the house as he searched room by room.

"You're making a mess, Carl," I said in a hollow tone.

"I'm not worried about it," he snarled. "Look at all this stuff. Where did you get it? And don't tell me your parents bought it for you. I mentioned something about all their gifts the other day and the blank looks on their faces told me all I needed to know. Lying seems to be the norm with you, doesn't it?"

I refused to answer, knowing I'd already convicted myself by my actions.

"What's in this? Where are the keys?"

Oh, dear heaven no! He's found the safe. I found myself starting to shake as I searched for another lie.

"I can't remember where I hid them."

My head swirled as I watched Carl pry open the safe. It only took a couple of minutes and he gasped when he saw the stack of bills inside. He started going through them one by one.

"I've counted twenty different credit card bills and they're all maxed out. Are you out of your mind, Heidi? How do you think we'll pay for these?"

"I just wanted to please you," I whined. "You like me to dress up and look beautiful, don't you?"

Carl rolled his eyes. "Get real," he snapped. "I never wanted this and you know it. You're just making up excuses for what you've done."

My husband was furious and deep down I knew I couldn't blame him. He sat on the floor amidst the pile of bills, looking as pale as the papers he read. It scared me to see him that way. Thinking to comfort him I reached down and touched his shoulder, but he pulled away.

"Don't touch me!"

He stood up, wadded up the bills, and tossed them on the floor. I followed him to our room, where he pulled three suitcases from the closet shelf.

"What are you doing?"

"What does it look like? I'm leaving you, because you're a liar and I can't take any more of it. Those cards are all in your name; I never signed or agreed to anything, so it's your problem. Find a good job. You'll need one."

He finished stuffing his clothes in the suitcases and slammed them shut. I stood in the doorway hoping he'd reconsider.

"Please don't go, honey. I love you. I know you love me, too. How can you do this?"

"I could ask you the same question. Good-bye, Heidi."

It took him two trips to get his stuff loaded into his truck, and then he was gone. My husband had left me and I was alone. How will I survive without him and pay my debts?

My fist hit the wall. How can he do this to me?

My screams turned to tears and I took an aspirin to quell the pain in my hand. Sleep eluded me that night and I got out of bed the next morning feeling like a truck had run over me. The doorbell rang just as I got out of the shower. I toweled off, threw on a robe, and ran to answer the door. It was Dad. His smile faded when he got a good look at my face.

"Heidi, what's wrong? You look like heck. What can I do to help?"

"He's left me. Carl's left me and I think he wants a divorce."

Dad held me as I wept. When I was through I pulled away and wiped my eyes on the tissue he handed me.

"Why would Carl leave you? I don't understand. He's a good man and this isn't like him."

"It's my fault, Dad. I lied to him and now that he's found out, he won't forgive me."

"Start from the beginning and explain all this to me so I can try to understand what's happening."

He led me to the couch and sat beside me as I gave him a tear-filled explanation. When I finished I turned away, unable to look my father in the eye.

"You must think I'm a terrible person, Dad."

"I don't think that, sweetie. But I do believe you need professional help."

"And this house, I can't afford it anymore. I'm going to be a homeless person, Dad."

Dad patted me on the shoulder. "It'll be all right, Heidi. You can move in with your mom and me. But first I want to set some ground rules."

"What . . . what are they?"

"I have an opening in my business and you can earn the money to start paying off your debts, but you can't have any credit cards. Is that clear?"

"Yes."

"And you'll have to see a therapist, someone who can help you learn to control this addiction of yours. It won't be easy, Heidi, but if you're willing to try, we'll be there for you every step of the way."

"Thanks, Dad," I said in a humbled tone.

Dad left me to go home and tell Mom what was going on. Mom came with him when he returned and they brought boxes to help me pack.

"My old room won't hold all of this stuff; do you think you, Janice, or Lisa might have room for some of it?"

Mom stopped what she was doing. "We don't have any place for all of it and neither do your sisters. Your father and I are here to help you pack and sort through this mess, but you'll have to get rid of most of it."

"She's right, honey. We can sell some of these clothes and use the money to reduce the credit card debt."

What could I say? I knew they were right, but it was difficult to get rid of my beautiful clothing. After I'd taken Mom on a tour of my closets and secret hidey-holes, she took a break. I think it was all a bit much for her seeing how much I'd bought.

"This is really unbelievable, Heidi. Why would you ever think you needed this much stuff? You could outfit half the women in this town and still have plenty to wear."

"Mom, would you mind if I borrowed one of your tranquilizers?"

"Don't you think you've borrowed enough? Yes, I know you've been swiping some of my pills and I've let it go on for too long. No more of my pills for you, my dear. I've stopped taking them anyway. When you see a therapist he may prescribe something for you, but until then you won't be taking anything. Not in my house."

The walls felt like they were closing in, but it was my own fault. I'd put myself there and I'd have to work hard to get myself out.

It took a week to sort through my belongings. It would've taken longer if my whole family hadn't pitched in to help. We packaged up several items and returned them for refunds, while others placed well in consignment shops. That still left me with an adequate wardrobe. The rest of my belongings were stored away for a future garage sale.

I remember cringing as I watched Dad toss a pile of catalogs into the recycling bin.

"It's necessary," he said softly. "They're part of the problem."

I nodded and looked down at the floor, willing myself to not cry. I'd done enough of that to last a lifetime.

My landlord refused to return my deposit, claiming I hadn't given him enough notice. I could've used the money, but there was nothing I could do about it. Dad advised me to cut my losses and move on.

He put me to work answering the phones at his office. "The sooner you start earning money," he said, "the quicker you'll get out of debt."

It took a month to get in to see a therapist and I began going once a week on my lunch break. Dad and Mom paid for my therapy, but told me I'd be paying them back.

Dad found out about my secret mailbox somehow and made me close it, saying, "There'll be no more secrets. Not under my roof."

He made me gather my credit cards and give them to him. Then he and Mom sat at the table cutting them up and checking to make sure they were all there.

"I know we appear hardnosed about this, dear, but you having a credit card is like an alcoholic with a bottle of whiskey. You just can't stop yourself from charging."

"I'm not that bad."

"Yes. You are."

Dad checked the mail every day for credit card offers. Any with my name on them ended up in the shredder. I don't know how many they threw out. They never told me and it was a good thing, for I still dreamed of having a credit card again. I had a long way to go to gain control of my shopping addiction and I'm pretty sure I know what would've happened if I'd wrapped my fingers around a credit card again.

I joined an online group for compulsive shoppers. Communicating with others that had the same problem helped. I didn't feel so alone in my struggle anymore. Maybe there is hope for me after all.

You'll probably laugh, but at night my dreams featured credit cards. They haunted me like ghosts. I dreamed of Carl, too, and happier times, wishing I hadn't ruined everything with my out-of-control spending. I expected the divorce papers to arrive any day, but they never came. I wondered why.

One evening about a year later, I was watching TV when the doorbell rang. Mom answered it and I heard her talking to someone. I went back to watching my show, thinking it was a salesperson.

"Heidi, there's someone here to see you."

"Carl! What are you doing here?"

I wanted to run into his arms and hug and kiss him, but I didn't dare. I couldn't bear it if he pushed me away.

"I heard that you're doing better. Your mom tells me that your therapist thinks you're starting to get better."

"I'm trying, but it isn't easy. I have to fight the urge to charge something every day. The good news is that each day it gets a little easier. And guess what? With Mom and Dad's help, I'm getting my debts paid."

"That's great! You're probably not aware of this, but I've kept in touch with your folks all along. I tried, but I couldn't go through with a divorce because I still love you. I came by to see if you'd like to give us another chance. Do you think that's possible?"

"I love you, too, Carl, but I'm not ready yet to work on our marriage. I'm still learning to control this monster inside me and I don't have time to work on us. Do you understand? When we get back together I want to devote my whole self to us. I'd be cheating you if we tried now."

"Thanks for being honest with me. Can I come by for a visit now and then? Would that be okay?"

"Sure, I'd like that."

Carl stayed for a while and we talked. Part of me wanted to tell him I'd changed my mind and would go home with him, but it wasn't right—not yet. It thrilled me to know he wanted me back and that gave me more incentive to get better.

How quickly time flies. My therapist gave me some wonderful news last week.

"I think you're well on the road to recovery now," he said with a smile.

That night in my room I closed my eyes and bowed my head. Thank You, Lord, for all of Your help.

Carl and I are talking about living together again. He's been very patient with me and I feel ready to be his wife again. I've learned the value of honesty and the damage lies can cause.

I'm truly blessed with a husband who's forgiven me, and a family who's stood behind me all the way. I'll never be totally free of my addiction, but I have all the support I need to help me keep it under control. Now it's up to me.

THE END

CONFESSIONS OF A NEGLECTFUL MOM
I Ditched My Kids To Run Wild With My Boyfriend

I felt a twinge of guilt as I dialed Kayla's number. But she was my best friend and, as such, she was always willing to help me out. I was asking her too much, of course, but who else could I ask? Mother had only met Ethan once and judged him within the hour, which I felt was terribly unfair. Dad wasn't any better. Really, how could anyone know what a person is like after being in their presence for one hour?

For a heart stopping moment I thought Kayla wasn't home, but she finally answered on the sixth ring. Her "hello" was breathless sounding. Out working in her flower beds, no doubt. Kayla was always doing something creative. I never could figure out where she found the time with four kids.

"It's me," I began gaily. "Vicki, your best friend!"

"I know," she responded and there was no answering gaiety in her voice. "If I'd known it was you, I'd have let it ring."

I felt my jaw drop in shock. Nice, gentle Kayla never took that tone with me. "What's wrong? Are you having a bad day?"

"My day was just fine, until now. You never call anymore unless you want something, and I'm wondering what it is this time."

I couldn't believe my ears. Kayla? I have known her for years. She was talking like I was someone she despised. I couldn't believe it. "I'm sorry you're not feeling well," I sympathized, trying hard to inject the proper amount of concern into my voice. "I need someone to watch my two urchins for the weekend. Are you up to it?"

Dead silence greeted my question. It went on and on. My heart started pounding. Something was wrong. "Hello," I sang. "Kayla, are you there?"

"Yes, I'm here!" It sounded like she was speaking through clenched teeth. "And no, I'm not taking care of your kids over the weekend again, so you can run off with your lover boy. I've taken care of them for the past three weekends, and it isn't going to happen again. Why don't you just put Lizzie and Kevin in a foster home, Vicki, and forget you're a mother? Get rid of the kids and just party with playboy Ethan."

My jaw literally dropped this time. Dad had called him the same thing: "playboy Ethan." But neglecting my kids? How dare Kayla suggest such a thing? "You're saying some pretty awful things, Kayla. I'm not a neglectful mother."

"Really!" my friend sneered. "You work, you're gone every weekend, you go out with lover boy how many times a week? When are you with your children, Vicki? When was the last time you helped them with their homework? When was the last time you cooked a meal for them and sat down and ate it with them? I think you're absolutely despicable, and I think your two kids should be taken away from you. Do you think Lizzie doesn't talk? That little girl knows what's going on and thinks you don't like her anymore, or Kevin. Ethan Harris is nothing but a womanizer; you're just another in his long list of women. Do you actually think he is going to marry you? You must be blind as a bat." By this time her voice was shaking. "Don't call again! I hope one day soon you get what you so richly deserve. Oh, if Nicholas could see you now!" She hung up the receiver so hard it hurt my ear.

Anger coursed through me. How dare she mention Nicholas! I suffered agonies over his death in an air force chopper, which was out on maneuvers. How dare she bring up his name! How dare she accuse me of the things she said? I am not a neglectful mother. Even as the denial raced through my mind, my conscience, so long stifled, rose up in protest.

I walked to my bedroom and looked at my opened suitcase. I was in the process of packing. I had taken off work early—again—but had left getting a babysitter until the last minute. Ethan would be picking me up at six, and I had no sitter for Lizzie and Kevin. I'd call him; maybe he knew of someone.

"Hello, darling," I said, once again voicing a gaiety that was false. "Problems. My usual babysitter can't sit. Have any ideas?"

He was annoyed; I knew this at once. "Now, isn't this the pits. Why did she back out the last minute?"

"Something else came up that she couldn't get out of," I lied. I would never tell Ethan I had only just asked. There were lots of little things like this I never told him. "Do you know of anyone?"

"Of course not!" His voice was brusque. "My friends have more sense than to have kids. Who wants to be tied down like that? Can't do a damn thing."

I bit my lip, my conscience rising up on two very strong legs. I knew Ethan had very little sympathy or interest in children, but he had never voiced it so blatantly before. "Well, Ethan, I'm one of those who never had much sense, I guess, because I have two."

"Can't you leave them with your mother?"

"Mom doesn't babysit except in an emergency," I said firmly. I could never tell him what my parents thought of him. Is it possible they could be right?

"Well," said the man I professed to love, "they'll just have to stay home alone, won't they?"

"Ethan, please," I protested. "Lizzie is only eight and Kevin is six. I can't leave them alone."

"Kids that age are left alone all the time."

"Maybe so, but it's not legal . . . and it's not right." An idea suddenly popped into my head. The kids at this moment were at the daycare where they went after school. Why not call Mrs. Blackmon, the director, and make some excuse about being late picking them up? They could stay with her over the weekend. I would get them Sunday afternoon, when I returned to town. "I've thought of something, Ethan. Pick me up at the scheduled time. Everything will be arranged."

"Good," was his brief reply, and he hung up with a bang.

I knew I was doing wrong as I dialed the daycare's number, but my own desires dampened down any misgivings that tried to rear their righteous heads. I wanted to be with Ethan. Nothing was going to stop me. Mrs. Blackmon could be talked around. I was good at that sort of thing. I was accustomed to getting my own way.

"Toyland Daycare," said a familiar voice.

"Oh, Mrs. Blackmon, this is Vicki Webb. An emergency has come up, and I'll be late picking up Lizzie and Kevin."

"You know the rules, Vicki," Mrs. Blackmon said in a no-nonsense voice. "Five dollars for every fifteen minutes over."

"Yes . . . yes, I know that," I bubbled glibly. What I planned to do was really awful, but it would be okay this one time. It had happened to Mrs. Blackmon a couple of times before and nothing drastic had happened. And why don't daycares operate on the weekends, for heaven's sake? It's so inconvenient. "Thanks, Mrs. Blackmon." She didn't say goodbye.

"So who is watching them?" Ethan asked after giving me a long kiss.

"The director of the daycare."

"That's cool of her. Maybe you can pay her some extra." He picked up my suitcase, and I followed him from the house and out to his Corvette, which didn't have room for children.

I would be paying Mrs. Blackmon a lot of money, but I wasn't telling Ethan. He wouldn't like that, either. Come to think of it, there was quite a list of things Ethan didn't like, as I was finding out. But he liked me—and wasn't that all that really mattered?

As we drove down the avenue, heading for the freeway, I tried to block my actions from my mind. I had changed a lot since dating Ethan, and the changes were not all good. In fact, if I were honest, none of the changes were good. I didn't want to think of any of this. Panic rose in my breast whenever I did. At the moment I wanted to be a party animal like Ethan. I'd had enough of responsibility, trying to raise two children all alone. I was tired of never having any fun, of counting pennies, of budgeting.

If spending lots of money has anything to do with pleasure, then I should have had a glorious time over the weekend. What interfered was the constant nagging at the back of my mind of what I had done to Mrs. Blackmon and Lizzie and Kevin. The nagging would persist, no matter how hard I tried to be cheerful and carefree. I should have called Mom and begged her to take the kids, but I was so tired of her sermonizing, deploring the changes in my life, my "neglect" of the kids, while I chased around like a besotted teenager. She was even worse than Kayla.

"What's wrong with you?" Ethan asked me sharply over dinner Saturday night. We were eating king crab from Alaska.

I glanced up, petrified he could read my thoughts. "Why do you ask?"

"You seem preoccupied. Don't you like the crab?"

"Of course I do; it's wonderful. I can't help wondering how my kids are getting along."

"Drop the kids!" he exploded. "I'll make sure my next girlfriend doesn't have any."

Icy fingers touched my heart, hampering my breathing. His "next girlfriend?" The words rang in my ears. I'm not permanent then? Already, while with me, he could think of the next woman in his life? But why was I surprised? He told me when we met he had never married and never planned to. "Being tied down" wasn't for him. I, of course, was going to change him, make him into something he wasn't and had no desire to be. In my own mind I already was Mrs. Ethan Harris.

"You're a beautiful woman, Vicki, but having two kids certainly doesn't enhance your image."

My smile was so stiff I thought all the muscles in my face might crack and hang in shreds from my face. I forced Lizzie and Kevin to the back of my mind and tried very hard to act happy, without a care in the world.

Like Ethan, who really didn't care about anything—including me.

This truth hit me between the eyes with such staggering force I felt lightheaded. For the past three months I had lived in la-la land and that night he brought me back to homespun reality with his careless remark.

I took a deep breath and smiled sweetly at him. The charade that I loved so much must go on for a few more hours.

We left the lakeside resort at four on Sunday afternoon. It was a two-hour drive to the city. Ethan wanted to stay until evening, but I finally found the courage to demand an earlier departure. He sulked for the first hour of the drive and every nagging doubt I'd ever had about this man in our three-month relationship came back full-force.

What had ever made me dream this man would ever, or could ever, be a father to children, to stepchildren? I was out of my mind; Dad was right. Ethan was a playboy, nothing more, nothing less, totally self-indulgent. A woman had no say in his life. This moment he was sulking like a wayward child because I had insisted on leaving earlier than he wanted to. I let him sulk.

The enormity of what I had done hit me as we drove home. I broke out in a sweat, my heart palpitated, I felt like I was suffocating. What excuse was I going to give Mrs. Blackmon? It had all seemed so reasonable, so uncomplicated Friday, before leaving town with Ethan. Now, in my panic, I tried to think of a reason to give her, but my mind, usually so agile, refused to cooperate. There was no reason I could give; I had abandoned my children for the weekend.

"You're awfully quiet," Ethan said finally,

I stretched on the luxurious leather seat and feigned happiness. "I'm just tired. We crowded a lot into a couple days."

He reached over and patted my thigh. "Yes, we did, didn't we, Vick? We'll do it again next weekend. You're a lot of fun to be with, and it's great to have the other guys envying me—me with such a gorgeous woman."

Two days ago I would have glowed under such a compliment. But not that day. I felt sick. My smile of thanks was forced, but he didn't seem to notice. He was full of himself and spent the next hour describing his plans for the following weekend. Not once did he ask if this was okay with me, nor did he ask what I would like to do. But why should he? Never once in our three-month relationship had I suggested a change, or offered the slightest resistance to anything. I had been like a robot, a zombie, a programmed Barbie doll in his hands, one who smiled and joked and said all the right things at the right time. What happened to me? I was never like this before in my life.

Had pleasure and money corrupted me? Was it the same with all his women? They floated along beside him for a time, but once they demurred about anything, or suggested something else, did he drop them like a hot rock and move on to another fool like me?

Ethan left me on my doorstep quickly and efficiently, with a quick kiss and a hurried "I'll call you at noon about tomorrow evening." He ran to his Corvette and roared off down the street. What was his hurry? I should have told him what I really did in order to spend the weekend with him. What a fool I had become. Now I was left alone to face the harsh reality. With growing fear I unlocked my front door and stepped inside with my suitcase. It was ten minutes after six.

I walked the floor for several minutes, trying to gather my courage, to think up an explanation to give Mrs. Blackmon. I thought of calling my parents first and rejected that idea.

My fingers were trembling as I dialed Mrs. Blackmon's number. Her husband answered the telephone. "This is Vicki Webb." My voice was a whisper.

"Oh, it's Vicki, is it, finally making an appearance? Your kids are with your parents; the police have been notified of your actions. Don't bother calling again, and you'll be getting our bill Monday, and we expect immediate payment." The receiver crashed in my ear.

Slowly I placed the receiver in its cradle. So Mom and Dad had Lizzie and Kevin. In a way I was relieved. I could talk my way around them surely and explain . . . something. It wouldn't be the same as telling my story to the police. Besides, the kids loved their grandparents and enjoyed going to their house. However, I was still filled with misgivings as I dialed their number. I let it ring and ring, but there was no answer. Well, maybe they were out to dinner. It was six-thirty.

I carried my suitcase into the bedroom and began unpacking. Any fleeting enjoyment experienced over the weekend evaporated under the pressure of a heavy foreboding. I willed myself to call my parents every fifteen minutes, when I wanted to dial and redial and redial. While waiting I paced the floor, consumed by fear.

My parents were not the kind to make idle threats. Both, I knew, were outraged at my behavior the past three months, but I went on my way glibly, obsessed with Ethan.

I'd never had a relationship with a man like him before—a man who lived for fun, for pleasure and excitement and with the money to finance that lifestyle. I was caught up in the exhilaration of it all, neglecting everything I once held dear: my children, my home, my job, my standards, my parents' concern, friends—everything. But, surely, I could be excused this once. I had been alone ever since Nicholas died, struggling between job and raising children alone, being lonely, desperate at times for someone to talk to, to share my thoughts, longings . . . everything else I missed as a single parent. It was dreadful, awful, so terribly unfair that Nicholas had to die the way he did.

At eight-thirty I resigned myself to the fact that if Mom and Dad were home, they weren't answering the phone, which meant I had to face them and their wrath. I gritted my teeth, got my purse, and walked out to my little car parked in the driveway. What a far cry my little second-hand Honda was from Ethan's Corvette.

My parents lived five miles from my house. I drove slowly. Yes, they were home. Dad's pickup was parked in front of the garage;

Mother's car was probably inside the garage. I pulled in behind his and sat for long moments, trying to collect my thoughts, but I didn't have any to collect. My mind was numb; I could think of no excuse for my actions, other than the reason: I wanted to go. I chose to go. It was all that mattered Friday afternoon. But I couldn't say that.

As I got out of the car Dad walked out the front door. He held a paper in his hand. I have never seen him look so grim, so cold, so unloving. Any words I was going to say died on my lips. "I suppose you think you've come to pick up your children." His voice matched his face.

"Yes," I said, not able to meet his eyes.

"Here." He thrust the paper at me. "Read this."

I took it and tried to glance over the printed sheet, but could make so sense of it. "What is it?"

"Due to your abandonment of your children over the weekend and your general neglect of them these past three months, your mother and I now have custody of Lizzie and Kevin. This is a restraining order. You are not to come near either of them at our house, or at school. If you want to know all the details about this weekend, you can visit the police station." He turned on his heel and walked back to the house, up the steps, and closed the door behind him.

I stood rooted to the ground, unable to move or think. I have no idea how long I stood there, an image in stone, stunned at the consequences of my behavior. All I could think of was, No, no, no. . . .

Finally I turned and walked the few steps to my car. I have no idea how I drove home.

I spent the night walking the floor, too numb to cry, wanting to die, having no idea what to do. Phoning Ethan wasn't even an option. And I thought I wanted to marry this man? For three months I had become insane. I could think of no other explanation. He would laugh in my face and say, "Good riddance, Vick. Why the hysterics?"

I was insane. How could I have let him control me like that? I was a thirty-year-old woman, the mother of two children. I held a responsible job. Nicholas, my husband, was gone, dead these two years. I had always accepted my responsibilities until I met Ethan Harris. Surely I wasn't going to be punished to this degree for making one mistake. I'd never make such a mistake again. There would be no more dates with Ethan; no more weekends spent together.

Sanity had returned, and I questioned that very sanity that allowed me to become insane for three months. Was it because of the pressure, being alone, juggling a full-time job? Maybe I'd never know. Maybe I'd just have to accept the fact that for three months I lost all my bearings and, as a result, lost my children . . . as well as my self-respect.

I could not lose my job; I could not. No matter how desperate I felt I had to show up for work at nine Monday morning and operate my computer and process car insurance claims. I had to.

Perhaps it was my job that helped save me in the end. I had to get up every morning and go to work; I had to dress properly; I had to eat a little. My fellow employees were concerned for me, not that they said much. We never had that kind of relationship. Each of us was alone in our little cubicle, staring at a monitor, breaking only for coffee and the lunch hour. But I looked like death warmed up. Some of the women knew I had a boyfriend, and I just told them he had jilted me. I never told them I lost my children. None of them knew Ethan, thank goodness. But they offered their sympathy and clucked their tongues at his unfaithfulness. It was a joke, but one I had to live through.

Ethan was gone, on to his next girlfriend. I did call him that Monday morning and told him the kids had been taken away from me. He had little to say, although he was surprised. "Bum rap" was the expression he used. He never called again, and I never called him. Sometimes I wondered if I should try and find out who his present girlfriend was and warn her. Would she listen? No, she would be like me, tied up in the excitement of what money can buy in the way of pleasure.

I got Mrs. Blackmon's bill: five dollars for every fifteen minutes over closing time, which was six. I wrote out a check, using my grocery money for that week. I didn't feel like eating, anyway.

I made an appointment with Children's Services, of course, and tried to explain what happened in a way that made sense. I was told I would get my children back, if I proved myself responsible and took a parenting class. They would monitor my progress. I swallowed my pride—did I actually have some left?—and took the evening class, which lasted two months. They didn't teach a thing I didn't already know and practiced until I got involved with Ethan.

A month after my last date with Ethan, I discovered I was pregnant and realized in stunned disbelief there is no such thing as "safe sex." I contemplated suicide; I contemplated an abortion. I lay awake at night, hating myself, hating Ethan, hating the world, hating the military that had taken Nicholas from me.

I finally rejected suicide and an abortion. They were both murder. I would carry the baby growing inside me and give it up for adoption. For the first time I was glad Lizzie and Kevin were gone. There was no one to see my morning sickness, my noon sickness, my evening sickness.

My next moves were carefully planned. I made an appointment with a local adoption agency, which set up an appointment with the doctor who would handle my case. It was all very easy. The hard part was carrying the baby full-term and hiding my pregnancy from everyone. Gradually, I changed my style of clothing to the baggy type with no waistline, the type of style I previously hated. Because I'm tall and have plenty of room to carry a growing fetus, my past pregnancies never showed much. This time it couldn't show at all. My mind was fiercely made up on this point.

At the end of my parenting class I was permitted to speak to my children once a week: Sunday afternoon at three. They called me; I did not call them because I did not want to talk to my parents. I knew I had done wrong; I didn't need Mom and Dad to add to my feelings of guilt. The authorities need not have been called, I reasoned, when I lay in bed at night, unable to sleep. Dad could have handled the situation by himself. I felt a deep anger and hurt toward my parents and didn't know if I'd ever feel the same toward them again.

After the weekly parental meetings were over, I met twice a month with a family counselor who made reports on my "progress" to the local judge. I was working toward getting my children back, and she offered hope and was really my only source of encouragement during this time of pain and regrets.

I had cut any former friendships, whether they had anything to do with my losing custody of my children or not. I felt it best to start all over again and, at the present time, I was in limbo, until the baby I was carrying was born. I knew instinctively that former friends would want to talk about Ethan, my behavior, my parents, my losing the children—all of it, and I was having none of their advice, sympathy, or anything else they had to offer.

Was I bitter? You bet! I was bitter and hurt and resentful and angry—at myself, at Ethan, at Nicholas for dying. I had a lot of things to work through, and I wasn't going to be encumbered with unwanted friendships while I worked through all these issues. Not even the family counselor knew I was pregnant; only the adoption agency and my doctor knew.

At first the calls with my children were terribly painful, but gradually, over the weeks the long silences disappeared and we had a lot to talk about. When they began asking, "When can we see you, Mommy?" I would hang up in tears. However, the day did come when we were permitted to see each other. I dreaded the day, thinking they might see a difference in me, in the way I looked, might ask about my dress. I was filled with all kinds of fears. They were needless.

I picked them up Sunday afternoon and returned them at five. Mom and Dad never made an appearance, thank goodness. I had no desire to see or speak to them—not yet—although I was certain Mother watched from a window. As long as the weather held good I bought a meal from a drive-in for us, then took them to a city park where we ate, sitting on the lawn.

"I did a terrible wrong," I told them simply the first time we were together, "and now I'm paying for it. But we will be together again, I promise you."

"It's nice living with Grandpa and Grandma," Lizzie told me solemnly, "but I'd rather live with you, Mommy. We don't ever have to see Ethan again, do we?"

I hugged her. "No, dear, never again do you have to see Ethan. I never will, either. I made a terrible mistake."

They never brought up the subject again, but told me about school, little pieces of information about Mom and Dad. I came to believe they regretted getting the authorities involved, too, but once they did, there was nothing they could do about it.

I was in my ninth month. It was then that I took my vacation and hoped and prayed the baby would be born then. God must have heard my desperate plea and was more forgiving than friends and family. My plans had all been carefully made, and it seemed they were going to work out. Labor pains started at midnight the second day of my vacation, and I drove myself to the hospital and registered under the assumed name the doctor and I had worked out. The adoptive parents were paying all of the medical bills, of course, and the adoption agency took care of all the legal matters. All I had to do was have the baby.

I gave birth to a little girl at six in the morning. I did not see her; I had no desire to see her. She was never to be a part of my life. She was born healthy and that was all that mattered to me. The birth was easy, no complications, and I was released the next day, even driving myself home.

I walked into my home, weak, but delivered of the burden I had carried for nine months, glad it was over, and I could get on with my life. I went to bed, to rest, to gain physical strength, to plan my future, but my mind kept straying to the newborn I had left in the nursery. I knew that little girl would haunt me for the rest of my life. That was another fact I had to accept.

I had two weeks before returning to work. I was to have a hearing before the judge in two weeks' time as well. Everything had worked out perfectly, for which I would be eternally grateful to God. I would be under probation for a year, after the children were returned to me. "I suggest you not date during this time," my counselor had advised.

"Date!" I almost screamed the word. "I will not date until the kids are grown up."

"Well . . . I'm not sure you have to take such drastic measures as that," she said, rather surprised at my vehemence, I guess. However, I was dead serious.

Two days later I wandered through the house, feeling empty and lonely. My arms had never held the child. I knew I'd always feel that emptiness, that loss. What made it doubly hard was not being able to share with anyone. I could not; I was too ashamed. Perhaps one day in the far distant future I'd get married again, if I could ever let myself trust another man. He would have to be someone like Nicholas, my husband, who had been a gem. My moment of madness was in the past; I'd never commit such an outrageous act again.

What I really wanted to do was move away, to a new place, make new friends, a new beginning. But I was on probation for a year and had to report monthly to my officer and counselor, and they had to turn in their "progress" reports to the judge.

But I could make plans, couldn't I, about moving? Would it be fair to the children, once I got them under my roof again, to deny them a relationship with their grandparents? Just because I held animosity against them was no excuse to deny them a relationship. And they did love Grandpa and Grandma, and I knew my parents loved them dearly.

Well, I would just have to wait and see what the future held, how my own feelings changed. I knew in my heart I had to forgive my parents; they had only done what they thought was right for the children. I'm sure they thought I might move in with Ethan, or even marry him, and the children would suffer terribly.

In the meantime I had to take good care of myself and recuperate as much as possible in the time left from my vacation, so I could return to work. No one would be aware I had lived through a major crisis; no one knew but the doctor and the adoption agency.

The telephone rang, and I went to answer it. It was Mrs. Nelson, my counselor. "I have good news for you, Vicki. The judge has approved the children returning to you the end of the month. Isn't this wonderful news?"

"Yes . . . yes, that is wonderful news. Why, that's only a week away! I'll have to see about getting their rooms fixed up, to welcome them back." Suddenly I was crying. "The house has been so empty and lonely without them. I made a terrible mistake, Mrs. Nelson, and you can be assured I'll never do such a thing again."

Her voice was calm and soothing. "I know, my dear. I have gotten to know you quite well, and it's my opinion they should never have been taken from you. Well, congratulations. I'll be picking them up—remember, we discussed this—and bring them to your house. So, see you in a week, Vicki."

I settled myself on the sofa and had a good cry. Another phase of my life was going to begin. Actually, one that should never have been interrupted. But, thank God, I was being given another chance. All parents are not this lucky.

I went to the kitchen to prepare myself some lunch and was

exasperated at my weakness. Refurbishing Lizzie's and Kevin's rooms would have to wait until I regained my strength. I didn't think they would mind. We would be together again, and that was all that really mattered. I would have time to find another babysitting service, too . . . one closer to our home and to the school.

Yes, everything was going to be fin, after all.
THE END

CONFESSIONS OF A MURDERESS
I Killed My Own Mother

I turned off the car engine, looked at the dark house—and burst into tears.

Mother had turned off all the lights again to save a few pennies on our electric bill. Just once I'd have liked to come home to a house that had a light glowing in the window to welcome me home. I'd have liked to walk inside and find the house a comfortable temperature instead of finding it as cold as a tomb.

We were what people would call lower middle class, but that wasn't true. We were really a few notches lower than that, but not quite down to the poverty line. We could get by and pay our bills.

I've supported my mother and myself for ten years. She claimed her social security paid for everything, but it didn't; in fact, she put most of her money in her own account to save for her "old age." Mom was seventy; I guess she expected to live to be a hundred. She'd probably make it, but I didn't think I'd live much longer, though.

Sometimes I felt like I was already dead and I was just a zombie walking around. I'm thirty-two years old. I was secretly married once for two months when I was seventeen years old. I thought I was pregnant and when I told my boyfriend, we eloped. Then it turned out I wasn't pregnant; my period was just late. His parents and my mother agreed the marriage should be annulled. The boy never spoke to me again; I guess he thought I'd purposely tried to trap him.

That happened fifteen years ago, but Mom still brought it up about once a week.

People always asked me why I didn't just move away and cut my mother out of my life. I wished I could. I guess there were two reasons why I didn't. For one thing, I'm really religious and the Bible says to honor your mother and father. The other reason was that I didn't have any other family. My father died when I was ten, and I don't have any brothers or sisters or cousins or aunts or uncles. I just had Mom.

She always said that it was the two of us against the world. That made us sound like we were a team, but we weren't.

In spite of everything, I did love her. I guess I thought if I loved her enough, she'd love me a little, too.

I unloaded the groceries out of the car and took them into the cold, dark house.

"Is that you, Nora?" she hollered from the living room, where the only light was coming from the television.

"Of course, Mom—who else would it be?" I said and turned on the light in the kitchen. She'd replaced the 100-watt bulb I had in the overhead light and put in a 60-watt bulb.

I put the groceries away and started dinner. I worked as a waitress in a small café. Mom was always asking me why I couldn't bring home food from the café. I told her it was against the law, otherwise I'd be bringing home wilted lettuce and stale bread every night.

I cooked dinner and sat down next to her and stared at the TV screen without really seeing it.

"The new preacher will be at church Sunday. I hope he doesn't try to change anything or have any new-fangled ideas," Mom said.

"I'm sure he'll be fine," I said.

"Well, we'll have to wait and see, now won't we? Unless you are some kind of fortune teller and you can see the future. Or maybe you're a genius and you know everything. Do you know everything?" she demanded.

"No, I don't know anything at all," I said. I was tired and I didn't want to argue that night. "I think I'll go take a bath and go to bed early."

"Don't fill the tub up all the way. I know you do that. I know you fill it up all the way. That is a waste of water and a waste of electricity to heat up all that water. You can get clean with a half of a tub of warm water," she said and adjusted her footstool.

"Is your knee bothering you?" I asked, hoping to change the subject.

"It always bothers me. The cold weather makes it worse." She rubbed her knee. "Ever since I fell and broke it last year it has never stopped hurting."

I bit my lip to keep from saying that if she'd turn up the heat, her knee might not hurt so much, but I knew it was a waste of time.

I took my steaming hot bath and filled the tub so full it almost ran over. It was a stupid thing, a small thing. My victories over my mother might seem small to other people, but they were big to me—a hot bath with the water up to the brim of the tub, 100-watt light bulbs, occasionally buying a brand name of something instead of buying the cheapest generic store brand.

"One of us has to die," I said as I closed my bedroom door and shoved the throw rug up against the door so she couldn't see the light under the door. I wanted her to think I was asleep. I bought a romance novel at the store and didn't want her to know it. For one thing, she'd have a fit if she knew I bought a book when there was a library two blocks away, where I could check out books for free. For another thing, she didn't approve of romance novels. She called them "sexy-dirty filth."

I read for three hours and turned off my light. I wanted to read the whole book that night, but then I wouldn't have anything to look forward to the next night, so I saved the rest of the book to read later.

"Yeah, one of us has to die," I said and fell asleep.

The next day was Sunday and we went to church like we did every Sunday for as long as I could remember. We'd outlasted three ministers and most of the congregation. We always sat in the second pew. No one dared sit in our place; it was as if there was a reserved sign hanging there. If we didn't make it to church because of the weather or because Mom wasn't feeling well, I'm sure our place remained vacant, as if our ghosts were sitting there.

The new minister approached the pulpit. He was middle aged, mostly bald, and had a bit of a belly, but he had a nice face.

"Good morning, my beloved friends," the new minister began. "I'm Pastor Reichman and I hope I'll be serving you for a long time. Today, my first sermon will be on the Fifth Commandment, honor thy father and thy mother."

I slumped down in the pew. How many times have I heard this sermon? I had hoped the new pastor would have something different to say. Mom sat up straighter and lifted her head up and smiled. Well, the pastor certainly got on her good side already.

"The Bible says we are to 'honor' our mother and father. It doesn't say we have to love them or even like them," the pastor said.

Several people in the congregation laughed. Now I sat up straighter and mother frowned.

"We are to respect our mother and father, to be civil and polite to them. God never said to love them. He didn't say to obey them—He said to be polite to them." He smiled.

More people laughed.

Mom didn't approve of laughing in church. She pressed her lips together into a line across her face.

The people were laughing, the pastor was laughing, the music was upbeat and happy. I'd never enjoyed church as much as I did that day and I decided to make an appointment with the pastor to talk to him about what I should do with Mom.

As we drove away from church I felt as light as a feather.

"We'll have to find a new church. That man is spouting blasphemy! He'll be struck down. He'll burn in hell—mark my words!" Mom was breathing so heavily her nostrils were flared. She hadn't been that angry in ages.

I wanted to laugh, but I didn't. I'd laugh later when I was alone.

On Wednesday I left work early and went to the church. I'd already

"Mom!" I screamed. "Oh, God, I didn't mean it! Don't let her be dead!"

I kept expecting her to get up and yell at me. The house was quiet. It was quiet for the first time in my life.

I ran to the phone and started to call 911. Then I froze.

An hour ago, I'd told Pastor Reichman that I hated my mother and wished she were dead. The last thing I'd said to him was, "I'm going to do it." I meant I was going to move out, but what if he thought I meant I was going to kill my mother?

Who would believe it was an accident? People would think I pushed her down the stairs. I'd spend the rest of my life in prison!

Oh, why didn't I move out yesterday, a week ago, a year ago, ten years ago? Why did I wait too long? Now it was too late.

She was dead and I should be free, but people would think I murdered her. Maybe I did kill her. I threw the penny at her. I should have known she'd try to pick it up. What if I did it on purpose? What if I really did mean to kill her? I killed my own mother for a penny!

I kept expecting her to get up, to yell at me. Her mouth was open, but she'd never yell at me again.

Crazy things started going through my head. What if I burned the house down? What if I just got in my car and drove away and just drove forever and changed my name and started over in another state? What if I buried her body in the basement?

I could do it. She wasn't that big. I could drag her down the stairs into the basement and bury her. The only time anyone ever saw her was at church. If we didn't show up, people would think we'd quit because we didn't like Pastor Reichman. If anyone called, I'd say her knee was worse and she didn't feel like going out—but I knew no one would call. We didn't have any real friends.

I didn't know what to do, so I did nothing.

I didn't call 911. I didn't bury her. I didn't run away.

Instead, I took off my coat and laid it over her head. I turned on all the lights in the house. I even turned on the television.

I went into the kitchen and opened up a can of tomato soup and fixed a grilled cheese sandwich. Then I sat at the table and ate it—and pretended my mother's body wasn't lying in the hallway.

I was going to go to prison for murder. Honor your mother . . . that means to respect your mother. It means . . . don't kill your mother.

"I'm sorry, I'm sorry, I'm sorry," I whispered as I washed my dishes. "I'm sorry. . . ." I kept repeating.

I paced the floor until midnight. Mother had been dead for six hours. I was going to prison and then I was going to die and I was going to hell.

I couldn't call the police. I'd waited too long now. They'd ask why

I'd waited six hours and why I'd eaten dinner while my mother's body laid there getting cold. I had only one person I could call. Maybe he'd pray to God to forgive me.

"Pastor Reichman?" I asked in a small voice. "This is Nora—we talked this afternoon."

"Yes, Nora, did you tell your mother you were moving out?" he asked.

"Yes," I answered.

"How did she take the news?" he asked.

"Not good," I answered, and a sob escaped me.

"Nora, are you all right?" he asked.

"No," I said.

"What happened?" he asked, his voice getting tense.

"I killed her. I threw a penny at her and I killed her," I confessed, and then burst into tears.

"Nora . . . Nora!" he yelled into the phone, but I hung up.

Seven minutes later he was pounding on the front door. "Nora, it's Pastor Reichman. Let me in! Please open the door!" he pleaded.

I opened the door and he stepped inside. "Oh, my God!" he said when he saw Mom lying at the foot of the stairs.

He pulled my coat off of her and took her pulse, but it was obvious she was dead.

"Did you call the police?" he asked.

"No, I was too scared. They'll arrest me and put me in prison. I didn't mean to kill her." I was shaking as if I were standing in a bucket of ice water.

"Let's go into the kitchen. You make some tea and tell me exactly what happened," he said. "Then I'll call the police."

"I killed her with a penny," I said, and put the tea kettle on to boil. I couldn't help thinking how nice it would have been if he had just come here for tea and to visit. Now I'd never have someone to have a cup of tea with. I shouldn't have called him. I should have killed myself.

We sat at the kitchen table and he insisted I drink a cup of tea, but he didn't touch his. Maybe he was afraid I had poisoned the tea. I was a murderer, after all. I wished I did have a bottle of poison; I'd drink it and die. I remembered the two bottles of aspirin and wondered if I could swallow two-thousand aspirin and if it would kill me.

"Nora, you didn't kill your mother. She fell. It was an accident. She was old, she had a bad knee, this is an old house, the stairs are steep. I can't believe you would or could ever hurt anyone. We do have to call the police—you know that. I'll do it for you. Just tell the truth, that's all—just tell the truth," he said, and picked up the phone.

"This is Pastor Reichman. I'd like to report a tragic accident at the house of one of my congregation. We need an ambulance and the police. An old woman tripped and fell down a flight of stairs and her daughter is in shock," he said.

I looked up into his soft, brown eyes and felt safe. I knew that no matter what happened, in my heart I knew it was an accident.

The ambulance came and the EMTs agreed with the pastor that I was in shock. Mom had broken her neck when she'd fallen down the stairs. The police questioned me several times over the next few days and then labeled it an accident.

I was free. I didn't want to be free this way, but I was free. Maybe my mother was free, too. Maybe she'd found peace at last.

I sold the house and moved into an apartment. I love my apartment; it's light and bright and sunny and warm. I have two kittens. I took some courses at a beauty school and now I work in a salon. It makes me feel good to help people look their best. It's important for people to feel good about themselves.

Pastor Reichman and I have dinner together once a week. It's not a romance; we're just friends—really good friends.

I go to church every Sunday, but I sit in a different pew now and a young, married couple sits where my mother and I used to sit.

I wish my mother could have been the kind of mother I could have loved, but all I can do is respect her for giving me life. When I have children of my own someday, I'll be a kind and gentle mother, a mother they can honor, respect—and love.

Until then, I'm living the best life I can live, helping as many people as I can, and finding joy in each and every day.

THE END

CONFESSIONS OF AN ESTRANGED DAUGHTER
"I Came Back For Mother's Day"

"Hey, let's go camping this weekend," Jake said, as we sat on his couch watching country music videos. He squeezed my hand. "The weather's going to be perfect. It may be a little cold at night, but all the better reason to share a sleeping bag." He winked at me. "Tomorrow's Friday, I could take the day off, get an early start."

I frowned. Normally, I loved going away with Jake for the weekend. We'd fish and hike, and cook burgers and s'mores over the campfire. Even though I grew up near the mountains, I never knew I liked doing that kind of stuff until I met Jake. He was the best boyfriend I ever had, and we'd been together nine months.

But I couldn't go away with him. Not this time. Not right now.

I blew out a long breath. "I can't. It's Mother's Day this weekend."

Jake leaned back and cocked his head. "Hannah, I thought you hadn't talked to your mother in years."

I shrugged. "I know. That's exactly why I need to go home this weekend. I just have this feeling." I shook my head, trying to chase the fear away. Maybe it was just my imagination, but I just felt like something was wrong. I didn't know Jake well enough to tell him that my bad feelings were almost always right. And that sometimes, my dreams came true. Not that I was psychic or anything, but weird things happened to me. And something was going on with my mother. I knew it.

"You never told me why you two don't talk," Jake said. "What happened?"

I waved my hand like it was nothing. "Just the usual mother-daughter stuff. Nothing important."

But that wasn't true. It wasn't true at all. I doubted there were very many mothers who knowingly left their daughters with a man who did horrible things to six-year-old girls, a man who scarred that little girl for life. There weren't very many mothers who would pretend those things never happened.

Jake stared at me. "This sounds important to you. We can go camping another weekend. Do you want me to drive you there? It's what, three hours away?"

I shook my head. "I'll be fine. And I don't know how long I'll be there. It's something I need to do. By myself."

He put his arm around me and kissed me. "Whatever you need, babe."

I pulled away from him and stood up to grab my purse.

"Where are you going? Aren't you staying over?" he asked. "It's not like you have to go to work tomorrow. See, that's another good thing about losing your job." He'd been trying to cheer me up about being laid off for weeks now.

I forced a smile. "I'm beat. I'm going to head home and pack tomorrow. Guess that's another good thing about being laid off. You can drop whatever you're doing and leave town."

"You'll find something soon. But I don't understand why you won't move in with me. It's not like I'm going to charge you rent or anything. It doesn't make sense to blow through your savings like you are. We could use that someday, for a house or something."

I pulled out my keys. "I'll think about it." I knew Jake was ready to take our relationship further, but I wasn't sure I'd ever have room in my heart for that. I think my heart had been damaged for good, by the one person who's supposed to heal such things: my mother.

I drove home in the rain and went right to bed.

But sleep didn't come easily. Each time I managed to doze off, I'd wake, short of breath and sweaty. Images of that man from so long ago kept waking me all night. His breath—that rotten breath that stank of cigarettes and coffee—seemed to breathe down my neck, even when I pulled the covers over my head. I could still imagine the feel of his calloused fingers on my skin, and my shame as I stood before him, doing the horrible things he told me to do.

"I'll tell your Mommy you were a naughty girl if you don't listen to me," he had threatened, grabbing my arm. And so, I would do as he commanded.

I caught a sob in my throat, as I lay in bed, beating back the memories. "It was over twenty-two years ago," I whispered to myself. "Knock it off!" But the tears came hot and fresh as if it happened to me yesterday.

I fell asleep at some point, but I woke with puffy, burning eyes. I covered my face with plenty of makeup and did my hair with shaking hands. I hadn't seen my mother since I drove away after my high school graduation.

I sent her a postcard when I moved to Syracuse to tell her I was fine and that I didn't want to see her again. But with no return address, she'd never responded. I'm not even sure she tried.

I stared at myself in the mirror. What will she see when she looks at me? A strong, independent woman who put herself through two years of school to become a radiation tech? Or a hardened, shriveled up soul who couldn't fully open her heart to anyone else?

I snapped my gaze away from the mirror. "It's your fault, Mom." Why was I even bothering to go back to her?

But that nagging ache in my stomach reminded me why I was going. Something was wrong, terribly, terribly wrong. And I might regret it forever if I didn't go see my mother right away.

I loaded my bags into my car, and headed north. It was such beautiful country along the foot of the mountains; it was hard to imagine anything horrible could happen in a place like that. I had tried long and hard enough to convince myself that it didn't really happen. Just like she had pretended. But acting like it didn't happen just hurt me more, like a wound burrowing deeper into your soul, until it pierced and devoured your heart.

When I pulled into town, I stopped and gassed up. Then I picked up a few things at the grocery store. Mom always loved those Pepperidge Farm cakes they sold in the frozen food aisle. I lingered in front of the display, the cool air pooling around me as I tried to decide between the chocolate or coconut flavor. It was always a special day when Mom brought home one of those fancy little cakes. But I wasn't certain I'd even be bringing it inside to share with her.

After my trip to the store, I drove to the park and skipped stones across the lake. I was like a little kid afraid to pull off the bandage. I was gathering courage with each familiar place I stopped, like I was plucking flowers from a field that would hopefully leave me with a bouquet of strength.

After I drove by our church and sat in the parking lot for a while, I took a deep breath, and drove down the main street toward Mom's home. My home. My past. The place I vowed I'd never return.

When I pulled in the driveway, her car was there. The same old Taurus she had when I left, with a little more rust and a new dent in the bumper. Curls of paint peeled off the siding of the tiny ranch house. Weeds outnumbered the flowers in the front garden.

I swallowed hard and decided to leave my stuff in the car. I wasn't sure I was going to stay.

I stood on the steps and rang the bell. Despite my anger at Mom, seeing my old house squeezed my heart a bit. Home had been a safe place. He had never touched me at this home. Mom would drop me off at his house so he could baby-sit me while she worked at the nursing home.

When no one came to the door, I rang the bell again. That's when I noticed the overflowing mailbox. I pulled out the envelopes. Her electric bill was postmarked a week ago.

I tried to peer through the window, but the blinds were shut. I walked around back, and looked in the empty kitchen. Dishes filled the sink.

My heart kicked up a notch. *Where is she without her car?*

I knocked on Mrs. Murphy's door one house over, but there was no answer. I decided to take a chance and stop at the nursing home. Maybe someone had picked her up for work.

I drove across town to the nursing home. I walked in and went to the front desk. A young woman looked up and smiled. "Can I help you?"

I let out the breath I'd been holding. "I'm looking for my mother. She works here. Susan Sharkey?"

The girl's eyes widened. "Honey, don't you know? She's in the hospital." She bit her lip. "Had a stroke, two weeks ago. She's at County General."

My throat was tight as I raced to the hospital. I was right. Something was wrong.

I was breathless when I ran up to the visitor's desk. "I need to see my mother, Susan Sharkey."

The old woman at the desk punched a few keys on the computer. "Room 437. Take the red elevator at the end of the hall."

I nodded and stepped onto the elevator just before the door closed. I drummed my fingers on my thigh. I stepped off the elevator on the fourth floor and tried to slow my breathing. I walked down the hall and lingered outside her room for a few moments.

A passing nurse stopped. "It's alright. You can go in. She's awake. Just had her dinner. Sweet thing, she is."

People always said that about my mother. "Sweet Susie," they called her. "Your mother is an angel," people would tell me. "The way she just picked up and carried on when your father died. She's amazing."

I nodded at the nurse. "Thanks," I whispered. I tapped on the door before I stepped in the room.

"Mom?"

Her eyelids fluttered open. She looked around and rubbed her eyes. "Hannah? Is that really you?"

I sat in the chair next to her bed. "Yeah. Hi, Mom. How are you?"

"Oh, I've been better. Had a stroke, as it turns out. How did you know? How did you know to come?"

I shrugged. "Just a feeling."

"Ah yes, you and those feelings of yours. Never understood that. Your father used to say he had dreams that came true. He claimed he had 'feelings,' too." She chuckled. "That's what he said when he proposed to me. That he just had a feeling I was the one. Guess that's something he passed on to you. That, and those green eyes of yours."

I swallowed hard. "You never told me that. About his feelings." I fiddled with the hem of my shirt.

She let out a long sigh. "Oh, there are lots of things I never told you, Hannah. Too many."

I looked up at the ceiling. "So what do the doctors say?"

She smoothed her hair back. "Oh, who knows? It doesn't matter. Tell me about you. Do I have any grandchildren?"

I smiled and shook my head.

"Are you married? Boyfriend?" Her blue eyes seemed sunken into her face. Her skin was creased with more wrinkles than a fifty-eight-year-old woman should have.

"There's a guy. Jake. I like him a lot, but—"

"But what? Is he good to you?"

I nodded. "Oh, yeah. But I just don't know if marriage is in the cards for me."

We sat there in silence for a few moments. "I'm sorry I just left like I did. I just had to get out of here. Too many memories."

She grabbed the railing of her bed and tried to sit up. "I know you did. I'm sorry. I wasn't there for you like I should have been."

I slouched in my chair and stared at my shoes.

"He's dead, you know. Uncle Terry."

I couldn't help it; a whimper slipped through my lips and before I knew it, I was sobbing, my forehead resting on the cold metal railing on Mom's hospital bed.

Mom's hand gently rubbed my head. "I didn't want to believe you. It was just one more horrible thing in my life I couldn't deal with. It was easier to pretend you were imagining things."

I let out a strangled cry. "How could a little girl come up with something like that?" I pulled away from her and dropped my head in my hands. I could hear her crying.

"Terry said you had seen part of an R-rated movie by mistake. He had answers for every question. And he was my brother! How could I ever believe my brother would do something like that?"

I sat up, my face hot with tears and rage. "I was your daughter! How could you not believe me?"

"Is everything alright in here?" The nurse I'd met in the hall poked her head in the door.

"It's fine, Denise. My daughter and I are just talking a few things out."

"Alright, then. You let me know if you need anything."

I refused to meet her gaze.

"Hannah, it was wrong of me, I know that now. I've known it all along. I tried so hard to convince myself you were wrong. If I believed you, that would have meant I failed you. And how could I possibly fix things if it was true?" She dropped her head back on her pillow.

"You did fail me! I have a hole in my heart that I don't think can ever be fixed. I don't think there will ever be room for anyone in there. My trust just leaks right out of that hole." I stood up and grabbed my purse.

"Don't go. Not when you just came back," Mom pleaded, reaching for me. Tears ran down her cheeks.

"I need some time. I need some space."

"Will you come back tomorrow?" She looked so small huddled under her white sheets and blankets.

"I'll think about it." I left the room and lingered in the hall, uncertain where I was going to go next.

"Excuse me, are you Mrs. Sharkey's daughter?" It was the nurse, Denise, who'd checked in earlier.

I nodded and wiped my runny nose with the back of my hand.

Denise handed me a tissue from her pocket. "We've been trying to find her people. She's got cancer. We haven't told her yet. We wanted her to have some family support when we broke the news."

I stumbled back and leaned against the wall. "Cancer? Aren't you treating her for it? What are you waiting for?"

Denise touched my arm. "It's stage-four pancreatic cancer. There is nothing we can do. At this point, we can only ease her pain. It's up to you if you want to tell her or not."

I wiped away a tear rolling down my cheek. "How long does she have?"

"Could be a few days, could be a month. Only the Lord knows."

I ran down the hall, down the stairs, and out to my car. I lay my head against the steering wheel and waited for my heaving chest to slow, but it didn't. I banged the steering wheel and let the tears roll out.

I was surprised to find myself at the cemetery. I wandered through the headstones, remembering my father's grave was near the back corner. I'd only been here twice before. It was too painful to see the small stone marking what had been his life.

I squatted next to the small rectangle nestled in the grass. "Charles Sharkey 1954-1984. Beloved husband and father."

I smoothed my fingers across the words. "I'm sorry I never came here, Daddy. It was just too hard. It was just easier to try and forget you. It was just easier to pretend it didn't happen."

I sucked in a breath when I realized what I had said: the very same words my mother sobbed out at the hospital. I hung my head, unwilling to let pity and understanding climb in my heart. But the feelings hung there, hovering in my chest.

She was a wonderful mother in every other way. Once Uncle Terry moved away, it never happened again. I never saw him again. And it only happened a handful of times, those things he did to me. Things did get better, but my mother just never could talk about it with me.

I kicked at the grass. "Just like I never talked about my father," I whispered to myself.

I looked at my watch. Visiting hours were over. I'd have to wait until the next day to see her. I checked into a hotel and put the little cake I'd bought in the mini-fridge.

My dreams that night weren't as horrific as they had been the night before. I floated in a warm blue ocean, riding the waves, and holding someone's hand. But I couldn't tell whose it was.

Visiting hours weren't until eleven. So, I went to Mom's house and bundled up her mail. I pulled the weeds from the garden and swept off her porch. Can I bring her home? I wondered. I wasn't sure what to tell her about her diagnosis.

I grabbed the cake from my hotel room and drove to the hospital. She was asleep in bed. I straightened her serving tray in front of her and set the cake down. "Look what I brought, Mom."

She shook herself from her sleep and smiled. "I haven't had one of those in years."

"Well, it is a special day. Tomorrow's Mother's Day, and I say we don't wait one minute to celebrate." I pulled out paper plates and forks I got in the cafeteria.

"You're right. I might not have one extra minute." She sat up and then her smile fell. "What changed? I thought I'd never see you again after you left yesterday."

"I just did a lot of thinking. I can understand why it was easier for you not to talk about things with me. I just wish you had tried to stop him," I said in a voice so quiet I wasn't sure she'd heard me.

She was quiet for a while, running her fingers along the smooth surface of the serving tray. "I did try to stop him. That's why I made Terry leave town. Told him I'd call the police if he ever came near you again, and if he was smart he'd disappear before I changed my mind."

My mouth dropped open, but nothing came out.

"I only know he died a few years back when his wife sent me a clipping from the paper." Mom scratched at something invisible on the tray.

"Why didn't you tell me you made him leave? If only I'd known you believed me. That you cared."

"It was stupid, I know. I thought it best just to leave things in the past. That once he was gone, you'd move on. Better than dragging up all that garbage."

I reached over and hugged her. Her weak arms circled me and she patted me back.

"This is reason to celebrate," she said. "Let's have some cake."

We served up slices of the chocolate cake, and I got little cartons of milk from the cafeteria. When Mom dozed off after lunch, I talked to the nurse about bringing her home.

"We won't be able to discharge her until tomorrow. We'll have to set up some in-home visits so we can monitor her. But you can go home tomorrow," the nurse said.

I beamed. Finally, I'd be going home.

I slipped back into the room, and Mom was awake, pressing her fingers against the paper plate to get the last of the cake crumbs. "I always did love the chocolate best," she said, licking her fingertips.

"Mom, I'm bringing you home tomorrow. But I want to go out for a bit." I hung my head. "I didn't get you anything for Mother's Day."

She held out her hand to me. "You sit right down. You gave me the best gift ever. You gave me my daughter back. You gave me a second chance."

I sat next to her and held her hand.

She dozed on and off throughout the day, and we watched old movies together on the TV in her room. "Your father would be so proud to see you now. I only hope he can forgive me, as you have. That's what I'm going to ask him, first thing when I see him. For forgiveness."

"Shh," I scolded, blinking back tears. "You're not going to see Daddy for a long time."

She squeezed my hand and fell asleep.

I clicked off the TV and pulled my chair closer to her bed. I reached back for her hand.

In my dreams, I was back in the blue ocean. The waves were calmer. This time, I was holding a hand in each of mine: my mother's and my father's. I smiled, and when I looked up, Jake was swimming for me.

Mom was dead when I woke up Mother's Day morning. There was a smile on her face, and cake crumbs on her chin.

My heart was heavy, but steady. At least I made it here on time. I looked up and smiled. Thank you for sending me that feeling, Daddy. I didn't realize how you've always been with me.

I pulled out my cell and called Jake.

"Hey, baby. You all right?" he asked.

"I am. I really am. But I need you here with me. I need you always and forever."

I now knew that my heart was ready to hold all the love he was waiting to give me.

THE END

CONFESSIONS OF A 1-900-NUMBER GIRL
If my husband ever finds out about "my job," I'm terrified of what he'll do!

"Unzip your pants really slowly, so I can hear it. Will you do that for me?"

I cradled the phone against my shoulder so that I could stir the noodles around in the pot of boiling water. The clock on the stove told me I had thirty more minutes before I could quit my . . . unusual job.

As it was, since my husband was due home in an hour—

This was cutting it pretty close.

As it was, I didn't want him to find out what I was doing until all of our bills were caught up.

Over the burbling, bubbling sound of boiling water, I heard the sound of a zipper being unzipped. I swear—no matter how many times I did it, I never ceased to blush at this point.

Thank God they can't see me!

"I hear you . . . that's right; pretend my hot, little hands are clenched around you. . . . Now I'm stroking it, and it's soooo hard, baby. . . ." Two weeks of experience and I was already becoming an old pro at predicting when they'd blow and I could hang up. This one was breathing heavy, so I knew it wouldn't take long.

Then the phone slipped—just as the heavy breather paying ten bucks a minute muttered something. Fortunately, I took a wild guess.

"What's that? You want me to put my mouth around you? Just exactly what I had in mind next, baby. Mmmm. . . . You taste so good. . . . Can you feel my tongue licking away, baby?"

Behind me, suddenly I heard a key turning in the lock. In my panic, I nearly dropped the phone, realizing: Kenyon's home early! Frantically, I whispered, "I'm sucking you hard," before I hit the mute button on my end. In my ear, I could hear my client peaking, his moans growing louder, harsher, until they reached a crescendo.

Honestly, it constantly amazes me—how much more verbal a man can be on the phone with a woman than he can be with his own woman in person.

Hey—not that I was a total slut before I married Kenyon.

But I've definitely slept with my fair share of men.

I closed the company-issued cell phone and stuck it in a drawer just seconds before my hunky man came into the kitchen. He came up behind me and slid his arms around my waist, nuzzling my neck.

"Mmmmm. You smell like tomato sauce," he said with a husky chuckle. "And I'm hungry, so that's a good thing."

I felt my nipples spring to action as I sensed the swell of his erection against my behind. It amazed me: I could talk the filthiest trash imaginable to more than a dozen "customers" a day, and yet only my husband could turn me on. And for that fact alone, I was, indeed, extremely thankful. As it was, I felt guilty enough about lying to my husband about my "job" without the added guilt of acknowledging that some small, naughty, dirty, secret part of me got turned on by it, as some of my coworkers claim they do.

"We're having spaghetti," I announced unnecessarily. My breath caught in my throat as Kenyon pressed his impressively thick length hard against me; I could feel him throbbing and all of a sudden I could not wait for bedtime!

Hopefully, I thought, he won't fall asleep on me before I can finish bathing our two-year-old daughter, Rashida, and getting her to bed.

"How did work go today?" Kenyon asked me, still nuzzling my neck and pressing against me. His hands wandered up to my breasts and he started playing with my rock-hard nipples, tugging on them and teasing them and making it really hard for me to concentrate.

"Work? Um . . . it went well," I lied. "I've got two more websites to design."

Hey—I do know how to design websites; that's just not what I was doing back then. You see, I discovered early on that website design doesn't really pay the bills unless you're part of a really big company, or extremely well established—neither of which I was.

"Smart and beautiful." Kenyon turned me around to face him, giving me one of his sultriest, sexiest smiles. "I'm the luckiest dude on earth."

"Damn straight you are," I returned playfully. "And, speaking of smart, beautiful girls . . . your 'other girl' needs someone to wake her up from her nap while I finish making dinner."

Kenyon's gorgeous, brown eyes glittered with mischief. "Maybe we should let her sleep for, oh, say . . . another fifteen minutes?"

I squealed as Kenyon hefted me up onto the kitchen counter and thrust his hips between my legs. I tapped him on the shoulder with my wooden spoon. "Don't start something you can't finish, Ken!"

"Oh, I can finish," he promised in a deep, thrilling voice. To prove it, he unzipped his pants and reached out to thrust my panties aside. He was in luck; I was wearing a skirt.

With one hard thrust, he was inside of me . . . and then I was lost. . . .

From the first moment I laid eyes on Kenyon, I knew he was my soul mate. I lusted for him now, five years later, just as much as I did when we first met and, as far as I'm concerned—

No woman could ever love any man more than I love my Kenyon.

Indeed, as far as I can tell, my man only possesses one flaw: Kenyon lacks ambition. You see—as it was, he was perfectly content to keep right on living in our midsize mid-rise apartment, but I wanted the whole enchilada. I wanted the house and the white picket fence and the golden retriever and 2.5 kids.

"God, you're sooo hot inside, baby," Kenyon growled, swiveling his hips and making me moan for more. The man definitely has his mojo goin' on, and he never fails to make me scream out my ecstasy before he even thinks about his own pleasure.

I bit my bottom lip, conscious of our two-year-old sleeping in the next room on the couch as, thrust after delicious thrust, Kenyon brought me closer to my orgasm. When he raked my blouse aside and latched onto my bare breasts, I went over the edge, locking my scream in my throat. He followed soon after, his strokes increasing in rhythm until a growling noise ushered forth from his throat. Then he threw back his head, his neck muscles taut and bulging, eyes closed in ecstasy.

I watched him then, wondering if the clients I seduced over the phone wore similar expressions when they came. It was a heady thought—

Although not without shame.

The spaghetti noodles had cooked to gooey pieces by the time we finished making love on the counter, so Kenyon suggested that we order a pizza. Since pizza's not only my favorite food, but Rashida's, as well, I readily agreed.

After supper, to my surprise and delight, Kenyon insisted that I take a leisurely bath while he played with Rashida. Believe it or not, having sex with a dozen men—even, albeit, over the phone—wears a body out, so I didn't argue with him. Besides, I was feeling a little . . . nasty.

As I sank into a mound of scented bubbles, I asked myself again if I was doing the right thing by not telling my husband the truth about "my new job."

You see—I didn't go looking for a phone sex job. It just sort of . . . fell into my lap. One day while I was shopping for Rashida to buy her some new sneakers, I ran into a girl I went to high school with. We started reminiscing and ended up having lunch, and the whole time I couldn't help but envy her pricey designer clothes and gorgeous head of expertly woven, honey-blond extensions. To top that, she had on Jimmy Choo shoes I could never afford, no matter how hard I saved.

"What are you, a hooker?" I finally asked jokingly as I gave Rashida a salad cracker.

I nearly fell out of my chair at Symone's response—not laughter, as I expected.

"Sort of," she said with a sly smile at my shocked reaction. "Only, I don't have to do guys for real. Just over the phone."

My eyeballs nearly popped out of my head. "You mean, like—phone sex?"

She nodded. "Yep. Like phone sex. Exactly like it, as a matter of fact. They don't see you; you don't see them. You don't even use your real name. And the kicker is: They just deposit your pay into your checking account or your savings account—whichever you prefer." Eyeing my cheap sweats and Rashida's hand-me-downs, she said frankly, "Looks like you could use a good-paying job, girlfriend."

"I could," I admitted, blushing even though I know she didn't mean to be nasty. "Kenyon works hard, but, well—you know how it is. . . . He's not exactly the most ambitious brother I've ever met—that's for sure!"

"Well, this is the job for you, then. Plus, you can do it at home, so you're not out a babysitter, and you don't have to worry that your baby girl's being mistreated by some stranger."

Needless to say—the job sounded more tempting to me by the minute.

Symone stabbed a shrimp from her salad and popped it into her mouth. She chewed, and then swallowed, before saying, "You don't even have to tell your man about the job, you know. You can just tell him that you're telemarketing or something from home."

"Kenyon wouldn't like it, that's for sure." In fact, as it was, I was fairly certain that if I even so much as suggested the notion to him, he'd give me a big, old, flat-out no.

But we really do need the money, I reasoned. Our credit cards are all maxed out and we need a vacation, a bigger home, a newer car. . . . The list was endless.

Licking my suddenly dry lips, I asked the all-important question: "How much do you make?"

When she told me—my jaw dropped.

"Seriously? You wouldn't lie to a sister, would you?"

She laughed. "No, I wouldn't. I know it's hard to believe, but there's a big market for phone sex these days, what with all of the diseases going around. To tell you the truth—I honestly think most of the men I talk to are married and ain't gettin' it at home, if you know what I mean."

Before I could think, I said, "Kenyon sure isn't one of them." Symone's delighted cackle made me blush.

"I hear you, sister. I hear you. And, hey—good for you. Cuz if you're that good at satisfying your man, just think about how good you'd be at this job!"

"Could I work my own hours?"

"Sure can. That's the beauty of it, girl. You work as much or as little as you like. It all depends on what kind of money you need." She pointed down, indicating her Rock & Republic jeans and Jimmy Choo shoes. "Me, now—I need a lot of it, girl, cuz, you see—I'm 'in between men' right now." She fished a business card out of her purse and handed it to me. "I get an extra grand for recruiting, so lunch is on me, sister."

"Gee—thanks!"

I stuck the card in my purse and began to wash Rashida's chubby, little hands with a napkin dipped in my glass of water. My mind was already running ahead as I thought of how quickly I could get us out of debt making the kind of money Symone claimed she made.

The next day I put the baby down for her morning nap and dialed the 1-800 number on the card I got from Symone. A cheerful-sounding woman led me through the "application process" and before I knew it, she told me I'd be getting a phone in the mail with my very own 1-900 number. She explained to me that whenever I wanted to "work," all I need do was turn the phone on and punch in a special number (my employee ID code). To end my "workday," I simply turned my phone off, essentially clocking myself out. I couldn't believe it was all that simple.

"Now," she said near the end of our conversation, "eventually, you understand, you'll attract repeaters—that's what we call our regulars, or you might want to think of 'em as real big fans—and you'll want to do your best to be available to them when they need their 'needs' met. We leave that entirely up to you, of course, but money-wise, it's a good arrangement on your behalf, and ours, building up a stable of sex-crazed, desperate, compulsive, lonely studs with lots of time on their hands and loads of credit."

I almost laughed out loud at her description. "After I get my phone, my paycheck will be direct-deposited?" I wanted to make absolutely sure that there would be no paper trail for my husband to stumble over. As it was, I figured if he found my phone, I could always tell Kenyon that I "found it," or was "just trying it out."

"Yes, ma'am. And if you have any more questions, that's what I'm here for, honey. Anyway, good luck, and welcome to the biz."

I got the phone a few days later via express mail, but it was almost a week before I got up enough nerve to actually clock in and "do" my first "job." To tell you the truth, at first—I couldn't even believe I was actually doing this! What would my husband think if he knew? I found myself wondering almost constantly. Would he be jealous? Disgusted? Mad? Turned on? I honestly didn't know, but if I'd had to guess, I'd have said my man would be humiliated by the thought of me essentially giving men verbal sex over the phone just to help him take care of our family. As it is, Kenyon definitely isn't short in the pride department, even if he's not the most ambitious person I know.

Finally, I called Symone from my landline. She laughed when I told her I couldn't work up enough nerve to open "the sex phone," as I'd already named it in my mind.

"How about you practice on me, girlfriend?" she finally generously suggested. "Pretend I'm your first customer. I promise I won't laugh, okay?"

"Well . . . okay. . . ." I chewed my lip. My face was on fire, but Symone couldn't know that and, as it was, Rashida was down for her long morning nap, so I knew I had two to three hours to myself.

"Just pretend that you and Kenyon are playing a game of phone sex. Show me how down and dirty you can get. Believe me, girl—the dirtier you get, the quicker it's over—which won't always be your objective, obviously, for the simple reason of your own financial gains and incentive, but it's okay for now."

I closed my eyes, thinking suddenly of our huge credit card bill coming due the following week . . . the bad tires on our car that needed to be replaced, and the clothes that Rashida was fast growing out of. . . . I swallowed hard and finally began in a low, husky voice, "Hey, baby. What can Hot Cocoa do for you?"

"That's good," Symone murmured. Then, in a falsely deep voice she said, "I love your name, sweetness. Describe your luscious body to me in great detail."

I forged ahead, gradually gathering confidence. "Well, um, let's see . . . my breasts are double D's, the color and taste of rich mocha chocolate with chocolate-covered-cherry nipples. . . . As a matter of fact, I'm rubbing a candied cherry over them right now . . . would you like to lick them?"

There was a pregnant pause, and then Symone made me blush as she squealed, "Woman, you are hot! You almost made me hot, and I don't even swing that way!"

She chuckled admiringly and I couldn't stop blushing with pleasure at her praise. But then she said something that sobered me up real quick.

"Speaking of swinging the other way—I guess I should forewarn you that you might occasionally get calls from other women."

I felt my jaw drop at the very thought. Mind you—it's not that I'm homophobic or anything; I simply never considered this aspect of "the biz."

"You're kidding—right? I mean . . . talking sex with a brother is one thing, but, well . . . I honestly don't even know if I can seduce a woman." The thought alone made my mouth go dry with trepidation. "Do I really have to take their calls?"

"Sorry, sugar, but you sure do. Don't you worry, though, girl; you can do it. Anyway, by the time it happens, you'll be an old pro."

An old pro.

I wasn't so sure I liked the sound of those words, but I realized then that I'd made my bed, so I'd have to lie in it—or at least talk filthy-dirty in it—till I could get myself free of the situation.

Unfortunately, it wasn't that simple—not after my first big paycheck hit the bank within two weeks.

Let me just say that instead of buying the cheap, serviceable tires, we were able to get a set of wheels that made my man's coworkers envy him. And when Kenyon's happy—

I'm happy.

After an exhausting day of shopping, we ate at an upscale restaurant that we can rarely afford—our favorite place, normally reserved for very special occasions. As far as Kenyon knew, though, this was just a regular night. I knew otherwise, of course; stuffed with lobster and crab cakes, I leaned back in my chair and let out a deep, satisfied sigh.

Kenyon reached across the table suddenly and grabbed my hand, looking at me with his hot, dark eyes. Making me shiver with lust.

"Baby, we are so blessed, aren't we? You finally hooked your dream job . . . we've got a nice apartment, a beautiful baby. . . . We should start going to church, huh?" He chuckled and took a sip of his Crown Royal on the rocks, looking supremely satisfied—and damn-fine sexy.

I wasn't expecting his last statement. Immediately, my face filled with heat at the thought of going to church after having phone sex with strangers all day long and I found myself wondering frantically, Is it the same in God's eyes as adultery, or even just plain fornicating?

I didn't know; I just knew that I wasn't comfortable with the idea, and that bothered me. Almost constantly, I found myself wondering, Am I doing something terribly wrong, morally speaking?

My mother once told me that when a person does something they're too ashamed to tell their mother about, then it's probably a sin. Well—there's no way I would ever tell my mother about my job—or even my sisters, Jameela and Karma. I don't think my sisters would judge me, but they'd definitely make fun of me.

That night, after a fire-filled, but tender bout of lovemaking, I lay awake, caught up in my moral nightmare of indecision.

Is fulfilling a man's fantasies over the phone such a terrible thing to do, when all is said and done? Is God frowning in disapproval—does He even care?

And then I allowed myself to really, honestly consider Kenyon's reaction if he found out or if I actually told him. As it was, I certainly fancied that I knew my husband well, and in admitting that to myself, I had to conclude that he would be disgusted, jealous, and tremendously hurt by my deception. Other brothers might find it hip, or even amusing to have their wives make good money through phone sex, but deep down in my heart, I knew Kenyon would be devastated.

He'd feel like I cheated on him . . . with dozens of guys.

I stared up at the ceiling, feeling a wave of horrible, sickening shame sweep over me. No—he'd never understand, no matter what spin I put on the situation, and he'd insist that I quit immediately, no matter how much we really do need the money.

Which left me with a choice to make: Do I continue to hide it from him—at least until we've paid off some of our debts and acquired a few luxuries that I want? Or do I quit right now, and never tell Kenyon the truth? Without my job, we certainly aren't really in danger of losing our apartment—and at least our used car's paid for.

We'd just have to keep struggling to make ends meet.

To quit, or not to quit—

That was the question.

And if I didn't quit, then I knew I had to come to terms with my guilt; I had to stop feeling guilty all the time and truly believe that my job was "just like any other job."

After all, I told myself, I work.

I get paid.

I satisfy the customers.

That last thought made me wince.

That's the whole point, anyway—isn't it?

It's how I satisfy them that's wrong.

The next morning I kissed my husband good-bye as he left for work, fed Rashida her breakfast, settled her into the playpen with her toys, and then went straight into the kitchen to start my day of phone sex.

As if to mock my decision to keep my job, the second call of the day turned out to be: a woman.

Inwardly, I groaned. My face heated up at the very sound of her voice and, indeed, I suspect I wasn't totally successful at hiding my uncertainty in those previously "uncharted waters."

Wouldn't you know it? I'm one of the so-called "few" (from what I hear from my galpals and who I know) women who—in direct contradiction to those women's magazine "statistics" that claim that "most" women "experiment" with being with other women during their college years or even during high school—never did any such thing! My one-and-only "experience" happened with a friend of mine who got drunk once and tried to kiss me. She didn't even remember a thing about it the next day—much to my relief! And I never told her or anyone else about the incident—until now, that is, I guess.

Anyway, I could hear the nervous quaver in my voice as I said into the phone, "Hey, there. Um, what can Hot Cocoa do for you today . . . baby?"

"Hot Cocoa, huh?" the woman replied, a hint of amusement in her voice.

I swallowed a sarcastic retort and said instead, "I can be anyone you want me to be, honey."

"You've never done this with a woman before, have you?"

She pegged me too quickly for comfort. I bit my lip, trying to decide if honesty was—or was not—the best policy in this situation. "Um, well—no, actually—I haven't. But I—I don't mind," I added hastily. After all, the last thing I wanted was for someone to complain about me and get me fired!

"Ah, a virgin, then," she purred with obvious satisfaction.

Whatever floats her boat, I decided, suddenly feeling up to the challenge. Which reminds me: Have I told you yet that I never back down from a dare? And right then—I felt like she was definitely daring me.

"Yes, okay; yeah—I'm a virgin . . . when it comes to women, at least," I admitted. "But that doesn't mean the idea doesn't get me . . . hot." Admittedly, this was a lie, but I figured: Who cares—as long as I convince her and earn myself some decent dough?

"I don't believe you."

So much for convincing. "Let me prove it, then." I dropped my voice to sound husky . . . desirable. "I want to start by undressing you, one piece of clothing at a time. . . ."

By the time I hung up the phone fifteen minutes later, I had the unsettling, yet somehow, reassuring, sounds of the woman's orgasm ringing in my ears. Strangely, my "success" made me feel . . . powerful.

I just satisfied my toughest customer, I kept telling myself.

Which is exactly why she called back two hours later and put me on three-way with her partner for a threesome of phone sex.

I pulled it off with flying colors—as if I were somehow suddenly born to this job.

Needless to say, as I fed Rashida her lunch of macaroni and cheese and then got her settled down for her afternoon nap, I took a moment to wonder about whether or not this was all an omen—some sort of "sign" that indicated that I should stay in my newfound "line of work"—since I was apparently so good at it, after all.

But doing that would mean I'd have to live a lie with my husband—and I honestly don't know if I could do that.

Then there was another, more reluctant question I forced myself to ask myself: Am I somehow already becoming addicted to phone sex? Can I really even quit now—if, indeed, I really and truly want to?

I've seen TV shows and movies where men get addicted to phone sex and online porn. . . . Can a woman get addicted in the same way? After all, I have to admit . . . it gives me a real sense of power, pleasing so many men—not to mention two women--in one day, knowing that I did it all just by talking to them.

I was still undecided by the time I took my last call for the day. While Rashida ate her afternoon snack in her highchair, I wandered into the living room so that she couldn't hear me. I knew she didn't understand what I was saying, but still—I always made sure she was well out of earshot.

"Hello. What can Hot Cocoa do for you today?" I asked in my usual husky purr.

"Hey, Cocoa. I missed you."

This was one of my "regulars." This one, I called "Zulu," since we never used real names. "Hey, Zulu. Back so soon?"

"I told you, I missed you," he replied gruffly. "So? When are we going to go out on a real date?"

Well, my customer might consider phone sex a date, but I sure don't. Naturally, I didn't say this out loud.

"I don't know, Zulu. . . . But if we could go out on a date, where would you take me?" I figured the longer I kept the customer on the phone, the more money I made. As it was, I got pretty good at "stretching things out."

Zulu was silent for a short moment. Finally, he drawled, "I'd take you on a picnic out in the countryside. Somewhere secluded."

Yum, yum. A picnic with ants and dirt and grass. Hardly my idea of a dream date. "Wow. Sounds nice." Now it's time to get down to business, I decided. "So . . . what would you do to me once we were there with nobody else around for miles and miles and miles. . . ?"

As he started describing his version of "our dream date" in increasingly graphic detail, I couldn't help glancing at the clock on the wall above our fridge. That's when I frowned, realizing that I was cutting it close—too close, in fact.

Kenyon will be home any minute now.

But since my customer was doing all of the talking—still rambling on in ever-more-lurid, breathless, horny, desperate detail, I went and opened the freezer, trying to decide what to make for dinner.

"So . . . do you think you'd like that, baby?"

"Hm? Oh. Yeah. Sure. I'd love it if you did that." Unfortunately— or maybe fortunately—I had no clue as to what he'd been saying. All that time, my mind was on: Chicken fingers or cheeseburgers?

"So, then . . . what would you do to me?" he asked, his voice breathless seeing as, no doubt, he was pleasuring himself like sex was gonna go out of style in the next three minutes.

"Um. . . ." I shoved the family-sized bag of frozen chicken fingers out of the way and dug deep for the three pounds of frozen hamburger meat. " . . . .I'd do whatever you wanted me to do, Zulu. . . ."

When I closed the freezer door, Kenyon came into view.

He looked positively livid.

I screamed and dropped the hamburger meat.

It hit the floor with a hard thud, scaring Rashida.

Immediately, she started to cry.

Meanwhile, on the other end of the phone line, Zulu sounded bewildered. "Who's crying? Is that a kid?"

I snapped the phone closed, ending the conversation and, essentially, anything else I might've had going on with Zulu.

My husband caught me red-handed.

Believe me—that's the only thought that was going through my mind—pounding through it, truth be known—in those desperate, fateful, terrifying moments.

"Kenyon . . . I—I can explain," I said, stumbling over my guilt-laden words. I reached for Rashida, pulling her out of her highchair and shushing her. She stopped screaming, at least, but continued to whimper and sniffle.

Kenyon's eyes looked like hard, black pieces of onyx in his stone-cold face. "Explain? I don't think there's any need for you to 'explain,' woman. After all—I think it's pretty damn clear you were talking to your lover, you cheating slut."

I sucked in a sharp breath as he advanced on me. "Kenyon—no! You've got it wrong—all wrong! I swear!"

"Wrong?" he asked with thick sarcasm. "You think I'm stupid?"

"It's not what you think!" I cried, scaring Rashida into crying again. Needless to say—this is not a conversation I wanted to be having while holding a hysterical toddler, but I didn't exactly have much choice, now, did I? After all, I knew I had to clear things up—and fast. "Kenyon—just listen to me, okay? Please!"

He didn't answer me, but at least he stopped advancing.

"This is, well—it's my job—okay? It's wh-what I've been doing for the p-past month." He continued to glower at me, so I realized he didn't understand. "I d-don't design w-web sites for a living. I w-work for a nine-hundred number."

His expression turned from glowering to incredulous. "WHAT?"

My mouth was bone dry. I tried to lick my lips, but they were dry, too. "Um, it's a nine-hundred number, Ken." I took a deep breath and blurted out the horrendous words: "Phone sex."

"Phone sex?" he bellowed, startling me into jumping back.

Rashida whimpered and clung to my neck; she sensed that her daddy was mad, all right.

"You mean to tell me you've been earning money talking dirty to guys on the phone?"

Well, when he puts it that way, it does sound dirty, I found myself thinking for about a millisecond. "It's j-just a—a job, Ken. It d-doesn't mean anything." I cringed as I uttered the lame words. "And—and . . . we're f-finally g-getting out of debt, honey."

Kenyon struggled visibly to calm down. "Take Rashida into the living room and put her in the playpen. Now."

I have to say that I was scared then. Kenyon never laid a hand on me in anger before, but at that moment, I admit—I wasn't entirely convinced that he wouldn't. For a second, I toyed with the idea of keeping Rashida in my arms; I knew he'd never hit me while I was holding our child. Then shame hit me as I realized I was thinking about using my precious Rashida as a human shield.

So I went and put her down in her playpen and then, so reluctantly and dismally, walked back into the kitchen like a lamb to the slaughter. With dread in my heart, I stood in front of my angry husband and waited for my punishment.

I deserve whatever he dishes out, I told myself. I've lied to him—connived behind his back to keep him from finding out what my real job really entails. I know I'd be utterly betrayed and devastated if he ever did the same things to me.

"Sit down," he ordered.

I sat. I put my trembling hands in my lap and hung my head in shame. "I'm sorry," I finally mumbled in the weakest-sounding voice you ever did hear.

"Sorry?" he asked, his voice full of hurt and bewilderment. "You know me, woman. You know damn well that I would never, ever go for anything like that—no matter how badly we needed the money!"

And, indeed, I did know. But I figured admitting it would only make things worse—much, much worse. So I let him berate me. After all—

I knew I had it coming.

"It hurts, baby—you know what I'm saying? It hurts so damn much, knowing that you lied to me—that you've been lying straight to my face all this time! It hurts knowing that you felt you had to go behind my back just so we can have extra money. Am I not making you happy? Is that what you're trying to tell me in some sick, convoluted, backhanded kind of way?"

"Of course you are! You always make me happy, Kenyon! You know that!" I said emphatically, responding to the sadness in his voice, thinking: Kenyon's my life! Doesn't he know at least that much by now? "I was wrong, Ken—dead wrong. I—I shouldn't have done it, and I am so, so incredibly sorry—sorrier than you may ever know, in fact! I'll quit right away!"

"Damn right you will," he growled. But, suddenly—he didn't sound as mad as before, which gave me hope. "Now, come here, woman."

I rose and went into his big, strong arms, my knees weak with relief as I began to realize: He isn't going to hit me, or leave me. He still loves me, regardless.

Thank You, Jesus.

He buried his hands in my hair—and that's when I realized that he was trembling all over. His voice was urgent with an aching sound as he said next to my ear, "My God, baby . . . you don't know what went through my mind when I heard you talking like that. I—I thought you'd—" He choked, took a deep breath, and continued. "I thought you'd—found someone else. Someone better."

"Never!" I cried fiercely, clinging to him—holding him as tightly as my arms would allow. "You're the only man for me, Kenyon—and don't you ever doubt that fact for a single second of the rest of our lives!"

He pulled back and looked me in the eyes, his own turning to liquid heat. "I'd better be. I'd damn well better be."

Needless to say, my stint as a phone sex operator ended.

Two weeks later I found a part-time job babysitting another little girl Rashida's age, and although the job doesn't bring in "the big bucks," every little bit helps.

Thank You, Jesus.

THE END

CONFESSIONS OF A STEPMONSTER
His Kids Hate Me!

My pulse strummed with excitement as I stepped off the plane onto the jet bridge. I was in a new state, starting a new life with the man I loved. I'd left my past behind—my job, my friends, and all that was familiar—to become part of his family.

That family included his two adorable children.

I slipped past businessmen holding cell phones to each ear. I eased by a passenger dragging a carry-on bag with a stuck wheel. I skipped ahead of a cluster of chattering teenagers.

And then there they were. Waiting at the arrival gate was Greg, balancing his daughter on his shoulders. His son clung to his side.

My heart leaped as our eyes met. Greg greeted me with a quick kiss. "Hi, sweetheart. Welcome to the West Coast."

"I'm so happy to see you," I said, returning his kiss. "And the children," I added, looking at them in awe. "Look how they've grown in just six months."

"Can't you say hello to Helen?" Greg asked, taking Cassandra down from his shoulders.

Both of them mumbled a greeting.

"Scott, don't you have something for Helen?" Greg asked.

The boy slowly produced a small bouquet of mixed flowers from behind his back. A few of them dangled from broken stems.

"How sweet," I raved. "They're just beautiful. Thank you."

Greg slipped an arm around my waist. "Let's grab your luggage, and then head for home."

Home. I liked the way that sounded. With his divorce well behind us, Greg and I would be together—this time for good.

Greg's condo is twenty minutes from the airport. We gave updates on our lives along the way. The shared child-custody arrangements he had with his ex-wife were still working out well, he said.

Sitting in the backseat, the children played with the toys I'd brought them—a doll for Cassandra and a toy airplane for Scott. In my backpack were some gourmet cookies that I'd surprise them with later. I wanted so much for them to like me. And, if our past relationship was any sign, the kids and I were going to get along just fine.

The evening sun cast a rim of light around Greg's profile as he drove. His hair was tousled, giving him that boyish look that I loved.

He pulled into a cluster of condos with attached garages. "Here we are; number forty-two." He took the garage door opener from the dash and handed it to Scott.

The boy pushed a button and the door opened, revealing a tidy garage with three bicycles mounted on the back wall. One was adult-sized. Two were for children.

My first official act as a stepmother-to-be was unbuckling Cassandra from her booster seat and helping her out of the car. She immediately scrambled through the kitchen door after her brother. Greg stood back, waiting for me.

"How am I doing with the kids so far?" I asked.

"Great," he said with kiss. "By the way, the kids will be spending the night with us. Their mom is attending her ten-year class reunion tonight."

I struggled to conceal an unwanted pang of disappointment. I like the kids, but it was my first night there and I was anxious to be alone with Greg.

"Don't worry," he whispered. "They'll be tucked in by nine."

His words rang with an innuendo that made me smile.

Inside, everything was in perfect order. The small kitchen sparkled. The living room, with its beige carpet and beige furniture, was neat and clean, but needed a woman's touch. The only pictures were photographs of the kids on a console that held the TV.

"What do you think?" he asked.

"I like it, but with you, I'd live in a chicken coop."

The kids sat on the floor, quietly playing with their new toys.

I sat down on the floor next to them like I used to. "What are you going to name her?" I asked Cassandra about her doll.

"Don't know," she said shyly.

"I remember how you used to like trucks," I said to Scott. "We used to make highways out of slanted boards so they'd roll by themselves, remember?"

He nodded without looking at me.

"They've turned shy on me," I told Greg.

"They'll warm up to you again."

While the kids played and watched cartoons, I helped Greg put together a spaghetti dinner. He'd made the sauce from scratch himself. It was the kids' favorite meal. It was clear that the kids were still a central focus of his life. Who couldn't love a guy who loved kids?

We gathered around the table, in the middle of which I'd placed a jar holding my welcoming bouquet. Cassandra sat on a booster seat. Scott, the self-proclaimed "big boy," sat peering over the tabletop.

Greg held up his wine glass. "Before we start, I'd like to propose a toast to our very special friend, Helen. May her future be filled with love and happiness."

I clinked my glass against his. "That's very sweet of you."

"When are you leaving?" Scott asked me.

I smiled. "I'm not. Isn't that great? I'm never leaving."

The boy's jaw dropped as if he'd just seen the boogieman. He looked at his sister in wide-eyed horror.

"What do you mean by 'never?'" his sister asked.

The wine I'd just swallowed didn't seem to want to go down. It had turned into one big, choking bubble. "When you love someone, you don't want to leave them. I love your daddy and I love you. I'm going to stay and be like a second mommy."

"You mean you're Daddy's girlfriend?" Scott asked.

A cold pang of shock with through me as I looked at Greg.

"Yes, Scott," he explained. "Remember we talked about Helen and how she and I were going to be together again? You remember her and how she used to play with you and take you to the park."

"I thought she was someone you worked with at your office," Scott said.

I experienced a sinking feeling.

"She and I work for the same company. We still do."

"I thought she was our babysitter when we were away from Mommy," Cassandra added.

Baffled, I looked at Greg.

Greg looked at me helplessly, as if he, too, had been caught by surprise. "No, honey. You probably were too little at the time to realize it, but she was my girlfriend."

"You can't be Daddy's girlfriend!" she burst out. "Mommy is his girlfriend!"

The temperature of the room seemed to plunge fifty degrees. What's going on?

"Cassandra, Mommy doesn't want to be my girlfriend. We've talked about this before."

"Honey, I'm not trying to take your mommy's place," I said soothingly. "No one ever could. No one could ever be more special to you than she is. But I love your daddy and I want us all to be friends. Don't you think we can do that?"

She stuck out her bottom lip and shook her head.

"Of course, we can," Greg interjected.

"Daddy, I'm not hungry anymore," Scott said.

"Go on and play," he said. "I'll save your plate for later."

"Can I go, too?" his sister asked.

"Yes," he said.

Both scrambled from their chairs and went back to the living room.

"I don't understand," I said, stunned, once they were out of earshot. "You didn't tell them that we plan to get married?"

He ran a hand over his forehead. "I told them that you were coming to live here. As for marriage, I didn't use that word exactly. I wanted them to get used to the idea gradually."

"But I thought they understood."

"I thought they did, too, but that was nearly seven months ago. Seven months is a long time ago for a five and a seven-year-old."

"I thought they liked me," I said with disbelief. "We had so much fun together. Now, they don't want anything to do with me."

He took my hand and squeezed it. "Kids change. Just be patient. Everything will work out."

Greg refilled my wine glass and we made conversation, but I couldn't stop thinking about how my stepchildren-to-be had turned on me. I'd moved halfway across the country with visions of taking up where we'd left off, with all of us holding hands on our way to the ice cream store. I was so sure that I'd won their hearts. What had happened?

It was actually because of one of the children that I had met Greg. It was a Saturday morning and I'd stepped inside a neighborhood bakery for a pastry and a cup of coffee. I'd just finished eating and was putting away the newspaper I'd been reading when a man with two young children approached me.

"Excuse me," he said. "Would you mind walking my daughter into the restroom? I can't very well go in myself, and you look like a decent and respectable person. I'll be standing right outside the bathroom door."

"I'll be happy to," I said.

Wow, some women have all the luck, I thought as I took the little girl's hand. Daddy is a head-turner and so are the kids.

The little girl was pretty independent and didn't need much help, but I had to hold her up so she could reach the sink to wash her hands. When we stepped out, Daddy made sure she thanked me.

She said it with an endearing little voice that made me think of a talking doll. Then she smiled shyly, showing little white teeth and a dimple in one cheek.

"What beautiful children you have," I said.

"Thank you, but all children are beautiful, don't you think?"

"I think you're right."

"Thank you for letting me impose on you," he said. "I saw that you were getting ready to leave. I hope you're not in a hurry."

"Not at all," I said as we exited the bakery. "I usually meet a girlfriend here on Saturday mornings, but she's out of town, visiting her parents."

"This is my visitation weekend with my children," he explained. "By the way, I'm Greg Garretson," he said, offering a hand.

"Helen North," I responded.

"Cassandra is four; Scott is six," he said. "Thanks again for helping out."

"You're quite welcome."

"I can swing higher than the sky. You want to see?" the boy asked.

I laughed, not sure what to say.

"We're on our way to the park," Greg said. "Why don't you join us?"

"I wouldn't want to intrude on a family outing."

"I've already intruded on your peaceful Saturday morning. Besides, Scott wants to show you what a swinger he is." The twinkle in his eyes was irresistible.

"Sure," I relented.

That was how it started. It was almost as if fate had provided a guiding hand. At the park, we sat on a bench while the kids took turns showing off for us. We talked as if we'd known each other forever.

He was a thirty-three-year-old quality control specialist. Eight years younger, I was an administrative assistant. Amazingly, we worked for the same large corporation, but our paths had never crossed. We also discovered that we both loved roller blading and Seinfeld reruns.

Then the kids began to tire and we said our good-byes. Greg gave no hint, outside of work, that we might ever see each other again. Realistically, I thought, why should we? I'd simply done him a favor. He'd been nice in return and that was the end of it. Yet, as I'd walked home, I'd felt that old, familiar yearning. Greg and his children represented the family I'd always dreamed of having.

My parents were killed in a plane crash when I was four. An only child, I was raised by my grandmother. She didn't have much money, but she provided a lot of love. Yet our house was quiet and sometimes a bit sad because there was just the two of us, but someday, I knew I'd have a family of my own—a devoted husband, two or three children, a dog, and a cat. We would live a white house with black shutters. Oddly enough, the man in those dreams had looked a lot like Greg. The only thing different about that picture was that our family wouldn't be ready made.

To my surprise, I got a call on my office phone a few weeks later. It was Greg. He asked if I'd like to go with him the following weekend to take the kids roller blading. Excitedly, I agreed.

The more I got to know the kids, the more I liked them. At Greg's apartment, I played trains with Scott and dolls with Cassandra. We made cookies together. I taught Cassandra how to doggie paddle and taught Scott how to throw horseshoes. I'd fallen in love with their father. I'd also fallen in love with them. I saw the children only twice a month, but if their enthusiasm for our activities was any indication, they liked me, too.

"You're great with them," Greg said. "It makes me sad to tell you what I'm about to say."

My breath caught in my throat. "What is it?"

"Their mother is moving to the West Coast to be near her parents. I asked the company for a transfer so I could be near the children. They approved it today."

Unwanted tears sprang to my eyes. "You're leaving?"

He pulled me into his arms. "I want to continue our relationship, although I know a long-distance relationship can be hard. A separation can be a good test for us."

I was too choked up and stunned to say anything.

"Let's take it a day at a time," he continued. "Then we'll see what comes next."

At first, I couldn't see the wisdom of what he was saying. I wondered if it was his way of easing out of the relationship. Maybe he secretly still cared for his ex-wife. Was I losing a family all over again?

But it didn't turn out that way. After he left, we kept in daily contact by phone and email. He sent pictures of himself and the children. If anything, I wanted him more than ever. Finally, he flew back to the Midwest so that we could spend a week together. "Why don't you see about getting a transfer so we can be together?" he asked.

I was overjoyed. It took two months to get the transfer approved. I sold my secondhand furniture and household goods and boarded a flight to the West Coast. All I had left were my clothes, a few boxes of books, and family mementoes. I was trading an old life for a new one, one that included the family I'd always dreamed of.

But now, two-thirds of this family suddenly had no use for me.

"Why don't I put the kids to bed so we can talk some more?" Greg suggested.

I quickly agreed. Maybe they were just tired. Maybe things would be better in the morning.

I said good night to them both as Greg hustled them off to bed. They said good night to me, only at his prodding. I held back from offering to read them a bedtime story as I had months before. I knew I couldn't push myself into their lives. I had to let things come naturally.

I was finishing the kitchen cleanup when Greg slipped up behind me and kissed the back of my neck. "Alone at last," he whispered.

I turned to him with a burst of love in my heart. "I'm so glad to be here with you, but I'm worried about the kids."

"I had a little talk with them. I reminded them of the fun we used to have together. You and I probably would have acted the same at that age. We just need to give them time." He pulled me closer. "Now, let's make up for some lost time."

That led to the bedroom. As we started to make love, our other worries faded away. His love and support made me feel that I could conquer anything.

Before we could get completely involved, there was a tap on our bedroom door. My heart thumped as we threw ourselves apart.

"Daddy?" Cassandra called.

"Just a minute," Greg called, grabbing his pajama bottoms from the floor.

Hastily, I tossed on my nightgown.

Greg got up and opened the door. "What is it, honey?"

"Can I sleep with you? I had a bad dream."

My breath caught in my throat.

He picked her up and walked toward the foot of the bed. By the streetlight filtering through the blinds, I could tell that she was staring at me.

"What was your dream about?" he asked.

"A mean dog was chasing me," she said tearfully. "A mean, mean dog. He had teeth like butcher knives. I tried to get away, but I fell down and he jumped on me. And then I woke up."

"Poor baby," Greg said soothingly. "But it was only a dream. There is no mean dog here. Come on. Let's go back to bed. Your brother will be there with you. Everything will be all right."

"But I want you, Daddy. I'm scared. Please? I want to get in bed with you."

Greg heaved an audible sigh. "All right. Just for a little while."

My heart sank.

Greg climbed into bed next to me and put Cassandra on the edge of the mattress next to him. Once she was settled, he turned and whispered in my ear: "I'm sorry. When you have kids, these things happen."

"I know." I tried to sound understanding, but I couldn't help but worry. Did she really have a bad dream, or was this her way of reclaiming her daddy? Then I felt ashamed of myself. Is a five-year-old really capable of such manipulation?

I had trouble going to sleep. The man I loved was next to me and all I could do was to lie close to him. But his arms weren't around me. They were around his daughter.

I kept waiting for him to get up and carry a sleeping Cassandra back to her bed. But after an hour, I could tell by Greg's breathing that he was deep asleep.

With my body still in sync with Central Standard Time, I awoke at what was five o'clock on the West Coast. Beside me, Cassandra still slept next to her daddy. I took a deep breath. Today is a new day, a chance to start over. I have to win the kids over. I was going to work at it until I got it right.

I slipped out of bed quietly, dressed, and went into the kitchen.

Poking through the cabinets and the refrigerator, I was happy to find a bottle of maple syrup and basic ingredients for baking. I'd surprise the kids with pancakes.

I had everything ready to go when Greg emerged from the bedroom with Cassandra on his shoulders.

"Good morning, everybody," I said as cheerfully as I could. "Who likes pancakes?"

"We love pancakes," Greg said, setting Cassandra on her feet. He gave me a quick kiss. "Is that what you're up to?"

"Yes, it is."

Scott appeared with half the hem of his sweatshirt inside out. He looked slightly disoriented.

"Hi, sweetheart," I said. "Ready for some pancakes?"

"Is Daddy making pancakes?" he asked.

"No, I am."

"Oh," he said as if he were disappointed.

"They're the world's lightest pancakes," Greg joked. "They're yummy scrumptious."

The boy managed a slight smile, but the girl seemed unimpressed.

"You seem to know a lot about my pancakes considering that you've never tasted them," I joked as we stood alone in the kitchen. The kids were seated at the table with glasses of orange juice.

"I know they're made with love. That's the best ingredient."

But the kids didn't see it that way.

Although they came out just right, Cassandra declared, "My mommy makes the best pancakes."

"I like Daddy's best," Scott asserted.

Their verbal darts landed with a double whammy right in the middle of my heart.

Greg squeezed my hand under the table. "I vote for Helen's."

I smiled at him, but there was a lump in my throat.

"They hate me," I said a little while later. The kids were in their room getting ready for their mother to pick them up.

"They don't hate you," he insisted. "They're just a little threatened by your presence. For the record, however, I'm not. I'm absolutely thrilled by it."

I melted into his arms. "I'm not sure what to do."

"Just go on being your sweet self. I'll let the kids know that it's not nice to hurt people's feelings."

"I hope it won't make them hate me more."

"I'll tread carefully. In the meantime, try not to worry about it. We'll have the next two weeks to ourselves. That will give the kids time to get more accustomed to their little world being rearranged."

The doorbell rang.

"That's probably Molly," he said, rushing to answer it.

Anxiety surged through me like a bolt of electricity as Greg's ex-wife stepped inside.

"Mommy, Mommy!" the kids yelled, rushing into her arms.

She hugged them, and then looked up. Our eyes met in one awkward moment. She was tall, slim, and pretty with straight blond hair that grazed her shoulders. She wore black Capri pants, ballet flats, and a pale, blue knit top that came almost to her knees. I suddenly felt frumpy in my faded jeans and sneakers.

"Molly, I'd like for you to meet Helen," Greg said smoothly.

She stepped forward and shook my hand with surprising warmth. "I'm happy to meet you. Greg has always had good taste in women. I can see that he still does."

The combination joke and compliment left me momentarily speechless. "Why, that's very nice of you to say."

"Welcome to the West Coast," she said.

"Thank you."

"I guess it's time to gather up my little urchins and go home. I hope they haven't been too much trouble for you."

"Not at all," I fibbed.

"How was your class reunion?" Greg asked.

"I had the best time. I met an old boyfriend. As it turns out, he's single now, too. We plan on getting together sometime."

"If you do, you can always drop the kids off here," Greg said.

"I know that, and I appreciate it. By the way," she said, reaching into her purse, "I have some tickets to a basketball game. A friend gave them to me, but I won't be using them. I thought the two of you might like to go."

Greg took them. "Thanks a lot. We just might."

"Got to run," she said. "It was very nice meeting you, Helen."

"It was nice meeting you, too," I said, dazed.

Greg kissed the kids good-bye and they were gone.

"I wasn't expecting her to be so friendly and relaxed about everything," I remarked afterward.

"Like I said, it was a friendly divorce."

"Maybe she was just being gracious. I mean, it would be strange to see your ex-spouse with someone else, wouldn't it? Some women would be resentful. She seems to be okay with it. How could that be?"

"Maybe it's because we went to the altar not as starry-eyed lovers, but as dutiful parents-to-be. She was four months pregnant with Scott."

I looked at him in surprise. "I thought you said it was basic incompatibility."

"It was, but now you know the root of it. Don't get me wrong; neither of us would trade those two kids for anything, but we became parents before we really knew each other. Later, Molly had a fling with another man. She was contrite about it, but things were never the same between us."

I heaved a sigh. "I'm so sorry. I had no idea."

"I hesitated to go into detail because, after all, she's the mother of my children. I didn't want you to think I was denigrating her. Now that you're here and our relationship has gotten to the stage that it has, you might as well know."

"So, you get along with her pretty well?"

"Oddly enough, we get along better divorced than we did when we were married," he said.

"What does she think about you and me?"

"As you can see, she's pretty accepting of it."

"I wish the same were true of the kids."

He held me close. "I'm sorry about last night. I'm sorry about this morning. But don't worry, things will get better."

During the next two weeks, I got settled in my job and in my new home. I hung my clothes next to Greg's and bought a small bookcase for my books. I added my signature to the living room by putting one of my most prized family mementoes on a chest by the entryway. It was a plate my mother had painted by hand not long after I was born. On it was a cradle and my name and date of birth. It sat on a special stand.

Greg and I got reacquainted. It was almost like a honeymoon. We made love at odd hours of the day and he treated me to his favorite restaurants. We even went to the basketball game, using Molly's tickets. Being alone with Greg reminded me of everything I'd instantly liked about him—his thoughtfulness, his sense of humor, and the fact that he was a good father. Now, I was worried about what kind of stepmother I was going to be.

Our two-week "honeymoon" was over much too soon. It was time for the kids to come back again to spend the weekend. Greg and I decided that keeping the kids busy with outside activities would help take the pressure off them and me. We planned on roller blading and a children's museum.

Nervously, I got everything ready for them. I changed the sheets on their twin beds, bought new coloring books and crayons, and rented some cartoon videos. But on Saturday morning, not long before they were due to arrive, Greg discovered he had a low tire and hurried to a nearby station to have it repaired. He had yet to return when Molly showed up with the kids.

"Where's Daddy?" Scott asked, looking around.

"He should be back any minute," I said.

"You kids be good for Daddy and Helen," Molly said, giving them quick hugs. As usual, she looked casually stylish.

"Bye, Helen," she said with a friendly wave. "See you Sunday."

When the door closed, I found myself face to face with my little detractors.

"Well, what's new with you two?" I asked with all the cheerfulness I could muster.

"Nothing," Cassandra said. She clutched her teddy bear backpack as if she were afraid I'd try to take it from her.

"When's Daddy going to be back?" Scott asked.

"Any minute now," I repeated. "Why don't you go to your room and put away your things? You can watch cartoons while you wait."

Scott trudged down the hall, followed by his sister. I checked in on them to make sure they were settled before went to the kitchen. Although it really didn't need it, I began cleaning the sink to help relieve my nervous energy.

A few minutes later, I heard giggles and thumping noises coming from their room. When I looked in on them, I found them jumping wildly on the beds I'd so carefully made. The spreads were in disarray and the pillows had been flung to the floor. The mattresses squeaked from the beating they were taking.

"Scott, Cassandra, please. No bed jumping," I said. "You could fall and hurt yourselves."

"No, we won't," Scott said, continuing to jump.

I took him by the arm. "I'm sorry, no bed jumping," I repeated firmly, leading him off the bed. Cassandra jumped down on her own.

Scott pulled away from me. "You're not our mother," he said angrily.

"No, I'm not. But we should all learn to respect each other because I hope to be your stepmother."

"No, you can't be," he said. "All you can be is a step-monster."

I struggled to conceal my shock. "It makes me unhappy to hear you say that. It hurts my feelings."

Scott stared at me in silence, but my amateur psychology didn't work on Cassandra.

"You're not taking our daddy away," she cried.

"Honey, no one is taking your daddy away. He's always going to be yours. He'll never belong to anybody the way he belongs to you." As soothing as I tried to sound, I knew it wasn't helping the situation much. I'd made myself even more of a villain by disciplining them.

When Greg walked through the front door about that time, I breathed a sigh of relief.

"Daddy!" they yelled, running toward him.

He lifted them both off their feet at the same time. "Are you ready to go skating?"

"Yeah, let's go," Scott said.

I kept up a happy front at the skating rink and later at a miniature golf course. The kids seemed to have forgotten about our encounter, but I had a hard time putting it behind me. As the kids circled the rink, they gravitated around their father, making me feel like a fifth wheel. I'd hoped my relationship with the kids would be improving. Instead, it was getting worse.

"Anything wrong?" Greg asked as we sat down. We'd stopped for refreshments and the kids were back on the rink.

"I'm just a little tired, I guess," I fibbed. This was his weekend with his children. I didn't want to spoil it.

Thanks to the back-to-back activities we'd planned, the weekend passed without another major incident. However, there were a couple of minor ones. Cassandra refused to let me help her with her coat. "I want Daddy to do it," she'd said stubbornly. Scott wanted to ride in the front seat with his father, but Greg had refused.

After they left, a wave of exhaustion fell over me. "I'm trying, Greg. I really am."

He sat down next to me and put his arm around me. "Rome wasn't built in a day."

"But your ex-wife seems so accepting of our relationship. It seems the kids would pick up on that."

"They're kids," he said.

When I told him what about the bed-jumping confrontation, his eyes grew even darker with concern.

"I'm sorry. I had no idea. I'll have a talk with them."

"If you do, I'm afraid they'll think I'm a snitch and resent me even more."

Greg sighed. "I wish, too, that things were going a little bit better. Let's not get discouraged. It's too early for that."

"But what if they don't?"

"Then we'll worry about that later. In the meantime, let's take it a day at a time."

But the experience left one nagging question in my mind: What if things don't improve? Would Greg still want to marry me?

In the days to come, I'd see happy families together. Can we ever be like them? I wondered despairingly.

I love Greg. He was always doing something sweet and loving, like leaving a love note in my purse or surprising me with a little gift. But his children were making my life miserable.

I checked out every book that I could find on stepparenting. These relationships can take years to build, the books said. But they offered no magic formulas or easy answers.

What bothered me most was that Scott and Cassandra once acted as if they really liked me. What had happened?

Two weeks later the children were back, turning me again into a bundle of anxiety. I felt pressured to mend our relationship, but I didn't know how. They spoke to me, but I could still detect resentment in their eyes.

Right away, the kids decided that they wanted to go bike riding. Greg agreed, but there was one problem: I didn't have a bike.

"Sorry. We'll have to get you one," he whispered as the kids ran toward the garage.

"It's okay. I understand," I said. But I couldn't help but wonder if the kids were purposely trying to exclude me.

At noon, Greg returned with the kids. Their faces were flushed from riding in the cool autumn air. Greg's sleeve and part of his hair were splashed with mud from a passing car.

"Daddy, can we go out again this afternoon, just you, me, and Cassandra?" Scott asked.

My cheeks stung with rejection as Greg gave me an apologetic look.

"What about Helen?" Greg asked.

Scott responded with silence.

"If you were having a party, you wouldn't want me to tell you that one of your friends couldn't come, would you?"

"No," the boy said meekly.

"Helen is my friend and she is part of this family. This afternoon, we're going to Space Station Play Park and we're going together. Now, I would like for you to apologize to her."

"Sorry," he said halfheartedly.

"I accept your apology," I said, forcing a smile.

"I'll tell you what," Greg said gently. "I'm going to hop in the shower to clean up from the bike ride. You and Cassandra get your coloring books and crayons and make some nice pictures for Helen."

Neither of them moved.

"Come on. Get going," he said, giving them playful swats.

They disappeared, and then returned to the living room. They sat on the floor and began coloring at the coffee table. Scott's strokes were wild and sloppy. Cassandra colored slowly and without enthusiasm. While they played, I phoned in a pizza order for lunch. I wasn't going to risk having my cooking compared to their mother's again.

I was emptying out the dishwasher when I heard shrieking and laughing in the living room. I looked to see what was happening and found Scott chasing Cassandra. He was holding something between his fingers.

"What's going on?" I asked.

Ignoring me, they kept running.

I took Scott's arm, forcing him to stop.

"He's trying to put a bug down my back," Cassandra whined.

I looked at Scott. "Let me see."

"It was just a joke," he said, putting his hand behind his back."

"Please don't run in the house. I don't want you to fall and hurt yourself, okay?" I tried to temper my words with a smile.

As soon as they settled back down, I went back to the kitchen and took a deep breath. Why are they always testing me?

Only a few seconds had passed before I heard a thump, followed by the tinkle of shattered glass. I bolted from the kitchen to find my prized heirloom plate shattered on the wooden floor. My heart lunged into my throat as I rushed to gather up the pieces.

"Who did this?" I demanded.

"He was chasing me again," Cassandra said with a frightened look in her eyes. "I didn't do it on purpose. I bumped into it."

"I thought I told both of you to stop running."

Neither of them said anything.

"Now look what's happened."

Greg appeared in the room. "What's going on?"

I held up two large pieces of my plate.

"Cassandra broke it," Scott said.

"It was Scott's fault," she countered. "He chased me."

Greg looked at me. "Is that what happened?"

"I didn't actually see it. I just heard a crash. They'd been running before and I asked them to stop."

Greg looked at them intensely. "Why didn't you listen to Helen?"

Both responded with silence.

"Why were you chasing your sister?"

"He was going to put a bug down my back," Cassandra interjected.

"Where's the bug?" Greg asked.

He held out a broken piece of black crayon. "It was just pretend."

Greg sighed. "That plate meant a lot to Helen. Her mother made it when she was a baby."

"She can get another one," Scott said.

"No, it wouldn't be the same."

Once again, Greg made the kids apologize. "We're going to have lunch, and then I'm going to take you home," he said.

"What about the play park?" Cassandra asked.

"You haven't been behaving yourselves. We'll go to the play park only after you learn to behave and to show respect for other people."

"I don't care," Scott sulked. "Mom will take us."

A muscle twitched in Greg's jaw. "I don't think so. I'm going to have a talk with her."

During lunch, Greg tried to act as if nothing had happened, but he wasn't that convincing. A dark cloud hung over the room. I tried to pretend that I'd put the incident behind me, but I secretly grieved the loss of the keepsake. I tried to minimize things by telling Cassandra that I knew she didn't do it on purpose, but it seemed like no matter how hard I tried with the kids, nothing helped.

Only when Greg left to take the kids home was I able to let my guard down. As I gathered up the pieces of the plate and put them in a box, tears stung my eyes. It was then that I noticed that the top drawer of the chest on which the plate had sat was slightly open. I opened it further to see if any pieces had fallen inside. To my surprise, I found a beautifully framed eight-by-ten picture of Greg's ex-wife. Her black, feathery gown showed off her bare shoulders and a good two inches of cleavage.

I stared at the glamour shot with incomprehension. What's it doing here? Why is Greg keeping a picture of Molly?

And there was more. Also in the drawer was an album of family pictures. I flipped through it to find Greg and Molly as they posed happily with their children, from birth to more recently.

I shoved both of them back in the drawer and slammed it shut as a sick feeling spread over me. I'd uprooted myself because I'd been so sure of Greg's commitment to me. Now, I felt like a fool. Not only did his children hate me, but also he still seemed to be harboring feelings for his ex-wife. I slumped down on the sofa with my head in my hands. What was I going to do?

Suddenly, the lock clicked in the front door. I quickly wiped my eyes and stood.

"I'm so sorry, Greg said, stepping into the living room. "I don't know what's gotten into those kids."

"I tried so hard," There was a lump in my throat.

He put his arms around me. "Don't blame yourself."

I pulled back. "Greg, I have to ask you something."

His eyes narrowed. "What is it?"

"Do you still care for Molly?"

"Other than the fact that she's the mother of my children?"

"Yes."

"Why do you ask?"

I pulled open the drawer and removed the picture. "Why are you keeping this?"

His lips parted in surprise. "I've never seen it before."

"How could you not? It was in this drawer, along with a family photo album."

"Molly gave me a copy of the album, so we could each have copies of the kids' baby pictures. But I don't know where the picture of her came from."

I looked at him with pained skepticism. "Greg, I don't think this is working out."

There was a stricken look on his face. "Don't you believe me?"

"There has been too much happening that doesn't make sense."

With my heart pounding in my throat, I rushed into the bedroom. I pulled my suitcases out of the closet and began tossing my clothes inside.

"What are you doing?" There was an undertone of alarm in his voice.

"I'm leaving. I don't belong here."

"No, please. . . ." he said, trying to put his arms around me. "Stop and think things out."

I pulled away and faced him squarely. "How is that going to change things? Your children hate me, and now I find out you're keeping a picture of your ex-wife. That was the last straw. I can't take it anymore."

I tossed the rest of my clothes into the suitcases as Greg stood by.

"I love you," he said. "You have to believe that."

"I don't know what to believe anymore." I snapped the cases closed and set them down in the living room. I refused Greg's offer to carry them.

"You can't just walk out like this," he said. "Where are you going?"

I picked up the box containing my broken plate. "There are plenty of motels." "Please, Helen, stay and we'll talk this out."

I laid my keys to the condo on the chest containing his ex-wife's picture. "Good-bye, Greg."

With my throat aching with repressed sobs, I loaded my things into the used car I'd bought and started the engine. As I backed away, the sight of Greg standing helplessly by the door sent hot tears trickling down my cheeks.

I called in sick the following Monday. I spent the day in my motel room staring at soap operas and daytime talk shows, but they offered little escape from my misery. I made tentative plans to return to the Midwest. I wanted to put everything behind me, but I knew it wouldn't be easy. Despite his children, despite his ex-wife, I'd never be able to get him completely out of my heart.

I managed to go back to work the next day, taking pains to avoid any area where I might run into Greg. When a coworker innocently asked me about him, it took all the self-control I had to keep from bursting into tears.

After work, I picked up something to eat from a Chinese carryout. I wasn't hungry, but I'd eaten so little for several days that my stomach was making a racket. I was just settling down to eat in my motel room when there was a knock on the door.

"Helen, it's me, Greg," came a muffled call.

My heart kicked. I scrambled off the bed and opened the door, leaving the chain in place. "How did you find me?" I asked.

"I followed you from the parking lot at work. Helen, I have to talk to you. What I have to say is important."

Hesitantly, I unlatched the chain and let him in. "If you just want to apologize again, there's no need. What's over is over."

He shook his head. "No, listen to me. I found out why the children were misbehaving."

I stared at him, puzzled. "What do you mean?"

"I took the kids last night because Molly and her mother were hosting a kitchenware party. Of course, the first thing the kids noticed was that you were gone. When I told them that you'd moved out, Cassandra said, 'Mommy will be glad.'

"When I questioned Scott about it, he admitted that Molly had told them that if they were mean, then maybe you would go away and Mommy and Daddy could get back together again."

I took a sharp breath. "She didn't."

He nodded sadly. "She admitted it."

I stared at him in shock. "What about the picture?"

"She put it in Scott's backpack and asked him to leave it in the drawer."

I sat on the bed weakly. "She really wants you back, doesn't she?"

"The way I see it, she acted out of need, not love. When you really love someone, you don't try to mess up their lives." He sat down beside me and put his arm around me. "I don't want her back. I want you. That is, if it's not too late."

I burst into tears. "No, it's not too late."

Greg and I are back together again and my relationship with the kids is much better. Scott and Cassandra decorated a new plate for me and Greg took it to a craft shop and had it fired. It says, "For our special friend, Helen." There are self-portraits of the kids on it.

They're in counseling now with their mother. As it turns out, Molly became depressed when the man she was having an affair with broke off their relationship. Then she began abusing tranquilizers and alcohol. She wanted Greg back, not because she still loved him, but because she didn't want to be alone. Life without Greg was more complicated than she'd bargained for. To hide her motives, she pretended to be supportive of our relationship.

I'd been naïve to think that I could just step in and become part of Greg's family overnight. Even under the best of circumstances, it can be a long process. By giving up too soon, I almost lost him.

I know that I've walked into a complicated situation, but my eyes are wide open now and I'm going to give it everything I've got. Greg is just as committed to make this work as I am. Since our love for each other has survived this, it's a very good sign for the future.

THE END

CONFESSIONS OF A COVER WIFE
"His Secret Is Safe With Me"

I had to swallow hard as Hank put a comforting hand over mine and handed me a tissue as the organist started to play a hauntingly sad funeral song. Thirty-one years of marriage and now it was time to say good-bye to Luke. How could I say good-bye to such a good and decent person? Tears started to stream down my face.

Hank, my husband's friend, shifted in his seat and wrapped an arm around my shoulder, pulling me closer and offering me strength to make it through the service. His body radiated warmth and vigor. As I took a deep, cleansing breath and exhaled, I nodded at him, indicating I was okay. He nodded back, and I thought—not for the first time—how lucky Luke had been to have Hank in his life.

I was Luke's first partner, but Hank was his last. Somehow we'd made it work and ended up a family. He had a right to be in the front pew of the church. The family pew. He's as much a part of Luke's life as any of the rest of us.

Nobody around us knew it, and that was the way my husband and Hank had wanted it.

I have to admit that at first, part of me wanted to hate Hank. After all, he's the man my husband fell in love with after twenty years of being married to me. But Hank has a way of getting into people's hearts, an un-showy way of knowing when it was the right time to step forward and be a friend.

Luke and I had a great life. We'd met as freshmen at the University of Miami, dated—well, mostly studied together—through college and then started getting serious shortly after graduation. Nobody was a bit surprised when we got engaged just a year later.

Luke's job as an accountant kept him busy in those early years of marriage, and so did my teaching job. But we made sure we found lots of time to be together, too.

When I had PTA meetings or teacher conferences, Luke would always be there when I got home, waiting up for me and with a warmed-up dinner on the kitchen table, along with the glass of red wine he knew I'd need.

And when tax season came around and he had to work sixteen-hour days, I made sure to pick up his favorite nutrition bars and stash them in his briefcase, knowing he might not have time for a decent meal.

We cared about each other and we knew how to have a good time in bed, too. From the minute we started dating to our first years of marriage, we made time to get physical.

I could be sitting on the sofa, enjoying an intense movie, and all he'd have to do would be to rub a certain vulnerable spot on my shoulder or nip at my earlobe and I could have been watching fuzz for all I cared.

All my attention would be redirected to the feelings elicited by his touch and the crazy way my body reacted. So many days were like that. We could be in the middle of something and just a shared look was enough to make us stop in our tracks and head to the bedroom.

Three years after we were married, we found ourselves expecting our first baby.

Luke was apprehensive and downright scared at first. I think he was worried about how we'd be able to afford a baby, but he was definitely happy. We both had good jobs and although we were just getting started in our careers, I knew we'd be perfectly fine financially and otherwise.

Months later, we were blessed with two wonderful children! Twins. Jonathan and Julia were our little bundles of joy.

From the moment the nurse handed little Julia to Luke seconds after she was born, I could tell that Luke was going to be a great dad. Tears were running down his cheeks and he looked deep into her eyes. He cradled her close, and I could see a protective instinct kick in.

I was right; we'd be just fine. We might not have a boatload of money to spend on our kids, but our love would help us make it through.

As any parent knows, the first few years of being a new parent are tough—especially when the work is doubled with twins. We were up many times through the night with feedings, diaper changes, and dealing with Jonathan's colic.

Unlike many of my friends, who constantly complained that their husbands didn't help enough with the kids, Luke did his share. I think that made both of us better parents because I was rested and ready for the day most of the time, and he was a huge part of their lives.

With all this work, sex took a backseat. When we weren't working, we were busy with the kids. When we weren't, well, catching up on our sleep seemed to be a bigger priority than anything else. We'd often nap in each other's arms or fall asleep cuddled together on the sofa.

The lack of sex wasn't obvious to me. We still enjoyed a lot of time together—reading, watching movies, going out to dinner—it just wasn't in bed. We found time occasionally for intimacy, but as the kids hit elementary-school age, we were probably only having sex once a month or so.

It wasn't until the kids were teenagers that I realized it. I was taking dinner out of the oven and Luke called to say he'd be working late and not to wait dinner for him.

Well, as most wives will tell you, there's a strange mental red flag that goes up when a husband says this often. Something in my gut told me there might be cause for concern. And, when pressed to think about it, I realized it had been a good three months or more since we'd had sex. I was no expert, but I had to admit this couldn't be a good sign. But still . . . I dismissed it.

Problem was, the reason I didn't focus on our lack of sex was because everything else was going so well. Luke and I got along great and we were always there if one of us needed the other. When the accounting firm he worked for closed down and he lost his job, I made sure he knew we'd be okay. While he was looking for work, I started tutoring to make extra income so we'd be able to pay our bills.

Then he decided to open his own tax firm. The kids and I did whatever we could to help him. We painted his new office during summer vacation, helped him start up a website, and I helped promote his new business by writing ads for the local paper.

Luke was there for me. When my mom was diagnosed with Alzheimer's, he was the one who insisted I take a leave of absence from work. Luke, the one who was always so worried about making ends meet, made sure I felt comfortable knowing my wages weren't as important as being there for my mom.

When she passed away just one short year after her diagnosis, the only thing I wanted after coming home from the hospital was Luke's shoulder and strong arms around me. He was my comfort, my friend, and the person who knew me so well that we almost didn't need words to communicate.

Luke's tax business was in a quaint shopping strip outside of town. Sometimes I'd swing by the office on my way home from school just to say hi or let him know about some after-school event that had just come up. Both Jonathan and Julia loved sports and they always had a game or match. Luke and I would drop everything to go cheer them on.

We had a great life. The kids were happy, doing well in school, and on their way to becoming successful high school students.

That's why, one Saturday when the kids were off at their friends' houses and Luke was working at the office, I almost dropped a dish I was washing when it suddenly hit me that I couldn't remember the last time we'd had sex. Sure, we slept together every night, and usually a quick peck good-bye in the morning and hello in the evening, but none of the hot and heavy stuff.

I set the dish down in the sink and absently looked out the kitchen window at the blooming pink dogwood trees in the yard and tried to calculate exactly how long it'd been since we were intimate.

At least six months. Between soccer games, family functions, and work, we'd stopped making time to be alone together. How can that be?

I moved to the table, feeling a sudden, overwhelming need to sit because my legs were shaky. This happens to other couples, doesn't it? I'd overheard plenty of conversations in the faculty lounge about sex slacking off after years of marriage. It isn't always a sign of trouble, is it?

We were happy. We were very happy. I loved Luke and I was pretty sure he still loved me. A little voice started nagging me. Another woman, it said. But wouldn't I feel it in my gut?

My gut told me one thing and one thing only: he loved me. He was constantly doing things for me, calling me from the office frequently, and would do anything I asked of him. If this isn't love, what is?

The only thing missing was a roll in the hay. So I'd have to make up for lost time. He probably hadn't even noticed the lack of alone time because he'd been so busy recently, too.

It just so happened that the kids both had plans that very evening.

With a smile on my face, I showered with my favorite vanilla-scented bath gel and took extra care to look my best. By the time he walked in the door after a long day at the office, the scent of his favorite beef stew filled the house and I was waiting for him with a big smile on my face, wearing a robe with nothing underneath.

"Mmm," he said, pulling me in for a hug and kissing my lips.

When I tried to make the kiss last longer than a peck, he wriggled and I could tell he felt uncomfortable.

"What's that great smell?" he asked, walking to the stove, not noticing the look of rejection on my face.

Or had he noticed it and decided to ignore it? Okay, I wondered what was going on.

I decided not to spoil the mood by whining. Maybe he'd had a long day. Dinner . . . and then we'd see what happened.

As I bent to light one of the candles on the kitchen table, my robe came open a little, revealing more than I'd anticipated. I couldn't help notice that he saw, but turned away. Really?

Again, I shoved the thought to the back of my head.

"I made your favorite beef stew," I said, tightening the belt on my robe and moving to the stove.

"Smells great," he said. "Where are the kids?"

"Jonathan's working on a project with two classmates and Julia's at the movies with some of her soccer team friends."

He nodded and took the bowl I held out to him. Feeling suddenly awkward next to the man I'd been married to for twenty years, I filled my bowl after he took a seat at the table.

He had to notice that I'd gone to extra trouble, so why wasn't he saying anything? The fact that I knew he noticed, but wasn't addressing the issue, made me very nervous.

He took bite of his stew and chewed, staring into the flame of one of the candles. Then he put the spoon down and turned to look at me.

When you're married to someone for twenty years, you get to know certain looks that your partner gives you. I was suddenly looking at the "I've got bad news" look. He had something to tell me and it wouldn't be good.

Taking a deep breath to brace myself, I figured we'd better get it over with, whatever it was.

"Okay," I said, blowing out the breath. "Let me have it."

I found myself wishing we had a bottle of wine in the house. My hands were shaking and I was craving a glass of wine.

He didn't even try to pretend that he didn't know what I was talking about. Nodding slowly, he pushed his bowl out of the way and covered my hand with his.

"You know I love you," he started.

And then my heart went crazy, pounding hard in my chest, and doing flips and turns that echoed down to my stomach. I was going to be sick. Those words could never be the precursor of good news.

"I've wanted to tell you for some time now, but I couldn't find the words."

He glanced at the candles, and then glanced at the gap in my robe and his meaning was clear. He had noticed all the trouble I'd gone to and he knew where I wanted this night to go.

"Jackie," he said, leaning forward and begging me with his expression to look into his eyes.

I couldn't take my gaze off his strong hand on mine. I didn't want to lose what we had. It wasn't until this very moment that I realized what people meant when they said someone was their soul mate. In that instant, I know that if he was going to tell me we were through—that there was another woman—my soul would be gone.

He reached to lift my chin with two gentle fingers, forcing me to meet his gaze. His eyes were watery and concerned. My heart lifted just a little knowing that his concern was genuine. He still cared about me. I had that at least.

"There's no easy way to say this," he said, keeping eye contact with me. "I love you."

Suddenly, I couldn't take it anymore.

"Just say it, Luke! Who is she?"

I felt the hot burn of anger creeping up my neck and he let his fingers drop from under my chin. I held fast, glaring into his sad eyes.

"Not she," he said, twisting his napkin in his hands. "He."

He couldn't have shocked me any more if he'd slapped me. Questions tumbled around in my head, but none of them made it out of my mouth. My head started pounding as if I'd hit it on cement.

Once Luke had gotten the words out, it seemed like he couldn't stop talking. Pushing his chair back from the table, he stood, looking down at me with tears dripping down his face and then turned to start pacing the kitchen floor.

"I didn't mean for anything to happen. I mean nothing happened yet," he said. "I didn't know what was happening at first, and then I realized it was love." He stopped just long enough to take a breath. "Not like the kind of love you and I have. It's more like, well, I don't even know how to explain it."

"How long?"

My words were shaky, but I managed to get them out all the same.

He shook his head and sat down again, pulling his chair close to mine so we were face to face. I knew I was in shock.

"I think I've known for a long time that I'm more interested in guys than women. But I've been trying to deny it."

"And now you've found someone?" I asked, fear gripping at my stomach.

Fear for the life changes that were ahead of me. Selfishly, I wasn't thinking about him and his struggle, I was wondering how this was going to affect our children and me.

He nodded his head slowly in answer.

"So you're leaving us for him?" I croaked, my voice cracking on the last words when tears started streaming down my face like Niagara Falls.

He leaned in to pull me into a hug. My traitorous body—instead of pushing him away for all the hurt he was causing me—fell into my old reliable mode and let my pain wash over his strong body.

He hugged me and let me sob for a full ten minutes. Even when I was finished, he kept running his hands over my back, soothing me. I hated myself for letting him comfort me, but he was my rock and I needed his strength.

I was the first to pull away and he stood, walked across the room, and returned with a box of tissues. Pulling one out and handing it to me, he sat back in his chair.

"I don't want to leave you, Jackie. I don't want to leave the kids."

I swiped at my tears and blew my nose, trying to process what he was saying. I found myself staring at the dripping wax on the romantic pink candles. Moving to lean forward, I blew out the candles with a loud breath and then plopped back in my chair. Romantic dinner. Yeah.

"I don't understand," I said.

"I know it's selfish of me," he started. "But I've been thinking. . . ."

I had no idea where he could be going. I felt myself go a little numb—probably some sort of self-protection mechanism kicking in. But again, the one thing that kept running through my mind was the question of what was going to become of me and how this was going to affect Jonathan and Julia.

"I still love you so much, Jackie. And I love the kids. This is very selfish, I know, but I was wondering if you would consider keeping things as they are."

"You want me to cover for you?" I blurted, unable to believe what he was asking.

With a shrug of his shoulders, he nodded.

"In a way I guess that is what I'm asking." He leaned forward to take both of my hands in his. "I don't want to lose you, but I'm not . . . well, I'm not interested in the things I used to be interested in anymore."

"Sex with a woman?" I said, hoping to hurt him, even though I regretted the words as soon as they came out of my mouth.

I could see that I'd hit the spot when he blinked several times and hurt filled his eyes. He nodded.

I pushed back my chair so hard that it almost flipped over. Instinctively, he reached out to catch it before gravity pulled it down.

"I'm going for a walk."

I started for the door.

"Jackie," Luke said, moving to block the exit. "You might want to change first."

In my haste to get away from him, I forgot I was wearing only a flimsy robe with nothing underneath.

I was so lost in my thoughts during my long walk that I must have ignored at least five neighbors.

By the time I came home, I had no more of an idea about what to do than I did before I left the house an hour earlier. If anything, as the words and meaning of our conversation sunk in, I was more confused than ever.

I pushed open the cheerful, red door of our white stucco house. The home we were so proud to be able to afford when the twins were five. It was in the best school district in the state and there were lots of great neighbors.

Neighbors! What are the neighbors going to say when they catch wind of the idea that Luke is gay? Will they blame me? Say I haven't done enough to keep my guy happy?

I shook my head as I realized that worrying about what the neighbors thought was going to be the least of my problems.

Luke walked out from the kitchen, dishtowel in hand. While I was gone, he'd cleaned up the mess from dinner and the warm scent of my favorite peach tea filled the kitchen. He knew me so well. Knew how to make me feel better, always had my best interests at heart.

So many of my friends complained about their husbands being selfish, but even after twenty years Luke treated me with respect and kindness.

Feeling the need to be held by him overtake me, I flew into his strong arms, watching as the dishtowel fluttered to the floor like a white flag symbolizing my need to surrender to my feelings. Giving me his full attention, he held me close. I choked on a sob, but no tears came.

"I'm sorry, Jackie. I'm so sorry," he whispered in my ear.

It took me about a week to come out of the daze his confession had put me in. I felt like a robot—making lunches, signing permission slips, and handing out worksheets to my second-grade reading class.

During a break at school, I found myself pulling out my cell phone and pressing the speed dial button for Luke. It was an old habit, and it was as if my fingers had a mind of their own. Before I could hang up, Luke answered.

"Jackie?" he asked, breathless.

From the talking in the background I could tell he had been in the middle of a meeting and had jumped up to take the call. As the sounds in the background disappeared, I could picture him closing the conference room door behind him and standing in the quiet hallway. Every time I called him, every time I needed him, he'd been there for me. From the moment we met, and even now. I was a priority in his life.

Tears welled in my eyes and I bit my bottom lip to keep from crying.

"Jackie?" he asked, quieter this time, as if he knew I was trying not to cry.

Yes, he'd been there for me every time I'd ever needed him. Sure, I'd been there for him, too. But he needed me in a big way now. And I was going to be there for him.

Feeling a weight drop off my shoulders, I smiled—a real smile, not a forced one like I'd been plastering on all week.

"Luke, let's stay a family."

I could almost feel his happiness through the phone.

The next few months went by with almost no changes. Luke and I still slept in the same bed, but that's all we did. We sat side-by-side at the kids' soccer games, ate dinners together, and even went out with friends.

Strangely, it felt like we'd fallen back into our old pattern. I could almost forget he had a lover. As time went on, I found myself wanting to know more about this man.

We were alone in the car, driving home from one of Jonathan's soccer games, when I decided I had to know.

"So, what's this other guy's name?" I asked, a little afraid he would get mad that I was poking my nose into his private business.

He grinned, staring straight ahead out the windshield.

"I was wondering when you'd ask about him."

It felt so weird to be joking about this. I mean my husband was gay and we were going to stay together and present ourselves to the world as a married couple. And our children . . . we weren't going to tell them anything about the arrangement. At least not yet.

I smiled, glancing over at Luke's profile. He was a good-looking man. Still had a full head of thick, dark hair. And he kept himself in pretty good shape, too. The few wrinkles he had were crinkles around his eyes—smile wrinkles.

"Hank has been asking about you," he said, glancing at me over his sunglasses as we pulled to a stop at a traffic light.

"Hank?" I asked. "Hank from the karate school?"

Luke nodded and watched for my reaction. The strip mall where Luke had his tax preparation shop also boasted a coffee shop, barbershop, and a karate school. All this time, I'd been picturing some stranger with my husband. And it was Hank.

I thought I'd feel jealous when I finally found out who Luke's partner was. What I really felt was surprise. Surprise that it was someone I already knew.

I'd met Hank a few times when I was in Luke's office. He'd stop by and have lunch with Luke, or stop in to chat before going in to teach his evening classes. He was a popular karate teacher whose wife had passed away many years ago.

I wanted to hate Hank, but it was impossible. We invited him over for dinner, introducing him as Dad's friend from work. It felt wrong lying to Jonathan and Julia, but I wasn't sure when the timing would be right to disclose the facts to them. That was something Luke and I were going to have to decide on together.

Hank fit in well with our family. He was interested in the same action movies that we all liked, loved to play soccer, and even taught Julia how to improve her tennis backhand. Neither of our kids had taken a liking to karate, but they loved how Hank showed them some cool karate moves.

One evening, after a cookout with some neighbors, I was in the kitchen washing some of the serving platters when Hank came in carrying some empty bowls.

"Another great party, Jackie," Hank said, a shy expression crossing his face.

Things were pretty awkward between us, but I guessed that was to be expected.

"Thanks."

I moved to the side of the sink so Hank could put the bowls in. I couldn't help but wonder if things would ever be normal between us. How can they be? I wasn't sure, but I guessed we were both doing the best we could.

The day after that cookout was one of the worst in my life. I was waiting to make a left at the intersection—an intersection I drove through every morning on my way to work—when a dump truck plowed into me from behind, forcing me into oncoming rush-hour traffic.

I don't remember much, but when I came to hours later at the hospital, my whole body was throbbing. Luke was by my side and jumped out of the orange vinyl chair beside my bed when he saw my eyes flutter open.

"Ouch," I said. A lame attempt at humor.

Luke's lips curved into a small smile.

"Oh, Jackie," he said, tears straining at the corners of his eyes. "Thank God you're okay. Do you remember anything?"

I started to shake my head, but it hurt too much.

"No," I said. "I'm so thirsty."

Luke picked up a cup of ice chips from the bedside table.

"This is all you're allowed to—"

"The kids!" I said, my throat hurting from the exertion.

"With Hank," Luke said. "He took them to the movies and then out to dinner." Then he laid a gentle hand on my arm. "You were hit from behind by a dump truck. The guy lost his brakes. He pushed you right into the path of an SUV."

"What's the prognosis?" I said, feeling tears well up in my eyes.

"It's good, baby, it's good," Luke said, rubbing his hand up and down my arm. "You have a steel rod in your tibia to repair a broken bone and a few broken ribs that need to heal on their own." He gave me a small smile and added, "You're going to be in a wheelchair for a few days, need some physical therapy, and then you'll move to crutches before graduating from the rehab program."

It took eight full weeks before I could walk without using a walker or cane. Eight long weeks. I had to take a leave of absence from work, which meant Luke had to work extra-hard at his office.

Hank stepped up to the plate and helped with everything. He drove me to doctor appointments, brought groceries, and cooked dinners. He took the kids out often, too, to help keep them occupied.

Although they were seventeen, they weren't completely independent. They were both still on their provisional licenses. Luke and I had no extended family. I have no idea how we would've made it through that crisis without Hank.

We eventually told the kids about Luke and Hank's relationship, and they told us they'd already figured it out.

Hank was officially part of our family.

Everyone who knew our family knew Uncle Hank. All they knew was that he was a family friend; one who'd lost his wife years ago. He vacationed every summer with us, ate at our house more often than not, and cried as many tears as Luke and I on Jonathan and Julia's graduation, and then later, their wedding days.

When Luke was diagnosed with cancer at age fifty-seven, Hank was there for us again. Even though the pain he felt was at least as intense as ours—after all, he'd been with Luke for over ten years—he was worried about Jonathan, Julia, and me.

After one particularly rough reaction to chemotherapy, Luke was recuperating in our bed. Hank was on one side of him, and I was on the other. He reached out with his left hand for my hand and with his right for Hank's.

Somehow, I knew what was coming next. He didn't want to fight any more. Treating this monster of a disease was becoming worse than the disease itself.

"I want to be here as long as I can," Luke said, his voice raspy.

The chemo always affected his voice. In fact, he said one of the things he hated the most about chemo was not that it made him nauseous, it was the fact that he couldn't sing along with his favorite rock songs on the radio when he was driving in his car. Every time he tried to sing, he ended up having a coughing spell.

"I want to be here," he repeated, "but not if I'm not myself. This is making me live longer, but it's sucking the life out of me."

Hank frowned, but I knew what Luke was trying to say.

Luke went off all treatments the following week. Hank tried to fight him on it, but he eventually gave in. In my heart, I knew Hank was terrified of losing Luke. So was I, but I understood Luke's point.

Hank moved in with us after that. It was easier to take shifts if he lived with us. Some nights I'd stay up with Luke, and some nights Hank would. Between us, we were able to handle all of his needs. It wasn't until the last week before he passed away that we needed a few visits from Hospice. By then, we knew the end was near.

We sat with him—Hank on his right, and me on the left side of his bed—when Luke took his last, labored breath. With a small smile on his face, a memory I cherish, Luke moved on.

Hank and I held onto each other for long moments after.

As the sad funeral song ended, Hank was next to me. Jonathan, Julia, and their beautiful spouses and children filled out the rest of the family pew. I took solace in the fact that Luke would be proud of his little extended family.

I was glad that Hank wasn't alone in mourning Luke. He didn't just have me, but also his "nephew" and "niece" and all of their children.

Hank and I had discussed it, and it made sense for him to continue living at the house. He's good company, there's plenty of room, and we have an unspoken bond. I knew that the one thing Luke would really love is that my husband's partner has become my friend for life.

THE END

CONFESSIONS OF A GRIEVING MOTHER
"It's My Fault!"

The hot sun beat mercilessly on me as I stood there. But I didn't complain about the sweltering heat. It had been hot that night, too, and the sweat I felt running down my back was only one more punishment—a minor one at that—for what I'd done. I welcomed the atonement, although I knew it could never be enough.

As I stared into to the gaping hole with its endless blackness, I was careful to maintain my guard over the tiny, white coffin. It contained the remains of my dreams of motherhood. And I was the only one responsible for this unbearable loss.

I recalled how I had stood over the baby's crib and marveled at our little miracle. He might be just one of millions of babies in the word, but he was ours. I reached toward the tiny fist curled near his cheek, but when I touched the delicate skin, it felt cold and clammy. I quickly drew my hand back. My heart jack hammered in my chest and I gasped in horror. This just can't be true!

My piercing scream rang through the quiet night. I stood in Joel's nursery, screaming over and over. Then Lucinda, my best childhood chum who lived next door, burst in.

"My heavens, Rachel, what is it?" she asked, clearly concerned. "I heard you scream."

In answer, I could only point a shaking finger at the crib. Lucinda went to the baby's crib and peered in. She couldn't understand my terror until she, too, leaned down to caress the baby.

"Oh, my God!" she exclaimed. "He's not breathing!"

Scooping the infant into her arms, she bounced him up and down, obviously hoping that she'd been wrong, that baby Joel was simply sleeping soundly. But I knew better.

There was no response. Lucinda laid Joel back in his crib and began to push rhythmically up and down on his chest, trying to revive him. Joel continued to simply lay there like a slumbering angel.

With one protective arm around me, Lucinda led me into my bedroom and picked up the phone. Dialing 911 quickly, she spoke in hushed tones to the person answering. "Please send help right away. I think the baby just died."

Hanging up, she embraced me. "Rachel, I know there's nothing I can say that will help. But you know how very, very sorry I am."

"It's my fault," I responded dully. "I should have checked on him earlier. But I just figured he was finally skipping the midnight feeding. The doctor told me that was probably the next one he'd drop."

"Oh, Rachel," Lucinda commiserated. "It's not your fault. Was Joel sick or something?"

"No!" I exclaimed. "That's just it. He was thriving. He'd figured out how to pull himself up in his crib and stand. Boy, you should have heard him crow when he did that!" I smiled at the memory, and then continued. "He ate all his oatmeal and ground chicken supper, had his nine o'clock bottle. He went to sleep right after I changed him and laid him down in his crib. He'd eaten all his supper; he's a big boy who loves to eat. He was fine when I put him down, I swear it!"

"Okay, okay," said Lucinda soothingly. "When does Andrew get home from his business trip?"

"Not until tomorrow night." I put my hands to my face and moaned. "How can I ever tell him? Joel was the light of his life! And my parents! He was their only grandchild. They'll be devastated!"

I began to sob, quietly at first and with shaking shoulders, then increasingly louder until I imagined everyone on the block could hear.

The chilling sound of a siren could be heard. Stopping at the curb by my house, the ambulance's whirling red and blue lights continued their mad spin as the two paramedics scrambled out of the vehicle. They came running up to the house and pushed their way through the front door, not waiting for someone to invite them in.

"In here!" Lucinda called. The men came into the room and followed Lucinda's nod toward the crib where I stood, rocking a silent Joel cradled in my arms, and crooning a lullaby softly to him.

"Ma'am, we'll take over now," said the paramedic, gently lifting Joel from my arms. Laying the baby on his changing table, he put his stethoscope on Joel's chest, picked up his tiny hand and held it for a minute, consulting his wristwatch as he did so. Then he, too, began the same chest-pumping maneuver Lucinda had tried and added rescue breathing. He had the same predictable result. After a few minutes, he shook his head to his partner and began to wrap Joel up in a blanket.

"I'm very sorry for your loss, ma'am. We have to take the baby down to the medical examiner's office. Someone will call you in a day or so to let you know when you can pick him up and have funeral services."

That time, my scream seemed loud enough to awaken anyone else that could possibly still be asleep. "No-o-o-o!" I wailed. "No-o-o! No-o-o!"

"I'm very sorry, ma'am, but the law requires we bring the baby in for an autopsy," said the attendant. He paused, moving from one foot to the next, clearly uncomfortable speaking. "And, although I'm sure this isn't the case here, we're also required to treat the house as a crime scene and bring in the police."

My face reflected the horror I felt. And then what I'd just been told hit me smack in the face.

"And you think a crime's been committed here? Are you saying you think someone killed my baby?" I screamed again, truly horrified.

"Again, I am very sorry," replied the EMT. "Please try not to take this personally. I don't think anything of the kind, but I have no choice. State law requires these things. But we'll get it over with just as soon as we can."

As if to prove his point, I saw headlights from another car arrive in my driveway. Two uniformed police officers headed for my front door, and came in immediately.

"I'm Officer Moran," said one. "And this is Officer Kirkwood," he added, pointing to the other officer. "What's happening here?" asked Moran.

Once of the EMTs stated the situation concisely. "We got a call from Dispatch that a baby was unresponsive. We got here just five minutes ago and discovered the infant was no longer breathing. We tried to bring him back, but no luck. So we called you guys." Moran avoided my eyes during his recitation, but his somber expression spoke volumes about his feelings.

"Ma'am, I'm sure this is an extremely painful time for you, but if I could please speak to you privately for just a moment, I'd appreciate it. That way, I won't have to bring you downtown for questioning."

He stepped toward the kitchen and I followed him numbly, grateful for the emotional anesthesia that was coming over me.

We spoke for about ten minutes, then the officer said, "I think I have everything I need. Thank you for your cooperation."

When Lucinda asked me what had happened in the interview, I could barely contain my shock.

"They asked me about everything!" I reported, incredulity and outrage in my voice. "Did Joel have a cough, did he vomit, was he constipated, did he have colic? They even had the nerve to ask me if there had ever been any investigation of child abuse!"

Lucinda patted my hand. "Now, Rachel, I'm sure they're just following their procedure. They don't think you ever deliberately hurt Joel."

"Who knows what they think?" I said.

Then we stood on the porch, watching as the police car drove off into the night, its sirens silent, on their way to the medical examiner.

Lucinda had a protective arm around my shoulders as we stared into the black night. When the taillights disappeared from sight, Lucinda led me back into the house. The police had taken Joel's body with them, to the medical examiner.

"Come on, Rachel," she said. "You're coming home with me. No way are you staying in this house alone." As I stood there like a statue, Lucinda gathered up some nightclothes and toiletries and put them in a grocery sack. Then she led me out the front door and across the lawn to her own home. There, she guided me to a guest room, helped me into my nightgown, and turned down the bedspread.

"Come on, get in," she said, plumping the pillow. "This bed is actually pretty comfortable."

I obeyed, my face remaining devoid of all emotion. Lucinda pulled the blankets up to my chin, leaning down to kiss my forehead. Then, as though fearful that the gesture was too much like tucking a child in bed for the evening and thus might be upsetting to me, she straightened up, and said briskly, "Sleep tight. See you in the morning, hon."

When morning came, it was obvious that I hadn't taken my friend's suggestion to heart. Red-rimmed, swollen eyes dominated my face, and I sat, hair uncombed, robe unbuttoned and slipper-less, at the breakfast table staring off at something unseen.

"Scrambled or fried?" asked Lucinda with forced good cheer, as though I were simply a houseguest ready for breakfast.

"What? Oh, sorry. Nothing for me, thanks. I'm not hungry."

Lucinda seemed to understand and sat down next to me, bringing her own cup of coffee to the table. Placing her hand on top of mine in a gesture of comfort, Lucinda spoke in a calm, low voice.

"This is not your fault," she said emphatically, her voice shattering the surreal stillness.

I started, as if slapped. "You don't know that!" I replied. "I should have checked on Joel sooner. Then maybe he'd still be alive."

Tears began to fall. This is easy enough for Lucinda, I thought bitterly. She had always been "Little Miss Perfect," getting good grades with little effort, being named Head Cheerleader and Prom Queen in the same year. She'd even pledged the top sorority at college, while I didn't even get a second invitation to rush. And now she's married to Kent, the class hunk, and they're always jet setting off to one exotic vacation or another. About the only thing I'd done ahead of Lucinda was to have Joel. And now I don't even have him!

"Okay, I guess we'll just have to wait for the medical examiner's report, then. But I'm sure he'll find out that Joel's death wasn't due to anything you did. You are a great mother!"

"Were, you mean," I replied, rubbing my temples in an effort to banish the headache that pounded inside my skull.

Lucinda's face flushed as she realized her blunder. "Have you called Andrew? Your folks? Do you want me to do it for you?"

"Andrew will be home tonight. That's soon enough to find out. You can tell Mom and Dad, though. That's one phone call I don't want to make!"

"Done," said Lucinda as she cleared away my untouched coffee cup with her own. "Why don't you go back to bed and see if you can get some rest? You look like you could use it."

But I remained as I was, staring off into space. I was still there, as though frozen, when Lucinda came back into the kitchen after cleaning the house all morning.

Alarmed at my seemingly catatonic state, Lucinda said, with forced brightness, "I'm going to run back over to your house and get you some changes of clothing. I think it would be a good idea if you stayed here for a few days."

She came back in half an hour to find me once again unchanged from the morning.

"I know what you should do," Lucinda said. "How about a nice, long soak in a bubble bath? That's sure to relax you."

She placed a hand under my elbow and half-guided, half-pushed me into the nearby bathroom. While I sat on the closed toilet lid and watched, unspeaking, Lucinda poured bubble bath lotion into the rapidly filling tub. As the bubbles began to form, she eased me out of my nightgown and helped me into the tub.

"Clean bath towels are on the counter," she said. "Relax, now." Leaving the room, she resumed her housework. By noon, she was ready for lunch and went to ask me to join her. But I was still in the bathroom, although I had moved from the now-cold bathtub and returned to my perch on the toilet seat lid. The towel was loosely draped over my shoulders.

"Rachel, you must be freezing!" Lucinda exclaimed, wrapping the towel more securely around me. "Come on and get dressed. It's time for lunch now. Do you want a tuna sandwich or a salami one?"

I looked at her blankly. "I told you before. I'm not hungry."

"But you didn't eat breakfast, either. You have to eat something or you'll get sick! And if Andrew comes home tonight and finds you in this condition, he'll only feel worse."

"All right. I'll try to eat a sandwich. But I really don't care what's in it."

I did indeed try to eat a sandwich, and I succeeded. At least, I managed two or three bites before putting it down and repeating, "I said I'm just not hungry."

Lucinda decided not to push the issue, reasoning that I had at least made an attempt.

The next few days passed in a merciful blur. Andrew came home and was just as shocked as I'd been when he learned of our son's death. But his natural protectiveness came to the fore when he saw my continued haggard appearance and tears. He tried to comfort me while dealing with his own not inconsiderable grief. I could feel his body tremble and wetness on his cheeks as he held me tightly.

Then, one day when Lucinda was over for yet another unwelcome visit, a call came from the medical examiner's office. Numbly, I took the phone from her outstretched hand and answered the questions I was asked. Hanging up the phone, I looked at my friend, stunned.

A few days later, I had my answer. "There was nothing wrong with Joel," the disembodied voice said without inflection. "It is our conclusion that he died of Sudden Infant Death Syndrome. Please accept our condolences."

"What's this 'sudden infant death' stuff mean?" I asked Lucinda, bewildered.

"My cousin's baby died of that," said Lucinda. "It's usually abbreviated 'SIDS.' It's rare, but not unheard-of. Jessie said the doctors still don't know why a baby who's been healthy would suddenly be found dead in his crib. They only said it was a good idea to have the baby always sleep on its back, not on its tummy, though."

"Joel was always put to sleep on his back," I said. "But he was a strong little guy and he often changed his position when he slept. He probably turned himself over."

"That sounds very possible," said Lucinda, ever the loyal friend. "You have got to stop thinking it was your fault!"

But that was far easier said than done. The day of Joel's funeral was blazing hot and sultry. It was all I could do to breathe in the muggy air. Maybe I should stop breathing, I thought. That would be only fair. Somehow I got through the service, although the sight of that tiny, white coffin just about undid me. Andrew stayed by my side and Lucinda did, too, but everyone else seemed to avoid me. I don't know if they just didn't know what to say, or if they secretly blamed me. If they did, that was fine with me. I deserved it, didn't I? What kind of mother was I if I couldn't even keep my own baby safe? God probably knew that it was better for Joel if He took him home.

When we finally got back, Andrew put the car away and I went inside, going where I was spending more and more of my time, lately. Andrew found me there, sitting in the rocker next to Joel's crib, rocking myself slowly back and forth, my eyes unfocused and staring.

"I remember when we brought him home from the hospital. He was so tiny! Do you remember how sweet he looked in that little blue onesie designed like a baseball player's uniform?" My tears started anew.

Andrew squatted down next to me and leaned over to kiss my cheek gently. "Of course I remember, Rachel. How could I ever forget?" His own sobs shook his muscular frame. "I don't know how we're going to survive this, but we will. I love you so much!"

Andrew's attempt at consolation not only didn't work, it spurred me to cry even harder. How in the world can we ever get over something so unspeakably awful?

"Honey, please!" Andrew said with a catch in his throat. "You've just got to stop coming in here and sitting by the crib. It won't bring him back, and you're not helping yourself, either."

I didn't resist when Andrew pulled me out of the chair and led me into the living room. I knew I'd be back in the nursery at the first opportunity. I felt so close to Joel there, as if he'd suddenly materialize in my empty arms.

Yet somehow we got through that day, and the next, and many days after that. After a week or so, Andrew returned to work. Lucinda kept coming over, uninvited, asking me to go to the movies with her, or go shopping, or she'd just sit and talk to me about things I can't remember now. The image of seeing Joel's limp little body in that crib haunted me during the day, and I dreamed of it at night. The police had not charged me with any crime and Joel's death had been officially recorded as Sudden Infant Death Syndrome, or, as it's more commonly known, SIDS.

But diagnoses didn't matter to me. All I could think of was that my little baby was dead, and that I was to blame. After all, who else was there? Joel had been my responsibility, and now he's gone. Clearly, I was an incompetent mother. I thought about that bottle of sleeping pills the doctor had given me. Would it be so terrible if I ended the pain with an overdose? The idea kept coming up, and I found increasingly myself drawn to it. Why not? I didn't know what was stopping me.

And still, that stupid Lucinda kept coming over, her blond ponytail just bouncing away as she flashed another of those stupid, perky smiles at me.

"C'mon, Rachel!" she said cheerfully, I've got two tickets for the new concert downtown. I know you're going to love it, so I bought the best seats in the house! But we've got to hurry and get you dressed! And I'm definitely not taking 'no' for an answer this time! These tickets were too hard to get for that!"

Like an unstoppable force of nature, Lucinda pulled me off the couch and half-dragged me to my bedroom closet. Opening it, she pulled out a pink knit pantsuit and a pair of cream-colored loafers. As I stood there like a department store mannequin, Lucinda dressed me in the clothes and ran a brush through my lank and unwashed hair. Fastening it with a tortoise-shell hair clip, she stood me in front of the mirror.

"What do you think?" she asked brightly.

But I didn't recognize the person I saw. Who could she be, this woman with the dead eyes, the gaunt body, and the pinched expression? I didn't know her and I didn't care one way or the other. What difference did it make?

Lucinda propelled me outside and into her car. We were going somewhere, but I didn't know where and couldn't have cared less. Sooner or later, she'd take me back home, where I could be alone with my memories. We sat through the concert, and I applauded politely at the end of every song. The rest of the audience, though, seemed enraptured at what they'd heard. As for me, the end couldn't come soon enough. On the way back to the car, I declined Lucinda's invitation to go out for coffee and pie, saying I was too tired and just wanted to get home. But when we got there, Lucinda suddenly grasped my wrist, preventing me from leaving.

"Look, Rachel, you know I love you and would do anything for you. It just kills me to see you sitting in that rocker all day long; usually wearing the pajamas you went to bed in the night before. You won't eat, you won't go out, and you won't talk to me. I just don't know what to do anymore!"

"Well, Lucinda, I'm very sorry if you're uncomfortable around me," I said acidly. "But I'm coping the best way I can. It's unfortunate that that's not good enough for you."

"Really, Rachel!" she exploded. "It's hardly a question of being 'good enough' for me. I just can't stand to see you wasting away like this!" Then she burst into tears and grabbed me, hugging me to her tightly. I was so startled that I hugged her back, and soon, I couldn't tell my own tears from hers.

"Oh, God." I wept. "Why me? Why Joel?"

Lucinda looked up at me, the harshness of her words tempered by a slightly running nose. "Look at it like this, Rachel. Why not you? What makes you so special that you deserve to escape all of life's tragedies?" Her face got that tight look that let me know she meant every word.

"Oh, right! That's easy enough for you to say, you who's always won every prize, who's had every bit of luck come her way without trying. How could you possibly understand what I'm going through?"

Lucinda looked at me strangely. Then she said, "You don't know everything about me, Rachel."

I didn't believe her. "I've known you since we were six years old! What deep, dark secret could I possibly not know?"

A small sigh escaped Lucinda's lips. "I guess I should level with you."

Despite myself, I was intrigued. "Yes, please do," I said with elaborate, feigned courtesy. What could she possibly say to me?

Lucinda sat back in the car seat and folded her hands in her lap. "Do you remember our sophomore year in college, when I told you I wasn't coming home for spring break? That I was going to go with some of my sorority sisters to Mexico for a week?"

I nodded, and she continued. "Well, what I didn't tell you was that even though I really didn't want to go to Mexico, I felt I had no choice. I'd been told that it was the best place to get an abortion."

I gasped in astonishment. "You got pregnant?"

Lucinda nodded, eyes averted. "Do you remember my dating Tyler Madison, the star basketball player? I always felt so lucky to be seeing him, and I knew I was the envy of every girl on campus." She smiled ruefully and added, "I cared about those things back then, I guess."

Transfixed, I said, "Go on, Lucinda. What happened?"

"Tyler kept pressuring me to go a little bit farther each time we made out. I didn't feel comfortable with it, but I also didn't want to lose him. So I cooperated. Then one night, after he scored all those points in the championship game, he begged me to let him 'experience all of me.' He said he loved me and he wanted to show me how much. Stupidly, I believed him, even when he promised that there was no way I'd get pregnant." Her crying grew heavier, but she still continued.

"Well, you can guess the rest. I did get pregnant and when I told Tyler, he insisted the baby couldn't possibly be his!" Lucinda was still indignant. "As if it could possibly be anyone else's! Well, needless to say, marriage wasn't in Tyler's immediate plans, which was fine with me, because I couldn't stand the sight of the jerk.

"Don't hate me, please!" she begged. "I would have had to drop out of college and get some two-bit job somewhere to support the baby and myself. My parents and everyone else would have just been mortified. So Tyler asked around and got the name of this so-called doctor just across the border.

"So I went, and I swore one of my sorority sisters to secrecy. She came with me, and took me back to our motel." She looked at me beseechingly. "I've never told anyone, Rachel, not even Kenny. Please keep it to yourself. I'm being punished enough already."

"What do you mean?" I asked, wondering what penalty she could be paying.

"My doctor here told me I could never have any kids," she said quietly. "The abortion took care of that."

"Oh, Lucinda," I commiserated. "I never guessed! I always thought you had it all together! You should have told me before."

"Why? And have you think I was a stupid slut who got what she deserved?"

"I'd never think such a thing," I said, gathering her up in my arms. It was my turn to provide comfort and support. We clung to each other like two survivors of a shipwreck, which maybe we were. As it grew darker outside, we reluctantly pulled away from each other and sat, each of us looking at each other in a way we never had before.

"So, now what?" I asked.

"So, now I guess we just keep on keepin' on. I don't see any other choice, do you?"

"Sounds like a plan to me," I agreed, and after one more strong hug, I got out of the car and walked back inside, turning back just once to wave to my brave friend.

It was several days later that I heard from Lucinda again. By some unspoken agreement, we gave each other space after that emotional evening. But when the phone rang, I was truly glad to hear from her.

"What's happening, girl?" I asked, trying to sound jaunty, if not cheerful.

"Is it okay if I come over, Rachel? I have someone I'd like you to meet."

I was puzzled, but said, "Sure, give me ten minutes to sweep up the biggest dust bunnies, then head on over."

When the doorbell rang awhile later, I found Lucinda on the porch accompanied by a pleasant-looking middle-age woman who smiled warmly as she was introduced.

"Rachel, I'd like you to meet Kerry Winthrop. She's a representative from First Candle, and she has some important information for you."

I stood aside to let the women enter, and offered tea and coffee. I hadn't baked for a long time, but I put some store-bought cookies that Andrew had brought home on a plate to go along with our beverages.

"What's First Candle all about?" I asked my new guest politely. "I don't think I've ever heard of it."

Kerry Winthrop smiled. "We're trying to stop being so unknown," she said. "First Candle has been around officially since the early Sixties. We started out as a support group for families who'd lost an infant to Sudden Infant Death Syndrome, or SIDS. Then, later, we expanded our mission to serve families whose babies had died of other causes as well, like due to stillbirth or miscarriage."

"I'm sure you're doing important work," I said, still concentrating only on being polite to my guest. "I'd be happy to make a contribution."

Kerry smiled. "Thank you, but I'm not here to collect money. I'd like to invite you to our next meeting."

My response was swift and civil, if not warm. "Thank you, but I don't think I'd fit in." The very last thing I wanted to do was spend an evening hearing other people's sad stories. They all were victims of a cruel fate, while I clearly was responsible for what had happened to Joel.

Lucinda spoke up at once. "Don't say that, Rachel. Not until you've gone to a meeting or two and tried it."

Kerry agreed. "Many parents feel as you do," she said. "At least, at first they do. But most who come to our meetings return. Please reconsider."

"All right," I said, as much to end the conversation as anything else.

"I'm so pleased to have you join us," said Kerry, as she wrote down a meeting time and location.

But before she could give it to me, Lucinda snatched it up. "I'll take that," my friend said. "That way, you won't misplace it or forget to go. I'll come along to keep you company."

True to her word, Lucinda showed up the night of the meeting, clearly intending not to accept my refusal to go with her. Andrew had managed to be gone on a walk. That didn't surprise me; he and I barely communicated those days. We weren't arguing, we just seemed to be living separate lives.

Lucinda and I walked into a church basement to find about two-dozen men and women milling about, coffee cups in hands.

A woman spoke from the lectern: "We're ready to begin, everyone. Please take a seat."

After listening to an admittedly interesting talk by a counselor on the typical grief reaction to a child death, the audience broke up into smaller groups of eight. One attendee, a man of about forty, with thinning hair and a sad face, began.

"I thought my life was over when Emily died," he said, wiping a solitary tear from his face. "Maggie and I just drifted apart after that." He brightened visibly. "I'm so glad I learned from you folks that couples often forget each other's grief and ignore each other, instead of comforting the other partner. Thank God we found that out in time." He squeezed the hand of the woman seated next to him.

Another woman spoke. "At first, I thought it was my fault that Jason died," she said. "Then I learned that Sudden Infant Death could happen to anybody. It's not predictable. There was nothing I could have done. But, still, it's been hard to not to blame myself."

"I blame myself, too," I blurted out. "I should have checked on him sooner."

"Your feelings are very understandable," another man said. "It's even harder to accept that you can't control things. But some things happen whether we want them to or not. They just happen," he finished.

Can he be right? I wondered. Without my willing it, I felt my heavy load grow just a shade lighter.

When the meeting ended, Lucinda and I walked back to the car. On the ride home, I was quiet. Lucinda dropped me off. I spoke quickly, before I could change my mind.

"Can we go next week?" I asked. "That was helpful. Maybe I can talk Andrew into coming along."

"I'll be there at seven to pick you up," replied Lucinda, waving as she drove off.

I walked into the house slowly. I still mourned Joel, of course. I probably always will. But I knew my husband was suffering as well. I walked a little faster, wanting to hold him in my arms and share some of the solace I'd just found. There are still rocky roads and many gray skies ahead of us, I know, but just maybe there was a chance of a sunny day, too.

THE END

CONFESSIONS OF A DISGRUNTLED EMPLOYEE
"I Want Revenge!"

"Hey, Samantha!" Donovan called.

I jumped, and banged my head on the magazine rack above where I was sorting through the mishmash of crossword puzzle and Sudoku magazines.

I rubbed my scalp and stood up, trying not to scowl at my friend as he came down the grocery store aisle towards me. "What?" It came out sounding crankier than I would have liked.

Donovan gave me a sheepish look. "Sorry to scare you."

"That's okay." I forced myself to smile to reassure him. "I hit my head on that thing all the time. I ought to wear a hardhat when I clean out the magazines."

"Yeah. Hey, don't forget to save me the food and cooking mags that don't sell. Anyway, have you heard the latest?"

"The latest what?" I'd been organizing magazines, books, and greeting cards all morning and hadn't talked to anyone.

"News." He waved a hand. "Or gossip, whatever."

"No, but I'm sure you'll tell me." Donovan always knew what was going on with everyone in the store. I figured this news was juicy, because he lowered his voice.

"We're getting a new store manager," he said.

I groaned. Store managers were always being replaced, and about six months previously we'd finally gotten one I really liked and respected. He understood the grocery business, unlike most of the rest of the people I'd been forced to report to. "What's happening to Tony?"

"He's getting promoted. Being sent to the corporate headquarters."

"Good for him, I guess." Most of the managers we'd lost had been fired. "I wonder who we'll get." I cocked my head. "Maybe they'll promote from within, for once."

Donovan shook his head. "Nope. I heard it's a stranger. But we'll be able to check him out because he's coming by to meet with Tony today."

I glanced back at my magazine rack. It was almost in order. Hopefully I could finish straightening by the time he got here, and make a good first impression.

But it wasn't to be. I returned from my lunch break to find my lower left side magazines scattered across the floor. I recognized the signs—a boy, probably twelve or thirteen and still small, had climbed up to get to the Maxims on the upper row of the top rack. I breathed a heavy sigh and sank to my knees to start collecting my merchandise.

Of course, that's when Tony brought the new boss around.

"Samantha, this is George Sturke. He starts as the new store manager next week."

I jumped to my feet, and my armload of Teen Peoples and Cosmo Girls slipped. Two of them slid to the floor. Resisting the urge to dive after the magazines, I instead studied George.

He was short and stout, with a paunch, but he looked like he'd probably been athletic in his youth. His hair was buzzed so short it was hard to tell what color it was. Gray, maybe? The look in his eyes was serious, and not at all welcoming.

"Nice to meet you." I tried to smile, and reached out my hand.

George took it, and squeezed so hard I wanted to shake off the pain once he finally let go. He glanced at the magazines on the floor with distaste. "What is it you do here, Samantha?"

"I handle sundries—what you see on both sides of this aisle," I explained, turning to point to each area as I spoke. "Greeting cards, books and magazines, gift wrap, seasonal, and other novelties."

"Samantha really knows this business," Tony said. "She's done a great job with sundries for almost three years." I gave him a grateful grin.

"I'll check out your numbers," George said. "We'll discuss them during a meeting I'm holding at the end of next week."

"Sure. Uh, welcome." I said, though something told me what he had to say might not be so welcome.

I was right. George called an all-hands meeting for the next Friday at six in the morning, before the store opened. Since my shift normally starts at ten, I wasn't too thrilled to have to go in so early, though I understood that the time choice kept customers from being inconvenienced. The meeting was to be held in the break room, and as I drove to the store I pictured neat rows of folding chairs set out for all of us, plus cardboard carriers of Starbucks as thanks for arriving so early.

But no, the break room was in its usual condition with only eight chairs—already occupied by the early birds—around two circular tables. No cardboard coffee carriers in sight. The break room's old coffee pot wasn't even going, and I couldn't help sighing. I shuffled to the back of the room near the corner and propped myself up against the wall.

Donovan arrived a few minutes later, and with a frown echoing my own, joined me in leaning against the wall.

"I have a bad feeling about this," he muttered.

I just nodded. Looking back, that was the point when I should have started looking for a new job.

George breezed in at five minutes after six with a sheaf of papers under his arm. He didn't apologize for his tardiness, just launched into "We're going to talk about each department first, then I'll give some general guidelines on how I want checkout and stocking to work."

"He couldn't have started with good morning?" Donovan whispered.

"It's not a good morning," I whispered back.

"Produce," George called out, and Donovan straightened at the mention of the section he managed. "Profits are down over last quarter," he stated, then just stood and glared at Donovan.

"It's the middle of winter," Donovan told him, sounding more patient than I would have. "Fresh produce profits always go down in the winter because we can't get things locally and it costs more to ship it in."

"We're going to cut back stock, then. Stick with the basics." He passed a piece of paper back to Donovan through the employees in between. "This is a list of items I want you to eliminate from the department."

I watched as Donovan examined the list. His eyes narrowed as they moved downward, and his face reddened. "I can't get rid of nectarines! And romaine lettuce? It's much healthy than iceberg!"

"Stick to the basics," George repeated. "Nectarines and romaine lettuce are too froufrou to be basics."

"What about the vegetable dips? People love those vegetable dips. I can't fill the shelves fast enough!"

George shrugged. "Profit margins not big enough. Get rid of 'em."

A vein in Donovan's forehead was sticking out, and I feared for his blood pressure, but he pressed his lips together and didn't say anything more. George moved on to the meat department.

About ten minutes later, after bashing meats and the bakery, George called out my name. My stomach flipped and my heart began to pound. I needed this job, and I'd grown accustomed to the bonuses for good service I was earning regularly. If George thought Donovan and the other section managers were doing a poor job, what would he think of me?

"Magazines and cards are not groceries," George said.

I stared at him, but he didn't say more. I guessed it was my turn. "Uh, technically no."

"Then why are they in a grocery store?"

My mouth dropped open. Was he seriously expecting an answer to that? Had he ever actually shopped in a grocery store? "For the convenience of our customers," I finally said. "Plus, they're great impulse buys and have high profit margins for the store."

"Do they, now?" George looked down at one of his papers.

"Looks to me like the things that sell have high profit margins, but the return rate is high, which cuts back earnings."

I shook my head. "Not really, if you're talking about books and magazines. We're credited on our next order for anything we return to the publisher."

"We're not credited for the time spent stocking things that don't sell and the postage to send items back."

I didn't know what to say to that. What he said was true, but it had never been a problem for any of my other managers. "It can't cost much to return stuff. We rip off the covers and just send the covers back, not the whole magazine or book."

George slammed his papers down on the table nearest him. I jerked, along with the people sitting around that table. "Zero returns from now on," he proclaimed.

My mouth formed an "O" as my brain struggled to form actual words. "That. . .that will cost us more, uh, sir. Once March's issues are out, we won't be able to sell any more Februarys, and if we don't return them, we'll have to eat the cost."

The determined expression on George's face didn't change a bit. "The solution is simple. Sell every February you order."

I took a deep breath, but it didn't calm me much. "I work hard to balance the orders so we'll have enough of each issue, and not too many extras, but I can try to do better--"

"Zero returns from now on," George repeated. "Anything you don't sell, you will buy. We'll deduct the cost right from your paycheck."

I took a couple steps forward. "You can't do that!"

George showed me his teeth. "Oh yes, I can."

I couldn't pay for all the magazines the store didn't sell! I could barely make ends meet as it was. My mother and I would be out on the street! My fists clenched and my eyes filled with tears, but I would not let this idiot see me cry.

I ducked my head and plowed through the crowd of my coworkers, away from the break room and all the way out of the store. I managed to get around the corner from the customer entrance before the tears rolled down my cheeks.

Donovan came out a few minutes later. Putting his hand on my shoulder, he said, "George's making stupid mandates for every department. I think we should go over his head. To whoever at corporate is in charge of the store managers."

I sniffled and wiped my nose with the back of my hand. "Do you know who that is?"

"No, but we can find out. Meet me in the break room at nine forty-five, before we begin our shift, and we'll look through the company directory."

We did find the right person, and sent him a carefully composed e-mail listing several of the "non-standard requests" George had made for his store, and asking if corporate supported those requests. We were pretty proud of ourselves for our wording and tact.

While we were waiting for a response, George made me cry again. The day after we sent the e-mail, he noted that one Time was mixed in with the Newsweek's on the rack, so he dumped the entire display and yelled at me to fix it right away.

Several customers had been browsing nearby, and they stared at us for a couple of seconds, eyebrows raised, before rushing from the aisle. I'd never felt so humiliated in my life. Fortunately, as soon as George made sure I dropped right to my knees to pick up my merchandise, he strutted away, so he probably didn't notice my tears. Even after I calmed myself down, I found myself gritting my teeth through the rest of my shift.

The day after that, Donovan and I got our e-mail back from corporate, and it was curt: "Mr. Sturke and I were in the army together. I trust his decisions. You may carry out his orders or find employment elsewhere." Signed, "Levi Dalton."

I let out a long, loud sigh and Donovan, reading over my shoulder, turned and punched the wall. "Jerk!"

"If George's ex-army, he's never going to change his mind on anything," I said. His background did explain the "my way or the highway" attitude, though.

Rubbing his knuckles, Donovan asked, "What's next?"

I pursed my lips for a minute, thinking. "Let's call Tony."

And at our next break, we did.

"How's the new job?" I asked him, as Donovan hung at my back.

"The pay's good, but I hardly ever get to talk to anyone. Strange after dealing with you schmucks every day."

My heart clenched with fondness and missing him. "Aw, you like us," I teased.

"Of course," Tony said, and I could hear the smile in his voice. "You made me look good enough to get promoted."

I made sure my sigh was audible. "The new guy seems to think we're all incompetent and stupid." I told him about some of the decisions George had made and how mean he was being. I tried to sound neutral, but I'm sure some whining did come through. I also told him about our e-mail conversation with George's boss.

When I was finished, Tony said, "Well, obviously I don't agree with his methods because I didn't run things that way."

"Right," I said, and hope burned in my chest.

"But Levi Dalton's above me in the chain of command, too. I have to accept his decisions just like you do."

"Oh, my God," I groaned. Donovan, apparently getting the picture without being able to hear Tony's side of the conversation, gave a little grimace and moved to sit down at one of the tables. "I'd better start looking for a new job now. I don't know how much longer I can stand this guy. I certainly can't afford to pay for the magazines that don't sell."

"I'm sorry."

I could tell Tony meant it, but was very disappointed he couldn't help us. I looked at Donovan with a question in my eyes. Was there anything else worth saying to Tony?

The question didn't matter, because George's bulk was filling the break room doorway.

"Break's over. Back to work."

Tony couldn't help but hear George's bellow even over the phone, so I didn't feel bad about just muttering, "See you," into the phone and hanging up. Trembling with frustration, I made a point of looking at my watch. "We've only been in here for ten minutes. We're entitled to five more."

I glanced at Donovan, whose eyes were wide. He probably hadn't thought I was capable of standing up to George. But Donovan wasn't inside my skin to feel how hard my hands were shaking and how sweaty my palms had become.

George smiled, and the look made chills run down my spine. "Want to play things by the book, huh? Well, okay, what about the day before yesterday when you left the store before the end of your shift?"

I gritted my teeth. "I left, like, two minutes early. As it was, I had to drive like a maniac to get my mom to her doctor's appointment on time, and I'd scheduled the last appointment of the doctor's day."

"Not my problem," George said with a shrug.

"Your employees aren't robots," Donovan said, standing up. "We do have lives outside the store that need tending to."

George looked at him like he was a bug he could squash. "Again, not my problem." He turned back to me. "I catch you leaving early again—even just thirty seconds—you're fired. Your department's just a luxury, anyway. Probably wouldn't even replace you."

My fists clenched. Donovan moved to my side, I guess trying to present a unified front. "What clock or watch will be used to make the determination of whether or not we leave early?" he asked.

George showed us his teeth again. "Mine, of course."

"Then we should synchronize watches. It's only fair." And—I couldn't believe it—Donovan reached out for George's arm.

Of course, George wouldn't stand for it. He snatched his hand—and his watch—away.

"Don't touch me!" The words came out as a growl, and I was

afraid he was going to deck Donovan. "Touching is a firing offense."

Donovan, all bravado gone, just stared with his mouth and eyes wide. Luckily, George pivoted and left the break room, so neither Donovan nor I had to figure out a way to calm him down.

"What a loon," I said. "Not only should that guy be fired, he should be locked up in a mental hospital."

Donovan swallowed, still looking scared. "We can only hope he'll get fired—and soon—like our other incompetent managers."

I shook my head. "I don't think he'll be fired. He's that Mr. Dalton's old army buddy. Probably how he got the job in the first place."

"They always fire the manager when the sales numbers go down too far. If we follow his mandates to the letter—like stop stocking romaine lettuce and nectarines—the numbers should plummet, don't you think?"

"Maybe, but not before I'm broke from paying for back issues of magazines."

Donovan put his hand on my shoulder. "No, do what George wants, but overdo it. If you normally order ten of a particular magazine and sell eight of them, just order five. The store will get three fewer sales, plus three unhappy customers. It will add up with time."

"I don't think I can wait," I said with a frown. "By the end of this month, I'll probably owe the store money, instead of vice versa."

"We have to start somewhere."

"I know." But I needed faster results. Donovan's produce department would lose sales under his plan, but he wouldn't have to pay for it out of his own pocket. He could afford to wait. I was losing money as we spoke.

I mulled things over for a few days, unable to get the unfairness of it out of my mind. Plus, every time I saw George, I wanted to scratch out his eyeballs, but had to settle for balling my hands into fists. I wanted things fixed at the store, but by that point I also wanted revenge on my boss from hell!

I finally came up with a plan, but the help and creativity of my coworkers would make it more effective. Donovan and I talked about it first, and then we both secretly shared our ideas with others we could trust. The beauty of our plan was that no one person would know every action taken, and none of us knew exactly who else was involved. When questioned, we could plead almost complete ignorance.

Not that we were doing anything illegal, because I don't think we were. But we did want to keep our jobs if at all possible. And we wanted George gone.

We began to see results in only two days. I was stocking the magazines at the express register, which happened to be the one closest to the produce section, when George led a customer over to Donovan.

"This lady is looking for cherry tomatoes."

I watched as Donovan turned and pointed. "They're in that bin in the corner, ma'am."

The customer and George both shook their heads. "It's empty," George said.

Donovan frowned. "I was afraid that might happen. Our shipment was due first thing yesterday, but we still haven't gotten it. Would you like a phone call when they've arrived?" he asked the woman.

I didn't bother to listen for her response, but asked Donovan about the late shipment as we ate lunch together. "What happened? You didn't even run out of oranges after that big hurricane in Florida. George must have flipped his lid."

"Oh, he did." Donovan looked like he'd just swallowed the proverbial canary. "He had me contact the vendor, and it was really strange. They had received a fax, complete with George's signature, canceling our order. They faxed us back a copy." He crossed his arms and whistled, the picture of ignorant innocence.

I grabbed his arm. "How many shipments did you cancel?" Laughter bubbled up in my throat, making it difficult to ask the question.

"Only all the ones for produce," he said, shrugging.

"That was a brilliant idea, and it worked fast! My plan's going to take a while."

Donovan propped his elbows up on the table. "Care to confide?"

"No problem." I could trust Donovan. I leaned toward him and spoke quietly. "I filled out subscription cards in his name for every magazine we sell. The romance club novels, too. Checked 'bill me' on every single one."

He offered me a high five. "Not bad!"

I nodded. "And they'll all be delivered to him here at the store, from Modern Bride to Guns & Ammo."

"He's got eclectic taste," Donovan said with a grin, but then glanced at his watch. "We'd better get back to work in case George's watch is fast." He rose from his chair. "This could be fun. Things will just get more and more interesting around here, I'm guessing."

And they did.

My coworkers and I did a good job, and I don't think I even noticed everything that went on. I do know that within a week the mailman started delivering the store's mail in bins rather than small packets held together with rubber bands. And I heard George mutter more than once about the huge number of strange e-mails he'd been receiving at his store address. Then there was the day about fifteen different people showed up at George's lunchtime, asking for him. I saw George stomp out of the break room, red-faced and yelling. Donovan found out later the visitors were all salesmen wanting our store to carry their products. That was an especially good one, and I wondered who had come up with it.

Our stock of feminine hygiene products, condoms, and athlete's foot cream tripled, while we ran out of staples like milk, bread, and orange juice regularly. And every time an order or order cancellation was produced, it displayed George's signature, which someone must have swiped and reproduced like crazy.

Finally, after two weeks of confusion, our fearless leader held another staff meeting. Not surprisingly, he was in an unhappy mood.

"What is going on around here?" he bellowed as an opening to the meeting. "This place is chaos."

As agreed, my coworkers and I played dumb. We just looked at each other, then back at George.

Finally, I asked, "What do you mean, sir? Maybe I'm just working too hard, but I haven't noticed anything unusual."

Donovan, who was sitting next to me, shook slightly, apparently trying to contain his laughter. Finally, he faked a coughing fit to cover.

George glared at Donovan for an instant before turning to me. "We keep running out of things because orders are mysteriously canceled. I'm drowning in paper mail and e-mail. There are more appointments on my schedule than I could attend even if I worked 24/7. The storeroom is buried in boxes of condoms and tampons." He started out explaining calmly, as if I were a small child and couldn't possibly understand, but by the end of his speech, his tone had turned accusatory. "I repeat, what is going on here?"

Donovan waved a hand in the air, and then said, "With all due respect, sir, you haven't been working here very long. But I think things are going fine. Normal."

I nodded and said, "yeah," along with my coworkers. Who'd have thought we were such good actors?

George continued to glower. "Order cancellations are normal?"

"I thought you cancelled those orders, sir," Donovan said so politely and sweetly I expected maple syrup to drip out of the corners of his mouth. "That's what the faxes said."

"You wanted to make changes," the pharmacy manager offered. "I just assumed the order changes were part of that."

"I didn't make any order changes." George's hands were balled into fists, and his face was blotchy red.

I raised my eyebrows. "I thought in our last staff meeting you said you wanted to change orders."

"I didn't change any orders. I told you all to change them."

Donovan exchanged glances with me and the other employees that were nearby. "Then I don't understand, sir. How are they getting changed?"

My looking at Donovan was a risk—laughing at that point would have ruined everything—but I couldn't resist checking out the calm, amazingly quizzical expression on his face. If I didn't know better, I would swear he had no idea what had caused all the problems in the store.

George shouted a long stream of obscenities, causing spittle to fly out of his mouth and onto the poor employees closest to him. A number of us jumped in surprise and, yes, fear. I found myself clutching my own arms as if that would protect me. We all just stared until George finished his tirade and stomped out of the break room.

Donovan's head swiveled toward the door. When he turned back around, he declared, "Great job, everyone," and smiled.

The rest of us smiled, too, but dared not applaud or cheer. After a few quiet high fives and fist bumps, we went back to work as if nothing had ever happened. I continued to rack my brain for further "issues" I could create that might make George run screaming, because I had a feeling if he didn't leave, my paycheck would be affected very soon.

I needn't have bothered. It seemed Donovan and I made a monster of one of our coworkers, and I can honestly state I don't know which one. Okay, maybe we didn't create a monster, but someone did go too far. I didn't have a problem with irritating George, even hurting the store's sales, but physical injury went too far.

Okay, here's what happened, and I was a witness, at least to the end result. George has a teeny, tiny office in the back of the store near the butcher shop. When he's not out on the floor harassing his employees, he spends a lot of time in his office. It's kind of a relief when we know he's back there, and none of us ever set foot in the office willingly. Of course, that fact made it clear what happened was a personal attack.

Anyway, Dante, our butcher, enjoys the magazine Bon Appetit so much that he—unlike Donovan—actually buys an issue if it contains a particularly good meat recipe. I had two issues left that were due to be replaced, so I'd taken one over to the butcher's counter to see if Dante would pay for it so I wouldn't have to.

Dante flipped through it, spending a few minutes muttering to himself about a Beef Wellington recipe, and I was getting a little impatient. When George was paged to Register Four, I wanted to flee whether Dante bought the magazine or not.

I edged away from the meat counter, but didn't manage to escape completely before George's office door opened and he came rushing down his little hallway. He hadn't reached the store proper, though, before he let out a yell and disappeared from my view for two or three seconds. Then I could see him again, sliding out of the hallway and into the store on his back, howling all the way.

I looked at Dante, whose eyes were wide in surprise, then he and I headed for where George lay, unmoving, on the floor. I had to use care; it quickly became clear something very slippery was spread across the floor.

Dante kneeled next to George, losing his balance once and then recovering. I bent and examined the mess, guessing from what I could see and smell that it was olive oil mixed with cat kibble. Those two items were shelved far apart in the store, so even then I had the feeling the spill was no accident.

When I looked back up, Dante had grasped George under the armpits and was attempting to lift him up. "Stop!" I cried. "If he's hurt his back, you could make it worse by moving him."

George groaned, and croaked, "No, I want to get up."

I looked Dante in the eye and shook my head. "I'll go call an ambulance." As I trotted away toward the break room, I heard Dante telling George he couldn't risk pulling him up on the slick floor, and I nodded in approval.

The paramedics came, strapped George to a backboard, and hauled him off to the hospital. A couple of police cars showed up, too. I couldn't remember exactly what I'd told the 9-1-1 operator, but apparently, I had mentioned that a slick mixture spread across the floor had caused George's fall and they'd taken the claim seriously.

Police officers questioned me and every other employee and customer that were in the store when the accident happened, but they never did figure out whom had hurt George. And hurt he was. He'd broken his tailbone and had whiplash.

The doctors declared he wouldn't be able to work for three months. That didn't matter, though, as soon as the police told George his fall had been no accident, he opened a personal injury lawsuit against the store, which meant he would never be back to work there. If the cops ever decided who had actually spread the oil mixture, I'm sure he would go after them, as well, but they still haven't figured it out.

I haven't figured it out, either, but I quickly decided I didn't want to work with anyone who would do such a thing, even to an awful person like George. I talked to everyone I knew, in the business and out, begged and pleaded, and managed to get myself a job managing the sundries section of a chain drugstore.

The pay is a little bit less, but the atmosphere is good, and my manager appreciates all that I do. Sales and satisfaction ratings for my section are up, and everyone is pleased. I only wish Donovan could have come with me, but drugstores don't sell produce. He's still back at the old place.

But—at least for me—no more boss from hell.

THE END

CONFESSIONS OF A SUSPICIOUS SISTER
Did She Kill My Brother?

There were fewer people at my brother's funeral than there were at the wedding of his grieving widow.

I faked a smile and struggled to keep my four-year-old still as she squirmed in my lap. I looked around at the crowd of people as they smiled and watched my former sister-in-law marry the plumber she'd been having an affair with long before my brother, Allen, died.

No one seemed concerned that he'd been dead less than a year. No one questioned why a well-balanced guy would suddenly kill himself without leaving a note. No one was bothered in the slightest by the fact that his widow was two hundred thousand dollars richer with my brother in the ground.

All they saw was a woman brave enough to love again after suffering a terrible loss. A woman who found a man to be a father to the children Allen left behind when he took his own life. To the crowd around me, today was a blessed day, a moment to lift away the dark cloud of sadness in Sarah's life and let her start new.

Why was I the only one that saw the truth?

I got the call in the early hours of the morning. That's never good. In my family, a late-night or early-morning phone call means one of two things: someone's dead or someone's dying. If it's neither of the two, someone's going to be dead for calling me at this hour.

It was my brother, John. He's the funny brother—a necessity of being the middle child. He was the happy-go-lucky, life of the party brother. He sounded like none of those things at that moment. I could tell by the tone of his voice it was something bad.

"What's wrong?"

He started to speak, but then his voice broke as the hysterical tears he'd been holding back just rushed out. I'd seen my brother cry a total of three times since he reached the age of ten, and always at funerals. First Grandpa's, then Dad's, and then Mom's funeral three years ago.

"What is it?" I asked again, my voice near hysterical.

This isn't good. It can't possibly be anything I really want to hear.

"Allen's dead."

John started crying again.

I was stunned speechless. There were no words that came to mind as the images of our older brother flew through my head. Allen couldn't possibly be dead. He was the responsible one. The stable one. He was the one that did everything right. Allen was the glue holding the fragile remains of our family together.

"What? How?"

Those were the only words I could form through the cloud of sleepiness and shock. A million questions started flying through my mind.

"They seem to think it was a suicide."

The last word hit a heavy blow to my gut. My brother had to be wrong.

"No," I argued. Allen would never do something that reckless and selfish. He had three children and a wife. Granted, things weren't great with his marriage, but it certainly wasn't bad enough for him to—"

"I found his body this morning when I came by to pick him up for work."

We live in a small West Virginia mining town where everybody knows everybody. The mine is the lifeblood of the community. If you don't work there, your spouse does. Both my brothers worked at the mine and often drove together when they were on the same shift. If they went for breakfast first, that meant a brisk, three o'clock in the morning pick-up time.

"That's not possible," I argued. "I mean, how? What happened?"

My mind raced as I tried to work it out in my mind, but I couldn't find an answer to fit. The truth was that my brother would not commit suicide. Period. So what's going on?

"I. . . ." he started, then stopped. "Can we talk about this in person? I feel like you need to hear this in person. Anyway, I'm sitting in his driveway watching the ambulance leave. I need to get out of here."

"Yeah," I didn't press him for more details although I desperately wanted to.

I eyed the clock. It was almost four. The local diner on Main Street stays open twenty-four hours to cater to the long, irregular hours of the miners.

"I'll meet you at Mae's at five?"

"Okay."

John hung up the phone before I could say anything else.

I slid into a booth at Mae's Diner in my finest sweat suit. I was lucky to be there at all. That morning, of all mornings, I wished I hadn't kicked Jerry out. He was a bum, but at least I could've left the kids sleeping with him at home. Instead, I had to drag my kids out of bed in their pajamas and take them to the lady who watches them for me. I'd have to come up with a little extra money for the pre-dawn drop off.

John wasn't far behind me, settling into the booth as the waitress filled up my coffee cup.

I didn't say anything. He knew full well where our conversation had left off. Allen was dead and I wanted answers. I arched a weary eyebrow at him over my coffee.

"Gas," he said, plainly. "He left the stove on and let the room fill up with carbon monoxide."

I tried to comfort myself by thinking it was at least a peaceful death. He would've just gotten sleepy and passed out. Then a panicked thought grabbed me.

"What about Sarah and the kids?"

"They're all fine. Allen was sleeping above the garage in the guest house."

Allen is handy. Was handy, I reminded myself. Right after he bought their house, he'd built a two-story garage in his yard. Downstairs he kept a workshop with the motorcycles he worked on and upstairs was a spare room for extra storage and the occasional guest. It was just big enough for a bed, a television, a small bath, and a mini kitchen. I was certain he never imagined that one day his wife would force him to live out there.

The thoughts whirled in my brain as I tried to process the information. Allen killed himself. Was there a sign? I hadn't seen any. Maybe I didn't pay enough attention. I was wrapped up in my own life drama, as any single mother is.

I didn't know what to say to John. I'm the youngest, the one more prone to flights of fancy. I'm the one that always says the wrong thing at the wrong time. I'm nothing like Allen, as my parents reminded me every day until their deaths.

The waitress returned and took our breakfast order, delaying me long enough to try to come up with something to say.

"I just don't understand it," John spoke before I could.

"What?" I asked, although I'd had the same thought several times already.

"We had dinner last night. He seemed fine. Good, actually. He was thinking about getting his own place. He was talking about going to see a lawyer next week about filing for divorce and getting custody of the kids. Allen seemed really upbeat. Meeting early for breakfast was his idea. I just can't imagine him making plans like that, then going home and killing himself."

It didn't make sense, but suicide rarely does.

"Maybe he wanted you to find him instead of one of the kids."

He had two sons and a daughter, two from his first marriage and the last from his current wife, Sarah.

"No," John insisted. "There's something just not right about this."

"He could've been hiding it, John. You know how he was. Just like Dad. He wouldn't want to burden anyone with his problems."

"I saw him almost every day. If I'd thought for a second that he might. . . ." His voice trailed off as he turned to stare out the window at the occasional passing car.

"This isn't your fault, John. There's nothing you could've done to stop him if he wanted to do it. Did he leave a note?"

John shook his head.

"Nothing."

That worried me even more. It was one thing for Allen to kill himself, but it was completely unlike him to do it and not leave an explanation or a good-bye to anyone—not even his kids. Those kids were his entire universe.

John sat silently, continuing to look outside as though he could ignore everything that was happening.

"They're going to do an autopsy to make sure that's what killed him. The cops are also taking prints and photos of the room in case. . . ."

John's voice faded again as he turned back from the window and finally looked me in the eye.

"In case of what?" I asked.

He leaned in and lowered his voice as though the three truckers in the diner cared about our conversation.

"In case they find something that would make them think perhaps it wasn't suicide."

Not suicide? That only leaves two options—an accident or murder. Allen was far too conscientious for his death to be an accident.

"What do you mean? You think someone might've killed him?" I choked the last few words out in a hushed whisper.

"Maybe."

That was crazy. "Who could possibly want to kill Allen?"

"Come on, Vick."

I said the words, but in my heart, he was right. I already knew. I was being kind when I said Allen was having marital problems. His marriage was in shambles. His wife was a shrew. Everyone knew she'd been having an affair with a coworker. Allen had refused to divorce her. He'd already divorced once and didn't want to "fail" at marriage a second time, although his first wife's meth addiction had nothing to do with him.

"I just can't imagine she'd be capable of something like that. I've never liked Sarah, but I'd never pegged her as being a murderer."

"She might not be. Maybe she didn't have the nerve. But I'll bet you that guy she's been seeing on the side does."

That hadn't occurred to me. The rumor was that she was involved with one of the plumbers at the company where she worked as a receptionist and dispatcher. I didn't know the guy, but I guess it was possible that one of them could've turned on the gas without Allen knowing.

"Certainly there's a better option than murder, right? If he were finally considering divorce, she'd get what she wanted. He'd probably even let her keep the house. They don't have any money for her to inherit. What would be the point of killing him?"

John shook his head, and then leaned back suddenly as a platter of eggs and pancakes were set onto the table in front of him.

"He really didn't want to divorce Sarah. He wanted to make it work. Maybe he thought threatening her with leaving and taking the kids would scare her straight."

"You think she did it to keep the kids?"

"I doubt it. The two oldest aren't even hers and she's never treated them as though they were. She'd probably be relieved for them to go back and live with their druggie mother if it wasn't for the social security checks she'd miss out on."

That wasn't nearly enough money to justify killing him.

"I still think she could've talked Allen into a divorce with joint custody if she was really that unhappy with him. Did he know about the plumber? If she flaunted it in front of him that might've pushed him to give in and file."

"I think he suspected something, but she never came out and admitted it. Sarah was somewhat discreet."

John attacked his eggs with gusto.

"Not if we knew about it."

There was just no good reason for any of this. Unless he had. . . . I took a bite of eggs and immediately wished I hadn't. They tasted like ash in my mouth. I took a swig of coffee to wash it away.

"Tell me," I said, swallowing the eggs and the lump in my throat, "he didn't have a life insurance policy."

John nodded, his brow furrowed.

"I'm pretty sure he bought one a few years ago when Kyle was born."

"Well, it wouldn't make any sense for him to kill himself, then. If it was suicide, wouldn't the insurance nullify?"

"Only if he killed himself within two years of buying it. Most policies have that clause. After that, it doesn't matter how you die unless your death is somehow linked to the beneficiary of the policy."

"So if Sarah killed him or had him killed, she wouldn't get the money."

I didn't like my sister-in-law, but I knew she was too smart to lose out on that money by doing something obvious.

"No, it would go in trust to the kids and their guardians if she went to jail. But if it looked like a suicide...." John's voice trailed off, leaving me to weave my own web of guilt.

Kyle turned two last month. Either Allen or Sarah had been waiting for the two years to be up so the life insurance policy would pay out for a suicide. It probably wasn't much money on a miner's salary, but in a little town like Rockport, even fifty thousand dollars could change your life.

I pushed my plate away. I really didn't even know why I'd ordered it. I wasn't hungry. John seemed to be the opposite, piling huge bites of pancake into his mouth to smother his feelings.

"Now what do we do?"

He swallowed and shrugged.

"I guess we wait to see what the cops say."

The coroner confirmed that Allen died from carbon monoxide poisoning and released the body to his wife the following day. Sarah made the funeral arrangements, rushing out to have Allen's body cremated immediately. I thought it was suspicious given the circumstances, but he'd mentioned wanting to be cremated in the past.

The memorial service was small, just close family and a few friends, held at the local funeral home. It was almost pitiful how few people came out to pay their respects. There's a stigma about suicides, sometimes, and even more so in a small town. Most people were ashamed or embarrassed for the family and just stayed home. Even the pastor seemed distant.

There wasn't a wake afterwards. Instead, the family gathered at Allen—I mean—Sarah's house. Allen's kids played outside with mine. John sat in the corner and sulked over his casserole. My Aunt Millie stayed in the kitchen, busying herself with making sure everyone was fed and the kitchen was cleaned, as any good Southern aunt would.

I kept to myself, my eyes appraising my sister-in-law for the slightest sign of a guilty conscience. So far, there was nothing to report. Sarah was appropriately bereaved all afternoon. She stuck close to her father, who was a sheriff in the next county. On occasion, she would burst into tears and run into the bathroom. I didn't feel like chasing after her to console her and wipe away her crocodile tears. Instead, I picked at Aunt Millie's peach cobbler and pretended not to notice.

If Sarah was guilty, she was doing a pretty good job at acting innocent. Over the next few weeks, I saw her several times, which was more than I usually did. She invited the kids and me over for dinner, admitting tearfully that she didn't want to be alone in the house. One night she gave me a box of some of Allen's things she thought I might like to have, mainly pictures of us together as kids.

It was very considerate of her, but even then I questioned her motives. Is she just trying to get all the evidence of her dead husband out of the house? Maybe looking at his pictures aggravates her guilty conscience.

The most impressive thing was that the rumors of her and the plumber vanished almost overnight. Sarah wasn't seen with him. He hadn't come around the house. She was good. She had this whole thing wrapped up in a neat, little package to keep from arousing suspicions. Everyone believed her husband had killed himself over the grief of their unhappy marriage. She was distraught and struggling to take care of their children. No one would ever suspect the tearful sheriff's daughter of being the conniving criminal that she was.

About a month after the funeral, Rick, the local sheriff, paid a visit to my place to ask a few questions about Allen and Sarah. I didn't really know what the point was. The death certificate was already done and printed with suicide by CO asphyxiation.

I had to admit it was nice to see Rick, although I wished the circumstances were different. I sat him down in the living room and offered him some tea, which he accepted gladly.

"So, what brings you here today, Rick?"

He hesitated, taking a sip of tea before he spoke.

"Well, I don't want to stir up anything, but I'm quietly looking into your brother's death. I just want to ask you a few questions to see if it doesn't clear up some issues for me."

"Did you find something unusual during your investigation?"

"Not unusual, per se. The pieces just don't fit quite right for me. I'm by no means an expert—we have fewer than five homicides in the three nearby counties per year combined. But, personally, things just don't add up here."

I knew what he meant. Rick and I had gone to high school together, so I felt comfortable enough to speak frankly to him.

"Between you and me, Rick, I don't think Allen killed himself. You knew him. Your sister and he dated for a while in school. It just doesn't seem like something he would do."

Rick nodded and circled the brim of his hat in his hands.

"I know. I keep thinking maybe it was an accident. I haven't got a single stitch of evidence to prove it was anything other than suicide. But it's still nagging at me."

"Did you find anything in the room he was staying in?"

Rick shook his head. "Nothing unusual there. No signs of struggle or forced entry. Nothing showed on the autopsy that would indicate he was drugged. There were no unusual prints on or around the stove or anywhere else."

"Did you find Sarah's?"

Rick's gaze snapped up from his hat to look me in the eye.

"Yes, but it's her house. There's nothing unusual about that." He narrowed his eyes at me. "What are you trying to say, Vicky?"

I was tired of tiptoeing around it.

"I'm saying Sarah never went up there and she most certainly didn't do any cooking if she did."

Rick took a deep breath and leaned back into his chair.

"That's a big insinuation."

"It's also a big insurance payout."

John is friendly with the local insurance agent where Allen had bought his policy. Over a beer, his friend confided in him that he'd cut Sarah a check for two hundred thousand dollars—fifty thousand for her, and each of their children.

"You're not saying she killed Allen for money, are you?"

"You tell me, Rick. I'm just a suspicious sister. You're the cop. What does your gut tell you?"

Rick shook his head. "My gut tells me not to go accusing a sheriff's daughter of murdering her husband unless I've got solid evidence to convict on."

He was right. Sarah's father would pull whatever strings he had to and get that whole investigation shut down—possibly taking Rick's career down with it. There wasn't enough to go on. There wasn't even enough evidence to turn over to the insurance company and they weren't nearly as picky.

"What about that plumber she's been sneaking around with?"

"I don't know much about that, but it wouldn't surprise me. Sarah's always had a way with men."

"Yeah and it looks like she's gotten away with murder, too."

Rick tensed beside me. He wasn't about to drag a fellow officer's daughter in for questioning on something that flimsy and I knew it.

"What about the kids, Rick? If she killed their father, she's got no business keeping them. The two oldest ones don't even belong to her."

"You got a better idea?"

I could tell by the look in his eyes that if he had a viable option, he'd take it.

"Anything is better than their father's murderer keeping them!"

"Keep your voice down, Vicky," Rick urged, despite the fact that we were alone in my apartment. "We've got no reason to think Sarah is a danger to any of the kids. There's no place for them to go and no grounds for me to have them removed."

"I could. . . ." I started to offer taking them myself, but I stopped. I looked around my apartment and knew I could barely manage with my two children, much less two or three more. "Never mind."

"You're a good person to even consider it, Vicky." He patted me on the knee for a moment, his hand lingering a moment too long before getting up. "Listen, I'm going to keep an eye on all this. If I find any evidence—and I mean any—to implicate Sarah in Allen's death, you'll be the first to know."

"Thanks, Rick."

I forced a smile and nodded at him. Rick is a good guy and I knew he'd do whatever he could. For a moment, I wondered why I'd never dated him in school or after we'd graduated. He'd never been married. He's leaps and bounds over Jerry and the others I'd wasted my time with.

"How about over dinner on Friday?"

The words came out of my mouth before I could stop them.

Rick stopped in the doorway and smiled as he slipped his hat back on. "It's a date."

Sarah and the plumber announced their engagement eight months after Allen died. Their wedding was five months later.

I fidgeted in the heat and wondered why on Earth I'd even come to the ceremony. Of course it was for my brother's children. Despite what Sarah may or may not have done to Allen, I would stay around for their sake. That's part of the reason I've kept my suspicions quiet. When they're older, I want to be able to tell them about how wonderful their father really was. If I started throwing around unfounded accusations, Sarah would make sure I'd never see them again.

Rick, now my fiancé, reached over and squeezed my hand as though he could read my thoughts. His comforting was bittersweet. He loves me and understands my suspicions about Allen's death, but as sheriff, his hands are tied without the evidence to charge her with murder.

One thing he could promise me was that he wouldn't give up. Criminals often slip up, especially years down the road once they believed they'd gotten away with it for good. If and when Sarah makes a mistake, Rick will be right there waiting.

They say that no one ever expects a loved one to commit suicide, and that it's natural for people to seek out other ways to make sense of it in my mind. As time goes by, I've begun to wonder if they're right. Do I see Sarah's guilt because I don't want to admit to being blind to Allen's pain? It's a question I may never know the answer to.

But at night, when I lie in bed and think about Allen, I can't help but believe that my sister-in-law got away with murder.

THE END

CONFESSIONS OF THE WORST MOM EVER
My story is so horrifying, I can hardly believe it actually happened to me....

When you read this story you'll probably think I should be in prison, but I need to tell it so that I can purge some of this horrific guilt from my heart. There are times when I wonder if it really happened, or if I'm only imagining it. Other times I see what took place as clear as day. I've never served a day behind bars for what happened—if it did, in fact, happen. But believe me when I tell you that I've paid over and over again with my soul—that I've been locked inside of a prison of my own making.

My father's a police officer who works the nightshift. An insurance office employs my mother. She was three months pregnant when she graduated from high school and they got married. Six months later I was born.

I wasn't very old before I realized that I messed up their lives—that they never would've gotten married if it weren't for me. Since they didn't want the same thing to happen to me, they were always very strict with me, right from the get-go. For instance, at a very young age, I was told, in no uncertain terms, that I absolutely could not date until I turned sixteen, if not older. But unbeknownst to them, I started going out with Colin Ferguson when I was fifteen and he was seventeen.

Considered pretty by my friends, I have long hair and blue eyes and I guess you could say I've always looked older than my age. But none of that's ever been important to me. You see, all I've ever wanted is to score points on the basketball court. And except for laying down the law, the times when I played basketball are the only times when my dad ever paid any real attention to me. He's a good ol' boy who loves sports and going out with his buddies. He goes to work at six at night and gets off at two in the morning. Afterward, he hits the bars, drinking and staying out until three or four in the morning. He and my mother fight and argue about it constantly.

One day a girl at school who played basketball with me invited me to a party she was having on the weekend. I could scarcely believe it, seeing as I didn't hang around with the same crowd she did.

Although I wasn't allowed to go out with boys, I was permitted to go out with my girlfriends or with a group of friends, and so, of course—that's what I told my parents I was doing that night. At the party, I felt out of place; I was younger than most of the other kids and few of them paid any attention to me except for this really cute guy, Colin Ferguson, who asked me to dance several times. He was a senior, captain of the football team, and every girl's dream hottie.

The next day he came up to me at school and asked if I would sit with him at lunch. I was so excited, I could scarcely speak, but somehow I managed to accept his invitation, and Colin and I ate lunch together every day that week, and then that Friday night, he asked me to go to a movie with him. As it was, already, I idolized the ground he walked on and I simply could not believe my good fortune. So, just as I did the night of the party, I told my parents that I was going to the movies "with a girlfriend."

After that first time, Colin and I left whatever event I told my parents I was attending with "one of my friends" and spent the evening making out in the backseat of his car. Sometimes we'd go out to the Dam, which is a favorite making-out place for teens where I live. Of course, shortly after we started dating exclusively, Colin started pressuring me to have sex with him. As it was, we'd kissed and done some of what my old-fashioned mom would call "heavy petting" on our previous dates, but I refused to "go all the way," even though I knew lots of kids were. Then one night when we were out at the Dam, after he threatened to start seeing someone else if I didn't put out—well, what can I say?

I finally gave in.

"You know I love you, don't you, Christy?" he asked.

I loved him, but no one—not even my own parents—had ever told me that they loved me before. My heart started pounding faster and faster as we began kissing, as he undressed me. I was too embarrassed to ask him if he was going to use a condom. All in all, I have to say that he was really sweet and gentle, and that it only hurt for a little while. And when it was over, he held me close and we cuddled some more before he took me home. Because there was such a complete and utter lack of affection in my home, I guess maybe that's why I always wanted my moments with Colin to go on forever and ever.

The next several times we went out we had sex, but those times Colin used condoms. Then one night, claiming he was "all out," we had sex without one again. I told myself that since he didn't use a condom the first time and I didn't get pregnant, it wouldn't happen this time, either.

Two months later I realized that my period was late—make that very late—and that's when I knew I was pregnant.

It felt like my whole world ended that day.

I could barely stand it until I told Colin. Afterward, he was silent for a long moment. Then:

"Are you sure?" he asked as we stood in the hallway at school with other kids laughing and chatting, walking all around us.

When I told him that I was pretty certain about it, he told me to buy a home pregnancy test at the drugstore, just to be sure.

I was terribly embarrassed just buying the test. Since we live in a fairly large city, I took a bus to another part of town where I didn't think I would run into anybody who knew me, and even then, I bought things I didn't really need—like mascara and shampoo and typing paper—so the cashier wouldn't pay as much attention to the home pregnancy test and the age of the person buying it.

As soon as I got home, I read the instructions and took the test. The time I spent waiting for the results seemed like an eternity; I was so nervous that I actually thought I'd die from the suspense. Then all of a sudden there it was—

And then I knew that my worst fears were confirmed.

When I called Colin and told him that I was pregnant, he flipped out on me. "This can't happen!" he burst out. "I'm going to college and then law school after I graduate! I can't be tied down with a wife and kid! And you're only a freshman! You can't take care of a baby! And what will your parents say if you tell them?"

"They'll kill me," I answered plainly. And I knew they would.

"Mine will do worse than that to me!" Colin snapped fearfully.

"So what are we going to do?" I asked him, my voice full of anguish.

He was quiet for a long time. Then finally, he said flatly, "We'll have to come up with something. In the meantime, we'll just go on as usual. I know a guy whose girlfriend had an abortion; I'll talk to him and find out where she went."

"You mean—kill the baby?" I exclaimed, stunned to the point of sickness. "But—we can't do that! My gosh, Colin—how could you even suggest such a thing?"

"Have you got a better idea?" he countered angrily.

I burst into tears. He was acting like I was to blame for everything; yet, it was pretty darn clear to me, even then, that he had a part in it, too—to say the very least. Between sobs, I reminded him that I was only fifteen, and that I couldn't have an abortion without my parents' permission unless I went to some backstreet butcher, where I might end up bleeding to death or being rendered sterile by some hideous infection or surgical error. "I won't kill this baby," I finally told Colin in a voice that was as empathic as I could be at that time.

"Okay, okay—whatever; just don't panic, okay?" Colin cautioned crossly. "And for God's sake—don't you dare get stupid on me and go telling anyone. We'll figure out something—some kind of a solution—before it's too late."

"I think I should tell my mother." As it was, though, I felt like I could already hear her screaming and my father threatening to disown me.

"Yeah, right. And get yourself kicked out of your house?" Colin mocked. "What will you do then?"

"I don't know!" I wailed. He was talking about how my pregnancy would affect his future, and all I could think was: What about my future? I'm the one who's going to have to go through it! I felt betrayed. All alone. "I'll have to tell my parents eventually," I reasoned hesitantly, dread forming a painful lump in my throat. "I mean, after all, at some point—they're going to notice."

"Don't do that!" Colin warned hastily. "No one will be able to tell for a while. By then, I'll think of something we can do."

"Like what?" I asked sarcastically. "Pretend it's not true?"

"Don't I wish," he muttered miserably.

I passed through the next few days at school in a fog. During the weeks that followed, Colin and I kept seeing each other, but he wasn't as interested in having sex with me as he was before I got pregnant. In fact, as it was, we spent almost all of our time together arguing and trying to figure out what to do about my pregnancy.

Then one afternoon when I got home from school, Mom was sitting at the kitchen table, her face all puffy and red from crying. She was usually at work when I got home, so I figured she was pretty much lying in wait for me. Thinking she'd found out that I was pregnant, I panicked.

"What's wrong?" I whispered fearfully. Then I waited for the ax to fall—for her to tell me to pack my bags and get out.

"Your father and I are getting a divorce," she said tearfully.

"What?" I was shocked, and yet relieved, that her woes had nothing to do with what I thought caused them. After all, a lot of my friends' parents are divorced, and although my parents fight all the time, I honestly never expected it to happen to them—

Just like I never expected to get pregnant.

"Your father's got a new girlfriend," Mom said in a voice that was bitter, frank, and full of tears. "He wants a divorce so he can marry her."

"You two fight all the time, but you always patch things up," I rationalized weakly. "Can't you patch this up, too?"

She shook her head firmly, her face taking on a hard, hate-filled expression of grim resolve. "It's too late for that. Your dad's new girlfriend is pregnant, it seems."

All of a sudden I felt like I would drop through the floor.

What if she knows that I'm pregnant, too?

That evening when Dad came home he told me to go to my room

and then he and Mom started yelling at each other, as usual. When I heard the front door slam, hesitantly, my heart filled to overflowing with dread, I went back downstairs.

What now? I wondered in the eerie, unsettling silence that was the aftermath of my father walking out on my mom. This means he's leaving me, too. And of course he is; what else did I expect? After all, I know he never wanted me to begin with, so why would he care about me now? And having a grandchild will only diminish the macho image he suddenly has of himself. Come to think of it—maybe he doesn't want the child his girlfriend's expecting, either. But it's certainly an excuse he can easily use to get away from Mom.

"He'll come back," I told her when I found her standing in front of the living room window, crying as she watched him drive away.

"I don't want him back!" she raged angrily, turning on me suddenly. "I hate him! I want him to drop dead!"

Right then, I thought of how weird it is—that everything can be "normal" in your life one minute, and the next minute, you're pregnant and your parents are getting a divorce because your father is having a baby with another woman and you aren't a family anymore.

Of course, my father never came back, and for the next several weeks Mom spent a lot of time in her bedroom crying, or sitting on the sofa, watching daytime television with unseeing eyes and a glass of vodka in her hand. As time went by, the glass graduated to a bottle, and she would pass out on the sofa almost every evening. Several times I considered telling her that I was pregnant, but I held back, realizing that I couldn't place another burden on her devastated shoulders.

As it was, I usually wore sweatshirts and sloppy clothes and I was active in sports. In order to hide my "condition," I kept right on doing both. I seldom suffered from morning sickness and I went to school every day. To hide my weight gain, I cut waaay down on my eating and stayed as close as I possibly could to a hundred and fifteen pounds. That weight might look okay on someone who's petite and five feet tall, but I'm five-foot-seven, and in spite of my pregnancy, I know I looked like a beanpole. Still, I doubted that anyone suspected a thing; in fact, sometimes I actually almost forgot that I was pregnant. And then reality would seize me, and I would remind myself that my "secret" could hardly remain a secret forever.

I desperately wanted to tell someone—anyone—about what was going on, but my mother was drinking more and more and she was seldom sober after work. How she was able to get up in the morning and go to work is beyond me, even to this day. Then one evening when Colin hadn't talked to me in days, realizing he had his life all planned out, and that it quite obviously did not include our baby and me, I started to cry. I felt used—abandoned like a stray puppy left along a roadside. Wiping my eyes, I went downstairs to tell my mother about my pregnancy and suffer the consequences, once and for all.

She was sprawled out on the sofa. A half-empty vodka bottle stood on the floor beside the cluttered coffee table.

"Well, if it isn't my little girl," she said drunkenly. "Your dad walked out on me; I suppose you'll be next."

I wanted to sit down and put my arms around her, but since there was little love expressed in our family, feeling awkward, I held back.

"We fight a lot—I know. But I—I love your dad," she said then, tears forming in her bleary eyes. "My parents—they made him marry me when he got me pregnant with you, or he would've dumped me when I was sixteen. . . . I guess I should just be grateful that it didn't happen until now, right?"

I didn't know what to say to that. Finally, tentatively, I managed, "If I had a baby . . . would you kick me out, or would you make the guy responsible marry me like your parents did?"

She struggled to sit up, then slouched against the arm of the sofa, her empty glass in her hand. She tried, unsuccessfully, to focus her gaze on me. "If you were pregnant, I wouldn't make the guy responsible marry you. Nah—Lord knows he'd only eventually end up leaving you, anyway, just like your father's left me." Lifting the vodka bottle, she tried to refill her glass, but most of the liquor spilled over the side and onto the sofa and the carpet. "Anyway, you'd better not be pregnant," she said threateningly, dropping the bottle back onto the floor with a thunk. "Because if you are, you might as well kiss your sweet life good-bye, sweetheart."

"But . . . what would you do if I were?" I persisted, needing to know.

She pointed a wobbly finger in the direction of the front door. "If you were pregnant, I'd say, 'There's the door, doll. Don't let it bang you in the ass on your way out,' just like my parents said to me. As it is, your father's made me the talk of the neighborhood. Everyone knew about his cheating even before I did!" She snorted bitterly. "I don't need any more crap heaped on me." Lifting the glass to her lips, she swallowed the vodka she'd managed to pour into the glass, then dropped it onto the floor and collapsed against the sofa cushions once more.

Over the next two months I kept asking Colin if he'd come up with anything yet—any kind of solution to my dire problem. He always told me no, but that he was "working on it." I tried to think of something on my own, but the only "solution" I could come up with was that when the time came, if Colin hadn't figured out something better, I would take a cab to another part of town, walk into a hospital and, using a false name, have my baby.

Surely, I reasoned, they won't turn me away. They couldn't possibly. And after it's born, I'll leave it at the hospital and just walk out the door. When no one claims it and they don't know its mother's identify, they'll put it in a foster home. That'll be better than living on the streets with a teenage mother who'd be homeless after she got kicked out onto the streets, just because her parents won't abide her unplanned pregnancy. I would think this, and then I'd start envisioning my baby and myself, living in a cardboard box by night while I spent the days begging for spare change with which to buy formula and diapers.

Then one Friday afternoon around two in the afternoon when I was about seven and a half months along, I started having pains off and on while I was in school. I endured them as long as I could, then finally went home, telling the school nurse that I had my period and couldn't bear the cramps.

I walked the three blocks to my house, stopping and holding my breath whenever another wave of pain swept over me. When I finally made it home, I staggered upstairs and collapsed on my bed. The pains kept getting worse until I could barely stand them; as it was, I was doubled over, holding onto my stomach and moaning in agony.

Mom was still at work and I was all alone in the house. Feeling like I needed to go to the bathroom, I went in and sat down on the toilet. Seized by a bearing-down sensation, I doubled over, moaning, sweating, and crying all at the same time, and pushed. There was one searing pain—and then I heard and felt this whooshing, watery sound and sensation between my thighs. When I finally stood and fearfully looked down into the toilet bowl, I saw something bloody and glistening floating in the crimson water.

Gasping in horror, I stared at it for a moment—and then realized that it was a baby—

My baby.

My God! I thought with mounting horror and utter disbelief. What am I going to do? Delicately fishing it out of the water with my bare, shaking hands, I took a hand towel from the rack and gently wrapped it around the newborn. Then I went to my bed, my jeans and panties still down around my knees, and carefully placed the infant on it. It was covered with blood and mucus and it wasn't making any noise; in fact, it wasn't even moving one bit.

At first, I didn't know what to do. Then I realized I had to cut the umbilical cord. Maybe that's why it isn't crying yet, I thought, and I suppose I was trying to console myself. So I found a pair of scissors in my nightstand alongside me and cut the cord, tying it off with a thin string of ribbon I also found in the drawer. Afterward, I wiped the baby's tiny face and delicate body with a corner of the towel. It looked so pathetic, and it wasn't making any sounds—it wasn't even breathing, as far as I could tell. I saw that it was a girl. Its features were petite and perfect, just like those you might see on one of those precious, collectible newborn dolls.

As I stared down at the tiny body, I was scarcely able to comprehend what had happened. Again, I wondered what I should do. Who could I go to for help? Colin said that we couldn't tell anyone—that if we did, his entire future would be ruined. And Mom had stated that if I had a baby, she'd kick me out of the house. As it was, I'd heard her stumbling around downstairs after she came home from work, though I figured, She's probably passed out by now. Not that it matters, anyway; she can't handle her own life, let alone what's happening in mine.

Carefully, I cleaned up the blood-spattered bathroom and myself. After changing clothes, I laid down beside the child. When I felt the placenta coming, I got up, squatted over a plastic-lined wastepaper basket and later, placed the liner and the placenta in the garbage bin outside the house.

Mom called me for supper at six-thirty. I considered telling her that I wasn't hungry, but I knew I had to act "normal," as if nothing had happened. Hoping the baby wouldn't wake up and cry until I called Colin and asked him what I should do, I put the baby, still wrapped in the towel, in a corner of my closet. Then I went downstairs, where I nibbled at the food on my plate. Explaining to my mother, who was only having a cup of black coffee, that I had homework to do, I returned to my room fifteen minutes later. There, I called Colin on my cell phone, finally getting him after several attempts. When I told him what had happened, there was a long silence.

"Is it making noise so your mother will hear it?" he finally asked.

I told him that it hadn't made any noises at all, and that I didn't even think it was alive.

"You mean it's dead?" he asked apprehensively.

"I . . . don't know," I stammered. "I t-think so."

"If it were alive, we could take it to a church and drop it off, but if it's dead and someone finds it in your room, they'll think whoever gave birth to it did something to it."

I began to sob helplessly. "What are we going to do, Colin? Maybe I should tell my mom—"

"No!" he snapped quickly. "She'll make us get married or make me support the kid! My parents will kill me."

"Mom won't make us get married," I said, shuddering and trembling as I tried to hold back my tears. "She told me as much."

"Yeah? Well, she could change her mind. And anyway, if it's dead, we can start over without anyone ever knowing about it."

Colin's words whirled around in my mind. What he said made sense to me at that time, but I started to cry again nevertheless. "How are we going to do that?"

"Calm down," he admonished. "I'll be over in a few minutes."

"What are you going to do?" I asked, frantically wondering, Is he going to throw the baby in a garbage can or Dumpster somewhere where someone could find it and call the police? What if someone noticed that I was pregnant and tells the cops they think the baby is mine?

"I'll tell you when I get there," Colin said. "I'll come over after your mother goes to sleep. Leave the door unlocked for me; I'll take care of everything."

He sounded so cold. "What do you mean by that?" I asked carefully after a moment's hesitation.

"I mean just what I said—I'll take care of it. Jeez! What do you want to do? Put an announcement in the newspaper? Have a baby shower? Ruin both our lives?"

"No!" I wailed.

"Look—you said yourself that you think it's dead," he pointed out adamantly. "What do they do with dead people—huh? They bury them."

I gasped in horror. "You can't just dig a hole and put it in the ground!"

"What do you want to do with it, then? You can't leave it in your closet."

An hour after my mother went to bed, I called Colin again, then crept downstairs and unlocked the door. When he entered my bedroom a half-hour later and I showed him the baby, he looked down at it for a long moment without saying anything. Then:

"Are you sure it didn't make any noise?"

I shook my head. "Not that I heard."

"It must've been dead when it was born," he reasoned. "I have a friend whose parents have a fishing cabin upstate; I'll take it up there and bury it in the woods."

Horrified by the scenario, I burst out, "You can't do that!"

He started to walk toward the door. "If you have a better idea, go for it."

"Don't leave!" I cried out. "What will I do?" As cold and uncaring as Colin was, even then, I knew he was all I had.

"You don't have much choice," he said, shrugging like we were debating whether I should go to college or not. "You can let me handle this, or you can face the consequences. Everyone will think you killed it, anyway, and you'll go to prison."

"But I didn't kill it—I didn't hurt it!" I cried, sobbing. "It just—

plopped out! Maybe it drowned in the toilet bowl before I got it out—oh, God, Colin—I don't even know!"

"Whatever," he said in the nastiest, most dismissive tone of voice. Then, seeing that I was panicking and about to burst into tears again, he tried to calm me. "Okay, okay. That's probably what happened, right? But you still might be blamed for its death. You don't want that to happen, do you?"

"No," I whispered harshly, envisioning myself peering out between prison bars, spending the rest of my life locked up for a horrendous, hideous crime I didn't even knowingly commit.

In the end, I found a plastic shopping bag in my closet and placed the baby, still wrapped in its towel, gently into the bag.

"Don't worry. Everything's gonna be okay," Colin told me as he reached for the bag.

I went to school on Monday just as if nothing happened. Colin was absent that day, but he was in class on Tuesday. When I asked him what he did with the baby, he told me that he buried it in the woods.

"What if the animals dig it up?" I despaired, a picture of tiny bones strewn about the ground, of animals gnawing on them, forming in my mind and making me shudder until I thought I would vomit or pass out—maybe both.

"I dug a deep hole and placed rocks on top of it," he told me. "No one or nothing will ever find it."

"I want you to show me where you buried it," I said, harshly wiping the tears from my swollen, blotchy cheeks. "I'd—like to put some flowers on its—its . . . grave."

"Are you nuts?" he burst out, glaring at me with obvious fury and distaste. "My friend's parents who own the cabin—they don't know I buried it there, and I don't want them to know—understand? Have I made myself perfectly clear, you idiot?"

Colin and I continued to see each other for several months after that, but we were held together by our secret, not by any affection that existed between us. Several times I heard rumors that he was seeing other girls, but when I confronted him, he denied everything.

When spring came I was sixteen and both of us found jobs and worked all summer. I tried to shove what had happened during the past year into the deepest recesses of my mind and close the door on those hideous, heartbreaking memories, but sometimes they slipped out, anyway. I wondered if the baby would've survived if I'd only told my mother and we'd taken it to the hospital right after it was born. Then I reminded myself that I hadn't seen a single doctor during my pregnancy, hadn't had any prenatal care, and since the baby was born prematurely, it probably had something wrong with it. I tried to justify what I did by telling myself that its death was God's will—that it might not have survived even if it had received timely medical attention.

Needless to say, Colin and I drifted apart. Perhaps what happened drove us apart; I don't know. But in the fall, he left for college and I didn't see him for months. I heard through the grapevine that he was dating someone else, but I honestly didn't even care that much anymore. It was as if that part of my life was over and done with, once and for all, and what happened was just a bad dream—the very worst kind of nightmare that I suppose any woman can have.

By this time my mother had met someone and stopped drinking. Three years went by, during which she remarried and I graduated from high school. I dated once in a while, but I was never seriously interested in anyone.

The following fall, I attended business college, majoring in accounting. I met George in the accounting firm where I went to work after graduating. George is the direct opposite of Colin in every way—thoughtful, considerate, and extremely supportive—the kind of man every woman dreams about.

One day when I was shopping at the mall, I looked up and saw a little girl smiling at me—a little girl with long, blond hair and the biggest, bluest eyes I've ever seen. That one look told me that she was about the same age my little girl would've been at that time, had she lived. When her mother took her hand and led her away, she waved back at me.

Suddenly the tears started trailing down my cheeks, and I felt a stabbing pain in my chest—and then in my gut. For one insane moment, I actually thought that our baby had lived and that Colin lied to me about burying it and instead, gave her away—that that little, beautiful, precious girl in the mall was, in fact, my daughter, own flesh and blood. Leaving my shopping cart in the center of the store and pushing shoppers aside, I made a dash for the door. Tears blinding my eyes, I fled outside to the parking lot and looked around wildly for my car, finally spotting it. Stumbling over to it, I opened the door and collapsed against the steering wheel.

I cried until there were no tears left inside of me. Then, in a daze, I drove back to the apartment I shared with a girlfriend.

I locked myself in my room and continued to cry for days on end. I refused to talk to my roommate when she knocked on my door—never even got out of bed except to go to the bathroom. I didn't comb my hair or wash my face or dress, and when I didn't go to work, George called me and I told him that I was sick. Finally, after my worried roommate called her, my mother came to see me. When she asked me what was wrong, I burst into tears again. After I refused to talk to her and even George's visits did no good, my mother took me to see a psychiatrist. I went with her like a mindless zombie with no control over its body.

The doctor diagnosed me as suffering from acute clinical depression. She prescribed antidepressants and we started therapy, but over the next few months, when the medication and the therapy sessions did little to help me and I continued to cry all the time, Mom took me back to get a second opinion from another doctor. Mom told her that I was experiencing a "nervous breakdown." The psychiatrist told my mother that I would get better faster if she knew, to the best extent that I could fathom and explain, what triggered my depression.

When Mom tried to get me to tell her what happened, I refused to talk to her—at first. Then finally, the whole wretched story came pouring out of me in sobs, wails, and seemingly endless tears.

While I talked, my mother just stared at me in horror. Finally, looking beyond stricken, she interrupted me by declaring, "There is no way on God's green earth that you could've been pregnant and I didn't notice it. You certainly couldn't have had a baby in your room without me knowing about it!"

"But I did," I protested dully, wiping my tears from my eyes and blowing my nose. "You can ask Colin if you don't believe me—your own daughter."

Which is exactly what she did—after obtaining his phone number from his parents. She didn't tell them what it was about—just that she was "an old friend" and wanted to "reconnect" with him.

When he answered the phone and my mother explained the reason why she was calling, Colin snidely told her that he "barely knew" me in high school, and that if I "had a baby or whatever," it sure wasn't his.

Cupping the mouthpiece with her hand, my mother relayed to me what he told her while I stood there beside her in our kitchen, biting my nails down to the quick and feeling like this hideous rehashing of the whole ordeal might truly be the end of me. I simply could not believe what Colin was alleging, but I could see right away that my mother did. She thought I was delusional. Making it all up.

I reached for the phone. "I want to talk to him, Mom. He's lying."

"Yeah? Well, there's only one way to find out for certain if what you're saying is true," Mom retorted harshly. "We're going to confront him face to face."

So before she hung up, Mom made arrangements to meet with Colin. At first he refused; then, still adamantly insisting that it "wouldn't do any good," he reluctantly agreed.

When we met at a small restaurant near his college a few days later, once again he denied the whole thing—our romance, my pregnancy, our dead or near-dead baby, its unholy burial—all of the hugely significant events that conspired to change my whole life in so many, many ways.

I stared at him in stunned disbelief. "Why are you lying like this, Colin?" I finally asked him when I had the nerve and found my voice. "After the baby was born, you took it away. You told me that you buried it near a friend's fishing cabin—in the woods somewhere. Admit it, Colin; you know that's exactly what happened—exactly what you did."

He glared at me, a frown furrowing his brow. "I don't have a clue about what you're talking about. Jeez! Will you just get a grip for once in your pathetic life and admit to your poor mother that I scarcely knew you back in high school? I mean, I dated a lot of girls and I may have taken you out a couple of times, but even if I did—I don't remember any of it. In fact, I barely remember you. So why the heck are you doing this insane crap to me? Are you still mad just because I wasn't interested in you and trying to get even? What do you want from me, anyway? Money? A date? Sex?"

"Of course not!" I retorted furiously, adamantly. "I just want you to admit the truth so everyone stops thinking I'm completely out of my mind and fixating on some 'made-up baby' that never even existed in the first place!"

He leaned back in his chair, sank down, and took a casual sip of his Coke, shrugging like we were debating the existence of the Loch Ness Monster. "There's nothing to admit to, babe. I don't know squat about no 'baby,' and I certainly didn't bury some dead newborn somewhere!" He turned to my mother. "I'm sorry, Mrs. Peyser, but I don't know a thing about what your daughter's talking about or why she's making these terrible, sick accusations." He snorted, giving me a derisive look of pure disgust and contempt. "Heck—I'll be damned if I even have a clue as to what her real problem is, but I'm sure it's huge." He peered at me for a moment then, shaking his head like he thought I was demented. Then he stood and walked away.

"Stop!" I cried out, hurrying after him. "You have to tell the truth!"

He kept right on walking.

"We'll talk to your father," Mom said when we returned home. "Maybe he'll know what, if anything, can be done about this."

"I don't think the baby was alive," I told her in a solemn voice—the sound of which chilled me to my core. Even just saying the words made me want to drop dead on the spot and go straight to Hell. "When it was born, it . . . it didn't . . . move . . . didn't act like it was alive. . . . I wrapped it in a towel and . . . and give it to Colin when he finally came over. I didn't know what—what else to do. . . . Colin insisted that he would 'take care of it.' "

Mom shook her head slowly, staring at me in disbelief. "For the love of God. . . . Why didn't you come to me?"

"I couldn't. You were . . . drunk . . . all the time. You told me if

I ever had a baby, you would kick me out of the house."

She flushed. "That was the booze talking! I didn't really mean it!"

"I thought you did," I told her. "And I knew Dad wouldn't take me in when we both know darn well that he never even wanted me in the first place. Besides, he has another kid now, and a new, young girlfriend. She's practically my age."

"We'll talk to him," Mom said. "Maybe he can tell us how to get to the bottom of this, because at this point, well—I simply have to know if you're telling the truth, or if it's all in your head."

It was apparent that she didn't believe a single word of what I'd told her. Suddenly, I wasn't sure if I believed any of it, either.

Could Colin possibly be right? I found myself actually starting to wonder, crazy as I'm sure it sounds. Did I imagine everything—become vengeful simply because he walked out of my life? The fact that I had a baby and he took it away and buried it sounded inconceivable, too sordid to be true.

And when we met my dad at a restaurant—Mom refused to go to his place—and I told my story to him, I could tell right away that he didn't believe me, either.

"You say you think the baby was stillborn," he said once I'd explained myself to him. "Do you know where this guy, Colin, buried it?"

I shook my head. "I asked him to tell me where, but he refused. All he told me was that he took it to a fishing cabin upstate—buried it in the woods nearby. I asked several of his friends if their parents own a cabin and every one of them refused to tell me a single thing."

"Well, I don't know it there's a home burial law in this state that permits a body to be buried on private property; I guess I'll have to check into it. But if there was no baby to begin with, of course, then naturally, no laws have been broken."

"There was a baby," I persisted emphatically. "Maybe we should report everything to the police."

He took a sip from his coffee cup, a puzzled frown creasing his brow. "Report what, exactly?"

What do I have to do to get through to him and Mom? I wondered desperately. Why can't they see that I'm telling the truth—that I would never lie about, much less make up, such a hideously inhumane scenario? "Report that I had a baby—miscarried a baby, I think—and that Colin took it away and buried it somewhere."

"And what good will that do?" Dad asked. "He denies doing it. And we have no body. No evidence of a crime. No crime scene. And since you claim that the baby was stillborn, no crime was committed." He made a flippant, dismissive gesture with his hands. "What do you want them to do? Lock you up and throw away the key just because you think all of this preposterous insanity took place? There's a little thing called proof, you know. And I haven't heard one single bit of it yet."

My hands tightened around the glass of iced tea in front of me. I lowered my gaze, then lifted it and looked directly into his eyes. "I don't have any proof, Dad. There's just my word to go by. And as your daughter, I should think that, in and of itself, would be good enough. God knows I would never, ever lie to you or Mom—or anyone else, for that matter—about something as serious and as personally painful as this."

I could tell by his expression that he didn't consider that worth much. "So what do you want from me?" he asked.

"I want you and Mom—someone, anyone—to believe me!" I beseeched.

My father snorted. "And you think the police will believe this ridiculous story—this deluded concoction you've fabricated out of your depression or whatever it is that's actually going on with you?"

"Probably not," I despaired. As it was, I knew if the police questioned Colin, no matter how much they grilled him, he would continue to claim that he had no idea what I was talking about. And I had nothing to prove to anyone that I was telling the truth.

His father's an attorney and Colin's a law student, while I'm just a pathetic nutcase under the care of a psychiatrist. Or so it seems to everyone else, I thought woefully.

"I could go to a doctor," I volunteered then, even though at that point, I was actually entirely unwilling to go. "A gynecologist will surely be able to tell if I've had a baby, and it will prove to everyone concerned that I'm telling the truth—that I've been telling the truth all along."

"So what if it does?" my father challenged. "Sure—a doctor will probably be able to tell if you've had a baby, but having a baby isn't a crime. How will that help if you can't prove what happened to it?"

After all I'd been through and what I did, I never thought I could get any lower. But right then, I felt my heart sinking to the very bottom of the deepest pit of despair.

"Does anyone else know about any of this?" Mom asked all of a sudden. "Did you tell any of your girlfriends?"

I shook my head, looking down at my hands, wringing them in my lap. "No. Colin and I never told a soul."

"Well, you know, if you keep pushing that young man without any proof whatsoever that anything at all ever even happened between the two of you, he'll take you to court and sue you to high heaven," my father admonished crossly. "Is that what you want, Christy? Is it really what you want out of all of this self-pitying, deluded nonsense?"

I shook my head again and again, and I found myself actually wondering, What if I really did imagine the whole thing—as my parents believe, as Colin insists? Lord knows, my hidden pregnancy and the child's birth were so traumatic for me that I tried to deny it all myself; I was certainly in shock for weeks—months, even—after it was born. Maybe what Colin's insinuated really is true. Maybe, for some strange reason beyond my own understanding, I really was angry with him for dumping me, and so I made up this awful, awful lie just to get even with him.

Later, after I explained to George what happened, he stuck by me through it all. When I told him that—no matter what anyone else thought—I knew that Colin was lying through his teeth, George told me that he was sure that that was the case, but also that we'd probably never get Colin to admit it, much less prove otherwise. "Like your father said," George pointed out, "if there's no baby and no evidence that it ever even existed in the first place, that ends any role Colin may have played in your heartbreak."

"If I hadn't listened to him and I told my mother when it was born," I rued, "none of this would've happened."

George took my hands in his then, stroking them tenderly. "You were just a scared kid back then, Christy—only fifteen years old, for Pete's sake!" he stressed. "You had no one to turn to for help, so when Colin offered you a chance to 'make it all go away,' you took it. I'm sure it was easy for him to convince you to let him 'take care of everything' once you fully realized just how helpless and alone you really were. But Colin was thinking more of himself than he was of you; all he ever really cared about was figuring out how he could get himself off the hook, once and for all."

Gradually, through my ongoing medication and therapy, I guess you could say that I "recovered" from my depression and went back to work. I'm sure George's unwavering support and my mother's concern (if only for my health, seeing as, to this day, she continues to doubt and dismiss my "story") had a great deal to do with that. Still, somehow—perhaps because therapy has allowed me to heal to some extent and move on from the terrors of my past—my mother and I are "close" (if you can call it that) for the first time in my life. Meanwhile, to this day, my own father stays as far away from me as he possibly can—I suppose out of some sick, selfish fear that whatever I "have" might rub off on him and his brand-new, happy, perfect family.

Immaturity and fear are no excuses for what I did. Although I truly believe my baby was stillborn, that's absolutely no excuse for denying it a decent burial. Sometimes I wonder if the reason why Colin denied burying our baby is because he discovered it was alive, after all, and left it at a church. I let myself think sometimes, in my darkest moments, that someone took my little girl and is happily raising her as their own—just because I guess I need to believe that much. As things stand, though, unless Colin is someday willing to disclose what he did with our baby—and I don't think that will ever happen—that thought will linger forever in my mind.

To this day, at times, I discover myself still wondering if the little girl I saw at the mall was my child. But I know I can't dwell on that thought or what happened all those years ago for, no matter how much I wish things happened differently, the past cannot be undone, much less changed.

Today, my secret—my crime—rests between God and me.

My punishment awaits me in His hands.

THE END

CONFESSIONS OF A FREEWHEELING BIKER CHICK

I may look tough, but deep down, I've got a real soft spot for men who know what it means to love a woman in the sweetest ways. . . .

On a sweltering day in the solid sunshine outside of Jimmy's Joint, a phoenix-like shadow spread over my hot back, causing a shivery shudder to slide down my spine. I sat up, breasts warmed by the chopper's gas tank, hooked my heels on the highway pegs, and put my hands on my hips, frowning.

"Listen, buddy," I growled, "when I can't ride, I tan, so move it—you're blocking my sun."

"So much fire. . . ." The shadowy man smiled. "Are you sure we can't share?" He laughed as I shook my head and climbed off of Jimmy's motorcycle.

Isn't my damn bike finished yet? For an old, beat up Harley, it's sure giving my master mechanic a hell of a ride. I brushed my double-Ds against the shadowy man's chest and felt electricity and fire rush through me like lightning.

I didn't notice before what a beautiful Native American he is—tall, dark, and probably Iroquois. My insides ached with desire, just thinking of all sorts of feats of nature this hottie might perform on me. I paused and took in some of his power. Then I smiled and winked at him.

Another shock of electric fire ran through me as he gently cupped my backside to guide me in front of him as we entered Jimmy's shop. He growled to seemingly thank me for the touch, and I felt that growl resonate from my ass to my backbone.

I picked up my step in escape; I wanted to speak to my mechanic before I weakened and took this Indian out back to show him what a woman like me can do for a man like him. Man, is he hot!

"What's the word, bro?" I asked Jimmy as he toiled over my little Sportster.

"'Screwed'" is the word, D.J.," Jimmy replied. "I won't have this bitch set for another two or three days, baby. I'm sorry."

"Can I borrow your chopper?" I pushed my double-Ds out and smiled my sexiest smile for Jimmy, hoping he'd remember what a good job I do. . . .

Once Jimmy stopped laughing, he slapped me on the ass and told me, "Not even for a sweet taste of you, Miss D.J.! What you need to do is find a sugar daddy with a collection. With the way you go through bikes . . . hell, you should just date the damn Harley dealer!" His roars echoed through the garage and hit me hard.

I turned toward the tall, beautiful, shadowy man, who was also smiling and trying hard not to laugh, and stomped back out of the garage.

"Why ride a Harley when you can ride an Indian?" the shadowy man asked.

"Shut the hell up, Jacy. The girl needs to concentrate on getting a ride!" Jimmy yelled from his office.

Jacy followed my sweet ass out to the garage front, and was once again, he softly cupped and caressed it.

I did nothing to stop Jacy; instead, I leaned into him, causing his growl to resonate through him to his groin, where fire and energy seemed to be flowing at a great and powerful speed.

"I'll give you a ride, D.J.," Jacy growled.

After a "behave yourselves" look from Jimmy, I jumped into the front seat of Jacy's old Ford truck. I slid across the bench seat to unlock his door, and then cozied up right next to his hot, brown body. My hands immediately found the center of his energy, and I began to casually caress him as he groaned and tried to speak.

"I think I have a bike you might want. . . ." Jacy said.

"I think you know what I want," I whispered in his ear as I nibbled and stroked. I could tell he wanted it badly, so I began to unbuckle his belt and release the hardening hammer.

"Oh, man. . . ." Jacy groaned. "Seriously, baby . . . I have a three-wheeler my buddy left me when he went into Attica. I want to ride you—I mean—ride it . . . with you. . . . Oh, man . . . bitch, you are crazy. . . ." The old Ford swerved a bit while I took his rigid length into my mouth, teasing it, coaxing it.

He drove like a bat out of hell to his farm, moaning utterances that had to be some kind of Native tongue—or horny gibberish—for I had no idea what Jacy was saying. From his rocking hips and squirming body, I could sure understand that he was having a pleasurable time.

I gave the ultimate tease and nibbled up his belly and to his ear, where I whispered, "I'm free right now. Let's go ride, Jacy."

Before long, the screech of the truck's tires, the tug of strong hands tangled in my hair, and the sound of an Indian's satisfied yells—signaled that we arrived. I sat up, smiled, and kissed his cheek. Then I climbed out of the truck to take a look around.

Jacy seemed to be having an out-of-body experience, so he stayed immobile in the truck for the next few moments. By the time he snapped out of it, I already found and uncovered the old VW trike.

"Holy shit!" I screamed. "Look at this! Start the bitch up, Jacy! I want to screw you on this trike. Let's go!"

And go (at it) we did!

It took a while to get the bike started. The battery had to be hooked up, but with a spray of starter fluid and a little magic of the hands, all three engines—Jacy's, the trike's, and mine—were hot and ready to ride.

Since the trike was automatic with ape hangers, I sat on the gas tank, feet on the running boards, and leaned down to stroke Jacy's magnificent member again. The engine was running, and before I knew it, the trike was slowly moving out of the garage and down a path, into the woods behind Jacy's barn. As soon as he was ready to go, I sat up and signaled to Jacy to stop for a minute.

Our eyes met, and the fire exploded between us. I slipped out of my jeans and top and threw them in the field, then lowered myself onto his lap. I carefully moved my feet onto the frame, grabbed the back of the bucket seat for leverage, and began to move slowly onto this beautiful, shadowy man's body, and he into me. I didn't realize that he started moving the trike again until we hit some fantastic bumps on the trail. My body stirred in response, and I cried out in pure and complete ecstasy.

It was a good thing Jacy knows this trail, for my body lost control, and I wasn't quite sure just how much he could see, with me straddling him. But Jacy didn't seem to mind.

He was chanting some beautifully rhythmic song in a language I could not understand, until I moved to the rhythm, and came again and again. Our groans and yells and curses frightened the woodland creatures into their dens for days, but the freewheeling, three-wheeling sweathouse of a sex ride we had that day was a beautiful act of nature sent from the Great Spirits themselves.

And, by the way, I still own that trike, and have still never driven—only rode.

THE END

CONFESSIONS OF A WOMAN
"Who's That In The Mirror?"

I stared at the woman staring back at me with dismay and disgust. The woman's gray hair looked like a child gone berserk with the scissors had hacked it off. Her cheeks sagged into wrinkles that drooped over her chin, and her eyes looked tired and dim, the light of interest and intelligence had gone out behind them.

As my gaze dropped downward it got worse. The neck looked like it belonged on a turkey and the shoulders hunched forward. The shapeless dress and stretched out sweater failed to hide the lumpy, out-of-shape body beneath it.

"Ugh! You can't be me!" I muttered to the image in the full-length mirror. "What happened to the attractive woman I used to be? What have you done with her?"

Tears blurred the image as I realized it was too late. The dark, shining hair, the piercing blue eyes that could command attention from across the room, and the perfect size eight figure were gone—all gone. I should have noticed when they began to disappear some time ago.

For the first time, I gave in to the pity party that had been threatening ever since my sixty-fifth birthday three weeks ago. I sat on the floor and let the bitter, self-centered tears flow unchecked until they ran dry and I was emotionally exhausted. For the first time I saw how a vain, prideful opinion of myself had directed my life.

Oh, yeah! I was really something, wasn't I? The girl who had everything: good looks, winning personality, quick mind, smart, handsome husband, and smart, beautiful children. I was the main cog that kept her family running smoothly while holding down a part-time job, plus a load of volunteer work that would stagger most people.

So what happened? Where did the uh—creature—in the mirror come from? How did I lose myself?

As I checked off all the ways my life had changed in the last few years, it became obvious how that person I used to be disappeared, and it seemed perfectly reasonable that I should be upset and distressed.

My two daughters grew up, married, and moved across the country to another state. Their lives were complete with good and loving men for husbands and with beautiful little replicas of themselves to fill their mortgage-heavy homes. They didn't need me anymore even though they tried to make me think that being Grandma was the most important job in the world.

Then, Jack, my husband of forty years, had the nerve to die before his time. I always planned on me going out first. I didn't see how I could exist without him. He was my protector, my friend, my lover, my rock, and my reason for being. And he was gone.

The part time job disappeared with the slow economy and some of the volunteer work with it. Increasingly aching joints made much of it unappealing or impossible. There was no enthusiasm left for the kind of social work I had enjoyed helping with.

What good was I to anybody anymore? What need was there for me?

Such was the state of my mind when I saw the old lady in the mirror and no telling where it would have led if the doorbell hadn't rung at that moment.

"Open up, Rose, I know you're in there!" yelled my best friend, Margaret. "Your car's in the driveway and I have something to tell you. Rose? Open the door."

I knew it wouldn't do any good to ignore her. She'd just stay and ring that stupid doorbell until I let her in.

"Okay, okay, I'm coming," I called.

"Hey, friend, guess what?" she asked, as soon as the door opened. "Uh, oh. Bad day? You've been crying." Her tone changed in an instant, from perky greeting to commiseration when she saw my red-rimmed, puffy eyes.

"Yeah, I guess," I admitted.

"Well, I've got just what you need. I just signed up for exercise time at the health club and I want you to come with me. It'll do us both good. A little stretching and sweating will sweep out the bad feelings and renew our energy."

I groaned. Just the thought of forcing my aging joints to do things they weren't used to made me hurt. And for what reason would I do such an unkind thing to my body? Who would care what I looked or felt like anyway?

"Oh, Margaret, I don't think so. I'm really not into exercise."

"I knooow," she drawled. "That's why it's such a good idea. Your life is not over, even though you pretend it is, and you need to get moving again. I've already signed you up for a month and paid for it so you have to come. Consider it a love gift. Hey, I know it won't be easy. Old age is not for sissies. We have to fight this thing, but if you still really hate it at the end of the month, I won't insist you continue."

Well, why not? I thought. Might as well be doing that instead of sitting around crying.

"Okay. For one month since you've already paid for it."

"Great! First session is tomorrow afternoon at five. Dig up those old workout clothes you used to walk in and be ready. I'll pick you up at four-thirty."

And she was out the door before I could change my mind. I tried to remember where I had put the workout clothes she referred to and finally realized they went into a Goodwill box a couple of years ago when I "outgrew" them.

Muttering seldom-used curses at life in general, I washed my face, brushed my hair, and took myself to Wal-Mart to find something suitable to exercise in. I was appalled at the jump in size that my "maturing" body now required and I avoided the revealing mirror in the dressing room as much as I could.

Must be one of those trick mirrors they have at traveling carnivals, I decided. Makes everything look bigger—and older.

After several tries, I finally found a loose-fitting black jumpsuit with stripes down the sides that helped to visually make me look a bit taller and less chunky.

The next day, I was ready for Margaret in spite of many false starts and second thoughts. The woman in the mirror convinced me that something had to be done.

The health club was crowded and the energy level high, with one room full of treadmills, all occupied and going at full speed. A bigger room of machines that worked out the upper body was nearly full, and the slap and thunk of weights being lifted gave a counterpoint rhythm to the steady beat of the treadmills next door. A hallway branched off to the right with who knows what kind of rooms behind its closed doors. I was pleasantly surprised to find that many of the women looked much like me—dumpy and old—not anywhere near the svelte and toned bodies the advertisements for the club suggested.

Margaret checked us in at the front desk and after a short wait, we were assigned to a couple of the treadmills already warmed up and vacated by people finishing their allotted time. The attendant showed us how to start and stop the machine and then hurried back to her desk and left us to it.

Okay, so far, I thought. This is not too bad. Walking is not hard.

After ten minutes, I began to change that opinion. My legs felt like cooked spaghetti and I was gasping for breath. I groped for the off button and then had to just hold on until my body got the message that it had stopped moving.

I guess Margaret was right. I really do need this.

After a few minutes on the weight machine, we called it enough for the first day and Margaret steered me into a small juice bar in the back of the building. There we had a snack of fruit juice and whole-wheat crackers to restore our energy.

"How do you feel?" Margaret asked.

"Not as bad as I expected," I said. "I'll reserve final judgment until tomorrow."

"We take tomorrow off and go back the next day. Every other day, three times a week."

"Right," I said to her, and silently to myself, "We'll see."

We fell into a rhythm that I, amazingly, began to look forward to. I did feel better. My energy was up and I could see the pounds slowly begin to drop off. The old lady in the mirror was still there, though, and I still couldn't see any good reason for her to exist.

Then, one ordinary Monday, the world shifted although I didn't realize it until much later. A tall, distinguished gentleman with a troubled expression in his dark eyes took the treadmill next to me. He looked to be about my age. He had abundant white hair, a slim body, which was a little heavy around the middle, and a strong jaw line that nicely compensated for the lines around his mouth and across his broad forehead.

He nodded at me when he saw me watching him and then began to plod through a twenty-minute jog on the machine. As our sessions progressed, he became a regular and I moved up to a slow jog instead of just a walk. One day he surprised me.

"I'm Andrew," he said. "Have you been doing this long?"

"Pleased to meet you, Andrew," I managed when I caught my breath. "I'm Rose and no, not too long. My best friend insisted I come with her, and I have to admit it does make me feel better."

"I hope you're right. So far, I don't see much improvement for my old joints. I think I waited too long."

I chuckled. "I know what you mean. It takes a while before improvement sets in. Hang in there. It'll happen."

After that, it was easy to exchange greetings and comments. I began to look forward to my workouts for reasons I had not anticipated. I could see Margaret's smug smile as she watched us from her treadmill and I noticed how she carefully stayed out of our way until it was time to go home.

One afternoon, as Andrew and I commiserated about new parts of our anatomy with aching muscles, a little girl hurried into the room, and stopped in front of my new friend.

"Grandpa, I have to go home. I forgot about a paper I have to have for school tomorrow," she said.

Andrew stopped his treadmill. "Okay, Julie, why didn't you remember this earlier? How long have you known about the paper?"

Julie looked at her feet, her cheeks flushed, then jerked her head up and said defiantly, "I knew about it last week. I just forgot, all right! But I have to get it done. It's important!"

"Okay, calm down. Give me a second to get my keys and we'll go," Andrew said, with barely-controlled patience. He stepped off the treadmill and hurried out of the room.

Julie looked at me nervously and quickly dismissed me. She was a pretty child with shiny blond hair and her Grandpa's eyes.

"I used to do that when I was your age," I said with a chuckle.

"What?" she asked, with a startled and defensive look at me.

"Forget to do homework 'til the last minute," I said. "It is easier if you get it done as soon as it is assigned."

"Yeah, I know," she said curtly, and turned her back on me.

Even while I was thinking, Poor Andrew, he's got his hands full with this one, I was feeling sorry for Julie. She had a desperate, frightened look in her eyes that no child should ever have. I made up my mind to find out why it was there. So, at our next session, I dived in heedless of how shallow the water might be.

"Did your granddaughter get her homework done in time?" I asked Andrew.

He sighed a heavy sigh and hesitated. I began to think I had hit the bottom.

"She did. Julie has a very bright mind, but absolutely no common sense," he finally said, and then the door flew wide open. "Honestly, Rose, I don't know what to do with her. Nothing I try seems to be right. Before Mary, my wife, died a year ago everything was going pretty good. Well, if you don't count the fact that Julie's parents don't spend much time with her. Our daughter, Chloe, lost her heart and her reason to a charming jerk who didn't want to be tied down with a child. With too much money and too little common sense, he wants to spend all his time traveling the world and he wants Chloe with him. She chose the husband over the daughter because she knew we would take care of Julie." I could see the pain in his eyes.

"I don't know how to do what she needs, Rose. Mary was the one who understood, who knew how to provide the love and discipline a girl-child requires. Recently, I tried seeing a younger woman from my office thinking she would know how to reach Julie, but it only made everything worse. Julie was stubborn and rude and refused every advance Pat tried to make. I have to admit, I don't know what else to do. I feel like such a failure."

"Is Julie with you permanently now?" I asked.

"Pretty much. Her parents have bought a villa in Italy and spend most of their time there. The jerk refuses to have Julie live with them and Julie is equally adamant about not living there. They visit here now and then and Julie goes there sometimes, but they see each other so little there is no bond between them. My heart breaks for my daughter and for Julie. Chloe has made some very poor choices for her life and Julie is paying for them."

"I'm so sorry," I murmured, my own heart crying for the wayward daughter and the abandoned child. Even when parents are not worthy to be parents and are seldom seen, they still have a powerful influence on a child.

"I started picking Julie up after school to keep her from drifting into the unhealthy after-school activities some of the kids there participated in. There is a yoga class for children here and I thought the exercise would do us both good. Today she hit me with the news that she needs six dozen cookies for class tomorrow. Something about a class picnic. Where can I find six dozen cookies that taste like they were homemade?"

I chuckled. "You can pick up six dozen cookies in any grocery store, but the homemade taste can only come from someone's kitchen. Tell you what. I've got to make some cookies for a woman's club meeting. Why don't you bring Julie over to my house this afternoon after we're through here and I'll let her help make them? It's hard for anyone to resist warm, chocolate chip cookies."

Andrew looked hopeful but uncertain. "Are you sure? I don't want to impose my problems on you. I shouldn't have turned my tongue loose like that. I'm sure there's a way we can manage."

"Don't be silly. I love to bake and I've found it has always been good therapy for me when I'm upset. Maybe it will help Julie, too. I'll expect you both around six-thirty. I'll give you my card with my address."

Andrew nodded and said nothing. I cut my work out a little short to give me time to go by the grocery store for a big bag of chocolate chips and, on impulse, a large pizza, and all the time wondering what on earth I had done. The fact that I loved to bake and it was good therapy was true enough, but the fiction of cookies for a woman's club meeting had popped into my mind and out my mouth before I could stop it.

Rose, you idiot, kept running through my thoughts like a broken record as I hurried to get ready for what seemed like an ill-conceived inspiration. I didn't tell Margaret why I was in such a hurry, and she looked suspicious and a bit hurt. I was grateful that I had been a little late to the workout session and had my own car.

"I'll explain later," I said to her questions. "It's probably a huge mistake."

As soon as I got home, I turned the oven on and quickly mixed up a batch of cookies so that there would be a wonderful smell when they arrived. For the umpteenth time, I said a prayer of thanks for my convection oven that Jack had insisted I get shortly before he died. It allowed me to put several pans of cookies in at once and have them all cook evenly.

The doorbell rang just as I took the cookies out of the oven. I quickly slipped in another pan full and added the pizza on the bottom rack. My efforts were rewarded with an enthusiastic sniff as they came in the door and the remark from both of them, "Ooh, something smells good."

"Since we have so many cookies to make, I went ahead and got started," I babbled nervously. "Come on in. There's plenty left to do."

I gave Julie an apron and a wooden spoon to stir with. I handed Andrew a cup of coffee and gave him a chair at the table so he could watch. Julie looked a bit rebellious, but she took the mixing bowl and began adding ingredients as I read them off. As she mixed and stirred, her eyes slowly lit up at the look and feel of the dough as it developed under her spoon. I told her that the brown sugar and just a hint of cinnamon were secret ingredients I had added to the basic recipe.

As she dropped the dough in spoonful's on a cookie sheet, her nose got a whiff of the pizza browning in the oven.

"I smell pizza!" she said, as she sniffed the air. "Are we going to have pizza?"

"You bet," I said. "It's your reward for doing a good job with the cookies."

She looked at me and smiled—a real, honest-to-goodness smile. "How did you know I love pizza?"

"Well, I love pizza and I figured most people your age do too. How about your grandfather? Does he love it, too?"

Andrew nodded vigorously and Julie giggled.

We took time out to eat between the next pans of cookies and by the time all the dough was cooked and we had warm, fragrant cookies cooling on all the countertops, Julie was happily scooping up cookie crumbs—just as a ten-year-old should be.

Andrew had a dazed look in his eyes and a silly smile on his face that wouldn't go away.

"I can't thank you enough," he said quietly, while Julie put the box of cookies in the car. "I haven't seen Julie this happy in a long time. Can we come again?"

"Of course. Any time," I sputtered around the lump in my throat. I felt excited and happily tearful all at the same time.

After that, Andrew and I found it easier and easier to exchange thoughts, doubts, and worries at our workout sessions. Margaret made herself more and more invisible at the workouts and she encouraged me on the way home.

I am sooo happy for you," she'd say with a hug. "I haven't seen you like this in a long time. Andrew is a dear, and, from what you tell me, so is Julie."

"You don't think I'm being too impulsive? Making a big mistake?"

"What mistake? You have a new friend who needs you as much as you need him. Be thankful and have faith. I think maybe God has arranged this."

I looked at her skeptically and then smiled. It was not often that Margaret expressed her deep, religious beliefs. I hoped, yes prayed, that she was right.

The next week, Andrew and Julie came again and I taught Julie the special joy of making bread. The way her hands patted and caressed the living dough, I knew that she had inherited a strong love of cooking. Teaching her brought back sweet memories of my own daughters growing up and learning life lessons in my kitchen.

As their visits became more frequent, I looked forward to making dinner for the three of us, and thinking up new cooking lessons for Julie, who was eager to learn. Sometimes, Julie would bring her homework, and after dinner, she would sit at the kitchen table and study while Andrew and I sat nearby, I with my latest needlepoint and he with the daily crossword. There was a growing understanding and comfort between us. We seemed to be connected on a lot of levels, and when one evening he kissed my cheek as Julie gave me a good-bye hug, it felt right and appropriate—a visit or two later, the kiss moved to my mouth and felt even better.

About a week after school was out for the summer, Andrew came to me with a special problem. Julie needed new clothes. She had hit a growth spurt in the last few months and had outgrown all her summer clothes—including underwear. His wife had always tended to this chore, and, as long as Julie was a small child, Andrew didn't mind helping. Now that she was developing into a young lady, it made both of them nervous and embarrassed for him to be choosing her wardrobe.

"I hate to have to ask you to do this, but it's becoming way out of both of our comfort zones for me to do this for her," he said regretfully.

I was secretly delighted. "Don't worry another minute. I would be happy to help her. We'll have a girl's day out and go shopping, and maybe to the beauty parlor for haircuts. Both of us could use a new hairdo."

I made an appointment with my hairdresser and set up a day at the mall for shopping, lunch, and a beauty makeover. It was the first time in a very long time that I had been excited by such an outing. I felt needed by someone I cared about again, and I began to care about myself as well. The regular exercise was doing wonders for my sagging body. I had lost enough weight, and inches, that I, too, needed new clothes, and I was thoroughly disgusted with my ragged hair and careless makeup.

The day started out a little nervously, but as we helped each other choose clothes and exchanged opinions of life in general, we found we thought a lot alike, and by lunchtime, we had achieved an easygoing relationship. The two hours in the beauty parlor cinched it. By the time we met Andrew for his treat of bringing us out to dinner, we had become friends. Julie's smile had blossomed, and with her new hairdo, she looked like a different child.

"Who are these two beautiful women?" Andrew exclaimed. "They are not the same ones I left at the mall this morning. They must have found a fairy godmother somewhere."

"Oh, Grandpa, it's us," Julie said between giggles. "This is how we're supposed to look."

Andrew pulled her into a hug and kissed the top of her head. "You're right about that, my dear child. Happy is how you are supposed to look."

The look he gave me was full of admiration and something more that had not been there before. There was love in it, and I felt my heart swell to near bursting with happiness.

This lovely state of euphoria lasted another whole week—until a letter from Julie's mother brought it to a jolting halt.

"Mom and Dad are coming for a visit," was the first thing out of Julie's mouth when she and Andrew arrived for supper.

Her words knocked the breath out of me, and wiped the smile off my face. "Oh. How do you feel about that?"

"I don't know," Julie said, looking confused. "It'll be nice to see them again. I know I should be thrilled, but. . . ."

Her words trickled off as a look crossed her face I had never seen on a child. Longing, hope, love, fear, guilt, and shame all struggled for dominance. I pulled her into a hug so she wouldn't see the sudden tears in my eyes.

"Don't worry. It'll all work out. I'll be glad to meet your parents. When are they arriving?"

"Early next week," Andrew answered.

"Well, then. We have a lot to do," I said matter-of-factly. I loosened Julie's hold on my waist and pushed her out in front of me. "We need to plan a menu to show off how well you can cook. Do you think they would like to come over here for dinner one night? I need to shine up my house in case they do."

My babbling didn't ease the tense, worried expression on her face, but she nodded. "Okay. I'll help."

"Me, too," Andrew added, looking at me with such intensity and suppressed anguish it nearly brought the tears out again.

The next few days were a whirlwind of planning, cleaning, cooking, and talking. The combined emotions of expectation and dread kept us all on edge. I felt as though I was on a severe caffeine high and couldn't come down. Julie, and even calm, steady Andrew were both jittery and short-tempered; Julie excited one minute and fearful the next that this would be another rejection or worse, tear her away from what had become safe and comfortable.

As the time of their arrival drew near, we tried to get used to the fact of their visit.

Maybe it won't be so bad, I thought. Maybe it will do Julie good to see her parents again. Maybe it will ease Andrew's pain for his daughter's neglect of her child for him to see her again. Maybe.....

The day they were expected we waited anxiously. Because they didn't know exactly when they would leave Italy or when they would get into town, they had insisted on renting a car and driving themselves the rest of the way instead of being met at the airport. I was at Andrew's house to help with the final clean up, meal preparation, and for emotional support. When we heard a car pull into the driveway, Andrew and Julie hurried to the door.

Chloe spilled out of the car almost before it stopped and Julie hit the porch running. I stood in the shadows of the front hall watching as Julie and her mother nearly smothered each other in an explosion of loving hugs. My heart clinched in a spasm of pain as I saw the strength of the bond between a mother and her child—even with a mostly absent and care-less mother.

Julie was much less enthused with her father. She gave him a quick hug, then wriggled out of his grasp. The appraising, un-fatherly look he gave her made my hackles rise and I fervently prayed that I had misjudged it.

Chloe came, a little shyly, to Andrew. "Hello, Dad. You look great," she said, as she embraced him. "I know I've been a terrible mother and left you with all the care of Julie, but that's about to change. I've got good news, but can we have something cold to drink first? I'm dying of thirst."

"Of course you can, but before the drink, I want you to meet someone," Andrew said, as he reached for my hand and pulled me forward. "This is Rose. I've told you about her in my letters. She means a great deal to Julie and me."

"Oh, yes. I remember. I'm glad to meet you, Rose," Chloe said, as she gave my hand a quick shake and then turned back to Julie and Andrew. "I've got so much to tell you! How about that drink, Dad? Have you got any iced tea? And a beer for Simon?"

"Nice to meet you, too," I murmured to the air, as she swept Julie and Andrew into the kitchen ahead of her. Simon put down the suitcase he'd carried in and followed them.

"Hi. I'm Simon, the Dad," he said, as he walked past me, his eyes on Julie. "She's growing up, isn't she? She's going to be beautiful like her mother."

While the words sounded light and complimentary, there was an undertone that made my flesh crawl. Simon hadn't seen his daughter in more than a year and before that it was only a short, occasional visit. According to Andrew, he had made it clear that he was not interested in being a father. I shivered as I wondered what else he wanted to be to his half-grown daughter.

I could see why Chloe was so enchanted with Simon. He looked like the hero on the cover of a popular romance book. Dark blond hair, big brown eyes, a superbly fit, sculptured body, a sweet smile that made you think you were the only person in the room, and an unexpected dimple in one cheek was enough to charm a fence post.

And Chloe was no fence post. Slim and lovely, she looked like how I pictured a sprite or nymph in my poetry books would look. Blond curls bounced around a delicate, heart-shaped face. Large, blue eyes, smiling innocently at the world between thick lashes, gave her a forever young, childlike expression.

As I caught sight of myself in the hall mirror, I was thankful for the time spent in the beauty parlor and the gym. Instead of a dumpy old lady, I looked more like a stylish, "mature" woman. I followed them into the kitchen and helped Andrew with the drinks.

"What's your news, Mom? Are you coming back here to live?" Julie asked, as soon as everyone had their drink. There was eagerness in her voice and an anxious look on her face that made me hold my breath.

Chloe let out a rippling stream of laughter. "Oh, my goodness, certainly not. Your father and I have decided it's time for you to come live with us in Italy. Isn't that wonderful?"

The room went dead silent, as if all the air had suddenly been sucked out.

"Oh," Julie said on a soft breath.

She looked at Andrew whose face had gone white as paper. She looked at me and I felt like a stone with no response for her need. She swiveled her eyes around to Simon who smiled and said smoothly, "Now that you are becoming a big girl, we thought it was time you came to live with your parents. Make us a family. We need to get to know our daughter better."

"What's wrong, honey?" Chloe asked. "We thought you would be thrilled. Italy is a beautiful place. You'll love it there."

"I'm surprised, that's all," Julie murmured.

Simon hooked his arm around her waist and pulled her onto his lap. "I guess it is kind of a shock. You'll get used to it."

Julie squirmed out of his grasp and ran out of the room. Chloe stood up and started after her, but Andrew stopped her.

"Leave her alone. She needs some time to think about it. We all do," he said, as he, too, left the room.

For the next three days we moved like zombies, doing what was necessary but with no heart in it. I felt like my world had collapsed again, and from the look on Andrew's tense face, I knew he felt the same.

I hated the thought of losing Julie, but I hated even more the way

Simon looked and acted toward her—the sliding touch of his hand when she came near him; the lust in the half-closed eyes that followed her around the room.

One day, Julie scurried into the kitchen where I was making supper with a miserable look on her face.

"What's wrong with me, Rose? I'm afraid of my father. He scares me when he hugs me. It feels bad."

I wrapped my arms around her. "It's not you who's wrong, Julie. Your father doesn't know how to be a father."

I clenched my fists in angry frustration. Didn't Chloe notice? Was she helpless to do anything against Simon's wishes? Against all Andrew's persuasions and objections she was adamant that Julie was to go with them.

The days flew by and at the end of the week, Chloe had Julie's clothes packed and ready to leave. Julie went around with a tight, sullen scowl not helping her mother and avoiding her father. My heart was breaking watching this disaster develop and not being able to stop it.

On the day of their departure, I had come over to Andrew's early to say good-bye. When it was time for them to leave, Julie came slowly from her bedroom, dressed in an old pair of jeans and a T-shirt Chloe thought unworthy to take to Italy.

"For heaven's sake why aren't you ready?" Chloe cried. "We'll miss our plane."

Julie sat down and crossed her arms. "I'm not going," she said firmly.

"Of course you are, honey. We've made this trip just to bring you home with us." Chloe's voice had a desperate note in it.

"I am home," Julie said. "And I intend to stay here."

An ugly look had replaced the charm on Simon's handsome face. "Look, missy, you are a minor and we are your parents. You have to do what we say."

"Maybe. But if you force me to go, I'll make your life miserable."

"Don't threaten me you little. . . .'"

"Stop it, Simon!" Chloe said in a choked voice. "She's right. I've felt all week that this wasn't going to work. She has to want to come to make it right."

With tears streaming down her face, she picked up her handbag, gave Andrew a quick hug, nodded to me and went to Julie. "When you're ready, just call. We'll come get you."

"Thanks, Mom," Julie said through her own tears. "I love you."

Chloe turned and walked to the door. "Let's go, Simon."

Simon looked furious and uncertain, but he picked up their suitcases and followed her out muttering curses under his breath. To my utter surprise, the nymph had recognized the problem and was clearly in charge.

With a great sigh of relief, Andrew put his arms around Julie and hugged her close. "My dear child, that was a very brave and hard thing you did. I pray I can make your life here worth it."

"There is something you can do to make that happen," Julie said.

"Tell me. I'll do anything in my power."

She backed away and glanced at me. "You can marry Rose so I can call her Grandma, and we can all live in the same house and be a real family."

Andrew looked stunned for a moment, and then he threw back his head and laughed. "I've had that thought in my heart for some time now. How about it, Rose? Will you marry me and make a home for this presumptuous child?"

I could feel the smile spread over my face and the burst of happiness in my heart as I stepped into their waiting arms. "Oh, my! I thought you'd never ask."

THE END

CONFESSIONS OF A POSTPARTUM MOMMY

Only psychiatric help will save my sanity and my newborn—and God help us both if I don't get it. . . .

Stan and I were about to celebrate our seventh wedding anniversary when I found out I was pregnant.

At first, I simply could not believe it; after all, as it was, we'd been trying to conceive for over five years. But after a battery of tests, the doctors assured us that there was no physical reason why we couldn't have a baby. They advised us to relax, to take romantic vacations, to basically forget about trying so hard to conceive—and then maybe nature would take its course.

Well, Stan and I did everything they suggested. We took a chunk of our savings and went on an exotic island vacation. We tried to forget about having kids and just rest and relax. But no matter what we did, my period came every month—like clockwork.

So, as our seventh anniversary approached, I was pretty much resigned to never having a child. I told myself my life was full and happy just the way it was. I had a wonderful, loving husband, a comfortable home, a job I enjoyed, and a few good friends. What more could a woman ask for?

When I realized my period was late, I thought it was because of the head cold I was fighting. But when two weeks went by, I bought a pregnancy test.

The result was positive for pregnancy, but I still didn't believe it. I called my doctor and begged for an appointment right away. As luck would have it, there was a cancellation, and two hours later, I was sitting in Dr. Niels's office, shaking my head in disbelief.

"I can't be pregnant! After all this time. . . .?"

Dr. Niels laughed. "Believe it, Hailey. You are definitely pregnant. Didn't I tell you it would happen?"

I could hardly wait to get home and call Stan. I knew he was going to be as thrilled and excited as I was.

But when I got home, I realized I didn't want to call Stan. I wanted to tell him in person and see the joy on his face when he realized we were finally going to be parents.

When Stan got home that night, I met him at the door wearing my favorite blouse and skirt and the perfume he got me for my birthday that year. I gave him a kiss I knew he wouldn't soon forget.

"Wow! What did I do to deserve that?" Stan asked with a big grin.

"How do you feel about becoming a daddy in about seven and a half months?" I asked. I knew I was grinning like an idiot, but I didn't care. It was the happiest moment of my life.

"What? Are you saying what I think you're saying? Are you sure?"

"Call Dr. Niels if you don't believe me, Daddy. He verified it just a few hours ago. We are most definitely pregnant!"

Stan grabbed me and swung me around, then just as quickly, he released me, with a look of complete terror on his face. "Oh, Hailey, baby—I'm sorry! Did I hurt you?"

I hugged Stan with all my might. "Don't be silly. We won't break. Your son or daughter is snug as a bug right here." I patted my still flat tummy happily.

To say that Stan and I were ecstatic would be an understatement. Both of us walked around in a daze for a few days, but gradually, with the onset of morning sickness, we began to believe we were really going to have a baby.

All I can say about the next few months is that it was one of the happiest times of my life. Stan and I shopped for furniture for the nursery and decorated a large, sunny room for the baby. We went to childbirth classes and parenting classes and our love for each other grew stronger with every pound I gained.

Dr. Niels said my pregnancy was textbook perfect. Aside from a little morning sickness in the first trimester, I felt great right up to the end, and I went into labor two days before my actual due date.

For a first baby, my labor was relatively short and easy. At eleven-thirty on August twelfth, Elizabeth Susana Parker was born—pink, plump, and beautiful.

"Wow! Eight pounds, three ounces—she's perfect, Hailey." Stan had tears running down his face as he watched the nurse clean and dress our new daughter.

"Is she really here?" I asked, almost afraid to believe it was true. Stan and I have a daughter; we're finally a real family.

We brought Lizzie home when she was two days old. It was a little scary to think of caring for her without the help of the nurses, but Stan took a week off from work to stay with us, so it wasn't too bad.

The first night, we hardly put her down. It still seemed like a dream, but it was definitely a happy one. Our baby daughter was so sweet, so tiny, and so helpless. Being a mom was an awesome responsibility.

The hard part was that neither of my parents was alive to see their first grandchild. Stan's parents retired to Florida and would be coming to visit as soon as Stan's dad's hip surgery allowed. But all of our friends and coworkers came to visit, bringing soft blankets and frilly, little dresses and gobs of advice. Those first days were exciting and exhausting.

"I wish I didn't have to go back to work and leave my two girls," Stan said Sunday evening. Lizzie was nine days old and doing well, but she woke several times a night and it seemed like I was tired all the time. And now that Stan was going back to work, I knew he wouldn't be able to help me as much at night.

"We'll miss you, Daddy," I said, smiling down at our little angel. Sometimes when she woke me in the middle of the night, I wasn't so sure she was an angel, but I told myself everything would smooth out in time. Lizzie would eventually sleep through the night and I would lose all my baby weight and life would get back to normal.

Despite the childcare classes Stan and I took, I couldn't believe how lonely and bereft I felt when Stan left for work the next morning. I was on my own, alone with Lizzie for the first time, and suddenly, I wasn't sure I was up to it. What if she gets sick? What if I do something wrong and hurt her?

I tried to take naps during the day when the baby slept so I wouldn't be so tired at night, but it seemed like something always happened to keep me up. The phone would ring, waking both me and Lizzie, or someone would ring the doorbell.

By the end of Stan's first week back at work, I was a walking zombie. He couldn't get up at night with Lizzie anymore because he had to go to work in the morning, so it was all up to me. Rationally, I understood that, and I also knew that it was only a temporary situation. Eventually I'd get Lizzie on a schedule, and she would begin to sleep through the night. And despite my exhaustion, having Lizzie was the best thing that ever happened to me. She was beautiful and precious, and Stan and I both adored her.

"What did we ever do to deserve such a beautiful baby?" Stan asked one night while he gave Lizzie her bottle. He was probably one of the best daddies in the world. He changed diapers and cleaned spit-up without complaint, and every time he held and cuddled Lizzie, my heart melted.

That's why it was so hard for me to understand why I was so resentful of him. Every morning when he left for work, I felt angry. Why does he get to go off to a quiet, peaceful office, while I'm stuck here with a noisy, demanding baby?

Despite the fact that Lizzie was physically beautiful and perfect, she was far from a perfect baby to care for. She had frequent bouts of painful gas, and she was very fussy and demanding. If I held her and walked around the house with her all day, she was pretty good, but there were times when I just had to put her down—and usually that brought on a round of screaming that made my head ache.

I discussed the situation with my pediatrician and she advised me to let Lizzie cry a little.

"As long as she is fed and dry and doesn't have gas, you can safely let her cry for a while. No one expects a new mother to hold her infant twenty-four-seven. Give yourself a break, Hailey. If you get overtired and stressed out, you won't do anyone any good."

I'm sure Dr. Nolan's advice is sound, but it didn't work for me. I couldn't stand to hear Lizzie cry. So inevitably, I'd end up picking her up and carrying her around with me while I tried to do laundry and clean the house.

When I complained to Stan, he told me to lighten up. "The house doesn't have to be in perfect order every minute of the day, Hailey," he said, nuzzling Lizzie's plump cheeks. "We have a new baby. Concentrate on that for a while. Soon enough, you'll be going back to work and someone else will be caring for Lizzie. Can't you just enjoy this time with her?"

I shook my head in disgust and walked away. Stan didn't understand. He had no idea what it's like to be stuck alone with a baby all day. He thought Lizzie was an angel, and that I was a shrew for complaining.

When I went for my six-week checkup with Dr. Niels, I tried telling him how stressed and exhausted I was, but like Stan, he laughed off my complaints. "Caring for an infant is a full-time job, and it's always exhausting during the first few months. Things will level out, Hailey. You'll see. Just try to relax."

I didn't bother to tell Stan that the doctor told me it was okay to resume marital relations. Does any new mother really have the energy for sex?

But I should have known that Stan would figure out that it was time for things to go back to normal.

That evening, when he came home from work, he had a beautiful bouquet of roses and a wide grin. "Tonight's the night, right, hon? Boy, I could hardly concentrate all day."

I stared at Stan as if he grew two heads. And as I looked at him, I felt myself swell with rage. "Are you crazy?" I screamed. "Do you actually think I'm going to have sex with you? I'm so tired I can hardly hold my head up, and you expect me to jump in bed with you?"

"Hey! What's going on, Hailey? I thought you'd be as anxious to get back to normal as I am."

"Nothing will ever be normal again," I muttered, still filled with anger.

Suddenly I saw a look of uneasiness on Stan's handsome face. "Hailey . . . honey, what's wrong? What have I done to make you so angry? Lately, you seem to be mad at me all the time. I know you're tired, but everything we're going through now is normal. It will get easier."

"Oh, sure, and when will that be? When Lizzie goes to school? In the meantime, all I'll do all day is change diapers, sterilize bottles, make formula, and try to comfort a crying baby. Can't you see how much fun I'm having, Stan? If I knew it would be like this. . . ."

I caught myself before I finished my sentence. I was about to say that I never should have had Lizzie.

"I don't understand, Hailey. We were so happy when you got pregnant. We both wanted a baby so much, and now it's like you don't even want our baby!" Stan's face was pale, and he looked about as unhappy as I felt.

For a moment, I felt some of the love Stan and I used to share. I did love my husband and my child, but everything was so hard. I was tired and fat, and I didn't even think the baby liked me. It seemed like Lizzie was all smiles whenever Stan held her, but when I picked her up, it was a different story. Sometimes she would stiffen up and act as if she wanted to get away from me.

"Maybe you should see a doctor, Hailey," Stan said quietly, running his hands through his hair nervously. "Maybe you need a little help."

"What? Do you think I'm crazy? Is that what you're saying?"

"Hailey, no! That's not what I meant at all. It's just that you're not yourself, and you're not happy. Having a baby is what we both wanted, isn't it? This should be a happy time for us."

I saw the unhappiness on Stan's face and suddenly, I felt terrible for acting so mean. "It is a happy time," I lied. "Or, it will be when I get some sleep. I think I'm just overtired. Forgive me?"

"Oh, baby, of course. There's nothing to forgive. I know that caring for an infant is hard work, and I know that sometimes Lizzie can be a little fussy, but all of this will pass. You'll see. Just try to relax, okay?"

I nodded. "I will, and I'm sorry for being so cranky. Be patient with me, will you?"

At that moment, I really meant it. I didn't want things to be the way they were. I didn't want to be tired all the time and resentful of Stan. And most of all, I wanted to love my baby girl and be a good mother. I'll try harder, I promised myself. I'll nap when Lizzie naps. I'll take vitamins and try to fit in some exercise. And everything will be fine.

But later that night, everything blew up in my face. After bathing and giving Lizzie her bottle, I put her down in the bassinet we kept next to our bed. "Please let her sleep," I whispered. "Please just let me rest for a few hours."

Stan came into the bedroom and put his arms around me. "I love you, Hailey," he said softly. "Everything is going to be okay. You'll see."

I let Stan kiss me, but when his kiss deepened, I pulled away. "I'm exhausted, Stan," I said. "I just need to sleep."

Stan looked disappointed, but he dropped his arms. "Sure. Get a good night's sleep and you'll feel better."

But a good night's sleep was not on the program. I couldn't have been asleep for more than an hour when I heard it—Lizzie's thin, reedy wail—a wail that would escalate into a full scale screaming fit if I didn't get up and tend to her.

But before I could swing my legs over the side of the bed, Stan got up. "Stay put, honey. I'll see what I can do."

I rolled over gratefully, praying that Stan would be able to settle Lizzie down. One good night's sleep, I told myself, and I'll feel a hundred percent better.

But Lizzie had other ideas. After hours of walking the floor with her, Stan gave up. "I'm sorry, hon," he said, "but if I don't get some sleep, I won't be able to go to work tomorrow. I've tried everything. I don't know what else to do."

I climbed out of bed wearily. "Go to sleep," I said. "I'll take her downstairs."

Lizzie's little face was red with the exertion of her crying, and she stiffened when Stan handed her to me.

"Do you think she's sick?" Stan asked.

No, not sick—just evil, I thought, looking down at Lizzie's red, angry face. Instead of a gift from heaven, I got an evil, little creature that's trying to destroy me.

I sat down on the sofa in the family room and tried to rock Lizzie. Surely, after hours of crying, she would get tired and fall asleep. This couldn't go on all night, could it?

My head was throbbing and my stomach felt like it was tied in knots, and it was all I could do to keep my eyes open. I wanted so badly to sleep. All I wanted was for the crying to stop.

When the rocking failed to calm Lizzie, I finally laid her down on the sofa next to me. I stared at her for a moment, feeling completely detached. This isn't my baby. This can't be the child Stan and I wanted so desperately. Instead, it's some sort of alien being, a creature sent to torture me.

I tried talking softly to Lizzie. I even massaged her tiny legs like one of my childcare books suggests—but nothing worked. She just continued to cry.

All at once, I knew I couldn't stand it anymore. Somehow, some way, I had to make Lizzie be quiet.

I don't remember much after that. But I do remember picking up the little throw pillow on the sofa. Just a few minutes of peace, I thought. Just a blessed few minutes of quiet....

I vaguely remember Stan screaming at me and ripping the pillow out of my hand. "Hailey! What are you doing? What's the matter with you?"

The next thing I knew, I woke up in the hospital—in the psychiatric ward. Stan was sitting beside my bed, looking pale and frightened, and some doctor I never saw before was standing at the foot of the bed.

"How do you feel, Hailey?" the strange doctor asked. "I'm Dr. D'Agostino, the staff psychiatrist here at Memorial. Do you remember anything about last night?"

I shook my head, feeling fuzzy and weak. "The baby . . . where's my baby? Did something happen to her?"

"Your baby is fine, Hailey, thanks to your husband's intervention." Dr. D'Agostino hesitated, and then he spoke the words that will haunt me for the rest of my life: "You tried to smother your baby, Hailey. Luckily, Stan caught you in time."

"No! I didn't . . . I couldn't! I love my baby. We waited so long for her! Why are you saying such terrible things?"

"You're suffering from postpartum depression, Hailey. It's very common in new mothers, no matter how much they want their babies. It's not your fault, and there's no way you could have controlled it. It's just unfortunate that it went undiagnosed for this long. There could have been tragic consequences."

"Please! Stan, tell this man it's not true! I love Lizzie! I'd never hurt her!"

Stan took my hand in his. "Under normal circumstances, I know you wouldn't, honey. But you're not yourself, and you haven't been since Lizzie's birth. You need help. I'm just sorry it took me so long to realize it."

"But...."

"It's alright, Hailey," Dr. D'Agostino said gently. "Everything is going to be alright. You're going to stay here in the hospital for a few days until we get your medication adjusted. When you're feeling better and are rested, you'll be able to go home and have outpatient therapy."

It was a lot to absorb, and it was actually several days before I was able to understand what happened to me.

At first I was filled with self-loathing when I thought of what I almost did to my precious, little girl. I wasn't sure I'd ever be able to forgive myself. I told Stan I didn't understand how he could even bear to look at me.

"What almost happened that night . . . that wasn't you, Hailey. I know that. You are one of the kindest, most loving people I've ever known, and I know how much you love our baby. I blame myself for not seeing that something was seriously wrong and getting help for you. Can you forgive me?" Stan's words melted me.

We cried together then, and when our tears were finally dried, I knew everything was going to be alright.

Stan took a leave of absence from work to care for Lizzie while I was being treated. Even though I felt a hundred percent better with medication, I continued with my therapy for several months. I wanted to be sure I was able to give my daughter all the loving care she needed.

At first, I was afraid to be alone with Lizzie, and although it was a financial strain, Stan arranged for us to have someone come in during the day and help me. Gradually, as my depression abated and my love for Lizzie grew, I was able to forgive myself.

Lizzie will be a year old soon and she is the prettiest, brightest, sweetest little girl in the world. Stan and I will celebrate Lizzie's birthday with full hearts, knowing how lucky we are to have her and each other.

It's painful for me to relive those first months of my daughter's life, but if it helps one new mother, it's worth it. Please, if you have a new baby and you don't feel the way you think you should—get help right away. Postpartum depression is more common than most people think, and it can be treated. Do yourself and your precious baby a favor and talk to your doctor—it could save a life.

THE END

CONFESSIONS OF A BATTERED WOMAN
"I faked my death to escape his torture"

The semi-tractor that was headed right for me on the rain-slicked road didn't scare me in the slightest.

Considering the hell that became my life—the thought of being hit by a truck actually seemed like it might be all right.

The hiss of air brakes and the screech of the enormous, rubber tires on that big eighteen-wheeler brought me to my senses, and I jumped back out of the way—right into the ditch I just ran out of. The sodden grass grabbed at me and rain poured onto my head, as I struggled to keep my footing in the muddy ditch.

The truck skidded to a halt only a few feet in front of me, the passenger door lining itself up perfectly with my position. I would have been roadkill if I didn't move in time.

"Isabel, where the hell are you? Get your ass back here!" The distant, angry voice coming from the dense woods behind me spurred me to action.

Without thinking, I leaped up onto the step of the tractor, my hand reaching automatically for the door handle, pulling it open. I barely had time to notice the driver's startled face as I jumped into the cab, pulling the door shut behind me as I crouched down below the window, out of sight. "Drive!"

If my command surprised the driver, he didn't show it. He simply shifted into gear and took off. A mile passed, then another. Finally, he spoke. "Where'd you get the shiners?"

Gingerly, I put a hand to my face, not surprised to feel pain as I touched the bruises around both of my eyes. Keith did a real job on me this time.

"My boyfriend didn't like the supper I cooked for him," I said, trying to make light of it. What I said was true, but the larger reality was that Keith terrified me.

I tried before to get away from him, and every time, he found me, dragged me home, and beat the living daylights out of me. Each time was a bit worse, his threats more believable, as the damage inflicted on my body increased. I knew the day would come when he'd kill me, and my body would simply disappear somewhere in the remote woods, where he had his ramshackle, little cabin. I had no family, no one to miss me. I was allowed into town so seldom that I doubted anyone even realized I was a full-time resident in the area and not one of the millions of tourists who pour in every summer.

But I'd been in town enough to recognize the driver and the rig he drove. My heart sank. This man is local.

In fact, Keith once worked for him and cursed him soundly on a daily basis. From what I gathered at the time, Keith was actually expected to work, and in Keith's estimation, that was unfair and uncalled for. One day, Keith came home in a towering rage. He said he quit his job working for "that SOB," but even at the time, I knew that the man I was riding next to must have fired him. I got one of the worst beatings of my life that night, as Keith soothed his frustrations with liquor and his fists.

I hoped, as I was running onto the highway, that I could hitch a ride with someone headed far away. But I doubted this guy would be going more than a few miles—not far enough to get me away from Keith for good. Now what can I do? I knew Keith would be hot on my trail. I could only hope he didn't see me get into the truck. If he didn't, there was still a chance I could escape.

I turned to the driver. "My name's Isabel Hewitt. I'd appreciate it if you forget you ever saw me."

After a brief hesitation, he responded, "Abe Middleton. I've already forgotten you were here. Where can I drop you off? The police station?"

"No!"

My outburst startled him, but he gave me a smile. "Where, then?"

I hesitated. I had nowhere to go. I couldn't go back to the women's shelter. They weren't able to protect me before, and that was the first place Keith would look. Then the nightmare would start all over again.

I knew where Abe lived. I saw his big, blue truck sitting in his yard when Keith brought me into town. Keith cussed a blue streak every time we passed. Abe's place was right outside of town, but surrounded by thick forest and a cemetery in the back. I could hide out there in the forest, wait for Keith to give up on finding me, and then make my way out of town.

I explained to Abe that I'd like to be dropped off near his house, and then I told him about my lame plan. I could see he wasn't too impressed, but he said nothing.

Sooner than I wanted, he downshifted and stopped, waiting in a turn lane. Still crouched in my hiding place by the dashboard, I knew from experience where I was. Abe's place was only a quarter mile away. We'd be there in no time, and I would be out in the cold and on the run again.

I had no chance to prepare this time. Opportunity struck without any warning, when Keith got drunk and went to sleep before he remembered to shackle me to the bedpost, as he usually did.

Finding myself free, I knocked over a chair in my haste to get away. The noise woke him up. Keith followed, but I was sober, and fear gave wings to my feet, so I easily outran him in the rain and the dense undergrowth.

I ran straight through the woods, following an old deer trail that crosses the highway two miles from Keith's cabin. At last, when I thought my lungs would burst and Keith's angry ranting faded in the distance—I found myself on the highway, just in time for Abe to nearly run me down.

I knew I must look like hell, but that was okay, because I felt like hell, too. The prospect of leaving the warmth and safety of the truck cab and trying to find an escape in the gathering darkness and the storm didn't thrill me. Suddenly, I just felt weary, spent.

The truck came to a halt in Abe's yard. He must have known how I felt, because without a word, he climbed down from his side of the truck and walked around to mine. Pulling the door open, he helped me down to the ground. My legs cramped and I nearly fell.

I started to protest as he helped me inside to his first-floor office and sat me down in the chair behind the desk. "Please, I have to go now. Keith will find me, and then he'll kill me!" I probably sounded irrational, but the threat was very real to me. Keith promised many times to kill me, and he explained in graphic detail how he would do it if I didn't quit trying to escape.

Abe shook his head. "Look outside." Lightning split the sky as if on cue, and rain hammered the window. "You can't go anywhere tonight. Just sit tight, and when I come back in, we'll decide what to do."

"We'll decide," he said. The shock of that silenced me. In more years than I could remember, no one included me in even the tiniest of decisions. Even if it's just an expression, suddenly, I decided that maybe Abe was a nice man—if there was such a thing.

He went back out into the storm, and I heard the hiss of air brakes and the revving of a diesel engine as the truck pulled away. Then the only sounds were the rain and thunder.

Soaked to the skin, I started to shiver, in spite of the warmth in the little office. Plan after plan formed in my head, each more pathetic and impossible than the last. I was alone. I had no money, no clothes, no one to turn to for help. I thought about getting a restraining order, but then I laughed at the thought. I knew a piece of paper would mean nothing to Keith. He'd just ignore it and kill me, anyway. The only hope was to get away.

I heard the sound of a big, overhead door closing somewhere in the darkness behind the office. Fear knifed through me. Keith somehow found me already! I just knew it was him sneaking up on me from within the building. Abe went out the front door; who else could it be but Keith?

I was too scared to realize that a potential murderer wouldn't bother to close a big garage door. Frantically, I searched the little room for a place to hide, but there was nowhere. I plunged into the kneehole under the desk as a voice softly called my name.

"Isabel?"

I couldn't answer. The voice didn't sound like Keith's. The actions didn't match, either. Keith would have stormed into the place, shouting threats and obscenities. But in my fear, I couldn't take the chance that it was someone else. Closing my eyes, I childishly hoped that would make me invisible.

"Isabel?" The voice was closer now—very close.

I jumped, whacking my head on the bottom of the desk as a hand touched my arm softly. The breath I was holding in exploded in a yelp, and I opened my eyes to find Abe bending down to look into my little sanctuary.

"Are you okay?" His voice sounded concerned, but his blue eyes sparkled. I suppose if I were watching myself, I'd have found me amusing, too. "You can stay there if you want, but I'm going upstairs to have supper. Aren't you hungry?" he asked.

I was famished. I followed him out of the office, through the big machine shop where the truck and trailer were now parked, and up the steps to a little apartment on the second floor. But at the doorway to his home, I couldn't bring myself to enter. Once I was inside, I'd be at his mercy, just like I was at Keith's. I couldn't do that again.

Abe went into the kitchen, not noticing whether I followed him or not. I heard him rummaging through pans in the cupboards, heard the sound of a refrigerator door opening and closing, and eventually, bacon sizzling. The smell hit me right in my empty stomach, which grumbled and complained that I had to trust someone, at least long enough to get something to eat.

"Isabel? How do you like your eggs?" Abe's voice, asking such an ordinary thing, brought me over the threshold and into his little living room. Softly, I closed the door behind me.

How do I like my eggs? No one gave me a choice in so long that I forgot what it's like to have one. "Any way but scrambled," I told him as I stepped into the light of the kitchen. Keith insisted I always make eggs scrambled, and that was the only way I was allowed to eat them—when I was allowed to eat at all.

Abe took one look at me and set down the egg he was about to crack on the counter. Without a word, he motioned me into a bedroom to the side of the kitchen.

Panic sliced through me. *He's just like Keith, after all! Men* only want one thing, Keith always said, and women are supposed to provide it without question; it's our function in life, the only real reason we were put on earth.

But Abe didn't act like a man in search of sex. He ignored me while he rummaged through a box at the bottom of a closet. Finally, he stood up with a pair of jeans and a sweatshirt in his hands and laid the clothes on the bed.

"You can have anything in those boxes," he told me. "There's probably some underwear and socks and stuff in there, and a couple of pairs of shoes. Just help yourself. I don't know if things will fit, but you have to get into something dry." He seemed embarrassed, so I didn't say anything, and in a second, he went back out to the kitchen, closing the door softly behind him.

I clicked the lock in place after him, not caring if he heard me. I wanted those dry clothes badly, but I wasn't about to have him barging in and attacking me while I changed.

In seconds, I changed clothes and felt almost human again. I decided to forego underwear for the time being, but I did find a pair of thick, wool socks and slipped them gratefully on my cold feet.

That first supper with Abe was the best food I've ever tasted. Fried eggs, potatoes, cantaloupe on the side, bacon, and cottage cheese could have beat champagne and caviar any day. I'm sure I sounded like a pig as I slurped down glass after glass of milk. Keith hated milk and I was never allowed to have it. I missed it terribly and couldn't get enough.

Abe didn't say anything about my guzzling, but I noticed him refilling my glass several times when he thought I wasn't looking. "You'd better stay here tonight, Isabel," he advised me during that wonderful meal. "You can sleep in the spare room. As you know, there's a lock on the door, so you'll feel safe."

I felt my cheeks color. So he did hear me lock him out.

"It's okay. You've been through a lot, and you have good reason not to trust me or anyone else. If a lock makes you feel better, then use it."

Tears rolled over my swollen, battered face. How many years has it been since a man showed me even the slightest kindness? I could imagine what would have happened if I ever dared snap a lock against Keith. He'd have broken down the door with an ax, and then hacked me to death with it. But there sat Abe, telling me to lock the door, only because he thought it would make me feel more secure, my comfort being his sole consideration.

I did lock the door that night. And I slept like the dead, feeling safe for the first time in years.

Abe was gone in the morning when I got up, even though it wasn't much past dawn. In the fall of the year, people in the construction industry were all scrambling to get their work done before winter.

Make yourself at home, the note on the kitchen table read. I'll be back around lunchtime. We're working on the state park project today, if you need to reach me. A phone number followed the message, underneath which Abe scrawled his name.

Another first. Men disappear for days at a time, with no explanation or clue of their whereabouts. And when they come home, they're rip-roaring drunk and looking for sex or someone to beat up—or both. At least, that was my experience all my life.

I took full advantage of my solitude. First I went through all the clothes in the boxes I was shown. Then, after choosing a comfortable outfit, I took a luxurious shower, something I wasn't allowed to do living with Keith. He insisted it cost too much money to heat water for me, so I had to take sponge baths and wash my hair in the sink. I felt guilty, draining the water heater completely of hot water, but it was worth it. The warmth soothed the bruises on my face and body, and once I was clean, I felt almost alive again. Surely, I'll figure out a way to escape Keith's clutches and have a real life someday.

I thought about stealing money and maybe a truck from Abe. The idea grabbed me so fiercely I couldn't even wait to get dressed. I went to the door of his bedroom, wrapped in a towel, to search for valuables—but I couldn't go in.

I concluded Keith was right—I was useless and helpless. I couldn't bring myself to steal, or even snoop. Abe was so kind to me; I couldn't betray him. Feeling good and bad at the same time, I hurried back to my room and dressed.

A scream tore from my throat as I rounded the corner of my bedroom door and ran straight into someone. Hands grabbed my arms, and I kicked out, landing a solid blow to a shin. I couldn't stop screaming until finally, a voice penetrated through my terror.

I found myself held in a bear hug. Soothing words flowed around me, and I started to cry. A massive hand stroked my hair, while another held my back. "It's okay. It's just me. It's just ol' Abe. Don't be afraid. Shhhh. There, don't cry, Isabel. No one's going to hurt you here." Abe felt like a mountain against my ear.

Slowly my sobs faded as I held myself stiff, my arms crossed over my chest. But I knew better than to try to get away. Keith was a small, wiry man, barely taller than I am, and yet he had the strength to beat me senseless. What could Abe do to me when he's a foot taller than I am and twice my weight at least? He'd crush me like a sparrow, that's what! My only hope was to hold still and let him do as he pleased. His soothing words meant nothing. It was just part of the game. If I took them to heart, they'd just be used against me sometime in the future, so I said nothing, absorbed nothing.

Abe's hand stopped moving. Gently, he pushed me back from

him and looked into my face. I'm not sure what he saw there, because I tried to remain expressionless. I knew that was best, never to show emotion—especially weakness. That always set Keith off.

"Shall we have lunch?"

Lunch! Panic sliced through me. Abe left me a note, telling me he'd be home at lunchtime! How could I have forgotten? Now he'll beat me for sure! After all, I'm supposed to have food hot and waiting at all times, in case Keith—no, Abe—comes home to eat.

Abe must have seen my fear. I felt like a trapped rabbit, waiting for the fox to strike, and it must have showed on my face.

He let me go. "Let's see what we can find," was all he said as he turned and headed for the refrigerator. I stayed where I was as he rustled up a couple of hamburgers. He sat down to eat without saying another word to me. I was still afraid his niceness was just a trap, so I stood by the door and watched him eat.

"Aren't you hungry? I made one for you." He gestured with his fork at the chair next to his, but I didn't move.

Understanding dawned in his eyes. Slowly, he shoved my food across the table to the space farthest from him, putting the table between us. Timidly, I slid into the chair. The hamburger tasted like heaven. Keith never fed me enough. Mostly, I survived on whatever I could sneak out of the pan while I cooked. Certainly, I was never invited to join him at the table.

Anger clouded Abe's eyes, and I recoiled. He saw my reaction instantly, and the anger in his eyes was replaced by curiosity. "You don't miss much, do you?"

I shrugged. "It's a survival skill." I made myself relax a bit and helped myself to the salad Abe set out and subtly pushed in my direction over the last five minutes.

"My wife left me."

The abrupt change of subject took me by surprise, and I made no comment.

"She didn't leave because I beat her, Isabel. She left because—well, it doesn't really matter why, but she did."

So that's where the clothes I was wearing came from.

"I don't beat women, Isabel. No real man does." The anger returned to Abe's eyes, but I sensed he wasn't angry with me, and I was able to beat back the fear his anger triggered in me before.

"I've been thinking about your problem, and I have an idea. But you'll have to stay here and lay low for a while, maybe even a few weeks. Would that be okay?"

Okay? I felt like he just handed me the key to the Pearly gates! "I don't know if I can take advantage of you that way," I said, as much as I wanted to.

Abe nodded, thinking. "Okay, how's this? What if I hire you? I could use a housekeeper."

I glanced around the immaculate room. He obviously did fine on his own.

"And a cook. And a laundress."

I just stared.

"It's my busy time of year." He shrugged. "I don't have time to be a housewife, too."

"What other—umm, duties—would I be required to do?" I could have kicked myself, but I had to be sure. The last thing I wanted was to jump from the frying pan into the fire.

Abe just looked at me for a long time, not comprehending. Then, slowly, a bright, red blush spread over his face. "Oh, no—nothing like that! I would never—you'd never be expected to—" Abruptly, he got up, put his plate in the sink, and left, muttering curses at Keith all the way out the door.

I never managed to embarrass a man right out of his own home before. The feeling of power it gave me made me smile all afternoon.

I wondered what Abe's plan was to solve my problem. I hoped it involved squashing Keith with that big truck I almost got killed by, then burying him so deep he'd never be found, with that enormous backhoe which was chained to the trailer behind the truck. But unfortunately, I finally accepted that Abe is not the violent type.

If only I could drive a semi. And operate a backhoe.

Thoughts of revenge helped assuage my fears that afternoon, although wondering what to say to Abe that evening kept me on edge.

The key rattled in the lock, and supper was on the table right on time. As my hero walked into the kitchen, I simply said, "I accept."

He grinned, and so did I. It didn't matter to me what the plan was. I'd do anything to get Keith Jennings out of my life for good.

Over supper, he explained his plan about how to get rid of Keith once and for all. It was so simple it took my breath away. It was underhanded and devious, which was the best part, but it didn't even involve anything illegal or unethical. I gave my enthusiastic endorsement to the plan, and Abe promised to set it in motion the very next morning.

People say women gossip. The classic stereotype is a bunch of little, old ladies sitting around a table with their coffee cups, cackling about all the happenings in town. But the reality is, if you want to hear or spread gossip, talk to a contractor. They all know each other and everyone else in town, and they work in people's homes all over the community, where they see firsthand what's going on. Naturally, they talk.

Abe took full advantage of that fact. Each day when he came

home, he told me about the progress we made in getting rid of Keith. I did my part and stayed out of sight. As far as anyone knew, I disappeared from the face of the earth. That's what we wanted everyone to believe—including the county sheriff.

It wasn't long before the gossip got back to him that I disappeared. And he went nosing around Keith's place. Keith claimed he had no idea where I was, that I just packed up and left one day and he was glad to be rid of me.

The sheriff saw my things still in the cabin, though, and came back with a search warrant when Keith wasn't home. They found blood on the floor of the kitchen, heightening suspicions of foul play. I remember the occasion well—I bled all over the place after Keith punched my nose because he didn't like the way I served his supper.

In a little town like ours, peace officers like to gossip, too. It wasn't long before the results of the sheriff's visit and the ensuing search warrant were known all over town. By then, Abe's original benign remarks about Keith and me, made at a local bar full of contractors after work one night, blossomed into speculation that Keith murdered me and disposed of my body. Rumors are rampant, repeated as fact, and people began calling for law enforcement to do something about the supposed murder.

Abe kept the pressure up with a few well-placed, carefully chosen comments, but he never lied. He didn't have to. Gossip takes on a life of its own after a while, and people tend to believe the worst, especially if it's interesting. Abe merely made subtle suggestions about my presumed disappearance, and people ran with it from there, the innuendo getting bigger and worse with each repetition.

The second time the sheriff went to Keith's place, he took along a warrant for his arrest on suspicion of murder—to find that the cabin was cleaned out, and Keith was gone.

Keith was a bully and a coward, and I know he figured he'd most likely be convicted of my murder, even without a body, just because of the rumors and because of his reputation as a troublemaker.

Abe's plan worked flawlessly.

Before things went any further, Abe called the sheriff and asked him to come to the apartment for some information regarding my disappearance. The sheriff sat at our kitchen table with his little notebook in front of him.

"I know who you are, Abe." He made a note in his notebook. "But who is this pretty lady, and what does she have to do with this case?"

No one ever called me a pretty lady before. The very idea made me giggle. I knew I blossomed under Abe's kindness. Good food put some much-needed weight on me. Security and freedom from fear brought back a sparkle in my eyes and a confidence that surprised me every time I caught a glimpse of myself in a mirror. For the first time in my life, I was happy, and I guess it showed.

I offered my hand to Sheriff Kelsey. As he shook it, I said, "I'm Isabel Hewitt, the deceased."

I'll never know if the shock on his face came from seeing me alive, or from realizing that he didn't recognize me. I came a long way from the cowering, bruised, terrified woman he once took to a women's shelter.

At first, he was upset about our little charade, but after I reminded him how he wasn't able to protect me in the past, he understood why we did what we did. Keith was gone, running from a non-existent murder charge; short of killing him myself, our plan was the only way to get rid of him for good.

Sheriff Kelsey spluttered a bit about wasting taxpayers' money on a false report of a crime, until Abe reminded him that no one ever actually reported a crime. He also pointed out that, had the money not been "wasted" on a false lead, chances were excellent that his office would have spent even more money on a real murder. Finally, the sheriff just shook his head ruefully and congratulated us on our sneakiness, wished us well, and let himself out. We heard him chuckling as he headed down the stairs.

Abe and I have been together nearly twenty years now. It took a long time for each of us to get over the emotional wounds our respective former mates inflicted on us. We lived together in a comfortable, celibate existence for nearly a year before Abe—my hero, my rescuer, my gentle giant—confided to me that he loved me, but he was afraid of me. That statement took my breath away. How could I ever hurt him, big as he is and little as I am?

"I never told you why my wife left, Isabel. She didn't want to be a dirt contractor's wife. She thought it was too blue collar, being married to a guy who makes his living digging basements and putting in septic tanks. At the least, she wanted to move to a big city. She thought our little town was too backward, not sophisticated enough. And in the end, that's what she thought about me, too."

The hurt in his voice would probably never go away, but I know my tears that evening helped wash away some of his pain. Goodness and kindness know no class, and it broke my heart that anyone could hurt a man whose heart is so pure and true.

Our relationship developed so slowly that I know the love has to be solid. But sometimes I catch Abe looking at me in a way that tells me he's not quite sure I won't leave, like his ex-wife did. And sometimes he startles me with just a sharp word or a sudden movement. I guess we can never truly rid ourselves of the past, but I feel so blessed to have learned we can get past our hurt and move forward into happiness and joy.

Abe and I will grow old together. Of that, I'm sure. His kindness and subtle manner saved my life, and I like to think I saved his in a way, too, by healing some of the emotional pain inflicted on him by a woman who looked only at what he does for a living, instead of who and what he is. The vows we made nearly eighteen years ago still mean as much as they did that very first day. He's still a good man, and he's helped me become a happy, confident woman.

I'll go to my grave proud to be this contractor's wife.

THE END

CONFESSIONS OF A RUNAWAY
Why I Left Home

I was fifteen years old and had been on the run for a little over four months. Up until that point I'd never used drugs of any kind. As I lay there on a bare mattress next to a man I didn't known prior to that day, I promised myself no one would ever make me use them again.

The overhead lights spun around and around like some miniature UFO. I closed my eyes and whispered, "It's just bare light bulbs with fly specks." I don't know how long I had slept. I didn't mean to sleep at all, but I only intended to wait until he fell asleep and then take my leave quickly and quietly. But then he poured the drink. I didn't know what the white powder was that he put in it, but I felt the affect right away.

A fan whirred close by, squeaking as it oscillated. The breeze barely touched my face. I grasped the ragged quilt and pulled it down tight against my naked body. The touch of it repulsed me, but it was real, something tangible to hold on to until my mind cleared.

I felt my stomach churn and I thought I was going to vomit. I rolled sideways and hung my head over the edge of the bed. I heaved once. My head weighed a thousand pounds. I thought it would serve him right if I threw up in his bed for making me drink the whiskey. The idea forced a giggle from my throat, but the sound came out more like a tortured sob.

The nausea finally passed and I fell back onto the pillow. When my head stopped spinning in time with the light bulbs I sat up and swung my legs over the side of the bed. The groaning of weak, rusty bedsprings grated in my ears. Several minutes passed before I could focus on anything in the room without it taking off to swirl across the walls.

My clothes and my backpack were draped across the only chair in the room. The chair stood beside a rickety table with one leg broken and propped beneath the corner. There was no curtain at the window, but the pane was so covered with grime that even the sunlight was dimmed as it searched out the dark corners of the hovel. A dresser stood against one wall, the drawers partially opened. I saw only a few tattered pieces of clothing.

I slid from the mattress, onto the floor, and then crawled across the short space to my clothes. I pulled them off the chair to the floor beside me. Two twenty-dollar bills fluttered down with the jeans.

I worked my legs into the underwear and then the jeans, my head wobbling the whole time. My fingers felt thick and they refused to move with the same urgency I felt to get out. After I got the T-shirt on, I pulled my long hair loose and let it fall down my back. It felt like a cape that I might somehow hide under. Sweat streamed from under my arms. My shirt was stained and dirty, but there wasn't any time to worry about that. I had a jacket to wear over it and cover the filth.

I had to hold on to the chair to pull myself upright. My legs shook and I had trouble getting my balance. I looked toward the single minor and my breath caught at the image reflected there. I used to be healthy and athletic. Now I looked like a discarded scarecrow.

I stuffed the twenties into my pocket and sort of shuffled toward the only exit. My heart pounded as I opened the door a crack and peeked into the hallway. I didn't see anyone, but I wasn't even sure anyone else even lived on that floor.

When I got outside the dilapidated hotel I felt like I'd just escaped a human trap and the feeling pumped adrenalin through my veins, pushing the effects of the drug further and further from my brain. I heard the sound of diesel trucks not far away and their roar became a beacon. Being on the road I'd learned that where there are trucks, there have to be truck stops; a safe haven with restrooms and showers! Revulsion again rippled through me, but not as bad as before.

"Hey, there, missy. You lost?"

The voice tore through my mental shield and I stumbled. In an alley between the musty buildings an old man sat leaned against the wall, a bottle of whiskey between his legs. A sly grin split his wrinkled and toothless face—a grin I had seen many times these last few months.

"No," I hissed. Halfway down the block the nausea came back. That time it won. I stopped long enough to vomit, leaning against the rough brick of another rundown hotel for support. I knew the old man was standing at the corner watching, a knowing grin pasted across his ugly face. I pulled together every last ounce of strength I had and forced my legs to run toward the roar of traffic on the highway.

Less than a half-mile down the interstate I saw the truck stop billboard. I slowed to a walk and searched the traffic for patrol cars. The truck stop turned out to be a second-rate place, but I didn't care. I made my way through the parked rigs at the back of the lot toward the flashing light over the door marked ladies shower room. Fortunately the shower rooms were not locked. As rundown as the place was, I guess they thought no one would want to shower there. The cold concrete floor was bare. Inside the shower stall the walls were covered with chipped and broken squares of porcelain.

I tossed my bag onto the shelf overhead and without waiting to undress, turned the nozzle and adjusted the water until it steamed. I stood under the spray gasping for breath while the water streamed over me. I stripped off my clothes finally and let them lay at my feet. I stood still for a long time, and then scrubbed at my skin, imagining the germs and filth that clung to my flesh. My tears tasted salty as they mingled with the shower spray that pelted my face and body. I clawed with long, ragged fingernails at the palms of my hands and my knees, remembering the grimy linoleum I'd so recently crawled across. My fair skin tuned pink under the hot water, hiding the red streaks and my efforts to scrape away the memory.

After a long time I turned off the water and dried off. I took the twenty-dollar bills from the wet jeans pocket and tossed the whole pile of clothes into the trash bin. I had one last pair of jeans and a T-shirt in my shoulder bag. There was a bra, but no panties. I'd discarded all the others. No matter. I could go without for one day. Just one more day. No more hitching rides, no more rooms or dirty alleys. No hiding, no more running. Forty dollars just had to be enough. I felt a sob building in my throat.

There was nothing left in the bag except the letter and a hairbrush. I straightened my hair and shoved the brush, along with the faded envelope, into my back pocket, dropped the bag into the trash container, and headed for the restaurant out front. I hadn't eaten since the day before and now the sun was falling low against the western horizon. I had missed so many meals recently, though, that food was secondary in my mind.

"Is there a bus depot near here?" I asked the woman at the cash register

"About a mile down the road, then two blocks right, honey. It's in Meeks' Drugstore. But it closed about fifteen minutes ago," she said after glancing over her shoulder at the clock on the wall. She had graying hair and a friendly face, but I felt coldness in her stare.

"Do you know how much it costs to go to Milford Springs?"

"Nope. Never been there."

The woman turned away, smiling at a burly pair who came toward the counter laughing.

"What do we owe you, Ruby?" the younger man asked. The older one had a toothpick in his mouth that he worked from one side to the other. He pulled out his wallet to pay, but he never took his eyes off me.

"Excuse me, dear," Ruby said, catching my attention. "These boys need some room here. Did you want to eat or you just passing through?"

The smell of food overwhelmed me. My mouth filled with saliva. "I'm going to eat," I blurted out. I wanted to find out about a ticket first, but hunger got the best of me.

"Then find a seat somewhere, honey. We have to get these truckers taken care of so that they can get back on the road."

I found a booth not far from the door and slid into it, hiding my trembling hands beneath the table. The nausea was coming back. My head felt light and it was difficult to keep my eyes focused. I figured the drugs and the whiskey hit me hard because of lack of food. Maybe something in my stomach would make me feel better.

The waitress approached and I was amazed that she didn't look any older than I was. "Just a hamburger," I told her quickly, and ducked my head. I was afraid she might see and recognize in my eyes the trouble I was in. She scribbled in her ticket book and asked if I wanted anything to drink.

"No, just water. Thanks."

The man in the booth across the aisle glanced over at me, but he seemed uninterested as he turned back to his food. He had a platter with the biggest steak I'd ever seen on it. It was smothered with ketchup and half-covered by a pile of French fries. I wished I'd thought of fries, but it was too late. Besides, I wasn't sure what the burger would cost. I hadn't even looked at a menu, but I knew it was going to take a chunk of what little money I had. I had to eat, though, or I'd pass out. I was too close now to do something stupid and have someone call the police. I didn't go halfway across the country to be sent back. I thought briefly of the reason I'd left home and shuddered.

Thirty minutes later and with a full stomach, I felt much better. I tensed up, though, when the big truck driver in the opposite booth gulped his coffee and got up right behind me. I paid my bill and nearly ran outside. Somehow I knew that his leaving at the same time I did was no coincidence.

"Wait up, kid!" he yelled as he came storming out the door. "I don't mean any harm. I just didn't want to attract attention in there."

"What do you want?" I asked over my shoulder without slowing down.

"Wait a minute," he called again. "You want me to start yelling about a runaway clear across the parking lot?"

Well, that got my attention and stopped me dead in my tracks. I turned to look back, then out to the highway again. It was too late to run. He was practically breathing down my neck. The sun was long gone and reaching toward full dark.

"Don't you dare touch me," I snarled. I tried to sound tough, but I couldn't control the quiver in my voice.

"I'm not going to touch you." He stopped walking and held his hands up in front of him. "Look, kid, I heard you asking about Milford Springs. I just want to help you. If you don't have enough money. . . ."

Here it comes, I thought. I can earn what I need. "I have money." I cut him off before he could say those ugly words. But then he really surprised me. He didn't sneer, or even grin. He just shook his head, took a deep breath, and said, "Don't be so defensive, kid. I just want to lend you the money to get home on."

I have to admit that one nearly got to me. Not one person in all this time had offered to help me—at least not without some favor attached. Even those folks I knew suspected I was a runaway didn't offer to help. They just saw an opportunity to get work from someone they could cheat out of a minimum wage, knowing I couldn't say anything. And they were right. I was always grateful to be able to earn a few dollars and then walk away with my self-respect.

"What makes you think I'm a runaway?" I hedged.

"It's written all over you, kid. You think you're the only one that's ever run away, then got scared and wanted to go back? It happens all the time."

Ha, I thought. Shows what you know.

"Let me help," he said.

"How?" He seemed honestly sincere, but they all did in the beginning. Even my stepfather. I couldn't help but be suspicious.

Another pair of truck drivers came out of the restaurant door and disappeared around the side, carrying overnight bags. I guessed they were headed for the showers. They tossed knowing looks our way. My big friend shifted his weight to one foot and looked me straight in the eye.

I'll either give you enough money to make sure you can get a bus ticket, which means you still have to wait 'till morning, or I'll give you a lift. It's against the rules, but I hate to see anyone your age, boy or girl, out here on the highway hitching. That's against the law. You know the cops will pick you up if they catch you."

"I'm real careful," I said.

"Look, I'm going right past Milford Springs. No questions, no strings."

I felt my face burn at the implication.

"You think it over, kid, but don't take too long. I'm going over to my truck, the green rig over there on the far side." He pointed to the last row. There were three trucks parked there, but it was getting so dark that I couldn't tell which one was green. While I was trying to tell the difference in the colors, he turned and walked away.

I bit my bottom lip and wondered what to do. Can I trust him? I was starting to feel conspicuous standing out there in the open, and going with him meant I would reach the end of my search twenty-four hours sooner. It would also mean I wouldn't have to hide out that night, staying awake to make sure some creep didn't make a move on me. That thought alone compelled me to walk toward the big diesel that rumbled and throbbed at the far end of the lot.

Within minutes I was a part of the roaring stream of traffic moving west. I was exhausted and on edge. I leaned against the door of the truck, as far from the driver as possible, and I intended to stay awake just in case. Apparently I was more exhausted than nervous, because when he yelled, "Wake up, kid," it jerked me out of a deep sleep.

The world outside was still black. I'd fallen asleep slumped against the door and my neck was stiff. My shoulder felt bruised.

"We're just outside Milford Springs," the truck driver said.

"We're there?" I saw streetlights scattered about like beacons on a dark path. I had no idea how far we'd gone. It was enough to know that I was there. The place my father had mailed the last letter from, begging my mother to let me come visit him. My stomach rolled up in a ball.

"We're there, kid. Where do you want off?"

As he spoke, we passed an exit sign with the same street name as the one on the envelope.

"Just anywhere here," I said quickly. "It's not far." At least I hoped it wouldn't be far. Fortunately, from the number of lights piercing the darkness, Milford Springs was hardly more than a community crossroad and situated along one side of the interstate.

I couldn't wait to get out of that truck, but I wanted to thank the driver somehow, the first person in four months to help me and ask nothing in return. He seemed to understand my uncertainty, and he helped me again by simply smiling and holding out his hand. I shook it and smiled back.

"Good luck, kid," he said.

As soon as the truck started moving back onto the highway I jerked the faded envelope from my pocket and started running.

Dawn lent a gray cast to the darkness by the time I located a small bungalow on the outskirts of town. A single lamp glowed from inside. It made me feel like he was expecting me.

My heart fluttered and my tongue turned to wood. What would I say? My hand reached out and pressed the doorbell involuntarily. When the door opened he stood in shadowed outline, the lamp behind him. He was tall, just like Mom said, slim, his hair slightly rumpled. A book lay open on the table across the room.

"Can I help you?" he asked when I didn't say anything. My mind was running, but my mouth wouldn't work. When the words finally did start, I couldn't stop them.

"I've come to stay with you," I stammered. "If you still want me." I shoved the envelope toward him. "I'm Tammy Delfino. I mean, not Delfino. Tamara Robinson, your daughter."

He didn't say anything. "I found your letter a long time ago and you said you wanted to see me. I've kept it hidden until I could get away. Mama wouldn't let me come then—"

"Tammy!" he interrupted me finally. "I think you. . . ."

I didn't hear the rest of what he said. I felt fear, anger, and the frustration of years come boiling up out of my soul and I burst into tears. Without knowing how it happened, I was inside the door with my arms around his neck, sobbing. His hands came up and settled on my shoulders and he just held me there until I stopped blubbering.

"Here," he said. "Come on over here and sit down." I sort of collapsed onto the overstuffed chair and took the handkerchief he held out. He squatted down on his knees in front of me.

"I'm sorry. I know this must be a shock, but I didn't know how to get in touch with you. It just got so bad at home that I had to leave." Maybe I shouldn't have sprung it on him so suddenly, because as soon as I said those words he leaned back on his heels. His mouth opened and he looked as surprised as if I had slapped him.

"You . . . you've run away?" The situation was becoming almost funny. I had found my father after a separation, and all we could do was stutter and stammer at each other. I tried to grin, but it felt lopsided. "Yeah," I said. "About four months ago."

"Your mother must be worried sick." I saw his eyes turn toward the telephone and it wasn't funny anymore.

"No! No, please. Don't call," I begged. The all-too-familiar feeling of panic started growing inside of me. "I can't," I said and hiccupped. "I won't go back. I'll run away again!" My voice rose and got louder as I spoke. My father, Nelson, took my hands in his. I inspected his hands through tears. His nails were so clean and trimmed. His fingers long and slender, like mine.

"Why can't you go back, Tammy?"

He asked the question in a real soft voice, so I answered in a whisper, like we were sharing a secret. Until then the secret had been mine, and it was a dark one. "My stepfather."

I heard him groan and then I was on the floor beside him, cradled in his arms. "Daddy, I had to do some awful things to get here. I didn't have any money."

"Don't cry. You're safe now. He patted my back and assured me that I was going to be okay. I felt safe for the first time in a long time.

Three years have passed since that night. I've grown up, turned eighteen last month. I'm going to go take my GED test. Nelson made sure I kept up my studies, even though I couldn't go to school and have them asking questions about transferring school records and all that. Then I'm going to call my mother. I promised Nelson I would as soon as I was sure she couldn't make me go back.

As strange as it all was, we laugh about that night now. You see, he told me the whole story after a while. This Mr. Robinson had only lived in that house one year. The real estate people told him the house had been empty for years. I have no idea where my father is. Maybe one day I'll even look for him again.

The Mr. Robinson I found had lost his wife and daughter in a car accident. He'd moved to Milford Springs to start life over again. We moved away from there to a place where no one knew us and we started over together. I still have a lot to learn about him. The main thing is, I know I'm still safe with him.

My father's name? Yes, it's Nelson Robinson, too. But this one? I just call him Dad.

THE END

CONFESSIONS OF A DESPERATE HOUSEWIFE
"I Ruined The Neighborhood"

I never meant to break my wedding vows. Never meant to alienate all of my friends. I only wanted to fill a need within my soul for fun and spontaneity.

Scott, my husband, and I were discussing my desire for a pool at dinner this past spring. I used to swim competitively in high school and college and wanted to be able to get in the water whenever the mood struck. The pool would appease me and encourage me to get back into shape, I told him.

Scott had a business buddy who installs in-ground pools during the summer. He owed Scott a favor, so Scott agreed to the pool and suggested that we hire Jake from down the road to do the landscaping for the backyard. Jake could always use extra cash, Scott said, because his wife stays home with their two toddlers since daycare is so expensive. I'd always liked Jake's family and it felt good to help them out.

At the beginning of the summer we had a neighborhood block party. Our neighborhood was close-knit for the most part, often having impromptu baseball games, scrapbooking parties, and progressive dinners. Every family was represented that day. That was when Jake's wife announced that she was three months pregnant.

I was happy for them, but also concerned. Three kids under four years old are a lot of work and a lot of crying. Jake didn't have a regular, year-round job. Another mouth to feed could be a burden.

I wanted to get ready for bathing suit season and knock Scott's socks off when he saw me. Regardless of the lack of interest on Scott's part, I wanted him to want me. I needed to be desired. Figuring it was the belly I'd acquired that turned him off, I was ready to work out.

The first thing I had to do was find a running buddy. I called on my friends in the neighborhood for support. I set up a schedule to run with Lisa three mornings a week, and when the weather was bad we did Tae-Bo in her basement.

When I wasn't exercising or planning healthy meals, I scrapbooked with three other women from the neighborhood. We all became great friends. I felt like I could call any of the women and ask them to watch our daughter, and I was available to return the favor.

When the pool was finally in the crystal, blue water sparkled in the late morning sun. Jake had been working full-time on the landscaping. He was bent over, adding stones to the landscaping, and I couldn't help but sigh at the sight of his naked back.

The affair started one afternoon after I returned home from shopping. Lisa and I went shopping as a reward for my twenty-pound weight loss. I was so excited about trying on new bathing suits. She picked out a bikini that was skimpier than anything I'd ever worn.

I tried it on and was pleased with what I saw in the mirrors. It wasn't half-bad and I impulsively bought it. A few more pounds and I'd actually allow myself to be seen in public wearing it. I tucked my purchase in the bottom of my sock drawer and went out to the pool in my tankini, still two pieces like a bikini, but way more coverage.

"Hi, Jake," I said, trying not to scare him.

We'd been talking every day while he worked. It was never about anything of substance and never about our families. It was like flirting from junior high school, but I never felt shy around him.

"Hi, yourself, Holly," he answered. "You look fantastic. Did you do something different?"

I shrugged. "Nothing special, just some shopping. Retail therapy always makes me happy."

"Come here. I want to show you something I found."

He motioned for me to join him near the edge of the patio. Leaning over, he pointed to an object in the dirt.

"See it?"

He put his arm over my shoulder and drew me toward him. He pointed.

I glanced at his face so close to mine, and then focused on what he was trying to show me. My heart was beating out of my chest. I knew feeling like that was wrong on so many levels, but just being so near a man who really saw me turned my insides to jelly.

It was some sort of coin.

"What is it?" I asked, turning to look at him.

He didn't move his arm and I didn't ask him to.

"I think it's a medallion."

"What's it doing here?" I whispered.

It was his turn to shrug. Our heads almost touched and I couldn't break eye contact with him. The heat from his body radiated and it felt like my skin would burn.

"Holly?"

"Yeah?"

"I want to kiss you."

And just like that, he did. It was thrilling, dangerous, and I knew it was wrong, but at that moment I didn't care. It was the most male attention I'd had in months. The medallion was soon forgotten as we started making out behind a full bush, out of sight of anyone driving past.

I'd never noticed Jake other than as our neighbor until that summer. Sure he's handsome, but so is Scott. It wasn't until Jake began to work at our house that I really got to know him. He was always getting calls from his wife, who I could hear whining on the other end of the line, or demanding Jake work faster and earn more money.

"I'm just so glad to be out of the house," he'd said as he added another plant around the pool.

I brought him snacks and cold drinks when I had time to chat for a while. He told me about the exciting things he used to do before he settled down, and I always heard the longing in his voice. I knew what he meant.

Before we'd had our daughter, Scott and I used to travel all over the country. We thought nothing about hopping a plane, then boarding a cruise to the Caribbean for a week. Now everything has to be planned around sports, school, and work. I love my daughter, so I don't mind sacrificing, but the excitement and spontaneity is gone from our relationship.

Maybe that's why Jake was so tempting. He was handsome and he noticed me. He commented when I got my hair styled differently, or when I started wearing lower-cut bathing suits to the pool. Scott didn't notice my hair until I mentioned it, and then he just rolled his eyes.

The weight was coming off and my body was getting toned in all the right places. I kept up my running and started lifting weights because the experts say it helps burn calories faster.

Guilt was my daily companion, but the thrill of the forbidden relationship with Jake was like a drug. I looked forward to his visits and I found excitement in his arms. Scott went to work at his safe job selling products for a paper company. My daughter spent her days at summer camp, leaving me free to hang around the house when I wasn't running errands or socializing. However, I found more and more reasons to stay close to home as the summer went on

It's not like I gave up on my marriage. Scott was a great guy. We'd been married for eight years. Things were just functional. The spark had died when our daughter was born and it never re-ignited. Granted, I'd gained some weight with the baby and maybe I wasn't as cute as I was before we got married, but I wasn't undesirable. Sex was once a month—maybe.

The day my new bikini fit, I'd never felt sexier. The outfit would be totally lost on Scott, who had left for work without saying goodbye. I know Jake will appreciate the effort, I thought.

It was the hottest day of the summer when I checked my bikini and slipped out on to the newly laid patio.

"Hiya, Jake. Need something cold to drink?"

Jake stood up quickly, spinning around toward me. He gave me the once-over and from the heat that registered in his eyes I could tell he approved of the new suit.

"Everyone gone?" he asked, gesturing at the house and moving toward me.

I nodded, excitement and guilt still warring in my head.

"Then how about a dip? I'm roasting already."

He ran his hand across his chest. I agreed to the dip and he threw off his tool belt and lunged at me, circling his arms around my waist and pulling me into the pool. He still had on his denim shorts, but he obviously didn't mind being wet and having his clothes cling to him. Playing and being spontaneous made the relationship extra-special for both of us. We were never awkward with one another.

We hit the water together and surfaced at the same time.

"Hey," I said. "I'm not sure this bathing suit is supposed to get wet."

"You bought a bathing suit that can't get wet?"

He roared with laughter, and then his eyes darkened. Jake swam closer and kissed me.

"Someday we'll be together."

"I know."

I believed that he was telling the truth. In moments like that I separated myself from my real life, from my husband and our seven-year-old daughter. Luckily, they knew nothing about my affair with our neighbor and landscaper.

Our affair had been going on for three months. Jake kept finding reasons to come over to tweak the landscaping and to see me. There was always a new bush to put in, more mulch where the rain washed it away, something to bring him to me during the day when Scott was gone. On that day, Jake was there to stabilize some rocks.

Jake pushed me into the corner of the pool. I couldn't wait for him to touch me. When he did, he sent shivers through my body.

After a little while, I broke away from our lovemaking to catching my breath.

"There's a big end-of-summer bash this weekend," I stated.

He already knew about it because I'd been talking to his wife about what they'd bring.

"How are we going to be able to be there without giving this away?" I asked, pulling him closer to me. "I could barely talk to your wife without coming clean to her."

"I don't know how we'll stay away from one another at the picnic. Stay with Scott and I'll stick to my family. Just don't wear anything too revealing or I won't be able to keep my hands off you."

My heart flipped. I'd wanted to be desired like that for so many years. He wants to leave his wife, I rationalized with myself. He just can't yet because of the baby. I wasn't sure I was ready to leave Scott, or if I would ever be ready. Talking about being together was different than breaking up our families and actually being together.

We played in the pool for a while before Jake climbed out and wrapped up in a towel that hung over the fence he'd installed. I stepped out of the pool and into the towel Jake held out for me.

I was at the kitchen table looking through pool catalogues when Scott arrived home that night. I kissed him lightly on the cheek he offered me and smiled.

"Did you have a good day?"

He started telling me about how one company wanted to steal his customers. I only half listened.

"I'm going for a swim," he said.

I nodded, but I didn't move.

"Wanna join me?"

"I've already been in today. Maybe Cassie would like to swim with you."

He nodded before leaving to search for Cassie.

"I think she's upstairs in her room."

"Holly, what's this?" he asked, returning a minute later.

Scott held out the wet bikini I'd left in the upstairs bathroom.

"It's my new suit. You like it?"

"There's not enough here to like. You didn't wear this in front of Jake, did you? Did he come over?"

I felt anxiety creep up my throat. I'd always wondered if Scott knew, or suspected, what Jake and I did all day.

"Of course not. What do you think I am, an exhibitionist?" I lied.

"No," he said. "But with your new body and a new suit, I don't know what to think."

I felt my insides well up with anger. He's noticed my new look, but he never said anything? I tears stung my eyes. I grabbed the bathing suit and I ran up to our bedroom.

Why he couldn't tell me those things when he noticed? Why do I have to get compliments from the neighbor? I pushed the pillows off the bed and screamed. I'd woven such a thick web of lies and deceit that I felt I would never recover. I began to plan what life with Jake would look like.

The day of the end-of-summer block party was sunny and hot. I wanted to wear something light and breezy, but Jake's words floated through my mind. "I won't be able to keep my hands off you." I wore a golf shirt with a collar, which I buttoned up. I looked like Cassie's very yuppie mother.

"You look nice," Scott commented, and then he kissed my cheek as we left. I wanted to throw my hands in the air and yell, "What gives!" but I didn't.

The party was hopping when we got there. I stopped to talk to a few friends, but I couldn't keep myself from scanning the crowd for Jake. Stop it. Not here.

"No, I haven't heard about Mrs. Tipton's hip replacement," I told one neighbor, who had to repeat every detail to me.

Scott left me with a kiss on my forehead halfway through the description of the surgery.

I excused myself after the mention of the follow-up visit, saying I had to check on Cassie. Well, Cassie was playing with her friends at some carnival games set up by one family. I hunted for Scott and spotted him deep in conversation with Jake. My heart thudded loudly and my stomach fell to my freshly painted toes.

I slid up to Scott, linking my arm in his.

"Hi, sweetie. What's going on?"

I shot a frightened look at Jake, but he reassured me with a smile.

"Your husband was just complementing me on the work I've been doing around your yard," Jake said.

"I'll add my compliments, too, then. It's like a tropical paradise out there, and very private."

I didn't want to go overboard, but the comment about privacy caused a reaction in Jake. His eyes dilated and I saw him getting uncomfortable.

Jake excused himself after that. He said he was off to find his wife and his rugrats.

"Do you think Jake is uncomfortable around you?" Scott asked.

"Why?"

"He couldn't get away fast enough once you showed up."

"He probably missed his wife. Some guys are like that."

I'd started to walk away when Scott reached for my hand.

"I miss you when I'm not home. I haven't been able to get that bikini off my mind. I haven't seen you wear anything like that in so long," he whispered in my ear. "Let's get out of here."

I looked over his shoulder into Jake's heated gaze.

"Sure, honey. I'll let Cassie know to come home when the party's over."

With the block party and summer behind us, Jake and I started sneaking away to hotels. Our yard looked like a jungle and Scott told Jake not to add any more plants. One weekend in the fall I booked a spa getaway in Arizona. Jake told his wife he had a landscaping conference in Phoenix at the tail end of my trip. Of course he didn't mention me.

We spent the weekend making love and laughing. There was no chance of us being discovered, so we made reservations at area restaurants and hung out by the hotel pool. I even packed the bikini that wasn't supposed to get wet. The pressure of being discovered was off and we were like honeymooners.

One afternoon, I dove into the pool to cool off when Lisa's husband walked past Jake.

"Hi, stranger. I didn't realize you were down here. Are you alone?"

My heart stopped for the full time it took Jake to answer.

"Yes. I came alone, but guess who I ran into? Holly from down the street. She's on some spa thing."

Greg scanned the area until his eyes rested on me and flickered to my barely there bathing suit. I smiled and waved.

"Small world," I said, trying to act casual.

"Sure is," Greg answered.

He mentioned a meeting and ran off after one more look from me to Jake.

Jake and I both started talking at the same time.

"What are the chances?"

"How in the world are we going to explain this?"

"It's a coincidence," he said. "Nothing more."

"We've got to stop doing this. You're wife's going to have the baby any day and she'll need you around. When we get back we have. . . ."

"Don't say it."

"I can't risk everyone finding out."

That night we made love like it was the last time we'd ever see one another, even though he lived down the road. We both realized that our relationship wasn't permanent. Jake wasn't going to leave his wife and things were starting to get better with Scott and me. Nonetheless, I couldn't help crying after he left my room that night.

I arrived home an hour before I saw Jake's car pull into his driveway. My heart was broken, but I knew ending it was for the best. What had started out as an infatuation and a break from the mundane had gone too far. I never wanted to hurt anyone, and almost getting caught in Phoenix was too close for comfort.

My phone rang and I answered it. A small part of my heart hoped it was Jake, begging me to reconsider.

"Did you hear about Jake?" Lisa asked without even saying hello.

"No, what about him?"

"He's having an affair."

I started choking on nothing. I coughed to clear my throat.

"No way."

I felt the heat crawl up my face. Did Lisa's husband say something?

"When does Jake have time to have an affair?"

My mind was reeling. What am I going to do?

"I don't know. Tammy called and she was crying. She'd locked herself in the bathroom. She's due any day and that can't be good for her. You saw Jake in Phoenix. Did you see him with anyone?"

I was surprised she couldn't hear my heart beating.

"No. I only saw him a couple of times and no one was with him. Maybe Tammy is suffering from pregnancy paranoia."

"Yeah, maybe."

Lisa laughed, but it sounded canned to my ears.

The affair has to be over now. The whole thing is so close to blowing up in our faces. Suspicions are swirling through the neighborhood like a snowstorm. I was afraid to say anything more for fear I'd incriminate myself with Lisa.

I suggested that our family try a new church in the next town over. I'd never been overly religious, but it seemed like a good time to start looking for divine intervention. Cassie could start Sunday school. As long as lightning didn't strike me when I entered the church, maybe I could repent for a few of my sins. Scott said he had to finish some paperwork, so Cassie and I went by ourselves.

Everyone was so friendly. The guilt pounded in my ears, but I ignored it. I tried not to think that the sermon about adultery was directed at me. I felt better as we left the church. God understands that we all make mistakes. I'll be fine as long as no one knows I'm the one Jake had been sleeping with.

It was the following Wednesday that I ruined the neighborhood. I knew going to Jake's house was a bad idea and risky, but his wife was in the hospital after having delivered their baby boy a few days earlier. I needed to see him, to make sure he was okay. We hadn't spoken since that last night, but whenever I saw him I couldn't help the lingering looks we exchanged.

Jake was on the lawnmower when I stopped by.

"How's it going?" I asked.

"Why don't you come inside?" he said, looking up and down the street.

I was tempted. When he added "please," I caved. He led me into the house with his hand on my back. There was no talk of us getting back together. I asked him how he was doing with the new baby and the other kids. He asked if we had closed the pool for the winter. We were sitting next to one another, holding hands over the corner of the table like old friends, when Lisa burst through the door.

"How could you do this, you tramp?" she screamed. "These are your friends!"

I jumped to my feet.

"What are you talking about?" I asked, fearing she was talking about exactly what I thought she was talking about.

"You and Jake? Sneaking around like a bunch of sex-starved teenagers? I've been watching you since my husband saw you two in Phoenix. It's disgusting."

I wanted to explain, but there were no words.

"It's not like that," I said, adding a silent "this time," but Lisa put up her hand to stop me.

"Shut up. We're done. I can't trust you ever again. No one in the neighborhood will trust you."

She turned and started to walk out.

"Wait, Lisa. I can explain."

"Does Scott know? Of course not. You wouldn't be here cheating on your husband the second Jake's wife gave birth to his third child! What about the sanctity of marriage? You both make me sick." She latched onto my hand and pulled me out of the house. "If you can't control yourself, I'm not leaving you there with him."

I was mortified. I wasn't a stupid kid who got caught in a compromising position with her boyfriend. The only thing I got caught doing was comforting a friend who was under a lot of stress. Our affair was over and done with. No one should have ever found out.

Within hours the neighborhood was abuzz with the gossip. Lisa told Jake's wife about me two weeks after the baby was born. My phone stopped ringing and Scott began to ask questions about why we weren't invited to the neighborhood Halloween party.

I still hadn't told Scott about the affair. I wondered if he'd heard the gossip when he was around town. He began to compliment me more and told me he loved me regularly. I considered telling him the truth, but it wasn't something that came up in everyday conversation. I had decided to forget about the whole thing.

The debate in my mind ended at church one Sunday, when Lisa and her family came to the service. She must have thought I'd already told Scott, because she confronted him.

"I'm so glad you stayed with Holly after what happened with Jake. It's a tragedy to see families break up over infidelity."

Scott's chin hit the floor. I'm sure I heard it. I was afraid to look at him, afraid to breathe, and I glared at Lisa. Guilt, remorse, and pure terror struck me. I left church that day not knowing what God had in store for me. I guess I deserved everything He punished me with.

I've attended church every Sunday since that day and I even volunteer to make snacks for coffee hour. Jake and I didn't speak again. When he saw me, he crossed to the other side of the road. Tammy kept him on a tight rein and I couldn't blame her.

I called her after the Halloween party we weren't invited to, but she never answered. I also emailed Lisa several times, but with no reply. I miss my friends and if I had to do it all over again, I'd spend more time with Scott working on our relationship and less time out by the pool.

Scott decided to stay with Cassie and me, even after he knew everything. We still shared a bed and I know he tried to trust me. My parents watched Cassie for a week while Scott and I took a spontaneous cruise to the Caribbean. I was excited and happy that we could get our relationship back on track. I arrived home more in love with Scott than I had been for many years.

Scott died in his sleep two weeks after we returned from the cruise. The neighbors told one another that Scott died of a broken heart, and that he was a saint to stay with someone as unfaithful as I was, even for a few weeks.

I was crushed at his death. Loneliness and sorrow drowned my very existence. I turned back to the church and the tentative friendships I'd started to form there. My neighbors never came around, although they did go to Scott's funeral.

Every so often I'd look out to the pool. I thought about the thrill I'd gotten from Jake's attention, but it didn't bring me comfort. I still felt bad that Tammy was punishing him, but I have my own demons to live with.

THE END

CONFESSIONS OF A WORKING GIRL
My Husband Forced Me To Be The Breadwinner

I frowned as I picked up the jar of spaghetti sauce from the counter. "This isn't the brand I usually buy," I said to Jordan, my husband. "I always get the kind with the chunks of tomato in it."

Jordan laughed. "Which costs almost a dollar more a jar," he replied a bit smugly.

"Don't worry, honey. I bought some ripe tomatoes at the farmers' market on the way home from the grocery store. If I cut those up and put them in the sauce, it will taste even better. And the kids loved seeing the farmers' market."

Jesse, one of the twins, walked into the kitchen and hugged his father's leg. "It was great!" he said enthusiastically "There were miles and miles of booths with all this food and this one lady gave me and Jared free apples! She said we were cute and looked like her grandsons."

I stared at him for a long moment. "You boys had a great time at the grocery store and the farmers' market?" I finally repeated in disbelief. "You always hate going shopping with me!"

Jesse shrugged. "Dad made it really fun," he replied matter-of-factly. "He gave us five coupons and we had to try and find the stuff in the grocery store. I found mine right away and then I helped Jared. Then we went to the new playground by the church."

"Wow, that sounds like a fun afternoon," I said, trying not to sound as bitter as I felt. I turned to look at Jordan. "But that didn't leave you much time to work on your resume or make any follow-up calls on those job leads you had."

Jordan's face grew serious and he took a deep breath. "I've been doing some thinking about that," he answered slowly. "Look, Rachel, we need to face the facts. There aren't going to be a lot of job opportunities out there for me, at least not in the computer field, and definitely not for the salary I was making. That's why I got laid off in the first place. The field is changing too fast for me to play catch-up. There are plenty of kids just coming out of college who are better trained than I am."

"I know all that," I replied gently. "But you're good at what you do. If you just keep looking, surely something will turn up. I know it's been frustrating, but you have to be patient."

"Maybe," he agreed evenly. "And I intend to keep sending my resume out and looking for work."

"So, what are you saying?" I asked, puzzled. "What have you been thinking about?"

He took a deep breath. "The twins are out of kindergarten in a month," he replied quietly. "Then they're out of school for the whole summer. Remember last summer, when you'd just started to work part-time? It was a nightmare! First Jesse got bronchitis and then Jared broke his wrist. We both had to take time off work and if your parents hadn't been around to help, one of us would've had to quit working! If I'm not working, that solves the childcare problem. I'd be here."

"You'd be here?" I repeated slowly, not really understanding. "At home with the twins? As in not looking for a job at all?"

He grinned and gave me a quick kiss. "As in being realistic about my life," he replied easily. "I've sent my resume out to every company in the state that might be looking to hire. I've told everyone I know, even called people I worked with right out of college. Sure, if a great job comes along I'll grab it. I'm just not too hopeful. In the meantime, we're lucky that you're working."

"But I make about half of what you used to," I said, shaking my head. "We have mortgage and car payments, and the insurance."

"Rachel, I said I'd been giving this a lot of thought," he answered, frowning slightly. "I've been looking over our budget and there are plenty of ways we can cut back. For starters, think of what we'll save just on daycare alone!

"And," he continued excitedly. "The grocery shopping is just a start! We never have time to do much cooking—or use coupons—or send in for refunds on things. I can start making more of the meals at home and we'll cut down on the takeout costs.

"And I can do most of the car repairs and paint the bathroom," he continued. "I can do all of the little things we keep putting off because we don't have the time to do them."

In my head, I knew that what Jordan was saying made perfect sense, but my heart was telling me something completely different. I hadn't planned on being the sole breadwinner of the family while my husband raised our children. That put a lot of responsibility on me, and I didn't like it.

Jordan looked at me expectantly. "Well?" he finally asked.

"Well, what?" I snapped impatiently. "It sounds like you've already decided what you're going to do about looking for a job. What do you want me to say about all this?"

He looked hurt. "I want you to say that it sounds like a good idea," he said quietly. "I want you to say that you think my staying home would be good for the kids and our family. It would make a more stable life for the kids."

Jordan was obviously upset and looking to me for reassurance. This last year had been hard on all of us, and I knew his self-esteem had suffered when his boss had told him he was no longer needed at the company.

"Honey, I'm sorry," I replied quickly. "It's just that it puts a lot of pressure on me. What if something happens to my job? I mean, I think it's fairly secure right now, but that could change at any time."

"Then we deal with that situation when it comes up," he interrupted quickly. "Look, Rachel, I'm not happy about not being able to get a job. I talked to Steve Lewis and he said he'd probably have a couple of consulting jobs for me in a few weeks. It won't bring in much money, but it will be something."

I'd obviously hurt Jordan's feelings and I felt bad about that. I knew it wasn't his fault that he had been laid off, and that the computer field had somehow jumped ahead without him. Still, I felt angry and bitter. I didn't want to be the only one working! It didn't seem right.

"I'm just tired," I said, giving him a quick kiss. "It was a long day at work and I'm exhausted. We can talk about this later."

Jordan nodded. "Why don't you take a nice, hot bath," he suggested gently. "The boys and I will start dinner. You've got plenty of time to relax."

A long, hot bath was exactly what I needed, and I knew I should be grateful that I had married such an understanding and thoughtful husband. But I wasn't feeling grateful at all. My world was slowly turning upside down, and I didn't know how to handle it.

As I sank into the hot, soapy water, I closed my eyes and sighed. I love Jordan with all my heart, but I couldn't stop feeling mad at him. I hated to admit it, even to myself, but I felt I was losing respect for him. It seemed like he was giving up and taking the easy way out. I didn't want to be with someone I didn't respect.

Of course it hadn't always been that way. When I first met Jordan, I thought he was probably the smartest man I'd ever known! We had a chemistry class together in college. I couldn't help but notice that he barely paid attention to the teacher, yet he always got a perfect score on the tests. Whenever he was called on in class, he seemed to know the answer, even before she'd finished asking the question! Finally, I'd stopped him after class one day.

"How do you do that?" I asked curiously. "You don't even listen to Professor Winston's lecture and you know everything she's going to ask in class. Are you just naturally that smart?"

He looked puzzled, then grinned at me. "I guess I am," he

answered matter-of-factly. "At least, I know more than she does."

I stared at him in amazement. "Really?" I asked, slightly taken aback. "You think you know more than a college professor?"

He shrugged. "I know I do," he answered calmly. "But I have to take this class to graduate. And, if you notice, she takes attendance pretty religiously. It's probably what she does best."

"Don't you think that's kind of, well, conceited of you?" I asked, shaking my head.

"I don't think so," he answered honestly. "She's not a great teacher. She's just reading from the textbook in front of her. I have the same book and I'm already done with it. I could tell you exactly what she's going to say tomorrow and what she'll put on the test. She's predictable. I don't even know why she's teaching."

I tilted my head to study him. "Well, maybe you could help me," I finally said. "I'm barely passing her class. She's not at all predictable to me."

He grinned again. "I think that would be fun," he said. "Do you have time for a cup of coffee now?"

Jordan was cute, and a genius. He helped me raise my chemistry grade to a B, and I had to admit I learned more from him than the professor. It didn't take long for me to fall completely in love with him.

He wasn't like the other guys I'd dated—always out to prove they were the strongest or the bravest or the smartest. Jordan was pretty content just being who he was. He never bragged, he simply accomplished things and let me discover what they were.

He was offered a job at one of the most prestigious electronics companies in the country before we'd even graduated. I was shocked when he told me how much they'd offered as a starting salary, and saddened when he said the job was in a different state. I could only stare at him for a long moment.

"It's so far away," I said finally. "At least three hours by car from here, you know."

He looked surprised. "I thought you'd be happy," he answered slowly. "It's a great opportunity. And I knew there wouldn't be many jobs right around here. I mean this is a college town basically."

I was shocked at how casual he sounded about taking a job so far away from me, and the future I thought we had together! "What about us?" I demanded, finally finding my voice. "I mean, I thought we had something special going on between us. Did you give any thought to me when you decided to take this job?"

His frown deepened. "You'll come with, of course," he answered, sounding a bit confused. "Won't you?"

"Go with you?" I repeated slowly. "Are you asking me to marry you or just tag along?"

He smiled. "I thought that was obvious," he answered. "We love each other. Of course we'll get married."

I didn't know whether to laugh or cry. It was probably the most unromantic proposal in history, but it was also just like Jordan to simply assume we were both thinking the same way and he didn't have to explain himself! That was actually one of the reasons I loved him so much.

"Of course I'll marry you!" I said, after thinking it over for all of half a second. "I love you!"

We got married a few weeks after we both graduated and barely had time for a honeymoon before Jordan started his job. I managed to find a job right away as well, but I was only making a fraction of Jordan's salary. I was proud of him, but I couldn't help the twinge of jealousy I felt. After all, we had both gone through four years of college. Why was his education worth so much more than mine?

Still, I couldn't deny that I liked the things his salary could buy. We both liked to eat out, and I'd always had a weakness for clothes and jewelry. We celebrated our second anniversary by putting a deposit on a beautiful home in a nice suburb. We weren't millionaires by any means, but we could afford nice furnishings for the house and we both drove new cars.

By our third anniversary, I was ready to start a family. Jordan agreed that having a baby sounded like a wonderful idea, and he was more than ready to start our family.

I frowned. "But I'll want to stay home with our baby," I continued slowly. "I mean, we have a lot of money in our savings account, and you make more than enough to pay the mortgage and our other expenses.

"I wouldn't need to stay home forever," I continued quietly. "Just until they start school."

Jordan laughed. "They?" he repeated. "Aren't we going to start out with just one baby?"

"Well, we don't want an only child," I replied matter-of-factly. "We have to have at least two."

Jordan gathered me up in his arms. "We can have twenty as far as I'm concerned," he said, kissing me. "In fact, let's get started on that project right now."

He carried me into the bedroom and made love to me tenderly and passionately. "Wouldn't it be great if we started the baby right now?" I whispered.

"You stopped taking the Pill about twenty minutes ago," he teased me lightly. "I don't think anything happens that fast."

But, in my own mind, I was hoping for exactly that. I was young and healthy and it never crossed my mind that I wouldn't get pregnant when I wanted to.

But I didn't get pregnant. I tried not to worry as month after month went by, but I couldn't help it. Suddenly, everyone around me seemed to be pregnant: sisters, girlfriends, cousins, and even complete strangers. What was wrong with me?

One night, I couldn't help but feel overwhelmed with sadness. I called my sister, Raylene, and started sobbing.

"Rachel, what is it?" she asked in alarm.

"Why can't I get pregnant?" I blurted out. "I want a baby more than anything in the world! I thought it would just happen and it's not!"

"Hey, slow down," she broke in worriedly. "You're working yourself up into a panic attack."

"Well, that's what I feel like," I replied unhappily. "I am starting to panic! Jordan and I love each other and we want a baby, but. . . ."

"Rachel, calm down," she interrupted sharply. "You're letting yourself get all worked up before you even know there's a problem."

I was surprised at her tone. "You sound like you're mad at me," I said, sniffling. "I thought you'd be sympathetic."

She sighed and her tone softened slightly. "I'm not mad at you, Rachel," she replied patiently. "But you always make such a big deal out of things! I remember when you didn't get the Christmas present you wanted in fourth grade. It was the doll that could cry tears, and—"

"Raylene, I can't believe you think this is the same thing!" I interrupted furiously. "I was a child then! This is a real baby I'm talking about, not a doll!"

She sighed again. "The point is, you got the doll you wanted on your next birthday," she answered. "It wasn't the end of the world and neither is this. But you can't just sit around feeling sorry for yourself. That's not going to help."

I was definitely getting angry. "I called because I thought you might try to be sympathetic," I said, a bit sulkily. "Not lecture on what's wrong with me."

She laughed merrily. "Rachel, I'm trying to tell you not to worry," she said calmly. "Look, there are all sorts of treatments for this kind of thing if you really are having trouble getting pregnant. I can give you the name of a good doctor who specializes in this."

"Okay," I said quietly. "But what if—"

"Rachel," Raylene interrupted, sounding exasperated. "At least wait until you talk to the doctor before you give up hope. You have to stop imagining the worst is going to happen."

"Okay," I managed to whisper. "I'll go see the doctor."

Raylene turned out to be absolutely right about everything. The doctor assured me that Jordan and I were perfectly healthy. "Just go home and try to relax," he said calmly. "And—"

"But surely there's something I can do," I interrupted, frowning. "I mean, I've heard there are techniques for helping things along."

Dr. Garrison smiled and shook his head. "Yes, that's true," he agreed. "But I don't think you and Jordan need concern yourself with anything that complicated right now. Sometimes, the best judge of the right time to have a baby is still Mother Nature."

I was glad that Dr. Garrison had found nothing wrong with us, but I was fuming by the time I got home. "Imagine saying something so ridiculous!" I said to Jordan. "Mother Nature? What is the point of all the research and technology if doctors are still going to say things like 'let nature takes its course'?"

"Honey, I agree with him," Jordan replied, frowning slightly. "You're getting yourself all worked up for nothing. The doctor said there was nothing wrong with us. Why can't you accept that and just relax?"

"I want a baby," I replied stubbornly. "I don't want to just sit back and relax."

Jordan couldn't hide his smile. "Well, maybe we should lie down and relax," he suggested, winking. "I mean, that is how babies are made, right?"

My eyes widened in fury. "I can't believe you're joking about this!" I said angrily.

Jordan sighed unhappily. "Rachel, I want a baby, too," he reminded me. "But you're making us both miserable when you act this way. I want to make love to you and you make it seem like some sort of chore you have to get through so you can get pregnant."

We fought and then made up over and over again. It was a horrible, tension-filled time, but I forgot everything the moment the doctor told me I was pregnant. I couldn't believe the joy that overwhelmed me!

I made Jordan a special dinner that night—steak, baked potatoes, and double chocolate brownies.

He looked at me suspiciously. "What's all this?" he asked. "These are all my favorites."

I kissed him. "We need to talk," I began softly. "I mean I need to talk and have you listen. I found out today that I'm pregnant. We're pregnant! And I want to apologize for how awful I've been to you. . . ." Jordan cut me off in mid-sentence by grabbing me and kissing me soundly.

"I love you," he said huskily. "Don't apologize, please. Everything is perfect! We're going to have a baby."

It was a magical evening. We ate and talked until late about the baby and all the things we would do. Finally, we fell asleep after making love. It felt like everything had fallen into place at last.

And I did feel blessed, but the pregnancy was far from easy. I worried about everything. I just wanted everything to go perfectly.

Then, another miracle. We found out I was carrying twins! I was thrilled and scared out of my mind. "Twins," I whispered, staring at the ultrasound.

Jordan was equally stunned. "Yeah," he said finally. "Two babies."

"Two babies," I echoed stupidly. "Not one."

The doctor laughed. "The reality of it will sink in soon," he promised. "And there's nothing to worry about. Both babies look just fine."

I managed to nod. "Thank you, doctor," I said, shaking my head. "It just took so long to get pregnant and now there are two babies."

"That's how it works sometimes," he agreed with a smile. "Well, you have six months to get ready for them."

Our family and friends were excited for us and I tried not to worry, but late at night, I wondered if I was ready to be a mother to two babies.

Jordan laughed at me when I told him of my fears. "Honey, you'll be a great mother," he assured me. "This is what you've been dreaming about your whole life and now it's happening. In fact, it's probably twice the experience you thought it would be. Can't you just relax and enjoy yourself?"

I nodded slowly. "You're right," I agreed. "I know I'm driving myself crazy for no reason. I'll try to just enjoy being pregnant for a while."

And there was a lot to enjoy about being pregnant. My body was changing constantly. I can't say I was happy about gaining so much weight, but the idea that two babies were growing inside me was absolutely thrilling.

I've always heard that women forget the pain of childbirth once they see their babies. I'm not exactly sure that's true, but the pain seemed a distant memory when I first saw my twin boys!

"Oh, Jordan," I said in awe. "Look at them! They're so beautiful. Can you believe how perfect they are?"

He nodded and grinned. "I would say you're prejudiced, but you're absolutely right!" he agreed proudly.

We had already agreed on the names Jared and Jesse after both of our fathers. The only hard part was remembering which one was which!

Those first few months were both wonderful and exhausting. I thought I was prepared to be a mother until I actually had the responsibility of two tiny lives. I worried constantly that I was doing everything right for them. Were they getting enough to eat? Was the room too hot or cold?

Jordan was always much more relaxed and calmer, and he tried to get me to stop fussing so much.

"Rachel, you're not enjoying Jared and Jesse," he cautioned me. "They're wonderful, healthy babies. They're not going to break."

I gradually realized that the babies were fine and growing just as they should. It was still exhausting, but wonderful. They were adorable children, and people often stopped to admire them.

There was no question, at least in my mind, that my place was at home with the twins and not at work. Jordan was supportive, but not as convinced, as I was that I needed to be home full-time.

"Honey, I think it's great that you want to be with them," he said slowly. "But they'd be fine in a daycare, too. In fact, they might learn to socialize a bit. I'm a little bit worried that they only play with each other."

The truth was, the twins did seem to have a language all their own that only they understood. I thought it was wonderful that they had each other, but I could see that Jordan was concerned. Still, I wanted to keep them close to me for as long as I could.

"When they turn two," I conceded. "Then they could start a preschool class."

But when they were two, I only enrolled them for a couple of hours a day, and it didn't make sense for me to try and find a job around those hours. When they were three, Jared and Jesse were in school all morning. It gave me a chance to get my errands done and clean the house, but I still didn't think it was the right time for me to go back to work.

Jordan was making a good living and I really didn't see the urgency of my working, too. But I think Jordan knew that his job was in jeopardy and didn't want to worry me. He never complained when I didn't find a job, but he did seem concerned about our finances. He would look at our bills and frown several times, but he never said anything.

My sister, Raylene, brought up the subject one day when we took the kids to the playground. She looked at me for a long moment and then frowned slightly. "Don't you ever miss the adult world?" she asked bluntly.

I was taken by surprise. "What?" I asked, startled. "What do you mean by that, 'missing the adult world?' I'm still here."

She shrugged. "I mean, I can see you love the boys," she replied. "But don't you miss wearing something besides jeans and a sweatshirt? Don't you want to go back to work again and get your hair done and talk about something besides what toy they're giving away with the kid's meal and what new cartoons are on?"

"No, I don't miss it," I answered stubbornly. "If I were at work, I'd just worry about the boys anyway."

"But you have to leave them sometime," she pointed out. "And the longer you wait, the harder it's going to be to get back into the job market."

"Jordan makes a good living. There's no need for me to work."

"Geez, Rachel, you're not living in the 1950s, you know," she answered, sounding amused. "There are other reasons to work besides money. You're good at what you do and you trained hard to be good at it. But the money wouldn't hurt, either. Do you have any idea what braces cost these days? Not to mention college tuition?"

The truth was, my old boss had called me a couple of times, asking me if I wanted to come back to work. I was tempted, but the time just never seemed right. What if the boys got sick? What if I couldn't balance working and being a mother?

Of course I knew that millions of women do it and are very happy. I twirled my hair around one finger absently and tried to remember the last time I had my hair done at a beauty salon. And I hadn't bought a new dress for myself since the twins had been baptized.

"Well, I suppose I could try going part-time," I said slowly. "It might be good for me to get out of the house a bit."

It was easy to get my job back, but not so easy making everything work. On the days I had to be in early for a meeting, I could almost count on the boys spilling milk on the kitchen floor or forgetting where their shoes were. When they were sick, Jordan and I tried to figure out a fair solution. Working part-time felt like full-time because I had all the shopping and cleaning to do on my days off.

But the good part was that I did love my job. I liked sitting at my computer figuring out problems and feeling like I was actually contributing to something important. The money was nice and I realized I had missed "the adult world."

And the timing couldn't have been better: within six months of when I went back to work, Jordan's department was downsized and he was laid off. It turned out that Jordan had heard the rumors of layoffs for months, but he didn't want to worry me.

I was mad at him for hiding it from me, but I could also understand. "Look, Jordan," I began calmly. "We just have to face this one day at a time. I'll ask my boss if I can go to work full-time. We can switch the insurance and benefits over and it will be okay. But I don't want you hiding things to protect me. We're partners, remember?"

Jordan had hugged me then and promised not to hide anything. That's funny, I thought now, because he'd certainly hidden the fact that he wasn't going to try and go back to work!

Dinner was delicious and I had to admit that the sauce was great. I also knew it was wonderful that Jordan and the boys got to spend so much time together. But, still, something was nagging at me. The next day, I called my sister and told her about everything that had happened.

"I think I'm jealous," I said finally. "I want to be the one at home having fun with the boys."

Raylene paused for a long moment, and then burst out laughing. "Are you kidding me?" she asked at last. "Rachel, honey, I love Jesse and Jared with all my heart, but the last weekend I babysat them it took me two weeks to recover! I had Matt make me a pitcher of daiquiris when I got home and I sat on the couch for three hours just chilling out! Your twins never run out of energy from morning 'til night and they're constantly in trouble! You're acting like Jordan would be on some kind of vacation and nothing could be further from the truth."

"It's not that," I began unhappily. "I think. . . ."

"No, it's not," she interrupted quickly. "The problem is you can't imagine Jordan doing as good a job with the kids as you can. Or you don't want him to for some reason."

"That's ridiculous!" I snapped angrily.

"Is it? Face it, Rachel! Somewhere in the back of your mind, you think that you should be the one at home raising the kids and Jordan should be out supporting you! But if you're really, really honest with yourself, you'll admit Jordan is just as capable as you are of taking care of the kids. He's a wonderful father and you know it."

I opened my mouth to protest, and then realized she was right. "Well, but don't you think it's a bit strange he even wants to stay home?" I asked uncertainly. "Shouldn't he want a career?"

"He's had a career," she pointed out. "And he'll have one again. But right now, he's also got two sons to think about. Rachel, who else would you rather have taking care of them?"

"No one," I admitted. "I know Jordan is great with them, but—"

"But you think something is wrong with this whole picture," she finished for me. "You want Jordan to support you while you raise the kids."

I nodded, feeling ashamed. "Part of me does feel that way," I agreed. "I guess I don't mind working so much as the idea that I'm supporting the family. It . . . it just doesn't seem right."

"Times have changed," she answered matter-of-factly. "Whether you like it or not, your job is more reliable right now. You make enough so you can live comfortably, at least until the boys are a little older. Is it so bad that you're the main breadwinner?"

Is it so bad? When Raylene phrased it that way, it made all my doubts seem petty and childish. Times have changed and more and more women are working, even supporting the whole family. Why am I being so unreasonable about the whole thing?

Over the next few weeks, I tried to think more positively about Jordan's decision to stay home with our boys. He's a great father and Jesse and Jared love being with him. Jordan is patient and loving and likes to play with the boys. He was teaching them how to play soccer and baseball, but he also let them do elaborate arts and crafts projects.

When I come home, dinner is always cooking and the house, while not as clean as I would have liked, was comfortable. Jordan insisted I take time to relax and look at the mail or take a bath when I got home.

In short, Jordan is the perfect husband and father and everything should've been ideal, but it wasn't. I felt like an outsider in my own home. Oh, of course I knew that Jordan and the boys love me, but nobody needed me. No, that wasn't true, either, and I knew it, but that's how it felt. Jordan had everything under control and the boys adored him.

I knew I sounded selfish, and Raylene just laughed at my complaints. "You're crazy, Rachel. You told me that this week alone he got the boys to their dentist appointment, signed them up for that art class at the community center, and took them to the park every day to play.

"Besides that," she continued before I could reply. "He does the dishes and laundry, cleans the house, and has dinner waiting for you when you get home. You have the ideal situation, but for some reason you want to find fault with it."

"You don't understand," I answered, hating how whiny my voice sounded.

Raylene's voice became serious. "No, I don't," she agreed simply. "You sound like a spoiled brat, Rachel. And this attitude of yours is going to hurt your marriage and your kids. They need to look up to their father, not think there's something wrong with him because he wants to stay home with them."

"I never said that!" I protested.

"You didn't have to say it," she replied coolly. "Your kids are young, not stupid. They can sense the tension you feel."

"Why is everything my fault?" I asked, feeling sorry for myself again.

"Because you're creating problems where there aren't any," she answered quickly. "Look, you can't change the economy or make someone hire Jordan. The situation simply is what it is. And if you stepped back and looked at it realistically, you'd see you've got a pretty good life."

I didn't know what to think anymore. I liked my job, but something didn't feel right about me being the one who was out earning a living while Jordan stayed home. Was it just that I was hopelessly old fashioned?

A week later, my boss called me into his office. "Rachel," he said, when he had closed the office door. "I'll get to the point quickly. Andrew Maxwell is retiring next month. That means Brad Horton will move into his position and that leaves a vacancy that I want you to fill. Regional manager."

I sat back in shock. "Me?" I finally managed to ask.

Mr. Gray laughed. "Not quite the reaction I expected," he replied in amusement. "But, yes, that's what I mean. It's a wonderful opportunity for advancement, but it has some drawbacks. For the first nine months, there would be quite a bit of travel and setting up the new branches in different cities. I need someone I can count on.

"I'm going to give you a few days to answer," he continued, frowning slightly. "But I need to have someone in place soon. There are going to be some long hours, but it comes with a substantial raise."

When he mentioned the amount, I gasped and Mr. Gray smiled. "And the job comes with some other perks, like a company car and an expense account. Go home and think about it, Rachel. Take the whole weekend and give me an answer on Monday."

I was still in a mild state of shock, but I managed to thank Mr. Gray before I walked out of his office. It was crazy to even consider the offer, I knew, but the extra money was tempting. But it would mean even more time away from Jordan and the boys! How could I even think about taking it?

Yet, deep inside, I was flattered that I was Mr. Gray's choice for the promotion. And I knew his confidence was well placed. I could do the job well. I'm good with the clients and I know how to deal with the problems of opening new branches. But what would this job do to my marriage?

I waited until the kids had gone to bed that night before I told Jordan the news about the promotion. He looked at me and frowned. "Are you taking it?" he finally asked. His voice sounded strained.

"I don't know," I replied honestly. "The money would be nice, but it's so much travel."

"Rachel, why don't you say what you really mean?" he asked coldly. "You don't want to take the promotion. If you did, you would have come home with a bottle of champagne and said, 'I'm going to be making twenty thousand more a year!' But you didn't.

"I get that you're ashamed of me," he continued, his voice turning bitter. "I'm not providing for you like a 'real man' would. What I don't get is why you're not proud of yourself for being offered the job."

"I am proud of myself," I began quietly. "But…

"You're ashamed of me," he finished for me. "Believe me, Rachel, I get it! I've done everything I can to make things comfortable for all of us, especially you. I've knocked myself out these last few months, but nothing has been good enough."

"Jordan, I—" I started weakly.

He shook his head. "No, let me finish," he interrupted. "If the situation were reversed and I was offered a promotion, how would you have felt if I considered turning it down because I wasn't sure I should take it? I'll tell you. You would be furious! You would've thought I was crazy or selfish to even think it! I always thought of you as my partner, Rachel, an equal partner, but that's obviously not how you see me.

"It's not how I envisioned my life turning out, either," he continued sadly. "But it's the way it is. I love you and the boys. But I'm not going to live like I don't matter anymore. If you can't accept things the way they are, then I don't think we have much of a chance."

To my surprise, Jordan grabbed his coat and left. I heard the car door slam and then he was gone! I burst into tears and sank back on the couch. Jordan was right about everything. He had been wonderful about taking care of all of us and I had only shown contempt for his efforts. What if it was too late to save the marriage?

My first instinct was to call Raylene and cry on her shoulder, but I stopped myself before I hit the last number. It wasn't fair to Raylene and she had already warned me that I was taking Jordan for granted. She'd told me I was acting like a baby and she was right. I was the one who had to fix my marriage.

I was wrong and I was willing to admit it, but would Jordan accept my apology? Did he even want to give our marriage another chance?

Jordan didn't come home until late that night and it was obvious he'd been drinking. I could see he was in no condition to talk, so I pretended to be asleep. He didn't reach for me at all, so I knew he was still mad.

The next morning, I got up early and took the boys to my parents' house. I told them that Jordan was sick and I didn't want the boys to catch it. "Leave them for the weekend," my mother insisted. "Just to be on the safe side."

I felt terrible lying, but I also didn't want to have to explain how much trouble my marriage was in.

I stopped at the bakery on the way home and picked up Jordan's favorite pastries. I made some strong coffee and carried two cups and the box of doughnuts into the bedroom. Jordan stirred softly.

"It's not champagne," I said gently. "But I thought we could celebrate anyway."

He frowned slightly, but took the cup of coffee. "Sorry about last night," he mumbled. "I didn't mean to. . . ."

"No, you said what you had to say last night," I interrupted firmly. "It's my turn. You were right about everything. I've been acting like an idiot and I don't know why. You have been wonderful and I've been an ungrateful jerk. I hope you can forgive me."

Jordan sat up, "What brought all this on?" he asked suspiciously.

"The thought that I might lose you," I answered honestly. "I want you to know I love you and I'm sorry for the way I've been acting."

Jordan reached for me then. "Let's make up," he said huskily. "And then we can talk."

We made love and talked for most of the next two days. I can't say we solved everything that was wrong in that short of a time, but it was a good start. The most important thing is that we acknowledged we were a "team" and that our family came first.

I ended up taking the promotion and it was one of the best things I ever did. Not only was the extra money nice, but also Jordan and the boys came with me on many of the business trips and we had a wonderful time exploring new cities and different restaurants and museums wherever we go.

Our marriage is stronger than ever and every day I thank God for Jordan. In these changing times, it's sometimes hard to define our roles in marriages and relationships. I think all people can do is rely on their love for each other and find out what works for them.

THE END

Printed in Great Britain
by Amazon